P9-DUT-261

*F*yodor *D*ostoyevsky

Fyodor Dostoyevsky

Selected Works

Fyodor Dostoyevsky

The Karamazov Brothers

A novel
in four parts
with an epilogue

In two volumes
Volume Two

Translated by *Julius Katzer*

Raduga Publishers Moscow

Translation from the Russian
Designed by *Vladimir Kireyev*

First published 1981
Second printing 1990
English translation© Progress Publishers 1981
© Raduga Publishers 1990

Printed in the Union of Soviet Socialist Republics

ISBN 5-05-002803-5
ISBN 5-05-002805-1

CONTENTS

PART THREE

BOOK SEVEN

Alyosha

1.

The Odour of Decay

Preparations for the burial of the deceased hieromonach Father Zossima proceeded in accordance with the established rites. As is common knowledge, the bodies of monks, especially of the strictest rite, are not washed: to quote from the Book of Common Prayer: "When a monk rests in the Lord, the monk appointed for the office shall wipe the body with warm water, first making the sign of the cross over the brow, the hands, and the feet and knees, using a sponge; nothing more should be done." All this was performed by Father Paissi himself, who, after sponging the body, clad it in the monastic habit, wrapping it in a cope slit somewhat, according to the rite, to allow it to be folded crosswise about the body. On the head he placed a cowl with an eight-pointed cross, and left open, the face being covered with black gauze. In the hands was placed an icon of the Redeemer. Thus arrayed, the body was transferred at dawn to a coffin, which had been prepared long in advance. It was intended that the coffin should remain all day in the cell, the first and larger of the rooms where the late *starets* had been wont to receive callers both monks and laymen. Since the deceased had been a hieromonach of the most rigorous rite, the reading at the coffinside was to be from the Gospels, not the Psalter, and conducted by hieromonachs and hierodeacons. The reading was begun by Father Iosif immediately after the office for the dead; as for Father Paissi, who had himself expressed a desire to continue the reading all day and all night, he was still very busy and worried, as was the Father Superior, for something most uncommon, a kind of unheard-of and "unseemly" excitement and eager expectation, had begun suddenly to appear and then build up both among the monks and the crowds of laymen who had come flocking from the monastery inns and from the town. Both the Father Superior and Father Paissi made every effort to pacify the wrongful agitation. As soon as full day had set in, townspeople began to bring their sick, especially children, just as though they had been waiting expressly for that particular moment, evidently pinning their hopes on the immediate healing power which, they believed, would not fail to manifest itself. Only now did it become apparent how much the people of our town had grown used to regarding the deceased *starets*, even during his lifetime, as an unquestionably great saint. Many of the arrivals were by no means of the humbler class. To Father Paissi this keen expectancy on the part of the faithful, displayed with such undisguised eagerness and even impatience, almost as a demand, seemed rank backsliding, which, though foreglimpsed by him long before, now actually exceeded his forebodings. He even upbraided those monks he met who revealed that excitement. "Such direct expectation of something extraordinary," he said to them, "shows a levity possible only in laymen, but unseemly in us." But little heed was paid to his words, as Father Paissi noted with some misgiving, though he himself (to speak the truth), discomposed as he was by such excessively impatient expectations, which he found thoughtless and vain, looked forward to, in the innermost recesses of his heart, with the same suspense as the agitated crowd, something he could not but admit to himself. Nevertheless, it was most unpleasant to him to come across some people who aroused certain premonitions and grave doubts in him. It was with aversion (for which he at once reproached himself) that he noticed among those who were thronging the dead man's cell the presence, for instance, of Rakitin, and the monk from distant Obdorsk, who was still staying on at the monastery. For some reason, Father Paissi felt a sudden suspicion of the two, though they were not the only ones he regarded in that light. The monk from Obdorsk stood out as the fussiest member of the excited crowd: he was to be seen everywhere, asking questions, listening, and whispering with a peculiarly mysterious air. The expression on his face was one of the utmost impatience and even resentment that what was being expected was so long in coming about. As for Rakitin, he, as it

9

later emerged, had arrived at the hermitage at so early an hour at the express wish of Madame Khokhlakov. No sooner had that amiable but weak-willed woman, who could not herself be allowed to enter the hermitage, learnt, on waking up, of the decease of the *starets* than she was overcome by such burning curiosity that she promptly sent Rakitin to the hermitage with instructions to be on the look-out all the time, and keep her informed by notes penned every half-hour or so of *whatever was happening.* She considered Rakitin a most pious and devout young man—so adept was he at getting along with people and presenting himself in whatever light he thought most to their taste, if only he saw the least advantage to himself from doing so. It was a clear and bright day, with many of the worshippers thronging about the graves, which were particularly numerous about the church itself, but were also scattered all over the territory of the hermitage. As he walked about the hermitage, Father Paissi suddenly thought of Alyosha, whom he had not seen for quite a while, not since that night perhaps. Scarcely had he called him to mind when he caught sight of him in the furthermost corner of the hermitage, at the railing, seated on the gravestone of a monk long dead and noted for his saintly works. He was sitting with his back turned to the hermitage and his face towards the railing, as though seeking refuge behind the tombstone. As he approached Alyosha, Father Paissi saw that he was shedding bitter but silent tears, his face buried in his hands, and his body shaking with sobs. Father Paissi stood over him for a while.

"Enough, dear son, enough," he said at last feelingly. "Why are you weeping so? Rejoice and weep not. Don't you realise that this is the greatest of *his* days? Where can he now be, at this moment? Think on that!"

Alyosha was about to glance at him, uncovering his tear-swollen face, just like a child's, but at once turned away without a word, and again buried his face in his hands.

"Perhaps it's better that way," Father Paissi said thoughtfully. "Weep if you must: Christ has sent those tears." "Your heartfelt tears will bring comfort to your soul and will help gladden your dear heart," he added to himself as he walked away from Alyosha, thinking lovingly of him. He made haste to leave, for he was on the verge of tears himself, as he looked at Alyosha.

Meanwhile, with the passage of time, the monasterial service and the prayers for the repose of the soul of the departed followed their due course. Father Paissi again relieved Father Iosif at the coffin to continue the reading from the Gospels. But it was not yet three o'clock in the afternoon when something took place, which I already mentioned at the end of the previous book, something so unexpected in our parts, and running so counter to what was generally looked forward to, that, I repeat, the reprehensible story is vividly recalled in detail in our town and its environs to this day. I would like to add a personal note at this point, to wit, that I find it almost revolting to recall this provoking and blameful event, one that was, in essence, perfectly natural and insignificant; I would, of course, have made no mention of it in my story had it not had a definite and powerful affect on the heart and soul of Alyosha, the focal *though future* personage in my narration, for it proved a crisis and turning point in his spiritual development, staggering his mind but tempering it for the rest of his days, and giving it a definite purposefulness.

And so back to the story. When, before the break of day, the body, which had been prepared for burial, was laid in the coffin and taken into the front room, the one used for receptions, the question arose among those who stood at the coffin: should the windows be opened? However, the question, asked by one of them in an incidental and casual sort of way, went unanswered and almost unnoticed, though some of those present may have noticed it unspokenly, but only in the sense that to expect decomposition and an odour of decay from the body of such a man was an utter absurdity which should evoke pity (if not scorn) for the lack of faith and levity in implied. For quite the opposite had been looked forward to. But then, soon after midday, there began something that was inwardly accepted in silence by the comers and goers, and even with an evident apprehension, in each of them, of passing on what had arisen in his mind. By three o'clock in the afternoon, the signs were so clear and unmistakable that the news spread rapidly throughout the hermitage and among all the visitors, and immediately reached the monastery, filling the inmates with amazement. Very soon the whole town learnt of the happening, the general excitement involving believers and unbelievers alike. The latter were delighted; as for the former, there were some among them who felt even more delight than the unbelievers did, for "people love to see the righteous man's downfall and his disgrace", as the *starets* himself had once said in a homily. The fact was that an odour of decay began to emanate from the coffin, gradually growing ever more marked until, by three o'clock in the afternoon there was no mistaking the cause, which made itself felt more and more. The sinful scandal that followed in the wake of this happening, even among the monks, had no parallel in the entire history of the monastery, such was its unbridled intemperance, quite unthinkable in any other circumstances. Even many years afterwards, the more sensible of our monks felt surprise and even revulsion when they recalled the details of that day's events and the extent of the sinful talk. For even previously, when certain monks who had lived lives of righteousness, God-fearing men whose saintliness had been generally acknowledged, had passed on, an odour of decay had come from their humble coffins, as it naturally does from all dead bodies, yet that had not given rise to any sinful talk, or caused the least stir. There had, of course, been some monks in former times whose memory had remained green at our monastery, for their relics, according to tradition, had revealed no decomposition at all. This had exerted an emotive and mysterious influence on our coenobites, who had cherished it as something refulgent and wondrous, holding out the promise of still greater future glory from such tombs if the right time for that should, by God's grace, arrive. One of these, whose memory was particularly revered, was the *starets* Job, an ascetic famous for his fasting and silence, who died in the early years of this century at the age of a hundred and five. His grave was reverently shown to all pilgrims on their first visit to the monastery, with mysterious mention of certain great expectations from it. (That was the very grave Father Paissi had found Alyosha seated on in the morning.) Besides this long-deceased *starets*, there was another—the great and comparatively recently departed hieromonach and *starets* Varsonofi—whose memory was also held in reverence. It was his mantle that had descended on Father Zossima, and in his lifetime he had been regarded as a fool for Christ's sake by the pilgrims. The two, tradition maintained, had lain in their coffins as though still alive, and had shown no signs of decay when they were buried, their faces even seeming lambently serene in their coffins. There were some who recalled with insistence that an unmistakable fragrance had been given off by their bodies. Yet, despite even such impressive recollections, it would be difficult to account for the direct cause of the so ill-considered, absurd and spiteful spectacle that unfolded itself at the coffin of the *starets* Zossima. It is my personal view that many other and varied causes were simultaneously at work: one of these, for instance, was the deep-lying antagonism against the *starets* institution as a harmful innovation, an attitude entrenched in the minds of many of the monks. Last and above all was the envy of the dead man's saintliness, a reputation so firmly established in his lifetime that any questioning of it was practically forbidden. For though the late *starets* had won many hearts, not so much by any miracles he had performed as by love, and had surrounded himself with a host of those who loved him, nevertheless—or rather for that reason—he had thereby aroused a good deal of envy, and then come to have bitter enemies, both overt and covert, and not only among the monastic fraternity but even among the laity. He had never done harm to anybody, yet it was asked, "Why was he considered so saintly?" That question alone, repeated more and more often, ultimately gave rise to a spite of implacable animosity. That was why, as I see it, many were boundlessly delighted when they noticed the odour of decay from his body, and so soon too, for less than a day had gone by since his death. Even among those who had been devoted to him and hitherto revered him there were some who felt almost outraged and affronted personally by what had happened. The course of events proceeded as follows.

No sooner had decomposition set in than one could tell from the very faces of the monks why they had come into the cell where the body of the deceased lay. They would enter, stay for a while and then leave to bear out to those waiting outside the truth of the report. Some of the latter would mournfully nod their heads, while others made no secret of their delight, which gleamed maliciously in their eyes. There were none to rebuke them and no kindly voices were raised, which was even strange, for most of the monks had been devoted to the deceased *starets*; God had evidently seen fit this time to allow the minority get the upper hand for a time. Very soon, members of the laity, for the most part of the educated class, began to enter the cell, also to spy out things. Few of the common people went in, though they crowded about the hermitage gates. It was beyond doubt that the stream of lay visitors grew considerably after three o'clock as a result of the scandalous news. Those who had had no intention of coming that day, or at all, now saw fit to call, including some of high rank. However, a show of propriety was maintained, and Father Paissi, his expression severe, went on reading from the Gospels in a firm and distinct voice, as though unaware of what was taking place, though he had long before noticed something out of the ordinary. But very soon voices began to reach his ears, very low at first but gradually growing firmer and more assured. "It shows the judgement of God is not that of man!" Father Paissi suddenly heard, the words coming first from a layman—a civil servant in the town, an elderly man known, by all accounts, for his piety; in saying so, he was merely repeating aloud what the monks had long been whispering in each other's ears. They had given expression to this dismal idea long before, the worst of it being that a triumphant undertone was becoming ever apparent with almost every passing minute. Very soon, however, even the show of propriety was gradually cast off, as though all present seemed to feel they were somehow entitled to act in that way. "How could *this* have come to pass?" some of the monks said, with a show of regret at first. "He was meagre and shrunken of body, practically skin and bone, so whence the odour?" "That means some portent from God," others hastened to add, their opinion being immediately accepted without demur, since, they went on to say, had the odour appeared in the natural order of things, as from any departed sinner, it would have done so some time later, when at least twenty-four hours had elapsed, but not so prematurely. This man had "anticipated the course of Nature", so it was the doing of God himself, whose finger was evident, and it was a sign. The argument struck home. An attempt was made by the gentle hieromonach Father Iosif, the librarian and a favourite of the late *starets*, to retort to some of the detractors; he told them that "it is not the case everywhere" and it was not a dogma of the Orthodox Church but merely an opinion that the bodies of the righteous should escape corruption, and that even in the most Orthodox parts, at Mount Athos, for example, they were in no wise put out by the odour of decay; there it was not bodily incorruptibility that was regarded as the main evidence that saintly men had won glory, but the colour of their bones many years after their interment, when they had even decayed: "If the bones are found as yellow as wax, that is the main sign that the righteousness of the deceased has won him glory in the Lord, but if they are found to be not yellow but black, that means that the Lord has not deemed them worthy of glory. That is how Orthodoxy is preserved at Mount Athos, that famed place where Orthodoxy has been maintained since times immemorial in all its pristine purity," said Father Iosif in conclusion. However, the meek Father's words had no effect and even produced the derisive retort, "That all comes of learning and innovations, so there's no point in listening," the monks decided among themselves. "We keep to the ancient tradition. Who cares for all these new-fangled ideas? Why should we imitate them?" others added. "We've had just as many holy fathers as they," the greatest of the jeers put in. "They've been living under the Turkish yoke and forgotten everything. Even their Orthodoxy became tainted a long time ago, and they no longer have church-bells," they went on. Father Iosif walked off sadly, the more so for having failed to voice his opinion forcefully, as though he himself had little faith in it. But he was distressed to see that something most unseemly was taking shape, and that defiance of authority was rearing its head. Little by little, all the sensible monks fell silent, as Father Iosif had done. It thus came to pass that all those who had loved the *starets* and had accepted with devout obedience the institution he represented suddenly took affright of something, and exchanged timid glances with each other when they met. As for the foes of the *starets* institution as an innovation, they now held their heads high. "Not only was there no odour from the deceased *starets* Varsonofi, but he gave off a fragrance," they recalled with spite, "and he was vouchsafed that, not because he was a *starets*, but for his life of sanctity." Following this, a flood of condemnation and even accusations descended on the deceased. "His teachings were unjust; he taught that life is a source of great joy, not a vale of tears," some of the more addlepated said. "His faith followed the vogue and denied the material nature of hell fire", others, even more addlepated, put in. "He was not strict enough as regards the fasts, and permitted himself to eat sweetmeats; he was fond of cherry jam with his tea, and used to be sent it by the ladies. Should a monk of the strictest rite be so fond of tea?" could be heard from the more envious. "He was puffed up with pride," the most malicious recalled vindictively. "He considered himself a saint and thought it his due when people bent their knees to him." "He misused the sacrament of confession," the bitterest enemies of the *starets* institution added in malicious whispers; among them were even some senior monks who were most rigorous in their observance of fasts and the vow of silence. They had kept silent during the lifetime of the late *starets* but now spoke out, which was reprehensible because of the impact of their words on the young monks, whose faith was still in the formative stage. All this was listened to most avidly by the visitor from Obdorsk, the little monk from the monastery of St. Sylvester, who kept heaving deep sighs and shaking his head. "Indeed, Father Ferapont was speaking the truth yesterday," he thought to himself. It was at that very moment that Father Ferapont appeared, as though expressly to aggravate the ferment.

I have already mentioned that he rarely emerged from his wooden cell by the apiary; even at church he was seen at long intervals. This was overlooked ostensibly for his being a fool for Christ's sake, on whom the common rules were not binding.

To tell the truth, however, such permissiveness was born of necessity, for it seemed improper to insist on the general discipline being imposed on so great a faster and man of silence, who prayed day and night (even falling asleep on his knees), if he himself did not see fit to obey it. "He's holier than all of us, and has assumed a self-discipline far stricter than what is required," the monks would have objected in that case. "As for his missing church services, he himself knows when he ought to attend them; he follows his own rules." It was to preclude the possibility of such unseemly murmuring that Father Ferapont was left alone. As was common knowledge, he had an intense dislike of Father Zossima, and now the news reached him in the cell that "the judgement of God is not that of man" and that the *starets* had "anticipated the course of Nature". It may well be supposed that among the first to come running with the news was the monk from Obdorsk, who had visited him on the previous day and left his cell terror-stricken. I have also mentioned that though Father Paissi, who was standing firm and unshakable as he read from the Gospels over the coffin, could not hear or see what was going on outside the cell, he had, in his heart, foreglimpsed its tenor, for he had an intimate knowledge of things at the monastery. Yet he maintained his composure, fearlessly awaiting what might come next, following with keen insight the future outcome of the agitation, which he could already see with his mind's eye. There suddenly burst upon his ears a loud noise which came from the corridor and manifestly disturbed all decorum. The door was flung open and Father Ferapont appeared on the threshold. Behind him, as could be noticed and even clearly seen from the cell, were a crowd of monks and some townspeople, who had come with him and stood in groups at the porch. However, they did not mount the steps or go in, but waited in expectation of what Father Ferapont would say and do next, for they had a presentiment, mixed with some apprehension, despite all their audacity, that he had come with something in mind. Halting in the doorway, Father Ferapont raised his arms; from under his right arm could be seen the darting and inquisitive eyes of the Obdorsk monk, the only one of the company whose overwhelming curiosity had made him run

17

up the steps after Father Ferapont. The rest, on the contrary, clustered closer together, retreating in sudden fright, the moment the door was flung open. Raising his hands skywards, Father Ferapont suddenly bawled:

"By casting out, I cast out!" and at once, turning in all four directions, began making the sign of the cross over each of the four walls and at all four corners of the cell in turn. The reason for his action was quite clear to those who had come with him: they knew he always behaved in that fashion whatever premises he entered, and that he would not take a seat or say a word until he had exorcised all devils.

"Satan, get thee behind me; Satan, get thee behind me!" he repeated each time he made the sign of the cross. "By casting out, I cast out!" he again bawled.

He was clad in his coarse cassock with a piece of rope as a girdle. From under his hempen shirt, his bare chest could be seen, with its matted grey hair. His feet were quite bare. When he began waving his arms, the iron chains he wore under the cassock to mortify the flesh jingled and clanked. Father Paissi interrupted his reading, stepped forward and stood confronting him to see what would come next.

"What have you come here for, good Father? Why should you disturb the peace? Why are you stirring up trouble in the meek flock?" he said at last, looking severely at him.

"Wherefore come I? Why dost thou ask? What is thy faith like?" the latter shouted, again acting the saintly fool. "I've come to exorcise your visitors, the vile devils, to find out how many you've gathered here in my absence. I want to sweep them out with a birch besom."

"You want to drive out devils, but perhaps you serve them yourself," Father Paissi went on fearlessly. "And who can say of himself, 'I'm holy'? Can *you*, Father?"

"I'm vile, not holy. I'll never sit me down in an armchair and expect adoration as though I were an idol!" Father Ferapont thundered. "Nowadays people are destroying the holy faith. That dead man, your saint," he went on, turning to the crowd and pointing a finger at the coffin, "said that devils did not exist and gave purgatives against them. That's why the de-

18

vils have multiplied here like spiders, and he himself has begun to stink today. In that we can see a great sign from the Lord."

He was referring to something that had really taken place in Father Zossima's lifetime. One of the monks had begun to see devils in his dreams, and later in his waking moments. Frightened out of his wits, he had confided this to the *starets*, who had advised continual prayers and strict fasting. When that had proved unavailing, he had advised the monk to continue his prayers and fasting and augment them with a certain medicine. Many had been shocked at the time by such things, shaking their heads as they discussed them, and Father Ferapont most of all, whom some of the detractors had hastened to inform of such "extraordinary" instructions on the part of the *starets* in so special a case.

"Leave this place, Father!" Father Paissi said, commandingly. "It is for God, not man, to pass judgement. Perhaps we see here a 'sign' that neither you, I, nor anybody else is able to understand. Leave this place, Father, and do not stir up trouble in the flock!" he repeated emphatically.

"He did not observe the fast as strictly as he should have, and that's why the sign has been given. That's quite clear, and it's sinful to conceal it!" cried the fanatic, carried away by his excessive and unreasonable zeal. "He was too fond of sweets, which the ladies brought him in their pockets; he was partial to sweet tea, pampering his belly, cramming it with sweetmeats and his mind with prideful thoughts—that's why he's been put to shame—"

"Unseemly are your words, Father!" said Father Paissi, raising his voice in his turn. "I admire your fasting and rigorous discipline, but your words are unseemly, befitting a lay youth, callow and inconstant. Leave this place, Father, I command you," Father Paissi roared in conclusion.

"Leave it I shall!" said Father Ferapont, somewhat subdued but with unabated animosity. "You scholars! Your overweening learning has made you look down on a nobody like me. I came here almost unlettered, and here I've forgotten what little I knew. The Lord Himself has protected my lowly self from your wisdom—"

Father Paissi stood over him, waiting resolutely. Father Ferapont was briefly silent and then suddenly looking woebegone and pressing his right hand to his check, pronounced in a sing-song voice, looking meanwhile at the coffin:

"They'll be chanting *Helper and Defender* over him tomorrow—a glorious canon—while all I'll get when I pass on will be *What Earthly Joy,* just a brief sticheron," he went on in tearful self-pity. "You're all puffed up with pride; this is a place of vanity!" he suddenly bellowed like a madman and, waving a hand, he rapidly turned away and descended the porch steps. The awaiting crowd seemed to waver: some followed him at once, while others lingered on, for the door of the cell was still open, and Father Paissi, who had followed Father Ferapont on to the porch, stood watching. However, the old man, still worked up, had not yet had his say. After walking away some twenty paces, he suddenly turned towards the setting sun, raised both hands above his head, fell to the ground like grass mown down with a scythe, and gave a mighty cry:

"My Lord has conquered! Christ has conquered the setting sun!" he raved, raising his hands towards the sun and then, falling prone, he burst into sobs like a little child. At this they all rushed up to him with exclamations and sobs of sympathy—a kind of frenzy seemed to have overcome them all.

"He's the one who is saintly! He's the righteous one!" some exclaimed, no longer afraid. "This is the one who should be a *starets*," some added with malice.

"He wouldn't agree—" others at once retorted. "He'd refuse—he wouldn't encourage that accursed innovation—he wouldn't ape their tomfoolery." It is hard to say what all this might have led to, had not the bell rung out for the service, at which all present at once began to cross themselves. Father Ferapont rose to his feet and, crossing himself too, made for his cell without looking back, meanwhile uttering cries that were already quite incoherent. A few followed him, but the greater number began to disperse, hurrying to attend the service. Father Paissi had Father Iosif take over the reading and went out. The frenzied outcries of the fanatics had not the least effect on him, but he felt a sudden sadness and even a heartache came over him. He halted. "Why do I feel so sad, and even dispirited?" he suddenly asked himself, and realised with surprise that this onset of melancholy was due to a special if minor cause: in the midst of the excited throng at the entrance to the cell he had noticed Alyosha, and recalled that the sight of him had evoked a kind of pang in his heart. "Can it be that the youth has come to mean so much to my heart?" he asked himself in sudden surprise. At that moment, Alyosha hurried past him, seemingly bound for some place other than the church. Their eyes met. Alyosha quickly looked away and then lowered his gaze to the ground. From his appearance alone Father Paissi realised what a striking change was taking place in him.

"Can it be that you, too, have gone astray!" Father Paissi exclaimed. "Are you, too, with those of little faith?" he added sorrowfully.

Alyosha halted, and regarded Father Paissi with a vacant kind of look; then he quickly turned his eyes away once more and dropped them. He stood sideways to the monk, without looking towards him. Father Paissi observed him attentively.

"Whither are you hurrying? The bells are ringing for the service," he went on but received no answer.

"Are you about to leave the hermitage? How can you do so without permission and a blessing?"

Alyosha suddenly smiled wryly, and cast a strange glance, a very strange glance, at his questioner, at him to whom his late guide and adviser—his beloved *starets,* the former master of his heart and mind—had entrusted him before his death; suddenly, again with no word of reply, he waved a hand as though he no longer cared to show any respect, and strode rapidly through the gateway out of the hermitage.

"You will surely return!" Father Paissi whispered, looking in mournful surprise at the retreating figure.

2.

The Right Moment

Of course, Father Paissi was not mistaken in deciding that his "dear boy" would return; he had gained even an insight (keen if not complete) into the real significance of Alyosha's spiritual state. Yet I frankly admit that it would now be very difficult for me to clearly convey the precise meaning of that strange and indeterminate moment in the life of the young hero of my story, whom I love so much. To Father Paissi's sorrowful question, "Are you, too, with those of little faith?" I could, of course, give a firm reply for Alyosha: "No, he was not with those of little faith." Moreover, the reverse was true: he was troubled because he was of such great faith. Indeed, Alyosha was troubled, and so agonisingly, that long afterwards he would recall that sad day as one of the most painful and fateful of his life. If, however, it were asked in a straightforward manner: "Could all that distress and alarm in him have been caused only by the body of the *starets* having shown signs of early decay instead of displaying healing powers?" I would unhesitatingly reply, "Yes, that was the case." I would only ask the reader not to hasten to ridicule my young man's purity of heart. Far from apologising for him or trying to excuse and justify his simplicity of faith on the ground of his youthful years, for instance, or the little progress in his schooling, and the like, I must, on the contrary, state emphatically that I entertain sincere respect for the qualities of his heart. No doubt, any other youth, cautious in accepting heartfelt impressions and capable of tepid and not ardent love, with a mind though true in its judgements but too rational for his years (and therefore cheap)—that kind of youth, I say, might have escaped what overtook my hero; in some cases, however, it is more praiseworthy to yield to some urge, even if unreasonable but springing from some great love, than not to submit to it at all. That is the more so in one's younger years, for a young man who is always and excessively rational is not to be depended on, and of little worth—that is what I hold! "But," sensible people may exclaim at this point, "it is not any youth that will give credence to such a superstition, so your young man can be no model to others." To that I shall again reply: "Indeed, my youth had faith, a faith sacred and unshakable, and I offer no apologies for him."

You see, though I declared above (perhaps somewhat hastily) that I would not try to explain or justify my hero's behaviour or apologise for him, yet that something has to be clarified for a further understanding of my narrative. Here is what I shall say: this was not a question of miracle-working. Here there was no impatient expectation of miracles. It was not for the triumph of any convictions of his that Alyosha stood in need of miracles at the time (that was certainly not the case); neither was it because of some former and preconceived idea that should speedily triumph over some other idea—oh, no, not at all. First and foremost, in all this there stood in the foreground before him a single figure and none other—that of his beloved *starets,* the righteous man he revered to the point of adoration. The gist of the matter was that the all-embracing love abiding in his young and pure heart at the time and over the previous year had been at times wholly concentrated, perhaps even mistakenly, on a single being alone, at least in the most powerful impulses of his heart—to wit, on his beloved *starets,* now departed. Indeed, that person had so long stood before him as an unquestionable ideal that all his young energies and their aspirations could not but be focussed exclusively on that ideal, so much so that at moments he lost sight of "everyone and everything". (He later recalled that on that dismal day he had completely forgotten his brother Dmitri, whom he had been so anxious for and so longed to see on the previous day; he had also forgotten to take the two hundred roubles to Ilyusha's father, something he had been so eager to do also on the previous day.) Again, I repeat, it was not miracles that he stood in need of but only the "higher justice" which, he believed, had miscarried, thereby dealing his heart so cruel and sudden a blow. What if that "justice" had, in Alyosha's expectations, inescapably assumed the form of miracles immediately expected of the ashes of his late beloved guide? The same thought and expectation had been harboured by all at the monastery, even by those whose minds Alyosha held in such high esteem, Father Paissi, for instance. That was why, unburdened with any doubts, Alyosha had cloaked his dreams in the same vestment as all the rest. All this had struck deep root in his heart long before, during his year of life at the monastery, and the expectation had grown habitual in that heart. It was not only miracles alone but justice,

justice, that he thirsted after! And now the man who, he believed, should have been exalted above all others in the whole world—that very man had been suddenly cast down and put to shame instead of getting the glory that was his due! Why? Who had passed that judgement? Who could have done so?—such were the questions that tormented his inexperienced and innocent heart. He could not tolerate without bitterness, without even deep resentment, that the most righteous of the righteous had become the target of such jeering and spiteful mockery from an unreasoning crowd so inferior to him in every way. Well, even had there been no miracles at all, nothing extraordinary had occurred, and the immediately expected had not come true—why should such indignity have been allowed, why such disgrace and that early decay "anticipating the course of Nature", as the malicious of the monks had said? Why that "sign", now so triumphantly acclaimed by them together with Father Ferapont, and why should they believe they were even entitled to acclaim it? Where was the finger of Providence? Why had it kept its finger concealed "at the most necessary moment" (Alyosha thought) and seemed freely willing to submit to the blind, mute and ruthless laws of Nature?

That was why his heart was bleeding, the prime cause, as I have already said, being that the man he had loved above anything in the world should have been "put to shame", and "disgraced"! My young friend's murmuring may have been thoughtless and unreasonable, but again I repeat for the third time (and I am willing to admit in advance that I may do so just as thoughtlessly) that I feel glad that he did not prove so rational at such a moment: the time to be reasonable will always come to the man of sense, but if no love is to be found in a young man's heart at so exceptional a moment, then when will it appear? I will not, however, fail to mention, at this juncture, a phenomenon, strange if fleeting, that visited Alyosha's mind at that fateful and confusing moment. That new and short-lived *something* consisted in a painful impression, persistently recurring to Alyosha, of his conversation with Ivan on the day before. Indeed, it came at that very moment. Oh, it was not that something had been shaken in the basic and, as it were, elemental beliefs in his soul. He loved his God and his faith in him was steadfast, though he had suddenly murmured against him. Yet some vague but painful and sinister impression of that conversation again stirred suddenly in his soul, insistently demanding a way into his consciousness. Darkness was falling when Rakitin, who was passing through the pine wood on his way from the hermitage to the monastery, suddenly noticed Alyosha lying prone, motionless and apparently asleep under a tree. He went up to him and called him by name.

"Is that you, Alexei? Can you have—" he began in surprise, but broke off. What he wanted to say was, "Can you have *come to this*?" Alyosha did not look up at him, but from a faint movement he made Rakitin at once realised that he had been heard and understood.

"What's the matter with you?" Rakitin went on in surprise, which soon yielded place to a smile smacking more and more of sarcasm.

"Look here, I've been looking for you for over two hours. You suddenly vanished from there. But what are you doing here? What nonsense is this? You might at least give me a look—"

Alyosha raised his head, and sat up, his back against the tree. He was not weeping, but his face was expressive of suffering, and irritation could be seen in his gaze, which was fixed, not on Rakitin but somewhere away from him.

"Your face has changed completely, you know. There's nothing left of that famous humility of yours. Are you angry with somebody? Has anybody offended you?"

"Let me alone!" Alyosha said suddenly with a weary wave of the hand, his gaze still turned away from Rakitin.

"So that's how it is? You've started to raise your voice just like other mortals, eh? What a come-down from the angels! You do surprise me, Alyosha, you really do. I say so in all earnest. For a long time nothing here has come as a surprise to me. But I always regarded you as a man of education—"

Alyosha finally gave Rakitin a look, but in a vague kind of way as though understanding little of what the latter was saying.

"Could you have come to this only because your old man stinks to high heaven? Did you actually believe he'd begin producing miracles out of the bag?" exclaimed Rakitin, again in utter astonishment.

"I did and do believe; I want to believe and I will!" Alyosha cried irritably. "What else do you want to know?"

"Nothing at all, old man. Damnation, not even a schoolboy of thirteen believes in such things nowadays. Still, damn it all—so you're angry with your God and risen up against him. It's all because the old man hasn't been promoted and his name's not on the Honours List! Why should you?"

Alyosha gave him a long look through narrowed eyes, in which a flash suddenly appeared—but not of anger against Rakitin.

"I haven't risen up against my God," he said with a sudden and wry smile, "only 'I don't accept the world created by him'."

"What do you mean by saying you don't accept it?" asked Rakitin after a moment's reflection. "What tommyrot!"

Alyosha made no reply.

"Well, enough of that nonsense! Let's get down to brass tacks: have you had anything to eat today?"

"I don't remember—I think I have."

"You need some nourishment, to judge from your face. Just looking at you is enough to evoke compassion. You didn't sleep all night either. I hear you were in conference there. And then came all that stupid mummery— I suppose a bite of the consecrated bread is all you've eaten. Well, I've got some sausage in my pocket. I've brought it along from town just in case, only you won't eat sausage—"

"Let's have it."

"Oho! So that's how it is now! Frank rebellion, complete with barricades! Well, old man, that's an opportunity we can't afford to miss. Let's go over to my place—I wouldn't say no to a nip of vodka myself just now—I'm simply fagged out. I suppose you wouldn't go as far as some vodka—or would you?"

"Let's have some vodka too."

"Well, well! You do surprise me, Alyosha!" said Rakitin,

giving him a wild look. "Well, one way or the other, vodka or sausage, it's a worth-while occasion we can't afford to let slip by. Let's be going!"

Without a word, Alyosha rose to his feet and followed Rakitin.

"What a surprise your dear brother Ivan would have if he could see all this! Incidentally, your brother Ivan Fyodorovich left for Moscow this morning: do you know that?"

"I do," Alyosha replied listlessly; then, all of a sudden, the image of his brother Dmitri flashed across his mind, but only momentarily, though it did remind him of some urgent matter that brooked of no delay, some duty, a frightful obligation; yet even that reminder made no impression on him or reached his heart, but immediately slipped from his memory into oblivion. The recollection was long to remain in Alyosha's mind.

"Your dear brother Ivan once declared I was an 'inept windbag of a liberal'. You, too, could not resist intimating to me, on one occasion, that I was 'dishonest'— So what? Let's now see what your giftedness and honesty will get you" (he went on under his breath). "Oh, hell," he continued aloud, "let's by-pass the monastery along this path and go straight to town— H'm. I really ought to call at Madame Khokhlakov's. Just fancy, I wrote to her about all the happening here and, would you believe it, she at once replied in a pencilled note (she just adores sending notes, the dear lady!) that she 'would never have expected *such behaviour* from so esteemed a *starets* as Father Zossima!' Yes, that was the very word she used: *behaviour!* She, too, is in high dudgeon. Oh, you're all much of a muchness, the lot of you! Stay!" he cried suddenly, halting and, taking Alyosha by a shoulder, making him stop too.

"D'you know what," he said, looking searchingly into Alyosha's eyes, and in the grip of a sudden new thought that had occurred to him, though, outwardly, he was smiling, he seemed afraid to voice the new thought of his, so hard did he find it to believe in the strange and unexpected mood he now saw Alyosha in. "Alyosha, do you know where we should go now?" he finally said with ingratiating timidity.

"What's the difference—let's go wherever you wish."

"We'll go to Grushenka's, eh? Will you come?" Rakitin said at last, even trembling all over in timid expectation.

"Right, let's go there," Alyosha at once replied calmly, which came as such a surprise to Rakitin—that is to say, so prompt and calm was the consent that Rakitin almost jumped backwards.

"Well, I say!" he began in astonishment, but suddenly, taking Alyosha firmly by an elbow he led him rapidly along the pathway, terribly apprehensive lest Alyosha's resolve should fail him. They walked along in silence, Rakitin even afraid to open his mouth.

"How glad she'll be, how glad—" he murmured at last but then relapsed into silence. Actually, it was not at all to please Grushenka that he was taking Alyosha along to her: he was a pragmatically minded person, who never undertook anything that was not to his advantage. He was now pursuing a twofold aim: in the first place, vengeance, i.e. to witness "the disgrace of one who was righteous", Alyosha's "downfall" from "saint to sinner", a prospect which he relished in anticipation; secondly, he was looking forward to a certain material purpose highly advantageous to himself, of which more will be said later.

"So the right moment has struck," he thought with gay malice, "and I'll do well to grab it by the scruff of the neck—that moment—for it is just what I need."

3.

An Onion

Grushenka lived in the busiest section of the town, near Cathedral Square, in the house of Mrs. Morozov, a merchant's widow, in whose courtyard she rented a small wooden outbuilding. The house itself was a large brick building on two floors, old and most unattractive in appearance, in which the elderly mistress lived in seclusion with her two unmarried nieces, both quite elderly too. There was no need for her to rent out the lodge, but it was common knowledge that she had let the place to Grushenka (some four years previously) solely to please the merchant Samsonov, a relative of hers and the girl's acknowledged protector. It was said that, in placing his favourite with Mrs. Morozov, the jealous old man's original purpose had been that the old lady would keep a sharp eye on the new tenant's behaviour. Very soon, however, those sharp eyes proved unnecessary, and it all ended in Mrs. Morozov seeing Grushenka even very rarely and ultimately stopped pestering her with her supervision. True, four full years had passed since the old man had brought to this house a timid, shy, slim, dreamy and sad girl of eighteen from the gubernia capital, and since that time much water had flowed under the bridges. Incidentally, little was known in the town regarding the girl's life, and that little was vague; little more had been learnt later, even when quite a number of people had come to take an interest in the beauteous creature Agrafena Alexandrovna had developed into in four years. Only it was rumoured that she had been seduced by someone at the age of seventeen—an officer, it was said, who had immediately jilted her. He had gone off and got married somewhere, while Grushenka had been left behind, disgraced and destitute. It was said that, though Grushenka had been saved from poverty by the old man, she came of a respectable family of the clergy, being the daughter of some insignificant deacon, or something like that. And now, in four years, the sensitive, injured and pathetic orphan girl had grown into a rosy-cheeked and buxom Russian beauty, a bold and resolute woman, brazen and proud, who knew the value of money, was acquisitive, cautious and closefisted; she was said to have amassed quite a fortune of her own by fair means or foul. The only thing there was general agreement on was that she kept herself aloof: with the exception of her elderly patron, there was no man who could boast of her favours during those four years. This was an unquestionable fact, for there had been a goodly number of aspirants, especially during the past two years. All their efforts, however, had been unavailing, many such aspirants having had to beat an undignified and even comical retreat because of the firm and mocking rebuff from so determined a young woman. She was also known to have engaged in somewhat shady business deals, in which she had demonstrated a marked aptitude, so that many people had come to call her no better than a Jew. Not that she lent out money on interest, but it was known, for instance, that, in partnership with Fyodor Pavlovich Karamazov, she had for some time been buying up promissory notes on the cheap, for one-tenth of their nominal value, and later recouping ten times the value of some of them. The old widower Samsonov, a sick man who had lost the use of his swollen legs during the previous year, possessing considerable means but a skinflint, relentless, and a tyrant over his grown-up sons, had nevertheless fallen under the strong influence of his protégée, whom he had at first kept on a short rein and treated with harshness, on "lenten fare", as the scoffers said at the time. But Grushenka had been able to assert herself, while instilling in him a boundless faith in her constancy. A shrewd dealer, this old man (now long dead) was quite a character and, above all, was niggardly and flinthearted, and though Grushenka had gained such an ascendancy over him that he could not do without her (especially in the last two years), he did not endow her with any sizable fortune; even had she threatened to give him up for good, he would have still remained adamant on that score. Yet he did make some small capital over to her, even that coming as a general surprise when it became known. "You're a girl who's nobody's fool," he said to her as he let her have some eight thousand roubles, "so you've got to fend for yourself. I also want you to know that you'll be getting nothing more from me except your annual allowance until I die, and there'll be no provision for you in my will either." He was as good as his word; when he died, he left everything to his sons who, together with their wives and children, had always been treated by him as nothing more than servants. He did not even mention Grushenka in his will. All this came to light subsequently. He did, however, help Grushenka considerably with advice on how she should turn her "own capital" to advantage and brought a good deal of business her way. Old Samsonov, who was already with one foot in the grave, was vastly amused when Fyodor Pavlovich Karamazov, who had got to know Grushenka quite by chance over some transaction, ended up by falling head over ears in love with her, much to his own surprise, and even seemed to have lost his head. Remarkably enough, during the whole of their acquaintance Grushenka was completely and even cordially frank with the old man, who seemed to be the only person in the world she treated in that way. However, he had of late been no longer amused when Dmitri Fyodorovich suddenly appeared on the scene, too, with his love. On the contrary, he gave Grushenka some stern and earnest advice on one occasion. "If you have to choose between the two—between father and son," he said, "make the old man your choice, but only on condition the old scoundrel marries you without fail, and settles at least part of his money on you in advance. But keep away from his son, the captain; that will get you nowhere." Those were the very words spoken to Grushenka by the old lecher, who felt that his end was near; indeed, he died five months after these words of advice. I shall note in passing that, though the absurd and unseemly rivalry between the Karamazovs, father and son, for the favour of Grushenka was common knowledge in the town, few could make out the actual sense of her attitude towards them both. Even her two servants (after the calamity I will speak of in due course) later testified in court that Grushenka received Dmitri Fyodorovich exclusively out of fear of him, because, they said, he had "threatened to murder her". One of the two servants was the cook, a very old woman, ailing and almost deaf, whom she had brought with her from her parental home; the other was the old woman's granddaughter, a spry young girl of twenty, who served Grushenka as her maid. Grushenka lived frugally, her place being anything but luxurious. She occupied only three rooms, with old-fashioned mahogany furniture in the style of the twenties, the property of her landlady.

It was quite dark when Alyosha and Rakitin called on her but there were no lights yet in her quarters. Grushenka was reclining in her drawing-room on a big, uncomfortable mahogany-backed sofa, hard and upholstered in faded leather, shabby and in holes. Under her head were two white down-filled pillows from her bed. Lying outstretched and motionless on her back, her hands behind her head, she was smartly dressed, as though expecting somebody to call, in a silk black dress, wearing a light-lace snood, which was most becoming; on her shoulders was a lace shawl fastened with a massive gold brooch. She was certainly expecting somebody, looking bored and impatient, her face somewhat pale, the eyes and lips hot, and restlessly tapping an arm-rest of the sofa with the tip of her right foot. Scarcely had Rakitin and Alyosha appeared when a slight commotion set in. From the passageway, Grushenka could be heard to jump up from the sofa and cry out in alarm, "Who's there?" But the callers were met by the maid, who at once called back to her mistress:

"It's not him; it's somebody else! It's all right. "

"What's the matter with her?" Rakitin muttered, leading Alyosha by an elbow into the drawing-room. Grushenka was standing at the sofa, still looking frightened. A thick coil of her heavy light-brown plait had escaped from under her snood and fallen on her right shoulder, but she took no notice of it and put it back only after she had had a good look at her callers, and recognised them.

"Oh, it's you, Rakitin! You did give me a fright! Who are you with? Who's come with you? Good Lord, so that's whom you've brought along!" she exclaimed on seeing it was Alyosha.

"Have the candles lit!" said Rakitin with the free-and-easy air of a close and privileged friend entitled even to give orders in the house.

"Candles—oh yes, candles— Fetch him a candle, Fenya— Well, you have chosen a fine time to bring him here!" she again exclaimed, nodding towards Alyosha and, turning to the looking-glass, she began rearranging her hair. She seemed displeased.

"Why, have I done the wrong thing?" asked Rakitin, with an almost injured look.

"You did give me a fright, Rakitin, you really did," said Grushenka, turning to Alyosha with a smile. "Have no fear of me, my dear Alyosha, you can't imagine how glad I am to see you here, my unexpected visitor. You did give me a turn, Rakitin; I thought it was Mitya trying to get into the house. You see, I fooled him, though I made him promise he'd trust me, and

I lied to him. I told him I'd be spending the whole evening with my old Kuzma Kuzmich, helping him till late in the night to keep count of his takings. I always spend one evening a week helping him keep his books. We lock ourselves in: he flicks the beads on the abacus while I make the entries: I'm the only person he trusts. Mitya thinks I'm still over there, while I've locked myself in here—expecting a message. How could Fenya have let you in? Fenya, Fenya! Run over to the gate, open it and take a good look to see if the captain is anywhere about. He may be lurking somewhere on the look-out—I'm dreadfully afraid!"

"There's nobody to be seen there, Agrafena Alexandrovna. I've just taken a good look around, and been peeping every minute through a crack. I'm all of a tremble myself."

"Are all the shutters barred, Fenya? And the blinds should be lowered—that's better." And she lowered the heavy blinds herself. "He may come rushing in if he sees a light. I'm afraid of your brother Mitya today, Alyosha." She was speaking in loud if uneasy tones, and seemed almost exultant over something.

"What makes you so afraid of Mitya today?" Rakitin inquired. "You don't seem timid when he's with you; you always call the tune, don't you?"

"I've told you I'm expecting some news—glorious news, so I don't need Mitya here at all. Besides, I feel sure he didn't believe I'd be going to old Kuzma. I suppose he's in hiding close by the bottom of his father's garden, on the watch lest I turn up. Well, if he's there, he won't be coming here—so much the better. But I have been to the Samsonov place. Mitya saw me to his house; I told him I'd be there till midnight; and asked him to be sure to come at that time to take me home. After he left, I spent some ten minutes with the old man and hurried back here. I felt terribly afraid so I ran all the way to escape meeting him."

"But why are you all dressed up then? Going out somewhere? That's a curious bonnet you're wearing!"

"How inquisitive you are, Rakitin! I tell you, I'm expecting a message. I'll be off and away the moment it comes, and you'll see no more of me. That's why I'm dressed up—to be ready."

"And where will you be off to?"

33

"Ask no questions and you'll hear no lies."

"Hark to her! All overjoyed— I've never seen you looking like that before. All dressed up as though you'll be attending a ball," said Rakitin, eyeing her from head to foot.

"What do you know about balls?"

"Do you know much?"

"I've seen one. It was two years ago when Samsonov married off a son of his, and I watched from the gallery. But why should I be talking to you, Rakitin, when I have such a very prince standing here? How welcome you are, Alyosha, my dear boy, I can't believe my eyes! Whatever could have brought you here? To tell you the truth, I never expected you to come and it never even occurred to me that you might call. Although this is not exactly the fittest moment, I'm terribly glad to see you! Sit down on the sofa—here—light of my eyes! I'm really all a flutter— Oh, Rakitin, you should have brought him yesterday or the day before!— Well, I'm glad anyway. It may be even better he's come at such a moment, and not the day before yesterday—"

She seated herself briskly on the sofa next to Alyosha, her eyes fixed on him in undisguised delight. She was, indeed, glad, and not lying in speaking so. Her eyes were aglow, and her lips were laughing, but kindly and happily. Alyosha had never expected to see so kindly an expression on her face—he had seen little of her till the previous day, his impression of her had been a frightening one, and he had been shocked by her malicious and treacherous attack against Katerina Ivanovna, so he was now greatly surprised to suddenly see a quite different and unexpected creature before him. However crushed he felt by his sorrow, his gaze involuntarily rested on her with attention. Her entire manner seemed also to have changed for the better since the day before: there was scarcely a trace of the honeyed voice or the daintily affected movements—it was all so artless and simple, her movements rapid, direct and trustful, yet she was greatly agitated.

"Goodness, how all things are coming true today," she babbled on. "And I simply can't say why I'm so glad to see you, Alyosha. I couldn't tell you even if you asked me."

"D'you mean to say you don't even know what makes you glad?" asked Rakitin with a grin. "Then, why were you always pestering me to get him to come here? You did have something in mind, didn't you?"

"I did have a different purpose in mind before, but that's gone and done with. This is not that kind of moment. I'll treat you to something—that's what I'll do. I've turned kinder, Rakitin. Won't you take a seat too, Rakitin, why are you standing? Oh, you're seated already, are you? Oh, he always takes care of himself, does Rakitin. So there he is, Alyosha, sitting there opposite us, looking injured because I didn't ask him to be seated before you. Oh, he's very touchy, is Rakitin!" Grushenka exclaimed with a laugh. "Don't get into a huff, Rakitin, I'm feeling kindly today. But why do you look so sad, dear Alyosha? Can you be afraid of me?" she asked, looking into his eyes in merry mockery.

"He's greatly grieved because no elevation has been forthcoming," said Rakitin in a booming voice.

"What do you mean?"

"His *starets* has turned smelly."

"Stuff and nonsense! I suppose you've simply got to say something silly and nasty. Shut up, you fool. Let me sit in your lap, Alyosha, like that!" She suddenly sprang up and nestled on his knees like a playful kitten, her right arm flung tenderly about his neck. "I'll cheer you up, my pious boy! Are you really going to let me sit in your lap without getting angry? Say the word and I'll jump up."

Alyosha said nothing. He sat there, afraid to move. He heard her say, "Say the word and I'll jump up", but made no reply, as though benumbed. But he felt nothing resembling what might have been expected or imagined by somebody like Rakitin, for example, who was looking on lasciviously from his seat. The great grief in his soul engulfed any sensation that might have arisen in his heart, and had he been able to analyse what he felt at the moment, he would have realised that he was clad in adamantine armour against all and any temptation or enticement. Yet, despite his vague inertness of spirit and his overwhelming grief, he could not help marvelling at a new and strange sensation that was welling up in his heart: far from arousing in him the terror he felt every time he thought of a woman, if such a thought ever flitted across his mind, this woman, this "dreadful" woman whom he had feared more than any other in the world and was now sitting in his lap and embracing him, aroused in him a quite different, unexpected and peculiar sensation, a sense of extraordinary, most intense and undisguised curiosity, and all that without the least fear or the least trace of his former horror—that was the main thing, that was what involuntarily came as a surprise to him.

"Oh, stop babbling all that nonsense," Rakitin cried out. "You'd do better to let us have some champagne, as you promised you would, didn't you?"

"Yes, it's your due. You see, Alyosha, I promised him the champagne on top of other things if he brought you here. Let's have the champagne, and I'll join you too! Fenya, Fenya, fetch the champagne, the bottle Mitya left behind him, and be sharp about it. I may be stingy but I'll stand you the bottle, no, not you, Rakitin, for you're a toadstool, while he's a prince of a fellow! Though I have other things on my mind, I'll join you, for I feel like having a fling!"

"What's the occasion, the 'message' you keep bringing up? May I inquire or is it some secret?" Rakitin asked in curiosity, pretending to ignore the snubbing he was being subjected to all the time.

"Oh, that's no secret, as you are very well aware," Grushenka said in a voice suddenly anxious. She turned her head towards Rakitin and drew somewhat away from Alyosha though she still sat in his lap, an arm about his neck. "The officer's coming, Rakitin, my officer's coming."

"I've heard he's coming, but is he so close at hand?"

"He's at Mokroye right now, and from there he'll send a message here. That's what he wrote in a letter I've just received. So here I am, expecting the messenger."

"Really? But why should he be at Mokroye?"

"It would take too long to tell, and you've heard enough, anyway."

"And what about Mitya—how is he going to take it? Does

he know, or doesn't he?"

"He know? Of course, not! If he did, he'd do me in. But that's something I'm not afraid of at all now—I'm not afraid of his knife. Be quiet, Rakitin, and don't mention Dmitri Fyodorovich to me! He's crushed all the heart in me. And I don't even want to think of all that at this moment. But I can think of dear Alyosha, and I'm looking at him now— Come on and smile to me, my dear boy, cheer up, smile at my foolishness and my joy— Look, he *has* smiled, he has actually smiled! And how kindly his look is. You know, Alyosha, I've been thinking all this time that you must be angry with me because of what happened the day before yesterday—because of that young lady. I was mean then, indeed, I was— Yet it was a good thing it worked out that way. It was both bad and good," she went on with a suddenly thoughtful smile, and a sudden suggestion of cruelty was to be seen in that smile. "Mitya told me she screamed out I deserved to be flogged. Of course, I did hurt her feelings badly. She called me over to her house with the intention of subduing me and winning me over with a cup of chocolate— Yes, it's good it happened that way," she smiled on. "But I'm still afraid you're angry with me—"

"Indeed she is," Rakitin put in, genuinely surprised. "She's really afraid of you, Alyosha, a fledgeling like you."

"It's only to you that he's a fledgeling, Rakitin—and that's because you lack a conscience! You see, I love him in my soul, that's how it is! Alyosha, do you believe I love you with all my soul?"

"You shameless woman! It's her way of saying she loves you, Alyosha!"

"So what? I do love him."

"But what about your officer? And the wonderful message from Mokroye?"

"That is one thing; this is another."

"Spoken just like a woman would!"

"Don't roil me, Rakitin," Grushenka retorted. "That is one thing; this is another. I love Alyosha in a different way. True, Alyosha, I did have designs on you once. I'm a base and violent creature, but at moments, Alyosha, I've looked upon you as my conscience. I've kept on thinking, 'He should now despise an evil woman like me.' I thought so the day before yesterday when I was hurrying home from the young lady's. I've looked on you in that way for a long time, Alyosha, and Mitya knows it, I've told him so. And he understands. Would you believe it, Alyosha, I sometimes look at you and feel ashamed, ashamed of myself— I don't know how and I don't remember since when I've come to think of you in that way—"

Fenya came in and placed on the table a tray with an uncorked bottle and three glasses of champagne.

"Here's the champagne!" Rakitin exclaimed. "You're all worked up, Agrafena Alexandrovna, and not yourself. You'll start dancing after you've had a glass of champagne. Oh, dear, they can't even do this properly," he added, examining the champagne. "The old woman filled the glasses in the kitchen, the bottle's uncorked and the champagne's warm. Well, let's have some anyway."

He walked up to the table, took a glass, emptied it at one gulp, and refilled it.

"It's not every day that one can get champagne," he said, licking his lips. "Come on, Alyosha, take a glass and show the stuff you're made of. What shall we drink to?— The gates of Paradise? Take a glass, too, Grushenka, and drink to the gates of Paradise, too."

"What do you mean—the gates of Paradise?"

She took up a glass. So did Alyosha; he took a sip and replaced the glass.

"No, I'd rather not," he said with a gentle smile.

"And you boasted you would!" Rakitin cried.

"Then I won't either," Grushenka put in. "Besides, I don't feel like it. You can drink the whole bottle on your own, Rakitin. I'll have some if Alyosha does."

"Oh, how mawkish!" Rakitin said tauntingly. "And you sitting in his lap, too! He has cause enough for grief, but what is there for you to be upset over? He's risen up against his God, and was about to gorge on sausage—"

"Why so?"

"His *starets* died today, Father Zossima, that holy man."

"So the *starets* Zossima's dead!" Grushenka exclaimed. "Good Lord, I didn't even know!" She crossed herself devoutly. "Goodness, and me in his lap!" She started as though in dismay, jumped off and sat down on the sofa. Alyosha gave her a long and wondering look, and his face seemed lit up.

"Rakitin," he said in a suddenly loud and firm voice, "don't taunt me with having risen up against my God. I don't want to feel malice against you, so you should be more kindly too. I've lost a treasure such as you've never possessed, and it's not for you to pass judgement on me. You should rather follow her example: did you see how she spared me? I came here expecting to find a wicked soul here—I felt drawn to evil because I was base and wicked myself, but I found a sincere sister instead, a treasure, a loving soul— She spared my feelings just now— I'm speaking of you, Agrafena Alexandrovna. You've just restored my soul."

Alyosha's lips were quivering; he stopped short, catching his breath.

"So she's saved you, has she?" said Rakitin with a spiteful laugh. "Yet she meant to swallow you up—d'you know that?"

"Stay, Rakitin!" said Grushenka, jumping up. "Be quiet, the two of you. And now I'll have my say: you keep quiet, Alyosha, because your words make me feel ashamed of myself, for I'm bad, and not kind-hearted—that's what I am. And you, Rakitin, keep your mouth shut, because you're a liar. I did have the mean intention of swallowing him up, but now you're lying; it's quite different now—and not another word from you, Rakitin!" All this was spoken in extraordinary agitation.

"Hark to them—gone out of their wits, the two of them!" hissed Rakitin, looking at them in amazement. "Quite crazy— I feel as though I were in a madhouse. They're both unbraced, and will start crying in a minute!"

"I shall, I shall!" Grushenka replied. "He called me sister, something I'll never forget! Only remember, Rakitin: I may be bad, but I did give an onion away."

"What onion d'you mean? Damn it all, they've really gone out of their minds!"

Rakitin felt surprise at their vehement emotion, and was

angrily annoyed, though he might have realised that each of the two was overbrimming with emotions rarely vouchsafed in life. But though he was highly sensitive to whatever concerned himself, Rakitin was thick-skinned when it came to understanding the feelings and sensations of his fellow-creatures, partly because of his youthful inexperience, and partly out of intense self-centredness.

"You see, dear Alyosha," said Grushenka, suddenly turning to him with a nervous laugh, "I was showing off to Rakitin when I said I had given an onion away, but I won't brag to you about that, and I'm going to tell you why, for quite a different reason. It's only a fable but it's a good one, which I first heard as a child from my Matrena, who is now in my service as a cook. It runs like this: 'Once upon a time there lived a very wicked old woman. When she died, she did not leave a single good deed behind her. She was seized by devils, who hurled her into a lake of fire, but her guardian angel tried hard to recall some good deed of hers to report to God. He remembered and said to God: She once pulled up an onion in her kitchen garden and gave it to a beggar woman. So God said to him: Take that onion and hold it out to her in the lake. Let her take hold of it and pull. If you can pull her out of the lake, she can enter Paradise, but if the onion snaps, she will stay where she is. So the angel hastened to the woman, and held out the onion to her: Take hold of it, woman, and pull, he said, and set about pulling with great caution. He was on the point of getting her out when other sinners in the lake, on seeing she was being pulled out, began taking hold of her so as to get out together with her. But she was a very wicked woman and began to kick them off. It's me that's being pulled out, she said, and not you. The onion's mine, not yours. No sooner had she said so than the onion snapped, and the woman fell back into the lake, where she's burning to this day. The angel went away in tears.' That's the fable, Alyosha; I know it by heart, for that wicked woman is myself. I was bragging when I told Rakitin I had given an onion away, but to you I'll say something different: in all my lifetime, I've given away nothing but a *single* onion, and that's the only good deed to my credit. After that, you shouldn't have praise for me or consider me good. I'm bad, terribly wicked, and you'll put me to shame if you start praising me. Since I've started, I might as well confess to everything. Listen, Alyosha, I was so eager to get you to come here and pestered Rakitin so much about it that I promised him twenty-five roubles if he brought you here. Stay, Rakitin, just a moment!" She took some rapid steps towards the desk, pulled out a drawer, took a purse out of it, and produced a twenty-five rouble note.

"What nonsense! What utter nonsense!" exclaimed the disconcerted Rakitin.

"Collect the debt, Rakitin. You won't hold back, I'm sure, because you asked for it yourself," and she threw the note to him.

"Why should I refuse?" Rakitin boomed, obviously abashed, but assuming an air of nonchalance. "The money will come very handy. It is to the profit of the wise that fools exist."

"And now hold your tongue, Rakitin, for what I'm going to say is not meant for your ears. Sit down there in the corner and keep quiet. You have no love for us, so hold your tongue."

"Why should I have love for you?" Rakitin snarled, making no secret of his malice. He pocketed the twenty-five roubles, feeling most awkward at Alyosha witnessing the act. He had counted on getting the payment later, without Alyosha's knowledge, and his sense of shame made him lose his temper. Until that moment, he had thought it highly politic not to contradict Grushenka overmuch, despite all her snubs, for she obviously exercised some control over him. But now he bristled up:

"There must be some reason for love to be felt, but what has either of you done for me?"

"You should feel love for no reason at all, just as Alyosha does."

"In what way does he love you? What has he shown for you that you should make so much of him?"

Standing in the middle of the room, Grushenka spoke with emotion, and there was a hysterical note in her voice:

"Hold your tongue, Rakitin, for you don't understand the least thing about us! And don't ever dare to speak to me with such familiarity, I won't permit it. Where have you picked up that brash tone of yours? Stay put in your corner and keep quiet, like the lackey you are to me. And now, Alyosha, I'm going to tell you the unvarnished truth, for you to see what a low creature I am! I'm saying this, not to Rakitin but to you alone. I wanted to corrupt you, and was determined to do so—honest to God, I was. I was so set on doing it that I bribed Rakitin to bring you here. But why did I want so much to bring that about? You had no suspicion of it, Alyosha, and always turned away from me, dropping your eyes if you happened to pass me in the street. But I looked at you a hundred times, and began to ask people about you. Your face had become engraved in my heart. 'He despises me,' I thought, 'and won't even want to look at me." I became so resentful that I finally wondered at myself: why should I be scared of such a stripling? I'll just swallow him up and laugh at him. I felt quite furious. Believe it or not, but nobody here would dare to say or even think of coming to me with evil intent. That old man is the only one I have anything to do with here: I'm tied hand and foot and sold to him, wedded by Satan. But there's been nobody else. As I looked at you, I made up my mind: I'll swallow him, swallow him and make mock of him. So you see what a wicked hag I am, whom you have called sister! And now the man who wronged me has come, and I'm awaiting a message from him. Can you imagine what that man was to me? When Kuzma brought me here five years ago, I would hold myself aloof from people so as not to be seen or heard. I was a silly slip of a girl, always in tears and lying awake at night, thinking: 'Where can be now the man who wronged me? I suppose he's with some other woman, making mock of him; I'll get even with him if ever I see or meet him again—yes, I'd pay him back!' I would lie in the darkness of night, sobbing into my pillow, brooding over the wrong done to me, and feeding my heart on malice: 'I'll get even with him; I'll show him!' Those were the words I would scream out in the dark. But when I would suddenly realise that I could do nothing at all to him, that he was probably laughing at me, and had most likely quite forgotten me, I would fling myself from the bed on to the floor, dissolve in helpless tears, and lie trembling till daybreak. In the morning,

I would get up in the most evil of tempers, ready to rend the world apart. And imagine, I then set about building up my capital, grew stone-hearted, and have grown plump—but do you think I've gained in wisdom? Nothing of the kind: nobody in the wide world sees or knows how—just as when I was a girl five years ago—I often lie in the darkness of night, gritting my teeth and in tears, thinking: 'I'll get even with him, I'll get even with him yet!' Well, have you taken it all in? And what will you have to say about me now: the letter I've told you of reached me a month ago, informing me he was now a widower and was coming because he wanted to see me. It quite took my breath away; goodness, I suddenly thought to myself: if he comes and just whistles to me, why, I'll go crawling back to him with the guilty look of a whipped cur! I couldn't believe myself as I thought in that way: 'Am I so despicable, or am I not? Will I go running back, or won't I?' Throughout the last month, I've been enraged with myself in a way far worse than five years ago. You can now see what a violent and furious creature I am. I've told you the whole truth! I amused myself with Mitya so as to escape running off to the other man. Shut up, Rakitin; it's not for you to call me to task; I'm not addressing you. Just before you came, I was lying here, waiting, brooding and trying to make up my mind as regards my future. You'll never learn what was going on in my heart. No, Alyosha, tell your young lady she shouldn't resent what took place the day before yesterday!— Nobody in the whole world knows the state I'm in now, and nobody ever will— That's why I may take a knife along with me when I go there today—I haven't decided yet—"

Before she could complete this "pitiful" statement, Grushenka suddenly broke down, hid her face in her hands, flung herself on the sofa cushions, and burst into sobs like a little child. Alyosha rose to his feet and went up to Rakitin.

"You shouldn't be angry with her, Misha," he said. "She's wounded your feelings, but that shouldn't make you angry. You heard what she just said, didn't you? One cannot expect so much of the human heart, compassion is more in place here—"

Alyosha said this at the irresistible prompting of his heart. He felt he could not but speak out, so he addressed Rakitin.

Had the latter not been there, the words would have been spoken to nobody in particular. But Rakitin gave him a look of mockery, at which Alyosha fell suddenly silent.

"You've been so primed up with your *starets* that you've simply had to let loose at me with him, dear Alyosha, mannikin of God," said Rakitin with a smile of hatred.

"Don't laugh, Rakitin, or jeer; say nothing of the departed: he stood head and shoulders above anyone in the world!" Alyosha cried out with tears in his voice. "I was not speaking to you as a judge, for I myself am the lowest of those who are under judgement. What am I as against her? I came here to seek my downfall, and said to myself, 'Let that come about! Let it!', and only out of faint-heartedness. But she, after five years of agony, has forgiven and forgotten everything and is now in tears the moment someone has come and spoken to her in all sincerity! As soon as the man who has wronged her turns up and sends word to her, she forgives him everything, and hastens joyfully to him, and she'll take no knife with her, I feel sure! No, I'm not made of such stuff. I don't know whether you are, Misha, but what I know for certain is that I'm not! That's the lesson I've been taught today, right now— Her love has given her a stature higher than ours— Did you ever hear from her what she's just told us? No, you didn't, for had you done so, you would have understood everything long ago—and the other woman, the one whose feelings she hurt the day before yesterday, should forgive her too! And she will when she learns everything—and learn it she will— This is a soul that is not yet at peace with itself, and calls for compassion— It may hold some treasure—"

Alyosha stopped, his voice failing him. Notwithstanding his sense of resentment, Rakitin gave him a look of surprise: never had he expected such an outburst from the mild Alyosha.

"How well you plead her cause! Have you actually fallen in love with her? Why, Agrafena Alexandrovna, you've made quite a conquest—our pietist is really in love with you," he exclaimed with a coarse laugh.

Grushenka raised her head from the cushion and looked at Alyosha, a radiant smile suffusing her tear-swollen face.

"Leave him alone, Alyosha, my sweet angel. You can see the kind of person he is. He isn't worth talking to. I was on the point of apologising to you, Mikhail Ossipovich," she said addressing Rakitin, "for having been so rude to you, but I've changed my mind again. Come over here, Alyosha, and sit down next to me," she said, motioning to him and looking him joyously in the face. "Like that: sit down here and tell me (she took him by the hand and looked smilingly into his eyes), tell me: do I love that man, or not—I mean the man who wronged me—do I love him or not? As I lay here in the dark before you came, I kept questioning my heart on that score. Decide for me, Alyosha, for the time has come: it shall be as you say. Should I forgive him or not?"

"But you've forgiven him already," said Alyosha with a smile.

"I have, indeed," said Grushenka meditatively. "How vile my heart is! I drink to that vile heart of mine!" and she suddenly snatched a wineglass from the table, emptied it at a gulp, raised it and dashed it on the floor where it tumbled into fragments. A hint of cruelty flashed into her smile.

"But perhaps I haven't forgiven him yet," she said in a kind of menacing tone, dropping her eyes and seeming to be talking to herself. "Perhaps my heart is only making itself ready to forgive. I shall have to grapple with it yet. You see, Alyosha, I've grown terribly used to my tears during these five years— Perhaps it's the wrong done to me that I actually love, and not that man!"

"Well, I wouldn't like to be in his skin!" Rakitin hissed.

"And you won't, Rakitin. You'll never be. You'll be my shoemaker, Rakitin. I'll use you for that purpose. You'll never get the likes of me—neither will he, perhaps—"

"Won't he? Then why are you all prinked up?" Rakitin sneered.

"Don't rebuke me for my dress, Rakitin, for you don't yet know what's going on in my heart! If I choose to, I'll tear it off at once, this very minute!" she shrilled. "You don't know why I've put this dress on, Rakitin! Perhaps I'll say when I meet him: 'Have you ever seen me looking like this before?' After all, I was a thin and consumptive-looking cry-baby of seventeen when he left me. I'll sit down by his side, fascinate him and get him all worked up. 'You see what I'm like now,' I'll say. 'Well, there's nothing more you'll be getting—there's many a slip 'twixt the cup and the lip, you know!' Perhaps that accounts for the dress, Rakitin," she concluded with a malicious laugh. "I'm unruly and wild, Alyosha, I'll tear off this finery, maim myself, destroy my beauty, scorch my face and slash it with a knife, and turn beggar. If I choose, I won't now go anywhere or to anybody; if I choose, I'll return to Kuzma, tomorrow, all the gifts he has ever given me and all his money and become a charwoman for the rest of my life!— You don't think I won't do that, Rakitin—that I wouldn't dare?— But I will, I will! I'm capable of doing that rightaway—only don't exasperate me—I'll send that man about his business with a flea in his ear—he'll never win the likes of me!"

She screamed out the last words hysterically, but again broke down, hid her face in her hands and buried it in a cushion, again shaking with sobs. Rakitin rose to his feet.

"It's time to leave," he said. "It's late as it is, and we won't be admitted into the monastery."

Grushenka jumped up from the sofa.

"Surely you're not leaving, Alyosha?" she cried in mournful astonishment. "What are you doing to me now? You've stirred up my feelings, tormented me, and now I'm again to be left alone all night!"

"He can't very well spend the night here with you, can he? Though he can if he wants to. I can go alone!" said Rakitin caustically.

"Keep your mouth shut, you spiteful fellow," Grushenka shouted at him in a fury. "You've never spoken to me as he has now done."

"What has he said that's so special?" Rakitin asked irritably.

"I can't say, I really don't know, but it has gone straight to my heart; he's wrung my heart—he's been the first, the only one, to take pity on me—that's what he's done! Why didn't you come sooner, my angel?" she cried falling on her knees before him as though in a frenzy. "All my life long, I've been wait-

46

ing for someone like you; I knew that someone like you would come and forgive me. I felt sure that I, too, would be loved, however vile I may be, and not only for shameful things!—"

"What is it I've done for you?" Alyosha replied, bending over her with a gentle smile and tenderly taking her by the hands. "I've only given you an onion, just a tiny little onion, and nothing more, nothing more!"

He burst into tears as he said this. At that moment, there was a sudden commotion in the passageway—somebody had entered the hall. Grushenka jumped up as though terribly frightened. Fenya came running noisily into the room.

"Mistress, dear mistress, the messenger has come!" she exclaimed joyfully, quite out of breath. "There's a *tarantass* for you from Mokroye, a troika driven by Timofei the coachman. The horses are being changed— A letter, a letter, ma'am, there's a letter for you."

She was holding a letter in her hand, and kept waving it in the air as she spoke. Grushenka snatched the letter and took it closer to the candle. It was merely a brief note of several lines, which she read in an instant.

"He's calling me!" she cried, her face pale and contorted in a rueful smile. "He's whistled—so I must go crawling back like a whelp!"

But it was only for an instant that she stood in indecision; then the blood rushed to her head and suffused her cheeks.

"I'm off!" she suddenly cried out. "Five years of my life! Good-bye! Good-bye, Alyosha, my fate is sealed—Leave me, leave me now, all of you, so that I'll never set eyes on you again!— Grushenka is flying off to a new life— Don't think badly of me either, Rakitin. I may be going to meet my death! Phew, I feel as though I was drunk!"

She left them suddenly, and ran into her bedroom.

"Well, she can't be bothered with us now," Rakitin snarled. "Let's go, or else we'll be hearing more of that caterwauling. I'm sick and tired of all these tearful outcries—"

Alyosha let himself be led out unresistingly. In the courtyard stood a *tarantass*; the horses were being unharnessed, and some men were fussing about to the light of a lantern. A fresh troika were being led in through the open gateway. No sooner had Alyosha and Rakitin descended the front steps than the bedroom window was flung open and Grushenka called out to Alyosha in a ringing voice:

"Alyosha, dear, give my best wishes to your brother Mitya and ask him not to think too badly of me, that thorn in his flesh. Tell him these words of mine: 'It is to a scoundrel that Grushenka has gone—not to a man of honour like you!' Add, too, that it was only for an hour, a single hour, that Grushenka loved him—so let him remember that short hour for the rest of his life. Say that Grushenka tells him to do so!"

She concluded in a voice full of tears. Then the window was shut with a slam.

"H'm, h'm!" Rakitin growled sneeringly. "She does brother Mitya in, and then tells him to remember it for the rest of his life. What a man-eater she is!"

Alyosha made no reply, as though he had heard nothing. He walked rapidly beside Rakitin, seeming to be in a terrible hurry, lost in thought and moving like an automaton. Rakitin felt a sudden twinge of pain as though a finger had touched an open wound. Things had not worked out as he had expected when he brought Grushenka and Alyosha together: something quite different from what he had been after had come about.

"He's a Pole—that officer of hers," he went on, but with some restraint, "but he's no longer an army officer. In fact he was an official in the customs in Siberia, somewhere on the Chinese border—probably some measly little Pole, I'm told he's lost his job. He's got wind of Grushenka being quite warm nowadays, so he's back again. That's all there is to it."

Again Alyosha seemed quite deaf, which made Rakitin cast off all restraint.

"Well, have you converted the Magdalene?" he asked with a spiteful snigger. "Returned the harlot to the path of righteousness? Cast out seven devils, eh? That's how the miracles we've been looking forward to have come to pass!"

"Do stop, Rakitin," Alyosha replied, stricken in spirit.

"So now you hold me in contempt for those twenty-five roubles, do you? Sold a true friend, so to speak. But you're no Jesus, and I'm no Judas."

"Goodness, Rakitin, I assure you I'd forgotten all about it," Alyosha exclaimed. "It's you who've brought the matter up—"

But Rakitin lost his temper completely.

"To hell with all and every one of you!" he screeched suddenly. "What on earth made me take you up! I want no more dealings with you. Be off on your own—go your own way!"

He turned abruptly into another street, leaving Alyosha alone in the dark. Alyosha left the bounds of the town and made for the monastery across the fields.

4.

Cana of Galilee

It was, for the monastery, a very late hour when Alyosha reached his destination, where he was admitted by the door-keeper, through a side entrance. It had already struck nine o'clock—an hour of general respite and rest after the anxieties of that day. Alyosha timidly opened the door and entered the cell of the *starets* where the coffin now stood. There was no one in the cell but Father Paissi, who was reading in solitude from the Gospels, over the coffin, and the young novice Porfiri, who, worn out after the discourse of the previous night and the disturbing happenings of the day, was sleeping the sound slumber of the young, on the floor of the adjacent room. Though he heard Alyosha come in, Father Paissi did not as much as look in his direction. Alyosha turned rightwards from the door towards the corner, fell on his knees and began to pray. His heart was full to overflowing, but in a vague kind of way, with no single sentiment standing out distinctly; on the contrary one succeeded another in a slow and even rotation. But there was sweetness in his heart and, strangely enough, that came as no surprise to him. Again he saw the coffin before him, the covered body of the man he held so dear, yet the tearful, gnawing and poignant heartache he had felt in the morning was no longer

49

there. On entering, he prostrated himself before the coffin as before a shrine, but a sense of joy, deep joy, shone in his mind and heart. One of the windows was open, and the air was cool and fresh. "So the odour must have grown stronger if they've decided to keep the window open," Alyosha thought, but even the thought of the odour of decay, which had but so recently seemed to him so awful and shameful, no longer aroused his previous sense of being lost and indignant. He began to pray quietly but soon felt he was doing so almost mechanically. Fragments of thoughts flashed through his mind, flared up like stars and died down again to yield place to others, but there reigned in his soul something complete, firm and comforting—he was conscious of that. At times, he began ardently to pray, for he yearned to give vent to his love and gratitude— But no sooner did he begin to pray than he suddenly went over to something else, sank into thought, and forgot all about both the prayer and what had interrupted it. He began to listen to what Father Paissi was reading but his fatigue made him doze off—

"*And the third day there was a marriage in Cana of Galilee,*" Father Paissi read, "*and the mother of Jesus was there. And both Jesus was called, and his disciples, to the marriage.*"

"Marriage? What can that be—a marriage—" was the thought that swept through Alyosha's mind like a whirlwind. "She, too, felt happiness—went to a feast— No, she took no knife with her—took no knife— That, too, was merely a 'pitiful' word— Well, 'pitiful words' have to be forgiven without fail. Pitiful words gratify the soul—without them people could not carry the burden of sorrow. Rakitin went off into the side-street. As long as he broods over the way he's been wronged, he'll always be going off into a side-street— But the road—the road is long and straight, lit up and as clear as crystal, with the sun at its end— Ah! What's being read here?"

"*And when they wanted wine, the mother of Jesus saith unto him, They have no wine,*" Alyosha heard.

"Ah, yes, I missed something there—I didn't want to, for I love that passage: it's Cana of Galilee, the first miracle— Ah, that miracle—that lovely miracle! It was not grief but men's joy that Christ visited when he worked his first miracle to help

50

create human joy— 'He who loves men will also love their joy—
That was what the dead man had constantly reiterated, it was
one of his main thoughts— One can't live without joy, Mitya
says— Yes, Mitya— Whatever is true and beautiful is always full
of all-forgiveness—that is also what he would say—"

"*Jesus saith unto her, Woman, what have I to do with thee?
mine hour is not yet come.*

"*His mother saith unto the servants, Whatsoever he saith
unto you, do it.*"

"Do it— Joy, what joy for some poor, very poor people—
Poor they were, of course, if they had no wine even for a wedding—The historians all say that the people settled about Lake
Gennesaret were among the poorest of the poor—And another
great heart, that of another great creature, his Mother, who was
there at the time, knew that it was not for his great and awesome sacrifice alone that he had descended: his heart was open
also to the simple and artless merriment of obscure creatures,
obscure and untutored, who had so warmly invited him to their
humble wedding. 'Mine hour is not yet come,' he had said with
a gentle smile (the smile could not but be gentle)— Indeed,
could it have been merely to create an abundance of wine at
weddings of the poor that he had descended to earth? Yet he
did go and do what she had asked him— Ah, he's going on with
the reading."

"*Jesus saith unto them, Fill the waterpots with water. And
they filled them up to the brim.*

"*And he saith unto them, Draw out now, and bear unto
the governor of the feast. And they bare it.*

"*When the ruler of the feast had tasted the water that was
made wine, and knew not whence it was, (but the servants
which drew the water knew,) the governor of the feast
called the bridegroom.*

"*And saith unto him, Every man at the beginning doth set
good wine; and when men have well drunk, then that which
is worse: but thou hast kept the good wine until now.*"

"But what can be happening? Why has the room suddenly
expanded so?— Ah yes—the marriage—the wedding—of course.
And here are the wedding guests, the bride and the bridegroom

and the merry-makers and—but where is the wise ruler of the feast? But who can that be? Who? The walls are receding again—Who is the man rising to his feet from the festive table. Why—Can he really be here too? But he's laid out in his coffin!—Yet he is here—he's stood up and sees me; he's coming over here—Good Lord!"

Indeed, it was to him, to him that he was coming up—a wisp of an old man, his face criss-crossed with wrinkles, joyous and laughing softly. The coffin was no longer there and he was dressed just as the previous day when he had been sitting there, with the callers gathered about him. His face was uncovered, the eyes shining. Could it have come to pass that he, too, was present at the feast, having been invited to the wedding at Cana of Galilee?

"Yes, my dear boy, I've also been called—called and chosen," the mild voice was saying above him. "Why do you keep in the background where you can't be seen? Come and join us too."

It was his voice indeed, the voice of the *starets* Zossima—Who else could it be; he was calling him. The *starets* held out a hand to help Alyosha, who rose from his knees.

"We are making merry," the wizened old man went on. "We're drinking wine that is new, the wine of a new and great joy. Do you see how numerous the guests are? Here are the bridegroom and the bride, as well as the wise ruler of the feast. He's tasting the new wine. Why are you looking at me in such surprise? I've made the offering of an onion; that's why I, too, am here. There are many here who have given away only an onion, a single little onion—What are our acts worth? And you, my quiet and meek boy, you, too, were able to pass an onion on to a woman in sore need. Set about your mission—begin it, my dear and meek boy! Can you see our Sun—do you see him?"

"I'm afraid—I dare not lift my eyes," Alyosha whispered.

"Fear him not. He is awesome in his majesty, terrible in his eminence, but infinitely merciful. He has become like one of us out of his love, and joins us in the merry-making, turning water into wine, so that the rejoicing of the guests may not be cut short. He is expecting fresh guests, and constantly calling new ones, and that for joy everlasting. Look, new wine is being brought—you can see them bringing the vessels—"

Something was aflame in Alyosha's heart, filling it to the point of pain; tears of ecstasy were gushing from his soul— He stretched forth his hands, cried out, and awoke.

Again before him was the coffin, the open window, and the low-keyed, measured and impressive reading of the Gospels. But Alyosha was not listening to what was being read. Strangely enough, he had fallen asleep as he knelt, but he was now standing; as though he had been jerked to his feet, he took three firm steps towards the coffin. His shoulder even brushed against Father Paissi but he was not aware of it. Father Paissi looked up briefly from the book but at once turned his gaze away, realising that something strange was happening to the youth. For half a minute, Alyosha kept his eyes fixed on the coffin, and the covered dead man as he lay still and stretched out, an icon on his breast and the cowl, with its eight-pointed cross, on his head. He had just heard his voice, which was still ringing in his ears. He was still listening, expecting more to come—but suddenly he turned on his heel and left the cell.

He did not pause on the porch but rapidly descended the steps. Brimful with rapture, his spirit thirsted after untrammelled freedom and spaciousness. High overhead was the boundless firmament with its host of softly twinkling stars. From the zenith to the horizon stretched the two faintly luminous bands of the Milky Way. The earth below was wrapped in the cool stillness of the night. Gleaming against the sapphire-blue sky were the white towers and golden cupolas of the cathedral. The luxuriant flowers of autumn were slumbering till morn in their beds. The hush on earth seemed merged with that of the heavens, the mystery of one blending with that of the other— Alyosha stood wide-eyed and suddenly fell prone onto the ground.

He knew not why he was embracing the earth and was unaware of the cause of his irresistible yearning to keep on kissing it, but he yielded to the urge, weeping and sobbing, watering it with his tears and vowing vehemently to love it for ever and ever. "Water the earth with the tears of your gladness and love those tears," the words resounded in his soul. Wherefore his tears? Oh, in his ecstasy he was weeping even over those stars that were shining down to him from the depths of space, and "was not ashamed of that ecstasy". It seemed as though all the threads from all those countless worlds of God's had all at once come together in his soul, which was tremulous as it "came into contact with other worlds". He longed to forgive all men and for all things and to beg forgiveness—no, not for himself but for others, for all and everything, for "others are begging for me too"—this re-echoed in his soul. With every passing moment, he clearly felt—almost tangibly—that something firm and unshakable, like the very vault of heaven, had entered his soul. It was as though some idea had become installed in his mind for the rest of his days, eternally. He had fallen to the ground a weak youth, but rose from it a resolute fighter for the remainder of his life: he suddenly realised and felt it, at the very onset of his ecstasy. Never afterwards, never for the rest of his life, could Alyosha forget that moment. "Someone visited my soul at that hour!" he would say afterwards with firm faith in the truth of his words—

Three days later he left the monastery in accordance with the behest of his departed *starets,* who had bid him to "go forth into the world".

BOOK EIGHT

Mitya

1.

Kuzma Samsonov

Meanwhile, Dmitri Fyodorovich, to whom, before setting forth on a new life, Grushenka had instructed Alyosha to convey her farewell greetings, telling him always to remember the short hour of her love for him, was in total ignorance of what she had gone through. He, too, was in a state of the utmost perturbation, full of care. During the past two days, he had been in such an unimaginable state that he might very well have contracted brain fever, as he himself later asserted. Alyosha had failed to locate him the morning before, and Ivan had been unable to arrange for a meeting at the tavern on the same day. At Dmitri's bidding, his landlord and landlady were keeping his whereabouts a secret. During those two days, he had been literally dashing from place to place, "grappling with my fate and trying to save myself", as he later put it; he had even left town for several hours on some pressing matters, though he was terrified of losing sight of Grushenka even for a moment. All this transpired afterwards in every detail and was borne out by documentary evidence, but we shall, for the time being, confine ourselves to the barest essentials of those two dreadful days of his life which preceded the dire disaster that was to overwhelm him.

Though Grushenka had, it is true, loved him truly and sincerely for a brief hour, she also at times tormented him with merciless cruelty. The worst of it was that he could never tell what her intentions were; to ascertain them by kindness or force was out of the question: she was quite unyielding, and would only have bridled up and turned away from him completely— that was something he was clearly aware of at the time. He had a well-grounded suspicion that an inner struggle was taking place within her, and she was in a state of the utmost irresoluteness, trying without success to arrive at some decision, which was why he felt, not without reason and with a sinking heart, that there were moments when she simply hated him and his passion. That might have been so, but he could not make out what was weighing on Grushenka's mind. As far as he was concerned, the agonising option was whether it was to be he, Mitya, or Fyodor Pavlovich, his father. At this point, incidentally, an unquestionable fact should be noted: he was quite certain that his father would without fail ask Grushenka to become his lawful wife (if he had not already done so) and he did not for a moment believe that the old lecher hoped to get off with only three thousand roubles. That was what Mitya had inferred with his knowledge of Grushenka and her nature. He therefore felt at times that all her distress and indecision arose only from her not knowing which of the two she should choose, and which of them would be more to her advantage. Strange to say, he gave no thought, during those days, to the impending arrival of the "officer", that is to say, the man who had had so ominous an influence on Grushenka's life and whose return she was awaiting with such fear and trepidation. True, she had made no mention of his arrival during the last few days. However, he had learnt from Grushenka herself of a letter she had received a month previously from her seducer, and knew something of its contents. At a moment of ill temper, she had let him see the letter but, much to her surprise, he had not attached the least value to it. It would be hard to say why: perhaps simply because, oppressed by the ugliness and the horror of the struggle he was waging with his own father for this woman, he was incapable of imagining anything more terrifying or dangerous to him, at least at the time. He simply did not believe that a suitor would suddenly appear from the blue after an absence of five years; still less did he believe he would arrive soon. Indeed, the "officer's" first letter, which was shown to Mitya, spoke most vaguely of the new rival's coming: the letter was ambiguous, very florid and full of nothing but effusive sentiments. Grushenka, it should be noted, had withheld from him the concluding lines of the letter, which spoke somewhat more definitely of his returning. Besides, as Mitya later recalled, he had, at that moment, discerned on Grushenka's face a certain involuntary and proud disdain for the message from Siberia. Grushenka, however, did not go on to tell Mitya anything of her further communications with this new rival. So Mitya had gradually come to completely forget the officer's existence. His sole thought was that, come what might and whatever turn the course of events would take, his impending and final clash with his father was at hand and had to be resolved first and foremost. He was all keyed up, expecting Grushenka's decision to come at any moment, and feeling sure it would be sudden and unpremeditated. What if she suddenly said to him, "Take me, I'm yours for ever"? That would clinch matters: he would snatch her up and at once carry her off to the end of the world. Oh, he would at once carry her off far away, as far away as possible—if not to the end of the earth, then at least to the furthermost end of Russia; he would marry her and settle down with her incognito, so that nothing would be known of them, here, there, or anywhere at all. Then, oh then, a quite new life would at once set in! That different, newly found and now "virtuous" way of life ("it must, without fail, be virtuous") was constantly in his thoughts: he yearned for it with a kind of frenzy. He was thirsting after that renascence and redemption. The loathsome morass he had sunk into by choice was past bearing, and, like very many in such a situation, he pinned his hopes on a complete change of environment: away from all these people, these circumstances, and the accursed place—then everything would be reborn and follow a new road! That was what he believed in and yearned for.

But that could come about only given the first, *the happy* solution. There was also another solution; he could envisage another outcome, but a terrible one. What if she suddenly said to him, "Go. I've just reached an understanding with Fyodor Pavlovich, and I'm marrying him. I don't need you—", and then—what would come about then, Mitya did not know, right to the very last, he did not know, and that must be admitted in all justice to him. He harboured no definite intentions, and was planning no crime. He was merely on the look-out, spying and agonising, yet he was preparing himself only for the first

57

and happy outcome of his dire problem. He even banished any other thought from his mind. But at this point there arose a quite different source of anguish, a circumstance quite new and extraneous, but just as formidable and even irresolvable.

For even were she to say to him, "I'm yours; take me away", how was he to do so? Where was he to find the money? It was just at this time that the allowance regularly doled out to him for so many years by his father was abruptly discontinued. Of course, Grushenka was well off, but Mitya displayed an access of fierce pride on this score: what he wanted was to take her away himself and begin a new life with her at his own expense, not at hers. The thought of taking her money never even occurred to him, the very idea causing him the utmost revulsion. I will not dilate on this or analyse the fact, but shall simply remark that such was his frame of mind at the moment. All this may have been caused indirectly and even subconsciously by his agonising qualms of conscience over the money he had misappropriated from Katerina Ivanovna: "I've acted the scoundrel with one of them, and now I'd again be a scoundrel with the other," he thought at the time, as he later acknowledged. "If Grushenka comes to hear of it, she'll have nothing to do with such a scoundrel!" So where was he to get the wherewithal, the fateful money? Without it, all was lost, and nothing would come about, "and all for the lack of the money—oh, the shame of it all!"

I shall run somewhat ahead: he may indeed have known where the money could be obtained, and perhaps even knew where it was to be found. I will not go into any details this time, for more will come to light later, but the main trouble was—and I shall say that, even if vaguely, at this point—that to get that money, to *have the right* to take it, he had first to return the three thousand to Katerina Ivanovna; otherwise, he decided, "I'm nothing but a pickpocket and a scoundrel, and I don't want to start a new life as a scoundrel." That was why he decided he would move heaven and earth, if necessary, to be able to return the three thousand to Katerina Ivanovna without fail, and *before anything else*. The decision had matured within him only, as it were, in the most recent hours of his life, that is to say, following his last meeting with Alyosha two days before, on the highway, on the evening Grushenka had insulted Katerina Ivanovna, when, on hearing Alyosha's account of the happening, he had acknowledged he was a scoundrel, and asked his brother to inform Katerina Ivanovna of it, "if that will in any way make things easier for her". It was on that very night, after parting with his brother, that he felt in his frenzy that it would even be better "to murder and rob somebody than fail to repay the debt to Katya". "I'd rather appear as a murderer and robber to my victim, confess to my crime in public, and be sentenced to penal servitude in Siberia than give Katya the right to say that I've deceived her, stolen her money and used it to make off with Grushenka and to begin a virtuous life! That's something I can't do!" Mitya said so, grinding his teeth, and had good reason to imagine at times that it would end in his falling ill with brain fever. Meanwhile, he continued to wage the struggle.

How strange it all was: one might have thought that, given such a decision, despair was the only recourse left open to him, for where was such money to be urgently obtained, particularly by one in such penury? Yet he kept hoping against hope that he would lay hands on the three thousand, that they would turn up somehow, fall from heaven, as it were. That is always the case with those who, like Dmitri Fyodorovich, spend their lives dissipating and squandering the money they come into, but have not the least notion how money is to be earned. A most fantastic turmoil of thoughts was seething in his mind right after he had parted with Alyosha two days ago, putting all his thoughts into disarray. It thus came about that he hit upon an utterly wild scheme. It is possibly in such situations that people of this kind see the most absurd and fantastic enterprises as highly feasible. He suddenly decided to call on the merchant Samsonov, Grushenka's protector, and propose a "plan" that would enable him to obtain the entire sum he sought. He had not the least doubt as to his "plan's" efficacy; only he was uncertain how Samsonov himself would look upon his artifice, were he to consider it apart from its business aspect. Though he knew the merchant by sight, he was not acquainted with him and had never even spoken to him. However, the conviction had long struck root in him that the old lecher, who practically had one foot in the grave, would not now object to Grushenka's turning respectable and marrying a "dependable" man. Not only would he raise no objections but actually wanted that to come about, and would be willing to help should the opportunity arise. Because of some rumours that had reached him, or some remarks dropped by Grushenka, he had inferred that the old man might prefer him to Fyodor Pavlovich as a husband for Grushenka. Many of my readers may think it showed a certain coarseness and lack of scruples in Dmitri Fyodorovich to count on such assistance and be prepared to accept his future wife from, so to speak, the hands of her protector. I shall merely remark that Mitya regarded Grushenka's past as something over and done with. That past evoked in him a sense of boundless compassion, and he resolved with all the ardour of his passion that the moment she told him that she loved him and would marry him a quite new Grushenka would at once appear and, together with her, a quite new Dmitri Fyodorovich, one already with no vices and full of every virtue: the two would forgive each other and turn over a new leaf. As for Kuzma Samsonov, he looked upon him as one who had exercised a fateful influence on Grushenka's remote past but had never been loved by her and—which was the main thing—was also "over and done with", so that he was practically non-existent. Besides, Mitya could not even regard him as a man, for it was common knowledge in the town that he was nothing but a decrepit wreck whose relations with Grushenka were, so to say, simply paternal, quite different from what they had been, and for quite a time—almost a year in fact. In this, Mitya was displaying a good deal of artlessness, for, with all his vices, he was a very simple-hearted man. Because of this simplicity of mind, he was, incidentally, quite certain that old Kuzma, with one foot in the grave, must feel sincere repentance for his past with Grushenka, and that she now had no protector or friend more devoted than this already harmless old man.

On the day following his talk with Alyosha in the field, after which Mitya had spent an almost sleepless night, he called at the Samsonov house at about ten in the morning and asked the servant to announce him. The house was old and gloomy, very spacious and on two storeys, with outhouses and a lodge in the courtyard. The occupants of the ground floor were Samsonov's two married sons and their families, his elderly sister, and his spinster daughter. In the lodge lived his two shopmen, one with a large family. The shopmen, together with the children, were cooped up in their close quarters, but the old man lived alone on the upper storey and would not permit even his daughter, who attended upon him, to live there; despite her long-standing shortness of breath, she had to dash upstairs to him at certain fixed hours and whenever he might call her. The upper floor contained a variety of reception and other such-like rooms furnished in the old-fashioned merchant style, with long and dreary rows of mahogany arm-chairs and chairs along the walls, cut-glass chandeliers shrouded in dust-covers, and gloomy pier-glasses. All these rooms were never used and were quite uninhabited, for the old man lived cooped up in a single small room, actually his bedroom, which was far removed from the others; there he was attended upon by an old domestic with kerchiefed hair, and a "lad" stationed on a long chest in the passageway. The old man could hardly walk because of his swollen legs, and on the rare occasions he did rise from his leather arm-chair it was with the aid of the old domestic who, supporting him under the arms, would conduct him a couple of times up and down the room. He was severe and taciturn even with this old woman. Told that the "captain" had called, he ordered that the visitor should be informed he was not at home. However, Mitya insisted on being announced a second time, at which Samsonov questioned the lad closely: what the caller looked like and whether he was drunk and disorderly. Learning that Mitya was sober but refused to leave, he told the lad to repeat he was not at home. Then Mitya, who had anticipated all this and purposely brought pencil and paper along with him, sent a message upstairs, consisting of a single clearly written line: "On a most urgent matter closely affecting Agrafena Alexandrovna." After some thought, the old man ordered that the caller be admitted into the reception room, and sent the old woman downstairs to summon his younger son upstairs at once, without a word. The latter, a man over six foot tall and immensely strong, who shaved his beard and dressed in the European fashion (the father wore the traditional caftan and a beard) appeared immediately and without a word. The entire household stood in awe of the old man. It was not out of fear of Dmitri that the father had sent for the young man, for he was far from timid by nature, but just in case he might need a witness. Accompanied by the servant lad and by his son, who supported him by an elbow, he finally waddled into the reception room. He was probably motivated by some keen sense of curiosity. The reception room where Mitya awaited him was a vast, gloomy and oppressive affair, with a gallery and two tiers of windows on either side, walls of imitation marble and three huge chandeliers wrapped in dustcovers. Mitya was sitting on a little chair at the entrance door, awaiting his fate in nervous impatience. When the old man appeared from the opposite door some twenty yards from Mitya, the latter jumped up from his chair and stepped out towards him with his long military stride. He was smartly dressed, his frock-coat buttoned up, his black-gloved hands holding a top-hat, exactly as he had been when he had called on the *starets* at the monastery three days before to attend the family meeting. The old man awaited his approach, standing with severe and dignified mien, so that Mitya at once felt he was being closely scrutinised as he drew near. Mitya was taken aback by Samsonov's face, which had swollen immensely of late: the lower lip, which had always been thick, was now quite pendulous, for all the world like some monstrous crumpet. He bowed to the caller in dignified silence, motioning him to an arm-chair at the sofa, on which he slowly lowered himself opposite Mitya, leaning on his son's arm and groaning painfully. Seeing his painful exertions, Mitya at once experienced some remorse and a regret born of delicacy: he felt deeply conscious of his insignificance as against so dignified a personage, whom he had put to so much trouble.

"What is your business, sir?" the old man asked slowly and distinctly, in a severe but civil tone, when he had finally seated himself.

Mitya started, jumped up somewhat from his chair, and then

resumed his seat. Then he burst into loud, rapid and nervous speech, gesticulating in an absolute frenzy. He had obviously reached the end of his tether, standing on the brink of ruin, clutching at the last straw, and ready even to end his life in case of failure. This was something old Samsonov at once realised, though his expression remained unchanged and as cold as a statue's.

"Most esteemed Kuzma Kuzmich, you've probably heard more than once of my differences with my father, Fyodor Pavlovich Karamazov, who has robbed me of the inheritance left to me by my mother—it's common knowledge in all the neighbourhood—it's the talk of the town here, where people simply won't mind their business— Besides, it might also have reached your ears from Grushenka—I mean, from Agrafena Alexandrovna—whom I hold in the highest esteem—" It was in such tones that Mitya began, and then stopped just as abruptly as he had begun. We shall not reproduce his speech verbatim but shall merely set forth its overall tenor. The gist of the matter, he went on, was that, some three months previously, he, Mitya, had with express intent (he used these very words, instead of saying "had found it necessary") consulted a lawyer in the gubernia city—"a distinguished lawyer, sir, Pavel Pavlovich Korneplodov—you may have heard the name. A noble brow, and the mind almost of a statesman—knows you, too, sir—and spoke of you in the highest terms"—Here Mitya stopped short a second time. However, such hiatuses could not check him: he would at once negotiate them, and gallop on and on. After questioning Mitya closely and examining the documents submitted (of such documents Mitya expressed himself hurriedly and in vague terms), that selfsame Korneplodov had offered the opinion that a suit could certainly be brought for the village of Chermashnya, which should be his property from his mother, and thereby put that old blackguard's nose out of joint, "for not all avenues have been blocked, and justice might yet find some loop-hole". In short, there was good reason to expect an extra six or even seven thousand roubles from Fyodor Pavlovich, since Chermashnya was worth at least twenty-five thousand, or rather twenty-eight thousand in fact—"no, thirty thousand, thirty thousand, Kuzma Kuzmich, but fancy, I've been unable to extract even seventeen thousand from that cruel man!" Well, he, Mitya, had given up the matter at the time, for he knew nothing of law, but, on returning home, he had been dumbfounded by a counter-claim presented against him (at this point Mitya again grew confused and made another plunge); "so won't you, excellent Kuzma Kuzmich, take over all my claims on that monster for a payment of only three thousand—You don't stand to lose anything, I assure you of that on my honour, on my honour, sir; quite on the contrary, you can make a profit of six or seven thousand, instead of three—" Above all, Mitya wanted the matter clinched that very day. "I'll have it arranged with a notary, or in some other way—" he went on. "In a word, I'm ready to do anything, let you have all the documents you ask for, and sign anything—we could have the paper drawn up at once, this very morning if possible— You could let me have the three thousand—for there's no other man of substance to compare to you in this town—and in that way, you would save me from—in short, you would save my poor head for a most honourable, a most high-minded act, if I may say so—for I harbour the most honourable sentiments for a certain person you know only too well and show paternal concern for. I would not have called if it were not paternal. And so, three lives have clashed, if I may put it that way, for fate is an awesome thing, Kuzma Kuzmich! One must be realistic, Kuzma Kuzmich, realistic indeed! Since you've long been out of the running, only two rivals now remain. I may be putting it somewhat bluntly, but I'm no man of letters. It's a choice between me and that blackguard. And it's for you to make the choice. It all rests with you—three fates and two lots to cast— Forgive me, I'm not making myself very clear, but you understand—I can see that from your esteemed eyes— But if you've failed to understand, then I'm a dead man—that's how it is!"

Mitya cut short his absurd speech with the words "that's how it is!" and, jumping up from his seat, awaited an answer to his inept proposal. As he spoke the concluding sentence, he suddenly and hopelessly realised that his scheme had fallen through, and, what was worse, he had been talking sheer nonsence. "How strange it is! Everything seemed quite all right on the way here, but now it's all claptrap!"—such was the thought that suddenly crossed his forlorn mind. While he was speaking, the old man sat motionless, watching him with an icy expression in his glance. After keeping him in suspense for a full minute, Kuzma Kuzmich said in a most decisive and chilling tone:

"You will excuse me, but we do not conduct that kind of business."

Mitya suddenly had a sinking feeling in his heart.

"But what am I to do now, Kuzma Kuzmich?" he muttered with the ghost of a smile. "It's all up with me—don't you think so?"

"You must excuse me, sir—"

Mitya remained standing, his stare fixed on Samsonov, and he suddenly discerned a slight movement on the latter's face. He gave a start.

"You see, sir, that's really not our line of business," the old man said slowly. "It means court hearings and lawyers—no end of trouble! But if you like, there's a man you might see—"

"Good Lord, who can it be? You give me fresh hope, Kuzma Kuzmich," said Mitya, his voice suddenly faltering.

"He's not a local man, and he's away just now. He is of the peasants and deals in timber—goes by the nickname of Lurcher. For the past year he's been bargaining with your father over your stand of timber at Chermashnya, but they can't come to terms over the price—you may have heard. He's back again and staying at the priest's in Ilyinskoye, some twelve versts from Volovya Station. He's written to me for advice in the matter—I mean that timber. Fyodor Pavlovich wants to go and see him himself. Well, if you get there before your father does and make Lurcher the same offer, he may well—"

"A splendid idea!" Mitya put in enthusiastically. "The very man—it will suit him fine! He's out to buy, but the price is too high, and here he's getting the title deed to the property—ha, ha, ha!" And Mitya went off into his abrupt and wooden laugh so unexpectedly that even Samsonov gave a start.

"How can I thank you, Kuzma Kuzmich?" cried Mitya effusively.

"There's nothing to speak of," said Samsonov, inclining his head.

"But you don't realise you've saved me! Oh, I had a feeling you were the right man to approach— And, now, off to the priest!"

"You don't have to thank me, sir."

"I'm off straight away. I'm afraid I've done your health no good, but it's something I'll never forget—a Russian is saying that to you, sir, a R-russian!"

"To be sure."

Mitya was about to seize the old man's hand to shake it but an ominous gleam came into the latter's eyes. Mitya withdrew his hand, but at once reproached himself for his suspiciousness. "He must be getting tired"—the thought flashed through his mind.

"It's for her sake! For hers, Kuzma Kuzmich! Don't you realise it's for her sake!" he suddenly cried out, then bowed, turned on his heel and, without looking back, strode out of the room with the same long and military stride. He was trembling with delight. "It all seemed doomed until my guardian angel stepped in," was the thought that ran through his head. "And if so businesslike a man as Samsonov (a most worthy old gentleman, and what deportment!) suggests such a course, then—it's sure to lead to success. I must rush off. I may be back before dark, or perhaps later, but the matter will be clinched. Surely the old man wasn't playing a joke on me?" Such were the impetuous thoughts that occurred to him as he made his way towards his lodgings; of course, he could imagine two alternatives: either the advice was most practical (coming from such a practical man), who had revealed much acumen and a knowledge of that Lurcher (what a strange name!), or else—or else the old man was making mock of him! Alas, the latter thought was the only correct one. Long, long afterwards, when disaster had descended, old Samsonov laughingly admitted that he had made a fool of the "captain". He was a spiteful, cold and sardonic man, who could harbour morbid dislikes. Whether it was the captain's effusiveness, or that "waster and spendthrift's" ridiculous conviction that he, Samsonov, could swallow the bait of his "plan", or jealousy of Grushenka, for whose sake that "whippersnapper" had applied to him with an absurd story to extract money from him—I cannot tell what it was that induced, the old man to act in the way he did; but at the moment Mitya was standing before him, with sinking heart and uttering incoherent exclamations that he was doomed—at that very moment the old man gave him a look of intense spite and decided to make a fool of him. When Mitya had left, Kuzma Kuzmich, his face pale with anger, turned to his son and instructed him to see to it that the pauper should never be admitted even into the courtyard, or else—

He did not finish his threat, but even his son, who had often witnessed his anger, started in fear. For a whole hour afterwards, the old man was shaking in fury, but by the evening, he had fallen ill and had the "leech" sent for.

2.

The "Lurcher"

So Mitya had to set out post-haste, though he did not possess a single copeck to pay for the horses. No, he did have two twenty-copeck coins, but that was all he had after so many years of prosperity! But at home he had an old silver watch which had long stopped running. He took it to a Jewish watchmaker, who kept a little shop in the market-place, and got six roubles for it. "More than I could have expected!" cried the overjoyed Mitya (whose rapture had not abated) and grabbing the six roubles, he made for home. There he augmented the sum with three roubles he borrowed from his landlord and the landlady, who were so fond of him that they willingly let him have it, though it was all the money in the house. The excited Mitya told them then and there that his fate was to be decided that very day and informed them, in hasty words of course, of practically the whole of the "plan" he had proposed to Samsonov, then of the latter's advice, his own hopes for the future, and so on and so forth. Even before that, he had kept them informed of many of his private affairs, which was why they regarded him as one of their *own circle,* a gentleman who was not at all prideful. Having thus collected the sum of nine roubles, Mitya had post-horses sent for to take him to Volovya Station. It was later recalled and established that "at noon of the day previous to a certain event Mitya did not have a single copeck and had to sell his watch to obtain some money and borrowed three roubles from the people of the house, all in the presence of witnesses".

I am taking note of the fact in advance, the reason for which will come to light later.

Though, as he set out for Volovya Station, Mitya was full of joyous hopes that he would at last bring "all these matters" to a successful close, fear was clutching at his heart: what would become of Grushenka in his absence? What if she were to decide that day to go to his father's? That was why he had gone off without telling her anything and had instructed his landlady not to disclose where he had gone should he be asked after. "I must—I simply must get back before dark," he kept repeating to himself as he was jolting along in the cart. "And I suppose I'll have to take that Lurcher man along with me—to draw up the deed of sale." Such were his eager expectations, though, alas, they were not fated to come about quite in accordance with his "plan".

In the first place, he was late because he took a rough country track from Volovya Station, which proved eighteen versts long instead of twelve. Secondly, he did not find the priest at home at Ilyinskoye: he had gone off to a village close by. By the time Mitya located him, travelling to that near-by village with the same tired horses, darkness was already falling. The priest, a timid and amiable-looking man, at once told Mitya that though Lurcher had originally put up at his house he was now at a place known as Sukhoi Poselok, where he would spend the night at the forester's cottage, for he was buying timber there too. He acceded, after some demur, to Mitya's urgent request to take him there and thus "save him, so to speak". His curiosity had evidently been aroused, but, unfortunately, he advised walking there since it was only a "little over" a verst away. Of course, Mitya at once agreed and set out with his long strides so that the poor priest almost had to run to keep pace with him. He was a very cautious little man, and not at all elderly. Mitya at once began to discuss his plans with him too, in excited and nervous tones, asking for advice in respect of Lurcher, and talking all the way. The priest listened with attention but was not forthcoming with advice. He was evasive in replying to Mitya's questions: "I wouldn't know—I really know nothing of such things—how can I know?" and so on. He grew alarmed when Mitya spoke of his differences with his father over his inheritance: he was dependent in some way on Fyodor Pavlovich. But he asked in surprise why Mitya called the peasant trader Gorstkin by the name of Lurcher, and obligingly explained that, though the man deserved his nick-name, he took offence when it was used, and should certainly be addressed as Gorstkin: "otherwise you can't do any business with him, for he won't even listen to you," the priest added in conclusion. Mitya somewhat hastily expressed surprise at this, explaining that Samsonov himself had called him by that name. On hearing of this circumstance, the priest at once changed the subject, though he would have done well to make his surmise known to Dmitri Fyodorovich, namely that if Samsonov had sent the latter to the peasant he had called Lurcher then he must have done so in jest, so there must be something suspicious in the matter. However, Mitya was in too much of a hurry to dwell on such "trifles". He pressed on hastily, and it was only on reaching Sukhoi Poselok that he realised they had walked not a verst or a verst and a half but a good three versts. This annoyed him greatly but he let the matter pass. They entered the cottage. One half of it was occupied by the forester, an ac-quaintance of the priest's, while the other and better half, entered through a passageway, was now occupied by Gorstkin. They entered it and lit a tallow candle. The place was overheat-ed. On a deal table stood a samovar that had already gone out and, by it, a tray with some cups, a half-empty bottle of rum, a partly drunk bottle of vodka and the remnants of some wheat bread. The visitor himself was lying stretched at full length on a bench, his head pillowed on his rolled-up overcoat; he was snoring stertorously. Mitya stood in perplexity. "Of course, he has to be awakened," he said agitatedly. "My business is too urgent. I've come here in such haste and I've got to hasten back today," but the priest and the forester stood in silence, without voicing any opinion. Mitya walked up to the sleeping man and set about waking him most energetically, but with no success. "He's drunk," Mitya thought, "so what am I to do? Good Lord, what am I to do?" In a fever of impatience, he suddenly set about tugging at the sleeping man's arms and feet, jolting him by the head, and pulling him up into a seated posture on the bench, yet all his exertions resulted in nothing but grunting noises and stream of violent and muttered oaths.

"You'd better bide your time," the priest said at last, "for he seems to be quite incapable."

"He's been drinking all day," the forester added.

"Good Lord!" Mitya exclaimed. "If you only knew how pressing the matter is and how desperate I am!"

"I think you'd better wait till the morning," the priest repeated.

"Till the morning? Good heavens, that's quite out of the question!" Driven by despair, he was on the point of again trying to waken the drunken man, but desisted, realising that his efforts would be in vain. The priest was silent, and the sleepy forester gloomy.

"What terrible tragedies the realities of life create for people!" Mitya cried in utter despair, drops of sweat running down his face. Availing himself of the opportunity, the priest observed, very reasonably, that even if the sleeping man could be awakened, his drunken state would still make him incapable of any coherent talk; "Your business is so important," he went on, "that you'd better put it off until the morning"– With a gesture of despair, Mitya expressed his agreement.

"I'll stay on here with a lighted candle, Father, and wait for the right moment. I'll begin as soon as he wakes up– I'll pay you for the candle," he said to the forester, "as well as for the night's lodging–you won't forget Dmitri Karamazov. But what about you, Father? Where will you sleep?"

"I'll be returning home, sir. I'll take his mare and drive

home," he said, pointing to the forester. "I must now bid you good-bye, and wish you every success."

So the matter was decided. The priest drove off, glad to be rid of the whole matter but uneasily shaking his head, wondering whether he should let his benefactor Fyodor Pavlovich Karamazov know early on the morrow of the curious happening, "or else", he thought, "he may take offence and cut off his favours". Scratching his head, the forester returned to his quarters in silence, while Mitya sat down on the bench to await the right moment, as he had put it. A sense of deep dejection enveloped his soul, like some thick fog—a deep and oppressive dejection! He sat in thought, but could not decide on anything. The candle was burning low, and a cricket was chirping; it was becoming unbearably close in the overheated room. With his inward eye he suddenly pictured the garden and the path at the bottom, a door furtively opening in his father's house, and Grushenka darting in through it— He jumped up from the bench.

"How tragic it all is!" he exclaimed, grinding his teeth and, walking mechanically towards the sleeping man, he studied his face. He was a lean, middle-aged peasant, with a very long face, curly light-brown hair, and a long, thin reddish beard. He was wearing a cotton blouse under a black waistcoat, from a pocket of which hung a chain to a silver watch. Mitya scrutinised the face with intense hatred, and for some reason or other he found the curly hair particularly odious. It was intolerably distressing that he, Mitya, who had come on such pressing business, was now standing over him, completely exhausted after so many sacrifices and such neglect of important matters, while that cad, "on whom all my fate depends, is snoring away for all he's worth, as though he's from some other planet. Oh, the irony of fate!" Mitya exclaimed, and losing all self-control, again frenziedly fell to rousing the intoxicated man, jostling and pushing him about, and even pummelling him, but he gave up his vain efforts after some five minutes and returned to his bench in helpless despair.

"How ridiculous it all is!" he cried, "and—how dishonourable!" he suddenly added for some reason. His head was beginning to throb awfully. "Shall I give it up and go away?"—the thought flashed through his mind. "No, I'll wait till the morning. I'll stay on expressly! After all, what did I come here for? Besides, I haven't got the fare, and the means to get away, so how am I to? Oh, the absurdity of it all!"

His headache was getting worse and worse. He sat there motionless, and gradually dozed off and fell asleep in his sitting posture. He must have been asleep for two hours or more, and was awakened by a headache so unbearable that he could have screamed. His temples were throbbing painfully and the crown of his head was aching; for a long time he could not make out where he was and what had been happening. At last he realised that the overheated room was full of fumes from the stove and that he might die of asphyxiation. Yet the drunken peasant still lay snoring; the candle was flickering out. With a shout, Mitya staggered out of the room into the passageway towards the forester's room. The man at once woke up, but, on learning that the other quarters were full of fumes, went to attend to the matter, albeit with strange unconcern, which surprised and annoyed Mitya.

"But he must be dead, quite dead—and then—in that case, what am I to do?" Mitya exclaimed in a frenzy.

They opened the door and the window, as well as the chimney damper, to get the flue working. Mitya brought a bucket of water from the passageway, first wetting his own head and then, finding some rag, dipped it in the water and applied it to the man's head. The forester still treated the matter with indifference and even contempt. Leaving the window open, he said gloomily, "It's all right as it is", and went back to bed, leaving Mitya the lighted iron lantern. For another half-hour Mitya attended to the gas-poisoned drunkard, moistening and changing the rag on his head. He was determined to sit up all night, but, utterly exhausted, he sat down for a moment to come to himself, but his eyes closed at once, he unconsciously stretched himself full length on the bench, and fell fast asleep.

It was dreadfully late when he woke up—about nine o'clock and the sun was shining bright in the two windows of the hut. On the bench sat the curly-headed peasant, fully dressed, and with a boiling samovar and another bottle of vodka before him. Yesterday's bottle stood empty and the new one more than half-empty. Mitya jumped to his feet, at once realising that the accursed peasant was drunk again, suddenly and irreversibly drunk. He glared at the man for some time, the man returning the gaze in crafty silence, with a kind of offensive composure and even contemptuous arrogance as it seemed to Mitya. He ran up to him.

"Excuse me—you see—I—I suppose you've heard from the forester here that I'm Lieutenant Dmitri Karamazov, a son of the old Karamazov whose timber you want to buy—"

"You're a liar!" the man suddenly said firmly and distinctly.

"What do you mean? Don't you know Fyodor Pavlovich Karamazov?"

"I've no idea who he is," said the peasant in a thick voice.

"He's the one you're bargaining with for a stand of timber—timber. Wake up and talk sense. Father Pavel from Ilyinskoye has brought me here— You wrote to Samsonov, who sent me here—" said Mitya in a choking voice.

"You're a liar!" the man repeated slowly and distinctly.

Mitya's heart sank into his boots.

"Goodness, I'm not joking! You may be in your cups, but surely you can talk and understand—otherwise—otherwise I'm quite at a loss!"

"You're a dyer!"

"Goodness, my name's Karamazov, Dmitri Karamazov, and I've come here with an offer—a most profitable one—regarding that timber."

The peasant was stroking his beard impressively.

"No, you've reneged the deal like the scoundrel you are. You're a scoundrel!"

"You're mistaken, I assure you!" cried Mitya, wringing his hands in despair. The man kept stroking his beard, and suddenly screwed up his eyes in a crafty expression.

"Now tell me this! Is there any law that permits underhand dealings? D'you hear? You're a scoundrel—d'you get that?"

Mitya retreated gloomily, and suddenly "something seemed

to strike me on the head", as he later put it. The truth flashed into his mind, "a light flared up and I realised it all". He stood dumbfounded, wondering how he, a man of some intelligence, could have landed in such a mess, become involved in such fool-hardiness for almost twenty-four hours, and wasting his time attending to that Lurcher man with a wet towel– "He's drunk, blind drunk, and he'll go on boozing for another week, so what's the use of waiting? And what if Samsonov sent me here on purpose? And supposing she– Good Lord, what have I done?"

The man sat there, watching him derisively. At any other time, Mitya could have killed the fool in a fit of fury, but he now felt as weak as a child. He walked quietly to the bench, donned his overcoat without a word and walked out. The fores-ter was not in his room, so he took some fifty copecks in small change out of his pocket and left it on the table to pay for the night's lodging, the candle and for the inconvenience he may have caused. As he left the hut, he could see nothing but forest all around. He struck out at random, not knowing which way to turn—right or left: in his haste on the evening before, he had paid no attention to the road. He did not feel vengeful towards anyone, not even to Samsonov. He strode aimlessly along the narrow woodland track with a lost feeling, the "idea" shattered, and he did not care whither he was going. A mere child could have overcome him, so suddenly weak did he feel in body and soul. He did somehow find his way out of the forest, only to see fields, bare after the harvesting, stretching as far as the eye could see. "What a dreary and deathlike view all around!" he kept repeating as he walked on and on.

He was saved by meeting an elderly merchant who was travel-ling along the rough track in a hired droshky. Mitya asked the way as it drew level with him, and learned that the passenger was bound for Volovya Station; after exchanging a few words, he agreed to give Mitya a lift there. They reached their desti-nation some three hours later. At Volovya Station Mitya at once ordered post-horse to drive to town. He suddenly realised that he was famished. While the horses were being harnessed, he had an omelette made for him, which he ate at once, as well as a thick slice of bread and some sausage, and then downed three glasses of vodka. Thus, fortified, he felt more cheerful and light-hearted. As he urged the driver to whip the horses into a spanking pace, a new and "irreversible" plan took shape in his mind as to how to obtain "that accursed money" that very day, before evening fell. "Just fancy—just fancy," he exclaimed contemptuously, "that a man's life can be ruined for want of a miserable three thousand! But I'll settle the matter today!" He might have felt quite cheerful again but for the constant thought of Grushenka and what may have happened to her. The thought of her pierced his heart every moment like a keen knife. They arrived at last and Mitya at once rushed off to see Grushenka.

3.

A Gold-Mine

That was the very visit Grushenka had spoken to Rakitin of with such terror. She had been expecting the "message" at the time and was very glad that Mitya had not been to see her on that day or the day before, hoping to God that he would not call until after her departure. Then he put in a sudden appearance. The rest we already know: to get rid of him, she at once persuaded him to see her to Kuzma Samsonov's, where, she said, she absolutely had to go to "do his accounts". When she was taking leave of him after he had taken her there, she made him promise to come for her after eleven to see her back home. Mitya, too, was pleased with this arrangement: "If she's at Kuzma's, she won't be going to Fyodor Pavlovich's—unless she's lying," he at once added. But he believed she was not lying. He was that kind of jealous man who, when he is away from the woman he loves, at once begins to think up all kinds of terrible things that may be happening to her, and how she is being "unfaithful" to him. But, when he hastens back to her, heart-broken and crushed, quite certain the worst has happened, and she has been unfaithful to him, at the first glance at her face—the woman's laughing, gay and affectionate face—he at once casts off all suspicion, his spirits soar again, and he reproaches himself in shamefaced delight for his jealousy. He rushed home after escorting Grushenka. Oh, there was so much to attend to that very day! But, at least, he felt a sense of relief. "Only I must find out at once from Smerdyakov whether anything happened last night, and whether by any chance she came to see Fyodor Pavlovich—damnation take it!"— That was the thought that flashed through his mind. So he had scarcely reached his quarters when jealousy began to stir again in his restless heart.

Jealousy! "Othello is trustful, not jealous," Pushkin observed, a remark which, even taken alone, testifies to our great poet's amazing insight. Othello's soul has simply been shattered and his entire outlook on life has become distorted because *his ideal has been destroyed.* But Othello will never resort to concealment, spying, or eavesdropping: he is a trustful man. The reverse is true: he had to be egged on, prodded and inflamed through extraordinary efforts to make him even suspect infidelity. Not so is the truly jealous character. One cannot possibly imagine the shame and the moral degradation a jealous man will tolerate without any qualms of conscience. And yet not all jealous men are sordid and vulgar of soul. Far from it: a most high-minded man, whose love is pure and most unselfish, may yet take to hiding under tables, bribing the vilest of people and putting up with the filthiest snooping and eavesdropping. Othello could never become reconciled to infidelity—he could forgive it but not become reconciled to it—though he was as gentle and innocent of soul as a babe. It is not so with the truly jealous character: it is hard even to imagine how much such people will tolerate, reconcile themselves to, and forgive! They will be the first to forgive—every woman knows that! The jealous man is capable of almost at once forgiving (of course, after a terrific scene) such things as almost proven infidelity, embraces and kisses he has himself witnessed, if, for instance, he can somehow be persuaded that it has been "for the last time", and that his rival will vanish from that hour on, depart to the end of the earth, or that he himself will carry her off to some place where that dreadful rival will never appear. That reconciliation will, of course, be short-lived because even if the rival has indeed vanished, he will invent another one on the morrow, and become jealous of him. What kind of love is it, it may be asked, that calls for such vigilance, and what is the worth of a love which has to be so carefully watched? That is something the really jealous character will never realise, though there are undoubtedly men of high principles among such jealous people. It is also noteworthy that those very noble-hearted people, while hiding in some closet to eavesdrop and spy, never feel any pangs of conscience at the moment, though they realise clearly enough in their "noble hearts" how low they have fallen of their own choice. Mitya's jealousy would vanish whenever he laid eyes on Grushenka, and for the moment he would become trustful and magnanimous, even despising himself for his evil sentiments. However, that merely meant that his love for her contained something far higher than he himself supposed, and not merely sensual passion, not merely the "curve of her body", he had told Alyosha of. But whenever Grushenka was away, Mitya at once began to suspect her of all the baseness and perfidy of infidelity. In this, he never felt any qualms of conscience.

And so jealousy seethed in him again. He had to make haste in any case. The prime object was to borrow at least a little money for the time being. Yesterday's nine roubles had all gone on travelling expenses, and, as is common knowledge, one cannot take a step unless one has the wherewithal. But, on his way back to town in the cart, he had, together with his new plan, given thought to how he could raise a short-term loan. He possessed a brace of fine duelling pistols complete with cartridges, and had never pawned them because he set such great store by them. He had long ago struck up a light acquaintance, at the Metropolis Inn, with a young civil servant who, he had learnt, was unmarried, well-to-do, and an avid collector of all kinds of weapons—pistols, revolvers and daggers, which he displayed on walls at his home; he would boastfully show them to friends, and was an expert in explaining how a revolver works, loads, fires, and the like. Without any ado, Mitya called on him and offered to leave the pistols with him for a deposit of ten roubles. The delighted civil servant tried to persuade him to sell them outright, which Mitya declined to do, at which the young man let him have the ten roubles, declaring that nothing could induce him to take any interest. The two parted on good terms. Mitya now hurried to get to the pergola bordering on his father's garden so as to summon Smerdyakov at the earliest opportunity. That was how it was established that, only three or four hours prior to a certain happening, of which more will be said anon, Mitya was penniless and had pawned a prized possession for ten roubles, while some three hours later, thousands of roubles were found on him— But I am running ahead somewhat.

At Maria Kondratievna's, Fyodor Pavlovich's next-door neighbour, he learnt the unexpected and disturbing news of Smerdyakov's illness. He heard of how the latter had fallen into the cellar and had an epileptic fit, this followed by the news of the doctor's visit and his father's anxiety. He also learnt with interest that his brother Ivan Fyodorovich had left for Moscow that very morning. "Then he must have driven through Volovya before I did," Dmitri Fyodorovich thought, but what worried him terribly was the news about Smerdyakov. "What am I to do now? Who will keep watch for me and keep me posted?" he thought. He began eagerly questioning the women whether they had noticed anything on the previous evening. They were fully aware what he wanted to learn and fully reassured him: no, there had been no callers; Ivan Fyodorovich had spent the night there, and everything was quite all right. Dmitri grew thoughtful, deciding that he would have to stand watch that night, but where? At his father's house or at the entrance to Samsonov's house? He would have to be on the look-out at both places according to circumstances, but meanwhile, meanwhile— The point lay in the new and fool-proof plan he had thought up during his return journey in the cart, and brooked no delay. He decided to devote an hour to the matter: "I'll settle everything within that hour," he thought. "I'll learn everything and then make first of all for Samsonov's to see if Grushenka's there, and come back here at once. I'll wait here till eleven, and then go to Samsonov's again to see her home." That was what he decided to do.

He dashed to his quarters, washed, combed his hair, brushed his clothes, got dressed and went to call on Madame Khokhlakov, on whom, alas, his "plan" hinged: he had made up his mind to borrow three thousand roubles from her. The main thing was that he had suddenly felt quite positive that she would accede to his request. It might perhaps seem strange that, in view of that certainty, he did not in the first place go to her, who belonged to his own social circle, instead of appealing to Samsonov, a man of an alien stamp, and one he did not even know how to speak to. The trouble, however, was that he had had practically no social contacts with the lady during the past month, theirs being a nodding acquaintance, and, besides, he was well aware that she could not tolerate him. The lady had taken a strong dislike to him from the very outset simply because he was affianced to Katerina Ivanovna, while she was, for some reason, dead set on the young lady throwing him over and marrying his brother Ivan Fyodorovich, who was "so charming, chivalrously refined, and with such excellent manners". As for Mitya's manners, she detested them. Mitya would even deride her and on one occasion expressed the opinion that she "is just as vivacious and brash as she is ill-educated". But, when he was being driven in the cart that morning, a most brilliant idea had occurred to him: "If she's so keen on my not marrying Katerina Ivanovna" (he knew she grew almost hysterical over the matter), "why shouldn't she lend me the three thousand for me to give up Katya and clear out for good? If some fancy idea enters the mind of some pampered society lady such as she is, she will spare no effort to achieve what she's after. Besides, she's so wealthy," Mitya argued. As for his "plan", it was the same as before, to wit, to offer his title deed to Chermashnya, but with no business inducement, as with Samsonov on the day before, with the prospect of doubling the initial outlay, but simply as seemly security for a loan. The more he elaborated his new idea, the more delighted Mitya felt with it, as was invariably the case with him whenever he took up some fresh initiative or arrived at some abrupt decision. His enthusiasm for any new idea bordered on the passionate. Nevertheless, a shiver of apprehension ran down his spine as he mounted the front steps of Madame Khokhlakov's house: it was only at that moment that he fully realised, this time with mathematical clarity, that this was his very last hope, failure leaving him no other choice in the world but "murdering and robbing someone for three thousand roubles". It was about half past seven when he rang the door-bell.

The beginning seemed auspicious—he was received with no delay as soon as he was announced. "Almost as though she was expecting me," was the thought that flashed through his mind. No sooner had he been shown into the drawing-room than the lady of the house came almost running in and declared she had been expecting him to call—

"Indeed, I've been expecting you! But you will agree I could never have even imagined you'd come. Yet you have come and you may well marvel at my instinctive feeling. All morning I felt certain you'd come today, Dmitri Fyodorovich."

"It certainly is remarkable, ma'am," said Mitya, awkwardly taking a seat, "but I've called on an important matter—one of the utmost importance to me, ma'am, to me alone and to nobody else, and I'm pressed for time—"

"I know you've come on some important business, Dmitri Fyodorovich, and this is not an instance of some presentiment, or some retrograde hankering after miraculous (you must have heard about the *starets* Zossima, I suppose?); this is simply a matter of mathematics: you could not avoid coming here after all that's happened to Katerina Ivanovna—you just couldn't, that was a mathematical certainty."

"One of the realities of life, ma'am, that's what it is! But you will allow me to explain—"

"Indeed, it's all part of the realism of life, Dmitri Fyodorovich. I'm all for realism now that I've learnt my lesson as far as miracles go. Have you heard of the death of the *starets* Zossima?"

"No, ma'am, this is the first time I've heard of it," said Mitya, somewhat surprised. Alyosha's image rose in his mind.

"It happened last night, and just imagine—"

"Madam," Mitya broke in, "the only thing I am capable of imagining is that I'm in a most desperate situation, and that, if you refuse to help me everything will go to rack and ruin, and I'll be the first to go. Forgive me the trite expression, but I'm all worked up and in a fever—"

"I know, I know you're in a fever. I know it all, and you could hardly be in any other state of mind, and, whatever you say, I know it all beforehand. I've long been giving thought to your future, Dmitri Fyodorovich, I've been watching and studying it— Oh, believe me, I'm an experienced doctor of the soul, Dmitri Fyodorovich."

"If you're an experienced doctor, ma'am, then I'm certainly an experienced patient," said Mitya with an effort to be affable, "and I have a feeling that, if you've been watching over my future, you'll help save it from ruin; if that is so, will you now permit me to set forth to you the plan I make so bold as to propose to you—and what I expect of you— I've come, ma'am—"

"You don't have to explain, that's of secondary consequence. As for help, you're not the first person I've helped, Dmitri Fyodorovich. You've probably heard of my cousin Mrs. Belmessov, whose husband was on the brink of ruin, rack and ruin, as you so characteristically put it, Dmitri Fyodorovich. Well, I advised him to take up horse-breeding, and he's simply prospering now. Have you any idea of horse-breeding, Dmitri Fyodorovich?"

"Not the slightest, ma'am—oh, not the slightest!" cried Mitya in nervous impatience, almost starting up from his seat. "I only entreat you, ma'am, to hear me out and let me have only two minutes of unbroken speech for me to first set everything forth to you, the entire project I've come here with. Besides, I'm pressed for time and in a terrible hurry!" Mitya cried out hysterically, feeling she would burst into speech again, and hoping to outshout her. "I've come here in a state of despair—sheer despair—to ask you for a loan, three thousand roubles, on good security, the very best, the firmest guarantee! Only let me explain—"

"That will come later, later!" Madame Khokhlakov said, waving a hand at him in her turn. "Indeed, I know in advance whatever you may say, I've already said so. You're asking for a loan, you need three thousand roubles, but I shall give you more, immeasurably more, I will save you, Dmitri Fyodorovich, but it is essential that you should follow my advice!"

Mitya almost jumped up from his seat again.

"Can you really be so kind, ma'am!" he cried in deep emotion. "Good Lord, you've saved me. You're saving a man from a violent death, from the pistol— My eternal gratitude—"

"I'll give you far more, infinitely more than three thousand!" cried Madame Khokhlakov, looking at the delighted Mitya with a beaming smile.

"Infinitely more? But I don't need so much. All that's necessary is that fateful three thousand, and for my part I've come to offer you firm security for that sum with boundless gratitude and I propose a plan which—"

"Enough, the matter is settled," said the lady, cutting him short with the virtuous jubilation of a benefactress. "I've promised to save you, and I will. I'll save you just as I saved Belmessov. What do you think of gold-mines, Dmitri Fyodorovich?"

"Gold-mines, ma'am! Why, I've never given them thought."

"But I've done that for you!—lots of thought. I've been keeping an eye on you for a whole month with that idea in mind. I've watched you a hundred times as you walked past, and kept saying to myself: that is the kind of forceful man they need at the gold-mines. I've even studied the way you walk and have made up my mind that you're a man who'll certainly find many gold-fields."

"From the way I walk, ma'am?" asked Mitya with a smile.

"Why not? One can tell from that, too. Can you deny that the way a man walks reveals his character, Dmitri Fyodorovich? That is borne out by the natural sciences. Oh, I've become a realist, Dmitri Fyodorovich. From this day on, after all that happened at the monastery, which has upset me so terribly, I've become an absolute realist, and I want to throw myself into practical matters. I'm cured. As Turgeniev has said, enough!"

"But, ma'am, what about the three thousand you so generously promised to lend me—"

"They will not pass you by, Dmitri Fyodorovich," Madame Khokhlakov interjected, "the money is as good as in your pocket, and not merely three thousand, but three million, Dmitri Fyodorovich, and in the immediate future! I'll tell you what you are to do: you'll locate the gold-mine, make millions, return here, become a public figure and guide us forward to good deeds. Is all this to be left to the Jews? You'll erect buildings and launch various enterprises. You'll help the poor, who will bless you. This is the railway age, Dmitri Fyodorovich. You'll win a reputation and be indispensable to the Finance Ministry, which is so hard up at present. The way the value of our paper rouble keeps dropping gives me no sleep at night, Dmitri Fyodorovich, people know little of me from that angle—"

"But ma'am, ma'am!" Dmitri Fyodorovich broke in with a kind of uneasy presentiment. "I shall perhaps make sure to take your advice, your wise advice, ma'am, and shall perhaps set out for those parts—the gold-mines—and call on you again to speak of such things—even many times—but at this moment the three thousand you so generously— Oh, how they would untie my hands, if only you could let me have the money today— You see I haven't an hour to lose—not a single hour—"

"Enough, Dmitri Fyodorovich, enough!" said Madame Khokhlakov, interrupting him emphatically. "The question is: are you setting out for the gold-mines, or aren't you? Is your mind made up? Answer with the utmost precision."

"I'll go but only later— I'll go wherever you want me to, ma'am, but at present—"

"Just a moment!" cried Madame Khokhlakov; jumping up from her seat, she ran to a magnificent bureau with an endless number of little drawers, which she began pulling out one after another, looking for something in the utmost haste.

"The three thousand," Mitya thought with bated breath, "and I'm to get it straightaway, without any security or formalities—oh, how ladylike! A wonderful woman! If only she were less talkative—"

"Here it is!" Madame Khokhlakov exclaimed joyfully, returning to Mitya. "Here's what I was looking for!"

It was a tiny silver icon on a cord, of the kind sometimes worn about the neck next to the skin, together with a cross.

"It comes from Kiev," she continued reverently, "from the relics of the martyred St. Barbara. Allow me to put it about your neck, with my blessing for a new life and new achievements."

Indeed she put the cord about his neck with the intention of inserting it under his dress. Greatly embarrassed, Mitya bent to help her, finally getting it under his necktie and shirt collar and on his chest.

"You can start out now!" said Madame Khokhlakov, resuming her seat with an air of gratification.

"I'm greatly moved, ma'am—I don't even know how to thank you for your kindly sentiments, but—if you only knew how pressed I am for time now!— The sum of money that I'm expecting so from your magnanimity— Oh, ma'am," Mitya exclaimed with sudden ardour, "if you're so kind to me, so touchingly magnanimous, you'll allow me to reveal—something you've known for some time—that I'm in love with another woman here— I've been false to Katya—to Katerina Ivanovna, I should say. Oh, I've behaved dishonourably, like a cad, to her, but I've fallen in love with somebody else—a woman, ma'am, you look down on perhaps, for you are probably in possession of all the facts, but I can't give her up on any account, which is why the three thousand—"

"Leave everything behind you, Dmitri Fyodorovich!" Madame Khokhlakov said, interrupting him with marked emphasis. "Everything, especially women. The gold-mines are your target, and you can't be taking any women along with you. Later, when you return rich and famous, you'll find yourself a girl after your own heart in the most elevated circles. She'll be a modern girl, educated and without prejudices. By that time the burgeoning woman's question will achieve maturity, and a new type of woman will emerge—"

"That's beside the point, ma'am, quite beside the point—" Mitya exclaimed, almost clasping his hands in supplication.

"It's very much to the point, Dmitri Fyodorovich, it's just what you need, what you're longing for unawares. I've no objection to the women's question of today, Dmitri Fyodorovich. The advancement of women and even their political involvement in the immediate future—such is my ideal. I'm the mother of a daughter, Dmitri Fyodorovich, and people know little of me in that capacity. I've written on the subject to the writer Shchedrin. I learnt so much from him, such a lot about woman's destiny that I sent him an anonymous letter of two lines last year. It reads: 'I embrace and kiss you, my dear author, for the woman of today; carry on the work." I added the signature "A Mother'. I was thinking of wording it "A Contemporary Mother', but on second thought I kept the first version because of its greater moral beauty, Dmitri Fyodorovich, and besides, the word contemporary would suggest the magazine *The Contemporary,* a bitter reminder to them in view of the present-day censorship— Goodness gracious, what's wrong with you?"

"But, ma'am," cried Mitya, finally jumping up and clasping his hands, in helpless entreaty, "you will reduce me to tears if you put off what you've so magnanimously—"

"Shed tears, Dmitri Fyodorovich, let them come! They spring from noble sentiments—you've such a long journey ahead of you! Your tears will give you solace; you'll return later and rejoice. You'll make a point of hastening back to me from Siberia to let me know of your joy—"

"But allow me to put in a word," Mitya bawled suddenly. "I beg you for the last time to tell me if you can let me have the promised sum today? If not now, when can I call for it?"

"What sum do you mean, Dmitri Fyodorovich?"

"The promised three thousand—that you magnanimously—"

"Three thousand? Do you mean roubles? Oh, no, I haven't got three thousand roubles," Madame Khokhlakov announced in a kind of mild surprise. This threw Mitya into a state of consternation—

"But you only just now—you said—you even declared the money was as good as in my pocket—"

"But no, you misapprehended me, Dmitri Fyodorovich. If that was your impression, you understood me incorrectly. I was speaking of gold-mines— True, I held out a promise of

85

more, infinitely more than three thousand, I recollect that now, but I had only a gold-mine in view."

"But what about the money? The three thousand?" Dmitri Fyodorovich exclaimed ineptly.

"Oh, if you had money in mind, I must tell you I haven't got any. I'm quite moneyless at the moment, Dmitri Fyodorovich. As a matter of fact I'm wrangling with my steward over money, and actually had to borrow five hundred roubles from Miusov some days ago. Indeed, I'm quite out of money. But you should know, Dmitri Fyodorovich, I wouldn't let you have any money if I had it. In the first place, I never lend money to anyone. Loans always end in quarrels. You're the last person I'd lend money to, and that out of love for you, a desire to save you; I wouldn't lend you any money because all you need is gold-mines—nothing but gold-mines, gold-mines!—"

"Damnation!" Mitya roared suddenly, bringing his fist down on the table with all his might.

"Oh, oh!" screamed the frightened Madame Khokhlakov, retreating hastily to the furthermost end of the drawing-room.

Mitya spat in disgust on the floor, and strode rapidly out of the room, out of the house, and into the darkness of the street! He walked as one possessed, beating his breast on the very same spot as he had done two days before, when he had last met with Alyosha on the road in the dark of evening. The significance of such blows *on that spot* and what he meant thereby—was, for the time being, a secret known to nobody in the world; he had not even revealed it to Alyosha. But it was a secret that spelt not only disgrace to him, but ruin and suicide, for he had made up his mind on that score should he fail to obtain the three thousand to pay his debt to Katerina Ivanovna and thus erase from his breast, "*from that very spot there*", the disgrace which he bore within it and which weighed so heavily on his conscience. All this will be fully explained to the reader in due course, but at that moment, when his last hope had vanished, this man, physically so strong, burst into sudden tears just like a child, after taking a few steps from the Khokhlakov house. In a state of stupefaction, he wiped his eyes with his fists as he walked on. Thus he reached the town square, and suddenly felt he had walked into something. There came a squeaking wail from an old woman he had almost knocked over.

"Lordie, you almost done me in! You should watch your step, you ruffian!"

"So it's you!" cried Mitya, who had recognised the old woman despite the dark. She was the elderly domestic who attended on Kuzma Samsonov, and at whose house he had noticed her only too well on the previous day.

"And who may you be, sir?" asked the old woman in quite a different voice. "I can't recognise you in the dark."

"You live at Samsonov's, don't you? You attend on him, eh?"

"Indeed I do, sir. I just ran over to Prokhorich's— But I don't seem to remember you."

"Tell me, my good woman, is Agrafena Alexandrovna at your place just now?" asked Mitya, beside himself with suspense. "I saw her to your house a short while ago."

"She did come, sir, but she stayed only for a while and then left."

"What? She left?" cried Mitya. "When was that?"

"Why, she left almost at once. She stayed for little more than a minute. Told the master a story that made him laugh and then ran off."

"You're lying, damn you!" Mitya screamed.

"Oh, oh!" the old woman shrieked, but Mitya had vanished. He hurried with the utmost despatch to the Morozov house, where he arrived a mere fifteen minutes after Grushenka had driven off to Mokroye. When the "captain" came dashing in, Fenya was sitting in the kitchen with her grandmother, the cook Matryona. She uttered a piercing scream on seeing him.

"What are you screaming for?" Mitya roared. "Where is she?" Without giving the terror-stricken Fenya time to answer, he suddenly fell down at her feet.

"Fenya, for the sake of our Lord Jesus Christ, tell me: where is she?"

"I don't know a thing, sir, nothing at all. I couldn't tell you even if you killed me," Fenya exclaimed in vehement denial.

"Why, you left together with her not long ago—"

"But she came back here!—"

"She didn't, sir. I swear by God that she didn't!"

"You're lying!" Mitya shouted. "I can tell from your fright where she's gone!—"

So saying, he dashed out, the terrified Fenya being glad to have got off so lightly, but she was well aware that things would have gone badly with her had he not been in such a hurry. But as he was leaving, he surprised Fenya and her grandmother by doing something quite unexpected. On the table stood a brass mortar with a pestle in it, a small brass pestle some seven inches long. On leaving, he had already opened the door with one hand when he suddenly grabbed the pestle with the other and thrust it into a side-pocket. Then he was gone.

"Good Lord!" cried Fenya, throwing up her hands. "He'll murder somebody!"

4.

In the Darkness

Where was he off to? Of course: "Where can she be except at Father's. She must have rushed there straight from Samsonov's, that's quite clear. All the intrigue, all the deception, is now obvious—" Such were the thoughts that went whirling through his mind. He did not make for Maria Kondratievna's yard, next to his father's. "No, I mustn't go that way—I really mustn't—that may raise the alarm—they'll tell on me at once and give me away— Maria Kondratievna's obviously party to the plot, so's Smerdyakov. They've all been bought!" He decided on another plan of action: he made a big detour about his father's house across the side-street, ran along Dmitrov Street and crossed the foot-bridge; that brought him into a deserted and uninhabited back-lane, with the wattle fence of a neighbour's kitchen garden on one side and, on the other, the tall and strong fence enclosing Fyodor Pavlovich's garden. There he chose a spot, evidently the same where, according to the story he knew so well, Smelly Lizaveta had once clambered over the fence. "If she was able to climb over it, I can do the same," was the thought that for some reason flashed through his mind. Indeed, he made a jump, grabbed hold of the top of the fence, pulled himself up vigorously and sat astride it. Close to the fence stood the bath-house, but from where he was he could see the lighted windows of the house. "Just what I thought: there's a light in the old man's bedroom, so she's there!" and he jumped down into the garden. Though he knew that Grigori was ill and so was Smerdyakov perhaps, so that there was nobody to hear him, he instinctively kept in hiding for a while, and then listened, with ears pricked. But there was a dead silence all around—a dead calm, as it happened, and without a breath of wind.

"And only the silence is whispering"—for some reason the line of poetry came to his mind. "But I do hope nobody heard me jump over the fence. Nobody seems to have, though." After standing still for a minute or so, he walked softly over the grass in the garden, skirting the trees and shrubs. His progress was slow and stealthy, and he listened intently to his every step. It took him about five minutes to reach the lighted window, below which, as he remembered, there were several tall and thick elder and guelder-rose bushes. The back-door into the garden, which was on the left-hand side of the house, was shut, as he made a point of verifying as he passed it. He finally reached the bushes and concealed himself behind them, with bated breath. "Now I'll have to wait," he thought. "Some time is needed for reassurance in case my footsteps have been heard and somebody is listening—only I mustn't cough or sneeze—"

He waited for a couple of minutes, but with pounding heart, almost choking at moments. "No, my heart won't stop throbbing, so I can't wait any longer." He was standing in the shadow of a bush lit up in front from the window. "The guelder-rose—how red are its hips!" he murmured, without knowing why. With noiseless steps, he stole up to the window and stood on tiptoe. He had a full view of all of his father's bedroom, a small affair divided into two parts by red screens, "Chinese", as Fyodor Pavlovich called them. "Yes, Chinese," flashed into Mitya's mind, "and Grushenka is behind them." He began to closely watch his father. He was wearing a new striped silk dressing-gown Mitya had never seen before, tied about with a tasselled silk cord. From under the collar of the dressing-gown there showed an expensive shirt of fine linen with gold studs. About his head was the same red bandage Alyosha had seen. "All dressed up," Mitya thought. Fyodor Pavlovich was standing not far from the window, apparently deep in thought. Suddenly, he pulled up his head with a jerk, listening attentively, but, hearing nothing, went up to the table, poured himself half a glassful of brandy from a decanter, and drank it. He then took a deep breath, again stood still for a while, walked absently to the pier-glass, raised somewhat, with his right hand, the red bandage from his forehead and began to examine the scars and bruises, which had not yet disappeared. "He's alone," Mitya thought, "in all probability, he's alone." Fyodor Pavlovich moved away from the mirror, turned suddenly towards the window and peered out, at which Mitya slipped into the shadow.

"Yet she may be there, behind the screen. Already asleep perhaps," he thought with a pang in his heart. His father turned away from the window. "He was looking for her through the window, so she can't be there. Why else should he be peering into the dark? It means he's consumed with impatience—" Mitya at once dashed to the window and looked in again. The old man was now sitting at the table, evidently quite dejected. Suddenly he propped his right elbow on the table, cupping his cheek in the palm of his hand. Mitya watched him closely.

"He's alone, quite alone!" he repeated. "He'd look quite different if she were here." Strange to say, her not being there aroused an acute and quite absurd feeling of vexation in his heart. "It's not because she isn't there," Mitya said to himself, at once realising why he felt that way. "It's because I can't tell for certain whether she's there or not." Mitya was later to recall that his thinking was extraordinarily lucid at the time, his perception taking in every detail, even the minutest. But a sense of anguish, an anguish, born of uncertainty and irresolution surged up in his heart. "Is she there, after all, or isn't she?" he asked himself in anger, and then he arrived at a sudden decision, stretched out a hand and tapped on the window frame, giving the signal agreed on between the old man and Smerdya-kov: two slow taps and then three in rapid succession—rat-tat-tat, indicating that Grushenka had come. The old man started, his head jerking up; he jumped up from his chair and made for the window. Mitya retreated hastily into the shadow. Fyodor Pavlovich opened the window and leaned out.

"Is that you, Grushenka? Can it be you?" he said in a kind of tremulous semi-whisper. "Where are you, dearie, my angel, where are you?" He was gasping for breath in extreme agitation.

"He's alone!" Mitya decided.

"Where are you?" the old man called out again, leaning even more out of the window, gazing in all directions, right and left. "Come to me; I've got a little gift in readiness for you. Come, I'll show it to you!"

"He means the envelope with the three thousand," flashed into Mitya's mind.

"But where are you?—At the door perhaps? I'll open it immediately—"

The old man was leaning almost completely out of the window, looking rightwards, in the direction of the door into the garden, and trying to discern her in the dark. In another moment, he would certainly have run to unlock the door, without waiting for Grushenka to answer. Mitya looked on from the side, without stirring. The old man's profile, which he loathed so much: his pendant Adam's apple, the hooked nose, all wrinkled in lecherous anticipation, his lips—all these were brightly lit up in the slanting rays of the lamp falling on the left from the room. A burst of fierce anger suddenly seethed up in Mitya's heart. "There he is, my rival, the tormentor of my life!" It was an onset of that sudden, vengeful and unbridled fury he had foreseen in his conversation with Alyosha in the pergola four days before, during which he had replied to Alyosha's question "How can you say that you'll murder Father?"

"I don't know—I don't know—" he had said. "Perhaps I won't, perhaps I will. I'm afraid he'll suddenly become hateful to me at *that very moment, with that face of his.* I hate his Adam's apple, that nose of his, those eyes, and his brazen snigger. I loathe the sight of him—that's what I'm afraid of. It may be too much for me to withstand—"

Thus physical detestation was growing unendurable, and Mitya suddenly pulled the brass pestle out of his pocket—

. . . .

"God was watching over me then," Mitya later said. It was at that very moment that the sick Grigori woke up. On the evening before, he had taken the treatment Smerdyakov had described to Ivan Fyodorovich, that is to say, he had rubbed himself down—this with help from his wife—with vodka mixed with a secret and exceedingly potent infusion of herbs, and had drunk what was left over to the accompaniment of a "certain prayer" whispered over him by his wife, after which he had gone to bed. Marfa Ignatievna had also partaken of the beverage and, unaccustomed to strong drink, had fallen sound asleep at her husband's side. However, Grigori quite unexpectedly woke up suddenly during the night, and lay awake turning things over in his mind; then he sat up in bed, despite an acute pain in the small of the back. He did some more thinking, got up and got dressed quickly. Perhaps he felt a twinge of conscience at being asleep while the house was unguarded "at such a time of danger". After his epileptic fit, Smerdyakov lay motionless in a near-by cubicle. Marfa Ignatievna did not stir. "The potion's been too strong for the woman," he thought as he looked at her, and then, with a groan, went out onto the porch steps, merely to have a look round, for the unbearable pain in his back and right leg made it hard for him to walk. But suddenly he remembered that he had not locked the wicket into the garden for the night. He was the most punctual and careful of men who kept to an established routine and the habits of years. Wincing from the pain, he limped down the steps and towards the garden. Indeed, the wicket was wide open. Quite mechanically, he went into the garden: he may have fancied something or heard some faint noise, but, casting a glance leftward, he saw that his master's window was open, with no one looking out of it. "Why is it open?" Grigori thought, "it isn't summer time." It was at that very moment he glimpsed something unusual: at some forty paces in front of him, a shadowy figure seemed to be running away very rapidly in the darkness. "Goodness!"

cried Grigori and, forgetting the pain in his back, he dashed forward to intercept the running man. He took a shorter path, evidently being more familiar with the layout of the garden than the stranger, who ran past the bath-house and made for the fence. Keeping him well in sight, Grigori followed him, straining every nerve, reaching the fence at the moment the fleeing man had got one leg over it. Quite forgetful of his pain Grigori uttered a loud cry, rushed at the man, and grabbed the other leg with both hands.

His presentiment had indeed proved true: he recognised the "monster of a parricide!"

"Parricide!" the old man shouted at the top of his voice, but no sooner had he done so than he was felled to the ground. Mitya jumped down and bent over the prostrate figure. He was still holding the brass pestle, which he now threw away mechanically into the grass. It fell within a couple of paces of Grigori, but not in the grass but on the pathway, where it was most conspicuous. For several moments he examined the lying man. The old man's head was all bloodstained; Mitya stretched out a hand and began to feel. He was later to recall that he felt most anxious at the moment "to find out for certain" whether he had crushed the skull or merely stunned the old man with the pestle. But the bleeding was profuse, terribly profuse, the hot flow drenching Mitya's trembling fingers. He remembered pulling out of a pocket the new white handkerchief he had provided himself with for his call on Madame Khokhlakov and applying it to the old man's head in a senseless attempt to wipe the blood from the forehead and the face, but the handkerchief, too, was at once soaked in blood. "Good Lord, why am I doing that?" cried Mitya, suddenly recollecting himself. "How am I to find out if I've bashed it in— But then, what difference does it make now?" he suddenly added hopelessly. "If I've killed him, the thing's done— Lie there if you've had yours!" he added aloud, and then made for the fence, which he scaled, and began to run along the street. The blood-soaked handkerchief was clenched in his right fist, and, as he ran, he thrust it into the back coat-pocket. He ran for all he was worth, and the few passers-by he encountered in the dark recalled afterwards that on that night they had seen a man running furiously. He rushed back to the Morozov house. As soon as he had left several hours earlier that evening, Fenya had hastened to Nazar Ivanovich, the head janitor, imploring him "for the love of Heaven not to admit the captain either that day or the next". The man agreed, but it so happened that he was suddenly summoned upstairs by the mistress of the house and, on the way there on meeting his nephew, a lad of twenty, recently arrived from the country, had told him to stand in for him but had forgotten to instruct him not to admit the captain. When Mitya knocked at the gate, he was at once recognised by the lad, whom he had tipped many a time. He at once unlocked the wicket, let Mitya in, and, with a welcoming smile, hurried to tell him obligingly that Grushenka was out.

"But where can she be, Prokhor?" asked Mitya, stopping in his tracks.

"She left for Mokroye a short while ago—it's two hours since. Timofei was driving her."

"But what for?" cried Mitya.

"That I can't say, sir, but I think she's gone to some army officer, who had horses sent for her from there—"

Mitya left him abruptly and ran into the house in search of Fenya, as though bereft of reason.

5.

A Sudden Decision

Fenya was sitting in the kitchen with her grandmother; the two were making ready to retire for the night. Trusting that Nazar Ivanovich would keep watch, they had not locked themselves in. Mitya came rushing in, and seized Fenya by the throat.

"Speak up! Where is she? Who is she with at Mokroye?" he yelled, quite beside himself.

The two women began to scream.

"I'll tell you, Dmitri Fyodorovich, I'll tell you everything right away! I won't hold anything back!" Fenya gabbled, frightened to death. "She's gone off to Mokroye, to her officer."

"What officer?" Mitya roared.

"The same officer, the one she used to be with five years ago until he jilted her and went off," Fenya gabbled.

Dmitri Fyodorovich released his grip on her throat.

He stood facing her, wordless and as pale as a sheet, but the look in his eyes showed that her words had struck home: he had realised everything, taken in the entire situation. The unfortunate Fenya was not, of course, capable, at the moment, of noting whether he had understood or not. She remained seated on the trunk just as she had when he had come dashing into the room: she was quaking with fear, her arms outstretched as though in self-defence, and had frozen in that posture. Her dilated, horror-stricken pupils were rivetted on him. To make matters worse, both his hands were smeared with blood: he had probably wiped off the sweat from his face when he had come running to the place, so that there were smears of blood both on his forehead and his right cheek. Fenya was on the verge of hysterics, while the old cook, almost unconscious with terror, had jumped to her feet, staring at him as though out of her mind. Dmitri stood stock-still for a moment and then sank unthinkingly on to a chair next to Fenya.

He sat there benumbed with fear. Yet everything was now as clear as daylight: that officer—he had known of him, had learnt everything about him from Grushenka herself; he knew that he had written to her a month before. That meant that for a month, a whole month, it had all been kept a dead secret from him right up to the return of this new rival, to whom he had never even given thought! But how could he have failed to do so? Why had he completely lost sight of the officer, forgotten him the moment he had learnt of him? That was the question that loomed before him like some hideous monster. And he was now regarding that monster with chill fear.

But then he suddenly began to speak to Fenya in a mild and gentle tone, just like an affectionate child, seeming quite oblivious of his having just now scared, offended and tormented her. He suddenly began to question her with a preciseness that was extraordinary and even astonishing for a man in his condition. And though she kept staring wild-eyed at his bloodstained hands, Fenya began to answer every one of his questions with the utmost willingness and alacrity, seeming eager to present him with the unvarnished truth. By degrees, and even as though glad to do so, she began a detailed account, not at all wishing to hurt him but, on the contrary, as though she wanted with all her heart to render him a service. She described the events of the day down to the minutest detail, Rakitin and Alyosha's visit, her having stood watch, her mistress's departure, and her having called out to Alyosha from the window, telling him to convey her regards to Mitya who should remember for ever how she had loved him for one short hour. Mitya gave a sudden wry smile on hearing this message, a touch of colour coming into his pale cheeks. It was at that moment that Fenya said to him without the least apprehension of being inquisitive:

"What's wrong with your hands, Dmitri Fyodorovich? They're all bloodstained!"

"They are," Mitya replied dully, looking at his hands absent-mindedly and at once forgetting all about them and Fenya's question. He again relapsed into silence. Some twenty minutes had passed since he had come running into the place. His recent fear had gone, and he seemed to be in the grip of some new and inflexible decision. He suddenly rose to his feet and smiled pensively.

"What has happened to you, sir?" said Fenya, pointing to his hands again. She spoke with compassion, as one standing very close to him in his grief.

Again Mitya looked at his hands.

"It's blood, Fenya," he said, giving her a strange glance. "Human blood, and, my God, why should it have been split? But, Fenya—there's a certain fence here—" (he looked at her as though setting her a riddle) "a high fence and frightful to the view but—when day breaks tomorrow, the sun hits the sky, Mitya will jump over that fence—You don't seem to understand, Fenya, what fence I mean, but never mind that—it makes no difference, you'll hear of it tomorrow and understand everything—and now, farewell! I won't stand in her way; I'll step down—I'll be able to do that. Live on, my darling—you loved me for a brief hour, but you'll remember Mitya Karamazov for ever. She always called me dear Mitya—d'you remember?''

So saying, he suddenly left the kitchen, which frightened Fenya almost more than the way he had come rushing in and fallen upon her.

Exactly ten minutes later, Dmitri Fyodorovich was calling on Pyotr Ilyich Perkhotin, the young civil servant he had pawned his pistols with. It was already half past eight, and Pyotr Ilyich, after his tea had just redonned his frock-coat and was preparing to leave for the Metropolis Inn for a game of billiards. Mitya intercepted him on his way out. At the sight of him and his bloodstained face, Perkhotin exclaimed:

"Good Lord! What's the matter with you?''

"Here's what,'' Mitya said rapidly, "I've come for my pistols and brought the money. And thanks very much. I'm in a hurry, Pyotr Ilyich, so please get them at once.''

Pyotr Ilyich was growing more and more surprised: he caught sight of a thick sheaf of bank-notes in Mitya's hand. What was most unusual was that he had entered, holding the money in a way Perkhotin had never before witnessed: the notes were all in Mitya's outstretched right hand as if for the world to see. Perkhotin's servant boy, who had met Mitya in the hallway, later said that he had entered the hall with the money in his hand, so it must have been the way he had held it before him in the street. They were all hundred-rouble notes in the grip of the bloodstained fingers. Questioned later as to the sum of the money, Perkhotin replied that it had been hard to estimate at a glance, but that it may have been two or perhaps three thousand; at any rate, it had been a thick wad. As he later testified, "Dmitri Fyodorovich was not quite himself either—not intoxicated, but elevated and very distrait, yet at the same time, he seemed absorbed in something he was giving thought to but could not unravel. He was in a great hurry, his replies being curt and very strange. At moments he seemed even cheerful, and in no way upset.''

"But what can be the matter with you? What has happened to you?'' cried the dumbfounded Perkhotin. "Where's all that blood from? From a fall? Just look at yourself!"

Taking Mitya by an elbow, he guided him towards the mirror. At the sight of his blood-smeared face, Mitya gave a start, and scowled.

"Dammit, that was the only thing lacking," he muttered in an angry voice. Then he rapidly transferred the notes to his left hand and jerkily pulled his handkerchief out of his pocket. However, the handkerchief was soaked in blood (he had used it to wipe Grigori's face and head). It had retained practically none of its original white; the blood had not yet dried but had turned the stiffened crumpled handkerchief into a sticky ball. Mitya angrily flung it on the floor.

"The deuce take it! Have you got some rag—to wipe myself with?"

"So you're not injured but merely smeared with blood? In that case, you need a wash," said Perkhotin. "The wash-stand is over there. Let me help you."

"A wash-stand? That's fine—but what am I to do with this?" asked Mitya, indicating the money in the greatest perplexity and looking inquiringly at Perkhotin, as though expecting the latter to decide what he, Mitya, should do with his own money.

"Put it in your pocket or leave it on the table here. It won't go astray."

"My pocket? Yes, I'll do that. Fine— But don't you see it's all nothing but sheer nonsense?" he exclaimed, as though emerging from his daze. "Look here, let's first settle the matter of the pistols. Let me have them—and here's your money—because I'm badly in need of them—and I haven't a single minute to spare—"

Peeling a hundred-rouble note from the wad, he held it out to Perkhotin.

"But I haven't got the change," said the latter. "Haven't you got a smaller denomination?"

"No, I haven't," said Mitya, again eyeing the money, and, as if uncertain of his own words, felt two or three of the upper-lying notes between finger and thumb. "No, they're all the same," he added, giving Perkhotin another questioning look.

"Where's all that sudden wealth from?" the latter asked. "Just a moment. I'll send my boy to the Plotnikovs. They close late and may be able to change it. Hi, Misha," he called into the hallway.

"To the Plotnikov shop—excellent!" cried Mitya as though struck by some thought. "Misha," he said, turning to the boy as he came in. "Look here, run along to the Plotnikovs and say that Dmitri Fyodorovich sends his compliments and will be along presently— Stay, stay: tell them to get some champagne ready—say, about three dozen and have them packed when I come, in the way they did when I went to Mokroye— I ordered four dozen that time," he explained, suddenly addressing Perkhotin. "They'll know—don't you worry, Misha," he went on, turning again to the lad. "Listen carefully: tell them to include cheese, Strasbourg pies, smoked salmon, ham, caviare, and all the rest they have in stock—a hundred roubles' worth, or a hundred and twenty, like last time— Stay: they are not to forget the goodies: sweets, pears, up to four water-melons—no, one will do; then, chocolate, fruit and mint drops, toffee—well, everything in the hamper they got up for me last time when I went to Mokroye—to the value of three hundred roubles with the champagne— Let them do the same this time. And remember, Misha—if that's your name—it *is* Misha, isn't it?" he said, turning to Perkhotin again.

"Just a moment," the latter put in, listening and observing with some perturbation, "you'd better go there and tell them yourself; he'll get it all wrong."

"He will indeed; I can see that! Oh, Misha, and I was going to embrace you for carrying my errand— Well, there's ten roubles for you if you don't get it wrong— Off with you and get going—the champagne—that's the main thing they should get ready, as well as brandy, and red and white wine, and all that sort of thing, like last time— They should know what I ordered then."

"Look here!" Perkhotin again put in, this time with impatience. "I tell you: let him run over there to change the note and tell them not to lock up, and then you'll go there yourself and order what you need— Now let me have that note. Misha, off with you and make it snappy!" Perkhotin evidently wished to get Misha away as soon as possible because the lad seemed rooted to the spot, his eyes fixed on the caller's blood-smeared face and the trembling bloodstained fingers clutching the wad of bank-notes, his mouth gaping in amazement and fear, and apparently understanding very little of Mitya's instructions.

"And now have a wash," said Perkhotin severely. "Put the money on the table or else thrust it in your pocket— That's right, take your frock-coat off."

And as he began to help him out of his frock-coat, he again exclaimed:

"Look, your frock-coat is bloodstained, too!"

"No, it's not the frock-coat— Just a little here on the sleeve— And that's only here where the handkerchief was lying. It has soaked through the pocket. I must have sat on the handkerchief at Fenya's, and the blood soaked through," Mitya at once explained with a kind of trustfulness that was amazing. Perkhotin listened with a frown.

"How on earth has that come about? You must have been involved in a fight with somebody," he muttered.

Mitya began to wash, with Perkhotin holding the jug and pouring the water. Mitya was in a hurry and did not soap his hands properly (his hands trembling, as Perkhotin later recalled). The host at once told him to use more soap and lather his hands more; he seemed more and more in command of the situation. We shall observe, in passing, that he was a young man of character.

"Look, there's still some blood to wash away under your nails. And now for your face—here, on the temples and by the ear— Are you going in that shirt? And where are you going? Look, your right sleeve cuff is all bloodied."

"So it is," Mitya remarked, examining the cuff.

"Then change the shirt."

"No time for that. I think," Mitya went on just as trustfully, now wiping his face and hands with a towel and donning his frock-coat, "I'll turn the cuff up at the wrist, like this, so it won't show from the sleeve— See?"

"And now tell how it came about? Have you been fighting somebody? At the tavern again, like that time? Was it the captain you beat up and pulled by the beard like that time?"

asked Perkhotin as if in reproach. "Who else have you thrashed—or murdered perhaps?"

"Rubbish!" said Mitya.

"What do you mean?"

"Don't ask me," said Mitya, and suddenly grinned. "I just knocked an old lady over in the city square just now."

"Knocked her over? An old lady?"

"No, an old man!" cried Mitya, with a laugh looking Perkhotin straight in the face, and shouting as though the latter was deaf.

"Dammit, who was it: an old man or an old woman?— You haven't murdered anyone, have you?"

"We made up. We had a fight and then made up. It happened at a certain place. We parted friends. A certain fool— but he's forgiven me—I hope he's forgiven me— He wouldn't have done so if he'd risen to his feet," said Mitya with a sudden wink. "Only, to hell with him, Pyotr Ilyich, to hell with him! No more of it— I don't want to discuss it just now!" said Mitya abruptly.

"I was asking because really you shouldn't pick quarrels with all kinds of people with little or no reason, just as you did with that captain. You've been in a shindy and now you're off for a spree—that's you all over. Three dozen bottles of champagne—what d'you want all that for?"

"Bravo! And now let me have my pistols. Really, I'm short of time. I'd love to have a chat with you, my dear fellow, but I haven't got the time. Besides, there's no need for that, for it's too late. But where's the money? Where have I put it?" he cried, turning out his pockets.

"It's lying on the table—you put it there yourself. Have you forgotten? You seem to treat money like so much dirt or water. Here are your pistols. It's so odd—your pawning them a little after five o'clock for ten roubles and now turning up with thousands. Two or three perhaps?"

"Three, I should imagine," said Mitya with a laugh, stuffing the money into a side trouser pocket.

"You'll mislay it that way. Are you an owner of gold-mines?"

"Mines? Gold-mines!" roared Mitya, bursting into laughter. "Would you like to set out for the gold-mines, Perkhotin? A local lady will fork out three thousand roubles if only you'll go. That's what she did for me—she's so much in love with gold-mines. D'you know Madame Khokhlakov?"

"I haven't made her acquaintance, but I've heard of her and seen her. Was it really she who gave you the three thousand—just like that?" asked Perkhotin with a mistrustful look.

"You'll call on this Madame Khokhlakov tomorrow as soon as the sun hits the sky—the eternally young Phoebus will rise, praising and glorifying the Lord. You will ask her yourself whether she forked out the three thousand, or did not. Find out from her."

"I don't know what terms she and you are on—but she must have given it to you if you are so positive about it. So you picked up the money but, instead of going off to Siberia, you'll just make ducks and drakes of it— But where are you actually off to now?"

"Mokroye."

"To that place? But it's night already!"

"One can fall from riches to rags, you know!" Mitya exclaimed.

"Rags? With all those thousands of yours?"

"I don't mean the thousands. To hell with them. I'm speaking of the ways of women:

> Wayward is the heart of woman,
> Fickle and unvirtuous.

I quite agree with Ulysses when he says that."

"I don't follow you."

"Do I seem drunk?"

"Not drunk, but something worse."

"I'm drunk in the spirit, Pyotr Ilyich, in the spirit, but enough, enough of that—"

"What's that you're doing—loading your pistol?"

"I am."

Indeed, Mitya had unfastened the pistol-case, opened the

powder flask, and poured and rammed in the charge into one of the pistols. He then took a bullet, and held it up between finger and thumb in front of the candle before inserting it.

"Why are you eyeing the bullet?" Perkhotin asked, watching him with uneasy curiosity.

"It's a fancy I have. Now would you, for instance, examine the bullet, or wouldn't you, if you loaded the pistol with the intention of blowing out your brains?"

"But why examine it?"

"If it's to enter my brain, it's a matter of interest to see what it looks like— However, all that's a lot of nonsense, fleeting nonsense. Now that's done with," he added, placing the bullet in the barrel and ramming home the tow wad. "My dear fellow, that's all stuff and nonsense; if only you knew what nonsense it is! Let me have a piece of paper, will you?"

"Here you are."

"No, just a clean sheet of ordinary note-paper. That's right." Taking a pen from the table, Mitya quickly wrote down two lines, folded the paper in four and put it in his waistcoat pocket. He then replaced the pistols in the case, locked it, picked it up, and gave Perkhotin a long and pensive smile.

"Let's be going," he said.

"Where to? No, stay a moment— You may well get the idea of sending that bullet into your brain—" said Perkhotin uneasily.

"That bullet's all rubbish! I want to live on, for I love life! You may be sure of that. I have a love for the golden-curled Phoebus and his glowing light— Are you capable of stepping down, my dear Pyotr Ilyich?"

"What you mean by that?"

"Giving way. Yielding way for a dear creature and for a hateful one. So that the hated shall become dear to you—that's what I mean! And being able to say to them: God be with you; go your way, pass by, while I—"

"While you?"

"Never mind. Let's be going."

"Really, I must tell someone to prevent you from going

there," said Perkhotin, eyeing him. "What should you be going to Mokroye for?"

"There's a woman there, a woman, and that's all you should know, Pyotr Ilyich. Quite enough!"

"Look here, you may be a wild man, but I've always liked you in a way—that's why I'm worried."

"Thank you, my friend. I'm a wild man, you say. Wild men, wild men! That's what I keep on saying: wild men! Ah, here comes Misha. I seem to have forgotten him."

The boy came dashing in with a fistful of small notes and reported that things were humming at the Plotnikovs', with bottles, fish and tea and the like being prepared for the hamper, which would be ready presently. Mitya took a ten-rouble note, which he gave to Perkhotin, and then another, which he tossed to Misha.

"Don't dare do that!" Perkhotin exclaimed. "Not in my house, for it sets a bad example. Put your money away. Put it here. Why should you squander it like that? It'll prove very handy tomorrow! You'll be coming to me to borrow the ten roubles. And why are you stuffing it all in your side pocket? You'll lose it!"

"Look here, my dear fellow, can't we go to Mokroye together?"

"Why should I go there?"

"Look here, if you wish, I'll uncork a bottle straightaway and we'll toast life. I feel like a drink, and especially with you. I've never had a drink with you before, have I?"

"Don't mind if I do. We can have a drink at the tavern. I'm setting out there at once."

"There's no time for that. We'll have that drink in the Plotnikov's back room. And now, may I set you a riddle?"

"Go ahead."

Mitya produced the piece of paper from his waistcoat pocket, unfolded it and showed it to Perkhotin. Written on it in a bold and clear hand were the words:

"I am passing sentence on myself for the whole of my life; I am punishing myself for the whole of my life."

"Really I must let someone know; I'll do that right now,"

said Perkhotin, on reading the note.

"You won't have the time, old man. Come along for that drink. Come!"

The Plotnikov shop was located only next door but one from Perkhotin's house, at the street corner. It was the leading grocery in our town, quite a good one, in fact. It stocked everything obtainable in the capital: groceries of every kind, wines "bottled by the Yeliseyev Bros. firm", fruit of every description, cigars, tea, sugar, coffee, and what not. It was always served by three shop-assistants and two errand boys. Though our parts had grown poorer, the landed proprietors had gone, and trade had slackened, the grocery remained just as prosperous as before, in fact more so with every year, for its stocks attracted customers all the time. Mitya's arrival was awaited there with impatience. They remembered only too well how, some three or four weeks previously, he had bought, all at one go, provisions and wine of every kind to the value of several hundred roubles paid in cash (for, of course, he was not granted any credit); it was also remembered that, just as on this occasion, he had been holding a fistful of hundred-rouble notes, which he had splashed all round, without any chaffering, and without thinking, or even bothering to think why he should need so much wines, provisions and the like. It was later the talk of the town that, having driven off with Grushenka to Mokroye, he had "poured three thousand roubles down the drain in a single night and the following day, returning to town from the spree down to his last copeck, and without a stitch on his back." He had brought in an entire Gypsy camp (staying in our neighbourhood at the time), who in two days had gulled him out of no end of money whilst he was in his cups, and drank most of his expensive wine. He was held up to ridicule, in reports about these happenings, for having made the yokels there drunk on champagne and feasted the village women and girls to satiety on sweets and Strasbourg pies. Much fun was poked, especially at the local tap house (not in his presence, of course, for that would have been somewhat dangerous), at Mitya's frank admission, made in public, that the only reward he had won from Grushenka for the entire "escapade" had been "permission to kiss her foot, and nothing more".

When Mitya and Perkhotin arrived at the shop, they found, at the entrance, a rug-covered cart with a belled and berib-boned troika harnessed to it, with coachman Andrei in the driver's seat awaiting Mitya. The hamper of provisions was prac-tically ready, and the shop people were only awaiting his arrival to load it on the cart. Perkhotin was greatly surprised.

"How did you get hold of this troika at such short notice?" he asked Mitya.

"I ran into Andrei on my way here, and told him to drive straight here to the shop. There's no time to be lost! I travelled with Timofei last time, but he drove off with a certain charmer just ahead of me. We shan't be far behind, shall we, Andrei?"

"They won't be more than an hour ahead of us at most, sir, perhaps less!" Andrei hastened to reply. "I helped Timofei harness his team, so I know the road he'll take. His pace can't compare with ours, Dmitri Fyodorovich, not by a long chalk. The difference will be less than an hour," was the retort put in by Andrei, a middle-aged coachman, lanky and carroty-haired, in an underjacket and a long peasant-style overcoat over his left arm.

"I'll tip you fifty roubles if you're only an hour behind."

"I can promise an hour, sir, Dmitri Fyodorovich, but we may make it in half that time!"

Though Mitya was fussing about giving orders, his speech was strange, somewhat disjointed, and hardly very consistent. He would launch out into some matter and then break off. Perkhotin found it necessary to come to his aid.

"Four hundred roubles' worth, no less just like last time," Mitya commanded. "Four dozen bottles of champagne, and not a bottle less."

"What do you need so much for? What's the idea? Stay!" Perkhotin bellowed. "What's in this basket? There can't be four hundred roubles' worth here!"

The bustling shop-assistants at once explained to him in the most mollifying of tones that the first hamper contained only half a dozen bottles of champagne, as well as "all kinds of initial necessities" such as snacks, sweets, fruit-drops and the like, while the more substantial foodstuffs would be packed and forwarded, as it had been on the previous occasion, by special delivery, also by a troika and within an hour of Dmitri Fyodorovich's arrival at his destination.

"And not more than an hour," Mitya insisted vehemently, "and with plenty of fruit-drops and fondants; the girls over there are very fond of them."

"The fondants are all right, but why four dozen bottles? One will do," said Perkhotin almost in anger. He began haggling, and demanded that the bill should be shown to him, and would not calm down. However, he could not trim the bill by more than a hundred roubles, it being finally agreed that only three hundred roubles' worth would be sent off.

"To the devil with you!" cried Perkhotin, seeming to think better of how he should act. "What has it got to do with me? You may pour your money down the drain if it's been so easily come by!"

"Come this way, you close-fisted man, and cool down," said Mitya, dragging him into a back room. "We'll be served a bottle of champagne presently, so we can have a drink. Look here, Pyotr Ilyich, come along with me, for you're a man after my own heart."

Mitya sat down on a wicker chair standing in front of a tiny table with a filthy table-cloth on it. Perkhotin took a seat opposite, and the champagne was immediately forthcoming. The two were asked whether they would like oysters—"first-class oysters, just received".

"To hell with oysters, I don't care for them. We need nothing else, anyway," Perkhotin snapped almost resentfully.

"There's no time for the oysters," Mitya remarked, "and I have no appetite anyway. D'you know, old man," he continued suddenly and with feeling, "I've never liked all this discord."

"Who does, after all? Gracious, three dozen bottles for muzhiks! It's enough to make anyone blow his top."

"That's not what I mean. I'm speaking of the higher harmony. There's no harmony within me, none of the higher harmony— But—all that's over and done with. It's no use agonising. Too late in the day, damn it! All my life's been marked by

107

discord, so it's time for bringing some accord into it. Sounds like a play on words, doesn't it?"

"You're talking through your hat, not playing on words."

"Glory to God in the Highest,
Glory to God in me!

The lines burst out of my soul once—more of a plaint than a verse!—I made them up myself—but it was not when I was dragging that captain by his beard—"

"Why do you have to bring that up now?"

"Why, indeed? That's all tommy rot! All things come to an end; all things are levelled down! Comes the summing up, and then the drop of the curtain."

"You know, I can't get those pistols of yours out of my mind."

"They're tommy rot too! Down your drink, and don't let your imagination run away with you. I love life, always have loved it excessively, even revoltingly so! Well, enough of that! Let's drink to life, old man, a toast to life! Why am I pleased with myself, as I am? I'm vile, but pleased with myself. Yet the thought that I'm vile but pleased with myself is worrying to me. I bless the Creation and I'm now ready to bless God and what he has created, but—I must exterminate a noxious insect to stop it from crawling about and ruining other lives— Let's drink to life, brother! What can be more precious than life? Nothing, nothing at all! Here's to life and a queen among women."

"All right, here's to life, and to your queen, if you so wish!"

They swallowed a tumbler each. Though he looked ebullient and expansive, Mitya was somehow sad as though the burden of some overwhelming care was weighing on his mind.

"Misha—so your Misha's come? Misha, my lad, come over here and drink this glass to Phoebus, the golden-haired of tomorrow morn—"

"Why are you letting him have that?" Perkhotin cried in exasperation.

"Oh, let me do it, please. It's a whim of mine."

"Oh, hell!"

Misha emptied the glass, bowed, and dashed off.

"It's something he'll remember," Mitya observed. "Woman, I just love woman! What is a woman? She's the queen of the earth! But my heart is sad, so sad, Pyotr Ilyich. D'you remember those lines in Hamlet: 'I'm very sorry, good Horatio!— Alas, poor Yorick!' Perhaps I'm a Yorick? Indeed, I am a Yorick, and the skull will come later."

Perkhotin was listening in silence. Mitya, too, was silent for a while.

"What kind of doggie is that?" he suddenly, if absent-mindedly, asked a shop-assistant on noticing a pretty lapdog with black eyes, sitting in the corner.

"It belongs to the mistress," the man replied. "She came here with it a short while ago, and has forgotten it. I'll have to take it back."

"I once saw one just like it—in the regiment," said Mitya pensively, "only it had a broken hind leg— Incidentally, Pyotr Ilyich, I'd like to ask you something: have you ever stolen anything in your life?"

"What a question?"

"Well, I was just asking. I mean something that wasn't yours—from somebody's pocket, you know? I'm not referring to government money because that's stolen by practically everybody, including you, of course—"

"Oh, go to hell."

"I mean something that isn't yours—straight from a pocket, from a purse, eh?"

"I did steal a twenty-copeck coin from my mother once. I was nine at the time. I took it from the table on the quiet, and clutched it in my hand."

"Well, how did it all end?"

"Nothing out of the ordinary. I kept it for three days, then felt ashamed of myself, owned up and gave it back."

"What happened then?"

"I was given a thrashing, of course. But what about you? Haven't you ever stolen anything?"

"I have," said Mitya with a sly wink.

"What was it?" asked Perkhotin inquisitively.

"A twenty-copeck coin from my mother when I was nine. Gave it back three days later." Having said this, Mitya suddenly rose to his feet.

"Isn't it time to make haste, Dmitri Fyodorovich?" Andrei suddenly called from the shop door.

"Are you ready? Let's be going then!" said Mitya, galvanised into activity. "Just a last word and—Andrei, have a glass of vodka for the road! Give him a glass of brandy on top of that! And put the pistol-case under my seat. Well, good-bye, Pyotr Ilyich, don't think ill of me."

"But you'll be back tomorrow, won't you?"

"Without fail."

"Will you pay the bill now, sir?" asked the shop-assistant, darting forward.

"Oh, yes, the bill! Of course, of course!"

And again he pulled his fistful of notes out of his pocket, peeled three one-hundred-rouble notes off the bundle, flung them down on the counter, and hurried out of the shop. All the assistants followed him, bowing and scraping, with effusive expressions of good wishes. Andrei grunted in appreciation of the brandy he had just swallowed, and was about to take his seat when Fenya quite unexpectedly came dashing up, quite breathless. With a cry, she clasped her hands in supplication and fell at his feet.

"Oh, sir, dear Dmitri Fyodorovich, do no harm to my mistress!— It's all because of me because I told you everything!— Do no harm to him either—he was once her lover! He'll marry my mistress now—that's why he's returned from Siberia. Oh, sir, dear sir, don't do away with another's life!"

"Aha, so that's how it is! Well, you're certainly heading for trouble!" Perkhotin muttered under his breath. "Everything's perfectly clear now, as clear as daylight. Look here, Dmitri Fyodorovich, let me have your pistols at once if you want to do the right thing," he exclaimed to Mitya in a loud voice. "D'you hear, Dmitri?"

"The pistols? Wait awhile, my dear chap, I'll throw them into the first ditch on the way," Mitya replied. "Get up, Fenya, don't kneel to me. Mitya would not do anybody in; this foolish man will never do any harm to anybody again. Listen, Fenya," he cried out to her as he seated himself. "I offended you a short while ago, so forgive the scoundrel, forgive and forget— And if you can't, what difference does it make? For nothing matters any more! Drive off, Andrei, speed along like the wind!"

Andrei started up his horses, to the jingling of their bells.

"Farewell, Pyotr Ilyich! My last tear of regret will be for you!—"

"He's talking bunkum though he's not drunk!" Perkhotin thought as he watched him drive off. He had had half a mind to stay on to attend to the forwarding of the rest of the provisions and wines (also by a troika), for he knew in advance that Mitya would be cheated and defrauded, but, overcome by a feeling of anger with himself, he swore under his breath and went off to his inn for a game of billiards.

"He's a fool though not a bad fellow—" he muttered under his breath as he walked along. "I've heard something of that officer—Grushenka's old flame. Well, if he's turned up— Oh, damn those pistols! But, hang it all, am I his keeper? Let things run their course! Besides, it'll all fizzle out. Just a lot of loud talk. They'll get drunk, start a brawl, and then make it up again. Are they serious people? And what's all this 'I'll step down', 'I'll punish myself'—it'll all come to nothing. He was yelling such loud words a thousand times while he was drunk at the tavern. But he isn't drunk now, though he says he's 'drunk in spirit'— how the rascals love resounding words. Am I supposed to be his keeper? He couldn't keep out of a brawl—his kisser was all bloodied up. Who was it with? I'll find out at the tavern. His handkerchief was also soaking with blood— The deuce take it— he left it lying on my floor— Well, I couldn't care less!"

On reaching the tavern very much out of humour, he at once made up a game of billiards, which improved his temper. He began another game, during which he suddenly told a partner that Dmitri Karamazov seemed to be flush again to the tune of some three thousand roubles; he had seen the money with his own eyes, and Dmitri had driven off to Mokroye for another spree with Grushenka. The news was received with almost unexpected curiosity by the company, who all began to discuss it most earnestly and without the least hilarity, even breaking off their games.

"Three thousand? But where could he have got the money?"

More questions were forthcoming, Madame Khokhlakov being discounted as a source of the windfall.

"Could he have robbed his old man?"

"Three thousand! There's something fishy about that."

"He did vow to do his father in, didn't he? All of us here heard that. And he did speak of three thousand roubles—"

Perkhotin listened to the talk, and then his replies to the questions asked him became terse and guarded. He made no mention of the blood on Mitya's face and hands, though he had meant to do on his way to the place. The third game was begun and the subject of Mitya was gradually dropped, but by the end of the game, Perkhotin felt he had enough, laid his cue down, and left the place, without having supper, as had been his intention. On reaching the town square, he stopped short in perplexity, feeling even surprised at himself. He suddenly realised that he felt an urge to go straight to the Karamazov house to ascertain whether anything untoward had happened there. "I shall awaken the entire household for some trifling reason, and create a disturbance. Dammit, am I supposed to be a kind of keeper to them?"

He made straight for home in the worst of humours, but suddenly recalled Fenya. "Why on earth didn't I question her," he thought with vexation. "I'd have learnt everything." He was suddenly overcome by so irresistible a desire to see her and find out things that, halfway towards home, he turned abruptly towards the Morozov house, where Grushenka rented rooms. He knocked at the wicket, the sound seeming so loud in the silence of the night that it served to somehow sober him and rouse his ire. Besides, there was no response from the sleeping house. "I'll be creating a disturbance here, too," he thought with a kind of pang in his heart but, instead of making off, he began banging at the wicket door with might and main, the noise resounding through the street. "Come what may, I'll get them on their feet!" he muttered, his fury mounting with each knock, yet redoubling his efforts.

6.

Here I Come!

Meanwhile Dmitri Fyodorovich was speeding towards Mokroye. It was a little over twenty versts to Mokroye, but Andrei's troika galloped along at a spanking pace that bid fair to get there in an hour and a quarter. Mitya seemed refreshed by the rapid motion. The air was cool and bracing, and the luminous stars were bright in the sky overhead. It was on that very night and perhaps at that very hour when Alyosha fell prone on the ground "vowing vehemently to love the earth for ever and ever". As for Mitya, his soul was unquiet, very unquiet and, though there was much to torment it now, all his being yearned for her alone, his queen, to whom he was speeding so as to look on her for the last time. There is one thing I can aver for certain: never for a moment was there even any uncertainty in his heart. I may perhaps not be believed if I say that this jealous man felt not the least jealousy of this new rival, this "army officer", who had materialised out of thin air. Were any other such a one to have appeared, that would have at once aroused his jealousy, and he might very well have steeped his terrible hands in blood again, but, as he sped along on his troika, he did not feel the least hostility—let alone jealous hatred—towards her "first lover"; true, he had not yet set eyes on the man. "This is a clear-cut matter," he thought, "something the two of them are entitled to; he was her first love, which has remained green these five years; consequently, she has loved him alone all those years, so where do I come in? Why should I come between them? Stand down, Mitya, and yield way! Indeed, what am I now? It's all over and done with, even apart from the officer. Even had he never shown up, everything would have been a dead letter anyway—"

Had he been capable of reasoning, he would have given vent to his feelings in words such as these. But at the moment, he was already incapable of reasoning. His present resolve appeared on the spur of the moment, quite involuntarily; it had been foreglimpsed and accepted in its entirety and with all it entailed, at Fenya's first words a short while before. Yet, despite all his resolve, his heart was troubled, even to agony: his resolve brought him no tranquility. There was so much behind him, and it tormented him. At moments, he found it strange: had he not passed sentence on himself and committed it to paper: "I am passing sentence on myself"? The paper was lying all ready in his pocket; the pistol was loaded; his mind had been made up on how he was to meet the first hot rays of Phoebus, the golden-haired, on the morrow morn, yet he felt unto anguish that he could not wipe clean the slate of his past, all that was behind him—and this was a source of torment to him, piercing his heart with a sense of despair. There was an instant during his drive when he felt an impulse to make Andrei stop, jump off the cart, pull out the loaded pistol and put an end to it all, without even waiting for the advent of dawn. However, the instant was gone in a flash. The troika galloped on, "devouring the versts" and the closer his destination drew, the more the thought of her, and her alone, rendered him breathless, to the exclusion of all the fear-inspiring phantoms from his mind. Oh, how he longed to see her, to catch a glimpse of her if only from afar! "She's with *him* now, so I'll just have a look at her with her former sweetheart—it's all I want." Never before had his heart been engulfed in so much love for that woman, who had so fateful an influence on his life; never before had he felt such new feelings, unexpected even to himself, bordering on a tender devoutness, complete self-abnegation. "And disappear from the scene I shall!" he suddenly decided in an onrush of almost hysterical ecstasy.

They had been galloping along for close on an hour. Mitya had been silent, and Andrei, though usually talkative, had not uttered a word either, as if fearful of speaking, and confined himself to urging his lean but spirited bays forward. Mitya cried in acute alarm:

"But Andrei! Supposing they're asleep!"

The thought occurred to him suddenly: it had not come into his mind before.

"That may very well be so, sir."

Mitya frowned darkly: he was hastening there with such feelings—and what if they were asleep—with him next to her perhaps—? A feeling of rancour welled up in his heart.

"Drive them flat out, Andrei! Whip them up! Faster!" Mitya cried in a frenzy

"P'raps they haven't gone to bed," Andrei surmised after a pause. "Timofei said there was quite a crowd over there—"

"At the posting-station?"

"Not over there, but at the Plastunovs', at the inn. They keep a livery stable, sir."

"I know that, but why do you say there's quite a crowd there. Where from? Who are they?" Mitya exclaimed, much put out at this unexpected piece of news.

"Timofei was saying they're all of the quality—two of them from our town, only I don't know who they are. Timofei was saying that two are local gentlemen, and two others seem to be strangers. There may be more besides, but I didn't ask him properly. He said they were playing cards."

"Cards?"

"Yes, sir, p'raps they haven't gone to bed if they're playing cards. It must be getting on for eleven o'clock, no later."

"Hurry up, Andrei, make it faster!" Mitya again cried nervously.

"There's something I'd like to ask you, sir," Andrei continued after some silence, "only I'm afraid it may make you angry."

"What is it?"

"Well, Fenya fell at your feet a short while ago, sir, and begged you to do her mistress no harm, or to somebody else too—so here's what, sir: I'm taking you there now. I'm sorry to be saying this; perhaps my conscience has made me say silly things."

Dmitri suddenly grabbed him by the shoulders from behind.

"You're a driver, aren't you?" he began in a fury.

"I am, sir—"

"Then don't you know you've got to yield way to others? What kind of driver is it, I ask you, that never yields way to others—look out, here I come! No, driver, you've no right to run over others! You mustn't crush others, or ruin their lives. If you've done that, inflict punishment on yourself—if you've ruined another's life, punish yourself and withdraw."

All this burst forth from Mitya frantically, as it were. Though taken somewhat aback, Andrei went on in the same vein.

"That's true, sir. You're quite right when you say one shouldn't crush or torment another, or even any living creature, for any creature, sir, is God's handiwork—a horse, for instance. But that's something many do—our coachmen, for instance—There's no holding them back, for they don't spare their horses."

"Driving where—towards Hell?" Mitya broke in, bursting into his sudden and abrupt laughter. "Andrei, you soul of simplicity," he went on, again grabbing Andrei firmly by his shoulders. "Tell me: will Dmitri Fyodorovich Karamazov go straight to Hell, or won't he? What do you think?"

"That I can't say. It depends on you, sir, for you're— You see, sir, when the Son of God was crucified and died, he came down from the cross straight into Hell, where he set free all the souls that were in torment there. Then a great plaint arose from Hell, because the devils were afeard that no more sinners would be arriving. So the Lord said to them, 'Complain no more, you there in Hell, for there will be coming to you notables, governors, chief justices and rich men of every kind, and you will be replenished, as you have been throughout the ages, until I return.' That's the truth, sir, just what He said—"

"What a splendid folk legend! Whip up the left-hand horse, Andrei!"

"So you see who Hell's for, sir," said Andrei, whipping up the horse, "but you, sir, are just like a little child—that's what we think you are— And though you are quick of temper, sir, the Lord will forgive your simplicity of heart."

"And you, Andrei, will you forgive me?"

"There's nothing I should forgive you for, sir. You've done me no harm."

"No, I mean all the others I have harmed: can you—here on the road and on your own, can you forgive me for all the others? Speak up, you simple heart of the common man!"

"Lordie! Your words are so strange that I feel afraid to be driving you—"

But Mitya gave no heed to his words. He was praying fervently and muttering feverishly to himself:

"Oh Lord, accept me in all my lawlessness, but do not pass judgement on me. Let thy judgement pass me by— Condemn me not, for I have condemned myself; condemn me not, for I love thee, O Lord! Vile though I am, I love thee: even if thou sendest me into hell, I shall love thee there too, and shall cry out from there that I love thee everlastingly— But let me go on loving—here and now, till the end, for another five hours until the first ardent ray of thy sun— For I love the queen of my soul. I love and cannot but love. Thou seest me what I am. I shall gallop up to where she is, fall at her feet and say, 'You are right to have passed me by— Farewell, and forget your victim, give no more thought to me!' "

"There's Mokroye!" cried Andrei, pointing ahead with his whip.

A solid mass of buildings scattered over a vast area suddenly loomed through the pale darkness of the night. Mokroye was a village of some two thousand inhabitants, who were already asleep at that hour, only a few lights flickering here and there.

"Make haste, make haste, Andrei!" cried Mitya as though in a fever.

"They're still up, sir!" said Andrei, pointing with his whip towards the Plastunov inn, which stood at the entry to the village, with the six windows giving on the street all lit up.

"Indeed, they are!" Mitya exclaimed joyfully. "Drive up with a dash, with all the noise you can! Make the horse-bells jingle for all they're worth, for all of them to know that I'm here. For here I come!" cried Mitya in a frenzy.

Andrei whipped his tired team into a gallop, and indeed had them dash with the utmost panache to the inn entrance, where he pulled up the steaming and outspent horses. Mitya jumped off the cart at the moment the innkeeper, on his way to retire for the night, came out on to the porch to find out who had arrived in so dashing a manner.

"Is that you, Trifon Borisovich?"

The innkeeper, bending down, peered into the darkness, and then came running down the steps with obsequious delight.

"Can it be you, Dmitri Fyodorovich, your honour? Is it you that I see again?"

This Trifon Borisovich was a burly man of medium height, with a somewhat fat face, severe and unyielding in appearance, particularly when he was dealing with the local peasants, but endowed with the ability to don a most obsequious mien when he sensed there was profit to be made. He dressed in the peasant style, complete with blouse and a full-skirted coat; he was quite well-to-do, but ceaselessly aspired to a better position in life. More than half of the local peasants were in his clutches, all of them being in debt to him. He leased or bought land from neighbouring landowners, which the peasants tilled to pay off what they owed him, something they were never able to do. A widower, he had four grown-up daughters, one of them had lost her husband; and now lived with him, with her two little children, as a daily help. Another daughter, a peasant woman, was now wife to a petty government official, who had won promotion from the ranks of the clerical staff. A miniature photograph of this civil servant, in uniform and with the appropriate epaulettes, could be seen among the family photographs on a wall in one of the inn rooms. When they attended church services or went out to pay calls, the two younger daughters donned blue or green dresses in the latest vogue, very close fitting at the back and with trains almost a yard long; early the very next morning, however, they would be back at their daily household tasks, sweeping the floors, emptying the slops, and cleaning up after the guests. Despite the thousands he had amassed, Plastunov enjoyed fleecing his guests whilst they were making merry. And now, recalling that less than a month had passed since he had made two if not three hundred roubles out of Dmitri Fyodorovich during the latter's wild party with Grushenka, Plastunov welcomed him with joyful alacrity, scenting more takings in the offing from the way Mitya came driving up to the inn.

"Can it really be you we shall be having here again, Dmitri Fyodorovich, your honour?"

"Stay, Trifon Borisovich," Mitya began, "first of all and most important: where is she?"

"You mean Agrafena Alexandrovna?" the host at once caught on, with a keen glance at Mitya's face. "She's—er—staying here, too."

"Who with? Who with?"

"With strangers to these parts— One's a civil servant, a Pole, to judge from the way he speaks. It was he who had the horses sent to bring her here. The other's a friend of his, or a fellow-traveller. Hard to say—they're both in mufti, sir—"

"Are they on a spree? Wealthy?"

"Hardly a spree, sir. Small beer, I would say."

"Small beer, eh? And the rest?"

"Two gentlemen from town— On their way back from Cherny, and stopping over. One of them's a young gentleman related to Mr. Miusov, I believe, but I've forgotten his name—I suppose you know the other one, too: he's a landowner named Maximov. He's been on a pilgrimage to your monastery, he says, but he's now accompanying that young relative of Mr. Miusov's—"

"Is that the lot?"

"That's all."

"Stay, Trifon Borisovich, and listen. Tell me the main thing: what of her? How is she?"

"Well, she only arrived a short while ago, and she's sitting with them."

"In good spirits? Laughing?"

"No, not very much, I think— Quite glum, as a matter of fact. She's been combing the young gentleman's hair."

"The Pole's? The officer's?"

"Oh, that man's not so very young, and he's no officer, either. No, sir, not his hair but the young gentleman's, Mr. Miusov's nephew—I forget his name."

"Is it Kalganov?"

"That's right—Kalganov."

"Good, I'll see for myself and decide. Are they playing cards?"

"They were but have stopped. They've had tea and the official has ordered liqueurs."

"Stay, Trifon Borisovich, stay, my dear fellow. I'll decide myself. Now tell me something important: are there any Gypsy singers to be found?"

"No, I haven't heard of any of late, Dmitri Fyodorovich. They've been expelled by the authorities, but there are some Jewish musicians here, nearby at Rozhdestvenskaya, who play the zither and the fiddle. They can be sent for, if you wish, rightaway. They'll come all right."

"Have them sent for; get hold of them without fail!" cried Mitya. "And get the village girls together like last time, especially Maria and Stepanida as well, and Arina. I'll pay two hundred roubles for a chorus!"

"For money like that I'll get the entire village on their feet, even if they've gone to bed already. But do the local peasants deserve such kind treatment, or the girls for that matter? Who spends money like that on such clodhoppers? Ought you to treat our bumpkins to cigars in the way you did? Why, they stink to high heaven, the vagabonds! And the girls—all of them—are crawling with lice. Why, I'll get my own daughters up for you without the least payment, so why spend all that money. No matter that they've gone to bed already: I'll kick them out of there and make them sing for you. You actually had the louts drink champagne last time, dash it all!"

The innkeeper with all his protestations had no concern for Mitya's pocket; he had held back half a dozen bottles of champagne on that last occasion and, besides, had picked up a hundred-rouble note from under the table, and kept it, clenched in his fist.

"I splashed plenty of money around last time—several thousand! Remember?"

"You certainly did, sir, so I can't have forgotten—three thousand as a matter of fact."

"I'll be doing the same now—see?"

He pulled the wad of notes out of his pocket and held it out right before the man's nose.

"And now listen and remember: the wine and the provisions—snacks, pies and sweets—will be here in an hour's time. Have them sent up at once. Do the same with the hamper Andrei's brought, have it opened, and serve the champagne straightaway— And, above all, see that the girls come—especially Maria—"

He made for the cart and pulled the pistol-case from under the seat.

"And now for your bill, Andrei! Here's fifteen roubles for the fare, and another fifty as a tip—for your readiness to oblige and your friendship— You'll remember your patron Karamazov!"

"I'm afeard, sir—" said Andrei hesitatingly. "A tip of five roubles will do fine, I don't want any more than that. Trifon Borisovich's my witness. P'raps I haven't put it proper, but no offence meant, sir—"

"What's there to be afraid of," said Mitya, looking him up and down, "but have it your way and to hell with you!" he cried, flinging five roubles to him. "And now, Trifon Borisovich, lead me upstairs quietly, and let me first get a good look at them, but unobserved. Where are they—in the blue room?"

The man gave Mitya a dubious look but hastened to do his bidding: he led Mitya cautiously into the passageway, himself entered first large room, which adjoined the one the guests were in, and brought lighted candle back with him. Then he quietly led Mitya into the room, and placed him in a dark corner, whence Mitya could watch unobtrusively the company in the adjoining room. However, he did not have to watch for long and could not: he saw her and his heart went pit-a-pat and a mist clouded his sight. She was sitting in an arm-chair standing sideways to the table, and next to her, on the sofa, was the youthful and handsome Kalganov. She was holding his hand and seemed to be laughing, while Kalganov, his eyes turned away from her and apparently annoyed, was saying something in a loud voice to Maximov, who sat facing her on the opposite side of the table. Maximov was laughing uproariously over something. *He* was sitting on the sofa and on a chair next to it, at the wall, was another stranger. The one sitting on the sofa sat sprawling, a pipe between his teeth, and Mitya got a fleeting impression of a stoutish and broad-faced man, apparently below medium height, who seemed angry about something. His companion, on the contrary, struck Mitya as being very tall, but he could make out nothing more. His breath was failing him. In a cold sweat, he lost all self-control, and, placing the pistol-case on a chest of drawers, he walked with sinking heart straight into the blue room towards the company.

"Oh!" gasped the frightened Grushenka, who was the first to notice him.

7.

Her First and Rightful Love

Mitya walked up to the table with his long and rapid strides.

"Gentlemen," he began in a loud voice that rose almost to a shout, yet stuttering at every word. "I—I mean no harm! Have no fear," he cried. "I'm not out to make any trouble," he went on, turning to Grushenka, who had shrunk back in her arm-chair towards Kalganov, clasping his hand tight. "I—I'm making off too. I am staying here only till the morning. Gentleman, will you mind a chance traveller being here with you—till the morning? Only till the morning, and for the last time, in this room?"

His final words were addressed to the stout gentleman with a pipe, who was sitting on the sofa. The man took the pipe from his lips, with an air of importance, and observed in a severe tone:

"Sir, this is a private room. There are other rooms available here."

"Why, can it really be you, Dmitri Fyodorovich?" Kalganov replied suddenly. "Why are you asking? Come and join us here. How are you?"

"Hullo, my dear—and most excellent fellow! I've always thought highly of you—" said Mitya in a warm and eager voice, at once holding out his hand across the table.

"Oh, what a grip you have! You've almost crushed my fingers," Kalganov laughed.

"He always does that, always!" Grushenka remarked gaily, though with a timid smile, seeming to have suddenly realised that Mitya had no intention of making a scene, and eyeing him with an intense curiosity that had some apprehension in it. There was something about him that surprised her greatly; she had not in the least expected that at such a moment he would walk in as he had done, and speak in the way he had.

"How d'you do, sir!" Maximov, too, put in from the left, in a cloying voice. Mitya hastened to greet him, as well.

"How d'you do. You're here, too, and I'm delighted you are! Gentlemen, gentlemen, I–" He again turned to the Pole with the pipe, evidently taking him for the most important person there. "I came hastening here–to spend my last day, my last hour, in this room, in this very room–where I, too, adored–my queen! Forgive me, sir!" he exclaimed in a frenzy, "but as I came flying here I made a vow– But have no fear, for this is my last night! Let's have a friendly drink, sir! The wine will be served presently– And I've brought this along." For some reason he suddenly produced his wad of notes. "Permit me, sir: I want to hear a lot of music, din and blaring, just like last time– And then the worm, the unwanted worm, will crawl off and will be no more! On this, my last night, I shall be recalling my day of joy!–"

He was almost choking: there was so much, so much, he wanted to say, but he could bring out nothing but incoherent exclamations. The Pole's gaze was fixed on him and his sheaf of notes, and then shifted to Grushenka. He was obviously nonplussed.

"If my queen permits–" he began.

"Do you mean me?" Grushenka broke in. "It's all so funny, the way you all speak. Do sit down, Mitya, and explain what you're talking about. And please don't try to frighten me. You won't, will you? If you don't, I'll be glad to have you here."

"Me, me, frighten you?" Mitya exclaimed, throwing up his hands. "You can all pass me by and go your way–I'll be no hindrance!"–And suddenly, he surprised them all, and himself

123

of course, by sinking on to a chair and bursting into tears, turning his face away towards the opposite wall and clasping the back of his chair as though embracing it.

"Come, come, you big silly!" Grushenka exclaimed reprovingly. "That's just how he would come to see me: he'd start talking in a way I couldn't make head or tail of. Once he burst into tears, and he's crying again now—for shame! Why should you be in tears? *There's not the least cause for that!*" she suddenly added enigmatically, stressing every word in a kind of exasperation.

"I—I'm not weeping— Well, hullo everybody!" Mitya said, turning round instantly on his chair and bursting into laughter—not his usual abrupt and hard laugh, but one that was silent, long, nervous and convulsive.

"There you go again!— Cheer up, do cheer up!" said Grushenka coaxingly. "I'm very glad you've come, very glad. D'you hear, Mitya? I'm very, very glad. I want him to be sitting here with us," she went on imperatively, apparently addressing the whole company, though her words were obviously meant for the man sitting on the sofa. "That's my wish! If he leaves, so shall I!" she added, her eyes flashing.

"My queen's wishes are law!" said the Pole, gallantly kissing Grushenka's hand. "Will you please join our company, sir," he said courteously, addressing Mitya, who again jumped up with the obvious intention of bursting into another effusion, but then things worked out differently.

"Let's fill our glasses, gentlemen!" he rapped out in lieu of a speech, this evoking general laughter.

"Good Lord! I thought he was about to make another speech," Grushenka exclaimed nervously. "Listen, Mitya," she went on with insistence, "don't go jumping up any more, but it's really nice you've brought some champagne with you. I'll have some myself, for I dislike liqueurs. Your coming here is better than anything else could be. I've been feeling dreadfully bored— But you haven't come for another spree, have you? Only put your money back in your pocket! How did you come by so much money?"

Mitya, who had all the time been holding in his hand the

crumpled sheaf of notes, on which all eyes, especially of the Poles, were rivetted, rapidly thrust the money back into his pocket; in his confusion he turned red. At that moment, the innkeeper came in with an uncorked bottle of champagne and some glasses on a tray. Mitya snatched at the bottle, but was so bewildered that he did not know what to do with it, so Kalganov took it from him and poured the wine into the glasses.

"Bring another bottle, another one!" Mitya cried to the innkeeper and, forgetful of his expressed desire to clink glasses as a token of reconciliation with the Polish gentleman, downed his glass in a single gulp, without waiting for anyone else. His face underwent a sudden change, the gloomy and even tragic mien with which he had entered yielding place to one that was almost childlike. He seemed to have grown timid and subdued, looking shyly and happily at the others and breaking into a nervous titter now and again with the fawning and guilty appearance of a lap-dog that has been punished and then readmitted to favour. He seemed to have forgotten everything and looked about himself rapturously, with a childlike smile. His gaze was fixed constantly on Grushenka, and he moved his chair closer to her arm-chair. He gradually studied the faces of the two Poles, although he could not as yet quite make them out. He was struck by the pompous bearing of the Pole on the sofa, his Polish accent, and especially his pipe. "So what? It's good that he smokes a pipe," he reflected. The Pole's somewhat flabby and middle-aged face, with its smallish nose, and the pencil-line, dyed and fiercely turned-up moustaches had not yet evoked the least questions in Mitya. Neither was he particularly surprised by the Pole's shoddy-looking wig of Siberian make, with lovelocks absurdly combed forwards over the temples. "I daresay it's all right if he wears a wig," he went on as he blissfully contemplated the man. As for the latter's compatriot, a younger man, who was sitting at the wall and staring insolently and defiantly at the company, to whose conversation he was listening with silent contempt, he impressed Mitya by his great height, which was such a marked contrast to the Pole on the sofa. "Why, he'll be a good six foot ten in his socks," Mitya thought to himself. It also occurred to him that the tall Pole was probably a friend and follower of the Pole on the sofa, a kind of bodyguard, and that the little Pole with the pipe was the one who gave the orders. Yet even that seemed terribly good and unquestionable to Mitya. All feeling of rivalry seemed to have died away in the lap-dog. He had not yet the least comprehension of Grushenka herself or of the enigmatic tone of some of her words; the only thing he did realise in his throbbing heart was that she was kind to him, had "forgiven" him, and let him sit by her side. He was beside himself with delight at seeing her sip at the wine, yet he felt somewhat taken aback by the silence of the company and began to examine them with expectant eyes. "Why are we just sitting about like this? Why don't you start something, gentlemen?" his smiling eyes seemed to ask.

"He keeps on talking drivel, which has made us all laugh," Kalganov suddenly began, as though divining his thoughts, and pointing towards Maximov.

Mitya gave a rapid glance at Kalganov and then at Maximov.

"Talking drivel? Ha-ha!" he went on, with his abrupt and hard laugh, seeming gladdened by something.

"Indeed, he does. Just fancy, he maintains that, during the twenties, our cavalry officers all married Polish girls. But that's downright nonsense, isn't it?"

"Married Polish girls?" Mitya repeated, this time with frank delight.

Kalganov was well aware of the relations between Mitya and Grushenka, and had some idea of what had existed between her and the Pole, but all that presented little or perhaps no interest to him. It was Maximov that interested him most. He had arrived there with Maximov quite by chance, and had met the two Poles at the inn for the first time in his life. He had met Grushenka previously and had even called on her once with someone; she had not liked him at the time. But here she had been quite affectionate towards him and prior to Mitya's arrival had even been making much of him, but he had remained somehow insensitive to her kindness. He was a young man of no more than twenty, well dressed, with a charming face, creamy complexion, and thick fair hair. What was remarkable about the handsome face was his beautiful light-blue eyes, with an intelligent and sometimes even deep expression quite surprising at his age, though he sometimes looked and spoke just like a child, something he was unashamed and even conscious of. He was highly individualistic, even whimsical, though always kindly. His face at times conveyed an expression of immobility and obstinacy: as he looked at you and listened, he seemed to be concentrating on some inner thought. At times he would be listless and lazy; at others, he would suddenly grow excited over apparently the most trifling matter.

"Imagine," he drawled, but speaking quite naturally and without the least affectation, "I've been taking him about with me the last four days, ever since your brother—you remember?— pushed him off the carriage and sent him flying. That got me interested in him at the time, so I took him along with me into the country. He's been talking such tommy-rot that I feel ashamed to be seen with him, so I'm taking him back—"

"You've never set eyes on a Polish lady, so what you say could never have happened," the Pole with the pipe said to Maximov.

The Pole with the pipe spoke Russian fairly well, at least far better than he had pretended to. However, he gave a Polish twist to the pronunciation of whatever Russian words he used.

"Why, I've been married to a Polish lady myself, sir," Maximov replied with a titter.

"But you weren't serving in the cavalry, were you?" Kalganov retorted. "You were speaking of the cavalry. Were you ever a cavalry officer?"

"Indeed, is he really a cavalryman? Ha-ha!" cried Mitya, who was listening avidly, his questioning glance moving rapidly to every new speaker, as though there was no knowing what was to be expected of each of them.

"Oh, no," said Maximov, turning to him, "you see, what I want to say is that those Polish girls—and very good-looking they are, too—when they dance a mazurka with one of our uhlans—I mean, sir, that as soon as one of them finishes a mazurka with an uhlan officer—she jumps on his lap like a kitten— a white little kitten—and her papa and mama look on permissively—yes, they permit it, sir—and, of course, on the very next day, the uhlan will call and ask for her hand in marriage—yes, sir, asks for her hand—tee-hee!" Maximov concluded with a titter.

"*Pan-łajdak!*"* the tall Pole sitting on the chair growled suddenly, crossing his legs. Mitya's eye was caught momentarily by the man's huge greased boot, with its thick and muddy sole. In fact, the clothes the two Poles wore looked rather shabby and shiny.

"So he's a cad, is he? Why should you be calling people names?" cried Grushenka, flaring up.

"*Pani Agrippino, pan widział w polskim kraju chłopki, a nie szlachetne panie,*"** the Pole with the pipe observed to Grushenka.

"*Możesz na to rachować,*"*** the tall Pole snapped contemptuously.

"What next: let him speak on! Why interfere while people are having their say? It cheers one up to listen to them!"

"*Ja nie przeszkadzam, pani,*"**** said the bewigged Pole importantly, with a long look at Grushenka, after which he relapsed into a dignified silence, again sucking at his pipe.

"No, no, the gentleman was speaking the truth," Kalganov again put in, as though it was all a question of no trifling significance. "Since he's never been there, how on earth can he speak of Poland? You didn't get married in Poland, did you?"

"No, it was in Smolensk Gubernia, sir. Only my future wife had first been brought to Russia from Poland by her uhlan, together with madam her mother, her aunt, and a female relative with a grown-up son from the very heart of Poland, and then he turned her over to me. He was a lieutenant of ours, a fine young man. At first, he meant to marry her himself, but didn't because she proved to be lame—"

"So you married a lame lady!" Kalganov exclaimed.

*You're a cad.
**Madame Agrippina, the gentleman saw only serf-girls, not well-born ladies, when he was in Poland.
***You can count on that.
****I'm not interfering.

"Indeed, sir, I did. The two of them kept it dark at the time, misled me as a matter of fact. I thought that her hopping—she kept hopping all the time—was out of sheer playfulness—"

"Was it because she was overjoyed to marry you?" Kalganov cried in a boyishly shrill voice.

"Yes, sir, as if she was really overjoyed. But the reason that emerged was quite a different one. On the very first evening after the wedding, she confessed and very touchingly begged for my forgiveness, telling me that she had once tried to jump across a puddle in her early years and damaged her leg, tee-hee!"

Kalganov went off into a fit of such boyish laughter that he almost collapsed on the sofa. Grushenka burst into laughter, too. Mitya was rapturous.

"He's speaking the truth now, you know!" Kalganov exclaimed, addressing Mitya. "He isn't fibbing. And d'you know, he's been married twice? He's been speaking of his first wife; his second wife made off and is still alive somewhere, you know."

"Really?" said Mitya, turning rapidly towards Maximov, his face expressive of the utmost astonishment.

"Yes, she did," Maximov confirmed modestly. "I did have that unpleasant experience. She made off with a Frenchie and, moreover, she first had all my landed property made over to her. 'You're a man of education,' she said, 'so you'll always make a living!' That was how she let me down. A most worthy bishop once observed to me in this connection, 'One wife of yours was lame, and the other was too light-footed', tee-hee!"

"Listen, listen!" cried Kalganov ebulliently. "If he does invent things—and he often does—it's just for fun, and there's no harm in that, is there? I find him quite likable at times, you know. He's awfully low, but it comes so natural to him, eh? What do you say to that? Some people behave in that way out of self-interest, but with him it's just in his nature— And fancy: he claims, for instance, that Gogol had him in mind when he wrote *Dead Souls*, and he insisted on that all day yesterday. In the story, if you remember, Nozdrev has a landowner, Maximov by name, flogged, and is taken to court for 'having caused bodily harm to landowner Maximov by having him flogged, this under the influence of drink'. You remember the passage? Well, just fancy, he claims that it was he that was flogged! How could that have been? Chichikov set out on his travels not later than the early twenties so the dates don't fit. So our Maximov couldn't have been thrashed at the time. He couldn't, could he?"

It was hard to make out what Kalganov was so worked up over, but his excitement was genuine. Mitya took sides with him whole-heartedly.

"But supposing he really got a flogging!" he cried, roaring with laughter.

"It wasn't actually a flogging," Maximov suddenly put in, "but only—"

"What do you mean? Were you flogged, or weren't you?"

"*Która godzina*?"* the Pole with the pipe asked, addressing his tall companion with an expression of utter boredom. The latter shrugged his shoulders: neither of them possessed a watch.

"Why shouldn't people have their say? Let them talk. Must they shut up if you're bored?" Grushenka exclaimed, again flaring up, evidently to provoke him. At this, a certain thought occurred to Mitya for the first time. This time the Pole made reply with obvious annoyance:

"*Pani, ja nic nie mówię przeciw, nic nie powiedziałem.*"**

"All right, then. Go on with your story," Grushenka cried to Maximov. "Why have you all fallen silent?"

"Why, there's nothing more to tell, for it's all so nonsensical," Maximov at once replied, somewhat fatuously, and looking quite pleased with himself. "Anyway, it's all by way of allegory in Gogol, because all his names are used allegorically. Nozdrev*** wasn't really Nozdrev but Nosov, while Kuvshinnikov bears no resemblance to anything, for he was actually Shkvornev. But Fenardi was really Fenardi, only he was no Italian but a Russian, Petrov by name, sir, and Mam'selle Fenardi

*What is the time?
**I'm not contradicting him. I haven't said anything.
***The surname Nozdrev (a character in Gogol's *Dead Souls*) comes from the noun *nozdrya* (nostril), while Nosov is formed from the Russian for nose (*nos*).—*Tr.*

130

was a taking creature, her legs very pretty in tights, and her skirt very short and all in spangles, and she kept whirling like a top, only for four minutes, not four hours—she was quite ravishing—"

"But why were you flogged? Why was it done?" Kalganov whooped.

"It was because of Piron, sir," Maximov replied.

"What Piron do you mean?" cried Mitya.

"The well-known French writer Piron. We were holding a jollification at the time, quite a big affair, at an inn, at that very fair. I was invited there, and I began by speaking in epigrams, for instance, 'Can that be you, Boileau? What queer toggery you're sporting.' When I had Boileau reply that he was going to a fancy-dress ball, that is, to a bath-house, tee-hee, they thought I had them in mind. So I followed up at once with another epigram—a caustic one—that all people of education know very well:

> *Indeed Sappho and Phaon are we!*
> *But it so oppresses me*
> *That you've lost your way to the sea.*

That offended them even more and they called me all sorts of names and, as ill luck would have it, I tried to mend matters by telling them another enlightened anecdote about Piron who, when he was black-balled for membership of the academy, wrote his own epitaph:

> *Ci-gît Piron qui ne fut rien*
> *Pas même académicien.*

So they gave me a flogging."

"But what for? What for?"

"For my being so educated. There can be all kinds of reasons for flogging a man," Maximov concluded with mild sententiousness.

"Oh, I've had enough!" said Grushenka, cutting them all short. "It's all so dull that I want no more of it. I thought it would be amusing."

Mitya gave a start, and at once stopped laughing. Rising to his feet and, with the disdainful air of a man who feels bored in a company he usually eschews, the tall Pole began to pace the room from corner to corner, his hands clasped behind his back.

"What a pacer he is!" Grushenka remarked, giving him a contemptuous look. Mitya felt uneasy, the more so because he noticed that the Pole on the sofa was watching him with some displeasure.

"Sir," cried Mitya, addressing him, "let's have a drink! That includes the other gentleman. A drink, gentlemen!" he went on, at once assembling three glasses and filling them with champagne.

"To Poland, gentlemen! I drink to your Poland, the Polish land!" cried Mitya.

"I'll be delighted to, sir!" said the Pole on the sofa with a dignified and condescending air.

"And the other gentleman, sir, what's his name? Hey, you, sir, take up your glass!" cried Mitya effusively.

"Wróblewski," the man on the sofa prompted.

Wróblewski went up to the table with a rolling gait and took his glass.

"To Poland, gentlemen, hurrah!" cried Mitya, raising his glass.

The three emptied their glasses. Mitya at once took the bottle and refilled them.

"And now to Russia, gentlemen, and let's fraternise!"

"Fill our glasses, too," said Grushenka. "I also want to drink to Russia."

"So do I," said Kalganov.

"I'll do the same if you don't mind–to dear old Russia, our old grannie!" Maximov tittered.

"Join us, all of you!" Mitya exclaimed. "Landlord, fetch some more bottles!"

The three bottles remaining from the supply Mitya had come with were fetched, and he filled the glasses.

"For Russia, hurrah!" he repeated. They drank their wine, all except the Poles, Grushenka tossing off hers at one gulp. The

Poles did not even touch their glasses.

"What about you, gentlemen?" Mitya exclaimed. "Why are you holding back?"

Wróblewski took his glass, raised it, and full-throatedly cried out:

"*Za Rosję, w jej granicach przed rokiem 1772!*"*

"*A to bardzo piękne,*"** cried the other Pole, and the two at once emptied their glasses.

"You're both damn fools, gentlemen!" Mitya blurted out.

"S-sir!!" the Poles shouted threateningly, bridling up for all the world like two game-cocks, with Wróblewski simply boiling.

"*Czyż nie można mieć słabość do swojego kraju?*"*** he shouted.

"Silence! Stop that squabbling! I won't have it!" Grushenka cried peremptorily, stamping her foot on the floor. Her face was flushed, and her eyes were flashing, clearly the effect of the glass she had just drunk. Mitya was terribly alarmed.

"Forgive me, gentlemen! I'm at fault, and it won't happen again. Wróblewski, *Pan* Wróblewski, I'm really sorry!"

"You, at least, should hold your tongue! Sit down, you stupid!" the exasperated Grushenka snapped at him.

They all sat down in silence, eyeing one another.

"Gentlemen, I've been the cause of it all," Mitya went on, who had failed to understand what was behind Grushenka's outburst. "What are we sitting here like that for? Let's do something about it—to enliven things and make us cheerful again!"

"Oh, it's anything but cheerful here," Kalganov mumbled lazily.

"Let's have another game of faro—" Maximov suddenly tittered.

"Faro? A splendid idea!" cried Mitya approvingly, "if only these gentlemen—"

*To *Russia* within her pre-1772 boundaries!
**Well spoken.
***Shouldn't one love one's country?

"*Późno, panie,*"* the Pole on the sofa said as though with reluctance.

"Indeed it is," Wróblewski agreed.

"What does your *późno* mean?" asked Grushenka.

"It means 'late', *pani*. The hour is late," the man on the sofa explained.

"It's always late with them and they never find anything possible!" cried Grushenka almost in a scream of vexation. "They feel bored so they want all the others to feel the same way. They were just as silent before your coming, Mitya, and kept turning up their noses at me—"

"My goddess!" the Pole on the sofa cried in Polish. "It will be as you command. I'm much put out and can't help feeling depressed by your displeasure. I'm ready, sir," he concluded, addressing Mitya.

"You begin, sir!" exclaimed Mitya, pulling the notes out of his pocket and placing two hundred-rouble notes on the table.

"I feel like losing a lot to you, sir. Take a pack and make the bank, will you?"

"The cards should come from the landlord, sir," the shorter Pole said with grave emphasis.

"*To najlepszy sposób,*"** Wróblewski agreed.

"From the landlord? Very good, I understand. Let him provide them—that's a good idea! A pack of cards!" Mitya ordered the landlord.

The man brought an unopened pack of cards, and told Mitya that the girls were getting ready and the Jews would be coming soon with their cymbals, probably very shortly; but the troika with the provisions had not yet arrived. Jumping up from the table, Mitya dashed into the adjacent room to give the necessary orders, but only three of the girls had come, Maria not among them. He himself did not know just what orders should be given or why he had dashed out like that, so he merely said that the sweetmeats in the hamper should be brought in and handed out to the girls. "And don't forget some vodka for An-

* It's a late hour, gentlemen.
** That will be best.

drei," he added hastily. "Some vodka for Andrei! I've been un-fair to him!" At that moment, he was tapped on the shoulder by Maximov, who had followed him at a run.

"Will you let me have five roubles?" he whispered. "I'd like to have a flutter at faro, tee-hee!"

"Fine! Excellent! Here's ten!" cried Mitya, again pulling his wad of bank-notes out of his pocket and peeling off a ten-rouble note. "Come again if you lose, come again—"

"How nice!" Maximov whispered joyfully and ran back to the reception room. Mitya at once followed in his wake, and apologised for having kept them waiting. The Poles, who had already seated themselves at the table and opened the pack of cards, now looked far more amiable and almost kindly. The Pole on the sofa had lit another pipe and was preparing to deal, with even a look of solemnity on his face.

"*Na miejsca, panowie!*"* Wróblewski cried.

"No more play for me," said Kalganov. "I've lost fifty roubles to them already."

"The gentleman has had a run of bad luck, and his luck may change," the Pole on the sofa observed to him.

"How much is there in the bank?" the excited Mitya ex-claimed. "Is there enough?"

"*Słucham, panie, może sto, może dwieście, ile postawisz.*"**

"A million!" said Mitya, bursting into laughter.

"*Panie Kapitan, słychał o panie Podwysockim?*"***

"Who?"

"In Warsaw, anyone can stake against the bank at cards, so this Mr. Podwysocki comes along one day, sees a thousand zlotys in the pool, and stakes against the bank. The holder asks him, 'Are you playing for cash or on your word of honour?' 'I'm staking my word of honour,' Mr. Podwysocki replies. 'So much the better, sir.' When the banker deals for the entire pool, Podwysocki wins the thousand zlotys. 'Just a moment, sir,'

---

*Be seated, gentlemen.
**That's according: perhaps a hundred, perhaps two—as much as you will stake.
***Perhaps the captain has heard the story about Mr. Podwysocki?

says the banker, who pulls out a drawer and hands him a million! 'Take this, sir, in full settlement!' There was actually a million in the bank. 'But I didn't know that,' says Podwysocki. 'Mr. Podwysocki,' says the banker, 'you pledged your honour, and so did we.' And that's now Podwysocki got his million."

"That's untrue," said Kalganov.

*"Panie Kałganow, w szlachetnej kompanii tak mówić nie przystoi."**

"As if a Polish gambler would give up a million!" exclaimed Mitya, but at once checked himself. "Forgive me, sir, I'm at fault again: of course he'll give it up—the million—if he's pledged his honour, the honour of Poland!" he went on with a Polish accent. "You hear how I speak Polish, ha-ha! And here's a stake of ten roubles; the jack leads."

"And I'm placing a rouble on the queen, the little queen of hearts, the pretty little lady, tee-hee!" Maximov tittered, pushing his card forward and then, moving up closer to the table, as if wishing to conceal it from the rest, he hurriedly crossed himself under the table for good luck. Mitya won, as did Maximov's rouble.

"A quarter-stake!" cried Mitya.

"And I'll stake another rouble, an ordinary little stake!" Maximov murmured blissfully, tremendously delighted to have won a rouble.

"It has lost!" cried Mitya. "A double stake on the seven."

The seven was trumped, too.

"Stop!" cried Kalganov suddenly.

"Double stakes, double stakes," cried Mitya, suiting the action to his words but any card he doubled invariably lost, while the rouble stakes kept winning.

"Double again!" shouted Mitya in a fury.

*"Dwieście przegrał, panie. Jeszcze postawisz dwieście?"*** the gentleman on the sofa inquired.

---

*Mr. Kalganov, such things are not said in decent society.

**You've lost two hundred already, sir. Will you stake another two hundred?

"What? Lost two hundred already? All right, then, another two hundred—double stake!" cried Mitya, pulling the money out of his pocket and casting two hundred on a queen. Kalganov suddenly covered the money with a hand.

"Enough!" he shrilled.

"What are you up to?" asked Mitya, fixing his eyes on him.

"Enough! I won't allow it! You won't play any more."

"But why?"

"Just because. To hell with it all. You'd better leave. I won't let you go on playing!"

Mitya regarded him in amazement.

"Stay, Mitya, he may be speaking the truth. You've lost a good deal as it is," said Grushenka, a strange note in her voice. The two Poles suddenly rose from their seats, looking deeply offended.

"*Żartujesz, panie?*"* asked the little Pole, eyeing Kalganov severely.

"*Jak się, pozwalasz to robić, panie?*"** said Wróblewski, raising his voice at Kalganov, too.

"Don't you dare, don't dare to shout like that!" cried Grushenka. "You turkey-cocks!"

Mitya looked at them all in turn. There was something in Grushenka's face that struck him, and at that very moment a new thought flashed into his mind—a new and strange thought!

"Madam Agrippina!" the little Pole began, his face all crimson, when Mitya went up to him and slapped him on the shoulder.

"A couple of words with you, sir!"

"*Czego chcesz, panie?*"***

"Let's step into that room where I'll tell you a couple of words, something nice that you'll find to your liking."

The surprised little Pole looked at Mitya with apprehension, but soon agreed, on condition Wróblewski went along too.

"Your bodyguard? Let him come as well because he's cer-

---

*Are you joking, sir?
**How dare you behave like that, sir?
***What is it you want, sir?

tainly needed too!" Mitya exclaimed. "Forward, gentlemen!"

"Where are you off to?" asked the alarmed Grushenka.

"We'll be back promptly," Mitya replied. A kind of boldness, an onset of unexpected confidence shone in his eyes; his expression was quite different from what it had been when he had entered the room an hour before. He led the Poles into a small room on the right, not into the large room where the girls' chorus was assembling and the table was being laid, but into a bedroom, complete with trunks and packages, and two big beds, each with piles of calico-covered pillows. A candle was burning on a little deal table in a corner. The little Pole and Mitya sat down at the table, with the huge Wróblewski at their side, his hands clasped behind his back. The two Poles looked severe but obviously curious.

"*Czym mogę służyć panu*?"* the little man muttered.

"To cut a long story short, sir, I want to offer you this money," he pulled the notes out of his pocket. "If you wish, take three thousand and be off, out of here, no matter where."

The Pole eyed him searchingly, his eyes fixed on Mitya's face.

"*Trzy tysią, panie*?"** he asked, exchanging glances with Wróblewski.

"Three, gentlemen, three! Look here, sir, I see you're a man of sense. Take the three thousand and make yourself scarce, taking your Wróblewski along with you, d'you hear? Only rightaway, this very minute, and for good, d'you hear me, sir? Go through that door and never come back. What have you left there—an overcoat or a furcoat? I'll fetch it here. I'll have a troika harnessed in a jiffy and— *Do widzenia, panie*!*** Eh?"

Mitya awaited the reply with confidence, for he had no doubt what it would be. Something expressive of the utmost resolve passed across the Pole's face.

"*A ruble, panie*?"****

*What can I do for you, sir?
**Three thousand, sir?
***Farewell, sir!
****And the money, sir?

"As for the money, we'll arrange that as follows: five hundred roubles on the spot for travelling expenses and as a deposit, and two thousand five hundred will be handed to you tomorrow in town—I give you my word of honour that I'll get it at all costs!" Mitya exclaimed.

The two Poles exchanged glances, the little man's face darkening.

"Seven hundred, seven hundred, not five hundred, straightaway, and cash down!" Mitya went on, raising the sum, for he sensed that the matter was taking a turn for the worse. "What do you say to my offer, sir? Don't you trust me? I can't very well let you have the three thousand all at once. If I do, you may very well return to her tomorrow— Besides, I haven't got the whole sum about me now. I've got it at home in town," Mitya gabbled, his speech faltering and his spirits sinking with every word he uttered. "I have it hidden there, I give you my word—"

The little Pole's face instantly assumed an expression of the utmost dignity:

"*Czy nie potrzebujesz jeszcze czegoś?*" he asked ironically. "*Fe, a fe!*"* He spat on the floor, his companion following suit.

"You are spitting, sir," said Mitya in despair, realising that his scheme had come to grief, "simply because you think you can get more out of Grushenka. You're just like a couple of capons, the two of you—that's what you are!"

"*Jestem do żywego dotknięty!** cried the little Pole, red with anger, and he stormed out of the room, intimating that he would no longer discuss the proposal. Wróblewski followed him with his rolling gait, with the dumbfounded and crestfallen Mitya bringing up the rear. He was apprehensive of Grushenka and had a presentiment that the Pole was about to raise an outcry. That was exactly what he did. He walked into the other room and struck a theatrical pose in front of Grushenka.

"*Pani Agrippino, jestem do żywego dotknięty!*"*** he be-

---

*Won't you ask for something more—faugh! Faugh!
**I'm most insulted.
***Madame Agrippina, I m most insulted.

gan, but Grushenka seemed to have suddenly lost all patience as though she had been stung to the quick.

"Russian, speak Russian! Not another word in Polish!" she yelled at him. "You used to speak Russian before. You can't have forgotten it in five years!" She was red with anger.

"*Pani Agrippino—*"

"My name's Agrafena, Grushenka! Talk Russian, or I won't listen to you!"

Swelling with pompous indignation and speaking in rapid but broken Russian, the Pole went on in the same pompous manner:

"*Pani* Agrafena, I came here to let bygones be bygones, to forgive and forget all that has happened until this day—"

"What do you mean: forgive? You've come here to give *me* your forgiveness?" Grushenka asked, cutting him short and jumping up from her seat.

"Exactly so, *pani.* I'm a magnanimous man, not narrow-minded. But I was surprised to see your lovers here. *Pan* Mitya actually offered to give me three thousand in that room, if I went away. I spat in his face."

"What? Did he offer to pay you money for me?" Grushenka cried hysterically. "Is that true, Mitya? How dare you? Am I a woman to be bought?"

"Sir, sir!" Dmitri cried out, "she's pure and untarnished, and I've never been her lover! You're lying—"

"How dare you defend me against him!" Grushenka shrieked, "it's not out of virtue that I've been pure, and not out of fear of Kuzma, but because I wanted to keep my pride and have the right to call this man a cad when I met him. Could he actually have refused to take the money?"

"But he accepted it; he agreed to take it!" Mitya exclaimed, "only he wanted the three thousand in a lump sum, while I offered him only seven hundred in advance."

"It's all quite obvious: he got wind of my having some money, so he came here to marry me!"

"*Pani Agrippino,*" the Pole cried, "*jam rycerz, jam szlachcié, a nie łajdak! Ja przybyem wziąć cię za żone, a widzę nową* *panią, nie to co kiedyś a upartą i bez wstydu!"**

"Well, get out to where you came from!" Grushenka cried in a fury. "I'll order you to be turned out of this place, and kicked out you'll be! What a fool I've been, what a fool, to have tormented myself these five years! No, it was not because of him that I tormented myself, but just to spite myself! But this man isn't him at all! Did he use to be like this? It could be his father! And where did you have that wig made? That man was an eagle, but this one is a gander. That man was full of laughter and songs for me— And—I've been shedding tears over him these five years! What an accursed fool I've been! I'm a low and shameless creature!"

She fell back into her arm-chair and covered her face with her hands. It was at that moment that the chorus of Mokroye girls assembled at last, burst into a rollicking dance song in the next room.

"*To jest Sodoma!*" Wróblewski roared suddenly. "*Gospodarzu, przegoń bezwstydnych!*"**

The innkeeper, who had for quite a while been watching with curiosity through the doorway, at once came in on hearing the raised voices and realising that a quarrel was in the air.

"What's all this hollering about?" he asked, addressing Wróblewski with a rudeness that was even hard to account for.

"*Bydło!*"*** the latter roared.

"A beast am I? And what kind of cards were you playing with only just now? I gave you a new pack, which you hid. You were using marked cards! D'you know, I can easily have you packed off to Siberia for playing with marked cards? It's just the same as passing counterfeit money—" He went up to the sofa, inserted his fingers between the back and the seat, and extracted an unopened pack of cards.

"This is my pack—unopened!" he said, holding it up for all to see. "From where I was standing I could see him slip my

---

*I'm a gentleman and a nobleman, not a cad. I came here to make you my wife, but I see a quite different woman, not the one I knew, but a wilful hussy!
**This is a regular Sodom. Innkeeper, tell the hussies to clear out!
***You beast!

141

pack down inside and replacing it with his own—you're a card-sharp and no gentleman!"

"I saw the other man cheat twice!" Kalganov exclaimed.

"Oh, how disgraceful, how disgraceful!" cried Grushenka, throwing up her hands and flushing for shame. "Good Lord, how low he's fallen!"

"I thought so, too," cried Mitya. Scarcely had he uttered the words when Wróblewski, taken greatly aback and flushed with rage, turned towards Grushenka and, shaking a fist at her, yelled:

"*Publiczna szelma!*"*

In a flash Mitya pounced on him, seized him with both hands, lifted him in the air and instantaneously carried him into the room on the right, the one he had led the two a few minutes before.

"I've put him on the floor in there!" he announced, returning at once and breathing heavily with agitation. "He fought back, the scoundrel, but I think he won't come out of there, no fear of that!—" Closing one half of the door and holding the other wide open, he called out to the little Pole:

"Honoured sir, won't you go in there, too? Kindly do!"

"Dmitry Fyodorovich, sir," exclaimed the innkeeper. "Take their winnings back—what you lost to them! Why, they practically stole it from you."

"I don't want my fifty roubles back," said Kalganov all of a sudden.

"Neither do I want my two hundred!" Mitya cried. "I won't take it away for anything. Let him keep it as a consolation prize."

"Splendid, Mitya! Good for you, Mitya!" Grushenka exclaimed, a note of intense malice sounding in her voice. Purple with fury but shedding none of his pomposity, the little man made for the door, but halted and suddenly addressed Grushenka:

"*Pani*, if you wish to come with me, do; if you don't, it's good-bye!"

_____
*You streetwalker!

142

And swelling with indignation and self-importance, he left the room. He was a man of character: even after what had taken place, he still hoped she would follow him—so high was the opinion he had of himself. Mitya slammed the door after him.

"Lock them out," said Kalganov, but the lock clicked on the other side of the door. They had themselves locked it.

"Fine!" Grushenka again exclaimed with ruthless spite. "Fine! It's good riddance!"

8.

Delirium

What began was almost an orgy, unbridled revelry. Grushenka was the first to call loudly for wine: "I want a drink, I want to get quite drunk, like that time—remember, Mitya, d'you remember how close we got last time?" As for Mitya, he seemed to be in a delirium in anticipation of "happiness", but Grushenka kept sending him from her side. "Go and have a good time! Tell them all to dance and make merry—to get things whizzing, just like that time, just like that time!" she kept exclaiming in a state of the utmost excitement. And again Mitya rushed to do her bidding. The singers had assembled in the next room. The reception room they had been sitting in provided cramped quarters, besides being partitioned into two by a chintz curtain, beyond which stood a vast bed topped with a well-filled feather-bed and a pyramid of chintz-covered pillows. Indeed, each of the four reception rooms had a bed standing in it. Grushenka seated herself in the doorway in an arm-chair expressly placed there by Mitya: she had sat also in the same place "that time", on the day of their first spree there, and from that vantage point had watched the dancing and the singing. The girls were the same as on that occasion; the Jews had also turned up with their fiddles and zithers, and the long-awaited troika cart had at last arrived with the wine and the provisions. Mitya bustled about. All kinds of other people—peasants and their womenfolk—had crowded into the room to look on: they had wakened from their sleep and were looking forward to the same kind of munificent treat they had enjoyed a month before. Mitya greeted and embraced all those he already knew and whose faces he remembered, uncorking the bottles and filling the glasses for all and sundry. Only the girls displayed a preference for champagne, the men opting for rum and brandy, but particularly hot punch. Mitya had hot chocolate made for the girls, and ordered that three samovars should be kept boiling throughout the night to provide tea and punch for any caller who wanted such refreshments. A scene of wild and absurd junketing ensued, but Mitya seemed quite in his element, and the more absurd everything grew, the more his spirits soared. Had some muzhik asked him for some money at the moment, he would have immediately pulled out his roll of notes and handed them out indiscriminately right and left. That was why, to protect Mitya, Trifon Borisovich, the innkeeper, kept hovering by his side almost all the time. He seemed to have given up the idea of going to bed that night, but drank very little (only a single glass of punch), keeping a sharp look out over Mitya's interests. Whenever the need arose, he would in- tervene obsequiously and mildly to dissuade Mitya from hand- ing out "cigars and Rhenish wine", or heaven forfend, money, as he had done on the previous occasion, and grew incensed at the wenches drinking liqueurs and eating sweetmeats. "They're a lice-infested lot, Dmitri Fyodorovich," he said, "I'd give them a kick on the backside and order them to consider that an honour—that's all they're worth!" Mitya again recollected And- rei and had some punch sent to him. "I hurt his feelings today," he kept reiterating in a weak and mild voice. Kalganov did not feel like drinking, and did not find the girls' singing to his liking at first, but after a couple of glasses of champagne, he mellowed greatly and strolled about the rooms, laughing and voicing admiration of everything and everybody, the songs and the music. The blissfully drunk Maximov never left his side. Grushenka, too, was growing tipsy. Pointing to Kalganov, she kept saying to Mitya: "What a darling he is, what a wonderful lad!" At this, the delighted Mitya dashed up to Kalganov and Maximov to embrace them. Oh, there was so much in store for him, he felt: she had said nothing as yet to justify his expectations, and even seemed to be purposely holding back the words, but from time to time she would give him an affectionate but ardent glance. Finally, she gripped his hand and drew him forcibly towards herself. She was sitting in the arm-chair in the doorway.

"The way you came walking in here! Goodness, how you looked then!— You did give me a fright! But how did it come about that you wanted to turn me over to him? Did you really want to?"

"I didn't want to ruin your happiness!" Mitya gabbled blissfully. But she stood in no need of his reply.

"Well, go—have your fling," she said sending him off again, "only don't get upset, for I'll call you back!"

And he would dash off, while she listened again to the singing and watched the dancing, her glance following him wherever he happened to be. She would call him back again some fifteen minutes later, which made him run back to her again.

"And now sit down at my side and tell me how you got to learn yesterday that I'd left for this place? Who was the first to tell you?"

And Mitya began to tell her everything, disconnectedly, incoherently, fervently but somewhat strangely, yet kept on, often frowning suddenly and breaking off his account.

"Why are you frowning?" she asked.

"Nothing of importance—I left a sick man behind me there. I'd give ten years of life if he's got well, or at least to learn that he'll get well!"

"Oh, never mind if he's ill. But did you really intend to shoot yourself tomorrow, you silly boy, and for what reason? Yet I love reckless men such as you are," she babbled on, her speech becoming somewhat thick. "So there's nothing you won't do for me, eh? Did you really intend to shoot yourself tomorrow, you silly? No, just wait a little, for I may have a little word to say to you tomorrow—no, tomorrow, not today. You'd like me to say it today, wouldn't you? No, I don't want to do that today— And now, run off again, and have a good time."

However, she did call him back once, looking perplexed and worried as she did so.

"Why do you look so sad? I can see that you do— Indeed, I can," she added, looking intently into his eyes. "You may be embracing the peasants and talking at the top of your voice, but I can see something's wrong. I want you to make merry. I'm enjoying myself, and I want you to do the same— There's someone here I do love—guess who it is?— Look, my little boy has fallen asleep, quite tipsy, the dear boy."

She was speaking of Kalganov, who was indeed somewhat drunk and had dozed off momentarily on the sofa. But it was not only the strong drink that had put him aslleep, but a sudden sense of some sadness or, as he put it, of "boredom". He had become depressed by the girls' singing, which grew coarser and lewder as the drinking proceeded. It was the same with their dances: two of the girls were dressed up as bears and Stepanida, a pert baggage with a stick in her hand, was playing the part of their leader and putting them through their paces. "Make it snappy, Maria," she cried, "or you'll taste the stick!" The two bears finally fell to the floor in a fashion far from seemly, to loud laughter from the closely packed crowd of men and women peasants. "Well, let them go it, let them," said Grushenka sententiously, a blissful smile playing on her lips. "Why shouldn't people have a good time when a rare day of merry-making comes round?" As for Kalganov, he looked as though something had besmirched him. "It's all so revolting—this hoggishness," he remarked moving off, "these spring folk games while they keep watch on the sun all through the short summer nights." He found most repugnant a "new-style" song set to a rollicking tune about a country gentleman who came to win the favour of the village girls:

The master came to ask the girls:
Will you love me? Or will you not?

However, the girls did not find him lovable:

> *He will beat me black and blue*
> *So can I be his heart-throb true?*

Next to come was a Gypsy, who, too, asked the girls:

> *The Gypsy lad did ask the girls:*
> *Will you love me? Or will you not?*

But he couldn't be loved either:

> *The Gypsy he will always steal*
> *So what but grief shall I always feel.*

A lot of men would come along to ask the same question, including even a soldier:

> *The soldier he did ask the girls:*
> *Will you love me? Or will you not?*

But he was also rejected with contempt:

> *The Soldier cannot with his knapsack part,*
> *So after him I'll go—*

This ended in an unprintable expression sung with the utmost outspokenness and creating a furor in the audience. The whole matter ended when a merchant turned up:

> *The merchant he did ask the girls:*
> *Will you love me? Or will you not?*

It appeared that they loved him fondly because:

> *The merchant he'll get rich on trade,*
> *And so his queen I shall be made.*

This made Kalganov positively peeved:
"It's one of these outdated songs," he observed aloud, "and

who are they written by, I wonder! It only remains for a rich railway builder or a Jew to come along and try his luck for all the girls; they would all fall for him." And almost as if it were a personal affront, he declared it was all a bore, sat down on the sofa, and immediately dozed off, his youthfully handsome face looking somewhat pale as his head fell back on the sofa cushion.

"How handsome he is," said Grushenka, leading Mitya up to him. "I was combing his hair when you arrived; it's just like flax and so thick—"

Leaning over him affectionately, she kissed him on the forehead, at which Kalganov instantly opened his eyes, gave her a look, sat up and, with a most worried mien, asked where Maximov could be.

"That's who he wants," said Grushenka with a laugh. "Sit here with me for a while. Mitya, run along and get him his Maximov."

Maximov, it appeared, could not tear himself away from the girls, only leaving them now and again to pour himself a glass of liqueur—as for chocolate he had already drunk two cups. His face was flushed, his nose crimson, and his eyes moistly amorous. He came running up to them and announced his intention of performing a clog-dance "to a certain delightful tune".

"You see, I was taught all these refined and fashionable dances when I was quite a boy—"

"Go, go along with him, Mitya, while I watch him dance from here."

"I, too, want to watch him," exclaimed Kalganov, thus naively declining Grushenka's invitation to stay at her side. So they all went to watch Maximov, who did perform his dance, without evoking any particular admiration in anyone excepting Mitya. The dance consisted in nothing but some high-stepping, skipping and hopping, Maximov smacking the upturned soles of his boots with the palm of his hands at each leap. Kalganov did not like it at all, but Mitya even embraced the dancer.

"Thank you, my dear fellow. You must be tired, I suppose. Why are you looking this way? Perhaps you'd like a sweet, eh? Or perhaps a cigar?"

"No, a cigarette."

"Would you like a drink?"

"I'll have some liqueur here— Haven't you got any chocolates?"

"Why, there's a whole heap there on the table. Choose any you like, my dear fellow!"

"I'd like one with vanilla—they're good for old people, tee-hee!"

"No, I'm afraid there's none of that kind."

"Listen," said the old man, bending down to whisper in Mitya's ear. "That girl over there—Maria, tee-hee! Couldn't I get introduced to her, of course, with your kind permission—"

"So that's what you're after! No, my friend, nothing doing."

"But I mean no harm to anybody," Maximov muttered dejectedly.

"All right, all right. But you see, old man, nothing goes on here except singing and dancing, yet, dammit, something might develop— For the time being, eat, drink and make merry. Need some money?"

"Later on, perhaps, sir," Maximov smiled.

"All right, all right—" Mitya's head was burning. He went out on to the wooden gallery which ran round part of the house overlooking the inner courtyard. The cool air refreshed him. He stood alone in a corner of the dark gallery and suddenly clutched his head in both hands. His scattered thoughts suddenly arranged themselves, his sensations merged, and everything became illumined by a fearfully dazzling light. "When, if not now, am I to shoot myself?" was the thought that flashed through his mind. "Why not go for a pistol, bring it here, and put an end to it all in this very dark and filthy corner?" For close on a minute he stood there irresolutely. When he had been travelling to this place post-haste, he had had, hard on his heels, a sense of disgrace, the theft he had committed, and that blood, all that blood!— But it had been far, far less oppressive at the time! Everything had been put paid to: he had forfeited her, given her up, and she was lost to him, gone—ah, the sentence he had passed on himself could be more easily carried out, it had, at least, seemed necessary and inescapable, for what was there

149

left to live for? But now! Were things the same as then? Now, at least, one spectre, so sinister, had been laid: the first and rightful lover, so fateful in her life, had vanished without a trace. The awesome spectre had turned into something small and comical—it had been carried bodily into the bedroom and locked in. It would never return. She could not but have a sense of shame now, and from her eyes he could clearly see who it was she now loved. Now was the time to clutch at life—yet life was now impossible, quite impossible—damnation take it all! "O Lord, restore life to him I struck down at the fence! Let that fearful cup pass from me! Hast thou not worked miracles for sinners such as I, O Lord? But what, what if the old man is alive? Oh, I can then erase the blot of that other disgrace, restore the stolen money, return it by all and any means— No trace of my shame will remain, except for ever in my heart! But no, no! Alas for my unattainable and faint-hearted dreams! Oh, damnation!"

Yet, through the darkness, a ray of fair hope seemed to shine. He dashed back indoors—to her, back to her, to his queen for ever! "Does not a single hour, a single minute of her love outweigh all the rest of my life, even if burdened with the torment of disgrace?" That agonising question clutched at his heart. "To her side, to her alone! I want to see her, listen to her and think of nothing else! I want to forget everything if only for this night, for an hour, a fleeting moment!"

At the entrance from the gallery into the rooms he walked into the innkeeper, who seemed gloomy and anxious, and was apparently looking for him.

"What is it, Trofim Borisovich? Is it me you're looking for?"

"No, sir, not for you," the man replied, looking disconcerted. "Why should I? But where—where have you been, sir?"

"But why are you so glum? Has anything displeased you? Wait a while, you'll soon be going to bed— What's the time?"

"Must be about three, perhaps past three."

"We'll soon be through, quite soon."

"There's no hurry, sir. Stay on for as long as you like—"

"What's wrong with the man?" Mitya wondered briefly as he ran back into the room where the girls were dancing. But she wasn't there. Neither was she in the blue room, which was empty but for Kalganov dozing on the sofa. Mitya glanced into the curtained-off partition—she was there, sitting on a trunk in the corner, her lowered head and her arms on the bed, and shedding bitter tears, trying hard to stifle her sobs to avoid being heard. When she saw Mitya, she beckoned to him, grasping his hand tight when he reached her.

"Mitya, Mitya, I once loved him!" she began in a whisper. "I loved him so much all these five years, all the time! Was it him that I loved, or only my sense of spite! No, it was him, yes, him! It's untrue that I loved my spite, not him! I was only seventeen at the time, Mitya, and he was so tender to me, so gay and full of song— Or it may have seemed so to a silly girl like me— But, good Lord, it's not the same man I've seen; he's quite different. The face is different, quite different. I didn't even recognise his face. I kept thinking on my way here with Timofei, 'How am I to meet him? What am I to say? How shall we look at each other?'— I was all expectancy, but when we met I felt as though a pail of slops had been emptied over me. He spoke to me like a schoolmaster, all so learned and pompous that I felt quite at a loss. I simply couldn't get a word in. At first, I thought he felt ashamed of his lanky Polish companion. As I looked at them I wondered why it was that I didn't know how I ought to speak to him now. I'm sure it was his wife who brought about all that change—the woman he threw me over for, and married— It must have been she who brought about such a change. Oh, Mitya, I feel so ashamed, so ashamed of myself, of my whole life! A curse on all those five years, a curse on them!" And, still clasping Mitya's hand, she burst into fresh tears.

"Don't go away, Mitya dear, for I want to say something to you," she whispered, suddenly raising her face towards him. "Tell me: who is it that I love? There is a man here that I love. Who is he? Tell me that." A bright smile appeared on her tear-swollen face and her eyes were shining in the half-dark. "An eagle came swooping down, making my heart sink. 'You fool, that's the one you love!' my heart prompted me. Everything began to sparkle when you came in. 'What is he afraid of?' I thought to myself. And, indeed, you were afraid, weren't you? Quite afraid, and struck dumb. It wasn't them you were afraid of, I thought, for is there anyone who can frighten you? 'It's me he fears,' I thought, 'me alone.' Fenya must have told you, you foolish boy, how I cried out to Alyosha from the window that I had loved Mitya for a short hour, and was now off—to love another man. Oh, Mitya, Mitya, how could I have been so foolish as to think I could love another man after you! Can you forgive me, Mitya? Or can't you? You do love me, don't you?"

Jumping up, she took him by the shoulders with both hands. Speechless with rapture, Mitya gazed into her eyes, at her face and her smile and, suddenly embracing her, began to shower kisses on her.

"Will you forgive me for tormenting you? It was out of spite that I tormented you all. It was spite that made me drive that old man out of his mind— D'you remember you smashing your glass while you were drinking at my house? I hadn't forgotten that, and today I, too, smashed my glass after drinking to my 'vile heart'. Why don't you kiss me, Mitya, my eagle? You've kissed me once, and now you've drawn back to look and listen to me— Why listen to me? Just kiss me, kiss me harder—like that! When one loves, it should be heart and soul! I'll be your slave now, your slave for life! Being a slave is so sweet!— Kiss me, strike me, torment me, work your will on me— Oh, how I deserve to suffer torment— But stay! Wait a while, that will come later, not here," she said, pushing him suddenly away from herself. "Leave me, Mitya, I'll go and have some wine, for I want to get drunk and dance! That's what I'm going to do!"

She tore herself away from him and slipped through the curtains, Mitya following her like one possessed. "Come what may, whatever happens I'll give the whole world for a single minute!" was the thought that flashed through his mind. Indeed, Grushenka tossed off another glass of champagne, which made her suddenly quite tipsy. She returned to her seat in the arm-chair, a blissful smile on her face. There was a high colour on her cheeks, her lips were burning, her sparkling eyes lost their lustre, and their passionate gaze was seductive. Even Kalganov's heart went pit-a-pat and he went up to her.

"Did you feel me kiss you when you were asleep?" she murmured to him. "I'm quite tipsy now— Aren't you? Why isn't

Mitya drinking? Mitya, why aren't you drinking? I have, but you haven't—"

"I am drunk! Drunk with you already, and now I'll be drunk with wine too."

He drank another glass and—though he found that strange—it was only that last glass that suddenly went to his head, for until then he had been quite sober, as he clearly remembered. From that instant, everything about him went into a whirl, like a delirium. He walked about, laughing and talking to all and sundry, without any awareness of what he was doing. Only a persistently burning feeling oppressed him unremittingly, "like a live coal in my heart", as he later recollected. He would go up to her, sit down at her side, gaze at her, and listen to her— For her part, she had grown very talkative, calling people to her side, beckoning to some girl or other to come up to her, whom she would kiss and then send away, or else make the sign of the cross over her. She was on the verge of tears, though she was greatly amused by the "geezer" as she called Maximov. The latter kept running up to her to kiss her hands and "every little finger", and finally did another dance to the tune of an old song which he himself sang, cutting capers with particular gusto to the refrain:

> *The piggie it did grunt and squeal,*
> *The little calf did bleat,*
> *The little duck did quack and quack,*
> *And the gosling it did cackle.*
> *The pullet goes strutting through the porch,*
> *Clucking for all she's worth.*
> *Clucking and clucking away.*

"Let him have something, Mitya," said Grushenka, "give him some gift—he's so poor, you know. Ah, the poor and humiliated!— You know, Mitya, I'll enter a nunnery, I really shall one day. Alyosha told me something today that will remain with me all my life long— Yes— But today let's dance. A nunnery tomorrow, but dancing today. I want to drown all care today, good folk, and why not? God will forgive me. If I were God, I'd hand out pardons all round. 'My dear sinners, I forgive

153

you all from this day on,' I'd tell them, and myself go out to beg forgiveness: 'Good folk, do forgive this silly woman.' I'm unbridled and savage, that's what I am, but I want to pray. I once gave an onion away. A wicked woman like me wants to pray! Let them go on dancing, Mitya, and don't stop them. All people in this world are good, all without exception. It's good to be in this world. We may all be a bad lot, but it's good to live in this world. We're all both bad and good, both bad and good— And now tell me: I shall ask you—come up to me, all of you, and I shall ask you: tell me why am I so good? I am good, after all, very good— So here's what: why is it that I'm so good?" It was in this vein that Grushenka babbled on, growing more and more tipsy, and she finally announced her intention of joining in the dancing. She staggered as she rose from her seat. "Mitya, don't let me have any more wine, don't, even if I ask for more. Wine brings no peace of soul. Everything's in a whirl— the stove and everything else. I want to dance. Let them all see how I dance—how well and how splendidly I dance—"

She was speaking in all earnest: from a pocket she pulled out a little cambric handkerchief, which she took by a corner in her right hand to wave during the dance. Mitya bustled about, and the girls quieted down, ready to burst into a dance tune at the first sign. On learning that Grushenka herself wished to dance, Maximov squealed his delight and set about skipping and prancing in front of her, singing:

Legs so slender and sides so trim,
Its little tail curled all tight.

But Grushenka waved him away with her handkerchief.

"Sh-sh! Mitya, why don't they all come? Let them all come— to watch. That includes the locked-up men— Why have you locked them in? Tell them I'm going to dance and want them to look on too—"

With drunken audacity, Mitya walked up to the locked door and began banging on it with his fists.

"Hi, you there—you Podwisockis: come out! She's going to dance and she's calling you to watch."

154

"You *lajdak*!" one of the Poles shouted in reply.

"And you're a good-for-nothing cad yourself—so much trash, that's what you are."

"You shouldn't jeer at Poland," Kalganov who had had a drop too much, observed sententiously.

"Keep quiet, my boy! If I call him a cad, that doesn't mean I am referring to all Poles. One cad doesn't make a Poland. Be quiet, pretty boy, and eat your sweets."

"The kind of men the two are! Hardly human beings. Why won't they make up and be friends?" said Grushenka, and went forward to dance. As the chorus burst into a popular folk song, Grushenka tossed back her head, half-opened her lips, smiled, waved her handkerchief, and suddenly, swaying violently, came to a standstill in the middle of the room, a bewildered look on her face.

"I feel too weak—" she said in a voice drained of all vigour. "Forgive me but I feel too weak—I can't— So sorry—"

She bowed to the chorus, and then began to bow to the whole company around her:

"I'm sorry— Forgive me—"

"The lady's a bit tipsy; the pretty lady's has had a drop too much," some voices said.

"She's lit up," Maximov explained to the girls, with a titter.

"Lead me away, Mitya—take me, Mitya," said Grushenka helplessly. Rushing up to her, Mitya snatched her up in his arms and flew behind the curtains with his precious burden. "Well, now's the time to be leaving," Kalganov thought and, walking out of the blue room, closed the two halves of the door behind him. But the revelry in the larger room thundered on with ever greater force. Mitya laid Grushenka on the bed and fixed his lips on hers in a passionate kiss.

"Don't touch me—" she murmured entreatingly. "Don't touch me till I'm yours— I've said I'm yours, haven't I, but don't touch me yet—spare me— We mustn't, with them so close by. He's here. It's vile here—"

"I shall obey! I wouldn't think of it—I worship you!" Mitya murmured. "Yes, it's vile here, abominable." And, without releasing her from his embrace, he sank on his knees at the bedside.

"I know your savage nature but you're honourable," said Grushenka, speaking with difficulty. "It's got to be honourable—it will all be honourable for the future—and we must be good and honest, not brutish, but kindly— Take me away from here, far, far away—d'you hear— I don't want it here, but somewhere far, far away—"

"Indeed, indeed!" cried Mitya, pressing her in his embrace. "I'll take you away—we'll fly away— I'd give my whole life for a single year now, if only I could learn about that blood!"

"What blood d'you mean?" the bewildered Grushenka asked.

"Nothing in particular!" said Mitya, grinding his teeth. "Grusha, you want everything to be decent and honest, but I'm a thief. I've stolen money from Katya— How disgraceful, disgraceful!"

"From Katya? From that young lady? No, you've stolen nothing. You'll return it—you'll take it from me— Why are you objecting so loudly? Whatever I have is yours now. What do we want money for? We'll squander it anyway— We're made that way. We'd do better to till the soil. I'll scrape the earth with these very hands. One must work with one's hands—d'you hear? Those were Alyosha's instructions. I'll be not your mistress but your devoted slave, who'll work for you. We'll go to the young lady, bow low to her, beg for forgiveness, and go away. We'll leave even without her forgiveness. You return her money, and love me— But don't dare love her. Love her no more. If you do, I'll strangle her— Scratch her eyes out—"

"I love you, nobody but you. I'll go on loving you even in Siberia."

"But why go to Siberia? But if you wish, let it be Siberia, it makes no difference—we'll work there. There's so much snow in Siberia, and I like driving on the snow—especially to the jingling of bells. But listen, do you hear the jingle of bells?— Where from? Somebody's coming here— The jingling's stopped—"

She closed her eyes helplessly, and seemed to doze off momentarily. Indeed, there had been the jingle of horsebells from somewhere in the distance, which suddenly stopped. Mitya let his head sink on her breast. He did not notice that the bells had stopped jingling, and that the singing had ceased abruptly, the songs and the drunken uproar yielding place to a dead silence throughout the entire house. Grushenka opened her eyes.

"What, did I doze off? Oh, yes—the bells. I've just had a dream about driving along the snow—with the bells jingling, and me in a doze. I was travelling with someone dear to me—with you—and going somewhere far, far away. I was embracing and kissing you, nestling close to you for I was feeling the cold, and the snow was sparkling— When the snow is sparkling, you know, and the moon is shining, it's like something out of this world— When I awoke, my darling was close to me—how sweet—"

"Close to you," Mitya murmured, showering kisses on her dress, her breast, her hands. Suddenly, a strange feeling came over him: she seemed to be gazing straight before her—not at him, or his face but somewhere over his head, in an intent and strangely fixed stare. Her face was expressive of sudden surprise, even fright.

"Mitya, who can it be looking here at us from over there?" she suddenly whispered. He turned round and saw that someone had indeed parted the curtains and was watching them. No, there seemed to be more than one person there. He jumped up and strode rapidly towards the watcher.

"This way, sir, step this way," said a voice, speaking in a low but firm and insistent tone.

Mitya stepped beyond the curtain and came to a sudden standstill. The room was full of people—not those who had just been there, but new-comers. A cold shiver ran down his spine, and he shuddered. He recognised all of them instantly. The tall, stout old gentleman in a greatcoat and cockaded cap was Mikhail Makarovich, the uyezd chief of police. That smartly dressed "consumptive-looking" man, "always in such highly polished top-boots" was the deputy public prosecutor ("He's got a chronometer worth 400 roubles, which he has shown me"). And that small and bespectacled young man—Mitya knew him but his name had slipped his memory—he was the court investigator, just out of the Faculty of Law, and was a recent arrival. Then there was Mavriki Mavrikievich, the rural police inspector—he knew him quite well. But why the others with the brass badges? And another two, peasants by the look of them— And there, in the doorway, were Kalganov and Trifon Borisovich, the innkeeper—

"What's this all about, gentlemen?" Mitya began, but, suddenly seeming not himself, he cried out at the top of his voice: "I un-der-stand!"

The bespectacled young gentleman stepped forward abruptly and, approaching Mitya, began in a dignified if hurried tone:

"We have something—in short, I shall ask you to step this way, this way to the sofa— There is an imperative need to question you."

"It's the old man!" cried Mitya frenziedly, "the old man and his blood!—I un-der-stand!"

He collapsed on to a chair standing close by.

"So you understand, do you? Monster and parricide, the blood of your old father cries out against you!" the old police chief suddenly roared, walking up to Mitya. Purple-faced and trembling all over, he was quite beside himself.

"This is most irregular!" cried the small young gentleman. "This will never do, Mikhail Makarovich. Will you please allow me alone to speak— I never expected such behaviour from you—"

"But this is nothing but delirium," the uyezd police chief exclaimed. "Just look at him: drinking at this time of night, with a disreputable woman, and his hands in his father's blood! It's unbelievable—delirium!"

"I shall request you most insistently, my dear Mikhail Makarovich, to curb your feelings," the deputy public prosecutor began in a hurried undertone, "for otherwise I shall be obliged to take—"

However, the little court investigator interrupted him. Addressing Mitya in a firm, loud and impressive voice, he said:

"Retired Lieutenant Karamazov, it is my duty to inform you that you are charged with the murder of your father Fyodor Pavlovich Karamazov, committed this night—"

He went on speaking, with the prosecutor putting in some words, but though he tried to listen, Mitya could make out nothing of what was being said. He stared at them with eyes full of consternation—

BOOK NINE

The Preliminary Investigation

1.

The Beginning of Perkhotin's Career in the Civil Service

Of course, Pyotr Ilyich Perkhotin, whom we left knocking with might and main at the locked strong gate of Mrs. Morozov's house, finally got himself heard. On hearing the furious banging on the gate, Fenya, still too worked up and upset to go to bed after her fright two hours earlier, was again on the verge of hysterics: she imagined that it was Dmitri Fyodorovich again knocking (though she had herself seen him drive off). Who else but he could be knocking so "audaciously"? She rushed to the janitor, who was already up and was going out to unlock the gate, and began to implore him not to open it. However, on questioning the caller—and learning who he was and that he wanted to see Fenya on a very important matter, the janitor finally decided to admit him. When he entered the kitchen (Fenya insisting that Perkhotin should allow the janitor to be present at their talk "just in case"), Perkhotin began to question her and at once elicited a vital fact: to wit that, when Dmitri Fyodorovich had rushed away in search of Grushenka, he had snatched up the pestle from a mortar, and had returned without it, with bloodstained hands. "The blood was still dripping from them, dripping all the time!" cried Fenya, her distraught imagination conjuring up the horrible fact. But Perkhotin had himself seen those bloodstained though not dripping hands, and had helped to get them washed. The question was not how long it had taken for the hands to get dry, but whither Dmitri Fyodorovich had made off with the pestle: had he actually gone to Fyodor Pavlovich's, and what positive proof existed to that effect? Perkhotin dealt in detail with this particular point and though he gained almost no firm information, he became almost convinced that Dmitri Fyodorovich could have dashed off to nowhere but his father's house and that *something* could not

159

but have taken place there. "And when he came back," Fenya added excitedly, "and I told him everything I knew, I began to ask him why there was blood on both his hands, and he answered that it was human blood and that he had just murdered someone: that's what he admitted, repenting of what he had done, and then suddenly he ran off like a madman. I sat down and began to wonder: where he had dashed off to like mad? He'll go to Mokroye, I thought, and murder my mistress there. So I ran to his lodgings to beg him not to kill her, but when I was passing the Plotnikov shop, I saw him about to drive off, and there was no more blood on his hands" (this was something that Fenya had noticed and remembered). The old grandmother bore out Fenya's words to the best of her ability. After asking several more questions, Perkhotin left the house in a state of greater perturbation than when he had entered it.

It would seem that the most direct and simple thing for him to do would be to go straight to Fyodor Pavlovich's to find out whether anything untoward had happened there, and if so, what exactly; only then, he firmly decided, would he call on the uyezd chief of police if there was sufficiently clear-cut evidence to go by. However, it was a dark night, the gate to Fyodor Pavlovich's house was a strong one so that he would again have to knock loudly, and he had but a nodding acquaintance with the master of the house. What if the gate was finally opened and he learnt that nothing at all had taken place? In his sardonic fashion, Fyodor Pavlovich would spread the story all over town: how a civil servant named Perkhotin, whom he scarcely knew, had come bursting into his house at midnight to find out whether someone had murdered him. That would certainly bring him into obloquy, something he abhorred more than anything else in the world. Yet so overwhelming was the feeling that had come over him that, though he stamped a foot in anger and had some harsh words to say of himself, he at once set out on a new course, only not to Fyodor Pavlovich's but to Madame Khokhlakov's. If, he decided, she denied having provided Dmitri Fyodorovich with three thousand roubles at such and such a time, he would at once call on the uyezd chief of police without going to the Karamazov house. If the reverse transpired, he would go home and let the matter rest till the morrow. It was obvious, of course, that Perkhotin's decision to make so late a call, almost at eleven o'clock at night, at the house of a lady he was not acquainted with, perhaps even getting her out of bed, with the purpose of asking her a question quite amazing in the circumstances, contained far greater probability of obloquy for the young man than even going to the Karamazov house. But that is what happens at times, especially in cases like the one in question, with such decisions being made by the most punctilious and stolid of people. And at that moment Perkhotin was very far from stolid! Till the end of his days, he would remember how an overwhelming feeling of anxiety had gradually overcome him to such an agonising degree that it had urged him on, even against his own will. Of course, he kept on castigating himself all the way for yielding to the impulse to call on the lady, but "I'll go through it to the bitter end!" he repeated for the tenth time, grinding his teeth. Indeed, he did carry out his intention of seeing things through.

It was exactly eleven when he entered Madame Khokhlakov's house. He was admitted into the courtyard fairly soon, but when he asked the janitor whether his mistress had retired for the night, the man could not say for certain, informing the caller that she usually went to bed at that time. "You'd better go upstairs and send in your name, sir," the janitor said. "If the mistress wishes to see you, she will; otherwise she won't." But Perkhotin ran into difficulties when he went upstairs. The manservant refused to announce him but finally called a maid. Perkhotin politely but insistently asked her to inform her mistress that a local civil servant, Perkhotin by name, had called on an urgent matter; but for its importance, he would never have made so bold as to call. "Tell her in these very words," he asked the girl. She left, leaving him to wait in the hall. Madame Khokhlakov had not gone to bed yet, though she was in her bedroom. Upset ever since Mitya's recent call, she had a presentiment that she would not that night escape the migraine she usually got after such happenings. She was much surprised by the maid's announcement, yet she irritably declined to receive a "local civil servant" she had never met, on so unexpected a visit at such an hour, though it definitely aroused her feminine curiosity. But Perkhotin revealed a mulish obstinacy this time, insisting most emphatically that the maid should convey another message, "in those very words": he had come "on a most urgent matter, and she may very much regret later if she declines to see me now". "I simply kicked over the traces then," as he later said. Giving him a close if surprised look, the maid went off to carry the second message, which produced a strong impression on Madame Khokhlakov, who, after some thought, asked the maid what he looked like, to be told that he was "very well dressed, young and ever so courteous". We shall observe, parenthetically and *en passant,* that Perkhotin was quite a handsome young man, and aware of the fact. Madame Khokhlakov decided to receive him. She was already in slippers and dressing-gown, so she cast a black shawl about her shoulders. The "civil servant" was shown into the drawing-room in which she had received Mitya shortly before. She emerged with an expression of severe inquiry on her face and without inviting the caller to be seated, she asked him pointblank: "What is your business?"

"I have ventured to disturb you, madam, on a matter relating to a common acquaintance of ours, Dmitri Fyodorovich Karamazov," he began, but hardly had he pronounced the name when a look of acute irritation came over the lady's face. She almost shrieked out, and interrupted him with fury.

"How much longer," she cried out, quite beside herself, "how much longer am I to be tormented by that horrible person? How dared you, sir, how could you have made so bold as to disturb a lady who is a complete stranger to you, at her home and at such an hour—with the aim of talking of a man who, in this very drawing-room and only three hours ago, came to murder me, and then stamped out of the place in a way no one leaves a decent house. I want you to know, sir, that I shall bring a complaint against you and will not let the matter pass, so please leave me at once— I'm a mother, and I—I—"

"Murder? Did he actually want to murder you too?"

"Why, has he committed a murder already?" Madame

Khokhlakov asked impetuously.

"If you will be so good as to listen to me for half a minute, madam," Perkhotin replied in a firm voice, "I shall explain everything to you in a few words. At five o'clock this afternoon, Mr. Karamazov borrowed ten roubles from me as from a friend, and I positively know that he had no money at the time, yet at nine o'clock this evening he came to see me, with a wad of hundred-rouble notes in his hand, probably totalling two or even three thousand roubles. His hands and face were all blood-stained, and he looked quite out of his mind. To my question where so much money had come from, he answered with pre-ciseness that he had just got it from you, a loan of three thous-and to enable him to leave for some gold-mine—"

A sudden look of utter and painful agitation came over Madame Khokhlakov's face.

"Good Lord! He must have murdered his old father!" she cried, throwing up her hands. "I never gave him any money, never! Oh, hurry, hurry!— Not another word! Save the old man—hasten to him at once!"

"Then you provided him with no money at all, madam? Do you clearly remember that you gave him no sum at all?"

"No, I didn't, I never did! I refused because he could not ever have appreciated it. He left in a fury, stamping his feet. He wanted to attack me but I escaped from him— I shall also tell you, for you're a person I'll now hold nothing back from, that he even spat at me—just imagine! But why are we standing? Do sit down— Forgive me, I— But better, hasten to save the un-fortunate old man from a horrible death!"

"But supposing he's murdered him already?"

"Good Lord, he may have done so! What are we to do now? What d'you think we should do?"

Meanwhile she made Perkhotin take a seat and sat down facing him. In terse and fairly clear terms, he gave her an ac-count of the affair, or at least the part he had been witness to, and told her of his visit to Fenya, as well, and about the pestle. These details had an overwhelming effect on the agitated lady, who kept crying out and covering her eyes with her hands—

"Just imagine, I had a premonition it would happen! I have

that faculty: whatever I anticipate comes to pass. Many were the times I looked at that dreadful man with the thought: this is a man who will end up by murdering me— And now, that's happened— I mean to say that if he's murdered not me but only his father, it's probably because I've been preserved by the finger of God; and besides, he couldn't bring himself to murder me because, at this very spot, I had placed about his neck an icon with some relics of Barbara, the sainted martyr— But how close I stood to death at the moment: I walked close up to him and he held out his neck towards me! D'you know, Pyotr Ilyich (forgive me, didn't you say your name was Pyotr Ilyich?)— d'you know, I don't believe in miracles, but the icon and the manifest miracle it worked with me—it's simply amazing, and I'm again ready to believe that anything is possible. You've heard of the *starets* Zossima, haven't you? But I'm afraid I don't realise what I'm saying— And just imagine, he actually spat in my face with my icon about his neck— True, he didn't murder me but merely spat at me—and so that's where he dashed off to! But where should we be going now—what are we to do? What do you think?"

Rising to his feet, Perkhotin announced that he would go direct to the uyezd chief of police to inform him of what it was all about; the official would take whatever steps he thought appropriate.

"What an excellent man he is, excellent indeed! I'm acquainted with Mikhail Makarovich. Of course, he's the right man to see. How resourceful you are, Pyotr Ilyich, and how well you've thought of everything. It would never have even occurred to me, you know!"

"Particularly since I'm myself quite well acquainted with the police chief," Perkhotin observed, who was still standing and was obviously anxious to get away from the impetuous lady, who seemed unwilling to let him take his leave.

"Yes, yes," she prattled on, "come and let me know what you've seen and found out—and whatever transpires—what will be decided and where he'll be packed off to. We have no capital punishment in our country, have we? Be sure to come, even if it's three o'clock in the morning, four or even half past— Have me awakened even forcibly if I don't get up— Oh dear, I don't think I'll be able even to fall asleep. But shouldn't I go with you? What d'you think?—"

"N-no, but it might prove quite useful were you to pen three lines now, in your own handwriting, just in case, to the effect that you never gave Dmitri Fyodorovich any money at all. It may be needed—"

"Without fail!" cried Madame Khokhlakov fervently, running up to her bureau. "And I must say that you really amaze me and even stagger me by your resourcefulness and your skill in such matters— You're in the civil service here, aren't you? It's so nice to learn that you are—"

As she spoke, she rapidly wrote the following lines in a bold hand, on a half-sheet of note-paper:

"Never in my life I lent the unfortunate Dmitri Fyodorovich Karamazov (for he is really unfortunate now) the sum of three thousand roubles, or any other sum, either today or at any other time—never! I swear that by all that is sacred in our world.

Khokhlakov"

"Here's the note!" she said, turning rapidly to Perkhotin. "Go and save him. It's a noble deed you're performing."

And she thrice made the sign of the cross over him, and then hastened even as far as the hall to see him out.

"I'm so grateful to you! You can't imagine how grateful to you I am for your coming to me in the first place. How is it we haven't met before? I'll be flattered to receive you at my home. And it's so nice to know that you're in the civil service here—and with such preciseness and resourcefulness. You should be valued here, and properly esteemed, and if there's anything I can do for you, believe me— Oh, I love our young people! I'm simply in love with them. Our young people are the foundation of our dear and now suffering country, her entire hope— Oh, now go, do go!—"

But Perkhotin had already made off, or else she would never have let him get away so soon. Yet Madame Khokhlakov had made quite an agreeable impression on him, which somewhat

165

allayed his disquiet over being involved in so nasty a business. As is common knowledge, there is no accounting for the extraordinary variety of tastes. "She isn't at all so elderly, after all," he thought with some pleasure. "On the contrary, I'd take her for her daughter."

As for Madame Khokhlakov, she was simply captivated by the young man. "Such skill, such competence in such a young man, and in our times, and all that together with such good manners and looks. And there are people who say that our present-day young people are a futile lot, but here we have an example of a young man who—" and so on in that vein. So she simply lost sight of the "dreadful affair", and it was only when she was getting into bed that she again recalled suddenly how "close to death she had been": "Oh, how dreadful, dreadful!" she said, as she sank into sound and sweet slumber. Incidentally, I would never have enlarged on such trivial and irrelevant details had not the eccentric meeting, just described by me here, between a young civil servant and a widow by no means elderly subsequently become the starting point of the future career of this precise and competent young man. To this day the story is recalled with astonishment in our town, and we, too, may have something particular to say about it when we conclude our long narrative about the Karamazov brothers.

2.

The Alarm

Mikhail Makarovich Makarov, our uyezd chief of police, a retired lieutenant-colonel, who had been awarded the appropriate rank in the civil service, was a widower and an excellent man. He had come to our parts only three years before, but had won widespread esteem mainly for his ability "to bring people together". He kept open house, and could not imagine living otherwise. There was always some one or other dining with him—he could never sit down to table without a visitor or two. He would give dinner parties on any pretext, sometimes most unexpected ones. If not exquisite, the food was always plenteous, the meat, fish or cabbage pies most toothsome, and the wines made up in quantity what they may have lacked in quality. The first room visitors entered contained a billiard table and was quite well appointed, that is to say, even with pictures of English thoroughbred horses in black frames on the walls, which, as is common knowledge, is essential in the *décor* of any unmarried man's billiard room. Cards were played every evening, if only at a single table. The best people in our town—including mothers and unmarried daughters—would assemble at the house quite often to dance there. Though a widower, Mikhail Makarovich lived with his family: a long-widowed daughter and her two girls, his grown-up granddaughters, just out of finishing school. They were vivacious girls and not at all bad-looking, and though all knew that they had no dowries, they attracted our young gentlemen to their grandfather's house. Though Mikhail Makarovich was not excessively intelligent, he performed his official duties in a manner no worse than many others did. In plainer terms, he was a man of little or no education, and was even lacking in a clear understanding of the terms of reference he enjoyed at his post. It was not so much his inability to fully grasp the significance of some of the reforms effected during the present reign, as the quite considerable errors he made in his interpretation of them; that stemmed, not so much from any particular incapacity as simply from his innate unconcern, for he could never find the time to delve into things. "At heart, I'm more of a soldier than a civilian, gentlemen," he would say of himself. He did not even seem to have arrived at any definite or firm understanding of the precise fundamentals of the peasant reform, and, so to speak, had, from year to year, accumulated some knowledge of it from practice and inadvertently, and yet he was a landowner himself. Perkhotin knew for a certainty that he would meet with some callers on Mikhail Makarovich, but could not know which in particular. As it turned out, the host was playing cards with the local public prosecutor, and Varvinsky, the district doctor, a young man who had recently taken up his duties after graduating *summa cum laude* from the St. Petersburg Academy of Medicine. Ippolit Kirillovich, the public prosecutor (actually the deputy public prosecutor, though known locally by the full title) was very much in the public eye in our parts: only thirty-five, somewhat consumptive, married to a very stout and childless lady, he was touchy and irritable, though highly intelligent and even kind-hearted. The trouble with him was that his opinion of himself was somewhat higher than his actual qualities warranted, which was why his behaviour always seemed restless. Moreover, he had pretensions to certain superior and even artistic faculties, for instance, a psychological flair, a special knowledge of the human soul, and a particular gift of insight into crime and the criminal. In this sense he always had a chip on his shoulder, considering he did not get the advancement he deserved in the service because of his superiors' inability to appreciate his true worth, and also because of the enemies he had. At his gloomier moments he even threatened to resign and become a criminal lawyer. The unexpected case of the Karamazov parricide seemed to come as a timely fillip: "This is a case that could come to the knowledge of all Russia." But I am running ahead in what I am saying.

Sitting in the next room in the company of the ladies was Nikolai Parfenovich Nelyudov, our young court investigator, who had come from St. Petersburg only two months previously. It was later remarked, with some surprise even, that all these persons should have assembled, as though intentionally, at the home of the chief local executive officer on the very evening of the "crime". Yet the reason was a very simple one, and everything happened in the most natural way: the public prosecutor's wife had had a bad toothache for the last two days and he had to seek refuge somewhere from her groaning; as for the doctor, his very essence precluded his spending an evening anywhere but at cards. Nikolai Parfenovich Nelyudov had been planning for three days to call on the Makarovs that very evening just by chance, so to speak, in order to slyly spring a surprise on Olga Mikhailovna, the elder Makarov girl, to wit, by divulging that he was aware of her secret: it was her birthday, a fact she had wished to conceal so as to avoid being obliged to give a dance for the occasion. He was looking forward to having a lot of fun and making dark hints at her age, and her fear of revealing it, and since he was now in possession of her secret, he could very well make it public on the very next day, and so on in that vein. The amiable young man was very frolicsome in such matters; our ladies had dubbed him "that naughty man", which seemed much to his liking. Incidentally, he was quite well born, of a good family, with breeding and worthy sentiments though he was a *bon vivant*, his pleasures were innocuous and always quite proper. In appearance, he was below medium height and of a frail and delicate constitution. Several bejewelled rings were always sparkling on his slender white fingers. However, he assumed an air of the utmost importance while performing his official duties, as though endowing his significance and his post with a kind of sanctity. He was most skilful at tripping up murderers and other malefactors of the lower orders during his interrogations of them, and if he did not win their respect he did evoke a kind of amazement.

On entering the house, Perkhotin was simply astonished to learn that the entire company knew what had happened; they had abandoned their cards and were all on their feet, discussing the affair. Even Nikolai Parfenovich had hurried away from the young ladies, and looked aggressively poised for action. Perkhotin was met with the astounding news that old Fyodor Pavlovich Karamazov had indeed been murdered at his home that very evening—murdered and robbed. The matter had just come to light in the following manner.

Though fast asleep in her bed, where she might well have gone on sleeping till the morning, Marfa Ignatievna, the wife of Grigori, who had been felled at the fence by Mitya, was suddenly awakened, probably by a dreadful howl emanating from Smerdyakov, who was lying unconscious in the next room, a sound his epileptic fits always began with, painfully frightening Marfa Ignatievna out of her wits. She could never get used to it. Still half-awake, she dashed into Smerdyakov's cubicle. But it was dark there, and all she could hear was the sick man's stertorous breathing and his convulsions. This made Marfa Ignatievna burst into screams and call her husband, but she suddenly realised that Grigori had not been by her side when she had got up. She ran back to her bed and began to grope about with her hands, but the bed was really empty. He must have gone outside then—but where? She hurried out on the front steps, whence she called him in a timid voice. There was no reply but she heard some distant groans in the silence of the night, seeming to come from the other end of the garden. She strained her ears: the groans were repeated, coming indeed from somewhere in the garden. "Lordie, it's just like it was with Smelly Lizaveta!" was the thought that came into her distraught mind. She fearfully descended the steps and noticed that the garden wicket was ajar. "He must be there, the poor dear," she thought as she went up to the wicket, and suddenly and distinctly heard Grigori calling her by name, "Marfa, Marfa!" in a dreadfully weak and moaning voice. "Good Lord, preserve us from evil," she whispered as she rushed to answer the call, and that was how she found Grigori, only not where he had been felled but at some twenty paces from the fence. It later appeared that, on coming to, he had crawled away and kept doing so for quite a while, losing consciousness several times. On seeing that he was all covered with blood, she began to scream at the top of her voice, while Grigori kept muttering faintly and incoherently, "He's committed murder—he's murdered his father—why scream, you fool—run for help—" But Marfa Ignatievna did not desist and went on screaming, then, suddenly noticing that the master's window was open and a light was burning inside, she ran there and began calling Fyodor Pavlovich. But when she looked in through the window, a dreadful sight caught her eye: her master was lying supine on the floor, quite motionless. His white shirt and light-coloured dressing-gown were soaked in blood. The blood and the dead man's still face stood out in the candlelight from the table. The utterly horrified Marfa Ignatievna made off, ran out of the garden, unbarred the gate and ran headlong along the back alley towards her neighbour, Maria Kondratievna. Both mother and daugher had retired for the night, but were awakened by the furious banging on the shutters and Marfa Ignatievna's desperate screams, and hurried towards the window. Though her shrieks made her speech incoherent, Marfa Ignatievna was able to convey the main fact, and call for help. As it happened, Foma the roamer was staying at their house for the night, so they got him up at once and the three made for the scene of the crime. On the way, Maria Kondratievna was able to recall that, at some time after eight that evening, she had heard a dreadful and piercing cry coming from their garden: it had, of course, been Grigori's shout of "parricide", as he grabbed at Mitya's leg when he was already sitting astride the fence. "Someone screamed and suddenly stopped," Maria Kondratievna said as they ran along. On reaching the place where Grigori lay on the ground, the two women were able, with Foma's help, to get him back to the hut. They lit a candle and discovered that Smerdyakov was still writhing convulsively in his cubicle, the whites of his eyes showing, and foaming at the mouth. Grigori's head was cleansed with a mixture of water and vinegar, which at once revived him. "Has the master been murdered?" was the first thing he asked. The two women and Foma then went to find out, and, on entering the garden, they saw that, besides the window, the door from the house into the garden stood wide open, too, though the master had himself locked up every evening during the past week and did not permit even Grigori to disturb him, whatever the pretext. On seeing the open door, the two women and Foma were afraid to enter thereby "to avoid future trouble". When they returned to Grigori, the latter told them to hasten at once to the uyezd chief of police. This was done by Maria Kondratievna, who raised the alarm there. She arrived only five minutes before Perkhotin, who brought with him not only his surmises and conclusions but was himself an eye-witness whose account only confirmed the generally held suspicion as to who the criminal could be (something he had, in his innermost thoughts, refused to give credence to until that very moment).

Energetic steps were decided on. The deputy chief of the city police was instructed to at once get hold of four witnesses to assist in the proceedings, and, in conformity with the rules for such action, which I shall not go into here, entry was effected into the Karamazov house and an inquiry started on the spot. The district doctor, new to this post and very keen at his job, had practically volunteered to accompany the police chief, the public prosecutor and the court investigator. I shall briefly summarise their finding: Fyodor Pavlovich was quite dead, with a fractured skull—but with what weapon? It was most probably the same as was later used against Grigori. The weapon was soon forthcoming, after Grigori, who had received all possible medical aid, gave them, albeit in a weak and faltering voice, a fairly articulate account of how he had been struck down. A search by lantern light produced the brass pestle lying conspicuously on the garden path near the fence. There were no particular signs of disturbance in the dead man's room, but lying on the floor at his bed behind the screens was a big office-type heavy envelope, which, on examination, revealed the following inscription: "A little gift of three thousand roubles to my angel Grushenka, should she wish to come", below which had been added, probably later and in Fyodor Pavlovich's hand, the words "and my little chick". The envelope carried three large seals of red wax, but it had been torn open and emptied: the money had gone. Also found on the floor was the narrow pink ribbon the envelope had been tied up in. What produced a strong impression on the two law officers was that part of Perkhotin's testimony which said that Dmitri Fyodorovich would most certainly shoot himself by daybreak, a firm intention he had announced to Perkhotin, in whose presence he had loaded a pistol, penned a note and had put it in his pocket, and so on and so forth. When Perkhotin had voiced some disbelief on that score and threatened to report him to prevent the suicide, Mitya had grinningly retorted, "You won't have the time to." Consequently, they had to go to Mokroye post-haste to take the criminal before he could carry out his threat. "It's clearly, quite clearly the way such hotheads behave!" the prosecutor kept reiterating excitedly. "I'll kill myself tomorrow, but I'll have a riotous time before I die." The account of the wines and provisions Mitya had ordered from the shop only served to work the prosecutor up even more. "You must remember, gentlemen, the fellow who murdered the merchant Olsufiev? After robbing him of fifteen hundred roubles, he went to have his hair curled, and, with no attempt at concealing the money—in fact, almost holding it in his hand—went off for a spree with the wenches." However, the inquiry, the search, the formalities and the like all took time, so, two hours in advance they sent on ahead the rural police officer Mavriki Mavrikievich Shmertsov, who had come to town on the previous morning to collect his pay. Mavriki Mavrikievich was instructed not to raise the alarm on reaching Mokroye, but to keep the "criminal" under constant surveillance until the proper authorities arrived, and also to have the witnesses, village constables and the like all ready. Shmertsov followed his instructions and concealed his identity, taking into his confidence, and only in part, the innkeeper, Trifon Borisovich, alone, an old acquaintance of his. The hour coincided with Mitya's walking into the innkeeper on the unlit gallery. The man had been looking for him, and Mitya at once noticed the sudden change that had come over his face and voice. Thus neither Mitya nor anyone else knew that they were being watched; as for the pistol-case, it has been taken away by the innkeeper for safe-keeping. It was only after four o'clock in the morning, almost at daybreak, that the uyezd chief of police, the public prosecutor and the court investigator arrived in two troika-drawn carriages, the doctor having stayed behind at the Karamazov house to perform the autopsy in the morning, but what was of the greatest interest to him was the condition of the sick servant Smerdyakov. "Such violent and protracted epileptic fits recurrent uninterruptedly for two days are rarely to be met—a matter of scientific interest," he declared agitatedly to his departing companions, who laughingly felicitated him on the discovery. The prosecutor and the court investigator distinctly recalled afterwards that the doctor had added most decisively that Smerdyakov would not live till the morning.

And now, after this lengthy but, I think, necessary explanation, we now return to that very point in our story at which we broke off in the preceding book.

3.

A Soul's Descent into Gehenna.
Ordeal the First

And so Mitya sat eyeing the people about him with consternation, without the least comprehension of what was being said to him. Suddenly he rose to his feet, flung up his hands, and cried in a loud voice:

"I'm innocent! I'm innocent of that blood! I'm innocent of my father's blood— I did intend to kill him, but I'm innocent! It wasn't me!"

Hardly had he uttered these words when Grushenka came rushing from behind the curtain and fell at the uyezd police chief's feet.

"It's me, me who's to blame, wretch that I am!" she shrieked in a heart-rending voice, the tears streaming down her face, and her hands outstretched. "It was because of me that he committed the murder!— It was me who tormented him and drove him to do it! I tormented the poor old man that's now dead, just out of spite, and led him up to it! I'm to blame—it's all my doing—mine first and foremost!"

"Yes, it is! You're the main culprit, you fury and vicious hussy! You're to blame most of all!" the police chief yelled, shaking a fist at her, but at this point he was rapidly and resolutely curbed, the public prosecutor even throwing his arms about him.

"This is most irregular, Mikhail Makarovich," he exclaimed. "You're positively hampering the examination—ruining the matter—" he went on, almost gasping.

"Steps must be taken without fail—they must be taken!" cried Nikolai Parfenovich Nelyudov, greatly worked up. "Otherwise, it's quite impossible to proceed!—"

"Put the two of us on trial!" Grushenka, still on her knees, went on in a frenzy. "Punish us together! I'll go by his side now even to the scaffold!"

"Grushenka, my life's blood, my sacred treasure!" cried Mitya, falling on his knees at her side and embracing her closely.

"Don't believe her!" he shouted. "She is quite guiltless of any blood, of anything!"

He was later able to recall being forcibly dragged from her side, and her being led away. When he came to himself, he was sitting at the table, with some men wearing the badges of village constables standing beside and behind him. Sitting on the sofa on the opposite side of the table was Nikolai Parfenovich Nelyudov, the court investigator, who kept trying to persuade him to drink some water from the glass on the table. "It will refresh you and help you to be calm. Have no fear and pull yourself together," he added most courteously. Mitya's gaze (as he later recollected) was suddenly drawn to the man's large rings, one with an amethyst, and another with a vivid yellow stone of fine water. Long afterwards he recalled with astonishment how he had been unable to tear his gaze away from the rings or forget them even throughout the dreadful hours of his interrogation, so irresistible was the attraction of something so incongruous in his situation. On Mitya's left, where Maximov had been seated earlier in the evening, the prosecutor now sat, while the seat where Grushenka had been was now occupied by a pink-cheeked young man in a kind of a well-worn hunting jacket, with an inkpot and paper before him, evidently the clerk whom the court investigator had brought along with him. The police chief was now standing at a window at the other end of the room, next to Kalganov, who too had taken a seat at the same window.

"Have a drink of water!" the court investigator repeated mildly, perhaps for the tenth time.

"I've had some, gentlemen, I've had, but—well, gentlemen, you may crush me, punish me, decide my fate!" exclaimed Mitya, his stare strangely fixed on the court investigator.

"You positively affirm that you are not guilty of the death of your father Fyodor Pavlovich, is that so?" asked the court investigator in a mild but insistent voice.

"It is! But I'm guilty of shedding another's blood, the blood of another old man, but not my father's. It's a cause of grief to me! I murdered, I actually murdered the old man, murdered and struck him down— But it's hard to have to answer for that misdeed with another's blood, a dreadful murder I'm innocent of— That's a terrible charge, gentlemen, which has stunned me! But who could have murdered my father, who has done that? Who could have murdered him if I didn't? It's something out of this world, absurd and utterly impossible!—"

"Indeed, who could have done it—" the court investigator began but Ippolit Kirillovich, the public prosecutor (actually the deputy public prosecutor, but we shall give him the full title for the sake of brevity) gave him a meaningful glance, and addressed Mitya:

"You don't have to worry about the old servant Grigori Vassiliev. You should know that he's alive; he's come to himself and, despite the severe beating you gave him, in accordance with your present testimony and his own—there's no doubt he will live. At least, that's what the doctor says."

"Alive? Actually alive!" Mitya cried out suddenly, throwing up his hands, his face beaming with joy. "Lord, I thank thee for the great wonder thou hast worked for me, sinner and evildoer that I am, in reply to my prayer!— Yes, yes, in reply to my prayer, for I was praying all night long!—" He crossed himself thrice. He was almost choking in his emotion.

"It is from that very man Grigori that we've received such important evidence concerning you that—" the public prosecutor proceeded, but Mitya suddenly jumped up from his chair.

"Just a moment, gentlemen, for God's sake, a single moment. I'll just run over to her—"

"I'm sorry, sir! But that's quite impossible at this juncture!" Nikolai Parfenovich almost shrieked, also jumping to his feet. Mitya was grabbed by the constables, but sat down of his own accord—

"What a pity, gentlemen! I wanted to see her for a single moment—I wanted to tell her that the blood that has been pressing so crushingly on my heart all night has been washed away and that I'm no longer a murderer! Gentlemen, she's my fiancée!" he said suddenly, ecstatically and reverently, looking around at them all. "Oh, I thank you, gentlemen! You've restored my life, made me resurrected in a single instant!— That old man—why, gentlemen, he used to carry me in his arms,

176

wash me in the tub when I was abandoned by everybody at the age of three. He was like a father to me!"

"So you—" the court investigator began.

"Gentlemen, give me another moment, please," Mitya broke in, putting his elbows on the table and covering his head with his hands. "Give me a moment to think and get my bearings, gentlemen. All this has been a shattering shock to me. A man's soul is not a sheepskin drum, gentlemen!"

"Have some water—" Nikolai Parfenovich murmured.

Mitya took his hands from his face and laughed. His look was composed, and he seemed to have instantly changed. His whole bearing was different: he was now again on a par with all these men, all these former acquaintances of his, just as if they had all met the day before when nothing had happened, at some social gathering. We shall observe here incidentally that, on his arrival in our town, Mitya had been welcomed at the uyezd police chief's house, but that later on, especially during the previous month, Mitya had hardly ever called there and, when meeting him in the street, the police chief looked angry and frowned, replying to Mitya's bow merely out of civility. Mitya had not been slow to notice it. His acquaintance with the public prosecutor was even more distant, but he sometimes paid courtesy calls on the prosecutor's wife, a nervous and fanciful lady, without quite knowing himself why he called on her, and she always received him cordially, taking an interest in him up to the last. He had not been able to make the acquaintance of the court investigator, though he had met and even spoken to him on one or two occasions, each time about the fair sex.

"You're a most skilful investigator, I can see, Nikolai Parfenovich," Mitya cried suddenly with a gay laugh, "but I'll do all I can to help you now. Oh, gentlemen, I feel risen from the dead and—take no offence if I address you so familiarly and frankly. Besides, I'm afraid I'm a little drunk, I tell you that frankly. I believe I have had the honour—er—the honour and pleasure of meeting you, Nikolai Parfenovich, at my relative Miusov's— Gentlemen, gentlemen, I don't lay claim to be on equal terms with you, I'm fully aware of my present position. If Grigori has given evidence against me, then I am—oh, of course—I am under a dreadful suspicion! It's horrible, horrible—I quite realise that! But let's get down to business, gentlemen, I'm ready, and I'm sure we shall get through with it all instantaneously, because—listen, gentlemen, listen! If I know that I'm innocent, then we can get through with the matter at once, can't we? Can't we?"

Mitya spoke with nervous and rapid effusion, as though absolutely certain that his listeners were his best friends.

"So for the present we shall record that you absolutely reject the charge brought against you," the court investigator said impressively and, turning to his clerk, he dictated to him in an undertone what to write.

"Record it? D'you want to record it? Why, by all means I don't mind, I give you my full consent, gentlemen— Only, you see— Wait, wait! Take this down: 'He is guilty of disorderly conduct, guilty of inflicting violent blows upon a poor old man—yes, he's guilty of that.' And, well, there's something else that I'm guilty of in my heart of hearts, but you needn't write that down (he turned suddenly to the clerk) for that, gentlemen, is part of my private life and has nothing to do with you, I mean what's in the recesses of my heart—But as for the murder of my old father—I'm innocent of that! The whole thing is absurd! Quite absurd! I'll prove it to you and you'll be convinced at once! You will laugh later, gentlemen, you will roar with laughter at your suspicion!—"

"Pray calm yourself, Dmitri Fyodorovich," the court investigator reminded him, as though wishing to overcome Mitya's frenzy with his own calmness. "Before continuing the interrogation, I'd like you, if you consent, to confirm that you seem to have disliked your father and to be having constant quarrels with him— At least, I believe you said a quarter of an hour ago, that you even wanted to kill him. 'I didn't murder him,' you exclaimed, 'but I wanted to!' "

"Did I say that? Oh, well, that may very well be so, gentlemen. Yes, unfortunately, I did want many, many times to murder him—most unfortunately!"

"You wanted to. Would you mind explaining the motives you were guided by in such hatred of your father's person?"

"What is there to explain, gentlemen?" said Mitya, morosely, shrugging his shoulders and lowering his eyes. "I've never concealed my feelings; it is common knowledge in the town, and all the people at the town inn know of it. Only a short while ago I spoke about it in the cell of the *starets* Zossima— and, on the evening of the same day, I fell on my father and nearly killed him and swore in the presence of witnesses to come back and kill him— Oh, there are thousands of witnesses! I kept shouting about it a whole month—lots of people will confirm it! There's direct evidence of that fact, it speaks, it shouts for itself, but, gentlemen, feelings—feelings are quite a different matter. You see, gentlemen," Mitya frowned, "it seems to me you have no right to question me about my feelings. You may be empowered to do so, I quite understand that, but it's my own affair, my private and personal affair— But since I haven't concealed my feelings before—at the town inn, for instance, where I've talked to everyone about it, I—I won't make a secret of it now. You see, gentlemen, I realise very well that the evidence against me in this affair is overwhelming: I've declared publicly that I'll kill him, and all of a sudden he's been murdered; therefore, it couldn't have been anyone but me, could it? Ha, ha! I don't blame you at all, gentlemen, I quite understand. You see, I'm completely mystified myself; for who, after all, could have killed him, if not me? Isn't that so? If not me, then who, who? Gentlemen," he exclaimed suddenly, "I'd like to know, gentlemen, indeed, I demand to be told where he was murdered? How was he murdered? How and what with? Tell me," he asked quickly, looking at the public prosecutor and the court investigator.

"We found him lying on the floor of his bedroom, lying on his back, with his head battered in," said the public prosecutor.

"How dreadful, gentlemen!" Mitya shuddered suddenly and, leaning on the table, covered his face with his right hand.

"Let's proceed," the court investigator interrupted. "What prompted you in your feelings of hatred? You declared in public, I believe, that it was jealousy, didn't you?"

"Well, yes, jealousy, but not only jealousy."

"Differences over money?"

"Yes, over money, too."

"There was, I believe, an argument over three thousand roubles, which you claimed was owing to you as part of your inheritance."

"Three thousand? Far more," Mitya cried excitedly. "Over six thousand, over ten thousand, perhaps. I've told everyone about it, actually shouted about it! But I made up my mind to let it go at three thousand. I needed the three thousand desperately—so that I regarded the envelope with the three thousand, which I knew he kept under his pillow ready for Grushenka, as simply stolen from me. Yes, gentlemen, I regarded it as belonging to me, as my own property—"

The public prosecutor glanced significantly at the court investigator and managed to wink at him unobserved.

"We'll return to that later," the latter said at once. "You will, I hope, let us now note and record this—er—little point, I mean, that you regarded the money in the envelope as your own property."

"Take it down, gentlemen, take it down. You see, I realise that it's just another piece of evidence against me, but I fear no evidence, and I bring it against me myself. Do you hear? Myself! You see, gentlemen, you seem to take me for quite a different kind of person from what actually I am," he added with sudden and gloomy sadness. "You're talking to a man of honour, a most honourable man, but above all—and bear that in mind—a man who's committed lots of mean acts, but who has always been a most honourable human being, as a human being, inside, at bottom, and well, in short, I—I'm afraid I don't know how to put it— I mean, what has made me so unhappy all my life is that I've yearned to be an honourable man, to be, as it were, a martyr to honour and to seek for it with a lantern, with the lantern of Diogenes, and yet all my life I've been acting meanly towards people, like all of us, gentlemen— I mean, like me alone, gentlemen, not like all, but like me alone. I'm sorry, I was wrong—like me alone, me alone!— Gentlemen, my head aches," he knit his brows in pain. "You see, gentlemen, I didn't like his appearance, there was something obscene about him, a braggart who trampled everything sacred under foot, derisive and impious—horrible! But I think differently now that he's dead."

"What do you mean—differently?"

"No, not differently, but I'm sorry I hated him so much."

"Do you feel repentant?"

"No, not repentant. Don't take that down. I'm not a very attractive man myself, gentlemen, that's the truth. I'm not at all a model, and that's why I had no right to consider him so repulsive. Yes, that's it! You may take that down."

Having said that, Mitya fell into a sudden melancholy. For some time now, as he kept replying to the court investigator's questions, he had gradually grown gloomier and gloomier. It was then that there was another unexpected scene. Though Grushenka had been removed, she had not been taken away very far, only to the room next but one to the blue room where the interrogation was taking place. It was a small room with a single window, next to the large room in which they had danced and feasted all night. She was sitting there alone, with only Maximov at her side, who was terribly confounded and scared, clinging to her as though seeking security. At the door of their room stood a constable with a metal badge on his chest. Grushenka was weeping, and then, suddenly, when her grief grew overwhelming, she jumped up, threw up her hands, and with a loud wail, "Oh, woe is me, woe is me!" rushed out of the room to him, to her Mitya, and so impetuously that there was no stopping her. Hearing her outcry, Mitya trembled all over, jumped to his feet, and with a yell rushed headlong towards her, quite beside himself. But again they were not allowed to meet, though they saw each other. He was violently seized by the arms: he struggled and tried to free himself so that it took three or four men to hold him. She, too, was seized and he saw her stretching out her arms to him as she was dragged, screaming, out of the room. When the scene was over, he found himself back in the same place as before, at the table, opposite the court investigator, and shouting at them:

"What do you want of her? Why do you torment her? She's innocent, quite innocent!—"

The public prosecutor and the court investigator did their

utmost to calm him. Thus, some ten minutes passed; at last, Makarov, who had been away all this while, returned hurriedly into the room, and said in a loud, excited voice to the public prosecutor:

"She's been taken downstairs. Will you permit me, gentlemen, to say a word to this unfortunate man? In your presence, gentlemen, in your presence!"

"Do, Mikhail Makarovich," replied the court investigator. "We have no objection."

"Now listen to me, Dmitri Fyodorovich, my dear fellow," Makarov began, addressing Mitya, and there was an expression of warm and almost fatherly compassion on his excited face. "I've taken your Agrafena Alexandrovna downstairs and entrusted her to the care of the landlord's daughters, with that old man Maximov at her side, all the time. I've reasoned with her—do you hear?—I've talked her round and calmed her, I've made her understand that you have to clear yourself and that she mustn't upset and hinder you, or you may get confused and say what you shouldn't—understand? Well, in short, I've spoken to her and she understands. She's an intelligent girl, old man. She's a good soul. She tried to kiss my hands in her eagerness to ask me to help you. She's sent me here herself to tell you not to worry about her, and I have to go, old man, I have to go and tell her that you are calm and easy in your mind about her. So, please compose yourself. Understand that I feel at fault to her, she's a Christian soul, yes, gentlemen, she's a gentle soul and she's not to blame for anything. So what am I to tell her, Dmitri Fyodorovich? Will you keep calm or not?"

The kind-hearted fellow had said a great deal he shouldn't have, but Grushenka's suffering, the suffering of a fellow-creature, had gone straight to his kind heart and tears even started to his eyes. Mitya jumped to his feet and rushed up to him.

"Forgive me, gentlemen, and permit me, oh, permit me!" he cried. "Yours is an angelic heart, Mikhail Makarovich, angelic, and I thank you for her! I will, I will be calm, I will be cheerful. Tell her, in the infinite goodness of your heart, that I am cheerful, quite cheerful, that I shall be laughing in a moment, knowing she has a guardian angel like you at her side. I shall get through with all this any moment now, and, as soon as I'm free, I'll join her. She'll see. Let her wait! Gentlemen," he said, turning suddenly to the public prosecutor and the court investigator, "I shall now open up my heart to you, I'll unburden myself to you, and we shall get it over in a moment. Let us get through with it with alacrity and—we shall have a good laugh when it is all over, shan't we? But, gentlemen, that woman is the queen of my heart! Oh, permit me to say that, gentlemen. That I must reveal to you now— For I can see that I'm dealing with most honourable men. She's the light of my eyes, whom I hold sacred—oh, if you only knew! You heard her cry 'I'll go to the scaffold with him'? And what have I given her, I, a penniless beggar? Why such love for me? Do I, an awkward and shameful wretch, with disgrace staring me in the face, deserve such love? Do I deserve that she should accompany me to penal servitude in Siberia? And a moment ago she was prone at your feet for me, she—a proud and innocent woman! How can I help adoring her? How can I help crying out and rushing to her as I did just now? Oh, forgive me, gentlemen! But now, now I am comforted!"

Sinking into his chair and, covering his face in his hands, he wept aloud. But those were happy tears. He pulled himself together at once. The old chief of the uyezd police seemed very pleased, as did the lawyers too: they felt that the interrogation was about to enter into a new phase. When the police officer was gone, Mitya looked positively happy.

"Well, gentlemen, I'm at your disposal now, entirely at your disposal. And—but for all these trifles, we'd come to an understanding at once. I'm speaking about trifles again. I'm at your disposal, gentlemen, but, I swear, there must be mutual confidence—you must trust me and I must trust you, otherwise we shall never get it over. I'm saying this in your interests. Let's get down to business, gentlemen, to business. Above all, don't probe into my heart like that, don't lacerate it with trifles. Just ask me about facts and about what has a direct bearing on this affair, and I'll satisfy you at once. To hell with trifles!"

So Mitya kept exclaiming. The interrogation was resumed.

4.

Ordeal the Second

"You can't imagine, Dmitri Fyodorovich, how your readiness is encouraging to us—" Nikolai Parfenovich Nelyudov began animatedly, an expression of satisfaction showing in his large, light-grey, protruding but shortsighted eyes, from which he had removed the spectacles a minute before. "And you were quite right about our mutual confidence, without which it is sometimes quite impossible to carry on in a case of such importance, provided, that is, the suspect really desires and hopes to clear himself, and is able to. For our part, we shall do all we can, and, indeed, you can see for yourself how we are conducting the case— You approve, Ippolit Kirillovich?" he turned suddenly to the public prosecutor.

"Oh, without the least doubt," the public prosecutor replied approvingly if somewhat dryly, compared with Nelyudov's impulsiveness.

Let me note, once and for all, that the court investigator who had arrived in our town only recently, had from the very outset developed an extraordinary esteem for our public prosecutor and felt almost an affinity with him. He was practically the only man in the locality to have implicit faith in the outstanding psychological and oratorical talents of our public prosecutor, who had been treated in "so unfair a fashion" by his superiors in the civil service, and he was fully convinced that the latter had really been given a bad deal. He had already heard of him in St. Petersburg. In his turn, our young Nikolai Parfenovich was the only man in the world our "unfairly treated" public prosecutor had taken a sincere liking to. On the way to the inn, they had managed to reach some understanding on how the present case was to be conducted, and now, as he sat at the table, the court investigator's keen mind was quick to perceive every indication and movement on the face of his senior colleague, from a half-uttered word, a look, or a wink.

"Gentlemen, if you let me tell my story in my own fashion and don't interrupt me with trifling questions, I'll tell you everything at once," cried Mitya excitedly.

"Excellent, sir. Thank you. But before we go on to your statement, you will, I hope, let me establish another fact which is of great interest to us, I mean the ten roubles you borrowed at about five o'clock yesterday, leaving your pistols in pledge with your friend Pyotr Ilyich Perkhotin."

"I pledged them, gentlemen, I pledged them for ten roubles. What more do you want to know? That is all. As soon as I got back to town, I pledged them."

"You came back to town? Had you been out of town?"

"I had, gentlemen, about forty versts out of town. Didn't you know that?"

Glances were exchanged between the public prosecutor and the court investigator.

"And, in general, what if you began with a systematic account of your movements since early yesterday morning? We would like to learn, for instance, why you left town, at what time you left, and returned—and all the facts—"

"You should have asked me that from the very outset," Mitya laughed loudly. "Why, if you wish, I should really start not with yesterday but with the morning of the day before. Then you'll understand where, how, and why I went. I left on the morning of the day before yesterday, gentlemen, to call on our local merchant Samsonov so as to borrow three thousand roubles on firm security—it was a pressing matter, gentlemen, most pressing—"

"Permit me to interrupt you," the public prosecutor put it courteously, "but why did you have such urgent need of that particular sum, I mean three thousand roubles?"

"Oh, gentlemen, I wish you wouldn't go into such trifles: how, when and why, and why I had to have just so much money or not so much, and all that gammon— Why, three volumes wouldn't be enough to take all that down, and an epilogue besides!"

Mitya said all this with the good-natured but impatient familiarity of a man eager to tell the whole truth and full of the best intentions.

"Gentlemen," he suddenly said, pulling himself up, "you

185

must take no offence at my being intractable. I beg you again: believe me I have the greatest respect for you and I understand the situation. Don't think I'm drunk. I'm quite sober now. Even if I were drunk, that would be no impediment. With me, you know, it's a case of:

> *Sober and wise—he's stupid;*
> *Drunk and stupid—he's wise.*

Ha, ha! But I see, gentlemen, it is yet improper for me to crack jokes with you—not, that is, until the matter is settled. Allow me also to maintain my sense of dignity, too, gentlemen. I'm aware of the present difference between us: you see me as a criminal and therefore far from being on terms of equality with you and it is your duty to keep an eye on me. Nor can I expect you to pat me on the head for Grigori, for one really can't go breaking old men's heads with impunity, can one? I suppose you'll bring me to court for that and keep me behind bars for six months or a year. I don't know just what the sentence will be, but I hope it will be with no deprivation of civil rights, eh, Mr. Prosecutor? So, you see, gentlemen, I'm quite aware of the distance between us— But you will also agree that you could fluster the Lord Himself with such questions as: where did you step, how did you step, when did you step, and what did you step on? If you go on like that, I'm sure to get flustered, and then you'll use every trifling remark I may make as evidence against me, and put it on record, so what will all lead up to? To nothing at all! And even if I've begun to speak balderdash, please let me finish it, and you, gentlemen, as men of honour and education, will forgive me. Let me end with a request: dispense with the hidebound procedure of interrogation, gentlemen. What I mean, is: starting with something trifling and petty, like: how I got up, what I had for breakfast, how and where I spat, and then, by catching the criminal off his guard, suddenly stunning him with the question: 'Whom did you murder? Whom did you rob?' Ha, ha! That's your official practice, isn't it? It's the rule with you, that's what all your craftiness is based on! But only peasants can be taken in with clever tricks like that; I won't. I know a thing or two, for I've been in the service myself, ha, ha, ha! You won't be angry with me, gentlemen, will you? You will forgive my impertinence?" he cried, looking at them in a good-natured way that was almost surprising. "It's only Mitya Karamazov who's said that, so you can forgive it, for what is unpardonable in a man of sense, can be forgiven in Mitya, ha-ha!"

The court investigator listened and laughed, too. The public prosecutor did not laugh, though, for he was watching Mitya intently, his eyes fixed on him as though reluctant to miss a single word, the least movement, a slightest tremor of a muscle on his face.

"But from the very outset," the court investigator said, still with a laugh, "we've never tried to confuse you with questions about how you got up in the morning and what you had for breakfast. As a matter of fact, we even began with questions of the utmost import."

"I understand. I realised and appreciated it, and I appreciate even more your present goodness to me, unparalleled goodness befitting your most generous hearts. We three here are men of honour so let everything be based on the mutual confidence of educated and well-bred people linked together by a common bond of noble birth and honour. Let me, at any rate, look upon you as my best friends at this moment of my life, at a moment when my honour is at stake! That doesn't offend you, gentlemen, does it?"

"On the contrary, Dmitri Fyodorovich, you've expressed it all excellently," the court investigator agreed with a look of dignified approval.

"And away with trivialities, gentlemen, away with all these pettifogging trivialities," Mitya cried warmly, "or goodness only knows what will come of it otherwise. Don't you think so?"

"I shall follow your sensible advice entirely," the public prosecutor suddenly interposed, addressing Mitya, "but I cannot forego my question. It is extremely important for us to know why you needed such a sum, I mean, just three thousand roubles."

"Why I needed it? Oh, for one thing or another—well, to pay a debt."

"Who to?"

"That I flatly refuse to say, gentlemen! Not because I can't, or daren't, or am afraid to tell you, because the entire matter is of no importance whatever, in fact, it's a quite trifling matter. But I won't tell you because it's a matter of principle: it's my private life and I will allow no invasion of my private life. That's a principle with me. Your question has nothing whatever to do with the case, but is part of my private life! I wanted to pay a debt, a debt of honour, and I'm not going to say who to."

"You will agree to our recording that, won't you?" said the public prosecutor.

"By all means. Just record that I flatly refuse to say. You may write, gentlemen, that I consider it even dishonourable to speak of it. Gracious, the time it takes to write things down!"

"Let me caution you, sir," the public prosecutor said with emphatic severity, "and remind you once more that you have a perfect right to decline to answer questions being put to you, and that we, for our part, have no right whatever to extort any answer from you, if for one reason or another you decline to do so. That's entirely up to you. However, in cases such as this, it is our duty to explain and point out to you the great detriment you will be causing to yourself by withholding any piece of evidence. You may now proceed."

"Gentlemen, I'm not angry—I—" Mitya muttered, somewhat disconcerted by the reprimand. "Well, anyway, you see, gentlemen, Samsonov to whom I went then—"

We shall, of course, not reproduce in detail his account of what is known to the reader. Mitya was eager to describe everything down to the slightest detail and, at the same time, get it over as soon as possible. But as his evidence was being taken down, they had to interrupt him continually. Dmitri Fyodorovich objected, but submitted; he grew angry at times, but did not lose his temper. It is true that he could not help exclaiming at times: "Gentlemen, this is enough to drive the Almighty Himself into a fury", or "Gentlemen, do you realise that it's no good exasperating me?" but even while reacting in this way, he retained his genially effusive mood. Thus, he told them how Samsonov had "cheated" him two days before. (He had fully realised by now that he had been deceived.) The sale of his watch for six roubles, to pay for his travelling expenses—something neither the court investigator nor the public prosecutor knew anything about—at once whetted their interest and, to Mitya's intense indignation, they thought it necessary to record the fact in detail as further confirmation of the circumstance that he had been practically penniless at the time. Mitya began to gradually sink into gloom. Then, after describing his journey to see that Lurcher, and the night he spent in the fume-laden hut, etc., he brought his story down to his return to the town, and here he began, without any prompting, to give a detailed description of the torments of jealousy he had endured on account of Grushenka. They listened to him with silent attention and seemed to be particularly interested in his long having had an observation post in Maria Kondratievna's house, at the back of old Karamazov's garden, to keep watch on Grushenka, as well as in Smerdyakov having kept him informed about the goings-on in the house: this they took special note of, and registered in detail his jealousy of Grushenka. He spoke with emotion and at length, and though inwardly ashamed to reveal his innermost feelings to the public view, he quite obviously tried to overcome his shame in order to be truthful. The dispassionate severity with which the court investigator and especially the public prosecutor viewed him as he told his story disconcerted him greatly in the end. "This stripling Nelyudov, with whom I exchanged some silly remarks about women only a few days ago, and that sickly public prosecutor do not deserve to hear what I'm telling them," he reflected sadly. "What a disgrace! But I must be patient, bear it all and keep my lips sealed," he thought in conclusion, so he pulled himself together again and went on with his story. When he came to tell of his call on Madame Khokhlakov, his spirits again rose and he was about to tell them an amusing little story about the lady, which had nothing to do with the case, when the court investigator cut him short and suggested courteously that he should pass on "to more important matters". Finally, after describing his despair and telling them how, on leaving Madame Khokhlakov, he thought that he would get the three thousand even if he had to murder someone, he was stopped again and they recorded that he had meant "to murder someone". Mitya let them write it down without protest. Finally, he reached the point of the story where he suddenly learnt that Grushenka had deceived him and had left Samsonov's house soon after he had taken her there, though she had told him herself that she would stay there till midnight. "If I didn't kill that Fenya then, gentlemen, it was only because I lacked the time," he blurted out at that point in his story. That, too, was carefully taken down. Mitya waited gloomily and went on to tell them how he had dashed to his father's garden, at which the court investigator suddenly stopped him and, opening his large brief-case, lying beside him on the sofa, took out the brass pestle.

"Do you recognise this object, sir?" he asked, showing it to Mitya.

"Oh, yes!" Mitya smiled gloomily. "I know it all right! Let me have a look at it— Oh, hell, you needn't show it to me!"

"You haven't mentioned it," said the court investigator.

"Oh, hell, I wouldn't have held it back from you, we'd have come to it, anyway, don't you think so? It simply slipped my memory."

"Please tell us exactly how you came to arm yourself with it?"

"Why, yes, gentlemen, of course."

And Mitya told them how he had taken the pestle and made off with it.

"But what was your object in arming yourself with such a weapon?"

"My object? I had none. I just grabbed it and made off."

"But why, if you had no object?"

Mitya was fuming. With a gloomy and malicious smile he fixed his gaze on the "stripling". In fact, he was beginning to feel more and more ashamed of himself for having told "such people" the story of his jealousy in so sincere and so effusive a manner.

"Damn the pestle!" he blurted out suddenly.

"But still—"

"Well, to keep the dogs off. Or because it was dark— Or just in case—"

"But have you ever, on any previous occasion, when going out at night, armed yourself, if you're so afraid of the dark?"

"Oh, damn it all! Really, gentlemen, it's literally impossible to talk to you!" cried Mitya, exasperated beyond endurance, and flushing with anger, he turned on the clerk and said to him rapidly, with a note of fury in his voice:

"Write down at once—at once—that I took the pestle with me because I wanted to go and murder my father—Fyodor Pavlovich Karamazov—by hitting him on the head with it! Well, gentlemen, are you satisfied now? Have you got what you wanted?" he said, glaring defiantly at the court investigator and the public prosecutor.

"We are only too well aware," the public prosecutor replied dryly, "that the testimony you've just given was merely the result of your annoyance with us and of your exasperation at the questions we put to you, questions which you, sir, consider trivial, but which are actually of prime importance."

"But, good Lord, gentlemen, what if I did take the pestle?— Why does one take up things at such moments? I don't know. I just grabbed it and made off. That's all. For shame, gentlemen, *passons*, or I swear I won't say another word!"

His elbows on the table, he cupped his chin in his palms. He was sitting sideways to them, staring at the wall, and trying to control his mounting exasperation. And, indeed, he felt a terrible urge to get up and tell them they wouldn't get another word out of him, even if he had to "swing for it".

"You see, gentlemen," he said suddenly, restraining himself with an effort, "you see. I listen to you and it seems to me that I'm having a dream—you see, I sometimes have one and the same dream—I often do, it keeps on recurring: that someone is chasing me, someone I'm terrified of, chasing me in the dark, at night, looking for me, and I hide somewhere from him behind a door or a cupboard, hide myself so humiliatingly, and the worst of it is that he knows perfectly well where I've hidden myself from him, but he seems to be pretending deliberately not to know where I am, so as to prolong my agony, to enjoy my terror to the full— That's what you're doing now! It's just like that!"

"Is that the sort of thing you dream about?" asked the public prosecutor.

"Yes, that's the sort of thing I dream about— Aren't you going to write that down?" Mitya smiled wryly.

"No, sir, we're not going to write that down. Still, I must say you have curious dreams."

"But this time it isn't a dream! This is real, gentlemen, a fact of real life! I'm the wolf and you're the hunters. Well, hunt the wolf down!"

"You shouldn't make such a comparison," the court investigator began very mildly.

"Yes, I should, I should!" Mitya flared up again, though, having evidently relieved his mind by his outburst of sudden anger, he was again growing more good-humoured with every word he spoke. "You may not believe a criminal or a man on trial, who is being tormented by your questions, but, gentlemen, you cannot disbelieve, you've no right to disbelieve an honourable man, the honourable impulses of the heart—I say it boldly!—but—

> ...O heart, be silent,
> Bear this all in silent humility!

Well, shall I go on?" he broke off gloomily.

"Kindly do," replied the court investigator.

5.

Ordeal the Third

Though Mitya had begun in a stern tone, he was obviously doing his best not to forget or omit a single detail of his account. He told them how he had climbed over the fence into his father's garden and walked up to the window, and about everything that had been at the window. Speaking clearly and precisely, with the utmost distinctness, he gave an account of the feelings that had agitated him during those moments in the garden when he had yearned so much to find out whether Grushenka was at his father's or not. But, strange to say, both the public prosecutor and the court investigator listened to him this time somehow with greatest reserve, regarded him coldly, asking far fewer questions. Mitya could gather nothing from their faces. "They're angry and offended," he thought. "Well, to hell with it!" But when he told them how he had finally decided to give his father *the signal* that Grushenka had come so that he should open the window, neither the public prosecutor nor the court investigator paid the least attention to the word "signal", as though they completely failed to grasp the significance of that word, which Mitya could not help noticing. When he finally came to the moment when the sight of his father leaning out of the window had made him seethe with hatred and pull the pestle out of his pocket, he suddenly stopped short, as though on purpose. He sat staring at the wall, aware that their eyes were fixed upon him.

"Well," said the court investigator, "you pulled out the weapon and—and what happened then?"

"Then? Why, then I murdered him—hit him on the head and cracked his skull!— That's what happened, as you see it, didn't it?" Mitya asked, his eyes suddenly flashing. All his smouldering anger suddenly flared up in his soul with extraordinary force.

"That's how we see it," the court investigator repeated. "Well, and how do *you* see it?"

Mitya dropped his eyes and was silent for a long time.

"As I see it, gentlemen, as I see it, here's what happened," he said quietly. "Whether it was someone's tears, or my mother entreated God, or a good angel kissed me at that moment—I don't know, but the devil was overcome. I dashed away from the window and ran back to the fence— My father took fright, he must have caught sight of me for the first time just then, and sprang back from the window with a cry—I remember that very clearly. And I ran across the garden towards the fence and—and it was there that Grigori caught me, just as I was sitting astride the fence—"

At this point he at last looked up at his listeners, who seemed to return his glance with absolutely unruffled attention. A spasm of indignation clutched at Mitya's heart.

"Why, you're just laughing at me at this moment, gentlemen!" he said suddenly.

"Why should you think so?" asked the court investigator.

"You don't believe a single word—that's why! I understand perfectly well that I've come to the crux of my story: the old man is now lying there with his skull smashed in, and I—after giving such a tragic description of how I wanted to kill him and pulled out the pestle—I suddenly run away from the window— A poem! Something in verse! As though you could take a man at his word! Ha, ha! You're making mock of me, gentlemen!"

And he swung round on his chair so violently that it creaked.

"And did you notice, sir," the public prosecutor suddenly began, as though disregarding Mitya's agitation, "did you notice, when you were running away from the window, whether the door into the garden at the other end of the house was unlocked or not?"

"No, it wasn't open."

"It wasn't?"

"On the contrary, it was shut. But who could have opened it? Oh, the door? Just a moment," he seemed to suddenly pull himself together and almost started. "Why, did you find it open?"

"Yes."

"So who could have opened it if you didn't?" Mitya asked, suddenly looking greatly surprised.

"The door was unlocked and your father's murderer quite certainly entered the house by that door and, after committing the murder, went out by it," said the public prosecutor, bringing out his words slowly, and stressing every syllable. "That is perfectly clear to us. The murder evidently took place in the room *and not through the window*, which is positively clear from the examination that has been made, from the position of the body, and from everything else. There can be no doubt whatever about it."

Mitya looked terribly taken aback.

"But that's impossible, gentlemen!" he cried, completely at a loss. "I—I never went in—I tell you positively I know for certain that the door was shut all the time I was in the garden and when I fled from it. I only stood at the window and saw him through the window. That was all, all— I remember everything down to the last instant. And even if I didn't remember, I'd know it just the same, because the *signals* were known only to me, Smerdyakov and the dead man, who would never have opened the door to anyone in the world without the signals!"

"Signals? What signals do you mean?" the public prosecutor cried with the keenest and almost hysterical curiosity, all traces of his dignified deportment gone. He asked the question as if he were furtively approaching a quarry. He sensed an important fact hitherto unknown to him, and was at once most apprehensive lest Mitya might be unwilling to disclose it in full.

"Oh, so you didn't know!" Mitya said, winking at him with a sardonic and malicious grin. "And what if I won't tell you? Who will you find it out from then? You see, only the dead man, Smerdyakov and I knew of the signals—that's all, I suppose. Heaven knew it too, but it won't let you know. And the fact is a most intriguing one, you could build goodness only knows what on it, couldn't you? Ha, ha! But have no fear, gentlemen, I'll reveal it, for you have sorts of silly ideas on your minds. You don't know the kind of man you're dealing with! You're dealing with a prisoner who gives testimony against himself, testimony that may be damaging to him! Yes, sir, for I'm a man of knightly honour, and you are not!"

The public prosecutor swallowed all these bitter pills, for he was trembling with impatience to learn of the new fact. Mitya gave a full and precise account of everything bearing on the signals which had been thought up by Fyodor Pavlovich Karamazov for Smerdyakov, he told them exactly what each tap on the window meant, even demonstrating the different taps on the table. The court investigator's question whether, when he had knocked on the window, he had tapped out the signal "Gru-shenka has come", Mitya replied unhesitatingly that it had been precisely what he had done.

"So that's that, now you can erect your tower of theory!" Mitya broke off, turning away from them with contempt.

"The signals were known only to your dead father, to Smer-dyakov and you? No one else?" the court investigator asked again.

"Yes, to the servant Smerdyakov and to Heaven besides. Take that down about Heaven. It may not prove superfluous. And, you'll stand in need of God yourselves."

Of course, all this was duly recorded, but while that was be-ing done the public prosecutor suddenly said, as though prompted by a new idea:

"But if Smerdyakov also knew of those signals and you po-sitively deny having had anything to do with your father's murder, couldn't it have been he who tapped out the agreed signals, made your father unlock the door and then—commit-ted the crime?"

Mitya looked at him sardonically, but at the same time also with intense hatred. He stared at him wordlessly so long that the public prosecutor began to blink.

"Caught the fox again!" Mitya said at last. "Got the rogue by the tail—ha, ha! I can see through you, Mr. Prosecutor! You thought that I'd swallow the bait at once, seize on your sugges-tion and scream at the top of my voice: 'Yes, it's Smerdyakov! Smerdyakov is the murderer!' Admit that's what you thought, didn't you? Admit it, and I'll go on."

But the public prosecutor admitted nothing. He kept wait-ing in silence.

"You're mistaken," said Mitya. "I'm not going to hollo 'It's Smerdyakov!' "

"You don't even suspect him at all?"

"Do you?"

"He, too, has been under suspicion."

Mitya fixed his eyes on the floor.

"Joking apart," he said, gloomily, "listen: from the very outset, almost from the moment I ran out to meet you from behind the curtain, the thought flashed through my mind: 'Smerdyakov!' Since I've been sitting at the table here and shouting that I am innocent of murder I've kept thinking: 'Smerdyakov!' I've been unable to get him out of my mind. And just now, too, the same thought occurred to me: 'Smerdyakov', but only for a second, for almost at once I thought: 'No, it can't be Smerdyakov!' It's not the sort of thing he'd do, gentlemen!"

"In that case, is there anyone else you suspect?" the court investigator asked cautiously.

"I don't know who or what person it could be, whether it was the hand of Heaven or of Satan but—not Smerdyakov!" Mitya declared emphatically

"But why do you affirm so firmly and so emphatically that it can't be he?"

"From my conviction. From my impression. Because Smerdyakov is a most despicable creature and a coward. He's not merely a coward, but the epitome of all the cowardices that exist in the world and walk on two legs. He was born of a chicken. Whenever he spoke to me, he trembled lest I should kill him, though I never raised a finger against him. He would fall at my feet and weep, literally kissing my boots, imploring me not to 'frighten' him. D'you hear? Not to 'frighten'—what an expression to use! And I even offered him money. He's a sickly, chicken-hearted, and feeble-minded epileptic, whom an eight-year-old boy could thrash. Is that a character? No, gentlemen, it was not Smerdyakov. Besides, he doesn't care for money. He wouldn't accept any gifts from me— Besides, why on earth should he kill the old man? You see, he's probably his son, his natural son, did you know that?"

"We've heard that legend. But, then, you're your father's son, too, and yet you told everyone yourself that you meant to kill him."

"*Touché*. And below the belt, too! But I'm not afraid! Oh, gentlemen, don't you think it's ignoble of you to say that to my face? Ignoble because it's something I've told you myself. Not only did I wish to kill him, but I could have done so, and, in fact, I told you of my own accord that I nearly did kill him! But, then, I didn't murder him. My guardian angel saved me—

that's what you haven't taken into account— And that's why it's ignoble of you, ignoble! For I didn't murder him, I didn't, I didn't! Do you hear, Mr. Prosecutor," he turned to the public prosecutor. "I did not murder him!"

He was almost choking. He had never been so agitated during the entire interrogation.

"And what has Smerdyakov told you, gentlemen?" he added suddenly, after a pause. "May I ask you that?"

"You may ask us about anything you like,' the public prosecutor replied with cold severity. "About anything that has any bearing on the facts of the case and, I repeat, we are even in duty bound to answer any question you ask us. We found the servant Smerdyakov, about whom you are inquiring, lying unconscious in bed in a very severe epileptic fit, which had perhaps recurred for the tenth time. The doctor who was with us examined Smerdyakov and even told us that he may not live till the morning."

"Well, in that case it must have been the devil that killed my father!" Mitya blurted out as though he had up to that very moment been debating within himself whether it had been Smerdyakov or not.

"We'll return to that later," the court investigator decided. "Wouldn't you like to carry on with your testimony now?"

Mitya asked for a respite, which was courteously granted. After an interval, he continued his testimony. But he was obviously in a miserable state. He was worn out, mortified and morally shaken. Besides, the public prosecutor kept exasperating him all the time, this with intent, by harping on "trivialities". No sooner had Mitya described how, sitting astride the fence, he had struck Grigori, who had been hanging on to his left leg, on the head with the pestle and then had at once jumped down to see how badly he was hurt, than the public prosecutor stopped him and asked him to describe in greater detail how he was sitting on the fence. Mitya looked surprised.

"Well, I was sitting like this, astride, one leg on one side of the fence and one on the other—"

"And the pestle?"

"The pestle was in my hand."

"Not in your pocket? You remember that clearly? Well, did you strike out with force?"

"I suppose so. Why are you asking?"

"Would you mind sitting on the chair just as you were on the fence then and demonstrating to us how you struck out and in what direction?"

"You're not making fun of me, are you?" asked Mitya with a haughty look at his interrogator, who did not even bat an eyelid. Mitya turned abruptly, sat astride the chair, and swung an arm:

"That's how I struck him! That's how I killed him! What more do you want to know?"

"Thank you. Would you mind explaining now why you jumped down, with what purpose? What exactly did you have in mind?"

"Well, damn it—I jumped down to look at the man I'd knocked down— I don't know why!"

"Agitated as you were? And making off?"

"Yes, agitated as I was, and making off."

"You wanted to help him?"

"How could I help him?— Well, I don't know. I may have wanted to help him, too. I don't remember."

"You mean, you were too worked up? Unaware of what you were doing, in fact?"

"But I was! I remember everything. Down to the slightest detail. I jumped down to have a look, and wiped the blood off his face with my handkerchief."

"We've seen your handkerchief. You hoped to restore him to consciousness, did you?"

"I don't know. I just wanted to make sure whether he was alive or not."

"Oh, I see. You wanted to make sure? Well, did you?"

"I'm no medico, I couldn't tell. I ran off thinking I had killed him, and now he has recovered."

"Excellent—thank you, sir," the public prosecutor concluded. "That's all I wanted to know. Pray proceed."

Alas, it never occurred to Mitya to tell, though he well remembered it, that he had jumped down from the fence out of pity and, standing over Grigori's prostrate body, even pronounced a few miserable words of regret: "Bad luck, old man—it can't be helped—well, you may as well lie here." The public prosecutor, however, could only draw a single conclusion, namely, that the man had jumped down "at such a moment and in such agitation" only to make sure whether *the sole* witness of his crime was alive or not. Which, of course, showed how great was the man's strength of mind, resolution, coolness, and prudence that even at such a moment—and so on and so forth. The public prosecutor felt pleased with himself: "the best way to get the truth out of a morbidly nervous man is to harass him with 'trivialities'."

Mitya went on with an excruciating effort, but he was immediately stopped again, this time by Nikolai Parfenovich.

"How could you have run to the servant Fenya with your hands so bloodstained and, as it appeared later, your face, too?"

"Why, at the time I never noticed that my hands and face were covered with blood!" replied Mitya.

"He's quite right," the public prosecutor said, exchanging glances with the court investigator. "It does happen like that."

"I never noticed it: you've put it very well, Mr. Prosecutor," Mitya said in sudden approval. But there followed the story of Mitya's sudden decision "to step down" and let the happy couple pass by. And he could not any longer as before make up his mind to open his heart again and tell them about "the queen of his heart". He felt nauseated at the thought of talking about her to these coldhearted people, who were "fastening on him like bugs". And so, in reply to their repeated questions, he declared briefly and curtly:

"Well, so I made up my mind to do away with myself. What was there left for me to live for? That was the question that stared me in the face. Her first and rightful lover had come back, the man who seduced her but had hurried back to offer her his love and to atone through marriage, after five years, for the wrong he had done her. So I realised that it was all over for me— And behind me was that disgrace and all that blood—Grigori's blood— What was there left for me to live for?

So I went to redeem the pistols I had left in pledge, load them and put a bullet through my brain at dawn—"

"And have a high time the night before?"

"A high time the night before. Oh, damn it all, gentlemen, let's get through with all that quickly. I was quite determined to shoot myself, not far from here, on the outskirts of the village, and I'd have done myself in at five o'clock in the morning. I had a note ready in my pocket—wrote it at Perkhotin's when I was loading the pistol. Here it is. Read it. It's not for your benefit I'm telling this!" he suddenly added contemptuously. He produced the note from his waistcoat pocket and flung it on the table. They read it with interest and, as is usual, added it to the material evidence.

"And you never thought of getting your hands washed even when you called on Mr. Perkhotin? So you weren't afraid of arousing suspicion, were you?"

"What kind of suspicion? Suspicion or not, I'd have come dashing here all the same and shot myself at five o'clock, and no one would have been able to do anything about it. For, if not what happened to my father, you wouldn't have learnt anything about it and you wouldn't have come here. Oh, the devil's been responsible, the devil has murdered my father, and it was through the devil that you found it out so soon! How were you able to get here so quickly? Extraordinary, fantastic!"

"Mr. Perkhotin has informed us that when you came to see him you were holding some money in your hands—your blood-stained hands—a great deal of money—a wad of hundred-rouble notes, and that his boy servant saw it too!"

"Yes, gentlemen, I remember that."

"Now, sir, another question presents itself. Would you mind telling us," the court investigator began very mildly, "where you got so much money from? For, as it appears from the evidence and even from a time calculation, you could not possibly have gone home for it?"

The public prosecutor frowned slightly at a question, put so point-blank, but he did not interrupt the court investigator.

"No, I didn't go home," Mitya replied, who seemed very calm, though his eyes were fixed on the floor.

"In that case, let me repeat my question," the court investigator continued in a stealthy voice. "Where could you have obtained such a large sum all at once when, on your own admission, at five o'clock that afternoon—"

"I stood in need of ten roubles and left my pistols in pledge with Perkhotin, then went to Madame Khokhlakov to borrow three thousand, which she did not let me have, and so on and all that sort of thing," Mitya interrupted sharply. "Yes, gentlemen, at one moment I needed money and the next I'd suddenly got hold of thousands—eh? You know, gentlemen, you're both in a funk now: what if he won't tell us where he got it? You're right, gentlemen, but I won't tell you, you won't find out," Mitya said emphatically and most resolutely.

The interrogators were silent for a moment.

"You must understand, Mr. Karamazov, that it is absolutely essential for us to know it," the court investigator said quietly and even meekly.

"I understand, but I won't tell you all the same."

The public prosecutor intervened and again reminded the suspect that, of course, he need not answer their questions, if he did not consider that to his advantage, and so on, but in view of the damage he might cause himself by his silence, especially in view of the great importance of such questions as—

"And so on and so forth, gentlemen! Enough, I've heard that reasoning before!" Mitya again interrupted. "I'm fully aware how important it is and that this is a most essential point, yet I'm not going to tell you."

"Well, sir," the court investigator said nervously, "What's that to us? It's your affair, not ours. You'll only be causing yourself damage."

"You see, gentlemen, joking apart," Mitya said, raising his eyes and looking intently at the two. "I had a presentiment from the very outset that we would be at loggerheads on this point. But at first, when I began to give my testimony, all that was still far off, concealed in a mist, everything was still uncertain, and, indeed, I was so naive that I began with a suggestion of 'mutual confidence' between us. I now see for myself that there could have been no question of such confidence, for we would have reached this stumbling-block all the same! And now we have reached it! I can't tell you, and that's all there is to it! Yet I do not blame you, for I can't expect you to take me at my word—I realise that!"

He relapsed into a gloomy silence.

"But couldn't you, without abandoning your decision to say nothing about the main point—couldn't you at the same time give us some slight hint as to the motives, which are so strong as to induce you to maintain silence at such a moment in your testimony so critical to you."

Mitya smiled sadly and somehow pensively.

"I'm much kinder than you think, gentlemen, so I'll tell you my reason and give you that hint, though you don't deserve it. I'm silent on that score, gentlemen, because it's a matter that casts disgrace on me. The answer to the question where I got the money from exposes me to such disgrace that it defies comparison with the murder and the robbing of my father, had I indeed murdered and robbed him. That's why I can't speak of it. I can't do it because that would mean disgracing myself. Why, gentlemen, you're not going to take that down, are you?"

"Yes, we'll have that down," the court investigator mumbled.

"You ought not to record that—I mean about the 'disgrace'. I told you that only out of the kindness of my heart, for I needn't have told you that at all. I've made you a gift of it, so to say, and you're at once turning it against me. All right, record anything you like," he concluded with contemptuous distaste. "I'm not afraid of you—I can still maintain my pride with you!"

"You couldn't tell us by any chance of the nature of that disgrace?" the court investigator murmured.

The public prosecutor frowned severely.

"No, no, *c'est fini*, don't bother. And, anyhow, it's not worth while soiling myself, for I've been soiled enough by you. You don't deserve it. Neither you nor anyone else— Enough, gentlemen. No more!"

This was said too flatly; the court investigator insisted no more, but at once understood from a look in the public prosecutor's eyes that the latter was still hopeful.

"Can't you at least tell us how much money you had in your possession when you went to see Mr. Perkhotin—how many roubles, I mean?"

"I can't tell you that, either."

"I believe you spoke to Mr. Perkhotin of having obtained three thousand from Madame Khokhlakov."

"Perhaps I did. Enough, gentlemen, I won't tell you how much I had."

"In that case, could you tell us how you came here and what you've done since your arrival?"

"Oh, you'd better ask the people here about that. Still, why not? I'll tell you."

He told them, but we will not repeat his story. He did so dryly and cursorily. He said nothing of his rapturous love, but did tell that "certain new facts" had made him abandon his decision to shoot himself. He told his story without going into motives or details. Besides, his interrogators did not badger him much this time: it was obvious that they attached no importance to the matter.

"We shall verify all that," the court investigator said, concluding the interrogation, "and we'll return to it during the examination of the witnesses, which will, of course, take place in your presence. Now, I should like to request you to place on the table everything in your possession and especially all the money you still have about you."

"My money, gentlemen? Very well, I understand it is necessary. Indeed, I'm surprised you showed no interest before. It's true I couldn't have gone away anywhere, for here I am for all to see. Well, here's the money. Count it, take it. That's all, I think."

He emptied his pockets down to the small change, and then produced two silver twenty-copeck pieces from his waistcoat pocket. When the money was counted, it was found to total eight hundred and thirty-six roubles and forty copecks.

"And is that all?" asked the court investigator.

"It is."

"You've stated in your testimony just now that you spent three hundred roubles at Plotnikov's shop, gave Perkhotin ten roubles, the coachman twenty, lost two hundred here at cards, then—"

The court investigator counted it all again, Mitya helping him readily. They recollected every copeck spent and added it to the total, which the court investigator quickly added up.

"With this eight hundred you must have had about fifteen hundred at first?"

"I suppose so," Mitya said sharply.

"Why, then, is it asserted that there was much more?"

"Let them say so."

"But you asserted it yourself."

"Yes, I, too, asserted it."

"We'll verify that again against evidence of persons not yet interrogated. Don't worry about the money, it will be attended to where—er—such things are usually taken care of, and will be at your disposal at the end of—er—this business if—er—it appears, or rather is proved, that you have an incontestable right to it. Well, sir, and now—"

Suddenly rising to his feet, the court investigator told Mitya firmly that it was his duty to make a thorough search of "your clothes and everything else—"

"Certainly, gentlemen, I'll turn out all my pockets if you like."

And he really began to do so.

"I'm afraid you'll have to undress."

"Undress? Is that what you want me to do? Damn it, can't you search me as I am? Can't you?"

"I'm afraid it can't be done, Dmitri Fyodorovich. You will have to undress."

"As you please," said Mitya, submitting gloomily. "Only not here please, but behind the curtain. Who's going to conduct the search?"

"Behind the curtain, of course," the court investigator said inclining his head in assent, an expression of the utmost gravity on his face.

6.

The Public Prosecutor Catches Mitya Tripping

What ensued came as a complete surprise to Mitya. Even a moment before, he could not have even imagined that such treatment could be meted out to him, Mitya Karamazov! And the worst of it was that there was something humiliating in it, and, on their part, something "arrogant and scornful". He would not have minded if it were only a question of taking off his frock-coat, but he was asked to undress further. Not asked, either, but actually ordered to—he understood that perfectly. Out of pride and contempt he submitted unprotestingly. Besides, the court investigator, as well as the public prosecutor, went behind the curtain, and there were also several peasants present, "to use force, if necessary, of course", thought Mitya, "and perhaps for something else".

"Well, have I got to take off my shirt too?" Mitya asked sharply, but the court investigator made no reply: together with the public prosecutor, he was absorbed in an examination of Mitya's frock-coat, trousers, waistcoat, and cap, and they were obviously very interested in what they saw: "They make no bones about it," thought Mitya, "and don't observe even the most ordinary civilities."

"I am asking you for the second time," Mitya said even more sharply and irritably, "do I have to remove my shirt or not?"

"Don't worry, we'll let you know," the court investigator replied in a rather peremptory tone or so, at least, it seemed to Mitya.

Meanwhile, the court investigator and the public prosecutor seemed deep in consultation conducted in an undertone. There appeared to be extensive bloodstains on the frock-coat, especially on the left skirt, at the back. They had gone stiff and dry, and had not yet flaked off. There were bloodstains on the trousers, too. In addition, the court investigator, in the presence of witnesses, passed his fingers along the collar, the cuffs, and all the seams of the coat and trousers, evidently looking for something—money, of course. They did not even bother to conceal from Mitya their suspicion that he was capable of sewing money up in his clothes. "They treat me as if I were a thief, and not an officer and a gentleman," Mitya muttered under his breath. Moreover, they exchanged thoughts in his presence with a frankness that was strange indeed. For instance, the clerk, who was also behind the curtain and who fussed about and helped them in their search, drew the court investigator's attention to Mitya's cap, which they were also fingering. "Do you remember Gridenko, sir? The rural district clerk?" the clerk observed. "Last summer he went to town to fetch the salaries for the entire office staff and when he came back he declared that he had lost the money while drunk. And where was it found, sir? Why, in just these pipings of the cap, the hundred-rouble notes screwed up in little rolls and sewn into the piping." They recalled Gridenko's case perfectly well, both the court investigator and the public prosecutor, so they put Mitya's cap aside, too, and decided that it would all have to be thoroughly re-examined later.

"I say," the court investigator suddenly exclaimed, noticing that the right cuff of Mitya's shirt was turned back inwards and soaked in blood, "I say, what's that—blood?"

"It is," Mitya snapped.

"I mean, whose blood, sir? And why is the cuff turned back inwards?"

Mitya told them how he had got his cuff soaked in blood while attending to Grigori, and had turned it inwards while washing his hands at Perkhotin's.

"We'll have to take your shirt, too. It's very important as—er—material evidence."

Mitya flushed and flew into a rage.

"Am I to remain naked?" he cried.

"Don't worry—we'll see what we can do about it. Meanwhile take your socks off, please."

"Are you joking? Is that really necessary?" cried Mitya with flashing eyes.

"We're in no mood for joking!" the court investigator retorted severely.

"Well, if it's necessary—" Mitya muttered and, sitting down

on the bed, he began taking off his socks. He felt terribly embarrassed: they were all dressed, while he was undressed and, strange to say, the absence of clothes in their presence seemed to arouse a sense of guilt in him and, what was worse, he felt almost convinced that he really was inferior to them all, and that now they were fully entitled to look down on him. "If all the others are undressed, you won't feel ashamed, but when you're the only one undressed and all eyes are fixed on you, it's degrading!" was the thought that kept flashing again and again through his mind. "It's something out of a dream. I've sometimes had dreams of being in such a humiliating situation." But it was even a torment to take off his socks: they were very dirty, and so were his underclothes, and that for all to see. But the main thing was that he disliked his feet and for some reason had all his life thought the big toes on both feet hideous, especially the coarse, flat, ingrowing nail on the right foot, and now they would all see it. His intolerable sense of shame suddenly made him deliberately ruder than ever. He tore off the shirt himself.

"You wouldn't like to look anywhere else if that doesn't make you feel ashamed of yourselves?"

"No, sir, not at present."

"Well, am I to remain naked like this?" he added fiercely.

"Yes, sir, I'm afraid it is necessary for the time being—Please sit down here for a while. Take a blanket from the bed and wrap yourself in it. I—I'll see to the rest."

All the articles were shown to the witnesses, a report of the search was drawn up and the court investigator finally left, and the clothes were carried out after him. The public prosecutor also went out. Mitya was left in the company of the peasants, who stood in silence, their eyes fixed on him all the time. Mitya wrapped himself in the blanket. He felt cold. His bare feet were sticking out and, try as he might, he could not cover them with the blanket. For some reason, Nikolai Parfenovich, the court investigator, was away for a long time. "An excruciatingly long time. Treats me as if I were a whelp," Mitya muttered, grinding his teeth. "That swine of a public prosecutor has also gone! Out of contempt, I suppose. Felt disgusted by the sight of a naked man." Mitya still believed that his clothes would be returned to him after being inspected somewhere. He grew indignant when Nikolai Parfenovich suddenly returned with quite different clothes, carried in after him by a peasant.

"Well, here are some clothes for you," he said in a casual tone, evidently well satisfied with success of his mission. "Mr. Kalganov has kindly provided them for this emergency, as well as a clean shirt. Fortunately, he had them all in his trunk. You may keep your socks and underclothes."

Mitya blew up.

"I won't have other people's clothes!" he cried menacingly. "Let me have my own!"

"It can't be done."

"Let me have my own! To hell with Kalganov and his clothes!"

It took a lot of time to talk him round. At last he was calmed down, somehow or other. It was pointed out to him that his clothes, being stained with blood, had to be added to the other material evidence and that they had not "even the right" to let him wear them "in view of the possible outcome of the case". Mitya finally realised this. Subsiding into a gloomy silence, he began to dress hurriedly, remarking, as he put on the clothes, that they were much more expensive than his old ones and that he would not like to "take advantage" of it. Besides, the coat was ridiculously tight. "Am I to play the clown in it for—your enjoyment?"

It was again suggested that he was exaggerating: Mr. Kalganov was only a little taller; perhaps the trousers alone might be somewhat too long. But the coat turned out to be really tight in the shoulders.

"Damn it, it's hard to button up," Mitya complained again. "Do me a favour and tell Mr. Kalganov at once from me that it was not I who asked for his clothes, and that it's not my doing that I've been arrayed like a clown."

"I'm sure he understands that very well, and regrets not the clothes but—er—the entire matter," Nikolai Parfenovich mumbled.

"I don't care a dam for his regrets! Well, where now? Or am I to go on sitting here?"

Asked to return into the "other room", Mitya went there scowling with anger and trying not to look at anyone. He felt quite disgraced in another man's clothes, even in the eyes of the peasants and the innkeeper, whose face for some reason suddenly appeared in the doorway and vanished again. "Came along to have a look at the mummer," thought Mitya. He resumed his former seat at the table, with a feeling of something absurd and nightmarish; it seemed to him that he was not in his right mind.

"Well," he said to the public prosecutor, grinding his teeth, "what are you going to do now? Are you going to have me flogged? There's nothing else left to be done." He had no desire to turn to Nikolai Parfenovich as though he disdained having even to talk to him. "He examined my socks a little too closely," he thought. "Even had them turned inside out, the scoundrel! He did that on purpose. Wanted to show everyone how dirty my underclothes were!"

"We'll now have to proceed to the interrogation of the witnesses," said Nikolai Parfenovich, as though in reply to a question from Mitya.

"Yes," said the public prosecutor thoughtfully, as though he, too, was reflecting on something.

"We've done everything possible in your interests, Dmitri Fyodorovich," Nikolai Parfenovich went on, "but since you flatly refuse to say where the money in your possession has come from, we are at present—"

"What kind of stone is that on your ring?" said Mitya, suddenly interrupting him, as though coming out of some reverie and pointing to one of the large rings adorning Nikolai Parfenovich's right hand.

"Ring?" Nikolai Parfenovich repeated with surprise.

"Yes, that one—on your middle finger—the one with the fine grains in it—what kind of stone is that?" Mitya insisted somehow irritably, like a stubborn child.

"It's a smoky topaz," said Nikolai Parfenovich with a smile. "Would you like to have a look at it? I'll take it off for you—"

"No, no, don't!" Mitya cried fiercely, recollecting himself

suddenly and angry with himself. "Don't take it off—there's no need to— Damn it! Gentlemen, you've defiled my soul! Do you really think that I'd have concealed the fact from you if I had really murdered my father, that I would dissemble, lie, and cover up anything? No, Dmitri Karamazov is not made of such stuff, he would never tolerate that. And, I swear, if I were guilty, I wouldn't have waited for you to come or for the sun to rise, as I intended at first, but would have destroyed myself before that, without waiting for the dawn! I know it for certain now. I couldn't have learned as much in twenty years of my life as I've found out during this damned night!— And would I have behaved like that tonight, at this moment, sitting here with you—would I have spoken like that, moved about like that, looked at you and the world like that, if I'd really been a parricide, when even the thought that I had killed Grigori by accident gave me no rest all night—and not because I was afraid, or feared your punishment! It was the disgrace! And you really expect me to be frank with such scoffers as you, men who see nothing and believe in nothing, blind moles and scoffers; you expect me to tell you of yet another mean action I've committed, another disgrace, even if that could save me from your charge? No, better penal servitude! The man who unlocked the door into my father's room, and went in through that door—that man murdered my father, that man robbed him. Who was he? I'm racking my brains, I'm at my wit's end trying to think who it could be, but I can tell you one thing for certain: it was not Dmitri Karamazov—and that's all I can say to you—and now enough, enough; don't badger me any more— Send me to Siberia, hang me, but don't exasperate me any more. I'll say no more. Call your witnesses!"

Mitya uttered his abrupt monologue as though he had quite made up his mind not to say another word again. The public prosecutor was watching him closely the whole time and, as soon as he fell silent, suddenly said with a very frigid and composed air, just as though it were the most ordinary thing:

"Well, about that open door you just mentioned: we are now able to inform you of a most interesting piece of evidence of the utmost importance to you as well as to us, which has been given by Grigori Vassiliev, the old man you injured. On recovering, he stated clearly and insistently in replying to our questions that when he went out on to the porch and heard a noise in the garden, he decided to enter the garden by way of the open wicket; on entering the garden, even before he caught sight of you running away in the dark from the open window at which, as you have told us, you saw your father, he cast a glance to the left and noticed that the window was open, but at the same time he noticed, much closer to himself, the wide open door, which, you claim, was shut all the time you were in the garden. Nor will I hold back from you that Grigori Vassiliev himself affirms and bears witness that you must have run out from that door, though, of course, he did not see you do so with his own eyes, for he noticed you for the first time at some distance from himself, in the garden, running away towards the fence—"

Half-way through this speech Mitya jumped up from his chair.

"Nonsense!" he yelled in a sudden frenzy. "A brazen falsehood! He couldn't have seen the door open because it was shut— He's lying!"

"I consider it my duty to repeat that he is absolutely firm in his statement. He doesn't waver. He swears to it. We've asked him again and again about it."

"Yes, indeed, I've questioned him several times about it!" Nikolai Parfenovich confirmed heatedly.

"It's untrue, untrue! It's either an attempt to pin the blame on me or the hallucination of a madman," Mitya went on shouting. "He simply imagined it all up in his delirium, when he came to, from loss of blood, from the wound— He's just raving."

"Well, sir, he noticed the open door, not when he recovered consciousness after being wounded but before that, as soon as he entered the garden from the lodge."

"But it's untrue, quite untrue! It can't be so!" Mitya gasped for breath. "He's accusing me out of spite— He couldn't have seen it— I didn't run out through the door."

The public prosecutor turned to the court investigator and said to him impressively:

"Let him see it."

"Do you recognise this object?" Nikolai Parfenovich asked, placing on the table a large and heavy envelope of the size used in government offices, with the three seals still intact. The envelope itself was empty and torn open at one end. Mitya stared goggle-eyed at it.

"I—I suppose it must be my father's envelope," he muttered. "The same that contained the three thousand roubles and—if there's an inscription—let me see, please— 'To my little chicken'—here, you see? Three thousand," he cried, "three thousand! You see?"

"Of course, we do, but we found no money in it. It was empty and lying on the floor near the bed, behind the screen."

For a few seconds Mitya stood as though thunderstruck.

"Gentlemen, it's Smerdyakov!" he suddenly shouted at the top of his voice. "It's he who murdered and robbed him! He alone knew where the old man had hidden the envelope— It's he—that's clear now!"

"But you, too, knew of the envelope and that it was kept under the pillow."

"I never knew it. I've never seen it before; this is the first time I've seen it, I only heard of it from Smerdyakov— Only he knew where the old man kept it hidden, I didn't know—" Mitya declared, almost choking.

"And yet, sir, you stated in your testimony a short while ago that the envelope was under your late father's pillow. You most definitely stated that it was under the pillow. So you must have known where it was."

"We've got it recorded!" Nikolai Parfenovich confirmed.

"Nonsense! It's absurd! I never knew it was under the pillow. It might not have been under the pillow at all— I said it was under the pillow unthinkingly— What does Smerdyakov say? Have you asked him where it was? What does Smerdyakov say? That's most important— I've told you lies against myself deliberately— I told you without thinking that it was under the pillow, and now you— Well, you know how one blurts something out without meaning it. Only Smerdyakov knew, Smerdyakov alone, and no one else!— He did not reveal even to me where it was! It was he, it was he! There can be no doubt at all now that it was he who murdered him. It's as clear as daylight to me," Mitya kept exclaiming more and more frenziedly, repeating himself incoherently, and growing more and more worked up and desperate. "You must understand that and arrest him at once, at once— It was he who committed the murder after I had run away and while Grigori was lying unconscious. It's clear now— He gave the signal and my father opened the door to him— He alone knew the signal, and without the signals my father would not have opened the door to anyone—"

"But," the public prosecutor observed with the same restraint, but with a note of triumph, "you again forget the circumstance that there was no need to give the signal if the door was already open while you were there, while you were still in the garden—"

"The door, the door," muttered Mitya, staring mutely at the public prosecutor. He sank back exhausted in his chair. They were all silent.

"Yes, the door!— It's a spectre! God is against me!" Mitya cried, staring vacantly in front of him.

"So you see," the public prosecutor said gravely, "and judge for yourself now, Dmitri Fyodorovich: on the one hand, there's this evidence of the open door, from which you ran out, a crushing fact both for you and for us. On the other, there's your inexplicable, obstinate, and almost obdurate silence about the origin of the money which appeared so suddenly in your possession, when only three hours earlier, according to your own statement, you pledged your pistols to obtain only ten roubles! In view of all this, decide for yourself: what are we to believe, and what are we to base ourselves on? And don't reproach us with being 'cold-blooded cynics and scoffers', incapable of believing in the noble impulses of your heart— Try to put yourself in our position—"

Indescribably agitated, Mitya turned pale.

"All right!" he cried suddenly. "I'll reveal my secret. I'll tell you where I got the money! I'll reveal my shame so as not to blame either myself or you afterwards."

"And believe me, Dmitri Fyodorovich," the court investigator cried in a kind of almost pathetic delight, "that every sincere and full confession of yours, and particularly at this moment, may later serve to immeasurably mitigate your fate and indeed, may also—"

But the public prosecutor nudged him under the table and he managed to stop in time. True, Mitya was not even listening to him.

7.

Mitya's Dark Secret Is Pooh-Poohed

"Gentlemen," he began, as agitated as ever, "about the money—I'd like to make a full confession—the money was *mine.*"

The faces of the public prosecutor and the court investigator looked disappointed: it was not at all what they expected.

"What do you mean: it was yours?" Nikolai Parfenovich murmured. "At five o'clock in the afternoon, on your own confession—"

"Oh, damn the five o'clock in the afternoon and my own confession, that's beside the point now! That money was mine, mine, I mean, stolen by me—not mine, that is, but stolen by me, and it amounted to fifteen hundred, and I had it on me, I had it on me all the time—"

"But where did it come from?"

"I took it off my neck, gentlemen, off this neck of mine—It was there, round my neck, sewn up in a piece of rag and hanging from my neck. I was carrying it about for a long time, for a whole month, round my neck, to my shame and disgrace!"

"But who did you—appropriate it from?"

"You wanted to say 'steal from', didn't you? You can speak frankly now. Yes, I consider that I had as good as stolen or, if you like, really 'appropriated' it. But as I see it, I stole the money. And last night I stole it in good earnest."

"Last night? But you've just said you—er—got it a month ago!"

"Yes, but not from my father, don't worry, not from my father. I didn't steal it from my father, but from her. Let me tell you the story, and don't interrupt me. It's not so easy, you know. You see, a month ago I was asked by Katerina Ivanovna Verkhovtsev, my former fiancée, to call on her— Do you know her?"

"Why, of course we do."

"I know you do. She's a most noble soul, the noblest of the noble, but she's hated me for a long, long time—and with good reason, yes, with good reason!"

"Katerina Ivanovna?" the court investigator asked with surprise. The public prosecutor, too, was amazed.

"Oh, don't take her name in vain! I'm a cad to drag her into all this. Yes, I'd seen that she hated me—long ago—from the very first, from our first meeting at my lodgings— But enough, enough, you don't deserve even to know of that—I mustn't talk of it at all— All I need to say is that a month ago she asked me to call on her and gave me three thousand roubles to remit to her sister and a relative of hers in Moscow (as though she couldn't have done that herself!) and I—you see, it was just at that fateful hour of my life when I—well, in short, when I fell in love with another woman, with *her*, my present fiancée, the one who's downstairs now—Grushenka— I took her here, to Mokroye then, and squandered half of that damned three thousand, that is, fifteen hundred in a matter of two days, keeping the other half on me. Well, I kept the fifteen hundred— carried about round my neck like an amulet and yesterday I opened the little bag and spent it. Except, that is, for the eight hundred which are in your hands now, Nikolai Parfenovich. It's what's left of yesterday's fifteen hundred."

"But how can that be? A month ago you spent three thousand here, not fifteen hundred. That's common knowledge."

"Who knows of that? Who counted the money? Who did I give it to to count?"

"But, good Lord, you told everyone yourself that you had run through exactly three thousand that time."

"Indeed, I did. I said that to all and sundry in the town, and it was the talk of the town, and everybody thought so, here and in Mokroye too, that it was three thousand. Nevertheless I spent fifteen hundred roubles, not three thousand, and I sewed what was left into a little bag. That's how it was, gentlemen. That's where I got the money yesterday—"

"This is almost like a miracle—" the court investigator murmured.

"May I ask you, sir," said the public prosecutor at last, "whether you told anyone about it before—er—I mean, that you kept the fifteen hundred a month ago?"

"I told no one."

"That's strange. Are you sure you told absolutely no one?"

"Absolutely no one. No one at all!"

"But why did you keep silent about it? What induced you to make such a secret of it? Let me put it more plainly: you've told us your secret at last, a secret which, according to you, was so 'disgraceful', though in fact—I mean, relatively speaking, of course, this action, that is, the appropriation of three thousand roubles which did not belong to you and, no doubt, only for a time—that action was, in my opinion at least, highly thoughtless, but by no means so very disgraceful, especially when one takes into consideration your nature— But even assuming it was a highly reprehensible action, let's admit it, it was indeed reprehensible, but not disgraceful— What I'm driving at is that many people here guessed during this last month that you had spent Miss Verkhovtsev's three thousand, even without your admitting it. I heard the story myself— Mr. Makarov, too, for instance, has heard it. So that it isn't really a 'legend' any more, but the talk of the whole town. Besides, there were indications that you, too, if I am not mistaken, confessed it yourself to someone, I mean, that the money was Miss Verkhovtsev's— That is why I am so surprised that till now, that is, up to this moment, you made such an extraordinary secret of the fifteen hundred which, you say, you kept hidden, endowing this secret of yours with a sense of horror— It seems to me incredible that confessing to such a secret should cost you so much distress, for—for you were just shouting that you'd rather be sentenced to penal servitude than confess it—"

The public prosecutor fell silent. He was all worked up. He did not conceal his vexation, almost anger, and gave vent to his accumulated resentment, without thought to the beauty of his style, that is, disconnectedly and almost incoherently.

"The disgrace was not with the fifteen hundred, but in my separating the sum from the three thousand," Mitya declared firmly.

"But," the public prosecutor said with an exasperated laugh, "what is there so disgraceful about having set aside, at your own discretion, half of the three thousand you had reprehensibly or, if you prefer it, disgracefully appropriated? Surely, the important point is that you appropriated the three thousand, not what you did with it. By the way, why did you do that, I mean, why did you put away that half? What did you do it for, what was your object in doing it? Can you explain it to us?"

"Oh, gentlemen, the motive was the nub of the matter!" Mitya exclaimed. "I put it aside because I was vile, or because I had a selfish reason for it, and to have a selfish reason in such a situation is vile— And that vileness went on for a whole month!"

"I don't understand."

"I'm surprised at you. However, I'll put it more plainly. Perhaps it really is difficult to understand. Now, listen carefully: I appropriate three thousand entrusted to my honour; I spend it on a wild spree, and, having spent it all, I come to her next morning and say: 'Katya, I'm sorry, I've squandered your three thousand.' Well, is that proper? No, it isn't. It's dishonest and cowardly and the man who does such a thing is a beast, with no more restraint than a beast. Isn't that so? But he's no thief yet, is he? Not a downright thief, not a downright one, you must admit! I squandered the money, but did not steal it! Now a more favourable alternative—please listen carefully or I may get confused again—I'm afraid my head's swimming—so, here's the other alternative: I spend here only fifteen hundred out of the three thousand, that is, half of it. The next day I go to her and bring her that half: 'Katya, take the fifteen hundred back from me, blackguard and thoughtless scoundrel that I am, for I've squandered half the money and may therefore also squander the rest—so take it and keep me from temptation! Well, what about that alternative? Anything you like—a beast and a blackguard, but not a thief, not entirely a thief. For if I were a thief, I would certainly not have brought the other half, but would have appropriated that too. Here she would see that since I returned half of her money, I'd bring back the rest, too, that is, the money I had squandered, that I'd seek that money for the rest of my life, would work, but find and get it. Thus, I'd be a blackguard, but not a thief, not a thief, whatever you may say!"

"I daresay there is a certain difference," said the public prosecutor with a cold smile. "But yet it is strange that you should regard it as such a crucial difference!"

"Yes, I do see a crucial difference! Anyone can be and perhaps is a blackguard, but not anyone can be a thief, for only an arch-blackguard can be that. Anyway, I'm afraid I'm not very good at these subtleties— Only a thief is viler than a blackguard, I'm convinced of that. Now, listen: I carry the money about on me a whole month. Tomorrow I may decide to give it back and then I'm no longer a blackguard. But the snag is that I can't make up my mind, though I try to every day and though I urge myself every day to do that: 'Make up your mind, you blackguard, make it up!' And yet for a whole month I can't make up my mind. Well, what do you think of that? Is that proper?"

"I suppose it's not so proper. That's something I understand perfectly well, and I don't want to argue the point," the public prosecutor replied with restraint. "Anyway, let's desist from all this wrangling about these subtleties and distinctions and, if you don't mind, let's get back to the point. And the point, sir, is that you have still not explained to us, although we've asked you, why, in the first place, you divided the three thousand into two equal parts, squandering one half and concealing the other? What exactly did you hide it for? What exactly did you intend to do with the fifteen hundred? I must insist on an answer to this question, Dmitri Fyodorovich."

"Yes, indeed!" cried Mitya, striking himself on the forehead. "Forgive me for being such a nuisance to you, but I haven't yet explained the main thing, or you'd have understood it at once. For it's in the motive, in the motive of it, that the disgrace lies! You see, it was the old man, my late father, who kept pestering Agrafena Alexandrovna, and that made me jealous; I was thinking at the time that she was hesitating between me and him. I kept asking myself every day: what if she were to suddenly make up her mind, what if she got tired of tormenting me, and were suddenly to say to me: 'I love you and not him, take me away to the other end of the world'? And I had only forty copecks to my name—so how could I take her away, what could I do? I'd be lost! You see, I didn't know her then, I didn't understand her; I thought she was after money and that she wouldn't forgive me my poverty. And so I craftily set aside half of the three thousand and coolly sewed it up with a needle, sewed it up intentionally, sewed it up before I got drunk, and having sewed it up, I was off to get really drunk on the rest! Yes, gentlemen, that was vile! Do you understand now?"

The public prosecutor laughed aloud. So did the court investigator.

"Well, in my opinion it was eminently sensible and highly moral of you to have curbed yourself and refrained from spending the lot," said Nikolai Parfenovich with a chuckle, "for really, what is there extraordinary about that?"

"Why, I have stolen it, that's what. Oh, Lord, your lack of understanding horrifies me! All the time I was carrying those fifteen hundred roubles sewn up on my chest, I kept saying to myself—daily and hourly I kept saying to myself: 'You're a thief! You're a thief!' That's why I've been in such a rage all this month, that's why I had that fight at the pub, that's why I fell on my father. It was all because I felt I was a thief! I dared not even tell my brother Alyosha the truth about the fifteen hundred: I felt I was a blackguard and a swindler! But I want you to know that as I was carrying the money with me, I at the same time kept saying to myself daily and hourly: 'No, Dmitri Fyodorovich, you may not be a thief as yet.' Why not? Because tomorrow you may go and give back the fifteen hundred to Katya. And it was only yesterday, on my way from Fenya's to Perkhotin's, that I made up my mind to tear the amulet off my neck. Up to that moment, I couldn't bring myself to do it, but as soon as I tore it off, at that very moment, I definitely and finally became a thief, a thief, a dishonest man, for the rest of my life. Why? Because together with the amulet I destroyed my dream of going to Katya and saying to her: 'I'm a blackguard, but no thief!' Do you understand now? Do you?"

"But why was it that you decided to do it just yesterday evening?" Nikolai Parfenovich put in.

"Why? What a strange thing to ask: because I had condemned myself to die at five o'clock in the morning—here, at dawn. 'What difference does it make,' I thought, 'whether I die a blackguard or a man of honour!' But it seems I was wrong. It isn't the same thing! Believe me, gentlemen, it was not that I had killed the old servant and that I might be sent to Siberia that tormented me most of all last night; and that at a time when my love was rewarded and Heaven was revealed to me again. Oh, that did torment me, but not so much, not as much as my damned awareness that I had at last torn the accursed money from my chest and squandered it and had therefore become a downright thief! Oh, gentlemen, I repeat to you, with a bleeding heart: I learnt a lot that night! I learnt not only that it was impossible to live as a scoundrel, but also that it was impossible to die as one— No, gentlemen, one must die an honest man!''

Mitya was pale. His face was haggard and he looked worn out, though he was intensely worked up.

"I'm beginning to understand you, Dmitri Fyodorovich," the public prosecutor said in a gentle and almost compassionate voice. "But say what you like, it all, in my opinion, comes from your nerves—your overwrought nerves—yes, that's what it is. Why, for instance, could you not have spared yourself all the anguish you suffered for almost a whole month, and gone to the lady who had entrusted the money to you and returned fifteen hundred roubles? After explaining everything to her, why could you not, in view of your position, which you have depicted as so awful, not have tried a solution which would so naturally have occurred to one, I mean, why couldn't you, after frankly admitting your errors to her, have asked her to lend you the sum needed for your expenses which she, with her magnanimity of soul and in view of your disturbed condition, would not have refused to do, especially if you had signed a promissory note or even offered the same sort of security as you did to the merchant Samsonov and Madame Khokhlakov? You still consider that security valuable, don't you?"

Mitya suddenly flushed.

"You don't really consider me such a thorough scoundrel, do you? You can't mean it seriously, sir!—" he said, with indignation, looking the public prosecutor straight in the face, as though unable to believe his ears.

"I assure you I do mean it seriously— Why do you think I

don't?" asked the public prosecutor, surprised in his turn.

"Oh, how base that would have been! Gentlemen, do you realise that you're tormenting me? Very well, I'll tell you everything. So be it. I'll tell you everything now, and confess in all my infernal make-up, just to make you feel ashamed of yourselves, and amaze you with the depth of baseness a compound of human feelings can sink to. Let me tell you that I had conceived that compound myself, I mean, the one you spoke of just now, Mr. Prosecutor. Yes, gentlemen, I, too, had that idea in my mind during the whole of that damned month, so that I almost made up my mind to go to Katya—I was so vile! But to go to her, tell her of my betrayal, and because of that betrayal, to carry it out, to cover the forthcoming expenses of that betrayal, to beg Katya herself for money (to beg, do you hear, to beg!), and then go straight from her and run off with another woman, her rival, a woman who hated and had insulted her— Why, Mr. Prosecutor, you must be out of your mind!"

"Well, not exactly out of my mind," the public prosecutor said with a grin, "But I admit, of course, that I was a little rash and did not quite take into account one woman's jealousy of another— if, indeed, there could be any question of jealousy here, as you say— Yes, yes, I suppose there is something of the kind here—"

"But that would have been infamous," cried Mitya, striking the table fiercely with his fist, "it would have stunk to high heaven! Why, do you realise that she was quite capable of giving me the money and indeed she would have done so—she would have quite certainly done so—just to avenge herself on me; she would have given it, just to enjoy her revenge, to show her contempt for me, for hers, too, is an infernal nature; she's a woman of great wrath! I'd have taken the money, oh, I'd have taken it all right, and then for the rest of my life—oh, God! I'm sorry, gentlemen, I'm shouting like that because I had that idea in my mind quite recently, only the day before yesterday, the night I was having all that trouble with the Lurcher, and yesterday, too. Yes, all day yesterday, I remember it. Right down to the incident—"

"What incident?" Nikolai Parfenovich put in, unable to suppress his curiosity, but Mitya was not listening.

"I've made a terrible confession to you," he concluded

gloomily. "You must appreciate it, gentlemen. And that's not enough, it's not enough to appreciate it. You must accept it on trust, for if you don't, and that fails to reach your hearts, then you simply have no respect for me, gentlemen, that's what I must tell you, and I'll die of shame at having confessed it to men like you! Oh, I'll shoot myself! Yes, I can see, I can already see that you don't believe me! Why, you're not going to take that down, too?" he cried, now in dismay.

"Yes, of course—everything you've just said," Nikolai Parfenovich said, looking at him in surprise. "I mean that, to the very last hour, you still intended to go to Miss Verkhovtsev to beg her for that sum— I assure you, Dmitri Fyodorovich, we consider that a very important piece of evidence, I mean, about your having wanted to go to her— It's of particular importance for you."

"But for goodness' sake, gentlemen," Mitya cried, throwing up his hands, "for shame, don't take that down, at any rate! Why, I have, so to speak, rent my soul open to you, and you take advantage of it and are probing with your fingers in the wounds in both the torn halves— Good Lord!"

He buried his face in his hands in despair.

"Don't take it so to heart, Dmitri Fyodorovich," the public prosecutor concluded, "everything that has been taken down will be read over to you afterwards and we'll alter anything you don't agree with. Now I should like to ask you a little question for the third time: are you quite sure that no one, positively no one, has heard from you about the money you sewed up? I must tell you it's quite unimaginable."

"No one, no one! I said so before, or you don't understand a thing! Oh, leave me alone!"

"Just as you please. This matter will have to be explained and there's plenty of time for it. But, meanwhile, I'd like you to think this over carefully: we have perhaps dozens of witnesses who will say that you yourself spread the story of the three thousand you had squandered, that you proclaimed it from the roof tops, and that the sum was three thousand, not fifteen hundred. And even this time, when you got hold of some money yesterday, you also gave many people to understand that you had brought three thousand along with you—"

"You've got not dozens but hundreds of witnesses, two hundred witnesses," Mitya exclaimed. "Two hundred people have heard me say that, a thousand have!"

"Well, you see, sir, all, all bear witness to it. And the word *all* must mean something, sir."

"It means nothing at all. I hoaxed them and they all swallowed the story."

"But why did you have to 'hoax them', as you put it?"

"The devil knows why. Perhaps to brag—of squandering so much money— Perhaps because I wanted to forget about the money I'd sewn up—yes, that's it!— Damn it, how often are you going to ask me that question? Well, I told a lie and that's all there is to it and since I'd lied, I didn't care to correct it. Why do people tell lies sometimes?"

"It's very difficult to decide, Dmitri Fyodorovich," the public prosecutor said impressively, "why people tell lies. Now tell me, though, was the amulet, as you call it, about your neck sizable?

"Oh, not very big."

"Approximately how big?"

"Like a hundred-rouble note folded in two—that was the size."

"Could you show us any shreds of it? You must have some on you."

"What nonsense, damn it—I don't know if I have them."

"But excuse me, can't you tell us where and when you took it off your neck? According to your own testimony, you didn't go home, did you?"

"I tore it off my neck and took the money out on my way to Perkhotin's from Fenya's."

"In the dark?"

"I didn't need a candle for that, did I? I did it with my fingers in a jiffy."

"Without any scissors? In the street?"

"In the square, I think it was. What did I want scissors for? It was an old rag and tore at once."

"What did you do with it then?"

"I threw it away."

"Where exactly?"

"Why, in the square, somewhere in the square! I'm damned if I know just where in the square. What do you want to know that for?"

"It's of the utmost importance, Dmitri Fyodorovich. It's material evidence in your favour, don't you see that? Who helped you to sew it up a month ago?"

"Nobody. I did it myself."

"Can you sew?"

"A soldier has to know how to use a needle. No special skill was required for that, anyway."

"Where did you get the material from, I mean, the rag, to sew the money up in?"

"Are you making fun of me?"

"Certainly not. We're in no mood for that, Dmitri Fyodorovich."

"I don't remember where I got the rag from. Must have picked it up somewhere."

"But, surely, you ought to remember that."

"Honestly I don't. I might have torn a bit off my linen."

"That's very interesting. We might find the thing at your lodgings tomorrow—a shirt, perhaps—you tore a piece off from. What sort of rag was it: cotton or linen?"

"I'm damned if I know. Just a moment, though— I don't think I tore it off anything, after all. It was a piece of calico— I believe I sewed it up in an old cap of my landlady's."

"An old cap of your landlady's?"

"Yes, sir. Stole it from her."

"Stole it? How?"

"You see, I seem to remember now that I actually mistook one of her caps for a rag, perhaps to wipe my pen on. I took it on the quiet because it was really just a rag of a thing. I tore it up and left the bits lying about somewhere. I sewed the fifteen hundred up in them— Yes, I think I did sew it up in that rag. It was a worthless old calico cap. Must have been washed thousands of times."

"You remember that for certain?"

"Not quite. I think it was the cap. Oh, what does it matter?"

"In that case, your landlady must have missed the thing?"

"I don't think so. She never did. It was an old rag, I'm telling you, an old rag, quite worthless."

"And where did you get the needle and thread from?"

"You won't get another word out of me," said Mitya, finally growing angry. "Enough of that!"

"And don't you think, it's rather strange that you should have so completely forgotten where you dropped that—er—amulet in the square?"

"Why not have the square swept tomorrow?" said Mitya mockingly. "Perhaps you'll find it. Enough, gentlemen, enough," he declared in an exhausted voice. "I can clearly see you don't believe me! You don't believe a word I've said. It's my fault, not yours. I shouldn't have told you anything. Why, oh why have I degraded myself by confessing my secret to you! It's just a laughing matter to you, I can see it from your eyes. It was you, Mr. Prosecutor, who have tested my patience! Sing your own praise, if you can— Damn you, you torturers!"

He dropped his head and buried his face in his hands. The public prosecutor and the court investigator were silent. A minute later, he raised his head and stared vacantly at them. His face expressed complete and hopeless despair; he seemed mute and forlorn, and sat as though unconscious of what was taking place about him. But the time had come for an end to his questioning: they had urgently to go over to the interrogation of the witnesses. It was eight o'clock already and the candles had long been put out. Makarov and Kalganov, who had been coming in and out of the room during Mitya's interrogation, had now both left again. The public prosecutor and the court investigator, too, looked very tired. It was a dull morning, the sky was overcast and it was pouring with rain. Mitya gazed blankly at the windows.

"May I have a look out of the window?" he suddenly asked the court investigator.

"Oh, as much as you like," he replied.

Mitya rose and went to the window against whose greenish little panes the rain came lashing. Beyond the window the muddy road could be seen; farther, in the rainy haze, stood rows and rows of black poor weatherbeaten and unsightly peasant huts, which looked even poorer and more weatherbeaten in the rain. Mitya recalled "Phoeubus the golden-haired" and how he had meant to shoot himself at its first rays. "I suppose it would have been much better on such a morning," he grinned and, suddenly, with a downward motion of his hand, he turned to his "torturers".

"Gentlemen!" he cried, "I can see that I'm done for. But what about her? Tell me about her, I implore you. Will she, too, be ruined together with me? She's innocent. She wasn't in her right mind when she cried out last night: 'It's all my fault!' She had nothing to do with it! Nothing at all! I felt so grieved as I sat with you all night— Can't you—won't you tell me what you are going to do with her now?"

"You needn't worry at all on that score, Dmitri Fyodorovich," the public prosecutor replied at once with obvious alacrity, "so far, we have no grounds whatever for troubling the lady you're so interested in. I hope it will be the same in the later stages of this case— On the contrary, we'll do everything in our power in this matter. You can set your mind completely at rest."

"I thank you, gentlemen, I knew you were just and honourable men in spite of everything. You've taken a load off my mind— Well, what are we going to do now? I'm ready."

"Well, we must certainly hurry up. We must proceed at once to the interrogation of the witnesses. All that must take place in your presence and therefore—"

"Oughtn't we to have some tea first?" the court investigator interrupted. "I think we've earned it!"

It was decided that, if tea were ready downstairs (the uyezd chief of police Makarov had certainly gone down "to have a cup"), they would have a cup, too, and then "carry on and on". A proper breakfast would have to wait for a more favourable opportunity. Indeed, the tea was soon prepared downstairs and brought up. Mitya at first declined the tea the court investigator politely offered him, but afterwards asked for some himself, and drank it avidly. He looked utterly worn out. One might have thought that a night of carousing, even if accompanied by the most violent emotions, would not have greatly taxed a man of his prodigious strength, yet he felt that he could hardly sit upright on his chair, and at times everything in the room began to swim before his eyes. "A little more and I'll go raving mad," he thought to himself.

8.

The Witnesses Testify. The Bairn

The interrogation of the witnesses began, but we shall not continue our story in such detail as we have till now. We shall therefore omit a description of how the court investigator impressed upon every witness his duty to tell the truth and nothing but the truth and that he would afterwards have to repeat his testimony on oath, or how every witness was required to sign his deposition, and so on and so forth. We shall merely note that the two officials repeatedly laid special stress on the main point, i.e. the three thousand, in other words, whether the sum spent by Dmitri Fyodorovich at Mokroye the first time he was there a month before had been three thousand or fifteen hundred, and whether Dmitri Fyodorovich spent three thousand or fifteen hundred on the previous night. Alas, the evidence given by every witness worked against Mitya; not one of them was in his favour; moreover, some of the witnesses introduced new and almost overwhelming facts in refutation of his statements. The first witness to be interrogated was the innkeeper. He appeared before the two officials without the slightest sign of apprehension; on the contrary, he had an air of stern and grim-faced indignation against the accused, which undoubtedly made him appear quite extraordinarily truthful and full of a sense of his own dignity. He spoke little and with restraint, waiting for the questions to be put to him and replying readily and after careful consideration. He testified firmly and without the least hesitation that a month before Mitya could have spent no less that three thousand, and that all the peasants could bear witness that they had heard of three thousand mentioned by Dmitri Fyodorovich himself. "The money he flung away on the Gypsies alone! I suppose they must have got over a thousand at least."

"I don't think I gave them as much as five hundred," Mitya commented gloomily. "Didn't count it at the time, though. I was drunk. A pity—"

This time, Mitya was sitting sideways, with his back to the curtains. He listened gloomily, looked tired and melancholy and seemed to be saying: "Oh, say whatever you like! It's all the same to me now!"

"You must have spent over a thousand on them, Dmitri Fyodorovich," the innkeeper objected firmly. "You were just throwing your money about and they were picking it up. They're thieves and rascals, the lot of 'em. Horse-thieves. They've been chased away from here or, I daresay, they'd have testified how much they profited from you. I saw the money in your hands myself, sir. It's true I didn't count it—you never let me, but from what I could see, I'd say it was much more than fifteen hundred— Fifteen hundred indeed! I've seen a lot of money in my time, I have, and I can judge—"

As for the sum Dmitri Fyodorovich had had on him on the previous day, the innkeeper declared forthright that as soon as he got off the cart Dmitri Fyodorovich had told him himself that he had brought three thousand with him.

"Come now, are you quite sure, Trofim Borisovich?" Mitya objected. "Did I say in so many words that I brought three thousand?"

"You did, Dmitri Fyodorovich. You said it in front of Andrei. Andrei is still here; he hasn't gone yet, so you can have him sent for. And while you were treating the chorus in the drawing-room, sir, you yourself shouted that you were leaving your sixth thousand here—together with what you spent before, that is, it must be understood like that. Stepan and Semyon heard it, and Mr. Kalganov, too, was standing next to you at the time. Perhaps he, too, remembers it—"

The testimony regarding the sixth thousand made a deep impression on the two officials. The new version was to their liking: three and three made six, which meant three thousand then and three thousand now—and there they had the six thousand—what could be clearer?

All the peasants mentioned by the innkeeper were then interrogated: Stepan and Semyon, and the driver Andrei as well as Pyotr Fomich Kalganov. The peasants and Andrei unhesitatingly confirmed the innkeeper's evidence. In addition, the officials recorded, word for word, Andrei's account of his talk with Mitya on the way and Mitya's remark to the effect: "Where am I going to get to—to heaven or to hell, and will I be forgiven or not in the next world?" The "psychologist", that is, the public prosecutor, listened with a sage smile and ended up by recommending that Mitya's remark about where he would get to should also be "adduced as evidence".

When he was called, Kalganov came in reluctantly, looking sullen and capricious, and spoke to the public prosecutor and the court investigator as though they were complete strangers, and no long-standing acquaintances he had been meeting practically every day. He began by declaring that he knew nothing about the matter and had no desire to. However, it transpired that he had heard of the "six thousand", and admitted that he had been standing next to Mitya at the moment. He could not specify "how much money" Mitya had had in his hands, but confirmed that the Poles had cheated at cards. He also explained, in reply to repeated questions, that, after the Poles had been turned out, Mitya's standing with Agrafena Alexandrovna had certainly taken a turn for the better and that she had said herself that she loved him. He spoke of her with respectful restraint, as though she were a lady of quality, and never once allowed himself to call her "Grushenka". Despite Kalganov's obvious repugnance to giving evidence, the public prosecutor interrogated him at great length and it was only from him that the public prosecutor learnt all the details of Mitya's "romance" that night. Mitya did not even once interrupt Kalganov. At last, the young man was allowed to leave, which he did with undisguised indignation.

The Poles, too, were questioned. Though they had gone to bed in their little room, they did not sleep all night, and on the arrival of the authorities they hastily dressed, realising that they would be sent for. They came in looking dignified, though rather apprehensive. The little Pole turned out to be a retired civil servant of the lowly twelfth class, who had served in Siberia as a veterinary surgeon. His surname was Musialowicz. Wróblewski proved to be a dentist in private practice. Though the questions were put to them by the court investigator, they both addressed their answers to the uyezd chief of police, who was standing aside, taking him, in their ignorance, for the superior officer in charge of the proceedings and addressing him at every step as "colonel". And it was only after doing that several times and at the instigation of the uyezd chief of police himself that they realised that they had to address their answer to the court investigator alone. It proved that they had quite a good command of Russian, except perhaps for the pronunciation of some words. About his relations with Grushenka, past and present, Musialowicz began to speak warmly and with pride, so that Mitya at once lost his temper and shouted that he would not allow the "blackguard" to talk like that in his presence. Musialowicz at once drew attention to the word "blackguard" and asked it to be put on record. Mitya flew into a rage.

"He's a blackguard, a dirty blackguard! You can take that down, too. Put down that, in spite of the record, I still say that he's a blackguard!" he shouted.

Though he recorded the expression, the court investigator revealed a most praiseworthy and business-like skill in dealing with this unpleasant incident: after reprimanding Mitya, he at once discontinued any further inquiries into the romantic aspect of the case and turned hastily to the essentials. That provided a piece of evidence from the Poles which aroused the keenest interest in the two officials: Mitya's attempt to bribe Musialowicz in the other room by offering him three thousand roubles if he gave up Grushenka, on condition that he agreed to take seven hundred down and the remaining two thousand three hundred "next day in town", assuring him on his word of honour that he had not that sum at Mokroye, but that his money was at the town. Mitya, in his excitement, objected that he had never said that he would let them have the money in the town for certain on the morrow but Wróblewski confirmed his friend's evidence. Mitya himself, after giving the matter brief thought, frowningly agreed that the Poles were probably right, and that he had been much worked up at the time and might really have said that. The public prosecutor literally pounced on that piece of evidence: it seemed clear to the officials (as, indeed, it later transpired) that half or part of the three thousand that had come into Mitya's possession could really have been concealed somewhere in town or, indeed, somewhere at the Mokroye inn, which might explain the fact, so awkward for the prosecution, that only eight hundred roubles had been found on Mitya so far—the only fact that, insignificant as it was, spoke somewhat in Mitya's favour. But even that single favourable piece of evidence now broke down. Asked by the public prosecutor where he would have obtained the remaining two thousand three hundred roubles he had pledged his word of honour to let the Pole have the next day, though he himself averred that he had only fifteen hundred, Mitya firmly replied that he had had no intention of offering "the dirty Pole" money, but would have conveyed to him the title of the estate of Chermashnya, the same he had offered to Samsonov and Madame Khokhlakov. The public prosecutor even smiled at Mitya's "innocent ruse".

"And do you really think that he'd have agreed to accept the 'title' in lieu of two thousand three hundred roubles in cash?"

"He certainly would have agreed," Mitya declared heatedly. "Why, he would have made not two but four or even six thousand out of it! He'd have put some pettifogging lawyers, Jews and Poles, onto the matter, and they'd have extracted not three thousand but the whole estate out of the old man."

The evidence given by Musialowicz was, of course, taken down practically verbatim, after which the Poles were allowed to leave. Their cheating at cards was scarcely mentioned; as it was the court investigator was too grateful to them, and he did not want to bother them with trifles, particularly as it had been nothing but a stupid quarrel between drunken men over cards. There had been enough wild drinking and shocking goings on that night— So the two hundred roubles remained in the pockets of the Poles.

Next to be sent for was Maximov, who came in timidly, went up to the table with little steps, looking very dishevelled and mournful. He had all the time found refuge downstairs with Grushenka, sitting mutely with her and "now and again", as Mikhail Makarovich later put it, "began whimpering and wiping his eyes with his blue check handkerchief", so that she had to soothe and comfort him. The poor old man at once said that he was sorry that, "being so poor", he had borrowed "ten roubles" from Dmitri Fyodorovich and that he was ready to pay them back— To the court investigator's direct question whether he had noticed how much money Dmitri Fyodorovich Karamazov had had in his hands, since he must have been able to see it better than anyone when he got the ten-rouble note from him, Maximov replied most positively: "Twenty thousand, sir."

"Have you ever seen twenty thousand anywhere before?" the court investigator asked with a smile.

"Yes, sir, I have, only it wasn't twenty thousand but only seven when my wife mortgaged my little property, sir. She just let me have a look at it from a distance, boasted to me about it, she did, sir. A very thick wad it was, too, sir, all rainbow-coloured notes. Dmitri Fyodorovich's too, were all rainbow-coloured."

He was soon allowed to go. Finally Grushenka's turn came. The public prosecutor and the court investigator were evidently apprehensive of the impression her appearance might produce on Dmitri Fyodorovich, and the court investigator even murmured a few words of admonishment to him, but, in reply, Mitya merely bowed his head in silence to intimate that there would be no "scene". The uyezd chief of police Makarov himself led Grushenka in. She entered with grave and sombre mien, looking almost composed and sat down quietly on the chair pointed out to her opposite the court investigator. She was very pale, and seemed to be feeling cold, for she kept wrapping herself closely in her beautiful black shawl. Indeed, she was beginning to feel a light feverish chill coming on, the onset of a long illness which she contracted that night. Her grave air, frank and earnest look, and quiet manner produced a most favourable impression upon all. The court investigator was even "taken" by her somewhat. He admitted himself, when talking about it later, that it was only then that he realised how "good-looking" a woman she was, for though he had seen her several times before, he had always considered her a sort of "provincial hetaera". "Her manners are quite refined," he exclaimed enthusiastically in the company of some ladies. However, his remark was received with great indignation and he at once was called "a naughty man", which was much to his liking. On entering the room, Grushenka only cast a cursory glance at Mitya, who in turn, looked at her uneasily, but her face immediately set his mind at rest. After the first usual questions and cautions, the court investigator asked her, somewhat hesitantly but with courtesy, of her relations with retired Lieutenant Dmitri Fyodorovich Karamazov, to which Grushenka replied quietly and firmly:

"He is an acquaintance of mine and it was as an acquaintance that I received him during the last month."

To further inquisitive questions, she replied simply and with absolute frankness that though she liked him, "at times", she was not in love with him, but tried to get a hold on him, as well as on the "old man" out of "sheer spite". She had seen that Mitya was very jealous of his father and of anyone else, but that had only amused her. She had never intended to go to Fyodor Pavlovich Karamazov, but had only been making mock of him. "I had no time to bother with either of them all this month. I was expecting another man, one who had wronged me— But," she concluded, "I don't think there's any need for you to inquire into that, or for me to answer your questions, for that's my own private concern."

The court investigator at once acted on these words: he again stopped insisting on the "romantic" aspects of the case and passed on to the substantive, that is, the main question about the three thousand. Grushenka confirmed that a month before, at Mokroye, three thousand roubles had been spent, and though she herself had not counted the money, she had heard from Dmitri Fyodorovich himself that it had been three thousand.

"Did he tell you that privately or in anybody's presence, or did you only hear him speak about it to other people in your presence?" the public prosecutor inquired.

To which Grushenka replied that she had heard it from him in the presence of other people, that she had heard him tell other people about it, and that she had heard it from him privately.

"Did he say it to you privately once or several times?" the public prosecutor inquired again, and was told that Grushenka had heard it several times.

The public prosecutor was well satisfied with this testimony. Further questions elicited the information that Grushenka knew where that money had come from: Dmitri Fyodorovich had got it from Katerina Ivanovna.

"And didn't you hear even once that a month ago Dmitri Fyodorovich had spent, not three thousand but less, and that he had kept half of that sum?"

"No, sir," Grushenka testified, "I never heard that."

It was further disclosed that, during that month, Mitya had, on the contrary, often told her that he was penniless. "He was always expecting some money from his father," concluded Grushenka.

"And—er—did he ever say in your presence—er—er—just in passing, or at a moment of exasperation, that he meant to make an attempt on his father's life?" the court investigator suddenly asked.

"Oh yes, he did!" Grushenka sighed.

"Once or several times?"

"He mentioned it several times, but always in anger."

"And did you believe he'd do it?"

"No, I never believed it!" she replied firmly. "I had confidence in his honourable character."

"Gentlemen," Mitya cried suddenly, "please let me say a word to Agrafena Alexandrovna, in your presence."

"You may," the court investigator assented.

"Agrafena Alexandrovna," Mitya declared, getting up from his seat, "believe me as you believe in God: I am not guilty of my father's murder last night!"

Having said this, Mitya resumed his seat. Grushenka rose to her feet, turned to the icon in the room and crossed herself devoutly.

"Thank God!" she said in a voice trembling with emotion, and without resuming her seat she turned to the court investigator and added: "Believe what he has just said! I know him: he may sometimes say something as a joke or out of stubbornness, but if it's against his conscience he'll never deceive anyone. He'll always tell the truth; you can believe that!"

"Thank you, Agrafena Alexandrovna. You've given me fresh courage!" Mitya said in a trembling voice.

Asked how much money Mitya had the day before, she declared that she did not know, but had heard him tell several people that he had brought three thousand with him. As to the question where he had got the money, he had told her alone that he had "stolen" it from Katerina Ivanovna; she had replied that it was not stolen money, and should be returned the next day. In reply to the public prosecutor's insistent question whether the money he claimed he had stolen from Katerina Ivanovna was the same he had spent yesterday or a month before, she declared that he had referred to the money he had spent a month before and that she had understood him thus.

Grushenka was at last allowed to leave, the court investigator telling her impulsively that she could go back to town any time she wished, and that if, for his part, he could be of any assistance to her, with horses, for instance, or if she would like an escort, he—for his part—

"Thank you very much, sir," Grushenka replied with a bow. "I'll return with the old man, the landowner, I'll take him back to town with me and, in the meantime, if you will permit, sir, I'll wait downstairs to hear what you decide about Dmitri Fyodorovich."

She went out. Mitya felt calm and even looked quite cheerful, but only for a minute. All the time, he had been feeling overcome by a strange physical weakness which grew more and more perceptible as time went on. His eyes were closing with fatigue. The interrogation of the witnesses ended at last and work was begun on the final draft of the official record of the evidence. Mitya got up, crossed over from his chair to the corner of the room by the curtain, lay down on a large rug-covered chest and fell asleep at once. He had quite a strange dream, which was entirely out of keeping with the place and the time. He seemed to be driving somewhere in the steppes, where he had served long ago, while he was still an officer in the army, and was being driven through the slush by a peasant on a cart pulled by a pair of horses. He felt very cold. It was early November, and snow was falling in large, wet flakes, which melted as soon as they reached the ground. The peasant was driving along briskly, wielding his whip with a will. He had a long, fair beard. He was not an old man, about fifty perhaps, and wore a peasant's grey homespun coat. They soon caught sight of a village, where he could see the grimy and weatherbeaten huts, half of them burnt down, only their charred beams to be seen. As they drove in, there were peasant women drawn up along the road, lots of women, a whole line of them, all haggard and thin with strangely brown faces. One woman in particular, at the very end of the line, was very tall and gaunt; she looked forty but may have been only twenty, with a long thin face, and in her arms was a crying baby; and her breasts were probably so withered that there was not a drop of milk in them. And the baby cried and cried, holding out its little bare arms with its little fists quite blue with the cold.

"Why are they crying? Why are they crying?" Mitya asked, as they dashed past them at a spanking pace.

"It's the bairn, sir," replied the driver. "The bairn's crying."

And Mitya was struck by the man having said "bairn", in the peasant fashion, and not "baby". And he liked the peasant's way of saying "bairn": there seemed to be more compassion in it.

"But why is it crying?" Mitya persisted stupidly. "Why are its arms bare? Why don't they wrap it up?"

"The bairn's chilled to the marrow, sir; its clothes are frozen and give no warmth."

"But why is that? Why?" Mitya still persisted stupidly.

"They're poor, sir, their home's been burnt down. Got no food, sir. They're begging because their homes have burnt down."

"No, no," Mitya still seemed unable to understand, "tell me why are the poor mothers standing there? Why are people so poor? Why's the bairn poor? Why's the steppe so bare? Why don't they embrace and kiss one another, why don't they sing songs of joy? Why are they so dark with bleak misfortune? Why don't they feed the bairn?"

And he felt that, though the questions he was asking were wild and meaningless, he could not help asking them and that, indeed, they had to be asked that way. And he felt, too, that strange emotions he had never experienced before were surging up in his heart, that he wanted to weep, wanted to do something for everyone so that the bairn and its withered mother should cry no more, that no more tears should be shed from that moment, and that he ought to do it now, now, without delay and regardless of everything, with all the Karamazovian recklessness.

"And I'm with you, too," he heard close to him the dear, deeply felt words of Grushenka. "I shall never leave you now, I shall be with you now for the rest of my life." And his heart flared up, surging towards the light, and he longed to live and go on living, to go on and on towards the new and beckoning light, and quickly, quickly—now, at once!

"Where am I? Where am I off to?" he exclaimed, opening his eyes and, sitting up on the chest, as though he had come to from a fainting fit, his smile bright. The court investigator was standing over him, asking him to listen to the statement, and sign it. Mitya realised that he had been asleep for an hour or more, but he did not listen to the court investigator. He was suddenly amazed to find a cushion under his head, a cushion which had not been there when he sank exhausted on the chest.

"Who put the cushion under my head? Who was that kindly man?" he cried with a rapturous feeling of gratitude and with tears in his voice, as though goodness only knows what great favour had been conferred on him. He never learnt who that kind man was. It may have been one of the witnesses, or the court investigator's clerk had, out of compassion, seen to it that a cushion was put under his head. But all his soul was shaken with tears. Going up to the table, he said he would sign anything they wanted him to.

"I've had a good dream, gentlemen," he said in a strange voice, looking transformed, his face radiant with joy.

9.

Mitya Is Taken Away

When the statement had been signed, the court investigator turned solemnly to the accused and read out a Notice of Committal to the effect that, on such and such a date and at such and such a place, the court investigator of such and such a district court, having examined so and so (that is, Mitya), who was accused of committing such and such crimes (all the charges were carefully stated), and since the accused, while pleading not guilty to the charges against him, had no evidence in his defence, whereas witnesses (so and so) and the circumstances (such and such) showed him to be guilty of the aforesaid charges, and acting in accordance with such and such paragraphs of the Criminal Code, etc. had decided: to deprive so and so (Mitya) of any means of evading further investigation and trial, the accused should be detained at such and such prison, of which the accused should be notified and a copy of the said Notice was to be sent to the deputy public prosecutor, etc., etc. Mitya, in short, was notified that he was in custody as of that moment and would be at once taken to town, where he was to be locked up at a very unpleasant place. Mitya listened attentively and merely shrugged his shoulders.

"Well, gentlemen, I'm not blaming you, I'm ready— I understand that there is nothing else you can do."

The court investigator explained to him gently that he would be taken to prison by the rural police officer Mavriki Shmertsov, who happened to be there—

"Just a moment, gentlemen," Mitya suddenly interrupted with a feeling somehow uncontrollable and turning to the people in the room, said: "We all are cruel and all monsters; we all make others weep, mothers and babes at the breast, but let that be clear once and for all—I am the most vile and despicable wretch of all! So be it! Every day of my life, while beating my breast, I've vowed to turn over a new leaf, and every day I've done one and the same vile things. I realise now that such men as I need to be stricken—stricken by fate, to be caught, though, with a noose and be caught by some external force. Never, never would I have risen of my own volition! But the lightning has struck. I accept the suffering of my accusation and of my public disgrace, I want to suffer and be cleansed by suffering! I will, perhaps, be cleansed, gentlemen, won't I? But listen to me for the last time: I am innocent of my father's blood! I accept my punishment, not because I killed him but because I wanted to kill him and, perhaps, might actually have killed him— But I swear to fight you all the same and I'm telling you that. I shall fight you to the very end, and then God will decide! Farewell, gentlemen. Don't be angry with me for having raised my voice at you—oh, I was still so stupid then— In another minute, I shall be a prisoner, but now, for the last time,

Dmitri Karamazov, as a free man, holds out his hand to you. I'm taking leave of you and thereby of all people!"

His voice trembled and he really did hold out his hand, but the court investigator, who stood closest to him, somehow suddenly hid his hands behind his back in a kind of spasmodic movement. Mitya noticed it at once and gave a start. He lowered his extended hand immediately.

"The investigation is not over yet," the court investigator murmured, looking a little embarrassed. "We shall continue in the town and, for my part, I'm ready to wish you every success—in—winning acquittal— I've always been disposed to consider you, Dmitri Fyodorovich, as a man who is, as it were, more unfortunate than sinful— All of us here, if I may express an opinion on behalf of us all, are ready to acknowledge you to be an honourable young man at heart, but one who, alas, has been swept along rather excessively by certain passions—"

The little figure of the court investigator was most impressive by the time he finished his speech. The thought struck Mitya that the "boy" might at any moment take him by an elbow, lead him to the other end of the room, and renew their recent talk about the "girls". But all kinds of irrelevant and stray thoughts sometimes come into the mind even of a criminal who is being led to the execution.

"Gentlemen, you are kind and humane,—may I see *her*? May I take leave of her for the last time?"

"Certainly, but in view of—in short, now it's no longer possible except in the presence of—"

"By all means, be present if you must!"

Grushenka was brought in, but their parting was brief, with few words spoken, which did not satisfy at all the court investigator. Grushenka bowed low to Mitya.

"I've told you I'm yours and I will be yours. I'll be with you for ever, wherever they may decide to take you to. Good-bye, dear, you've ruined yourself through no fault of your own!"

Her lips quivered and the tears flowed from her eyes.

"Forgive me for my love, Grusha, for ruining you with my love!"

Mitya had something more to say but suddenly stopped short

240

and went out. He was at once surrounded by people who now kept a constant watch on him. At the front steps, to which he had driven up in such style the night before, in Andrei's troika, two carts were already waiting. Mavriki Mavrikievich Shmertsov, the local police officer, a stocky man with a fat and flabby face, who was exasperated by something, some unforeseen irregularity, was short-tempered and shouting. He told Mitya a little too sternly to get into the cart. "In the past, when I would stand him drinks at the town inn, his face was quite different," thought Mitya as he climbed onto the cart. Trifon Borisovich, the innkeeper, too, came down the front steps. At the gate stood a crowd of peasants, women and drivers, all staring at Mitya.

"Farewell, good folk!" Mitya suddenly called out them from the cart.

"Farewell and forgive us," two or three voices replied.

"Farewell, too, Trifon Borisovich!"

But the innkeeper did not even turn round; he may have been busy, also shouting and fussing about something. It seemed that everything was not quite ready in the second cart, in which two rural constables had to accompany the local police officer. The little peasant who had been ordered to drive the second cart was donning his homespun coat and kept arguing back that it was not he but Akim who should by rights be driving. But Akim was not on the spot, and was being looked for. In the meantime, the little peasant persisted and begged them to wait.

"You see what our peasants are like, sir," cried the innkeeper, addressing the police officer. "They've no shame! Akim gave you twenty-five copecks the day before yesterday, which you've spent on booze, and now you're shouting. I'm really surprised at your kindness to our vile peasants, sir. That's all I can say."

"But," Mitya interposed, "what do we want a second cart for? Let's go in one, Mavriki Mavrikievich," he addressed the police officer. "Don't worry, old man, I won't give you any trouble; I won't try to escape. What do you want an escort for?"

"When speaking to me address me as 'sir', if you don't

know that yet! I'm not 'old man' to you. And keep your advice for some other time!—" cried the police officer, turning fiercely on Mitya as though glad to vent his anger on someone.

Reduced to silence, Mitya turned red. A moment later he felt terribly cold. The rain had stopped, but the dull sky was still overcast, and a cutting wind was blowing straight in his face. "I may have caught a chill," thought Mitya hunching his shoulders. At last the police officer, too, got in, sat down heavily and, as though not noticing it, pushed Mitya to the edge of the cart. It is true, he was in a bad mood and disliked the task assigned to him.

"Good-bye, Trifon Borisovich!" Mitya shouted again, but felt that he had spoken not from good nature, but out of spite and against his will. But the innkeeper stood proudly, his hands behind his back and staring straight at Mitya. He looked stern and angry, and made no reply.

"Farewell, Dmitri Fyodorovich, farewell!" cried Kalganov, who had suddenly appeared from somewhere. Rushing up to the cart, he held out his hand to Mitya. He was capless. Mitya had just enough time to press his hand.

"Farewell, my dear fellow, I shan't forget your magnanimity!" he cried warmly. But the cart started, parting their hands. The bell jingled. Mitya was taken away.

Kalganov ran back into the passageway, sat down in a corner, buried his face in his hands and wept. He sat like that for a long time—he wept as though he were a little boy, not a young man of twenty. Oh, he was almost sure of Mitya's guilt! "What sort of people are they?" he kept exclaiming incoherently, in bitter desolation and almost in despair. "What sort of people are they after that?" At that moment he had no wish to go on living. "Is it worth while? Is it worth while?" the distressed young man exclaimed.

PART FOUR

BOOK TEN

The Boys

1.

Kolya Krasotkin

It was early November; the temperature had stood at eleven degrees below zero in our town and the ground was covered with glare ice. Some powdery snow had fallen on the frozen ground during the night, and a biting wind was lifting and blowing it along the dreary streets of our little town and especially along the market square. It was a dull morning, but the snow had stopped. Not far from the square, close by the Plotnikov shop, stood a small house, very neat inside and out, belonging to the widow of the civil servant Krasotkin. He had died long ago, almost fourteen years previously, but his widow, a quite comely lady in her early thirties, enjoyed a comfortable income at her neat little home. She led a secluded and exemplary life and was of an affectionate and cheerful disposition. She was about eighteen when her husband died after but one year of marriage, and had borne him a son. Since then, from the day of his death, she had dedicated herself entirely to bringing up her treasured Kolya and, though she had loved him to distraction during those fourteen years, she had, of course, had far more trouble than joy from him: trembling and dying with fear almost every day, lest he fall ill, catch cold, be naughty, climb on a chair and fall off it, and so on. When Kolya's schooldays began, the mother began to brush up all the subjects so as to help him with his homework. She made the acquaintance of his teachers and their wives, was nice to Kolya's schoolchums and curried favour with them so that they should leave him alone, and not tease or beat him. She went so far that the boys really began making fun of him on account of his being "a mother's darling". But the boy was able to stand up for himself. He was a plucky little fellow, "terribly strong" as was rumoured and then confirmed in his class; he was nimble, headstrong, daring and resourceful. He was good at his lessons, and it was even said that he could beat even their teacher Dardanelov both at arithmetic and world history. But though the boy looked down on his fellows, his nose in the air, he was a good pal and not at all stuck up. He accepted his schoolmates' esteem as his due, but was friendly towards them. Above all, he knew where to draw the line, hold himself in check when necessary and, in respect of the school authorities, he never crossed a certain inviolate and sacred borderline, beyond which any prank turns into a riot, a rebellion, and a breach of the law, and is not to be tolerated. And yet he was as fond of mischief at the least opportunity as any street arab, not so much for the sake of the mischief as to excel in doing something out of the ordinary, "extra-special", to dazzle, and show off. Above all, he was very prideful. He was able to make even his mother submit to him and treated her almost despotically. She submitted to him; oh, she had learnt to do that long ago, and her one unbearable thought was that her boy did not "love her enough". It always seemed to her that Kolya was "unfeeling" to her and there were times when, weeping hysterically, she began reproaching him for his indifference. The boy did not like that, and the more she demanded heartfelt effusion of him, the more unyielding he became. But all this was not so much deliberate as involuntary— such was his nature. His mother was mistaken: he loved her, but disliked her "sloppy sentimentality". There was a bookcase in the house with a few books that had belonged to his father. Kolya was fond of reading and had read several of them on his own. That did not worry his mother, though she could not help wondering sometimes why, instead of running out to play, her boy spent hours at the bookcase engrossed in some book. In that way, Kolya read some things he should not have been allowed to at his age. However, more recently the boy, though he was not given to overdoing his pranks, had begun to do things which frightened his mother in good earnest; true, there was nothing vicious in them, only something reckless and unbridled. It so happened that summer, in July, during the school holidays, that mother and son went off to another uyezd, some seventy versts away, to spend a week with a distant relative, whose husband was an official at the railway station (the same one closest to our town, whence Ivan Fyodorovich Karamazov was to leave for Moscow a month later). There Kolya began with a detailed inspection of the railway, making a study of the rules and regulations, in the hope of impressing his schoolmates, on his return, with his newly acquired knowledge. But there happened to be other boys there at the time with whom he made friends. Some of them lived at the station and others close by—boys between twelve and fifteen, altogether about six or seven of them, two of whom happened to be from our town. The boys played games and pranks together, and on the fourth or fifth day of Kolya's stay they made a quite absurd wager for two roubles: Kolya, who was practically the youngest of them and was therefore somewhat looked down on by the others, volunteered out of vanity or sheer recklessness, to lie down between the rails when the eleven o'clock train was due to arrive, and lie there motionless while the train passed overhead at full speed. True, a preliminary inspection showed that it was quite possible to lie prone and lengthwise between the rails and remain untouched by the train, but doing so was no easy matter! Kolya firmly maintained he could do it. The boys at first laughed at him and called him a little liar and boaster, which he found quite unendurable and it spurred him on even more. The main thing was that the fifteen-year-olds turned up their noses at him and at first did not even wish to consider the "urchin" a fit playmate, which he could not put up with. So they decided to go that evening to a spot about a verst from the station, so that the train would gather full speed after leaving the station. The boys assembled. It was a moonless night, not simply dark but almost pitch-black. At the time fixed, Kolya lay down between the rails. The other five, who had taken on the wager, waited at first with sinking hearts in the bushes below the embankment, and finally with fear and remorse. At last there came from the distance the rumble of the train leaving the station. Two red lights gleamed in the darkness and they could hear the roar of the approaching monster. "Get off the rails!" the terror-stricken boys shouted to Kolya from the bushes, but it was too late: the train rolled overhead and thundered past. The boys rushed up to Kolya, who lay motionless. They began pulling at him and tried to lift him up. Kolya suddenly got up and descended the embankment in silence. He then declared that he had lain there pretending on purpose that he was unconscious to give them a fright, but the fact was that he really had lost consciousness as he confessed to his mother long afterwards. Thus it was that his reputation of a desperate character now stuck to him for good. He returned to the station as white as a sheet. On the next day, he had a slight attack of a nervous fever, but was in high spirits, happy, and well pleased with himself. The incident became known, not immediately but after their return to our town when the whole school learnt of it, as did the authorities there. However, his mama hurried to plead for her son, and ultimately Dardanelov, one of the most respected and influential masters, exerted himself on his behalf and the affair was hushed up. Dardanelov, a far from elderly bachelor, had been passionately in love with Mrs. Krasotkin for many years, and about a year before, faint with fear and the delicacy of his sentiments, made so bold as to ask for her hand very respectfully; but she had flatly rejected him, considering that her consent would be a betrayal of her boy, though certain mysterious signs may have suggested to Dardanelov that he had grounds to believe he was not entirely objectionable to the charming but excessively virtuous and loving young widow. Kolya's mad prank seemed to have broken the ice, and Dardanelov's intercession had brought in its train a hint that there was some hope in store for him, true, at some distant time. To Dardanelov, who was a paragon of purity and delicacy, that hint was enough to make him quite happy for the time being. He was fond of Kolya, though he would have considered it humiliating to curry favour with him. He therefore treated him with exacting severity in class. Kolya, too, kept him at a respectful distance, did his lessons well, was second from the top in his class, and treated Dardanelov with reserve; the whole class firmly believed that Kolya was so good at world history that he could easily "beat" Dardanelov himself. In fact, when Kolya one day asked Dardanelov who Troy had been founded by, the master replied in general terms about the movements and migrations of peoples, the remoteness of the times, and legendary stories, but failed to reply to the question who Troy had been founded by, the names of its founders, and for some reason even found the question idle and of no significance. But the boys remained convinced that Dardanelov did not know the answer. Kolya had read about the founders of Troy in Smaragdov, whose history was among the books in his father's bookcase. In the end, everyone, even the boys, became interested in the question of who had founded Troy, but Kolya would not reveal his secret, and his reputation for learning remained unshaken.

After the incident on the railway track, a certain change came over Kolya's relations with his mother. When Anna Fyodorovna learnt of her son's exploit, she nearly went out of her mind from horror. She had such terrible attacks of hysteria, lasting with intervals for several days, that Kolya, frightened in good earnest, gave her his solemn word of honour that he would never again engage in such pranks. He swore on bended knees before the icon and by the memory of his father, at the demand of Mrs. Krasotkin herself, and, overcome by his "feelings", the "manly" Kolya burst into tears like a six-year-old boy, and mother and son spent the whole of that day rushing into each other's embraces and sobbing their hearts out. The next morning Kolya woke up as "unfeeling" as ever but became more reticent, reserved, severe and thoughtful. True, he got into hot water again about a month later and his name even reached the ears of our Justice of the Peace, but it was quite a different kind of prank, foolish and ridiculous, and it would seem that he was not responsible for it, but was merely indirectly involved in it. But of that later. His mother continued to be worried and to tremble for him, and the more troubled she became, the more did Dardanelov's hopes increase. It must be noted that Kolya understood that and was aware of Dardanelov's hopes, and, quite naturally, despised him greatly for his "sentiments". He had even been indelicate enough to reveal his contempt to his mother, hinting vaguely that he understood very well what Dardanelov was up to. But after the incident on the railway track, he changed his behaviour in this respect, too: he permitted himself no more hints, even the vaguest, and began speaking more respectfully of Dardanelov in his mother's presence, which the sensitive Mrs. Krasotkin at once appreciated with infinite gratitude in her heart; but at the least and quite inadvertent mention of Dardanelov by some visitor in Kolya's presence she would blush pink. At such moments, Kolya either stared frowningly out of the window or became absorbed in looking for holes in his boots, or else began to yell for Perezvon, the rather big, shaggy, and mangy dog which he had acquired somewhere a month before, brought home and kept for some reason secretly indoors, without showing it to any of his friends. He bullied it terribly, teaching it all kinds of tricks, and reduced it to such a state that it howled whenever he was away at school and squealed with delight when he came home, rushed about like mad, begged, lay down on the ground and pretended to be dead, and so on, in fact, showed all the tricks it had been taught, no longer at a word of command but solely out of the ardour of its rapturous feelings and grateful heart.

Incidentally, I forgot to mention that Kolya Krasotkin was that very boy whom Ilyusha, the son of the retired Captain Snegiryov, already known to the reader, had stabbed with a penknife, in defence of his father, whom the schoolboys had taunted as "tow-beard".

2.

The Kiddies

And so, on that frosty, cold, and damp November morning Kolya Krasotkin was at home. It was Sunday and so he had no classes. But the clock had struck eleven and he simply had to go out on some "very pressing matter", yet he had been left alone in charge of the house, for it so happened that, because of some special and singular happening, the grown-ups were all out. In Mrs. Krasotkin's house, across the passageway from her own flat, was another small flat of two rooms, let out to a doctor's wife and her two little children. The doctor's wife was of the same age as Mrs. Krasotkin and a great friend of hers. Her husband, the doctor, had gone to Orenburg a year before, and from there to Tashkent, and for the previous six months there had been no news of him at all, so that but for her friendship with Mrs. Krasotkin, which somewhat allayed the misery of the forlorn wife, she would have dissolved in a flood of tears. And it just had to happen that, to round off the good lady's woes, Katerina, her only maid, had unexpectedly informed her mistress on the previous evening that she proposed to give birth to a baby the very next morning. How that could have escaped the general notice was a complete mystery. The astonished doctor's wife decided to take Katerina, while there was still time, to an establishment kept in our town for such emergencies by a midwife. As she highly valued her maid's services, she promptly carried out her plan, took her there and stayed on with her. In the morning, Mrs. Krasotkin's friendly sympathy and help were urgently required, for she could, if necessary, give her moral support or ask someone else to take an interest in the case. Both ladies were therefore out that morning, and Agafya, Mrs. Krasotkin's old maid-servant, had gone to the market. And so Kolya was temporary in charge of the "kids", that is, the little boy and girl of the doctor's wife, who were on their own. Kolya was not afraid to take care of the house and, besides, he had Perezvon, who had been ordered to lie flat on the floor under the bench in the hall "without moving" and who for that very reason shook his head and gave two loud and ingratiating taps on the floor with his tail every time Kolya, walking through the rooms, came into the hall; alas, there was no summoning whistle. Kolya looked sternly at the unhappy dog, who relapsed into catalepsy. The only thing that worried Kolya was the "kids". Of course, he had the greatest contempt for Katerina's chance escapade, but he was very fond of the abandoned "kids" and had already brought them a children's book. Nastya, the elder, a girl of eight, could already read, and the younger boy, the seven-year-old Kostya, was very fond of listening to her reading to him. Krasotkin could, of course, have found them something more amusing, that is, he could have made them stand side by side and play at soldiers or hide-and-seek with them. He had done that many times before and was not above doing so, so that even at school the news spread that Krasotkin played horses with the little lodgers at home, galloping and bending his head like a trace horse in a troika; but Krasotkin proudly parried this thrust, pointing out that to play horses with boys of one's own age, boys of thirteen, "in our days, would certainly be disgraceful", but that he did it for the "kids" because he was fond of them, and no one had a right to demand to render an account for his sentiment. That was why the two "kids" simply adored him. But he was in no mood for games at the moment. He had some very important matter of his own to attend to, something almost mysterious, and meanwhile time was passing and Agafya, to whom the children could be entrusted, had not yet decided to return from the market. He had several times crossed the passageway, opened the door of the doctor's wife's flat, and looked anxiously at the "kids", who, as he had instructed them, were sitting over a book. Every time he opened the door, they grinned at him, expecting him to come in and do something nice to amuse them. But the worried Kolya did not go in. At last, the clock struck eleven and he firmly decided that if that "damned" Agafya did not turn up within ten minutes, he would leave without waiting for her, making the "kids" first promise not to be afraid or naughty, and not to cry from fright. With that intention in mind, he donned his warm winter overcoat with the sealskin collar, slung his satchel over his shoulder and, despite his mother's constant entreaties to be sure to put on his galoshes "in such cold weather", he merely gave them a contemptuous glance as he walked the length of the hall, and left wearing only his boots. Seeing him dressed to go out, Perezvon began tapping loudly on the floor with his tail, his whole body quivering nervously, and even emitted a plaintive whine, but Kolya, seeing his dog's eager impatience, decided that it was bad for discipline, and kept him lying under the bench till the very last moment. It was only when he opened the door into the passageway that he suddenly whistled for the dog, which leapt up like mad and began bounding before him rapturously. Crossing the passageway, Kolya opened the door to have a look at the "kids", who were both still sitting at the table, no longer reading but arguing heatedly about something. They very often discussed all sorts of exciting problems of everyday life, Nastya, as the elder, always getting the better of the argument; if Kostya did not agree with her, he always appealed to Kolya Krasotkin, whose decision was accepted by the two contending sides as final. This time, Krasotkin grew quite interested in the discussion and halted in the doorway to listen. On noticing this, the children continued their argument with ever greater excitement.

"I shall never, never believe," Nastya was saying heatedly, "that midwives find babies among the cabbage beds in the kitchen garden. It's winter now and there are no cabbage beds, and the old woman couldn't have brought Katerina a baby daughter."

Kolya whistled under his breath.

"Or perhaps they do bring them from somewhere but only to those who get married."

Listening closely and thinking hard, Kostya looked intently at Nastya.

"Don't be so silly, Nastya," he at last said firmly and calmly, "how can Katerina have a baby if she isn't married?"

Nastya got all worked up.

"You don't understand the least thing," she snapped irritably. "Perhaps she has a husband, only he is in prison, and now she's having a baby."

"But are you sure her husband's in prison?" the positive Kostya inquired gravely.

"Or perhaps," Nastya interrupted impulsively, having rejected and forgotten her first hypothesis, "she had no husband— you may be right there—but she wants to get married, and she's been thinking how to get married, and she's been thinking and thinking about it so much that she's got herself not a husband but a baby."

"Oh, well, it may have been like that," Kostya, completely subdued, agreed. "Why didn't you say so before? How was I to know?"

"Well, children," said Kolya, stepping into the room, "I

can see you're a dangerous lot!"

"Have you got Perezvon with you?" asked Kostya with a grin and began snapping his fingers and calling Perezvon.

"Look here, kids, I'm in a fix," Krasotkin began importantly, "and you must help me. I expect Agafya must have broken a leg, for she isn't back yet. I'm sure she must have. But I've simply got to go out. May I?"

The children looked anxiously at each other. Their grinning faces began to betray some unease: they did not yet quite grasp what was expected of them.

"You'll behave while I'm away, won't you? You won't climb on the cupboard and break your legs? You won't start crying because you're frightened when you're alone, will you?"

A look of terrible anxiety came over the children's faces.

"If you promise to be good, I'll show you something nice— a little copper cannon which fires with real gunpowder."

The children's faces lightened at once.

"Show us the little cannon," said the beaming Kostya.

Krasotkin put his hand in his satchel and, pulling out a little bronze cannon, placed it on the table.

"That's what it's like! Look, it's on wheels," he said, rolling the toy along the table. "It can be loaded and fired."

"Could it kill anyone?"

"It can kill anybody once aimed properly," and Krasotkin explained where the powder had to go, how the pellets should be inserted and where the little hole for the priming was; he warned them of the recoil. The children watched with intense interest. What caught their imagination was the cannon recoiling after being fired.

"And have you got any powder?" Nastya inquired.

"I have."

"Show us the powder, too," she begged with an imploring smile.

Krasotkin dived again into his satchel and pulled out a small bottle with a little real powder, and some pellets, too, in a screwed-up bit of paper. He even pulled the cork out of the bottle and shook a little powder into the palm of his hand.

"One must be carefull there's no flame about, or it will

explode and kill us all," Krasotkin warned them to enhance the impression.

The children looked at the powder with awe-stricken alarm, which intensified their enjoyment. But Kostya liked the small shot most of all.

"The shot don't burn, do they?" he asked.

"No, they don't!"

"Give me a few pellets," he said in an imploring little voice.

"I will give you a few—here you are, only don't show them to your mother before I get back or she'll think it's gunpowder and die of fright and give you a hiding."

"Mummy never punishes us," Nastya at once remarked.

"I know. I only said that because it sounds good. And don't you ever deceive your mother except this time—until I come back. And so, kids, can I go out or not? You won't be frightened and cry when I'm gone, will you?"

"We'll cry!" Kostya said, on the verge of tears.

"Yes, yes, we're sure to cry!" Nastya put in with timid haste.

"Oh, children, children, you're at such a dangerous age! Well, little ones, I suppose I'll have to stay with you for goodness knows how long. And dear me, how time does fly!"

"Please, tell Perezvon to pretend to be dead," asked Kostya.

"Well, I suppose I'll have to get Perezvon to do some of his tricks, too. *Içi*, Perezvon!" And Kolya began giving orders to the dog, which went through all the tricks he knew. Perezvon was a shaggy, medium-sized mongrel with a kind of greyish-lilac coat. He was blind in the right eye and his left ear was ragged for some reason. He yelped and jumped, begged, walked on his hind legs, threw himself on his back with his four paws in the air, and lay motionless, pretending to be dead. During his last trick the door opened and Agafya, Mrs. Krasotkin's fat maid, a pockmarked peasant woman of about forty, appeared in the doorway, back from the market with a bag of provisions held in a hand. She stood watching the dog and holding the bag in her left hand. Anxious as he had been for her to return, Kolya did not interrupt the performance, and, after keeping Perezvon dead for a certain time, at last whistled to him: the dog jumped up and started prancing about in his joy at having done his duty.

"Some dog!" Agafya said sententiously.

"And why are you late, woman?" Krasotkin asked severely.

"Woman, indeed! Get along with you, you urchin!"

"Urchin?"

"Yes, sir, urchin! What does it matter to you if I'm late or not? If I'm late, I've good reason for it, you may be sure," muttered Agafya, bustling about the stove, but in no way displeased or angry; on the contrary, she seemed quite glad of the opportunity to exchange a few bantering words with the good-natured young master.

"Listen, you flighty old woman," Krasotkin began rising from the sofa. "Can you solemnly promise by all that's sacred in this world, and even more, that you'll keep an eye on the kids while I'm out? I'm leaving."

"But why should I give such a promise?" Agafya laughed. "I'll look after them anyway!"

"Oh, no, only if you swear by the eternal salvation of your soul. I shan't go otherwise."

"Well, don't. What do I care? It's freezing cold outside, so you'd better stay at home."

"Kids," Kolya turned to the children, "this woman will stay with you until I come back or until your mother comes back, for your mother, too, should have been back long ago. She will give you some lunch, too. You will give them something, Agafya, won't you?"

"That I will."

"Good-bye, little ones, I leave with my heart at ease. And you, granny," he said gravely in an undertone as he walked past Agafya, "won't, I hope, start telling them all your usual old wives' tales about Katerina. Spare their tender years. _Ici_, Perezvon, to heel!"

"Oh, get along with you," Agafya snapped back at him, really angry this time. "Funny, aren't you? You deserve a sound drubbing for speaking like that—you really do!"

3.

The Schoolboy

But Kolya was not listening, for he could leave at last. At the gateway, he looked round, hunched up his shoulders, and saying, "It's freezing!" walked straight ahead along the street and then turned to the right into a side-lane towards the market square. On reaching the last house but one before the square, he stopped at the gate, took a whistle out of his pocket and blew it with all his might—a kind of prearranged signal. He had to wait no more than a minute when a red-cheeked boy of eleven rushed through the gate and ran up to him. The boy was also wearing a warm, neat, and even smart overcoat. It was Smurov, who was in the preparatory class (Kolya was two classes higher), the son of a well-to-do civil servant. His parents must have forbidden any dealings with Krasotkin, who had a reputation for daring escapades, so that Smurov had evidently escaped from the house on the quiet. Smurov, as the reader will remember, was one of the group of boys who, two months before, had thrown stones across the ditch at Ilyusha and who told Alyosha Karamazov about the latter.

"I've been waiting for you for an hour, Krasotkin," Smurov said emphatically, and the boys stepped out towards the market square.

"I am late," replied Krasotkin. "There have been circumstances. You won't be thrashed for coming with me, will you?"

"The idea of it! I'm never thrashed! Got Perezvon with you?"

"Yes."

"Taking him there, too?"

"I am."

"Oh, if only we could have Zhuchka!"

"No Zhuchka. It doesn't exist. Zhuchka's vanished, without a trace."

"Oh, but couldn't we do it this way?" said Smurov, coming to a sudden standstill. "You see, Ilyusha says that Zhuchka was a shaggy, smoky-grey dog like Perezvon, so couldn't we say that this is Zhuchka? He might believe it."

"Schoolboy: spurn lies—that's the first thing; even in a good cause—that's second. I hope you've said nothing there about my coming—that's the main thing."

"Good Lord, no. I quite understand. But you won't comfort him with Perezvon," Smurov sighed. "I tell you what: his father, the captain—the tow-beard, I mean—told us that he's bringing him a puppy today, a real mastiff pup, with a black nose. He thinks that will comfort Ilyusha. But will it?"

"And how is Ilyusha himself?"

"Oh, he's in a bad way! I think he's got consumption. He's quite conscious, but he has difficulty in breathing. The other day, he asked to be allowed to walk round the room. They put his boots on and he tried to walk, but he kept falling. 'Oh,' he said, 'I told you, Daddy, that my boots were no good. The old ones—I couldn't walk in them either.' You see, he thought he was falling over his feet because of his boots, but it was only because he was too weak to stand up. He won't live another week. Herzenstube comes to see him every day. They are rich again now—they've lots of money."

"The quacks!"

"Who do you mean?"

"The doctors and the whole dirty medical profession, generally speaking, and, of course, individually. I'm against medicine. A useless profession. I'll make a study of the matter. What's all this sentimental nonsense about, though? The whole class seems to be going there!"

"No, not the whole class. Just about a dozen of our boys go to see him every day. It's all right."

"I'm surprised at the part Alexei Karamazov is playing in all this: his brother's going to be tried tomorrow or the day after for such a crime, and yet he finds so much time to waste on being sentimental with boys!"

"There's nothing sentimental about it. Aren't you, too, going to make it up with Ilyusha now?"

"Make it up with him? What a ridiculous expression! Still, I allow nobody to analyse my actions."

"Ilyusha will be so pleased to see you, I must say! He has no idea you are coming. Why didn't you want to come all this time? Why?" Smurov suddenly exclaimed warmly.

"My dear boy, that's my business, not yours. I'm going of my own free will, while you've all been dragged there by Alexei Karamazov, so there's a difference, you see. And how do you know? Maybe I'm not going to make it up with him at all. A silly expression!"

"It wasn't Karamazov, it wasn't him at all. It's simply that our chaps started going there by themselves. At first, of course, with Karamazov. And there's been nothing of that sort—no silliness. First one went, then another. His father was awfully pleased to see us. You know, he'll simply go out of his mind if Ilyusha dies. He can see that Ilyusha's dying. And he's so glad we've made it up with Ilyusha. He's asked after you, Ilyusha has. He didn't say anything, though. He just asks about you and says nothing more. I'm sure his father will go mad or hang himself. He behaved like a madman before, too. He's a very nice man, you know. It was all a mistake then. It was that parricide's fault—the one who beat him up then."

"All the same, Karamazov is a riddle to me. I could have got acquainted with him long ago, but there are cases where I prefer to have my pride. Besides, I've formed a certain opinion of him which has still to be checked and explained."

Kolya fell into an impressive silence. So did Smurov, who, of course, worshipped Kolya Krasotkin and never even dreamed of placing himself on a par with him. At that moment, his interest was greatly aroused because Kolya had said that he was going "of his own free will", for he could not help feeling that there must be some mystery in Kolya's taking it into his head to go to see Ilyusha that very day. They were walking across the market square, which was that day full of all sorts of country carts and lots of poultry for sale. The market women were selling buns, thread, etc., on their covered stalls. Such Sunday markets are naively known in our town as country fairs, and there were many such fairs in the year. Perezvon ran about in high spirits, rushing hither and thither in order to sniff at something. Whenever he met other dogs, he sniffed them all over with extraordinary zeal, according to all the canine rules and regulations.

"I like to observe life, Smurov," Kolya said suddenly. "Have you noticed how dogs meet and sniff at each other? It seems to be a general law of nature with them."

"Yes, it's a funny one, too."

"Well, no, not funny. You're wrong there. There's nothing funny in nature, however much it may seem so to man with his prejudices. If dogs could reason and criticise, they would, I'm sure, have found many, if not more, things that seemed funny to them in the social relationships of men, their masters—if not more. I repeat that because I'm quite sure that we have a great many more silly features. It's Rakitin's idea. A remarkable idea. I'm a socialist, Smurov."

"And what is a socialist?" asked Smurov.

"It's when all are equal, all hold property in common, there are no marriages, and religion and laws are according to everyone's liking, and, well, all the rest of it. I'm afraid you're too young to understand that. It's cold, though."

"Yes, twelve degrees below zero. Daddy looked at the thermometer a short while ago."

"And have you noticed, Smurov, that in the middle of winter, when it's fifteen or eighteen degrees below zero, it doesn't seem to be as cold as it is now, for instance, in early winter when it's suddenly twelve degrees below zero, as it is now, and there's scarcely any snow. That means that people haven't got used to it yet. Everything is a matter of habit with people—everything, even their social and political relations. Habit is what keeps things moving. What a funny-looking man, though!"

Kolya pointed to a peasant in a sheepskin, with a good-natured face, who was standing at his cart clapping his bemittened hands to warm them. His long fair beard was covered with hoar-frost.

"The peasant's beard is frozen over!" Kolya cried teasingly in a loud voice as he passed him.

"Lots of people's beards are frozen over," the peasant replied calmly and sententiously.

"Don't tease him," said Smurov.

"Nonsense, he won't get cross. He's a good fellow. Good-bye, Matvei!"

"Good-bye, sir."

"Is your name really Matvei?"

"Yes, sir. Didn't you know?"

"No. I just guessed."

"Did you? You're a schoolboy, I suppose?"

"Yes."

"Do they thrash you?"

"Just a little."

"Does it hurt?"

"I'm afraid it does."

"Oh dear, what a life!" the peasant heaved a deep sigh.

"Good-bye, Matvei!"

"Good-bye. You're a good lad. Yes, sir."

The boys walked on.

"That's a fine peasant," said Kolya to Smurov. "I like to talk to peasants and I'm always glad to give them their due."

"Why did you tell him a lie about our being beaten at school?"

"Well, I had to say something he'd like."

"What d'you mean?"

"You see, Smurov, I don't like being asked the same question twice if I'm not understood the first time. It's difficult to explain some things to people. As peasants see it, schoolboys are thrashed and have to be. What sort of schoolboy are you, if you're not thrashed? That's what they think. And if I told him that boys were not thrashed at our school, that wouldn't be to his liking. Still, I don't suppose you understand that. One must know how peasants should be spoken to."

"But don't tease them, please, or there'll be a row again, like the one over that goose."

"Are you afraid?"

"Don't make fun of me, Kolya. Of course I'm afraid. Daddy will be awfully angry. I've been strictly forbidden to go out with you."

"Don't worry. Nothing will happen now. Good morning, Natasha," he shouted to a market woman at a stall.

"I'm not Natasha, I'm Maria," the market woman, who was quite young, answered shrilly.

"I'm glad you're Maria. Good-bye."

"Oh, you little scamp; he's just a shrimp and he's at it already!"

"Sorry, I'm in a hurry," Kolya waved her away as though she had been pestering him, and not the other way round. "You'll tell me all about it next Sunday."

"What am I going to tell you next Sunday? You started it, not me, you impudent little rascal," Maria yelled. "You should be whipped, you should! You always go about insulting people, you do!"

There was some laughter among the other market women who had stalls next to Maria's. Suddenly an angry-looking man rushed out from the nearby arcade. He was not a local tradesman, but a sort of merchant's clerk, who had come to the fair. He was quite young, with a long, pale, pock-marked face and dark-brown curly hair and was wearing a long blue coat and a peaked cap. He seemed to be in a state of stupid excitement and at once began shaking his fist at Kolya.

"I know the likes of you," he shouted irritably, "I know what you are!"

Kolya stared at him. He, somehow, could not remember when he could have had a row with him. But he had been in so many scrapes in the streets that he could scarcely remember them all.

"Do you?" he asked him ironically.

"I know you! I know what you are!" the merchant's clerk kept repeating foolishly.

"So much the better for you. Sorry, I'm in a hurry. Good-bye!"

"Why are you up to your tricks again?" the man shouted. "You're always making mischief! I know the likes of you! You're up to your mischief again!"

"It's none of your business, my good man, whether I'm making mischief or not," said Kolya, stopping and continuing to scrutinise him.

"None of my business?"

"None at all."

"Whose is it then? Whose? Well, whose?"

"It's Trifon Nikitich's business, not yours."

"What Trifon Nikitich?" the man stared at him with idiotic surprise, though still as worked up as ever. Kolya eyed him gravely.

"Have you been to the Ascension service?" he suddenly asked him sternly and emphatically.

"What service? Whatever for? No, I haven't," the man said, taken somewhat aback.

"Don't you know Sabaneyev?" Kolya went on still more sternly and emphatically.

"What Sabaneyev? No, I don't know him."

"Well, to hell with you then!" Kolya suddenly snapped and, turning sharply to the right, went quickly on his way, as though thinking it beneath his dignity to talk to a blockhead who did not even know Sabaneyev.

"Wait, you—hey! What Sabaneyev?" the man recollected himself, getting all excited again. "Who is he talking about?" he turned suddenly to the market women, staring stupidly at them.

The women laughed.

"A smart boy," said one of them.

"What Sabaneyev did he mean?" the man kept repeating furiously, waving his right arm.

"I suppose that must be the Sabaneyev what worked for the Kuzmichovs, that's who it must be," one woman suddenly suggested.

The man stared wildly at her.

"Kuz-mi-chov?" another woman repeated. "But his name ain't Trifon! He's Kuzma, not Trifon. And the lad called him Trifon Nikitich, so it ain't him."

"That's not Trifon, that ain't. And not Sabaneyev, neither," a third woman, who had been silent till then, listening gravely, suddenly joined in. "He's called Alexei Ivanovich. Chizhov, Alexei Ivanovich."

"Aye, it's Chizhov all right," a fourth woman confirmed.

The bewildered man kept looking from one to the other.

"But why did he ask, why did he ask, good people?" he exclaimed, almost in despair. " 'Do you know Sabaneyev?' How the devil am I to know who Sabaneyev is?"

"Why, you stupid fellow, I tell you it ain't Sabaneyev but Chizhov—Alexei Ivanovich Chizhov—that's who it is!" a market woman shouted at him impressively.

"What Chizhov? What? Tell me if you know!"

"Why, the lanky one. The one whose nose is always running. He was trading in the market a short while ago."

"But what's your Chizhov got to do with me, good people, eh?"

"How do I know what Chizhov's got to do with you?"

"I'm sure I don't know what he's got to do with you," another woman put in. "You ought to know yourself what you want him for, if you keeps hollering like that. He was telling you and not us, you silly man. Don't you really know him?"

"Who?"

"Chizhov."

"Oh, to hell with Chizhov and with you too! I'll give him a hiding. I will. He was pulling my leg!"

"Give Chizhov a hiding? Take care he don't give you one! You're a fool, that's what you are!"

"Not Chizhov, not Chizhov, you evil woman, you! I'll give the boy a hiding. I'll get him, I will—he was making fun of me!"

The women roared with laughter. But Kolya was striding along a long way off, a triumphant look on his face. Smurov walked at his side, looking back at the shouting crowd in the distance. He, too, was in high spirits though he was still afraid of getting involved in some scrape with Kolya.

"What Sabaneyev did you ask him about?" he asked Kolya, knowing very well what his answer would be.

"How do I know? They'll be screaming their heads off till evening now. I like to shake up fools in every class of society. Here's another oaf—that peasant there. Mind you, people say 'There's no one stupider than a stupid Frenchman', but you can recognise a Russian fool too by his face. Now, just have a look at that one—can't you see it's written on his face that he's a fool?"

"Leave him alone, Kolya. Come on."

"Not for anything in the world. I'm starting right away. Hey, there, good morning, peasant!"

A sturdy-looking peasant with a round, simple face and a greying beard, who was walking slowly past them and seemed to have had a drop already, raised his head and looked at the boy.

"Good morning if you mean it," he replied unhurriedly.

"And if I do?" laughed Kolya.

"If you do, you do. It don't matter to me. I don't mind, I'm sure. There's no harm in a joke."

"I'm sorry, old chap. It was a joke."

"Well, the Lord will forgive you."

"Do you forgive me?"

"Yes, I forgive you all right. Run along now."

"I must say, you seem a clever peasant."

"Cleverer than you are," the peasant replied unexpectedly and as gravely as before.

"Hardly," Kolya said, taken aback a little.

"Aye, it's true all the same."

"I suppose it is."

"Yes, sir."

"Good-bye, peasant."

"Good-bye."

"There are all kinds of peasants," Kolya observed to Smurov after a short pause. "How was I to know that I'd come across a clever one. I'm always ready to recognise intelligence in the common people."

In the distance, the cathedral clock struck half past eleven. The boys hurried along and rapidly covered the rest of the way to Captain Snegiryov's house, almost without further talk. Twenty paces from the house, Kolya stopped and told Smurov to go on ahead and ask Karamazov to come out to him.

"I must sniff around first," he remarked to Smurov.

"But why call him out?" Smurov objected. "Go on; they'll be awfully glad to see you. Why do you want to meet him out here in the cold?"

"I myself know why I want him out here in the cold," Kolya cut him short despotically (which he was very fond of doing with "small boys"), and Smurov ran off to carry out the order.

4.

Zhuchka

Kolya leaned against the fence with a self-important air, waiting for Alyosha to appear. Yes, he had wanted to meet him for a long time. He had heard a lot about Alyosha from the boys, but till now he had always assumed an air of contemptuous indifference every time they spoke to him about Alyosha, and even "criticised" the latter whenever he heard about him. But in his heart of hearts he wished very much to get acquainted with him: there was something likable and attractive in all the accounts he had heard about Alyosha. The present moment was, therefore, important; to begin with, he must do his best not to lose face, and to show his independence: "Or else he'll think that I'm just a boy of thirteen and take me for the same sort of boy as the rest. And what does he want of those boys? I'll ask him when we can become friends. It's bad, though, I'm so short. Tuzikov is younger than me but half a head taller. I have an intelligent face, though; I'm not good-looking, I know I've an ugly face, but it's intelligent. I must be careful, too, not to show how keen I am to be friends with him, for if I take to him at once, he may think— Oh, it will be horrible, if he does!—"

So Kolya kept worrying, trying his utmost to assume a most independent air. The thing that upset him most was being so short, not so much his "mug" as his stature. At home, on a wall in the corner, he had made a pencil mark a year before to indicate his height, and since then he would stand anxiously against the wall to measure his height every two months to see how much he had grown in the meantime. But, alas, he grew very slowly, which simply threw him into despair at times. As for his face, it was not at all a "mug"; on the contrary, it was rather attractive, with a fair, pale and freckled complexion. His grey, small, but lively eyes had a fearless look in them, and often glowed with feeling. His cheekbones were a trifle too broad, his mouth was small, his lips rather thin, but very red; his nose was small and most definitely turned up: "Absolutely

265

snub-nosed, absolutely snub-nosed!" Kolya muttered to himself every time he looked into the mirror, and always turned away from it with displeasure. "I don't suppose it's an intelligent face either," he thought sometimes, uncertain even of that. Still, it would be wrong to suppose that his anxiety about his face and his height occupied him to the exclusion of everything else. On the contrary, however caustic the moments before the looking-glass, he quickly forgot all about them, and for a long time, too, "devoting myself entirely to ideas and the realities of life", as he himself defined his activities.

Alyosha soon appeared and rapidly walked up to Kolya, who noticed even before he came up to him that Alyosha looked very happy. "Is he so glad to see me?" Kolya thought with pleasure. Here, incidentally, we must note that Alyosha had changed very much since we last saw him: he had discarded his cassock and was now wearing a well-cut frock-coat, a round felt hat, and his hair had been cut short. All this was very becoming, and he looked quite handsome. His charming face always wore a cheerful expression, but his was a gentle and quiet cheerfulness. To Kolya's surprise, Alyosha came out without an overcoat, evidently in a great hurry. He held out his hand to Kolya at once.

"Here you are at last! We were all expecting you!"

"There have been reasons you will learn of presently," Kolya murmured, a little breathlessly. "Anyway, I'm glad to meet you. I've long been waiting for an opportunity. I've heard a lot about you."

"Why, we should have met anyway. I've heard a lot about you too, but you've been tardy in coming here."

"Tell me: how are things in there?"

"Ilyusha is in a bad way. I'm afraid he's sure to die."

"Really? You must admit, Karamazov, medicine is a low-down swindle," Kolya cried warmly.

"Ilyusha has often, very often, mentioned you, even in his sleep, in delirium, you know. One can see you used to be very, very dear to him before—before that affair with—the knife. There's another reason, too— Tell me, is that your dog?"

"Yes, Perezvon."

"It isn't Zhuchka?" Alyosha looked sadly at Kolya. "Has that dog got lost for good?"

"I know you'd all like this dog to be Zhuchka, I've heard all about that," said Kolya with a mysterious smile. "Listen, Karamazov, I'll explain it all to you. That's the actual reason why I've come and why I've asked you to meet me here out-side—to get the whole thing straightened out before we go in," he began animatedly. "You see, Karamazov, Ilyusha entered the preparatory class last spring. Well, you know what the boys in the preparatory class are—just kids. They began ragging Ilyusha at once. I'm two classes higher and, of course, I was watching it all from a distance. I could see he was a small and weak boy, but he wouldn't give in to them; he even fought them, a proud boy that, with plenty of spunk. I like boys like that. But they kept ragging him more than ever. The worst of it was that he was so poorly dressed: a shabby overcoat, his trousers too short, and his boots wanted mending. They teased him about that, too. Humiliated him. Well, I don't like that, and I took his part at once and let them have it good and proper. You see, I gave them a thrashing, yet they just love me. Did you know that, Karamazov?" Kolya boasted effusively. "But I'm very fond of kids, as a rule. I have two little ones on my hands at home—it's they who made me so late today. Well, so they stopped knocking him about, and I took him under my wing. I could see he had his pride, I tell you, but he grew devoted to me like a slave, did everything I told him, obeyed me as though I were God Almighty, and tried to imitate me in everything. He used to join me at once at playtime and we'd go about together. On Sundays, too. The boys at our school make fun of an older boy growing very pally with a kid, but that's a prejudice. It's nobody's business but my own—don't you think so? I teach him things, and develop his mind. And why, tell me, shouldn't I, if I like him? You, Karamazov, have made friends of all those little fellows, haven't you? And that means that you want to influence the younger generation, develop their minds and be useful to them, doesn't it? And I don't mind telling you that this feature in your make-up—something I've heard of—has caught my interest, and now back to my story: I began to notice that the boy was growing sentimental, and, you know, from my earliest days I've been downright against sloppy sentiments. Besides, there were those contradictions: he was proud and yet slavishly devoted to me—slavishly devoted, but all of a sudden his eyes would flash and he'd violently disagree with me. He'd argue till he was blue in the face. At times I would bring various ideas; it wasn't that he did not agree with them, but I could simply see that he was up in open rebellion against me personally because I treated his sentiments with coolness. So to keep him in check, I grew all the cooler, the more he showed his attachment to me. I did so on purpose, out of conviction. I was out to give him some backbone, lick him into shape, make a man of him—well, and so on—you get my meaning, don't you? I suddenly noticed that for three whole days he was upset and depressed over something, but not because of the way I kept him at a distance, but about something else, something more important, and higher. Well, I thought, what's all this tragedy about? So I kept pressing on him and found out what was the matter. You see, he seemed to have made friends with Smerdyakov, your late father's servant (your father was still alive at the time), and Smerdyakov taught the little fool a silly trick, I mean, a beastly trick, an abominable trick—to take a piece of soft bread, stick a pin inside it, and throw it to some stray dog, the kind that will gobble down anything because it's starving, and see what will happen. Well, so they got it all ready and threw a piece like that to Zhuchka, the shaggy dog they're now making such a fuss about, a watchdog that was never fed by its owners and that kept barking all day long. (Do you like that stupid barking, Karamazov? I can't stand it.) Well, the dog pounced on the bread, swallowed it, began to squeal and twist round, then ran off yelping all the time, and disappeared. That was how Ilyusha described it to me. He told me all about it and kept crying and crying, hugging me and trembling all over: 'He ran off, yelping all the time,' he kept repeating—the sight must have made a deep impression on him. Well, I could see he was sorry. I took a serious view of the matter. You see, I was set on teaching him a lesson for his past behaviour, so I was wily and pretended to be far more indignant than I actually was: 'What you've done is mean,' I said to him. 'You're a cad. I shan't tell anyone about it, of course, but I'll have nothing more to do with you for a while. I'll think the matter over and let you know through Smurov (the boy who has just come with me and who has always been devoted to me) whether I'm going to have anything to do with you in future or whether I'll give you up for good as a cad.' That took him quite aback. I must confess I at once felt I had perhaps gone a bit too far, but there was nothing to be done: that was what I thought at the time. A day later, I sent Smurov to tell him that I was not on speaking terms with him any more—which is the way we put it when two chums break off all relations. Secretly I meant to cold-shoulder him only for a few days and then, when I saw signs of repentance, hold out my hand to him again. That was my firm intention. But what do you think he did? When he heard Smurov's message his eyes flashed suddenly: 'Tell Krasotkin from me,' he shouted, 'that from now on I'll be throwing bits of bread with pins inside them to all the dogs, all, all of them!' 'Ah,' I thought to myself, 'so he's making a show of independence! We'll soon drive that out of him!' So I began showing the utmost contempt for him and every time we met I turned away or smiled sarcastically. And then that incident with his father took place—you remember?—the tow-beard. You must understand that his outburst had been prepared by what had gone before. Seeing that I'd given him up, the boys all set on him and began ragging him by shouting: 'Tow-beard! Tow-beard!' And it was then that fights broke out between them, for which I'm terribly sorry, for I believe that on one occasion he was given a sound drubbing. One day he flew at them in the courtyard as they were coming out of school. I was standing some ten paces away from him, looking at him. I swear I don't remember laughing at him at the time; on the contrary, I felt very sorry for him and in another minute I should have gone to his help. But he suddenly saw me looking at him; what came into his mind I don't know, but he pulled out his penknife, rushed up to me and jabbed me in my thigh with it—just here, above my right leg. I did not budge. I don't mind saying, Karamazov, that I can show pluck sometimes. I just looked at him with contempt, as though to say, 'If you'd like to stab me again for all my kindness to you, then go ahead!' But he did not give me another stab. Couldn't bring himself to. Got the wind up, threw his knife away, burst into tears and ran off. I was not, of course, going to tell on him and I told all the boys to keep mum, so that it should not reach the masters. I didn't even say a word to Mother till the wound had healed. It wasn't much of a wound, anyway. Just a scratch. Then I was told that he'd been throwing stones the same day and bit your finger—well, you can understand what a state he was in! But there was nothing to be done about it. I behaved stupidly: even when he was taken ill, I didn't go to forgive him—I mean, to make it up with him, and I'm sorry for it now. But then I had a special reason. Well, that's all there is to it—only I'm afraid I've behaved foolishly—"

"Oh, what a pity," Alyosha exclaimed feelingly, "I didn't know what terms you were on previously or I should have come to you myself long ago and asked you to go to him with me. You know, he spoke about you in his delirium, when he was feverish. I had no idea how much you meant to him! And haven't you really found the dog Zhuchka? His father and all the boys went looking for it all over the town. You know, since he's been taken ill, he's told his father tearfully three times in my presence: 'It's because I killed Zhuchka, Daddy, that I'm ill now. God is punishing me for it.' You can't drive the thought out of his mind! I can't help thinking that if you could have got hold of Zhuchka now and showed him that it wasn't dead it would make him so happy that he'd recover. We've all been counting on you."

"But tell me what reasons you had to count on my finding the dog, I mean, to think I'd be the one to find it?" Kolya asked, with intense curiosity. "Why should you have counted on me and not on someone else?"

"There was a rumour that you were looking for it and that when you'd found it you'd bring it over. Smurov said something of the kind. We are doing our best to make him believe that Zhuchka is alive and been seen somewhere. The boys got him a tame rabbit from somewhere, but he just looked at it, smiled and asked them to set it free in a field. That's what we did. His father has just come back and brought him a mastiff puppy which he got from somewhere, thinking it would soothe him, but I believe it made things worse—"

"Tell me something else, Karamazov: what do you think of his father? I know him, but would you call him a clown, a buffoon?"

"Oh, no. There are people who feel deeply but have been somehow downtrodden. Such buffoonery is merely a kind of bitter resentment against those he dare not speak the truth to because of his long-standing and humiliating timidity of them. Believe me, Krasotkin, that kind of buffoonery can be very tragic. Ilyusha is the centre of his world, and if he dies, his father will go out of his mind with grief or else commit suicide. I'm almost sure of that when I look at him now!"

"I understand you, Karamazov," Kolya said feelingly. "I can see you have a good idea of human nature."

"And as soon as I saw you with a dog, I thought that you had brought that very Zhuchka along."

"Wait, Karamazov, perhaps we'll find it, but this dog's name is Perezvon. I'll let him in now and perhaps he will amuse Ilyusha more than the mastiff pup. Just a moment, Karamazov, perhaps you'll find out something soon. Oh dear, why am I keeping you here?" Kolya cried impulsively. "You're wearing nothing but a thin little jacket in such bitter cold, and I'm keeping you out here! You see how selfish I am! Oh, we're all selfish, Karamazov!"

"Don't worry. It's true it's cold, but I don' t catch cold so easily. Let's go in, though. By the way, what's your name? I know you're Kolya, but that's all."

"Nikolai Krasotkin, or as they say officially, Krasotkin Junior," Kolya laughed for some reason, but suddenly added: "Of course, I hate my name Nikolai."

"But why?"

"It's so trivial, so official—"

"You are thirteen, aren't you?' asked Alyosha.

"Fourteen, really. I shall be fourteen in a fortnight. Quite soon. I'd better confess to a weakness of mine, Karamazov.

I don't mind telling you of it at the very beginning, for I'd like you to see at once what kind of fellow I am: I hate being asked my age, hate it more than anything else— And, another thing—there's a false story going round about me that last week I played robbers with the boys of the preparatory class. Now, it's quite true that I did play that game with them, but it's simply not true that I played it for my own amusement. I have reason to believe that you've heard that story, but I wasn't playing for myself, but for the sake of the kids, because they couldn't think up anything by themselves. But they're always telling silly stories round here. I can tell you that the people in this town are interested in nothing but gossip."

"So what if you were playing for your own amusement?"

"It makes a difference— You wouldn't be playing horses, would you?"

"Look at it this way," smiled Alyosha. "Grown-up people, for instance, go to the theatre, where all sorts of adventures take place on the stage, sometimes there are robbers and fighting—well, isn't it the same thing, in its own way, of course? And youngsters playing at coppers and robbers during playtime is also the beginning of some art, and awakening need of art in a young soul, and such games are quite often much better than theatrical performances, the only difference being that people go to the theatre to see the actors, while here the young people themselves are the actors. But that's only natural."

"You think so? Is that really your opinion?" Kolya asked, looking intently at him. "You know, you've put quite an interesting idea across. I'll think it over when I get home. I must say I knew that one could learn something from you. I've come to learn from you, Karamazov," concluded Kolya in a voice full of deep feeling.

"And I from you," smiled Alyosha, pressing his hand.

Kolya was extremely pleased with Alyosha. What struck him most was that Alyosha treated him as an equal and spoke to him as though he were "quite grown up".

"I'll show you a trick or two presently, Karamazov, a sort of theatrical performance, too," he laughed nervously. "That's what I've come for."

"Let's go in first to the landlady's, on the left. That's where the boys leave their overcoats, because it's a small room and it's hot in there."

"Oh, but I'm only going in for a moment. I won't take my overcoat off. Perezvon will stay here in the passageway and lie doggo. *Ici*, Perezvon, lie doggo! You see, he's dead now. I'll go in and look round first and then I'll whistle to him at the right moment and you'll see he'll dash in like mad. I must see, though, that Smurov doesn't forget to open the door at the right moment. I'll arrange it all, and you'll see my trick—"

5.

At Ilyusha's Bedside

Already familiar to us, the room retired Captain Snegiryov's family lived in was at the moment both stuffy and full of visitors. Several boys had come to see Ilyusha that day and though all of them, like Smurov, were prepared to deny that Alyosha had brought them and Ilyusha together in reconciliation, that was precisely the case. The skill he had displayed in this consisted simply in his having got them and Ilyusha together one by one, without any mawkish sentimentality, as though with no particular design, but by sheer chance, as it were, and to Ilyusha, it brought great relief from his suffering. When he saw the almost tender affection and sympathy shown to him by all these boys, his former enemies, he was deeply moved. Krasotkin alone was missing, a heavy weight on his heart. The bitterest of all Ilyusha's bitter memories was perhaps the episode with Krasotkin, his only friend and protector, whom he had attacked with a knife. That was also the opinion of the clever little boy Smurov, who was the first to make it up with Ilyusha. But Krasotkin himself, when Smurov hinted to him that Alyosha would like to see him "on a certain matter" at once cut him short and put an end to the approach, instructing Smurov to tell "Karamazov" that he knew best what to do and wanted no advice from anyone; if he came to see Ilyusha, he himself knew when to do so because he had his "own reasons". That had been about a fortnight before that Sunday, which was why Alyosha had not gone to see him as he had intended. However, though he waited, he did send Smurov to Krasotkin again on two occasions, but each time Krasotkin had met him with a most determined and curt refusal, making it quite clear to Alyosha that if the latter were to come in person he, Krasotkin, would never go to see Ilyusha and that he did not want to be bothered any more. Up to the very last day, Smurov had no idea that Kolya had made up his mind to come to Ilyusha's that morning, and it was only the evening before that Kolya, on parting from Smurov, told him brusquely to expect him the next morning, because he'd like to go to the Snegiryovs with him, but that he was not to tell anyone about his coming, as he wanted the call to come as a surprise. Smurov obeyed his instructions. He had gained the idea of returning the lost dog Zhuchka from some words dropped casually by Krasotkin, to the effect that "they're a lot of silly asses, all of them, not to have found the dog, if it's alive". But when Smurov, taking advantage of a favourable opportunity, timidly hinted at his surmise about the dog, Krasotkin flew into a terrible rage: "Do you think I'm such an ass as to go looking for somebody else's dog all over the town when I've got my Perezvon? And could anyone really believe that a dog could be alive after swallowing a pin? Sloppy sentimentality, that's what it is!"

Meanwhile, Ilyusha had been confined to his little bed in the corner of the room, under the icons, for close on a fortnight. He had not been to school ever since the incident when he had met Alyosha and bitten his finger. As a matter of fact, he had fallen ill the same day, though for a month afterwards he managed to get up occasionally and walk about the room and the passageway. But at last he grew so weak that he could not take a step without aid from his father. The latter was terribly anxious about him; he even gave up drinking and was almost out of his mind with fear that his boy might die. Often, especially after taking his boy for a walk round the room on his arm and putting him to bed again, he would suddenly dash out into the passageway and, with his forehead pressed against the wall, in a dark corner, he would burst into wailing sobs, which shook his body and which he stifled lest his boy hear them.

On returning to the room, he usually began doing something to amuse and comfort his precious boy, telling him tales or amusing stories, or mimicking all sorts of funny people he had happened to meet, even imitating the funny howls or cries of animals. But Ilyusha hated to see his father pulling faces and clowning. Though the boy did his best not to show how much he disliked it, he was painfully aware of his father's humiliating position in society and the memory of the "tow-beard" and of that "awful day" kept recurring time and again in his mind. Nina, Ilyusha's quiet, gentle, crippled sister, also disliked seeing her father playing the fool (his eldest sister Varvara Nikolayevna had long departed to St. Petersburg to resume her studies at the university), but his half-witted mother was vastly amused and laughed happily when her husband began mimicking someone or pulling all sorts of funny faces. That was the only thing that would cheer her up; for the rest of the time she was always grumbling and complaining that she had been forgotten, no one had any respect for her, her feelings were being hurt, and the like. But she, too, seemed to have changed completely during the last few days: she kept looking into the corner of the room where Ilyusha lay, and seemed lost in thought. She was less talkative and quieter and if she started crying, she did so softly, so as not to be heard. Snegiryov noticed the change in her with bitter bewilderment. At first, she disliked the boys' coming, which made her angry, but later their merry cries and stories began to amuse her and she came to like them so much that she would have become terribly depressed if they had stopped coming. When the children began telling some story or playing games, she would laugh and clap her hands. She would call some of them to herself and kiss them, becoming particularly fond of Smurov. As for Snegiryov, the appearance of the children who had come to cheer up Ilyusha filled his heart with rapturous delight from the very outset, and he now even hoped that Ilyusha would get over his depression and perhaps soon recover.

Up to the last few days, he never doubted for a moment that, despite his anxiety for Ilyusha, his boy would suddenly get well. He would meet the little visitors with reverence; he followed them about, waited upon them, was ready to give them a ride on his back and actually did so, but Ilyusha did not like those games and they were given up. He began buying presents for them, ginger-bread and nuts, gave them tea and buttered their sandwiches. It should be noted that he had plenty of money all the time. He had accepted the two hundred roubles from Katerina Ivanovna just as Alyosha had predicted. Later, on learning more about their circumstances and Ilyusha's illness, she called on them herself, made the acquaintance of the family and even succeeded in charming the captain's half-witted wife. After that, she was lavish in her acts of kindness, and Snegiryov himself, terrified at the thought that his boy might die, pocketed his former pride, and humbly accepted her alms. All this time, Dr. Herzenstube, called in by Katerina Ivanovna, came to see the patient punctually every other day, but his visits were of little avail, though he kept dosing him with medicines. But on that day, that is to say, on Sunday morning, a new doctor was being expected, a famous Moscow specialist. Katerina Ivanovna had sent for him for a large fee—not for Ilyusha, but with some other purpose, of which more will be said later and in due course, but as he had come, she asked him to see Ilyusha, too, and Snegiryov had been told to expect him. He had not the slightest idea that Kolya Krasotkin would be calling, although he had long wished that the boy, who had caused so much torment to his son, would come at last. At the moment Krasotkin opened the door and came into the room, all of them, Snegiryov and the boys, crowded round Ilyusha's bed, examining the tiny mastiff puppy which had just been brought. It had only been born the day before, though Snegiryov had bespoken it a week ago in order to comfort and amuse Ilyusha, who was still pining for the vanished and, of course, now dead Zhuchka. Ilyusha, who had heard three days before that he was to be given a puppy, and no ordinary one, but a mastiff puppy (which was, of course, terribly important), was anxious to spare his father's feelings and pretended to be pleased with the gift, but his father and the boys could not help noticing that the new puppy merely stirred up more violently in his little heart memories of the hapless Zhuchka he had so tormented. The puppy lay moving about restlessly beside him, and he, smiling painfully, stroked it with his thin, pale, wasted little hand. It was evident that he liked the puppy, but—it wasn't Zhuchka. Zhuchka was not there! If he could have had both Zhuchka and the puppy, he would have been quite happy!

"Here's Krasotkin!" one of the boys, who was the first to see him enter, cried suddenly. His coming caused a general stir and the boys parted and stood at either side of the bed, so that he had a full view of Ilyusha. Snegiryov ran eagerly to meet Kolya.

"Do come in, do—we're so glad you've come!" he mumbled. "Ilyusha, Mr. Krasotkin has come to see you—"

But Krasotkin, shaking hands with him hurriedly, at once showed his good manners. He first of all turned to Mrs. Snegiryov, who was sitting in her arm-chair (and who was, at the moment highly displeased with the boys, grumbling that their standing between her and Ilyusha's bed prevented her from seeing the puppy) and very courteously scraped a foot and bowed to her and, then, turning to Nina, he made her, as a lady, a similar bow. This act of courtesy produced a most favourable impression on the half-witted lady.

"One can at once recognise a well-brought-up young man," she said aloud, spreading her hands. "Quite unlike our other visitors, who come in on top of each other."

"Surely not on top of each other, Mother! You can't mean that!" Snegiryov murmured affectionately, but a little apprehensive of how "Mother" might behave further.

"That's the way they come riding in. They jump on each other's backs in the passageway and prance in pick-a-back, and this in a respectable family, too! What strange visitors!"

"But who came riding in like that, Mother? Who?"

"Why, that boy there came in today on that one's back, and this on that one's—"

But Kolya was already standing at Ilyusha's bedside. The sick boy, who had turned visibly pale, sat up and looked at him intently. Kolya had not seen his former little friend for two months and stood struck by what he saw: he could never have imagined that he would see such a wasted yellow face, such feverishly burning eyes, which seemed suddenly to have grown so huge, and such thin little hands. He observed with mournful surprise that Ilyusha was breathing so heavily and rapidly, with his lips so parched. He stepped close to him, held out a hand and, almost overcome with confusion, said:

"Well, old man, how are you?"

But his voice failed him, his jauntiness all gone; his face seemed to twitch suddenly, and the corners of his lips quivered. Ilyusha smiled ruefully at him, still unable to utter a word. Kolya suddenly raised his hand and for some reason stroked Ilyusha's hair.

"It'll be all right!" he murmured softly to him, perhaps to cheer him up but possibly because he did not know what to say. For a moment they were silent again.

"Hullo! What's that? A new puppy?" Kolya asked suddenly in a most unfeeling voice.

"Ye-es!" replied Ilyusha in a long whisper, gasping for breath.

"A black nose, which means that it'll be aggressive—a good watchdog," Kolya observed gravely and firmly, as though the puppy and its black nose were all-important. In fact, he was still trying hard not to burst into tears "like a cry-baby", and coping very poorly. "Yes, you'll have to keep it on a chain when it grows up. I'm sure of that."

"It'll be a huge dog!" one of the boys cried.

"Of course, it's a mastiff. It'll be enormous, as big as that, like a calf," several small voices cried all at once.

"As big as a calf, as big as a real calf!" Snegiryov said, rushing up. "I got one like that on purpose. A very fierce one, and his parents are also huge and fierce, as high as that from the floor— Do sit down here, on the bed beside Ilyusha, or here on the bench. I'm glad you've come. We've been expecting you for a long time— Have you come with Mr. Karamazov?"

Krasotkin sat down at the foot of the bed. Though he may have given thought, while on his way, to how he would broach the conversation, he did not know how to begin.

"No—I've come with Perezvon— I've got a dog now—Perezvon. A Slavic name. It's waiting for me outside the door. I have only to whistle—and it will dash in. I, too, have brought a dog, old man," he turned suddenly to Ilyusha. "Remember Zhuchka?" he suddenly asked, flabbergasting Ilyusha.

Ilyusha's little face quivered and he gave Kolya an agonised look. Alyosha, standing at the door, frowned and signalled stealthily to Kolya not to speak of Zhuchka, but Kolya did not or would not pay any attention.

"W-where is—Zhuchka?" Ilyusha asked in a broken voice.

"Well, old man, your Zhuchka's disappeared! Your Zhuchka's done for!"

Ilyusha said nothing, but just looked very intently at Kolya again. Alyosha, having caught Kolya's eye, again signalled to him vigorously, but Kolya again looked away, pretending not to have noticed.

"Must have gone off somewhere to die—of course, after such a meal!" Kolya went on pitilessly, and yet for some reason he seemed breathless himself. "But I've got Perezvon—a Slavic name. I've brought it to you—"

"I don't want it!" Ilyusha said suddenly.

"No, no, you must see it— It will amuse you. I brought it on purpose—it's as shaggy as the other one—You won't object to my calling in my dog, will you, ma'am?" he suddenly turned to Mrs. Snegiryov with quite inexplicable agitation.

"I don't want it, I don't want it!" Ilyusha cried with a catch in his voice. There was reproach in his eyes

"Perhaps you'd better—" Snegiryov said, suddenly jumping up from the chest by the wall, on which he had been sitting, "you'd better—er—perhaps some other time, sir," he murmured. But Kolya, in hurried persistence, suddenly shouted to Smurov: "Smurov, open the door!" and blew his whistle, the moment it was opened. Perezvon came bounding into the room.

"Jump, Perezvon, jump! Beg, beg!" bawled Kolya, jumping up from the bed. Rising on its hind legs, the dog stood erect in front of Ilyusha's bed. Then something no one had expected happened: Ilyusha started, lurched forward violently, bent over Perezvon and looked at it speechlessly.

"But it's—Zhuchka!" he suddenly cried in a voice breaking with suffering and joy.

"And who did you think it was?" Krasotkin yelled with all his might in a ringing, happy voice and, bending over the dog, lifted it up to Ilyusha.

"Look, old man, you see it's blind in one eye and its left ear is torn, exactly as you described to me. That's how I identified it! I found it almost on the same day. Didn't take me any time at all. You see, it did not belong to anyone, to anyone!" he kept explaining, turning quickly to Snegiryov, to Mrs. Snegiryov, to Alyosha, and then back again to Ilyusha. "It was living in Fedotov's back-yard. Made its home there, but they didn't feed it. It was a stray dog; it must have run away from some village— So I found it— You see, old man, it didn't swallow your piece of bread after all. If it had, it would most certainly have died. Most certainly! So it must have spat it out, since it's still alive. You didn't notice it. Well, it did spit it out, but pricked its tongue—that's why it squealed. It ran away yelping, and you thought that it had swallowed it. It could not help squealing loudly, for the inside of a dog's mouth is very tender— much tenderer than a man's, much tenderer!" Kolya kept exclaiming frantically, with burning face and beaming with delight.

Ilyusha could find no words. He gazed open-mouthed at Kolya with his big eyes, which seemed almost to start out of their sockets, and was white as a sheet. And if only the wholly unsuspecting Krasotkin knew what a devastating effect such a moment might have on the sick boy's condition, nothing would have induced him to play such a trick on him. But Alyosha was perhaps the only person in the room who realised that. As for Snegiryov, he seemed to have been transformed into a little boy himself.

"Zhuchka? So this is Zhuchka?" he cried blissfully. "Ilyusha, darling, this is Zhuchka, your Zhuchka! Mother, look—this is Zhuchka!" He was almost in tears.

"And I never guessed!" Smurov cried regretfully. "Well done Krasotkin! I said he'd find Zhuchka and he has!"

"He's found it!" some other boy put in joyfully.

"Well done, Krasotkin!" a third voice rang out.

"Well done, well done!" all the boys cried and began to clap their hands.

"But wait, wait," Krasotkin tried to make himself heard above the din, "let me tell you how it all happened. You see, the whole point is how it happened—that's the most important thing! I found it, took it home, hid it at once, locked it up and showed it to no one up to the last day. Only Smurov found it out a fortnight ago, but I made him believe that it was Perezvon and he never guessed. And in my free time I taught it all sorts of tricks. You should see the tricks it knows! You see, old man, I taught it everything so as to bring you a dog well trained and in fine condition and to be able to say to you, 'See, old man, what your Zhuchka looks like now!' You haven't got a piece of meat, have you? He'll show you a trick that'll simply make you die of laughter. Just a little bit of meat—haven't you got any?"

Sengiryov rushed across the passageway towards the landlady's kitchen where their cooking, too, was done. Not to waste precious time, Kolya, in desperate haste, shouted to Perezvon: "Doggo!" The dog spun round and lay motionless on its back, all four paws in the air. The boys laughed and Ilyusha watched with the same agonised smile. It was "Mother", however, who most liked the way the dog "died". She burst out laughing, and began snapping her fingers and calling: "Perezvon! Perezvon!"

"It won't get up for anything in the world, not for anything in the world," cried Kolya, triumphantly and with justified pride. "You can shout as much as you like, but if I call it'll be up in a jiffy. *Ici,* Perezvon!"

The dog jumped up and began bounding about, yelping with delight. Snegiryov ran in with a piece of boiled beef.

"It's not hot, is it?" Kolya inquired hastily and in a businesslike tone of voice, taking the meat. "No, it isn't. You see, dogs don't like their food hot. Now then, watch all of you, watch, Ilyusha, old man, come on, why don't you watch? I've brought it here, and you aren't even looking!"

The new trick consisted in making the dog stand pat, with its nose thrust forward, and putting the tempting bit of meat on its nose. The poor dog had to stand motionless, with the piece of meat on its nose, for as long as its master chose to keep it like that, even for as long as half an hour if need be. But Perezvon was kept thus for only a few seconds.

"Take it!" cried Kolya, and the piece of meat literally flew from Perezvon's nose into its mouth. The audience, of course, expressed their surprise and admiration.

"And did you actually stay away all this time only because you wanted to train the dog?" Alyosha cried in involuntary reproach.

"Yes, just because of that," Kolya cried most ingenuously. "I wanted to show it at its best!"

"Perezvon! Perezvon!" Ilyusha called suddenly, snapping his thin little fingers to attract the dog's attention.

"That's quite all right. Let it jump on the bed. *Içi*, Perezvon!" Kolya slapped the bed with the palm of his hand and Perezvon flew to Ilyusha like an arrow. Ilyusha impetuously threw both his arms round the dog's head, and Perezvon in a flash began to lick his cheek. Ilyusha clung to it, stretched himself out in the bed and hid his face from everybody in its shaggy coat.

"Oh dear, oh dear!" Snegiryov kept exclaiming.

Kolya again sat down on the bed near Ilyusha.

"Ilyusha, here's something else I've got to show you. I've brought you a little cannon. Remember I was telling you about it and you said, 'Oh, how I'd love to see it!' Well, I've brought it along."

And Kolya hurriedly pulled his bronze cannon out of his satchel. He was in such a hurry because he was feeling so happy: at any other time he would have waited for the impression created by Perezvon to wear off, but now he was too impatient to give thought to such things: "You're happy as it is, so I'll make you happier still!" He himself was absolutely delighted.

"I spied this thing out for you long ago at the civil servant Morozov's house. It's for you, old man, for you alone. He had no use for it. He got it from his brother. So I exchanged it for a book from my father's bookcase: *Mohammed's Relative, or Salutary Folly*. The book came out in Moscow a hundred years ago, when there was no censorship—and Morozov has a great liking for such things. He thanked me for it too—"

Kolya was holding the little cannon in his hand for all to see and admire. Ilyusha sat up and, his right arm still round Perezvon, gazed in admiration at the toy. The effect produced reached its peak when Kolya declared that he had some powder with him, and that he could fire the gun at once "if it won't frighten the ladies". Mrs. Snegiryov at once asked to be allowed to look closer at the toy, and her request was immediately granted. She liked the cannon with its wheels very much, and began rolling it about in her lap. Asked whether she would mind its being fired, she gave her full consent at once, without, incidentally, the least idea of what she had been asked. Kolya showed them the powder and shot. Snegiryov, as former military man, loaded it himself, priming it with a minute quantity of powder, and asking that the shot be put aside for another time. The cannon was placed on the floor, its muzzle pointing towards an empty part of the room, three grains of powder were put into the touchhole and a match was applied to it. The report that followed was absolutely magnificent. Mrs. Snegiryov started, but at once laughed with joy. The boys looked in speechless triumph, but the happiest of them all was Snegiryov as he looked at Ilyusha. Kolya picked up the gun and immediately made a gift of it to Ilyusha, together with the powder and shot.

"It's for you, for you!" he repeated overflowing with happiness. "I've had it ready for you a long time."

"Oh let me have it! You'd better give me the little gun!" Mrs. Snegiryov began begging like a small child. Her face was expressive of piteous anxiety for fear that she might not get it. Kolya felt embarrassed. Snegiryov fidgeted agitatedly.

"Darling Mother, darling Mother," he cried, running up to her, "the little cannon is yours, yours, but let Ilyusha have it now, because it was given to him, but it's yours all the same. Ilyusha will always let you play with it. It will be yours and his, yours and his—"

"No, I don't want it to be mine and his," "darling Mother" went on, on the verge of tears. "I want it to be all my own and not Ilyusha's!"

"Keep it, Mother, keep it!" Ilyusha cried. "Krasotkin, may I give it to Mother?" he asked turning imploringly to Krasotkin, as though afraid to hurt his feelings by giving his present to someone else.

"Of course, you may!" Krasotkin at once agreed, and taking the little cannon from Ilyusha, he handed it himself with a polite bow to Mrs. Snegiryov, who was so overcome that she burst into tears.

"Dear Ilyusha really loves his mother," she exclaimed deeply moved, and at once began rolling the gun about in her lap.

"Darling Mother, let me kiss your hand," her husband rushed up to her and at once did so.

"And this kind-hearted boy is the nicest young man here!" said the grateful lady, pointing to Kolya.

"And I'll get you as much powder as you like, Ilyusha. We make the powder ourselves now. Borovikov knows how to make it: twenty-four parts of saltpetre, ten of sulphur, and six of birchwood charcoal; it's mixed together, and well pounded. Water is added to make a paste, which is strained through a fine sieve and the gunpowder is ready."

"Smurov has told me about your powder already," said Ilyusha, "but Daddy says it's not real powder."

"Not real?" Kolya reddened.. "Well, it burns all right. I don't know, though—"

"No sir, I didn't mean that," Snegiryov rushed up suddenly with a guilty expression. "It's quite true I said that powder was not made like that, but that's nothing. It can be made like that, too."

"I don't know. I suppose you should know better. We lit some in an earthenware jar and it burnt beautifully. It all burnt away, leaving only a little ash behind. But that was only paste but if we'd put it through a strainer— However, you know better. I don't know— Have you heard that Bulkin's father gave him a hiding for our powder?" he said turning suddenly to Ilyusha.

"I have," replied Ilyusha, who was listening to Kolya with immense interest and delight.

"We'd made a whole bottle of powder and he kept it under

his bed. His father saw it. You could have blown us up, he said. And he thrashed him on the spot. He was going to lodge a complaint against me at the Gymnasium. He's no longer allowed to go about with me. No one is allowed to go about with me. Smurov isn't allowed to, either. I've got a bad name with everyone. They say I'm a 'desperate chap'," Kolya smiled contemptuously. "It all began with the railway incident."

"Oh, we've heard all about that happening, too!" cried Snegiryov. "How could you lie still there between the rails? And weren't you at all afraid, lying there under the train? Weren't you scared?"

The captain was buttering up to Kolya.

"N-not particularly," Kolya replied nonchalantly. "It's that damned goose that damaged my reputation more than anything else," he went on, turning to Ilyusha again. But though he tried to look nonchalant, he could not quite control his excitement and seemed to have difficulty in maintaining his tone.

"Oh, yes, I heard about the goose, too!" Ilyusha laughed, his face beaming. "They told me, but I didn't quite understand. Did you really have to appear in court?"

"Oh, it was a most stupid and trifling matter but, as usual, they made a mountain out of a molehill," Kolya began casually. "I was just walking across the market square one day when some geese were driven in. I stopped to look at them. Suddenly I noticed a fellow, Vishnyakov by name—he's working as an errand-boy at Plotnikov's now—looking at me. 'What are you looking at the geese for?' I looked at him: a round, stupid face, the silly ass must be twenty. But you know, I never have anything to say against the common people. I like to be with them— We've lagged behind the common people, that's obvious— I believe you're laughing, Karamazov?"

"Good Lord, no, I'm listening to you with great interest," Alyosha replied with a most good-humoured air, and the suspicious Kolya was at once reassured.

"My theory, Karamazov, is clear and simple," he again hurried on at once happily. "I believe in the common people and I'm always glad to do them justice, but without pampering them—that goes without saying— But I was talking about the goose, wasn't I? Well, then, so I turned to that fool and answered: 'I'm trying to think what the goose is thinking about.' He stared at me quite stupidly: 'And what is the goose thinking about?' he asked. 'Well, you see,' I said, 'there's a cart full of oats. The oats are dropping out of the sack and the goose has stretched its neck right out under the wheel and is pecking at the grains—see?' 'I see it all right,' he said. 'Very well,' I said. 'Now if we push the cart a wee bit forward, the wheel will snap the goose's neck, won't it?' 'Indeed, it will,' he said, a grin of delight spreading over his face. 'Well, then,' I said, 'come on, my lad, let's do it!' 'Let's,' he said. And it didn't take us long to fix it. He took up a stand on the quiet at the bridle while I stood from the side to shoo the goose. The owner was busy elsewhere at the time, talking to someone, so that I didn't have to guide the goose at all: it just stretched out its neck for the oats under the cart, straight under the wheel. I gave the fellow a wink and c-crack, the goose's neck was snapped in half! It so happened that we were noticed at that very moment by some peasants, who raised an outcry: 'You done that on purpose!' they yelled. 'No, I didn't.' 'Yes, you did!' Well, so they clamoured: 'Have him hauled to the Justice of the Peace!' they cried. They took me along too. 'You were in it, too,' they shouted. 'You were helping him! The whole market-place knows you!' And you know," Kolya added, with some pride, "all the market people do know me for some reason. So we all went off to the court and they took the goose with them, too. The young fellow got the wind up and began to blubber for all he was worth, just like a peasant woman. The man in charge of the geese kept shouting: 'They could destroy any number of geese that way!' Well, of course, there were witnesses. The Justice of the Peace dealt with the matter in no time. The owner was to be paid a rouble for his goose and the fellow was to keep the goose and warned not to play such tricks again. The young fellow kept complaining like some peasant woman. 'It wasn't me,' he said, 'it's him who talked me into it,' and he pointed to me. I replied very coolly that I hadn't suggested anything to him but had merely expressed the basic idea, and had spoken in the abstract. The Justice of the Peace, Nefedov, first smiled and then grew angry with himself at once for having done so. 'I shall at once report you to your school authorities,' he said to me, 'so that you won't go in for such theories in future, but will sit at your books and do your lessons.' Well, he didn't report me to the school authorities; it was said in jest. But the news did get round, even to the authorities, who have long ears, you see! Our classics master, Kolbasnikov, was particularly outraged, but Dardanelov got me off again. Kolbasnikov is furious with all of us, the silly ass. You know, Ilyusha, he's just got married. Got a dowry of a thousand roubles from the Mikhailovs, and his bride is as ugly as sin. The boys in the third class at once made up an epigram on the occasion;

> *Astounding news has reached the class:*
> *Even in marriage he's been an ass*

and so on. It's very funny, I'll show it to you later. I have nothing against Dardanelov: he's a man of some learning. Yes, most decidedly, of some learning. I respect such men, and not only because he got me off—"

"But you got him tripping about who founded Troy," Smurov suddenly put in, decidedly proud of Krasotkin at the moment. He was particularly pleased with the story about the goose.

"Did you really?" Snegiryov exclaimed, flatteringly. "You mean about who founded Troy? Yes, we heard how you'd scored off him. Ilyusha told me about it at the time—"

"He knows an awful lot, Daddy; he knows more than any of us!" Ilyusha, too, put in. "He only pretends to be like that, but he's first in all subjects—"

Ilyusha gave Kolya a look of ineffable happiness.

"Oh, that thing about Troy was all nonsense," Kolya said with dignified modesty. "I consider the matter of no importance whatever." He had by that time completely resumed his usual tone, though he was still a little uneasy: he realised that he was all worked up and that, for instance, he had told the story about the goose with somewhat too little self-restraint, while Alyosha had been silent all the time and had looked grave. The proud boy was beginning to feel uncomfortable. Had Alyosha been silent because he despised him and because he thought that he, Kolya, was expecting praise from him? If he dared to think anything of the kind, he, Kolya, would—

"I think the matter of no importance whatever!" he snapped, again with some pride.

"But I know who founded Troy," a boy, who had not yet spoken a word put in quite unexpectedly. He was a good-looking boy of eleven, called Kartashov, a shy and reticent boy, who was sitting at the door. Kolya gave him a look of dignified surprise. Indeed, the question of the founders of Troy had become a mystery to all the boys at the school, the key to which was contained in the Smaragdov book, which no one but Kolya possessed. On one occasion, however, while Kolya's back was turned, Kartashov quickly opened Kolya's book and at once found the passage about the founders of Troy. This had taken place long ago, but he was somehow too embarrassed to bring himself to declare that he, too, knew who had found Troy. He was afraid of what might come to pass and that Kolya might somehow put his nose out of joint. But now he just could not resist the temptation to speak. Besides, he had wanted to for a long time.

"Well, who did found it?" Kolya asked, turning to him with arrogant condescension. He had understood from the look on Kartashov's face that the boy really knew the answer, and, of course, immediately decided how he would react. A certain dissonance had come into the overall atmosphere.

"Troy was founded by Teucer, Dardanus, Ilias, and Troas," came the pat reply, the boy blushing so violently that it was pitiful to see. All eyes were fixed on him for a whole minute, and then suddenly, turned to Kolya, who continued to eye the audacious boy from head to foot with disdainful composure.

"What do you mean by calling them the founders?" he finally deigned to retort. "And what, generally speaking, does the foundation of a city or a state mean? Did they actually lay a brick each?"

Some laughter ensued, making the poor boy turn from pink to crimson. He made no reply, and was on the verge of tears.

Kolya kept him in suspense for a whole minute.

"To talk of such historical events as the founding of a nation," he went on incisively in an instructive tone, "you should first realise what is meant. Incidentally, I, for one, attach no significance to such old wives' tales, and don't think very highly of world history," he added casually, this time addressing no one in particular.

"World history?" Snegiryov inquired almost in alarm.

"Yes, world history, which is nothing but the study of man's follies. Maths and natural science are the only subjects I hold in esteem," said Kolya self-assertively with a glance at Alyosha, whose opinion alone he feared. But Alyosha kept silent and grave. Had he spoken, that would have ended the matter, but he was silent and "his silence may speak of his contempt", which made Kolya more and more worked up.

"Again, the classical languages we have to learn: it's sheer madness, nothing more— You seem to disagree with me again, Karamazov, don't you?"

"I do," Alyosha smiled restrainedly.

"If you want to know my opinion, the teaching of the classical languages is a police measure. That's the only reason why they've been introduced," Kolya said gradually becoming breathless again. "They were introduced because they are boring and blunt the mind. Things were as dry as dust even before, so what had to be done to make them even more boring? They were meaningless before, so what had to be done to make them even worse? That was why the classical languages were thought up. That's my full opinion of them which I'll never change, I hope," Kolya concluded sharply, two red spots appearing on his cheeks.

"That's true!" Smurov, who had been listening attentively, assented suddenly, with ringing conviction.

"And yet he's top at Latin himself!" a boy shouted.

"Yes, Dad, he says that and yet he's first in his class at Latin," Ilyusha, too, chimed in.

"So what?" Kolya thought it fit to speak, though the praise was pleasant to him. "I swot Latin because I have to, and because I promised Mother to do well at school. Anything one does is worth doing well, but at bottom I have the utmost contempt for classical studies and all that tommy rot— You don't agree, Karamazov, do you?"

"But why tommy rot?" Alyosha smiled again.

"Why, all the classics have been translated into all languages, so it's not for classical studies that Latin is taught, but as a police measure designed to stunt the development of our minds. That's why it's all so low-down."

"But where have you learned all this?" Alyosha cried at last, with a look of surprise.

"First of all, I'm quite capable of understanding it myself without being taught, and, secondly, let me tell you that Kolbasnikov himself said to the third form what I said just now about the classics having been translated—"

"The doctor's come!" Nina, who had been silent all the time, cried suddenly.

And indeed, Madame Khokhlakov's carriage drove up to the gate. Snegiryov, who had been expecting the doctor all morning, rushed out to meet him. Mrs. Snegiryov sat up, straightened her dress and assumed a dignified air. Alyosha went up to Ilyusha and adjusted his pillows, with Nina watching anxiously from her arm-chair. The boys made a hurried departure, some of them promising to come again in the evening. Kolya called Perezvon, and the dog jumped off the bed.

"I won't be leaving," Kolya said hurriedly to Ilyusha. "I'll wait in the passageway and come back when the doctor has gone. I'll be back with Perezvon."

But the doctor was already on his way in—an important-looking figure in a bearskin coat, with long, dark side-whiskers and a blue close-shaven chin. On crossing the threshold, he suddenly stopped, as though taken aback, probably imagining that he had come to the wrong address. "What's this? Where am I?" he muttered, without removing his fur coat and his sealskin cap with its peak of the same fur. The crowded room, its poverty, the washing hanging on a line in a corner of the room, disconcerted him. Snegiryov was bowing low to him.

"This is the place, sir," he murmured obsequiously. "It's here, sir, you were supposed to come, to my house, sir—"

"Sne-gir-yov?" the doctor said in a loud and dignified voice. "And you Mr. Snegiryov?"

"Yes, sir. That's me, sir."

"Oh!"

The doctor cast another disdainful glance about the room and threw off his fur coat. The high decoration round his neck flashed for all to see. Snegiryov snatched up the fur coat, and the doctor took off his cap.

"Where's the patient?" he asked peremptorily, in a loud voice.

6.

Precocity

"What do you think the doctor will say to him?" Kolya asked rapidly. "What a nasty dial he has, though, don't you think? I simply loathe medicine!"

"Ilyusha will die," Alyosha replied sadly. "I feel certain he will."

"They're all quacks! Medicine's a fraud! I'm glad, though, to have met you, Karamazov. I've wanted to meet you for a long time. I'm only sorry we had to meet on such a sad occasion—"

Kolya would have very much liked to say something warmer and more effusive, but something about Alyosha seemed to hold him back. Noticing that, Alyosha smiled, and pressed his hand.

"I've long learned to respect you as a rare creature," Kolya murmured again, hesitant and confused. "I've heard you are a mystic and have been in a monastery. I know you are a mystic but—that hasn't put me off. Contact with reality will cure you: it's always like that with people like you."

"Whom would you call a mystic? What will that cure me of?" Alyosha asked, looking a little surprised.

"Well—God and all that."

"Why, don't you believe in God?"

"On the contrary, I've nothing against God. Of course, God is only a hypothesis—but—I admit that he is necessary for orderliness—for world order and so on—and if there were no God he'd have to be invented," Kolya added, turning red. He suddenly fancied that Alyosha might think he wanted to show off his knowledge and let him see that he was grown up. "And I don't want to show off my knowledge to him at all," Kolya thought indignantly. Suddenly, he felt annoyed.

"I must say, I don't like being caught up in all these arguments," he said flatly. "One can love humanity without believing in God—don't you think so? Voltaire didn't believe in God, yet he loved mankind, didn't he?" ("I'm at it again!" he thought to himself.)

"Voltaire did believe in God, but not, I suppose, deeply, and I can't help thinking that he didn't love mankind so very much, either," Alyosha said, with quiet restraint, and quite naturally, as though talking to someone of his own age, or even much older than himself. Kolya was at once struck by Alyosha's apparent diffidence regarding his own opinion of Voltaire and by his seeming to leave the question for him, little Kolya, to decide.

"Have you read Voltaire?" asked Alyosha, in conclusion.

"Well, not exactly— I've read *Candide*, though, in a Russian translation—old, bad and ridiculous translation—" ("At it again!")

"And did you understand it?"

"Oh yes, everything—that is—why do you suppose I shouldn't understand it? There are, of course, a lot of dirty words in it— I'm certainly quite capable of understanding that it is a philosophical novel, and written to bolster an idea—" Kolya had got thoroughly muddled by now. "I'm a socialist, Karamazov, an incurable socialist," he broke off suddenly for no obvious reason.

"A socialist?" Alyosha laughed. "But when have you had time to become one? You're only thirteen, aren't you?"

Kolya winced.

"First of all, I'm fourteen, not thirteen. I'll turn fourteen in a fortnight," he declared, flushing. "And, secondly, I can't see what my age has got to do with it? What matters is my convictions, not my age. Don't you agree?"

"When you're older, you'll understand how one's age affects

one's convictions. It also seemed to me that you were not expressing your own ideas," Alyosha replied quietly and modestly, but Kolya interrupted him hotly.

"Why, is it obedience and mysticism you're after? You must admit that Christianity, for instance, has been of use only to the wealthy and well-born, to keep the lower classes in slavery. Isn't that so?"

"Oh, I know where you've read that," exclaimed Alyosha. "And I'm sure someone must have taught you that!"

"Good Lord, why should I have read it? And no one has taught me anything. I can do my own thinking. And, if you like, I'm not against Christ. He was quite a humane person, and if he were alive today, he would most certainly have joined the revolutionaries and would, perhaps, play a leading part— I'm quite sure of that."

"Where have you got all that from? What fool have you had dealings with?

"Of course, the truth will out. It's true that I often talk to Mr. Rakitin in connection with a certain matter, but— I'm told, old Belinsky used to say that too."

"Belinsky? I don't remember that. He hasn't written of that anywhere."

"Even if he hasn't, it's something he's said, and I've heard— well, no matter who from—"

"And have you read Belinsky?"

"To tell you the truth—I haven't—but I have read the passage about Tatyana—why she didn't go off with Onegin."

"Didn't go off with Onegin? Why, do you already understand—such things?"

"Good Lord, you must take me for that little fellow Smurov," Kolya grimaced irritably. "Still, you mustn't think I'm such a terrible revolutionary. I often disagree with Mr. Rakitin. If I mentioned Tatyana, it was not because I'm in favour of women becoming emancipated. I think that a woman is a subordinate creature and must practise obedience. *Les femmes tricottent,* as Napoleon said," Kolya grinned for some reason, "and in that, at least, I fully share the opinion of that pseudogreat man. Then I believe, for instance, that to be off to

America from your own country is mean, and even worse than mean—stupid. Why go to America when we can do a great deal of good for humanity in our country, too? Especially now. A frightful amount of fruitful activity. That's what I replied."

"Who did you reply to? What do you mean? Has anyone already asked you to go to America?"

"I must say that there have been attempts to talk me into it, but I've refused. That's, of course, between you and me, Karamazov. Not a word to anyone about it, do you hear? I'm telling this to you alone. I haven't the least wish to fall into the clutches of the Secret Political Police and undergo instruction at their headquarters at the Chain Bridge in St. Petersburg.

> *That building which at Chain Bridge stands*
> *Is linked with memory with iron bands.* *

You remember? That's splendid! But why are you laughing? D'you think I've been inventing things?" ("And what if he finds out that there's only a single issue of *Kolokol* in Father's bookcase and that I've read no others?" Kolya thought fearfully.)

"Of course, I don't! I'm not laughing at anything, and I don't think you've been inventing things. The trouble, you see, is that I don't think so because it is all only too true, alas! But tell me, have you read Pushkin, I mean *Onegin*— You spoke of Tatyana just now—"

"No, I haven't read it yet, but I want to. I have no prejudices, Karamazov. I want to hear both sides of the matter. Why are you asking?"

"Just like that!"

"Tell me, Karamazov, do you despise me very much?" Kolya asked abruptly, drawing himself up to his full height as though taking a firm stand. "Do tell me quite honestly."

"Despise you?" said Alyosha, looking at him with surprise.

*The lines come from a poem published in *Polyarnaya Zvezda* (The Polestar) in 1861. It was quoted in 1866 in *Kolokol* (The Bell), which was published abroad by Herzen and Ogarev, and brought illegally into Russia. The newspaper enjoyed considerable popularity among Russian progressives.— *Tr.*

"Why should I? I'm only sorry that an attractive nature such as yours should have been perverted by all this crude nonsense on the threshold of life."

"Don't worry about my nature," Kolya broke in, not without some self-satisfaction, "but it's quite true that I'm very sensitive. Stupidly and crudely so. You gave an ironical smile just now so I imagined that you—"

"Oh, I was smiling for quite another reason. I was recently reading what a German who had lived in Russia thought of our students of today. 'Show a Russian schoolboy,' he wrote, 'a stellar chart he has no idea of and he'll return it to you with corrections next day.' No knowledge and boundless conceit—that's what the German wanted to say of the Russian schoolboy."

"Oh, how true it is!" said Kolya suddenly bursting into laughter. "*Verissimo!* Hit the nail on the head! Bravo, you German! But the damn foreigner did not notice the good side, eh? What do you think? The conceit is there: it's a sign of youth that will be corrected, if it has to be, but, on the other hand, there's also an independence of mind almost from childhood, and boldness of thought and convictions, and not their vulgar spirit of servility to authority— But all the same, the German put it well! Good for him! Yet all Germans should be squashed. They may be good at the sciences, but they should be squashed all the same—"

"But why on earth squash them?" smiled Alyosha.

"Oh, well, I've been talking nonsense, I agree. I'm quite a kid at times, and when something is to my liking I can't keep myself in check, and blab a lot of nonsense. Look here, we're talking about all sorts of trifles here, while that doctor has been taking his time in there. However, he may be examining the mother and the poor cripple Nina as well. You know, I like that Nina. She whispered to me suddenly as I walked past her: 'Why didn't you come before?' And with such reproach in her voice! I think she's awfully kind-hearted and so pathetic."

"Indeed, she is! And if you start coming here, you'll see what a nice girl she is. It'll do you a lot of good to meet such people, for it will teach you to appreciate many things you can learn from knowing them," Alyosha observed warmly. "That more than anything will make you a different person."

"Oh, I'm so sorry for not coming sooner!" cried Kolya with some bitterness.

"Yes, it's a pity. You saw for yourself how overjoyed the poor child was to see you! And how upset he was at your failing to come!"

"Don't say so! Why rub it in like that? Still, it serves me right: I didn't come out of pride, selfish pride, and a mean desire to boss others, which I can never get rid of, though I've always tried hard to change. I can see now that I've been a cad in lots of ways, Karamazov!"

"No, yours is a charming nature, though it's been marred a little, and I quite understand how you've come to have such an influence on this magnanimous but excessively vulnerable boy!" Alyosha retorted warmly.

"And you say that to me!" cried Kolya, "you know, I've often thought—I thought so just now—that you despised me! If only you knew how highly I value your opinion!"

"But are you really so sensitive? At your age! You know, that was just my impression, while I watched you telling your story in there, that you must be morbidly sensitive."

"Did you? You see what an eye you've got! I bet it was when I was speaking about the goose. It was at that very point that I fancied that you must look down on me for being in such haste to show off; that made me feel a sudden hatred for you and talk a lot of rot. Then I fancied (it was just now, here) that when I said that if there were no God he had to be invented, that I was too hasty to display my education, particularly as I had read that sentence in a book. But I swear I was so keen to show off not out of vanity but—well, I really don't know why—out of joy, perhaps, yes, I do believe it was out of joy—Though I admit it's most discreditable to fall on somebody's neck out of joy, perhaps, yes, I do believe it was out of joy— Though despise me and that it's all my imagination. Oh, Karamazov, I feel terribly unhappy. I sometimes imagine goodness knows what, that I'm a laughing-stock to all and sundry, and then I'm simply ready to destroy the whole order of things."

"And you torment those about you," Alyosha smiled.

"And I torment those about me, Mother especially. Tell me,

Karamazov, am I making myself look very ridiculous now?"

"Give no thought to that, none at all!" cried Alyosha. "And what do you mean by ridiculous? Does it matter how many times a man is or seems ridiculous? Besides, today almost all people of ability are terribly afraid of making themselves ridiculous, and that makes them unhappy. Only I'm surprised that you should be feeling that so early, though I've noticed it for some time now and not only in you. Even those who are little more than children have begun to suffer from it today. It's almost a kind of madness. The devil has assumed the shape of this vanity and invaded an entire generation—yes, the devil," added Alyosha, unsmilingly, just as Kolya, who was staring at him, thought he would. "You're just like all the rest," Alyosha concluded, "that is, like many others. Except that one should not to be like everyone else. That's how it is."

"Although all are like that?"

"Yes, even although all are like that. Be the only one who isn't like that. In fact, you are not like all the rest: you weren't ashamed to confess a moment ago to something bad and even ridiculous. And who confesses to such things nowadays? No one. People do not any longer even feel the need to condemn themselves. So don't be like all the rest, even if you're the only exception."

"Excellent! I haven't been mistaken in you. You have the gift of consoling others. Oh, I was so keen to meet you, Karamazov! I have wished to for such a long time! Have you really given me thought too? You did say just now that you had thought about me, too, didn't you?"

"Yes, I've heard about you and thought about you—and if it's partly vanity that has made you ask, it's all right."

"You know, Karamazov, our talk has resembled a declaration of love," said Kolya in a weak and bashful voice. "That isn't ridiculous, is it?"

"Of course not, and even if it were, it wouldn't matter because it's so good," Alyosha smiled brightly.

"But, you know, Karamazov, you will admit that you too feel a little ashamed now—I can see it from your eyes," Kolya smiled slyly, but also with something akin to happiness.

"What is there to be ashamed of?"

"Well, why are you blushing?"

"Why, it's you who made me blush!" laughed Alyosha and, indeed, he really did. "Well, yes, I am a little ashamed. Goodness knows why, I'm sure I don't know why—" he muttered, almost embarrassed.

"Oh, how I love and value you at this moment just because you too feel ashamed for some reason! Because you're just like me!" Kolya exclaimed with genuine delight. His cheeks were flushed and his eyes sparkled.

"You know, Kolya, you'll be very unhappy in life," said Alyosha suddenly, without really knowing why.

"I know that, I know." Kolya at once agreed. "But how do you know it all in advance!"

"Yet on the whole, you will bless life all the same."

"Indeed, I shall! Hurrah! You're a seer! Oh, we shall be good friends, Karamazov. You know what I admire so much in you is that you regard me as an equal. But we are not equals, no, we're not. You stand higher than me! But we shall be friends. I want you to know that during the past month I've been saying to myself: 'We shall either become friends at once and for ever, or we shall part enemies to the grave after our first meeting!'"

"And, of course, when you said that, you loved me already!" Alyosha laughed gaily.

"Yes, I did, I loved you terribly. I'd been loving you and dreaming about you! And how is it that you know everything beforehand? Ah, here comes the doctor. What will he say, I wonder. Just look at the expression on his face!"

7.

Ilyusha

The doctor was about to leave the cottage, all muffled up in his fur coat, and with his cap on his head. His face was almost angry and disdainful, as though he were afraid of besmirching himself. He cast a brief glance about the passageway and, as he did so, gave Alyosha and Kolya a severe look. Alyosha signalled to the driver from the door and the carriage the doctor had arrived in drove up to the door of the house. Snegiryov rushed out after the doctor and, bowing obsequiously, stopped him for a last word. The poor man looked broken and frightened.

"Sir, sir—isn't there—?" he began, but didn't finish, merely throwing up his hands in despair, while still looking at the doctor in mute entreaty, as though a word from him might change the poor boy's death sentence.

"I'm afraid there's nothing I can do. I'm not God Almighty," the doctor replied off-handedly, though with his habitual impressiveness.

"Doctor— Your Excellency—and will it happen soon?"

"Be pre-pared for anything," the doctor said, emphasising every syllable and, dropping his eyes, was about to cross the threshold and enter the carriage.

"Your Excellency, for the love of Christ," Snegiryov stopped him again, looking frightened, "can nothing at all, nothing at all save him now?—"

"That doesn't de-pend on me now," the doctor said impatiently. "However—h'm," he stopped suddenly, "if—er—you could perhaps—er—send your patient—at once and without delay" (the words "at once" and "without delay" were uttered not so much severely as almost angrily, so that Snegiryov even gave a start) "—to Sy-racuse, so that the new and favourable climatic conditions there may—"

"To Syracuse, Your Excellency?" cried Snegiryov, as though unable to understand anything.

"Syracuse is in Sicily," Kolya blurted out to explain matters. The doctor gave him a look.

"To Sicily! But, Your Excellency," said Snegiryov, completely at a loss, "you've seen!—" he waved his hands as though to draw his attention to the surroundings. "And what about my wife, sir, my family?"

"N-no, your family should go not to Sicily but to the Caucasus in the early spring. Your daughter—to the Caucasus and your wife after—er—after spa treatment also in the Caucasus for her rheumatism—after that at once to Paris to the clinic of the famous psychiatrist, Dr. Lapelletier. I could let you have a note to him—and then there might be—"

"But, doctor, don't you see?" said Snegiryov again waving his hands, and pointing in despair at the bare log walls of the passageway.

"That's no concern of mine," the doctor smiled wryly. "I've only told you what sci-ence could do as a last resort—for your family. As for the rest, I—to my regret—"

"Have no fear, doc, my dog won't bite you," Kolya snapped out in a loud voice, noticing the doctor's rather uneasy glance at Perezvon, who was standing in the doorway. There was an edge of anger in Kolya's voice. He had used the word "doc" *intentionally* and, as he declared afterwards himself, "as an insult".

"What do you mean?" said the doctor, rearing his head and staring in surprise at Kolya. "Who's this?" he turned suddenly to Alyosha, as though demanding an explanation.

"I'm Perezvon's owner, doc. You don't have to feel concern as to who I am," Kolya said calmly.

"Zvon?*" the doctor repeated, who had not realised that Perezvon was the dog's name.

"But he can't say whence the sound. Good-bye, doc. We'll meet again in Syracuse."

"Who's this? Who's this?" cried the doctor, flaring up.

"He's a schoolboy here, doctor," Alyosha said, frowning and speaking rapidly. "He's a mischievous boy. Pay no attention to him, sir. Kolya," he cried to Krasotkin, "hold your tongue! Take no notice of him, doctor," he repeated a little more impatiently.

"He should be flogged—that's what he needs!" cried the doctor, stamping a foot in fury.

"You know, doc, my Perezvon might bite after all!" said Kolya in a trembling voice and turning pale, his eyes flashing. "To heel, Perezvon!"

"Kolya, if you say another word I'll break with you for good!" Alyosha cried peremptorily.

"Doc, there's only one man in the whole world who can order Nikolai Krasotkin about and that is the man," said Kolya indicating Alyosha. "I'll obey him. Good-bye!"

*Zvon is the Russian for the sound of bells, while perezvon means the clanging of bells. Kolya is quoting from the Russian nursery rhyme: He's heard a bell but can't say whence the sound.—Tr.

He made for the door, pulled it open, and went quickly into the room, Perezvon running after him. The doctor stood motionless for five seconds more, staring at Alyosha as though rooted to the spot, then he spat and went out quickly to the carriage, repeating in loud voice: "This—this—this—I don't know what this is!" Snegiryov rushed after him to help him into the carriage. Alyosha followed Kolya into the room. The boy was standing beside Ilyusha's side, who was holding his hand and calling for his father. A minute later Snegiryov, too, returned.

"Daddy, Daddy, come here—we—" Ilyusha murmured in violent agitation, but, apparently unable to go on, suddenly flung both his wasted arms round Kolya and his father, holding them, as well as he could, in a close embrace and hugging them. Snegiryov suddenly shook all over with silent sobs, and Kolya's chin and lips began to twitch.

"Daddy, Daddy! Oh, I feel so sorry for you, Daddy!" Ilyusha moaned bitterly.

"My dear boy—the doctor said you—you'd be all right and—we'll be happy—the doctor—" Snegiryov began.

"Oh, Daddy, I know what the new doctor said to you about me— I saw!" cried Ilyusha, again hugging both of them and hiding his face on his father's shoulder.

"Daddy, don't cry and—and when I die, find a good boy—another one—choose one yourself from all of them, a good chap, call him Ilyusha and love him instead of me—"

"Shut up, old man, you'll get well!" Krasotkin cried suddenly, as though in anger.

"And never forget me, Daddy," Ilyusha went on. "Visit my grave—and please, Daddy, have me buried near the big stone, where we used to go for our walks, and come to me there with Krasotkin in the evening— And Perezvon too— And I'll be expecting you— Daddy, Daddy!"

His voice failed him, and all three of them, united in a single embrace, were silent. Nina, too, was crying quietly in her chair, and Mrs. Snegiryov, seeing them all crying, burst into tears herself.

"My darling Ilyusha, my darling Ilyusha!" she kept exclaiming.

Krasotkin suddenly freed himself from Ilyusha's embrace.

"Good-bye, old man," he said rapidly. "Mother's expecting me for dinner. I'm very sorry not to have told her! She'll be awfully worried— But I'll be back at once after dinner, for the whole day, the whole evening, and I'm going to tell you ever so many things, ever so many! And I'll bring Perezvon along. But I'll take it along with me now, because it'll start howling if I'm not here and be a nuisance to you. So long!"

And he ran out into the passageway. He tried to hold back his tears, but in the passageway he cried all the same. Alyosha found him in that condition.

"Kolya, be sure to keep your word and come, or else he'll be terribly upset," Alyosha said emphatically.

"I will! Oh, how I hate myself for not having come earlier," Kolya murmured, crying unashamedly.

At that moment, Snegiryov seemed to leap out of the room and at once closed the door behind him. His face was contorted and his lips quivering. He stopped short before the two of them and flung up his arms.

"I don't want a good boy! I don't want another boy!" he said in a wild whisper, grinding his teeth. "If I forget thee, O Jerusalem, let my tongue—"

He did not finish, the words dying on his lips, and sank helplessly on his knees beside the wooden bench. Clutching his head in his fists, he burst out sobbing, now and again whimpering absurdly, but doing his utmost not to be heard from the room. Kolya rushed out into the street.

"Good-bye, Karamazov! Will you be coming back?" he asked Alyosha with cross brusqueness.

"I'll be back for sure in the evening."

"What was he saying about Jerusalem?— What did he mean?"

"It's from the Bible: 'If I forget thee, O Jerusalem', that is to say, if I forget all that is most precious to me, if I exchange it for anything, then—"

"I understand. That's enough! Be sure to come. *Ici*, Perezvon!" he shouted fiercely to the dog and made for home almost at the run.

BOOK ELEVEN

Brother Ivan Fyodorovich

1.

At Grushenka's

Alyosha set out towards Cathedral Square, making for Mrs. Morozov's house where he was to see Grushenka, who early that morning had sent an urgent message by Fenya to call on her. From Fenya Alyosha learnt that her mistress had been greatly distressed since the day before. During the two months after Mitya's arrest, Alyosha had often called on Grushenka, both of his own accord and at Mitya's request. Three days after Mitya's arrest, Grushenka had fallen seriously ill, and was ailing for close on five weeks, during one of which she had been delirious. She was greatly changed—thinner and paler—though now for nearly two weeks she had been well enough to go out. But to Alyosha her face seemed much more attractive than before and he liked to meet her gaze when he called, for an expression of new firmness and purpose had come into her eyes. There were signs of some spiritual change in her, of a resolve unchangeable and meek, but salutary and irrevocable. A small, vertical line had appeared between her eyebrows, this lending her charming face a look of concentrated thoughtfulness, almost severe at first glance. There was, for instance, no trace of her former frivolity. Alyosha also found it strange that Grushenka had not lost her former youthful gaiety, despite the misfortune that had befallen the poor woman, the betrothed of a man arrested for a terrible crime almost at the moment she had promised to marry him, and despite her subsequent illness and the almost inevitable verdict hanging over him at the impending trial. There was a soft light in her once proud eyes, and yet—and yet they blazed with an ominous fire at times, too, when her heart was visited by an old care, which, far from abating, had grown ever more. The reason was always the same: Katerina Ivanovna, whom she had named again and again during her illness and even in her delirium. Alyosha was aware that she was terribly jealous of her, though Katerina Ivanovna had never visited Mitya in prison, something she could well have done whenever she wished. All this presented a difficult problem to Alyosha, for he was Grushenka's only confidant and constant source of counsel; yet he sometimes felt quite at a loss what to say.

It was with a sense of concern that he entered her flat. She was at home, having returned from a visit to Mitya half an hour before. From the way she jumped up from her arm-chair at the table to meet him, he concluded that she had been expecting him impatiently. There were playing cards on the table, some of which had been dealt out for a game. On the other side of the table a bed had been made up on a leather sofa, and on it lay Maximov, in a dressing-gown and a cotton nightcap, half-reclining, and evidently ill and weak, though he was smiling ingratiatingly. On his return with Grushenka from Mokroye two months before, the homeless old man had stayed on at her house, as a kind of fixture. On arriving with her in the rain and slush, he had sat down on the sofa, soaked to the skin and frightened, and stared wordlessly at her with a timid, beseeching smile. Grushenka, who was terribly begrieved and already feverish, had been so busy in the first half-hour after her arrival that she had almost forgotten all about him. Suddenly she caught sight of him and looked at him intently: he raised his eyes and gave a pitiful and forlorn little snigger. She called Fenya and told her to give him something to eat. All that day, he remained rooted to his seat, almost without stirring. When it grew dark and the shutters were closed, Fenya asked her mistress:

"Is the old gentleman going to stay the night, madam?"

"Yes, he is," Grushenka replied. "Make up a bed for him on the sofa."

On questioning him in more detail, Grushenka learnt that he really had nowhere to go. "Mr. Kalganov, my benefactor," he said, "told me forthright that I would not be received again at his place, and gave me five roubles." "Well," Grushenka decided in her grief, smiling compassionately at him, "I suppose you'd better stay on." The old man was deeply moved by her smile and his lips quivered with gratitude as he barely held back his tears. And so the wandering hanger-on had stayed at her place. He did not leave even when she was ill. Fenya and her grandmother, Grushenka's cook, did not turn him out, but gave him his meals and made up a bed for him on the sofa. Grushenka had grown so used to him that, on returning from her visits to Mitya (whom she began visiting regularly even before she had completely recovered), she would sit down and begin talking to "old Maximov" about all sorts of trifling matters, just to get over her depression and keep her mind off her troubles. She discovered that at times the old man was rather good at spinning yarns, so that ultimately he became essential to her. Except for Alyosha, who did not, however, call every day and who never stayed long, Grushenka scarcely received anyone. Her old merchant was already seriously ill at the time—"at death's door", as they said in the town, and, indeed, he did die a week after Mitya's trial. Three weeks before his death, feeling the end was near, he called for his three sons and their wives and children and told them to leave him no more. From that moment, he gave strict orders to his servants not to admit Grushenka and to tell her, if she came, that he wished her long life and happiness and asked her to forget him. Grushenka, however, had his health inquired after almost every day.

"You've come at last!" cried Grushenka, throwing down the cards and greeting Alyosha joyfully. "Maximov kept frightening me by saying that perhaps you wouldn't. Oh, I need you so badly! Sit down at the table. Well, what will you have—coffee?"

"Oh yes," said Alyosha, sitting down at the table, "I'm awfully hungry."

"I thought so," Grushenka cried. "Fenya, some coffee! It's been ready for you. And bring some pies, Fenya, and mind they're hot. Just a moment, Alyosha. Before you say anything, I must tell you that we've had an awful row over those pies today. I took them to the prison for him, and he—would you believe it?—he threw them back in my face. He refused to eat them. He threw one pie on the floor and actually stamped on it. I told him I would leave them with the warder. 'If you don't eat them before the evening,' I said, 'then it means that it's your malicious spite alone that keeps you going.' With that I left. We've had another quarrel, you see. We quarrel every time I come."

Grushenka said all this in a single breath, greatly agitated. Maximov at once grew frightened and, dropping his eyes, went on smiling.

"What did you quarrel with him about this time?" asked Alyosha.

"Something quite unexpected. Just fancy, he felt jealous of the 'first one'. 'Why,' he asked, 'are you supporting him? So you've begun keeping him, have you?' He's always jealous. Jealous of me all the time! Jealous of me when he eats and sleeps. He was even jealous of Kuzma one day last week."

"But he knew about your first one before, didn't he?"

"Of course he did. He's known about it from the very outset. But today he suddenly got up and began to carry on. I'm ashamed to repeat what he said. The fool! Rakitin came to see him as I was leaving. Perhaps it's Rakitin who's egging him on. What do you think?" she added somehow absently.

"He loves you—that's what it is. He loves you very much. And, besides, his nerves are on edge now."

"I should think so. The trial begins tomorrow. I came there today to say something to him about it, for, Alyosha, I tremble to think what's going to happen tomorrow! His nerves are on edge, you say. And what about mine? Aren't they on edge too? And he has to bring up the Pole! What a fool! I suppose he isn't jealous of Maximov, or is he?"

"My wife was very jealous of me, too," Maximov put in.

"Was she really?" said Grushenka with a mirthless smile, "Who was she jealous of?"

"The parlour maids."

"Oh, do be quiet, Maximov! I'm in no laughing mood; I feel quite angry. Don't keep staring at the pies, I shan't give you any. They're not good for you. And I won't give you any of my home-made liqueur, either. How do you like that?" she laughed. "I've got him on my hands, too, just as if I kept an alms-house!"

"I don't deserve your benefactions, worthless creature that I am," Maximov said in a tearful voice. "You'd better lavish them on others who are of more use than me."

"Oh, everyone has some use, Maximov, and how's one to tell which of us is of most use? I wish that Pole had never existed, Alyosha. He, too, has gone and fallen ill. I've been to see him, too. Well, I'm going to send him some pies, too—on purpose! I hadn't intended to, but Mitya's accused me of sending him some, so I'm going to now on purpose, on purpose! Oh, here's Fenya with a letter! Yes, just as I thought! It's from those Poles again. Asking for money again!"

Pan Musialowicz's letter was indeed a lengthy one and couched in his usual florid style; in it he asked for a loan of three roubles. Enclosed was a receipt for the money, with a promise to repay it within three months; it was signed by Pan Wróblewski, too. Grushenka had received many such letters from her "first one", with similar receipts. The letters had begun arriving a fortnight before, as soon as Grushenka had recovered from her illness. She knew that the two Poles had also called to inquire after her health during her illness. The first letter was a very long one, written on a large sheet of note-paper with a big family crest on the seal. So obscure and florid was the style that Grushenka read only half of it and threw it away, unable to make head or tail of it. Besides, she could not be bothered with letters at the time. The first letter was followed by another the next day, in which Musialowicz asked for a loan of two thousand roubles for a very short period. Grushenka did not reply, and there followed a series of letters, which arrived regularly every day, all written in the same pompous and flowery style, but gradually reducing the amount requested, dropping to one hundred roubles, then to twenty-five, to ten, and at last Grushenka received a letter asking for only one rouble and enclosing a receipt signed by the two. It was then that Grushenka suddenly felt sorry for them and, at dusk, went round herself to see them. She found the two Poles in great penury, almost destitute and without food, fuel and cigarettes, and in debt to their landlady. The two hundred roubles they had won at cards from Mitya in Mokroye had soon gone. What surprised Grushenka, however, was that the two Poles had met her with an air of arrogance and independence, and with the greatest punctilio and orotund speeches. Grushenka just laughed it all off, and gave her "fist one" ten roubles. The same day, she laughingly told Mitya about it, and he was not at all jealous. But since then the Poles had attached themselves tenaciously to Grushenka, bombarding her daily with begging letters, and she had always sent them a little money. And now Mitya had suddenly took it into his head to grow fiercely jealous of her.

"Like a fool I went to see him too, just for a moment, on my way to Mitya, for, you see, he too is ill, my first one, my Pole," Grushenka began again, in nervous haste. "I told Mitya jokingly about it. 'Can you imagine,' I said, 'that Pole of mine has taken it into his head to sing me his old songs, to the guitar. He thinks I'll be moved and marry him!' Well, Mitya jumped up and began to heap abuse on me— Well, then, if he carries on like that, I'm jolly well going to send them the pies! Fenya, have they sent that little girl over? Here, give her three roubles and wrap a dozen pies up and tell her to take along. And you, Alyosha, don't forget to tell Mitya that I've sent them the pies."

"I wouldn't do that for anything," said Alyosha with a smile.

"Oh, you don't think he worries about it, do you?" Grushenka said bitterly. "He was pretending to be jealous on purpose. He doesn't care a bit."

"What do you mean—on purpose?" asked Alyosha.

"You're stupid, Alyosha dear, and, for all your cleverness, you don't understand the least thing. I'm not offended by his being jealous. I would have been offended if he wasn't. I'm like that. I'm not offended by jealousy, I have a cruel heart myself, I can be jealous too. If I'm offended, it's because he doesn't love me at all, and was jealous *on purpose*. Do you think I am blind? Don't I see? He starts talking to me all of a sudden about that Katya of his. That's the kind of woman she is, he says. She's sent for a doctor from Moscow, he says, to save him, and has engaged the most eminent and learned Moscow counsel as well. So I suppose he must love her if he keeps on praising her to my face, the shameless wretch! He's brought all this trouble on me, so now he must attack me and shift the blame on me alone. You were with that Pole before me, so why can't I do the same with Katya? That's how it is! He wants to put all the blame on me. He's provoking me on purpose, I'm telling you, on purpose, but I'll—"

Grushenka did not complete her threat, but hid her eyes in her handkerchief and burst into sobs.

"He doesn't love Katerina Ivanovna," said Alyosha firmly.

"I'll soon find it out for myself, whether he loves her or not," Grushenka said with an ominous note in her voice, taking the handkerchief from her eyes. Her face was distorted. Alyosha saw with distress how her face, so gentle and quietly happy a few moments before, now became sullen and spiteful.

"Enough of this nonsense!" she snapped. "I didn't ask you to come for that. Alyosha dear, what's going to happen tomorrow? That's what is tormenting me! And it seems to torment me alone! I look at them all, and no one seems to be concerned about it at all. Do you, at least, give thought to it? He's to be tried tomorrow! Tell me, how will he be tried? Why, it's the servant, the servant who murdered him! Good Lord, is he to be sentenced for something the servant did, and is there no one to take his side? They haven't even disturbed the servant, have they?"

"He's been cross-examined severely," Alyosha observed thoughtfully, "but they all decided that it wasn't he. Now he's very ill. He's been ill ever since that attack of epilepsy. He is really ill," added Alyosha.

"Oh dear, why don't you go to that lawyer yourself and tell him everything in confidence. I understand he's been brought from St. Petersburg at a fee of three thousand roubles."

"We got the three thousand together, Katerina Ivanovna, Ivan, and I but she got the doctor from Moscow for two thousand herself. The counsel Fetyukovich would have charged more, but the case has created a sensation all over Russia and has made the headlines in all the papers and journals. Fetyukovich agreed to come more for the kudos it'll bring him, for it's become so sensational a case. I saw him yesterday."

"Well? Did you tell him everything?" Grushenka asked hurriedly.

"He listened and said nothing. He merely said that he had already formed a definite opinion. But he promised to take my words into account."

"Into account! Oh, the scoundrels! They'll ruin him! But what about the doctor? Why did she send for him?"

"As an expert. They want to prove that my brother is insane and committed the murder in a state of diminished responsibility for his actions," Alyosha smiled gently. "Only Mitya won't agree to that."

"Oh, but it would be quite true if he had killed him!" cried Grushenka. "He was mad then, quite mad, and it's all, all the fault of a wretch like me! But, then, he didn't do it, he didn't! And they're all set against him. The whole town are sure that he did it. Even Fenya's evidence seems to show that he did it. And the people in the shop, and that civil servant, and, before, the people at the inn all heard him threaten to kill his father! They're all—all against him. They're all screaming that he's guilty."

"Yes," Alyosha said gloomily, "the evidence against him has piled up."

"And Grigori, Grigori insists that the door was open. Sticks to his story that he saw it. He can't be shaken. He was quite rude when I spoke to him."

"Yes, that's perhaps the strongest evidence against him," said Alyosha.

"As for Mitya being mad, he certainly seems to be now," Grushenka began suddenly, with a kind of mysterious anxiety. "You know, Alyosha, dear, I've been meaning to tell you about it before: I see him every day and simply can't help being surprised at him. Can you tell me what he keeps on talking about? He talks and talks, and I can't make head or tail of what he says. I keep on thinking he's talking about something very clever a fool like me can't understand. Only he starts talking to me about some bairn, that is, about some little baby. 'Why,' says he, 'is the bairn so poor? It's for the bairn that I'm going to Siberia now. I didn't do it, but I must go to Siberia!' What do you think it's all about? What bairn is he talking about—I couldn't make any sense of it at all! I just burst out crying when he said it, because he spoke so nicely. He cried himself, and I cried, too. And then, he suddenly kissed me and made the sign of the cross over me. What's it all about, Alyosha? Please tell me what bairn it is."

"I expect it must be Rakitin, who's been seeing him often lately for some reason," Alyosha smiled. "And yet—I don't think it is Rakitin. I didn't see Mitya yesterday, but I shall be seeing him today."

"No, it's not Rakitin. It's his brother Ivan Fyodorovich who's been getting him all confused. He's been seeing him and it's him, I'm sure of it—" said Grushenka, and suddenly stopped short.

Alyosha stared at her dumbfounded.

"Ivan? Has he been to see him? Mitya told me himself that Ivan hadn't come at all."

"Oh dear, I am a fool! I've let it slip out!" cried Grushenka, looking embarrassed and turning red. "Stay, Alyosha, don't say anything! Very well, having said so much, I'll tell you the whole truth. He's seen him twice, the first time as soon as he arrived—he came hurrying back from Moscow at once before I was taken ill. And the second time was a week ago. He told Mitya not to say anything to you about it, nor to anyone either, as a matter of fact. He came to see him secretly."

Alyosha sat pondering deeply, turning something over in his mind. He was obviously taken aback by the news.

"Ivan doesn't discuss Mitya's case with me," he said slowly, "and, in general, he's spoken very little to me during the last two months. He looked so displeased whenever I called, that I haven't been to see him during the last three weeks. H'm— If he visited him a week ago, then—some sort of change has really come over Mitya this week—"

"Yes, it has! It has!" Grushenka put in quickly. "They're sharing some secret! They have a secret! Mitya told me himself that there was a secret and, mind you, it's one that gives Mitya no peace of mind. He used to be so cheerful before, and, indeed, he still is but when he starts tossing his head like that and pacing the room and rubbing the hair on his right temple with a finger,

I know something's worrying him—I know! He used to be so cheerful before—and he was cheerful today, too!"

"But you said he was irritable!"

"Well, yes, he was irritable and cheerful at the same time! He would be irritable for a minute, and then cheerful, and then irritable again. And, you know, Alyosha, I just can't help being surprised at him: there's this horror he has to face, and yet sometimes he roars with laughter at such silly things, just as if he were a baby himself."

"But is it true that he told you not to tell me about Ivan? Did he actually say: not a word to him?"

"Yes, he did. You see, it's you Mitya's really afraid of. Because there's some secret here. He told me so himself— Alyosha, dear, do go and find out what their secret is and come and let me know," Grushenka suddenly besought him excitedly. "Do it for my sake, for me to know my fate! That's what I wanted to see you about."

"You think it concerns you in some way? But then he wouldn't have told you anything about the secret."

"I don't know. Perhaps he wants to tell me, but doesn't dare to. Maybe he's just warning me. There is a secret, but he won't tell me what it is."

"What do you think yourself?"

"What I think? It's the end for me, that's what I think. They've been arranging my end, the three of them, for that Katerina woman is in it, too. It's all her doing. It all comes from her. He calls her a fine woman, which means that I'm not. He's letting me know in advance. He's warning me. He's thinking of jilting me—that's the whole secret. They've planned it together, the three of them—Mitya, Katya, and Ivan Fyodorovich. Alyosha, I've been meaning to ask you a long time: a week ago he suddenly told me that Ivan was in love with Katya because he calls on her so often. Was he telling me the truth or not? Tell me honestly—don't spare me!"

"I won't lie to you: Ivan is not in love with Katerina Ivanovna. That's my opinion."

"Well, that's what I thought, too! He's lying to me, the brazen man—that's what it is! And he was jealous of me just now so as to put the blame on me afterwards. You see, he's a fool: he can't keep anything back for long–he's so outspoken– Only I'll show him! I'll show him! You know what he said to me? 'You think I did it!' That's what he said. That's what he reproached me with! Oh well, I don't mind! But I'll let that Katya have it good and proper in court! I'll say something there that– I'll tell them everything there!"

And again she shed bitter tears.

"Now this I can tell for certain, Grushenka," Alyosha said, getting up. "First, that he loves you. He loves you more than anyone in the world, and only you, believe me. I know. That I do know. Second, I must tell you that I do not want to worm the secret out of him, and if he does tell me today, I'll tell him frankly that I've promised to let you know. Then I'll come to you today and tell you. Only–I can't help thinking that Katerina Ivanovna has nothing to do with it at all, and that the secret is about something else. It's probably like that. And it's not likely to be about Katerina Ivanovna. That's what I think. And now–good-bye!"

Alyosha pressed her hand. Grushenka was still crying. He saw that she had little faith in his consolation, but, at any rate, she felt better for having told him what was worrying her, and got it off her chest. He was sorry to leave her in such a state, but he was in a hurry. He had a lot of things to attend to.

2.

The Bad Foot

The first of these was a call on Madame Khokhlakov, so he hurried there to get through with the matter as quickly as possible and not be late for Mitya. Madame Khokhlakov had not been feeling well for three weeks: her foot had for some reason swollen up, and though she was not in bed, she was half-reclining on a settee in her boudoir in an attractive but decorous *déshabillé*. Alyosha had on one occasion said to himself, with an ingenuous smile, that despite her illness Madame Khokhlakov was almost keen on showing off her clothes—topknots, ribbons, and flowing blouses, and he had some idea of the reason, but dismissed such thoughts as frivolous. Among the other callers, the young civil servant Perkhotin had become a very frequent caller during the past two months. Alyosha had not called for four days, and, on entering the house, was about to go straight upstairs to Lise's room, for it was her he wanted to see. Lise had sent a maid to him the day before with an urgent request to come and see her at once on "a very important matter", which for certain reasons, had interested Alyosha very much. But while the maid had gone to announce him, Madame Khokhlakov learnt of his arrival from someone and at once sent to ask him to see her "just for a moment". Alyosha decided that he should first meet the mother's request, for, if he did not, she would be sending someone to Lise's room every other minute while he was there. Madame Khokhlakov was lying on the settee, dressed very elegantly and evidently in a state of extraordinary nervous excitement. She greeted Alyosha with cries of delight.

"It's ages, ages since I saw you last! A whole week—my goodness! Oh, I'm sorry, you were here only four days ago, on Wednesday. You've come to see Lise, and I'm quite sure you wanted to tiptoe straight to her room, so that I shouldn't hear you. Dear, dear Alexei Fyodorovich, if only you knew how worried I am about her! But of that later. It may be the most important thing, but of that later. My dear Alexei Fyodorovich, I trust you completely with my Lise. Since the death of Father Zossima—God rest his soul," (she crossed herself) "I look upon you as a monk, though you do look charming in your new suit. Where did you find such a tailor in these parts? But no, no, that's not the main thing, that can wait. Forgive me for calling you Alyosha sometimes, do! I'm an old woman and I can permit myself such things," she smiled coquettishly, "but that can wait too. The main thing is that I mustn't forget the main thing. Please, remind me of it yourself the moment I begin to wander from the point. You must say to me: 'And what about the main thing?' Oh, but how am I to tell what the main thing now is? Ever since Lise withdrew her promise—her childish promise,

Alexei Fyodorovich, to marry you—you've realised, of course, that it was only the playful fancy of a sick girl who has so long been confined to her wheel-chair, but she can walk now, thank goodness. That new doctor Katya got from Moscow for your unfortunate brother, who will go on trial tomorrow— But why talk of tomorrow? I'm ready to die at the very thought of tomorrow! Mainly out of curiosity— In a word, the doctor was here yesterday and saw Lise— I paid him fifty roubles for the visit. But that's not what I want to talk to you about, again it's not that— You see, I'm all in a pother. I'm in such a hurry. But why am I in such a hurry? I'm sure I don't know. It's awful how I simply don't now know why I do things. Everything seems to be tangled up in a kind of skein. I'm afraid I bore you so much that you'll jump up and dash out of the room, and I shan't see you again. Oh dear! But why are we sitting here, and—first of all—coffee! Yulia, Glafira, coffee!"

Alyosha hastily thanked her and said that he had just had coffee.

"Where?"

"At Agrafena Alexandrovna's."

"At—at that woman's! Oh, it's she who's brought ruin upon everybody, and yet, I don't know. I'm told she's turned religious, though somewhat late in the day, I would say. She should have done that earlier when it would have been of some use. But what's the use of it now? Not a word, not a word, dear Alexei Fyodorovich, for I've got to tell you so many things that I'm afraid I shan't tell you anything. This dreadful trial—I shall certainly attend it, I'm getting ready for it. I'll have to be taken there in my chair. I can manage to sit up and, besides, I'll have people with me. You know, of course, that I'm one of the witnesses. How am I to speak there? Goodness, how am I to speak? I simply don't know what I'll say. You see, I'll have to take the oath. I will, won't I?"

"Yes, but I don't think you'll be well enough to appear."

"I can sit up. Oh, but you're confusing me! This trial, this brutal act, and then they'll all be sent to Siberia, others are getting married, and all this is happening so quickly, so quickly, and everything's changing, and everything ends in nothingness, people grow old and stand on the brink of the grave. Well, that can't be helped. Oh, I feel so tired. This Katya—*cette charmante personne*—has shattered all my hopes: now she's going to follow one of your brothers to Siberia, and your other brother will follow her and live in a neighbouring town, and they'll all be tormenting one another. It drives me out of my wits. But worst of all is the publicity: they've been writing about it scores of times in all the St. Petersburg and Moscow papers. Oh, by the way, they've been writing about me, too, can you imagine? They've been saying I was your brother's *chère amie*—I can't utter the horrid word. Imagine it! Just imagine it!"

"That's impossible! Where and what did they write?"

"I'll show it to you presently. I got it yesterday—read it yesterday. Here, in the St. Petersburg paper *Rumours*. The paper began to appear this year. I'm awfully fond of rumours, and I've subscribed to it and that's what I got it for, that's the sort of rumour it is. Here, here, read this."

And she held out to Alyosha a sheet of newspaper which she had kept under her pillow.

She was not so much upset as somehow at a loss, and perhaps everything really had become tangled up in her head. The newspaper item was very typical and, of course, must have affected her in a highly embarrassing way. But, fortunately, she was incapable of concentrating on any single subject at a time, and so might forget all about the newspaper paragraph in a minute and switch over to something else. Alyosha had known for some time that the dreadful trial had become a *cause célèbre* all over Russia, and the Lord alone knew what wild reports and newspaper stories about his brother, the Karamazovs and even about himself he had read during those two months among other truthful reports! One paper even reported that he had been so horrified by his brother's crime that he had entered a monastery and become a hermit; another refuted this report and stated that he and Father Zossima had "absconded" with the monastery funds. The report in *Rumours* was headlined: "From Skotoprigonyevsk* (alas, that is the name of our town,

*Literally: a centre of the cattle trade.—*Tr.*

316

which I have so long concealed): the Karamazov Trial". The brief item did not mention Madame Khokhlakov by name and, in fact, no names were mentioned at all. It was merely stated that the accused, whose impending trial had created such a sensation, was a retired army captain of arrogant manners, a bully, and a feudal-minded idler, who engaged in all sorts of love affairs and had a special fascination for "certain ladies pining in solitary boredom". One such lady, a pining widow, who did her best to look young though she had a grown-up daughter, had been so fascinated by him that, only two hours before the murder, she had offered him three thousand roubles provided he made off with her to the gold-mines. But the villain had preferred to murder and rob his father and so get the three thousand he needed so badly, hoping to escape punishment rather than make for Siberia with the bored lady, with her middle-aged charms. This playful report concluded, as was to be expected, by expressing the correspondent's high-minded indignation at the parricide's immorality and the recently abolished institution of serf-ownership. Alyosha read the story with interest and, folding the sheet, returned it to Madame Khokhlakov.

"Well, it is me, isn't it?" she prattled on, "it must be me, for almost an hour previously I suggested the idea of gold-mines to him, and now this sudden mention of 'middle-aged charms'! That wasn't why I suggested it to him, was it? The correspondent acted on purpose! May the Eternal Judge forgive him for 'the middle-aged charms' as I forgive him, for it is—you know who it is, don't you? It's your friend Rakitin."

"Perhaps," said Alyosha, "though I've heard nothing about it."

"It's he, he, there's no 'perhaps' about it! You see, I told him I'd never be at home to him— You know the story, I suppose."

"I know that you've told him you won't be at home to him any more, but why you did so I—I didn't hear it from you, at any rate."

"Oh, so you heard it from him! Well, does he abuse me? Does he abuse me very much?"

"Yes, he does, but then he abuses everybody. But I haven't

heard from him why you turned him out. I don't see him often now, anyway. We are not on friendly terms."

"Well, in that case I'll tell you all about it and, I suppose, I may as well confess that, on one point, I'm at fault myself. But, mind, only on one small point, so minor that it's hardly worth mentioning. You see, my dear Alyosha" (Madame Khokhlakov suddenly assumed a rather playful air, a charming if enigmatic smile playing about her lips), you see, I suspect—I'm sorry, Alyosha, I'm talking to you like a mother—oh, no, no, I'm talking to you as if you were my own father—because a mother is quite out of place here— Well, let's say just as I would to Father Zossima at confession. Yes, that's it, that fits the occasion very well. I called you a monk just now—well, that poor young man, your friend Rakitin (oh dear, I simply cannot be angry with him! I am angry and mad at him, but not very), in short, that thoughtless young man—just fancy!—suddenly took it into his head to fall in love with me. I noticed it later, only later, but at first, that is, a month ago, he began calling on me more often, almost every day, though we were acquainted before. I didn't suspect anything and—and suddenly the whole thing dawned on me and I began to notice things, to my astonishment— You know that two months ago I began receiving Pyotr Ilyich Perkhotin, that modest, charming, and worthy young man, who is in the civil service here. You met him here many times yourself. And he is a serious and worthy young man, isn't he? He usually calls once every three days and not daily (though I wouldn't mind him coming every day)—and he's always so smart. I'm generally very fond of young people, Alyosha, talented and modest young people, just like you, and he has the mind almost of a statesman. He talks so charmingly, and I'll certainly, most certainly, put in a good word for him. He's a budding diplomat. On that terrible day, he practically saved me from death by coming to see me at night. Well, your friend Rakitin would always come in such awful boots, and he would stretch his legs out on the carpet— In short, he even began making all sorts of hints, and one day, as he was leaving, he suddenly squeezed my hand very hard. And just as he did so, I felt an awful pain in my leg. He had met Pyotr Ilyich before

318

and, you know, he was always jeering at him, always jeering at him. Just growled at him for some reason. I just used to watch them carrying on together and couldn't help laughing inwardly. Well, one day, as I was sitting here alone, no, I mean, lying down alone, Mr. Rakitin came in suddenly and—just fancy!— brought me some verses, a short poem on my bad foot. I mean, a description of my foot in a poem. Stay, how did it run:

> *O little foot, so captivating,*
> *Why should you feel so aching?*

or something like that. I'm afraid I can never remember. I've got it here somewhere, I'll show it to you later. Oh, charming, so charming! And it was not only about my little foot: it was a very edifying too, with a most charming idea, too, only I've forgotten what. In fact, it was just the thing for an album. Well, I naturally thanked him and he seemed flattered. I'd hardly time to thank him when in came Mr. Perkhotin, and Mr. Rakitin suddenly looked as black as thunder. I could see that Mr. Perkhotin had upset his plans, for he certainly wanted to say something after reciting his poem to me. I had a feeling he would, and it was just at that moment that Mr. Perkhotin entered. I at once showed Mr. Perkhotin the poem without telling him who had written it. But I'm sure, quite sure, that he immediately guessed, though he won't admit it to this day, but keeps saying that he didn't know. But he says that on purpose. Well, Mr. Perkhotin immediately burst into laughter and began criticising it: 'What doggerel lines!' he said. 'Must have been written by some seminarist.' And, you know, he was most unsparing! Instead of taking it in good humour, your friend flew into a rage— Good gracious, I thought to myself, they're going to have a fight! 'I wrote it,' Mr. Rakitin said, 'I wrote it as a joke, for I consider the writing of poetry degrading— But my verses are good. There's a plan to erect a monument to your Pushkin for his verses on women's feet, but my verses contain an idea, while you,' he said, 'you're a supporter of serf-ownership. You lack all humane sentiments. You hold none of the modern enlightened ideas; present-day political development has passed

319

you by,' he said. 'You're a civil servant,' he said, 'and you accept bribes!' Well, at this point I raised my voice and begged them to desist. But, you know, Mr. Perkhotin, who is far from timid, suddenly adopted a most gentlemanly tone: he looked sarcastically at him, listened and apologised: 'I'm sorry,' he said, 'I didn't know it was you. Had I known, I'd have praised it. Poets,' he said, 'are all so susceptible—' In short, such derision and delivered in a most genteel way. He later explained to me that he had said it all ironically, and I thought he really meant it! Well, as I lay there, just like now, I thought to myself: would it or would it not be ladylike if I turned Mr. Rakitin out for being so boorish to a caller at my house. And—would you believe it?—I lay with closed eyes thinking whether it would be ladylike or not, and could not make my mind up: it was such a torment; I was tormented and my heart was beating so, but I just couldn't make up my mind whether to scream or not. One voice kept telling me: 'Scream,' and another: 'No, don't scream!' But the moment the other voice had said it, I suddenly screamed and swooned. Well, of course, there was a terrible to-do. Then I got up and said to Mr. Rakitin: 'I'm sorry but I don't be at home to you in future.' So I turned him out. Oh, dear Alexei Fyodorovich! I know I was wrong. I was lying, for I wasn't angry with him at all. But I suddenly fancied, yes, suddenly—that's the main thing—that it would make such a wonderful scene— Only, you know, the scene was quite natural, because I even burst into tears, and I cried for several days afterwards, and then, after dinner one day, I suddenly forgot all about it. So he has not called during the past fortnight, and I can't help wondering whether he will call again. That was yesterday, and in the evening the *Rumours* arrived. I read it, and gasped. Who could have written it? Why, he, of course. He went home that afternoon, sat down and wrote it, sent it off and—it was published. You see, it only happened a fortnight ago. Only, Alyosha, goodness, what am I saying? What I say is horrifying, but I don't say what I should, do I? Oh dear, I just can't help it!"

"I simply must hurry off to see my brother," Alyosha murmured.

"Of course, of course! You've brought it all back to me! Listen, what is meant by 'of unsound mind?'"

"What unsound mind?" asked the surprised Alyosha.

"I mean a plea of unsound mind. The kind for which all is forgiven. Whatever you do—you are acquitted at once."

"What do you mean?"

"Here's what I mean—that Katya— Oh, what a charming girl she is, only I can't for the life of me make out who she is in love with. She came to see me recently and I couldn't get anything out of her. Particularly as she only speaks to me so superficially nowadays, I mean, such things as my health and nothing else, and in such tone, too. Well, I said to myself: 'All right, let it be if that's what you want—' Oh yes, the plea of unsound mind: that's why the doctor has come. You know that a doctor has come, don't you? Of course, you do, he's a specialist in mental disorders; you sent for him yourself, I mean, no, not you, but Katya. It's always Katya! Well, you see, a man may be perfectly sane, and suddenly he has an attack of temporary insanity. He may be fully aware of what he is doing, and yet he's of unsound mind. Well, you see, Dmitri Fyodorovich was probably of unsound mind at the time. You see, as soon as our new courts were set up, they at once discovered all about temporary insanity. That's a great benefit conferred by the new law-court system. The doctor came to see me and he kept questioning me about that evening, about the gold-mines, I mean: what was he like then? Why, of course, he was of unsound mind at the time: he came in and started shouting: 'Money, money, three thousand, let me have three thousand!' And then he went away and suddenly committed the murder. 'I don't want to commit murder,' he said, and off he went and did it. That's why he'll be acquitted—because he was trying to overcome the urge, and yet committed murder."

"But he didn't murder him," Alyosha interrupted her a little sharply. He was getting more and more overcome by a sense of unease and impatience.

"I know. It's the old man Grigori who killed him—"

"What d'you mean? Grigori?" cried Alyosha.

"Yes, yes! It was Grigori. He got that knock on the head

321

from Dmitri Fyodorovich, and then got up, saw the open door, went in and murdered Fyodor Pavlovich—"

"But why, why?"

"Because he was of unsound mind. Dmitri Fyodorovich hit him over the head; he came to, suffered an attack of temporary insanity, went and killed him. And if he says he didn't, it's perhaps because he doesn't remember. Only, you see, it will be better, much better, if Dmitri Fyodorovich murdered him. As a matter of fact, that's who did it, though I say it was Grigori, but it was certainly Dmitri Fyodorovich and it's better so, much better! Oh, it isn't better because a son has killed his father: I'm not in favour of that at all: children should, on the contrary, honour their parents. But it's better all the same if it should be he, for then you'll have no cause for mourning, for he did it without being aware of what he was doing, or rather, aware of everything but without realising what was happening to him. Yes, let them acquit him: it's so humane, and besides it's good for people to see the benefits of the new legal system. I knew nothing about it, but I'm told it's been in force for quite a long time and when I learnt of it yesterday, I was so struck by it that I wanted to send for you at once. And if he's forgiven, bring him straight from the courtroom to have dinner with me, and I'll invite my friends and we'll toast the new courts. I don't think he'd be dangerous, do you? Besides, I'll invite a large number of friends, so that if he does start something, he can always be taken away, and then he may perhaps become a Justice of the Peace or something in another town, for people who've been in trouble themselves make the best judges. And, anyway, who is not of unsound mind nowadays? You, I, and everyone else is of unsound mind, and there have been so many examples of it: here a man is singing a love song: suddenly something displeases him, he pulls out a pistol and kills the first person he meets, and then he's forgiven completely. I read about that recently, and all the doctors confirmed it. The doctors are doing that now; all of them are confirming it. Why, my Lise is also temporarily of unsound mind. She reduced me to tears yesterday and the day before, but today I realised that she was simply temporarily insane. Oh, Lise makes me so unhappy! I'm sure she must be quite insane. Why has she sent for you? Did she send for you, or have you come to see her on your own?"

"Yes, she sent for me and I'm going to her now," said Alyosha, getting up resolutely.

"Oh, dear, dear Alexei Fyodorovich, that is perhaps the main thing," cried Madame Khokhlakov, suddenly bursting into tears. "God knows that I can trust Lise with you and it doesn't matter a bit that she sent for you without telling her mother about it. But I'm sorry to say I don't trust your brother Ivan Fyodorovich with my daughter so easily, though I still think him a most chivalrous young man. And yet, you know, he's been to see Lise and I knew nothing about it."

"Has he? When? How?" Alyosha asked, looking greatly surprised. He did not resume his seat, but listened standing.

"I'll tell you, for, perhaps, that's why I've asked you to come; you see, I don't really know myself why I've done so. What happened was this: Ivan Fyodorovich came to see me only twice after he returned from Moscow. The first time was simply a courtesy call, and the second call was quite recent. Katya was here and he came because he heard she was here. I naturally did not expect him to call so often, for I knew how busy he was, as it is; *vous comprenez cette affaire et la mort terrible de vôtre papa,* but all of a sudden I learnt that he'd been here again, only to see Lise, not me. That was six days ago. He came, and left five minutes afterwards. I learnt of it three days later from Glafira, so it came as a great shock to me. I sent for Lise at once, but she just laughed it off: he thought, she said, that you were asleep, so he came to ask me how you were. Well, that's what it was, of course. Only Lise, Lise, goodness, how she upsets me! Just fancy, one night, four days ago, just after you had left the last time you saw her, she suddenly had a fit. Cries, screaming, and hysterics! Why don't I ever have hysterics? The next day she had another fit, and the day after another and yesterday, yesterday that attack of temporary insanity. She suddenly shouted at me: 'I hate Ivan Fyodorovich and I demand that you shouldn't receive him! I want you to tell him never to call again!' I was dumbfounded at such an unexpected outburst and I said to her: 'Why should I refuse to receive such an excellent young man who is, besides, so knowledgeable and so unhappy?' For, after all, such experiences are a misfortune rather than happiness, aren't they? She suddenly burst out laughing at my words and, you know, so offensively. Well, I was glad, because I thought I had made her laugh and her fits would pass off, particularly as I myself had a mind to tell Ivan Fyodorovich not to call again, on account of his strange visits without my consent, and to demand an explanation. Only this morning Lise woke up and was annoyed with Yulia and—just fancy!—struck her across the face. But that's monstrous, for, you know, I'm always very civil to my servants. Then, suddenly, an hour later, she was embracing Yulia and kissing her feet. And she sent a message to me that she wasn't coming to see me and would never come to see me again, and when I dragged myself off to her, she started crying and kissing me and, while kissing me, pushed me out of the room without saying a word, so that I couldn't learn anything. Now, dear Alexei Fyodorovich, I pin all my hopes on you, and it goes without saying that my life is entirely in your hands. I simply beg you to go to Lise now, find everything out from her as only you know how to, and come back and tell me, her mother. For, you understand, I shall die, I shall simply die, if this goes on, or I shall run away from home. I can bear it no longer. I have some patience, but it may run out, and then—then something horrible may happen! Oh, dear me, here's Mr. Perkhotin at last!" cried Madame Khokhlakov, beaming, as she saw Perkhotin enter the room. "You're late! You're so late! Well, do sit down, please. Speak, put me out of my suspense. Well, what is that lawyer doing now? Where are you off to, Alexei Fyodorovich?"

"To see Lise."

"Oh, yes! So you won't forget what I asked you, will you? So much depends on it."

"Of course I won't forget if only it's possible—but I'm afraid I'm terribly late as it is," murmured Alyosha, beating a hasty retreat.

"No, you must, you must come and tell me, and not 'if

it's possible', or it'll be the death of me!" Madame Khokhlakov called after him, but Alyosha had already left the
room.

3.

The Little Imp

On entering Lise's room he found her half-reclining in the
easy chair she had been wheeled about in while still unable to
walk. She did not attempt to rise to meet him, but her keen
eyes were fixed on him intently. They were somewhat inflamed
and her face was pale and sallow. Alyosha was surprised to see
her so changed in three days: she even looked thinner. She did
not hold out her hand to him. He himself touched her long,
slender fingers which lay motionless on her dress, then sat
down silently opposite her.

"I know," Lise said sharply, "that you are in a hurry to get
to the prison, and that Mother has kept you for two hours and
has just been telling you about me and Yulia."

"How do you know that?" asked Alyosha.

"I was eavesdropping. Why are you staring at me like that?
If I want to eavesdrop, I do so. There's nothing bad about that.
I have no regrets at all."

"Are you upset over something?"

"On the contrary, I'm very pleased. I've just been thinking
for the hundredth time how lucky it is that I've rejected you
and won't become your wife. You're no good as a husband:
if I were to marry you and give you a note to take to the man I
fell in love with after you, you'd take it and most certainly deliver it and come back with his reply. And even when you're
forty, you'd still be carrying such notes for me."

She suddenly laughed.

"There's something spiteful and at the same time naive about
you," Alyosha smiled at her.

"The only thing that's naive about me is that I feel no
shame with you. Moreover, I don't want to feel ashamed with

you, you in particular. Alyosha, why don't I respect you? I love you very much, but have no respect for you. If I respected you, I wouldn't have said that without being ashamed, would I?"

"You wouldn't."

"And do you believe that I'm not ashamed of you?"

"No, I don't."

Lise again laughed nervously. She was talking very rapidly.

"I sent your brother Dmitri Fyodorovich some sweets in prison. Alyosha, you know, you're so nice! I'll love you awfully for having so quickly permitted me not to love you."

"Why did you send for me today, Lise?"

"I wanted to tell you a certain wish of mine. I wish someone would rend me to pieces, marry me and then rend me to pieces, and then jilt me. I don't want to be happy!"

"Have you developed a liking for disorder?"

"Oh, what I want is confusion. I keep wanting to set fire to the house. I keep imagining how I'd go and set fire to it by stealth. Yes, it must be done by stealth. They'll be trying to put it out, but it will go on burning. And I'll know and say nothing. Oh, what nonsense! And how boring it is!"

She waved her hand with disgust.

"Yours is too pampered a life," Alyosha said quietly.

"Would it be better if I were poor?"

"Yes, it would."

"That's what your late monk told you. It's not true. So what if I'm rich and all the rest are poor? I'll be eating sweets and drinking cream and give nothing away to anyone. Oh, not a word!" she waved her hand; though Alyosha never opened his mouth, "don't say anything; you've told me all before, I know it all by heart. It's such a bore. If I'm poor, I'll murder someone—and if I'm rich, I'll do the same. What's the use of sitting about and doing nothing! And you know what I want? I want to reap, to reap rye. I'll marry you and you'll become a peasant. A real peasant. We'll keep a colt. Would you like that? Do you know Kalganov?"

"I do."

"He's such a dreamer. He says: what's the use of actually

living; it's much better to dream. One can dream the gayest things, while to live is a bore. And yet he's going to be married soon. He had already made declaration of love to me. Can you spin peg-tops?"

"I can."

"Well, he's just like a peg-top: wind him up and make him spin, and then keep lashing at him, keep lashing at him with a whip. If I marry him, I shall spin him round and round all his life long. You're not ashamed to sit with me, are you?"

"No."

"You're awfully angry because I don't talk about sacred matters. I don't want to. What awaits you in the world to come for the greatest sin? You should know all about it."

"God will punish you," Alyosha said, looking at her closely.

"Well, that's just what I want. I'd come and be punished, and I'd suddenly burst out laughing in their faces. Oh, I do so want to set a house on fire, Alyosha, our house. You don't believe me?"

"Why not? There are children of twelve who long to set fire to something. And they do. It's a sort of disease."

"It isn't true! It isn't true! There may be such children, but I'm not talking about that."

"You take evil for good: it's a passing crisis. Your former illness may be the reason."

"So you do despise me, after all! I simply don't want to do good. I want to do evil. And it has nothing to do with my illness."

"But why do evil?"

"For nothing to be left anywhere. Oh, how nice it would be if nothing was left! You know, Alyosha, sometimes I think of doing a lot of evil and everything that's bad, and I'd do it for a long time by stealth, and suddenly everyone would learn of it. They would all surround me and point at me, and I'd look back at them all. That would be very nice. Why would it be so nice, Alyosha?"

"Oh, I expect it's just a craving to crush something good or, as you said, to set fire to it. That, too, happens."

"I wasn't merely saying it: I'm going to do it."

"I believe you."

"Oh, how I love you for saying that you believe me. And you're not lying. You're not lying at all. Or do you think perhaps that I'm saying all this to you on purpose, just to tease you?"

"No, I don't think so—though, I daresay, there's a little of that, too."

"There is a little. I shall never lie to you," she said, a strange flash in her eyes.

Alyosha was more and more struck by her earnestness: there was not a trace of mockery or jesting in her face now, though gaiety and jesting had never deserted her even at her gravest moments.

"There are moments when people just love crime," Alyosha said thoughtfully.

"Yes, yes! You've expressed just what I think. They all love it; they always love it, and not only at moments. You know: it's as though everyone once agreed to lie about it, and they have been lying about it ever since. They all say they hate evil, but in their heart of hearts they all love it."

"And you still read evil books?"

"Yes, I do. Mother reads them and keeps them under her pillow and I steal them."

"And aren't you ashamed to be destroying yourself?"

"I want to destroy myself. There's a boy here who lay down on the railway track and the train passed over him. What a lucky boy! Listen, your brother is being tried for murdering his father, but they all love his having killed his father."

"Love his having killed his father?"

"Yes, they all love it! They all say it's horrible, but in their hearts they love it. I, for one, love it."

"There's some truth in what you say about them all," said Alyosha quietly.

"Oh, what wonderful thoughts you have!" Lise shrieked in delight. "And you a monk! You can't believe how I respect you, Alyosha, for never telling a lie. Oh, I'll tell you a very funny dream I had! I sometimes dream of devils. It's night, I'm in my candle-lit room, and suddenly there are devils everywhere, in all the corners and under the table, and they open the doors, and behind the doors there are crowds of them, and they all want to come in and seize me. And they are already coming near and taking hold of me. But suddenly I cross myself and they all draw back in fear, only they don't go away, but stand near the door and in the corners, waiting. And then I'm suddenly overcome by a desire to begin cursing God in a loud voice, and I begin cursing Him and they all rush at me again in a crowd. They're so pleased, and they're again about to lay hands on me, and I cross myself again—and they draw back at once. It's great fun. Oh, it's breath-taking."

"I've had the same dream, too," Alyosha said suddenly.

"Have you?" Lise cried in surprise. "Listen, Alyosha, don't make fun of me—it's awfully important: is it possible for two different people to have the same dream?"

"I suppose it is."

"Alyosha, I'm telling you this is awfully important," Lise went on in a kind of intense astonishment. "It isn't the dream that is important, but that you should have had the same dream as me. You've never lied to me, so don't lie to me now. Is it true? You're not joking?"

"It's true."

Lise was so struck by something that she was silent for half a minute.

"Alyosha, do come and see me, come and see me more often," she said suddenly in a beseeching voice.

"I shall always come to see you, all my life," replied Alyosha firmly.

"You see, I'm telling this to you alone," Lise began again. "I'm telling it to myself and to you. To you alone in the whole world. And more readily to you than to myself. And I feel no shame with you, none at all. Alyosha, why is that? None at all! Alyosha, is it true that Jews kidnap children at Easter and kill them?"

"I don't know."

"I read it in a book about a trial somewhere, and that a Jew cut off a four-year-old child's fingers on both hands, and then crucified him, nailed him to a wall, and then said at his trial that the boy died soon, within four hours. Soon, indeed! He said the boy kept moaning and that he stood there enjoying it. That's good!"

"Good?"

"Good. I sometimes imagine that it was I who crucified him. He would hang on the wall and moan and I'd sit opposite him and eat pineapple compote. I'm awfully fond of pineapple compote. Are you?"

Alyosha looked at her in silence. Her pale, sallow face became suddenly distorted and her eyes glowed.

"You know, when I read about that Jew, I shook with sobs all night. I kept imagining how the little boy screamed and moaned (four-year-old boys understand, you know), and the thought of that pineapple compote kept hammering in my brain. Next morning I sent a letter to a man, telling him that he *must* come and see me. He did and I told him about the boy and the pineapples, told him *everything, everything,* and said that it was 'good'. He suddenly laughed and said that it was really good. Then he got up and left, after staying for only five minutes. Did he despise me? Did he? Tell me, tell me, Alyosha, did he or didn't he despise me?" she asked with flashing eyes, sitting up straight on the settee.

"Tell me," Alyosha said agitatedly, "did you send for that man yourself?"

"Yes."

"You wrote to him?"

"I did."

"Just to ask him about that, about the child?"

"No, not about that at all. Not at all about that. But when he came, I asked him at once. He replied, laughed and went away."

"That man behaved decently to you," Alyosha said softly.

"But did he despise me? Did he laugh at me?"

"No, because I suppose he believes in the pineapple compote himself. He, too, is a very sick man, Lise."

"So he does believe in it!" cried Lise with flashing eyes.

"He despises no one," Alyosha went on. "He merely doesn't believe anyone. But if he doesn't believe, that expresses his contempt too."

"So he despises me, too? Me?"

"You, too."

"That's good," Lise cried, grinding her teeth. "When he went out and laughed, I felt that it was good to be despised. And the boy with the cut-off fingers is good, and it's good to be despised."

And she laughed in Alyosha's face with a sort of feverish malice.

"Do you know, Alyosha, do you know, I'd like— Alyosha, save me!" she cried, suddenly jumping up from the settee and, rushing up to him, she flung her arms tightly round him. "Save me," she almost moaned. "Would I have said what I told you just now to anyone else in the world? And I was speaking the truth, the truth, the whole truth! I'll kill myself because everything is so loathsome to me! I don't want to go on living because everything is so loathsome to me! Everything is loathsome to me, everything! Alyosha, why don't you love me at all?" she concluded in a frenzy.

"I do love you!" Alyosha replied warmly.

"And will you weep for me? Will you?"

"I will."

"Not because I didn't want to be your wife, but simply weep for me? Simply?"

"I will."

"Thank you! All I want is your tears. Let the others punish me and trample me underfoot, everyone, everyone, with *no* exception! Because I love no one. You hear, no one! On the contrary, I hate. Go now, Alyosha, it's time you went to see your brother!" She suddenly tore herself away from him.

"But how can I leave you like this?" Alyosha said almost in alarm.

"Go to your brother. The prison will be closed. Go! Here's your hat. Give Mitya my love. Go, go!"

And she almost pushed Alyosha out of the door. Alyosha looked at her in mournful perplexity, when he suddenly felt that a letter had been thrust into his hand, a little note, folded up tightly and sealed. He looked at it and instantly read the inscription: "To Ivan Fyodorovich Karamazov". He glanced at

Lise, her face grew almost stern.

"Give it to him! Be sure to give it to him!" she ordered him in a frenzy, all of a tremble. "Today! At once! Or else I'll take poison! That's why I sent for you!"

And she slammed the door. The bolt was shot violently. Pocketing the letter, Alyosha went straight downstairs without going to see Madame Khokhlakov, indeed forgetting all about her. As soon as Alyosha was gone, Lise unbolted the door, opened it a little, inserted a finger in the crack and, slamming the door, got her finger squeezed there with all the force at her command. Releasing the finger some ten seconds later, she went back to her chair slowly and quietly, sat up erect in it, and began intently to examine her blackened finger and the blood oozing from under the nail. Her lips quivered, and she whispered rapidly to herself:

"What a low-down creature I am, quite, quite low-down!"

4.

A Hymn and a Secret

It was very late (the days are short in November) when Alyosha rang at the prison gate. Dusk was falling. But Alyosha knew that he would be admitted to Mitya without difficulty. Things in our town are just like anywhere else. At first, of course, after the preliminary investigation, certain formalities were still observed in admitting relatives and a few other people to see Mitya, but later it was not so much that the formalities were relaxed as certain exceptions were made for at least some visitors to Mitya. Indeed, even the interviews with Mitya in a room set aside for the purpose sometimes took place without any warder being present. However, there were not many persons who enjoyed the privilege: only Grushenka, Alyosha, and Rakitin. But the uyezd chief of police Makarov was very favourably disposed towards Grushenka: the old man could not forgive himself for having yelled at her in Mokroye. Then, on learning everything, he had completely changed his opinion of her.

And, strange to say, though he was firmly convinced of Mitya's guilt, he had begun regarding him more and more tolerantly since he had been taken into custody. "He's probably a good fellow at bottom," he thought, "but he has ruined himself with drinking and a disorderly life!" His former abhorrence yielded to pity. As for Alyosha, the uyezd chief of police was very fond of him and had known him a long time; Rakitin, who had taken to visiting Mitya very frequently, was a close friend of Makarov's daughters, his "young ladies", as he called them, and was always to be found at their house. Furthermore, he gave lessons at the home of the prison governor, a good-natured old man, though a great stickler for formalities. Alyosha, on the other hand, was an old and particular friend of the prison governor, who liked to discuss "elevated" subjects with him. The prison governor, for instance, did not so much respect as fear Ivan Fyodorovich Karamazov, and, chiefly, his opinions, though he was a great philosopher himself, having reached his conclusions "through his own reasoning". But he, somehow, felt powerfully drawn to Alyosha. During the last year the old man had happened to devote himself to the study of the Apocrypha and he constantly discussed his impressions with his young friend. He had even got used to seeing him at the monastery and talking to him and the monks for hours on end. In short, even if Alyosha were late, he had only to go and see the prison governor and everything would be arranged. Besides, everyone in prison, down to the last warder, had got used to Alyosha. The sentries, of course, did not interfere with him so long as he had official permission. Whenever summoned from his cell, Mitya always went downstairs to the room where interviews were held. As he was entering the room, Alyosha ran into Rakitin, who was about to leave Mitya. The two were talking loudly. Mitya was roaring with laughter as he was seeing Rakitin out, while the latter seemed to be grumbling. Rakitin had avoided meeting Alyosha, especially of late; he scarcely spoke to him and even bowed to him stiffly. When he saw Alyosha coming in, he frowned and looked away, as though absorbed with buttoning his big warm fur-collared overcoat. Then he began looking for his umbrella.

"Mustn't mislay anything," he muttered, simply to say something.

"Don't forget somebody else's things," Mitya joked and at once burst out laughing at his own witticism.

Rakitin flared up at once.

"Give such advice to your Karamazovs, you spawn of a serf-owner, and not to Rakitin!" he cried suddenly, trembling in rage.

"What's the matter? I was only joking!" cried Mitya. "Oh, to hell with it! They're all like that," he said addressing Alyosha, and nodding towards Rakitin, who had rushed out of the room. "A moment ago he was sitting here, looking cheerful and laughing, and now he suddenly flies into a rage! Didn't even nod to you. Have you fallen out with him completely? Why are you so late? I've not been so much waiting as longing for you all morning. But never mind! We'll make up for it now."

"But why does he come to see you so often?" asked Alyosha, nodding towards the door through which Rakitin had disappeared. "You haven't become so friendly, have you?"

"Friendly with Mikhail? No, not really. And, besides, he's a bloody swine! Thinks I'm— a blackguard. Such people can't see a joke, either. That's the main thing about them. Never see a joke. And they have arid souls, too, arid and drab, just as mine was when I was being driven up to the prison and looked at the prison walls. But he's a smart fellow, quite smart. Well, Alexei, it's all over with me now!"

He sat down on the bench, seating Alyosha beside him.

"Yes, the trial opens tomorrow. You haven't given up all hope, have you, Mitya?" asked Alyosha, timidly.

"What's that?" asked Mitya, looking rather vaguely at him. "Oh, the trial! Oh, to hell with it! Till now you and I've been speaking about all kinds of trivial things, that trial, for instance, but I said nothing to you about the most important thing. Yes, the trial begins tomorrow, but I didn't have the trial in mind when I said it was all over with me. It's not I who am done for, but what's in me that's gone, finished, done for. Why are you looking me in the face so critically?"

"What do you mean, Mitya?"

"Ideas, ideas, that's what it is! Ethics. But what is ethics?"

"Ethics?" Alyosha repeated in surprise.

"Yes. Is it a science?"

"Yes, there is such a science—only I'm afraid I can't tell you what kind of science it is."

"But Rakitin knows. He knows a lot, does Rakitin, damn him! *He* won't become a monk. He's planning to go to St. Petersburg. There, he says, he'll be working as a critic, but a critic with an elevated trend. Well, I suppose he may prove useful and make a career for himself, too. Oh, they're all great at making careers! To hell with ethics! It's all over with me, Alexei, you godly fellow! I love you more than anyone else. My heart aches for you—that's how it is. But who was Karl Bernard?"

"Karl Bernard?" Alyosha was surprised again.

"No, not Karl—my mistake! Claude Bernard. What was he? A chemist or what?"

"He's some kind of scientist, I suppose," replied Alyosha. "Only I'm afraid I can't tell you much about him, either. I've heard he was a scientist, but I don't know what kind."

"Well, to hell with him, too," Mitya swore. "I don't know, either. A blackguard of some sort, most likely. They're all blackguards. But Rakitin will worm his way through; he'll crawl through a crack—he's just another Bernard. Oh, these Bernards! They exist in their thousands!"

"But what's the matter with you?" Alyosha persisted.

"He wants to write an article about me, about my case, and so launch his literary career. That's what he comes here for, he told me so himself. He wants to write something with a definite trend: 'He couldn't help committing a murder, for he was a victim of his environment', and so on. He explained it to me. It will have a dash of socialism, he says. Well, damn him. If he wants that dash, let him add it, I don't care. He dislikes Ivan, hates him, in fact, and he is not particularly nice about you, either. Well, I don't kick him out, because he's a clever chap. Thinks a lot of himself, though. I was telling him just now: 'The Karamazovs aren't cads, but philosophers, for all genuine Russians are philosophers, but no matter how much you may have studied, you're not a philosopher, but a menial fellow.' He laughed back. Maliciously. And I said to him: *De ideabus non est disputandum—de ideabus* is good, isn't it? At least, I've taken up classical studies too," Mitya suddenly burst out laughing.

"But how is it all over with you? Wasn't that what you said just now?" Alyosha put in.

"Why is it over with me? H'm! Well, as a matter of fact, if—if you take it in its entirety—I feel sorry for God, that's why!"

"What do you mean—sorry for God?"

"Well, imagine: the nerves, in the head, I mean, the nerves in the brain (oh, damn 'em!) have sort of little tails, and, well, as soon as these little tails start wiggling—that is, you see, if I look at something with my eyes, like that, and they start wiggling—the little tails, I mean—and as soon as they begin wiggling, an image appears, not at once but after an instant, a fraction of a second, a kind of moment comes—no, not a moment—to hell with the moment—an image, that is, an object or an event, or whatever it is—damn it—so that's why I contemplate and then think—all because of the little tails, and not at all because I have a soul, and have been created in somebody's image and likeness—all that's nonsense. That's what Rakitin explained to me yesterday, and it simply flabbergasted me. Splendid, Alyosha, there's science for you! A new man is emerging. That I understand— Yet I do feel sorry for God!"

"Well, that's a good thing, at least," said Alyosha.

"My feeling sorry for God? That's all chemistry, brother, chemistry! Can't be helped, your reverence, move up a little, make way for chemistry! Rakitin doesn't love God—oh, how he dislikes him! That's the sorest spot with all of them! But they conceal it: they lie and make pretence. 'Well,' I asked him, 'will you develop these ideas in your critical articles?' 'I don't think I'll be allowed to,' he said, laughing. 'But,' I asked, 'what's to become of man then? Without God and without a future life? Why, in that case, everything is permitted. You can do whatever you like!' 'Didn't you know that?' he said and laughed. 'A clever man,' he said, 'can do whatever he pleases. A clever man knows how to make his way. But you,' he said, 'have made a mess of things; you've committed a murder and you're rotting in prison!' He says that to me, the swine! I used to kick such fellows out, but now I listen to them. You see, much of what he says makes sense. Damn clever at writing, too. A week ago he began reading an article to me and I copied three lines out of it. Just a moment. Here it is."

Mitya took a piece of paper hurriedly out of his waistcoat pocket and read out:

" 'To solve this problem, one must first of all bring one's personality into opposition with one's reality.' Do you understand that?'

"No, I don't," said Alyosha.

He gazed closely at Mitya and listened to him with curiosity.

"I don't understand it, either. It's unclear and obscure, but damn clever. 'They all write like that,' he says, 'because such is the environment.'—They fear the environment. He writes poetry, too, the scoundrel. He's written one in praise of Madame Khokhlakov's little foot, ha, ha, ha!"

"I've heard of it," said Alyosha.

"Have you? And have you heard that miserable poem?"

"No."

"I've got it. Here it is. I'll read it to you. You don't know, for I haven't told you, but it's quite a story. The rogue! Three weeks ago he set about nettling me. 'You,' he said, 'have got yourself into a hell of a mess like a fool, and all for three thousand roubles, but I'm going to rake in a cool hundred and fifty thousand. I'm going to marry a young widow and I'll buy a big house in St. Petersburg.' And he's told me he's paying court to Madame Khokhlakov, who hadn't much sense even in her youth, and now at forty had lost what little sense she ever had. 'Yes,' he says, 'she's very sensitive and that's how I'm going to hook her. I'll marry her, take her to St. Petersburg and start a paper there.' And there was such disgusting and lickerish spittle on his lips—his mouth was watering, not for Madame Khokhlakov but for her hundred and fifty thousand. And he made me believe in it. He really did. Came to see me every day. 'She is giving way,' he kept saying, actually beaming with delight. And then all of a sudden he was shown the door: Perkhotin

337

got the better of him, stout fellow! I mean, I could kiss that fool of a woman for having kicked Rakitin out! Well, it was while he was visiting me that he made up that feeble little poem. 'It's the first poem I've soiled my hands with writing,' he said. 'But it's to win a woman over, and, therefore, for something useful. Having got hold of the silly woman's fortune, I'll be able to be of some use to my fellow-citizens.' You see, such people justify every abomination they commit by referring to their duty to society! 'And anyway,' he said, 'it's a sight better than anything Pushkin ever wrote, for I've managed to shovel civic appeal into my ridiculous poem.' I understand what he means about Pushkin. So what if he really had talent and wrote about women's feet! And how he preened himself on his stupid verses! The vanity of these fellows—the vanity! *On My Dear One's Recovery from a Bad Foot*—that's the sort of title he thought up—quite a playful fellow is he!

> *A captivating little foot—how sweet!*
> *But swollen and tender and red.*
> *The doctors call and seek to treat—*
> *The quacks, it must be said.*

> *'Tis not for the feet that I dread,*
> *Let Pushkin their praises sing:*
> *What gets me under is her head*
> *And the ideas that no bells ring.*

> *For the worse the foot, strange to say,*
> *Her thinking begins to wane.*
> *It's for some remedy that I pray*
> *To restore both foot and brain.*

A swine, a regular swine, but he's put it very playfully, the rascal! And, to be sure, he did shovel in 'the civic appeal'. And how furious he was when she kicked him out! He was grinding his teeth!"

"He's had his revenge already," said Alyosha. "He's sent in a story to a paper about Madame Khokhlakov."

And Alyosha told him briefly about the report in the *Rumours*.

"It's him, him!" Mitya agreed, frowning. "It's him all right! These newspaper stories—I know—the horrible things that have been written about Grushenka, for instance! And about the other one—about Katya—h'm!"

He paced the room, looking much concerned.

"I can't stay long, Mitya," said Alyosha after a pause. "Tomorrow will be a great, an awful day for you: the judgement of God will be pronounced on you and—and I can't help feeling surprised at you. You pace the room and instead of talking of what really concerns you, you go on talking about goodness only knows what—"

"No, don't be surprised at me," Mitya interrupted impulsively. "What do you want me to do? Talk about the stinking cur—the murderer? We've talked enough about it already. I don't want to talk any more of the stinking son of Smelly Lizaveta! God will kill him, you will see. But enough of that!"

All worked up, he went up to Alyosha and, suddenly, kissed him. His eyes were shining.

"Rakitin wouldn't understand it," he began, in a kind of exaltation, "but you, you will understand everything. That's why I longed for you so much. You see, I've been wanting to tell you so much for a long time here, within these peeling walls, but I haven't said a word about the most important thing: the time was not ripe for it, somehow. Now the time has come at last for me to reveal my soul to you. During these last two months, brother, I've felt the burgeoning of another man in me—a new man has arisen in me! He was hemmed in, but he would never have emerged but for this bolt from the blue! It's fearful! And what does it matter if I spend twenty years in the mines breaking ore with a pick? I'm not afraid of that at all. It's something else I fear now—that the new man that has arisen within me may depart from me! One can find a human heart there too, in the mines, underground, at your side, in another convict and murderer, and make friends with him. For there, too, one can live and love and suffer! One can revive the frozen heart of such a convict; one can care for him for

339

years and years and at last bring up from that den of evil to the light of day a lofty and long-suffering soul which has become aware of its humanity, restore life to an angel, resurrect a hero! And there are so many of them, hundreds of them, and we are all at fault to them! Why did I dream of that 'bairn' that time? 'Why is the bairn so poor?' That was a sign to me at that moment! It's for the 'bairn' that I'm to suffer. For we are all at fault for everybody and everything. For all the 'bairns', for there are little children and big children. We are all bairns! And I'll accept suffering for all, for someone has to. I did not kill my father, but I've got to accept it. I do so! It all came to me here—within these peeling walls. And there are many of them, hundreds of them there, those who work underground, with picks in their hands. Oh yes, we shall be in chains, and we shall not be free, but then, in our great sorrow we shall arise anew to joyousness, without which man cannot live or God exist, for God gives joy. That's his privilege, his great privilege. O Lord, may man melt in prayer! How can I be there underground without God? Rakitin's lying! Even if God is banished on earth, we shall meet him below the earth! A convict cannot exist without God, even less than a non-convict can! And then we, men of the underground, shall sing forth, from the bowels of the earth, our tragic hymn to God, in whom there is joy! All hail to God and His joy! I love him!"

Mitya was almost gasping for breath in making this wild speech. He was pale, his lips were quivering and tears were streaming down his cheeks.

"No," he began again, "life is overbrimming; there is life even underground! You can't believe, Alexei, how much I want to live now, what a thirst for life and awareness has arisen in me within these peeling walls! Rakitin doesn't understand that. All he wants is to build a house and take in tenants. But I've been awaiting your coming. And, after all, what is suffering? I have no fear of it, however boundless it may be. I have no fear of it now, though I used to. You know, I may not reply to their questions at the trial. And there seems to be so much of that strength in me now that I shall overcome all things, all suffering, so as to say, repeat to myself all the time: I exist! I exist in thousands of agonies; I exist even on the rack! Even in the dungeon I exist; I see the sun, and even if I do not, I know that it is there. And knowing that the sun exists is already the whole of life. Alyosha, my angel, all these different philosophies will be the death of me—to hell with them! Brother Ivan—"

"What about brother Ivan?" Alyosha interrupted, but Mitya was not listening.

"You see, I never had any of these doubts before—they were concealed within me. Perhaps it was just because of all the unfamiliar ideas seething within me that I drank and fought and raged. I fought so as to subdue and crush them. Brother Ivan is not a Rakitin: he harbours an idea. Brother Ivan is a sphinx, and is silent, always silent. But God's tormenting me. That's the only thing that is tormenting me. But what if He doesn't exist? What if Rakitin is right that He is an artificial idea in mankind? For if He doesn't exist, then man is the master of the earth, the universe. How magnificent! But how can he be virtuous without God? That's the question! I'm always returning to that. For who will he love then—I mean man? Who will he be thankful to; who will he sing his hymn to? Rakitin is a mocker. He says that one can love humanity even without a God. Well, that's something only a snotty-nosed runt can assert. I don't understand it. It's easy for Rakitin to go on living: 'You should better give thought to the extension of civil rights,' he said to me today, 'or at least to keeping down in the price of beef. Thereby you'll be showing your love for humanity more simply and directly than by all this philosophising.' To that I retorted: 'But without God, you'll raise the price of beef yourself, given the opportunity, and make a rouble on every copeck.' That made him really angry. Now tell me, Alexei: what is virtue? It means one thing to me and another thing to a Chinese—it's a relative thing. Or isn't it? Isn't it relative? A slippery question! You won't laugh if I tell you it kept me awake for two nights. I only wonder now how people can go on living and not give it thought. It's all vanity! Ivan has no God, but he's got an idea. An idea that is beyond me. But he is silent. I think he must be a freemason. When I ask him—he is silent. I wanted to drink from his fount, but he is silent. Only once did he say something."

"What did he say?" said Alyosha quickly taking up the question.

"I said to him: 'Then everything is permitted, if that's so?' He frowned. 'Our dear father, Fyodor Pavlovich Karamazov,' he said, 'was a swine, but his reasoning was right.' That's the outrageous thing he said, nothing more than that. That's going even farther than Rakitin."

"Indeed," Alyosha agreed bitterly. "When was he here?"

"Of that later. I've something else to tell you now. I've said almost nothing to you about Ivan till now: I've put that off until the end. When my business here is over and the sentence is handed down, I'll tell you something—I'll tell you everything. Something dreadful is brewing here—and you'll be my judge in that. But don't start asking me now, not a word about it. You talk of tomorrow, of the trial, but believe me I know nothing about it."

"Have you spoken to your counsel?"

"Oh, him! I've told him about everything. A suave rogue from St. Petersburg. A Bernard! Only he doesn't believe a word I say. He thinks I did it—imagine! I can see that. 'Why, then,' I asked him, 'have you come to defend me in that case?' To hell with them all. They've also got a doctor from St. Petersburg. Want to prove I'm insane. I won't permit it! Katerina Ivanovna wants to do her 'duty' to the last. Whatever the effort!" Mitya smiled bitterly. "The cat! As hard as nails. She knows I said of her in Mokroye that she is a woman of 'great wrath'! She was told of that. Yes, the facts against me are as numerous as the sands of the sea! Grigori sticks to his story. Grigori is honest, but a fool. Many people are honest because they are fools. That's Rakitin's idea. Grigori's my enemy. There are people that are better to have as enemies than as friends. That refers to Katerina Ivanovna. I'm afraid, oh, terribly afraid, she'll tell them in court about how she bowed low to me after those four thousand five hundred! She'll return that debt down to the uttermost farthing. I don't want her sacrifice! I'll be put to shame at the trial! Oh, well, I'll endure it, somehow. Go to see her, Alyosha, and ask her not to speak of it in court. Or can't you? Oh, to hell with it! It doesn't matter, I'll put up with that, too! I'm

342

not sorry for her. She's asking for it herself, and she'll get what's coming to her, I'll have my say, Alexei." He smiled bitterly again. "Only Grushenka—Grushenka, good Lord! Why should she have to suffer so much now?" he cried suddenly, with tears in his eyes. "It's Grushenka, the thought of her, that's driving me to despair! She came to see me today."

"She told me. She was very much upset by you today."

"I know. Damn my temper! I was jealous! I felt sorry as she was leaving, I kissed her. But I didn't ask for her forgiveness."

"Why didn't you?" exclaimed Alyosha.

Mitya suddenly laughed almost gaily.

"God forfend, my dear boy, your ever asking forgiveness of a woman you love, if you happen to be in the wrong! Particularly from a woman you love. Yes, particularly, however much you may be in the wrong! For, my dear fellow, the devil alone knows what kind of creature a woman is! I know something of them, at any rate. But try to tell a woman that you're in the wrong: 'I'm sorry, it's my fault, forgive me, please'—and you'll get a stream of reproaches! She'll never forgive you simply and frankly, but will grind you into the dust, bring up things that have never even happened, recall any trifle and petty thing, forget nothing, add something of her own, and only then will she forgive you. And that's how the best of them, the best of them, will behave! She'll drag up everything and heap it on your head; they're prepared to flay you alive, I tell you, every one of them, every one of these angels without whom we cannot live! You see, my dear fellow, I'll put it to you in plain and simple words: any decent man has to be under some woman's thumb. That's my conviction—not a conviction, but what I feel. A man must be magnanimous, and that is no disgrace. It won't disgrace even a hero, even a Caesar! But all the same, don't ever ask her forgiveness for anything. Remember this rule: it was given you by your brother Mitya, who's come to ruin through women. No, I'd better make it up with Grushenka somehow without asking for her forgiveness. I worship her, Alexei, I simply worship her! Only she doesn't see it. No, she doesn't believe I love her enough. And she torments me, torments me with her love! It was different before. I used to be

343

tormented only by those infernal curves of hers, but now I've taken all her soul into my own and through her I've become a man myself! Will they marry us? If they don't, I'll die of jealousy. I keep imagining things every day— What did she tell you about me?"

Alyosha repeated everything Grushenka had said to him that day. Mitya listened attentively, asked for a number of points to be repeated, and was satisfied with what he heard.

"So she's not angry with me for being jealous," he exclaimed. "Just like a woman! 'I have a cruel heart myself!' she thinks. Oh, I love such cruel women though I can't stand any jealousy of me! Can't stand it! We'll have our squabbles. But I shall love her—I shall love her infinitely. Will they marry us? Are convicts allowed to marry? That's the question. I can't live without her—"

Mitya frowned as he took a turn round the room. It was getting almost dark in it. He suddenly grew terribly worried.

" 'So there's a secret,' she says, 'a secret? I have the three of them plotting against me,' she says, 'and that Katya woman is involved?' No, Grushenka, old girl, you're on the wrong track. You've made a bloomer here, the usual silly bloomer a woman makes! Alyosha, my dear fellow, oh, all right! I'll tell you our secret!"

He looked round, hurried up close to Alyosha, who was standing before him and began whispering to him with a mysterious air, though actually they could not be overheard: the old warder was dozing in a corner on a bench, and the sentries were too far off to hear anything.

"I shall tell you all our secret!" Mitya whispered hurriedly. "I meant to tell you later, for how could I decide on anything without you? You mean everything to me. Though I say that Ivan stands superior to us, you are like an angel to me. Your decision alone will decide the question. Perhaps it's you who really stands superior to us, and not Ivan. You see, it's a matter of conscience, a matter of supreme conscience—the secret is so important that I could not possibly cope with it myself and I've put it off till I saw you. Still, it's a little too soon to decide now, because we have to wait for the verdict:

as soon as the verdict is given, you will decide my fate. Don't decide now. I'll tell you all about it now; you'll hear me out but don't decide. Just stand and say nothing. I won't tell you everything, just the idea, without any details, and you say nothing. No questions, and no gestures. Agreed? But, good Lord, what shall I do about your eyes? I'm afraid your eyes will betray your decision, even if you are silent. Oh dear, I'm afraid of that! Alyosha, listen: Ivan has suggested that I should *escape*. I won't tell you the details: everything has been taken into account, everything can be arranged. Don't say a word—make no decision. I'll escape to America with Grushenka. I can't live without her! But what if they won't let her go with me? They don't allow convicts to marry, do they? Ivan says they don't. And without Grushenka what can I do there underground with a pick? I could only bash my skull in with a pick! But, on the other hand, what about my conscience? I should have run away from suffering! There was a sign and I rejected it; there was the road of purification and I turned my back on it. Ivan says that, given a good inclination, one can be of more use in America than working underground. But what about our underground hymn? What is America? America is vanity again! And I daresay there's a lot of swindling going on in America, too. So I must run away from my cross! I'm telling you this, Alexei, because you alone can understand it and no one else; to others it's all nonsense, delirium. I mean, all I've told you about the hymn. They'll say that I've gone out of my mind or that I am a fool. But I haven't gone out of my mind and I'm no fool, either. Ivan, too, understands about the hymn, oh, he understands it all right, only he says nothing—he's silent. He doesn't believe in the hymn. Not a word, not a word, I see your expression—you have already decided! Please, don't, spare me, I can't live without Grushenka, let's wait for the trial!"

Mitya concluded, like one in a frenzy. He clutched Alyosha by the shoulders with both hands and stared intently at him with yearning and feverish eyes.

"Convicts aren't allowed to marry, are they?" he repeated beseechingly for the third time.

Deeply shaken, Alyosha listened with intense surprise.

"Tell me something," he said. "Does Ivan insist on it very much? Who was the first to hit on the plan?"

"It was he; he thought of it first, and he insists on it! He never came to see me all the time and then, a week ago, he suddenly came and began straight with it. He insists on it vehemently, not as a request but as a command. He is sure I will do as he tells me, though I opened up my heart to him as I did to you, and spoke to him about the hymn, too. He told me how he was going to arrange it; he has gathered all the information, but of that later. He's dead set on it. The money's the main thing: he's promised to give me ten thousand to escape and twenty thousand for America. 'For ten thousand we'll arrange a wonderful escape for you,' he says."

"And he told you not to let me know on any account?" Alyosha asked again.

"To tell no one, but especially you. Not to tell you on any account! I suppose he's afraid you may confront me as my conscience. Don't tell him I've let you know. For heaven's sake, don't!"

"You're right," Alyosha decided. "No decision is possible before the verdict. After the trial, you'll decide for yourself. Then you'll discover the new man within yourself, and he will decide."

"The new man of a Bernard who'll decide in his Bernard fashion! For it seems to me I'm a contemptible Bernard myself!" Mitya smiled bitterly.

"But have you really lost all hope of proving your innocence?"

Mitya shrugged his shoulders convulsively and shook his head.

"Alyosha, my dear fellow, it's time you were going!" he said, with sudden haste. "I hear the superintendent has called out in the courtyard, and he'll be here soon. We're late and it's against the rules. Embrace me quickly, kiss me and make the sign of the cross over me. Make the sign of the cross over me, my dear, for the cross I have to bear tomorrow—"

They embraced.

"And Ivan," Mitya said suddenly, "has advised me to make

346

a getaway, but he himself believes that I committed the murder!"

A sad smile hovered over his lips.

"Have you asked him whether he believes it?" asked Alyosha.

"No, I haven't. I wanted to, but I couldn't, I couldn't bring myself to. But it made no difference, I could see from his eyes. Well, good-bye!"

They kissed again hurriedly. Alyosha was on the point of leaving when Mitya suddenly called him back.

"Stand here in front of me, please, like that—that's right."

And he again seized Alyosha firmly by the shoulders with both hands. Even in the almost dark room, the ashy pallor that had come over his face was dreadfully discernible. His lips twitched and his eyes were fixed on Alyosha.

"Alyosha, tell me the whole truth as you would to God: do you believe that I did it, or not? Do you believe it in your own heart? The whole truth, don't lie to me!" he cried frantically.

Everything seemed to Alyosha to be heaving and he felt a sharp pang in his heart.

"Good Lord, what are you saying?—" he murmured, quite at a loss.

"The whole truth, and nothing but the truth! Don't lie to me!" Mitya repeated.

"Not for a moment have I ever believed that you are the murderer," the words came tumbling out of Alyosha's breast in a shaking voice, and he raised his right hand as if calling on God to witness that he was speaking the truth. A look of intense happiness suddenly lit up Mitya's face.

"Thank you!" he said slowly, as if sighing after a swoon. "You've made a new man of me— Believe me, till now I dreaded asking you this, you of all people! Well, go, go! You've given me fresh strength for tomorrow, God bless you! Well, go now. Love Ivan!" he cried in parting.

Alyosha left in tears. Such mistrust in Mitya, such lack of confidence even in him, in Alyosha, suddenly revealed to him a depth of hopeless grief and despair in his unhappy brother's soul as he had never suspected before. He was suddenly overcome by feeling of profound and infinite compassion, a feeling that drained him of all strength in an instant. His pierced heart was aching terribly. "Love Ivan!"—he recalled Mitya's recent words. And now he was going to see Ivan. He should really have gone to see Ivan the first thing in the morning. He was anxious for Ivan no less than for Mitya, and more than ever now, after his interview with his brother.

5.

It Wasn't You! It Wasn't You!

On his way to Ivan's, he had to pass the house Katerina Ivanovna lived in. The windows were lit up and he suddenly stopped and decided to go in. He had not seen Katerina Ivanovna for over a week. It now occurred to him that Ivan might be with her, especially on the eve of such a day. He rang the doorbell and, as he walked up the stairs, dimly lit by a Chinese lantern, he saw a man coming down and, as they met, he recognised his brother. So Ivan had been to see Katerina Ivanovna.

"Oh, it's only you," Ivan Fyodorovich said dryly. "Well, good-bye. Are you going to see her?"

"Yes, I am."

"I shouldn't advise it. She's quite in a state, and you'll upset her even more."

"No, no!" a voice suddenly called from a door that was flung open upstairs. "Have you come from him, Alexei Fyodorovich?"

"Yes, I've been to see him."

"Has he given you any message for me? Come in, Alyosha, and you, too, Ivan Fyodorovich. You must, you must come back! Do you hear?"

There was such a peremptory note in Katerina Ivanovna's voice that Ivan Fyodorovich, after a moment's hesitation, decided to go up again together with Alyosha.

"She was eavesdropping!" he said irritably in an undertone, which Alyosha heard.

"You won't mind my keeping my overcoat on, will you?" said Ivan Fyodorovich, entering the drawing-room. "I won't sit down either. I'll only stay for a moment."

"Sit down, Alexei Fyodorovich," said Katerina Ivanovna, remaining standing herself. She had changed little during this time, but there was an ominous gleam in her dark eyes. Alyosha later recalled that she seemed extraordinarily beautiful at the moment.

"What did he ask you to tell me?"

"Only one thing," said Alyosha, looking straight into her face. "That you should spare yourself and say nothing in court about"—he faltered a little—"what passed between you—at the time of your very first meeting in—in that town—"

"Oh, he means that I bowed down to the ground to him for that money!" she said with a bitter laugh. "Well, is he afraid for himself or for me? He said I should spare—whom? Him or me? Speak up, Alexei Fyodorovich."

Alyosha was watching her closely, trying to understand her.

"Both you and him," he said softly.

"That's it!" she snapped spitefully and suddenly blushed. "I'm afraid you don't know me yet, Alexei Fyodorovich," she said menacingly, "and I don't think I know myself either. You may want to trample me underfoot after my interrogation tomorrow."

"You will, I'm sure, give your evidence honestly," said Alyosha. "That is all that's required."

"A woman is often dishonest," she said, grinding her teeth. "Only an hour ago I thought I'd be afraid to touch that monster—as though he were a reptile but—it seems I was wrong: he's still a human being to me! But did he do it? Did he?" she suddenly cried hysterically, turning quickly to Ivan. Alyosha at once realised that she had put the same question to Ivan perhaps only a moment before his own arrival, and not for the first but for the hundredth time, and that they had ended by quarrelling.

"I've been to see Smerdyakov— It was you, Ivan—it was you who persuaded me that he was a parricide. I believed only you!" she went on, still addressing Ivan. A forced smile came over his

349

lips. Alyosha started at her use of the familiarity, for he could not even have suspected such a relationship between them.

"Well, I think that will do," said Ivan cutting her short. "I'm leaving. I'll come again tomorrow." And turning on his heel, he left the room and walked straight to the staircase. Katerina Ivanovna suddenly seized Alyosha by both hands with an imperious gesture.

"Go after him! Overtake him! Don't leave him alone for a moment!" she said in a rapid whisper. "He's a madman. Don't you know that he's gone mad? He is in a fever, a nervous fever! The doctor told me so. Go, run after him—"

Alyosha jumped up and rushed out after Ivan, who was only about fifty paces ahead of him.

"What is it you want?" asked Ivan, who, seeing that Alyosha was overtaking him, turned round suddenly. "She told you to run after me because I was mad. I know it all by heart," he added irritably.

"She's mistaken, of course," said Alyosha, "but she is right about your being ill. I was looking at your face just now. You look quite ill. You look very ill, Ivan!"

Ivan walked on without stopping, with Alyosha following him.

"But do you know, Alexei, how people go mad?" asked Ivan in a voice that was suddenly quiet and not at all irritated, a voice in which there was a sudden tinge of the most good-natured curiosity.

"No, I don't. I imagine there are all kinds of insanity."

"And is it possible to observe how one is going mad oneself?"

"I don't think it's possible to observe oneself clearly in a case like that," Alyosha replied with surprise.

Ivan was silent for about half a minute.

"If you want to talk to me about anything," he said suddenly, "please change the subject."

"By the way, I've just remembered I've a letter for you," Alyosha said shyly and, taking Lise's letter out of his pocket, he held it out.

They had just walked up to a lamppost. Ivan recognised the handwriting at once.

"Oh, it's from that little imp!" he laughed spitefully and, without opening the envelope, he suddenly tore it into bits, which he threw in the air to be scattered by the wind.

"I don't think she's sixteen yet, but she's already offering herself!" he said contemptuously, striding along the street.

"Offering herself? What do you mean?" cried Alyosha.

"Just as wanton women do, of course."

"What are you saying, Ivan? How can you?" Alyosha protested heatedly but with sorrow. "She's just a child. You're insulting a child! She's sick, very sick, she, too, may be going mad— I had to deliver her letter— I was expecting to hear something from you— I mean, something that might save her."

"You will hear nothing from me. She may be a child, but I'm no nurse-maid to her. No more of that, Alexei. Don't go on. I'm not even giving it a thought."

They were again silent for about a minute.

"She'll now be praying to the Mother of God all night for guidance on how to act in court tomorrow," he said sharply and spitefully again.

"You—you mean Katerina Ivanovna?"

"Yes. Whether she should save or ruin Mitya? She'll be praying for inspiration from on high. You see, she hasn't made up her mind yet. Hasn't had the time. She, too, takes me for a nurse-maid. Wants me to sing lullabies to her!"

"Katerina Ivanovna loves you, Ivan," Alyosha said sadly.

"Perhaps. Only I'm not keen on her."

"She's suffering. Why, then, do you sometimes say—things to her that give her hope?" Alyosha went on, with timid reproach. "You see, I know you've given her hope. Forgive me for saying so," he added.

"I can't behave here as I ought to—break with her and tell her so frankly!" Ivan said irritably. "I must wait till sentence has been pronounced on the murderer. If I break with her now, she'll ruin that rotten scoundrel in court tomorrow so as to avenge herself on me because she hates him and she knows it. It's all a pack of lies here, lies piled on lies! But as long as I don't break off with her, she can still hope and she won't ruin that monster, knowing how anxious I am to get him out of the mess he's in. And when will that damned sentence be handed down!"

The words "murderer" and "monster" echoed painfully in Alyosha's heart.

"But how can she ruin Mitya?" he asked, pondering over Ivan's words. "What could she say in her evidence that could ruin Mitya?"

"You don't know that yet. She has a document in Mitya's own writing proving beyond any doubt that he did murder Father."

"That's impossible!" cried Alyosha.

"Why impossible? I've read it myself."

"No such document can exist!" Alyosha repeated heatedly. "It can't, because he is not the murderer. It was not he who killed Father, not he!"

Ivan came to a sudden halt.

"Who, then, is the murderer, in your opinion?" he asked, somehow coldly, with even a suggestion of arrogance in his tone.

"You know that yourself," Alyosha said in a low and fervent voice.

"Who? You mean the story about that crazy idiot, the epileptic? About Smerdyakov?"

Alyosha suddenly felt that he was trembling.

"You know who it was," the words escaped him involuntarily. He felt he was choking.

"But who? Who?" Ivan cried almost fiercely, all his restraint suddenly gone.

"I only know," Alyosha said, still almost in a whisper, "that it was *not you* who murdered Father."

" 'It wasn't you?' What do you mean by saying 'It wasn't you?' " said the dumbfounded Ivan.

"It wasn't you who murdered Father," Alyosha repeated firmly. "It wasn't you!"

They did not speak for about half a minute.

"I know myself it wasn't me," said Ivan, with a pale and

twisted smile. "Are you raving?" His eyes were fixed on Alyosha. The two were again standing under a street-lamp.

"No, Ivan. You've told yourself several times that you were
the murderer."

"When did I say that?— I was in Moscow at the time— When
did I say that?" Ivan muttered in utter confusion.

"You said it to yourself many times, when you were alone
during these dreadful two months," Alyosha went on, as quietly
and distinctly as before. But he spoke, not of his own volition
but, as it were, obeying some imperative behest. "You've accused yourself and confessed to yourself that you alone are the
murderer. But you did not do it. You are mistaken: you are not
the murderer, do you hear? It wasn't you! God has sent me to
tell you this."

They were both silent for a full minute, gazing into each
other's eyes. Both were pale. Suddenly Ivan, trembling, gripped
Alyosha by a shoulder.

"You've been at my place!" he said in grating undertone.
"You were at my place the night he came— Confess—you saw
him, didn't you?"

"Who are you talking about?— Mitya?" asked the bewildered
Alyosha.

"No, not about him! Damn that monster!" Ivan shouted,
quite beside himself. "Do you really know he comes to see me?
How did you find out? Tell me!"

"Who is *he*?" the terrified Alyosha faltered. "I don't know
who you're talking about."

"Yes, you do—how else could you—it's impossible for you
not to know—"

But suddenly he seemed to pull himself together. He stood
motionless, seeming to be pondering over something. His lips
were twisted in a strange smile.

"Ivan," Alyosha began again in a trembling voice. "I said
that because you'll believe me. I know that. I told you that
it was not you! Because I want you to remember it for the rest
of your life. Do you hear? For the rest of your life. And it was
God who put it into my heart to tell you so, even though you
may hate me for ever from this hour—"

But Ivan had now apparently regained complete control of himself.

"Alexei Fyodorovich," he said with a cold, ironical smile, "I can't tolerate prophets and epileptics. Especially messengers from God. You know that only too well. From this moment, I shall have nothing to do with you, and, I think, for good. I ask you to leave me at once at this place. Besides your lodgings are down this lane, aren't they? And beware of calling on me today! Do you hear?"

He turned away and walked straight ahead, with firm step, without looking back.

"Ivan," Alyosha shouted after him, "should anything happen to you today, think of me in the first place!—"

But Ivan made no reply. Alyosha stood by the street-lamp at the cross-roads till Ivan had disappeared in the darkness. Then he turned and walked slowly down the lane towards his lodgings. Both he and Ivan occupied separate quarters: neither of them wished to live in their father's empty house. Alyosha rented a furnished room with a tradesman's family; Ivan lived at some distance from him, occupying a large and fairly comfortable flat in the wing of a house belonging to a civil servant's well-to-do widow. The only person to wait on him was a rheumatic and completely deaf old woman, who retired at six in the evening and got up at six in the morning. Ivan had become strangely undemanding during the last two months, and liked very much to be left quite alone. He even himself tidied the room he lived in, and very rarely went into the other rooms in his flat. On reaching the gate of his house and taking hold of the bell handle, he suddenly halted. He felt that he was still trembling in fury. Suddenly he let go of the bell, spat, turned on his heel, and walked rapidly towards the other end of the town, to a very small and tumbledown wooden house, about two versts away from his flat. The house was occupied by Maria Kondratievna, Fyodor Pavlovich Karamazov's neighbour, who used to come to his kitchen for soup and for whom Smerdyakov had once sung his songs and played on the guitar. She had sold their cottage and was now living with her mother in little more than a peasant's log cabin, and Smerdyakov, ill and almost dying, had lived with them ever since Fyodor Pavlovich's death. It was to see him that Ivan was now going, impelled by a sudden and irresistible impulse.

6.

The First Encounter with Smerdyakov

It was already the third time Ivan Fyodorovich had gone to talk to Smerdyakov, since his return from Moscow. The first time, after the murder, he had seen and talked to him on the very day of his arrival; then he had called again a fortnight later. But his calls had ended after this visit, the second, so that over a month had elapsed since he had seen him, during which he had scarcely heard anything of the man. Ivan Fyodorovich had returned from Moscow on the fifth day after his father's death, so that he was too late for the funeral, which took place on the day before his arrival. The delay was due to the fact that Alyosha, who did not know his Moscow address, asked Katerina Ivanovna to send a telegram. However, she did not know his address either, so she telegraphed to her sister and her aunt in the hope that Ivan Fyodorovich would visit them immediately on arriving in Moscow. But he called on them only on the fourth day and, of course, on reading the telegram, at once set off post-haste to our town. The first person he met was Alyosha, and was greatly surprised to learn that Alyosha did not even want to suspect Mitya at all, but pointed directly at Smerdyakov as the murderer, which was quite contrary to the opinion generally held in the town. Having next seen the uyezd chief of police and the public prosecutor and learnt all the details of the indictment and the arrest, he was even more surprised at Alyosha, whose opinion he ascribed to his greatly enhanced feeling of sympathy and compassion for Mitya, of whom, as Ivan knew, he was very fond. Incidentally, a few words about Ivan's feelings for his brother Dmitri Fyodorovich, so as thus to put a closure to the matter once for all: he disliked Mitya intensely, though at times he felt compassion for him, but even that was intermixed with a great contempt, bordering on loathing. He found Mitya's person and even his very appearance repellent, and viewed Katerina Ivanovna's love for Mitya with indignation. He did, however, go to see Mitya in prison, also on the first day of his arrival, a meeting which strengthened rather than weakened his conviction of his brother's guilt. He found Mitya in a state of anxiety and nervous agitation. Mitya had been very talkative though in a distrait sort of way, and wandered from subject to subject. He spoke in very sharp terms, accused Smerdyakov, and was terribly muddled. He spoke mostly about the three thousand roubles which he claimed had been stolen from him by the dead man. "The money belonged to me, it was mine," Mitya kept repeating. "Even if I had stolen it, I would have been within my rights." He did not question the evidence against him, and if he did interpret some facts as being in his favour, he did so incoherently and absurdly, just as though he did not even wish to justify himself to Ivan or anybody else; on the contrary, he lost his temper, dismissed the charges against him scornfully, was agitated and used violent language. He merely ridiculed Grigori's testimony about the open door and declared that "the devil had opened it", but could offer no coherent explanation of the fact. He even managed to insult Ivan at their first interview, telling him sharply that it was not for those who maintained that "everything is permitted" to suspect and question him. In general, he was most unfriendly to Ivan on that occasion. It was immediately after this meeting with Mitya that Ivan went to see Smerdyakov.

Already while returning by train from Moscow, Ivan kept thinking of Smerdyakov and of his last conversation with him on the evening before his departure. There was much that puzzled him, much that seemed suspicious. But, in his testimony to the court investigator, Ivan made no mention of that conversation for the time being. He put that off till he had seen Smerdyakov, who was in hospital at the time. In reply to Ivan's persistent questions, Dr. Herzenstube and Dr. Varninsky, whom he met at the hospital, declared firmly that there could be no doubt that Smerdyakov's epileptic fits were genuine and were even surprised by Ivan's question whether Smerdyakov had been shamming on the day of the disaster. They intimated that the fit was of exceptional severity and kept recurring for several days, presenting a threat to the sick man's life; only now, after all the necessary measures had been taken, it could be definitely said that the patient would survive, though it was quite likely, Dr. Herzenstube added, that his mind would remain partially impaired "if not permanently, then for quite a considerable time". To Ivan's impatient question whether that meant he was now mad, they replied that it was not quite the case in the full sense of the word, but that "certain abnormalities were to be observed". Ivan decided to find out for himself what those abnormalities were. At the hospital, he was at once allowed to see the patient. Smerdyakov was lying on a cot in a separate ward. Near him was another cot occupied by a very sick townsman, swollen with dropsy, who would obviously die in the next day or two; he could therefore be no hindrance to their conversation. On seeing Ivan, Smerdyakov grinned mistrustfully and at first seemed even frightened; that, at least was Ivan's fleeting impression. But it was only momentary; for the rest of the time, on the contrary, Ivan was almost amazed by Smerdyakov's composure. From the very first glance, Ivan had no doubt whatever that Smerdyakov was very ill: he was very weak and spoke slowly, as though he had difficulty in using his tongue; he had grown very thin and sallow. During all the twenty minutes of their talk, he complained of headaches and pain in his limbs. His eunuch-like and shrivelled face seemed to have grown very small, the hair on his temples was tousled and his quiff yielded place to a thin tuft of hair on top of his head. But the screwed-up left eye, which seemed to be insinuating something, revealed the former Smerdyakov. "Talking to a clever man is always worth while," Ivan at once recalled. He sat down on a stool at the foot of the bed. Smerdyakov stirred painfully on his bed, but was not the first to speak; he was silent and did not appear to be particularly interested now.

"Can you talk to me?" asked Ivan. "I won't tire you very much."

"Yes, sir, I very much can," Smerdyakov mumbled in a weak voice. "Been here long, sir?" he added condescendingly, as though encouraging an embarrassed caller.

"No, I arrived only today— To clear up the mess you've all made here."

Smerdyakov sighed.

"Why are you sighing? You knew all about it, don't you?" Ivan rapped out.

At first, Smerdyakov was stolidly silent.

"How could I help knowing it, sir," he then said. "It was quite clear in advance. Only how was I to know, sir, that things would work out like that?"

"What d'you mean by that? Come, drop your wily tricks. You did foretell you'd have a fit as soon as you went down into the cellar, didn't you? You yourself made a direct reference to the cellar."

"Have you mentioned that in your testimony?" Smerdyakov inquired calmly.

Ivan flared up.

"No, I haven't yet, but I certainly shall. You'll have to explain a lot to me now, my dear man. And I warn you I'm not going to let you play about with me!"

"But why should I, sir, seeing as how I place all my trust in you as in the Lord?" said Smerdyakov just as calmly, merely closing his eyes for a moment.

"First of all," Ivan began, "I know that it's impossible to foretell an epileptic fit. I've made inquiries, so don't you try to twist and turn. The day and hour cannot be foretold. How, then, did you tell me the day and the hour beforehand, and that it would happen in the cellar? How could you have known in advance that you would fall down the cellar steps in a fit unless you deliberately staged such a fit?"

"I had to go down into the cellar anyhow, sir," Smerdyakov drawled unhurriedly. "Several times a day, in fact. I fell from the attic ladder exactly like that a year ago, sir. It's quite true you can't foretell the day and hour of an epileptic fit, but you always have a kind of presentiment."

"But you actually foretold the day and the hour!"

"You'd better ask the doctors here about my illness, sir. Ask them whether my fit was real or not. I've nothing more to say to you on that score."

"And the cellar? How could you know beforehand about the cellar?"

"You keep on harping on that cellar, sir! As I was going down into the cellar that day, I was full of fear and doubts; more in fear because you were away and I could expect no protection from nobody in the world. So I went down the cellar steps, thinking to myself: 'It's sure to come now, it's sure to strike me down. Am I going to fall to the bottom or not?' And it was because of my doubts that the spasm that always comes before a fit caught me by the throat and—and, well, sir, down I flew. All that, sir, and all the talk I had with you at the gate the evening before, when I told you of my fears and the cellar— all that I told Dr. Herzenstube and Mr. Nelyudov, the court investigator, and they took it all down in my testimony. And Mr. Varvinsky, sir, the Zemstvo doctor, made a special point of that. It was just the thought of it, he told them, that brought it on. Just because of my fearfulness, that is, that I might have a fall. Yes, that was why the fit came on that day. And, sir, they took down, sir, that it was bound to happen, seeing I was so terrified."

After these words, Smerdyakov drew a long breath as though utterly exhausted.

"So you told them all that in your testimony, did you?" asked Ivan, somewhat taken aback. He had meant to frighten him by threatening to tell about their conversation that evening, but it seemed that Smerdyakov had already told them everything himself.

"What have I to be afraid of, sir?" Smerdyakov said firmly. "Let'em take the whole truth down."

"And did you also tell them every word of our conversation at the gate?"

"No, sir. Not down to the last word."

"And did you tell them that you can actually throw a fit, as you boasted to me that time?"

"No, sir, I didn't tell them that, neither."

"Now tell me why you sent me to Chermashnya?"

"I was afraid you might go to Moscow, sir. You'd have been

359

nearer in Chermashnya, anyway."

"You're lying. You yourself suggested that I should go away. Get out of harm's way, you said."

"I said that, sir, just out of friendship and out of true devotion to you, foreseeing trouble in the house and feeling sorry for you. Only I felt even more sorry for myself, sir. I told you to get out of harm's way to make you understand that there would be trouble at home, so that you should stay behind to protect your father."

"Why didn't you say so more directly then, you fool!" Ivan suddenly flared up.

"How could I have said so more directly, sir? It was only out of fear that I spoke to you, and, besides, you might have got angry. I might, of course, have suspected that Dmitri Fyodorovich would make a row and carry off that money, for he looked upon it as his own, but how was I to know that it would end up in murder? All I thought, sir, was that he'd carry off the three thousand in an envelope under the master's mattress. But he went and did him in. You couldn't have guessed it yourself, sir, could you?"

"But if you say yourself that it couldn't be guessed at, then how could I have foreseen it and stayed on? Why are you mixing things up?" Ivan said, thinking it over.

"Why, sir, you could have guessed it because I asked you to go to Chermashnya instead of to Moscow."

"How on earth could I have guessed it from that?"

Smerdyakov, who seemed very tired, was again silent for a minute or so.

"You should have guessed that I wanted you to be at hand, sir, because I was trying to persuade you to go to Chermashnya, not to Moscow. For Moscow, sir, is a long way off, and your brother, seeing that you weren't far off, would not have felt so encouraged. And in case of anything happening, you could be back very soon so as to give me protection, too, for that was why I warned you of Grigori Vassilievich's illness and told you about my being afraid of a fit. And the reason why I told you of the knocks that could get you into your father's house and said that Dmitri Fyodorovich knew all about them through me was because I thought you'd guess yourself, sir, that he'd be quite sure to do something and that you wouldn't go even to Chermashnya but decide to stay on."

"He's talking very coherently," thought Ivan, "though he does mumble. What sort of impairment of his mental faculties was Herzenstube talking of?"

"You're trying to be foxy with me, damn you!" Ivan cried angrily.

"And I don't mind admitting, sir, that I thought at the time that you had guessed it all," Smerdyakov parried with a most artless air.

"I'd have stayed on if I'd guessed it!" cried Ivan, flaring up again.

"Well, sir, I thought that, having guessed it all, you was most anxious to get away so as to escape trouble and save yourself out of fear."

"You thought all other people were as cowardly as you?"

"I'm very sorry, sir, but I did think you was just like me."

"Well, of course, I should have guessed that," said Ivan excitedly, "and as a matter of fact I did guess that you'd be up to something vile— Only you're lying, you're lying again," he cried suddenly recalling something. "Do you remember coming up to the carriage and saying to me, 'Talking to a clever man is always worth while'? So you must have been glad I was leaving, since you praised me!"

Smerdyakov sighed again and again. Some colour seemed to come into his face.

"If I was glad, sir," he said a little breathlessly, "it was only because you agreed to go to Chermashnya and not to Moscow. For, say what you will, sir, it certainly is nearer. Only I spoke those words to you by way of reproach, not in praise, sir. You got me all wrong there, sir."

"Reproach for what?"

"Why, for leaving your own parent behind because you expected some misfortune and being unwilling to protect us, for, you see, sir, I might be picked up at any moment for stealing the three thousand."

"The devil take you!" Ivan swore again. "Stay: did you tell

the court investigator and the public prosecutor about those signals, those knocks?"

"I told them everything as it was, sir."

Again Ivan Fyodorovich could not help feeling surprised.

"If I did think of anything at the time," he began again, "it was only that you might do something vile. Dmitri might commit murder, but I never believed at the time that he could steal— But I expected you to play any vile trick. You told me yourself that you could sham an epileptic fit. Why did you say that?"

"I said that, sir, only because of my simplicity of mind. Besides, I've never pretended to have a fit on purpose in my life. I only said it to show off. It was sheer stupidity on my part, sir. I had got to like you very much then and I was just acting natural-like with you."

"My brother accuses you of murder and theft."

"Well, sir, what else is there for him to say?" Smerdyakov grinned bitterly. "And who's going to believe him with all that evidence against him? Grigori Vassilievich saw the open door, so what more can be said? But never mind him! He only is trying to save himself and is all of a-tremble—"

He fell silent and then suddenly, as though thinking of something, added:

"You see, sir, it's the same thing all over again: he wants to put the whole blame on me, says it's my doing—I've heard that already. And now you, sir, say that I'm good at shamming epileptic fits. But would I have told you beforehand that I could do so if it was really my design to murder your father just then. Had such a murder been my design, I wouldn't have been such a fool as to give such evidence against myself beforehand, and to his son, too! Would I, sir? Does that look probable? Could such a thing happen, sir? Why, of course not, sir. Now, take this conversation between you and me, sir. No one hears it except Providence itself. But if you, sir, was to tell the public prosecutor and Mr. Nelyudov about it, you'd provide me with the best defence you could think of. For what kind of evil-doer is it, sir, who's so simple-minded beforehand? That can be easily understood."

"Listen," Ivan Fyodorovich interrupted, getting up and greatly impressed by Smerdyakov's last argument, "I don't suspect you at all and, indeed, I consider it ridiculous to accuse you— On the contrary, I'm grateful to you for setting my mind at ease. I'm leaving but shall return. Good-bye for the present. Get well. Is there anything you need?"

"Thank you for everything, sir. Marfa Ignatievna, sir, does not forget me and lets me have anything I want. Very good she's always been to me, sir. Good people visit me every day."

"Good-bye. By the way, I shan't say anything about your being able to sham a fit and—I should advise you not to say anything about it, either," Ivan added suddenly for some reason.

"I quite understand, sir. And if you don't say nothing about it, sir, I won't say anything of that conversation of ours at the gate, either—"

At this point it so happened that Ivan Fyodorovich suddenly left the ward, and it was only after he had gone some ten paces along the corridor that it suddenly occurred to him that Smerdyakov's last sentence contained some offensive meaning. He was on the point of going back, but the idea had only flashed through his mind, so muttering "Nonsense!", he rapidly left the hospital. What pleased him most, he felt, was a sense of relief that the guilt lay not with Smerdyakov but with his brother, Mitya, though, it would seem, he should really have felt the reverse. He did not want to analyse why he should have felt that way; indeed, he felt revulsion at analysing his own feelings. He seemed to wish to put something quickly out of his mind. Then, during the following few days as he got acquainted more thoroughly with the damning evidence against Mitya, he grew absolutely convinced of the latter's guilt. There was the evidence of the most insignificant people, such as Fenya and her grandmother, for example, not to mention Perkhotin, the people in the town inn and at Plotnikov's shop, and the Mokroye witnesses. It was the details that were so damning. The information about the secret "knocks" impressed the court investigator and the public prosecutor almost as much as Grigori's testimony about the open door. In reply to Ivan Fyodorovich's question, Grigori's wife, Marfa Ignatievna, declared unhesitatingly that Smerdyakov had been lying all night behind the partition, "within a few feet of our bed" and that though she had slept soundly, she woke up several times, hearing him moaning. "He was moaning the whole time, moaning continually." Talking it over with Herzenstube, Ivan Fyodorovich told him that, in his opinion, Smerdyakov was not at all mad, but only very weak. But that merely evoked a faint smile from the old man. "Do you know how he spends all his time now?" he asked Ivan Fyodorovich. "Learning French words by heart. He had an exercise book under his pillow, with French words written out for him in Russian characters by someone, ha, ha, ha!" Ivan Fyodorovich finally cast any doubt aside. He could no longer think of his brother Dmitri without loathing. One thing, though, was strange: Alyosha insisted that Dmitri was not the murderer, but that, in all probability, Smerdyakov was. Ivan always felt that Alyosha's opinion meant much to him, which was why he felt perplexed by his younger brother. Another strange thing was that Alyosha did not even seek to speak to him about Mitya; he never himself began talking about Mitya, but merely replied to questions. That, too, had caught Ivan Fyodorovich's close attention. Incidentally, he was at the time very much preoccupied with quite another matter: on returning from Moscow, he at once yielded entirely to his mad and consuming passion for Katerina Ivanovna. This is not the place to deal with this new passion of Ivan Fyodorovich's, which was to leave a deep impression on the rest of his life: all this could provide the background for another story, another novel, which I do not know if I shall ever attempt. Yet I cannot dismiss the fact that when, on leaving Katerina Ivanovna that night with Alyosha, Ivan Fyodorovich, as I have already related, said to him: "I am not keen on her", he was telling a downright falsehood: he was madly in love with her, though it is quite true that at times he hated her so much that he could have killed her. There were many reasons: Katerina Ivanovna, shattered by what had happened to Mitya, had thrown herself at Ivan Fyodorovich, who had returned to her, as her only saviour. She was hurt, insulted, and humiliated in her feelings. And now a man had reappeared on the scene, who had loved her so much before—oh, she was only too well aware of that—and of whose mind and heart she had formed so high an opinion. But a girl of such high moral principles did not fully yield to him, despite the Kara-mazovian violence of her admirer's desires and the fascination he exercised over her. At the same time, she was continually tormented by remorse for having been unfaithful to Mitya, and during her violent quarrels with Ivan (and there were many of them) she told him so plainly. That was what, in his conversation with Alyosha, he had called "lies piled on lies". And, indeed, there were a great many untruths in their relationship, this angering Ivan Fyodorovich more than anything else— But of all that later. In short, he almost forgot Smerdyakov for a time. And yet, a fortnight after his first visit to him, he again began to be vexed by the same strange thoughts as before. It will suffice to say that he began continually asking himself the question: why did he, on the last night before his departure, steal downstairs in his father's house and listen to what his father was doing in his rooms? Why did he later recall it with revulsion; why had he suddenly felt so miserable the next morning, during the journey, and, on arriving in Moscow, had said to himself: "I am a blackguard"? And now it seemed to him that all these tormenting thoughts might drive Katerina Ivanovna out of his mind, so powerful was their grip on him! It so happened that, thinking thus, he met Alyosha in the street. He stopped him and suddenly asked:

"Do you remember that day when Dmitri burst into the house after dinner and fell upon Father? I told you afterwards in the yard that I reserved 'the right to have wishes'—tell me, did you think then that I wished for Father's death or not?"

"I did," Alyosha replied softly.

"Well, you were not mistaken, and there was really no need to engage in surmising. But didn't you think then I really wished that 'one viper should devour the other', that is, that Dmitri should kill Father, and as soon as possible, too, and— and that I didn't mind helping to bring it about?"

Alyosha paled a little and looked in silence in his brother's eyes.

"Speak up!" cried Ivan. "I must know what you thought at

the time. I really must know the truth, the truth!" He drew a long breath, looking with a kind of malice at Alyosha even before the latter had time to reply.

"I'm sorry, but I did think that, too, at the time," Alyosha whispered and fell silent without adding a single "extenuating circumstance".

"Thanks!" Ivan snapped and, leaving Alyosha, walked off. Since then, Alyosha had noticed that his brother had taken to avoiding him rather pointedly and even seemed to have taken a dislike to him, so that he, Alyosha, stopped calling on Ivan. But at that very moment, immediately after his meeting with Alyosha, Ivan Fyodorovich went straight to see Smerdyakov again, without first going home.

7.

The Second Call on Smerdyakov

By that time, Smerdyakov had been discharged from the hospital. Ivan Fyodorovich knew his new address: a rickety little log house partitioned by a passageway into two halves, one occupied by Maria Kondratievna and her mother, with Smerdyakov in the other half. Goodness knows by what arrangement he had taken up his quarters there: whether he paid them rent or not. It was generally believed later that he had been accepted as Maria Kondratievna's intended, and was living there rent-free for the time being. Both daughter and mother held him in the highest esteem and regarded him as vastly superior to themselves. On being admitted, Ivan Fyodorovich entered the passageway and was directed by Maria Kondratievna straight to the "parlour" on the left occupied by Smerdyakov. There was a tiled stove in the overheated room. The walls were covered with blue paper, which was, it is true, in shreds and infested with cockroaches in all the cracks, producing a constant rustling. The room was practically bare of furniture; there were two benches along the walls and two chairs by the table, which, though of plain deal, was covered with a pink-patterned cloth. There was a pot of geraniums on each of the two little window-sills, and icons in a corner of the room. On the table stood a battered little copper samovar and a tray with two cups. Smerdyakov had already had his tea and the samovar had gone out– He was sitting on a bench at the table and, consulting an exercise book, was writing down something with a pen. There was an ink-well in front of him, as well as a flat iron candlestick, with a stearin candle. From Smerdyakov's face Ivan Fyodorovich at once concluded that he had quite recovered from his illness. It was much fresher and fuller, his quiff brushed up and the hair on his temples plastered down. He was sitting in a multicoloured quilted dressing-gown, which was, however, very dirty and rather threadbare. He had spectacles on his nose, which Ivan Fyodorovich had never seen him wear. That most trifling circumstance seemed suddenly to redouble Ivan Fyodorovich's anger: "A creature like that and wearing spectacles, too!" Smerdyakov slowly raised his head and gazed intently at his visitor through his spectacles; then he slowly removed them and half-raised himself on the bench, but not in the least respectfully–almost lazily, in fact, just enough to meet the barest requirements of civility. All this flashed through Ivan's mind; he noticed it instantly and at once took it all in–and particularly Smerdyakov's unmistakably spiteful, surly, and even disdainful look: "What do you mean by barging in like that?" it seemed to say. "Everything's been settled between us, so why have you come here again?" Ivan Fyodorovich could hardly keep himself in check.

"It's hot here," he said, still standing, and unbuttoned his overcoat.

"Take your coat off, sir," Smerdyakov permitted.

Ivan Fyodorovich took his coat off, threw it down on a bench, took a chair, his fingers trembling, rapidly pulled it up to the table and sat down. Smerdyakov had already resumed his seat on the bench.

"First of all, are we alone here?" Ivan Fyodorovich asked severely and impulsively. "Can we be overheard from the other room?"

"No, sir, no one can't hear nothing. You've seen for yourself: there's the passageway."

"Look here, my man: what was it you blurted out as I was leaving the hospital, I mean, that if I said nothing about how good you were at shamming an epileptic fit, you wouldn't tell the court investigator everything about our conversation at the gate? What did you mean by *everything?* What did you have in mind then? You weren't threatening me by any chance, were you? You don't imagine I've entered into any kind of pact with you, do you? You don't think I'm afraid of you, do you?"

Ivan Fyodorovich said it all in a fury, openly and deliberately letting Smerdyakov know that he scorned any beating about the bush and that he was putting his cards on the table. Smerdyakov's eyes flashed spitefully, his left eye blinked, and, as was his custom, he at once replied with slow deliberation, as if to imply: "You want plain speaking, don't you, so you'll get it."

"What I meant, sir, and why I said it then, was that you, knowing beforehand that your father would be murdered, left him to his fate, and I promised not to tell the authorities, so that people shouldn't think nothing bad about your feelings and, perhaps, of something else, besides."

Though Smerdyakov spoke unhurriedly and with apparent self-control, yet there was a note of insistent firmness, malice and insolent defiance in his voice. He stared impudently at Ivan Fyodorovich, who felt almost dizzy for a moment.

"What? What did you say? Have you gone out of your senses?"

"No, sir, I'm quite sane."

"But did I *know* of the murder then?" Ivan Fyodorovich cried at last, striking the table with his fist. "What do you mean by 'something else, besides'? Speak up, you scoundrel!"

Smerdyakov said nothing and continued to stare impudently at Ivan Fyodorovich.

"Speak up, you stinking villain, what is that 'something else, besides'?" he yelled.

"By 'something else, besides' I meant just now that you, too, sir, were probably eager for your father's death at the time."

Jumping to his feet, Ivan Fyodorovich punched Smerdyakov on the shoulder, so that he fell back against the wall. In an instant, the tears were rolling down his cheeks, and, with the words, "You ought to be ashamed to hit a sick man, sir", he suddenly covered his face with a very dirty blue check handkerchief and began crying softly. A minute or so passed.

"Enough of that. Stop!" Ivan Fyodorovich finally ordered, sitting down on his chair again. "Don't make me lose all patience!"

Smerdyakov removed the rag from his eyes. Every line on his wrinkled face reflected the insult he had just received.

"So you thought, you rascal, that I wanted to murder my father as much as Dmitri did?"

"I didn't know what thoughts you had in your mind then, sir," Smerdyakov said in a hurt voice. "That's why I stopped you as you were entering the gate, to sound you out on that point."

"To sound out what? What?"

"Why, sir, on that very matter: whether you wanted your father murdered as soon as possible, or not."

What Ivan Fyodorovich resented most of all was the insolently insistent tone which Smerdyakov stubbornly refused to abandon.

"It was you who murdered him!" he exclaimed suddenly.

Smerdyakov smiled contemptuously.

"You know very well, sir, that I did not kill him. I should have thought there was no need for a clever man to go on saying that."

"But what, what led you at the time to suspect me?"

"Well, sir, it was simply out of fear, as you already know. For I was in such a state then that, shaking with fear, I suspected everybody. I decided to sound you out, too, sir, for I thought that if you, too, wanted what your brother did, then it was as good as done, and I, too, would be squashed like a fly."

"Look here, you said something quite different a fortnight ago."

"I meant the same thing when I was speaking to you at the hospital, only I thought you'd understand without me putting it into words. You see, sir, I thought that a clever man like you wouldn't care to talk of it directly."

369

"Did you? But answer me, answer, I insist: what could I have said or done to put such a base suspicion into your mean soul?"

"If you mean murder, sir, then, of course, you couldn't have done it, and you didn't want to, either. But you did want someone else to do it. Yes, sir, that you did."

"And how coolly, how coolly he says it! But why should I have wanted it? Why the hell should I have wanted it?"

"What do you mean, sir: you could not have wanted it? And what about the inheritance, sir?" Smerdyakov asked venomously and even somehow vengefully. "Why, sir, after your father's death, each one of you three would have got forty thousand at least and perhaps even more, but if your father married that woman, Agrafena Alexandrovna, she would have had all his capital made over to her immediately after the wedding, for she's certainly nobody's fool, so that you wouldn't have got as much as two roubles, the three of you, after his death. And how far were they from a wedding? Not a hair's breadth, sir. The young lady had only to move her little finger and he'd have dashed off with her to church with lolling tongue."

Ivan Fyodorovich restrained himself with a painful effort.

"Very well," he said at last, "as you see, I haven't jumped up, I haven't struck you, and I haven't killed you. Go on: you mean to say that I had intended my brother Dmitri to do it and had counted on him, eh?"

"Why, sir, you couldn't help counting that he'd do it. For if he murdered him, he'd forfeit all his rights as a nobleman, as well as his rank and property, and be sent to Siberia. His share of the inheritance would be shared equally by you and your brother Alexei Fyodorovich. Which means, sir, that each of you would get sixty, not forty thousand. Yes, sir, you certainly did count on your brother Dmitri Fyodorovich."

"The things I have to tolerate from you! Listen, you scoundrel, if I had counted on anyone at the time, it would have been on you, not on Dmitri and, I swear, I had a feeling then that you were up to something vile— I—I remember my impression!"

"I thought, too, at the time and for a moment that you was counting on me too," said Smerdyakov with a sarcastic grin. "That was how you gave yourself away to me. For if, as you say, sir, you had such a feeling about me and yet went away, you as good as said to me: you can murder my father; I won't stand in your way."

"You villain! So that was how you understood it?"

"And it was all because of Chermashnya, sir! Why, good Lord, sir, you was going to Moscow and you flatly refused to go to Chermashnya no matter how much your father asked you to! And suddenly you agreed to go there just at a foolish word from me! And why, sir, did you have to agree to go to Chermashnya that time? You must have expected something from me, if you didn't go to Moscow, but for no reason went to Chermashnya instead, just because of just one thing I said to you."

"No, I swear, I didn't!" Ivan yelled gritting his teeth.

"Didn't you, now? But, you see, sir, as a good son you should have turned me over to the police at once and have me flogged for such words—or, leastways, have me thrashed good and proper there and then. But, good Lord, sir, you did nothing of the kind. You was not a bit angry and you acted upon my words friendly-like at once. At a foolish word from me you went off, which, if you don't mind me saying so, sir, was very stupid of you, for you should have stayed on to protect your father's life— So what was I to understand by that?"

Ivan sat scowling, both fists pressed convulsively on his knees.

"Yes, I'm sorry I didn't give you a thrashing then," he said with a bitter smile. "I couldn't have taken you to the police, for who would have believed me and what charge could I lay against you?— But I could certainly have given you a hell of a thrashing. A pity I didn't think of it. Though it's forbidden to beat up a servant, I'd have made a mess of your ugly mug."

Smerdyakov looked at him almost with enjoyment.

"Under ordinary circumstances," he said in the self-satisfied doctrinaire tone he used to taunt Grigori and argue with him about religion at Fyodor Pavlovich's table, "under ordinary circumstances, the thrashing of a servant is really unlawful nowadays, and, indeed, sir, people no longer do it, but in exceptional circumstances people still go on beating their servants, not only in our country but anywhere in the world, even in the fullest of republics, the French, just as in the time of Adam and Eve, sir. And they will never give it up, but you, sir, didn't dare beat me up even in an exceptional case."

"What are you studying French words for?" asked Ivan, nodding towards the exercise-book on the table.

"And why shouldn't I study them, sir. So as to improve my education in case I might one day find myself in the fortunate places in Europe."

"Listen, you monster," cried Ivan with flashing eyes, trembling all over, "I'm not afraid of your accusations. Say what you like about me, and if I won't thrash you within an inch of your life right now, it's only because I suspect you of the crime and I'm going to see that you're brought to trial for it. I'll expose you yet!"

"And in my opinion, sir, you'd better keep quiet. For what can you accuse me of, seeing as how I'm completely innocent? And who will believe you? Only if you start anything, I will tell everything, too, for I have to defend myself, haven't I?"

"Do you think I'm afraid of you now?"

"Well, sir, even if the court don't believe all I've said to you just now, the public will, and you'll be put to shame, sir."

"Talking to a clever man is always worth while—is that what you mean—eh?" snapped Ivan, grinding his teeth.

"You've hit the nail on the head, sir. And you'd better act cleverly, sir."

Ivan Fyodorovich got up, trembling with indignation, put on his overcoat, and, without replying to Smerdyakov and without even giving him a look, rapidly left the house. The cool evening air refreshed him. The moon was shining in the sky. A terrible nightmare of thoughts and sensations was seething in his soul. "Go and tell the police at once about Smerdyakov? But what can I tell them? He's innocent, all the same. On the contrary, he will accuse me. And, really, why did I set out for Chermashnya then? What for? Whatever for?" Ivan Fyodorovich asked himself. "Yes, of course, I was expecting something, and he's quite right—" And again he recalled for the hundredth time how, on his last night at his father's house, he had listened on the stairs for some noise in his father's rooms, but he now recalled it with such anguish that he stopped dead as though stabbed to the heart: "Yes, it is true, I was expecting it then! I wanted the murder, I wanted it! Did I want it, did I? – Smerdyakov has to be killed! – Life is not worth living unless I muster the courage to kill him now!" Without returning home, Ivan Fyodorovich now went straight to Katerina Ivanovna's house, frightening her by his appearance: he was like a madman. He told her of his conversation with Smerdyakov, down to the last detail. He could not be calmed, however much she tried, but kept pacing the room, talking abruptly and strangely. At last, he sat down and, leaning his elbows on the table and resting his head on his hands, delivered himself of a strange aphorism.

"If Smerdyakov, and not Dmitri, murdered Father, I'd be as guilty as he, for I put him up to it. I don't know yet whether I put him up to it or not. But if he, and not Dmitri, murdered Father, then, of course, I am a murderer, too."

At this, Katerina Ivanovna got up from her seat without a word, went up to her writing table, opened a box standing on it, took out a piece of paper and laid it before Ivan. This was the document which, as Ivan later told Alyosha, was "mathematical proof" that Dmitri had murdered his father. It was a letter written by Dmitri to Katerina Ivanovna when he was drunk on the evening he met Alyosha outside the town, when the latter was returning to the monastery after the scene at Katerina Ivanovna's, where Grushenka had insulted her. On leaving Alyosha, Mitya had rushed to see Grushenka; whether he saw her or not is not known, but that night he found himself at the Metropolis Inn, where he drank himself into oblivion. It was then that he asked for pen and paper and wrote a document which was to have important consequences for himself. It was a frantic, wordy, and disconnected letter, in fact, a "drunken" letter. It was reminiscent of the way a drunken man, on returning home, begins heatedly to tell his wife, or one of his household, how he had just been insulted, by what scoundrel, and what a fine fellow he is himself, and how he will pay that scoundrel back—and he goes on and on, incoherently and excitedly, banging his fists on the table and shedding maudlin tears. The piece of paper they gave him to write his letter on at the inn was a dirty sheet of cheap note-paper, with a bill scribbled on the back of it. There was apparently not room enough for his drunken outpourings, and Mitya not only filled the margins, but had written the last lines across the rest of his letter. It ran as follows:

"Fateful Katya: Tomorrow I'll get the money and return your three thousand to you, and good-bye—woman of great wrath, but good-bye my love, too! Let's put an end to it! Tomorrow I'll try and raise it from someone or other, and if I can't get it from them, I give you my word of honour, I shall go to my father, bash his head in and take the money from under his pillow, if only Ivan goes away. I'll return your three thousand even if I'm sent to Siberia for it. And to you—farewell! I bow down to the ground to you, for I've treated you like a scoundrel. Forgive me. No, you'd better not forgive me: it will be easier so for you and me! Better Siberia than your love, for I love another woman, and you've found out the sort of woman she is today, so how can you forgive me? I shall kill my thief! I shall go away to the East from you all so as not to know any of you again. Not *her,* either, for you're not the only one who torments me; she does too. Farewell!

"PS. I am writing in curses, but I adore you! I hear it in my breast. One string remains and it jingles. Better let my heart break in two! I'll kill myself, but first of all that cur. I'll tear the three thousand out of him and fling them to you. Though I've been a scoundrel to you, I'm not a thief! Expect the three thousand. It's under the cur's mattress, tied up in a pink ribbon. I am no thief, but I'll kill my thief. Katya, don't look so disdainful: Dmitri is no thief, but a murderer! He has murdered his father and ruined himself to be able to stand up to you and not have to tolerate your pride. And not to love you.

"PP.S. I kiss your feet, farewell!

"PP.PS. Katya, pray to God that I get the money from someone else. Then I won't have any blood on my hands, but if I don't get it—I shall! Kill me!

Your slave and foe
D. Karamazov

When Ivan had read this "document", he rose from the table, convinced. So it had been his brother, and not Smerdyakov. And if it was not Smerdyakov, then it was not he, Ivan, either. The letter suddenly assumed the nature of a mathematical certainty. So far as he was concerned, there could no longer be any doubt of Mitya's guilt. Incidentally, he had never suspected that Mitya might have committed the murder together with Smerdyakov. It was not in keeping with the facts either. Ivan felt completely reassured. The next morning he thought only with contempt of Smerdyakov and his jibes. A few days later he actually wondered how he could have been so deeply wounded by the man's suspicions, and he decided to dismiss him from his mind with contempt and forget him. Thus a month passed. He made no further inquiries about Smerdyakov, but happened to hear once or twice that he was very ill and had gone out of his mind. "He'll end up by going mad," the young doctor Varvinsky said about him once, and Ivan remembered the words. During the last week of that month, Ivan himself began to feel very ill. He had already been to see the Moscow specialist who had been sent for by Katerina Ivanovna shortly before the trial. And it was just at that time that his relations with Katerina Ivanovna became acutely strained. They seemed like two bitter but enamoured enemies. Katerina Ivanovna's momentary but violent reversions to Mitya drove Ivan to the uttermost frenzy. Strange to say, until the very last scene just decribed by us, when Alyosha brought Katerina Ivanovna the message from Mitya, he, Ivan, had never during the whole month heard her voice any doubt of Mitya's guilt, despite all her "returns" to him, which he hated so much. It is no less remarkable that, while feeling that he hated Mitya more and more with every day, he realised at the same time that he hated him, not because of Katerina Ivanovna's "reversions" to him but *because he had murdered his father*! He felt and fully realised it. Nevertheless, he went to see Mitya ten days before the trial, and proposed a plan of escape, a plan that he had apparently thought over long before. In addition to the main reason prompting him to take such a step, he was also driven to it by the wound in his heart left by Smerdyakov's remark that it was to his, Ivan's, advantage that his brother should be convicted, since that would increase his and Alyosha's inheritance from forty to sixty thousand each. He therefore decided to sacrifice thirty thousand of his own money to arrange for Mitya's escape. On returning from the prison, he felt utterly depressed and disconcerted: he suddenly began to feel that he was so anxious for Mitya to escape, not only because his wound would be healed by his sacrifice of thirty thousand, but for quite another reason. "Is it because at heart I, too, am just such a murderer?" he asked himself. Deep, deep inside, something seemed to sear his soul. And, what was worse, his pride suffered terribly all through that month, but of that later—When, after his talk with Alyosha, Ivan decided, on his own doorstep, to go and see Smerdyakov, he did so in obedience to a sudden and peculiar upsurge of indignation. He suddenly recalled how Katerina Ivanovna had only a few minutes before shouted to him in Alyosha's presence: "It is you, only you who persuaded me that he (that is, Mitya) was the murderer!" Recalling this, Ivan was dumbfounded: never in his life had he tried to persuade her that Mitya was the murderer; on the contrary, after he had returned from Smerdyakov, he had told her that he might be guilty of his father's murder himself. It was *she,* she who had placed the "document" before him and proved his brother's guilt! And now she suddenly exclaimed: "I've been to see Smerdyakov myself!" When had she been to see the man? Ivan knew nothing of it. So she was not at all convinced of Mitya's guilt! And what could Smerdyakov have said to her? What, what had he said to her? His heart was full of a terrible anger. He could not understand how he, half an hour before, could have let her words pass without at once protesting. He let go of the bell and rushed off to Smerdyakov. "This time I shall, perhaps, kill him," he thought on the way.

8.

The Third and Last Encounter with Smerdyakov

When he was half-way to Smerdyakov's abode, a dry and biting wind that had been blowing early that morning arose again, and a thick, fine, dry snow began to fall, to be driven about in the wind until it became a blizzard. The streets in the part of the town where Smerdyakov lived were poorly lit, so Ivan Fyodorovich walked along in the darkness, disregarding the blizzard, and picking his way instinctively. His head ached and his temples were throbbing painfully. His hands, he felt, were twitching convulsively. Quite close to Maria Kondratievna's little house he suddenly came across a solitary drunken little peasant, in a patched homespun coat, zigzagging along the road. He was grumbling and swearing, and suddenly leaving off swearing and beginning to sing in a hoarse and drunken voice:

> *Vanya's gone off to St. Petersburg,*
> *So I won't be expecting him!*

But he kept breaking off at the second line and resuming the swearing, and then, again, suddenly began the same song all over again. Ivan Fyodorovich suddenly grew aware of the fierce hatred he felt for the man, even though he had scarcely given him a thought. He at once felt an irresistible urge to hit the little peasant and knock him down. It was at that moment that he overtook him. The little peasant, swaying perilously, suddenly lurched heavily against Ivan, who pushed him back furiously, sending the man flying so that he fell like a log on the frozen ground with a plaintive moan: "Oh-h!" and was silent. Ivan stepped up to him. He was lying on his back, quite motionless and unconscious. "He'll freeze to death!" thought Ivan and walked on to Smerdyakov's.

In the passageway Maria Kondratievna, who, candle in hand, ran out to open the door, whispered to him that Pavel Fyodorovich (that is, Smerdyakov) was very ill: it was not as if he was laid up, but he did not seem to be in his right mind, even ordering her to take the tea things away—he wanted no tea.

"He's not violent, is he?" Ivan Fyodorovich asked roughly.

"Why, no, sir! On the contrary, he's very quiet. Only," Maria Kondratievna begged him, "don't talk to him too long, sir—"

Ivan Fyodorovich opened the door and stepped into the room.

377

It was as hot as during his last visit, but certain changes could be seen in the room: one of the benches at the side of the wall had been taken out and an old mahogany sofa had been put in its stead. A bed with fairly clean white pillows had been made up on it. Smerdyakov was sitting on the bed, wearing the same dressing-gown. The table had been moved up to the sofa, so that the room seemed cluttered up. A thick book in a yellow cover lay on the table, but Smerdyakov was not reading it. He seemed to be sitting there without doing anything. He greeted Ivan Fyodorovich with a slow, silent gaze and apparently not at all surprised at his coming. He had changed greatly: his face had grown very thin and sallow, the eyes were sunken and there were blue pouches under them.

"You really are ill, then?" said Ivan Fyodorovich, stopping short. "I'm not going to keep you long. I won't even take off my coat. Where can one sit down here?"

He walked to the other end of the table, moved up a chair and sat down.

"Why are you looking at me in silence? I've come with a single question and I swear I won't leave without an answer: has the young lady Katerina Ivanovna been to see you?"

There was a long silence, Smerdyakov still gazing calmly at Ivan. But all of a sudden he gave a despairing wave of the hand and turned his face away.

"What's the matter?" exclaimed Ivan.

"Nothing at all."

"What do you mean—nothing at all?"

"Well, she's been here. What's that to you? Leave me alone."

"No, I won't leave you alone! Tell me when she was here."

"Why, I've forgotten all about her," said Smerdyakov, with a contemptuous smile, and, suddenly turning his face to Ivan again, he glared at him with eyes full of frenzied hatred, just as he had done at their encounter a month before.

"Seems to me you're ill yourself, sir," he said to Ivan. "Your cheeks are sunken. You look pretty bad."

"Never mind my health. Answer my question."

"And why are your eyes so yellow? The whites are quite yellow. Your conscience is in a bad way, isn't it?"

He grinned contemptuously and suddenly laughed outright.

"Listen, I said I wouldn't go away without an answer!" Ivan cried in intense exasperation.

"What are you pestering me for? Why do you torment me?" Smerdyakov said, with suffering in his voice.

"Oh, hell, I don't give a damn for you. Just answer my question and I'll go."

"I've nothing to tell you!" Smerdyakov said, looking down again.

"I assure you I'll make you answer!"

"What are you so worried about?" Smerdyakov asked, giving him another stare, not so much of contempt as revulsion. "Is it because the trial starts tomorrow? But nothing's going to happen to you, you may rest assured of that! Return home, go to bed and don't worry. Have no fear of anything."

"I don't understand you—what have I got to be afraid of tomorrow?" Ivan said in surprise, and suddenly chill fear did enter his soul. Smerdyakov measured him with a glance.

"So you don't un-der-stand?" he drawled reproachfully. "Don't you, now? Fancy a clever man like you trying to put one over me like that!"

Ivan looked at him in silence. The quite unexpected and incredibly arrogant tone this former lackey was addressing him in was extraordinary in itself. Even during their last encounter he had not spoken in such a way.

"I tell you you've got nothing to fear. I'm not going to say a thing against you. There's no evidence. Just look how your hands are trembling. Why are your fingers moving about like that? Go home: *it was not you who murdered him.*"

Ivan gave a start: he recalled Alyosha.

"I know it was not me—" he murmured.

"You know, do you?" Smerdyakov again put in quickly. Ivan jumped up and seized him by the shoulder.

"Tell me everything, you hound! Tell me everything!"

Smerdyakov was not in the least frightened. He merely glared at him with eyes full of insane hatred.

"Well," he whispered furiously, "it was you who murdered

him, if you really want to know!"

Ivan sank back on to his chair as though he had realised something. He smiled maliciously.

"You mean the same old thing? What you were talking about last time?"

"Yes, that time, too, you was standing before me, and understood everything. You understand it now, too!"

"All I understand is that you're mad."

"Aren't you tired of harping on that? Here we are, the two of us, sitting alone in a room, so what's the use of fooling ourselves, and making pretence? Or do you really want to put the whole blame on me to my face? You murdered him. You are the chief murderer. I was only your accomplice, your servant, and I done it because you told me to."

"You did? Did you murder him?" Ivan froze with horror.

Something seemed to give way in his brain and he began trembling all over. Smerdyakov himself now looked at him in surprise: the genuineness of Ivan's horror must have struck him at last.

"Did you really know nothing about it?" he muttered mistrustfully, staring at him with a wry smile.

Ivan kept looking at him; he seemed dumbfounded.

> *Vanya's gone off to St. Petersburg,*
> *So I won't be expecting him!*

suddenly echoed through his head.

"D'you know what? I'm afraid you're a dream, a spectre sitting before me," he murmured.

"No, sir, there ain't no spectre here, except the two of us, and somebody else, besides. No doubt he's sitting here between the two of us, the other one."

"Who is he? Who's here? Who's the somebody else?" Ivan cried in terror, looking hastily into every corner of the room in search of somebody.

"The other one's God, sir. Yes, Providence itself. Here next to us, sir. Only you needn't look, for you won't find it."

"You've lied that you murdered him!" Ivan cried frantically. "You're either mad or you're taunting me as you did last time!"

Smerdyakov watched him as searchingly as before, without the least fear. He still could not overcome his feeling of mistrust; it still seemed to him that Ivan "knew everything", but was merely making pretence so as "to put the whole blame on me to my face".

"Just a moment, sir," he said finally in a weak voice and, suddenly, dragging his left leg from under the table, he began rolling up his trouser leg. He was wearing long white socks and slippers. Smerdyakov unhurriedly removed the garter and put his hand into the bottom of his sock. Ivan looked at him and suddenly began to tremble in a convulsion of fear.

"You madman!" he yelled and, jumping up from his seat, he drew back so violently that he knocked against the wall and seemed glued to it, drawn up stiffly to his full height. He gazed horror-stricken at Smerdyakov, who, quite unaffected by his fright, was still fumbling about in his sock, as though trying to get hold of something with his fingers and pull it out. At last, he succeeded in extracting what Ivan saw was some papers or a sheaf of papers. Smerdyakov pulled it out and put it on the table.

"Here it is, sir!" he said quietly.

"What?" asked Ivan, trembling.

"Take a look, sir," Smerdyakov said, still in the same low voice.

Ivan stepped up to the table, took up the sheaf and began unfolding it, but suddenly pulled his hand away as though it had come into contact with some loathsome reptile.

"Your fingers keeps trembling, sir, just as if they was in convulsions," observed Smerdyakov, and unhurriedly unfolded the sheaf himself. Under the wrapper were three rolls of rainbow-coloured hundred-rouble notes.

"It's all here, sir, all the three thousand, you needn't trouble to count. Take it," he said to Ivan, nodding towards the notes. Ivan sank down on to his chair, as white as a sheet.

"You frightened me with—with your sock—" he said with a strange grin.

"Didn't you really know it till now?" Smerdyakov asked again.

"No, I didn't. I had Dmitri in view all the time. Brother! Brother! Oh God!" He suddenly clutched his head in both hands. "Listen, did you kill him alone? With or without my brother?"

"Only with you, sir. I killed him with your help, sir. Your brother's quite innocent, sir."

"All right, all right— We'll talk about me later. But why do I keep on trembling?— Can't utter a word."

"You was brave enough then, sir. Everything, you said, is permitted, and see how frightened you are now!" Smerdyakov murmured in surprise. "Won't you have some lemonade, sir? I'll ask for some at once. It's wonderfully refreshing, sir. Only I'd better cover this with something first."

And he nodded again towards the sheaf of notes. He was about to go to the door and ask Maria Kondratievna to make some lemonade and bring it in. But, looking for something to cover the money with, for her not to see it, he first pulled out his handkerchief, but as it happened again to be very dirty, he took up the big yellow book that Ivan had noticed on entering the room and put it over the notes. Ivan just had time to make out the title of the book: *The Saying of the Holy Father Isaac the Syriac.**

"I won't have any lemonade," he said. "We'll talk about me later. Sit down and tell me how you did it. Tell me everything—"

"You'd better take your coat off, sir, or you'll be all in a sweat."

Ivan, as though he had only just thought of it, tore his coat off and flung it on the bench without rising from his chair.

"Speak up, please speak up!"

He seemed to calm down and waited confidently, knowing that Smerdyakov would tell him *everything* now.

"About how it was done, sir?" Smerdyakov sighed. "It was

---

*A seventh-century Christian theologian; born in Nineveh; author of seven volumes of religious writings.— Tr.

done in a most natural way, sir, just as you said—"

"We'll come later to what I said," Ivan interrupted again, but no longer shouting as before, but pronouncing each word distinctly, as though he had regained full control of himself. "Tell me in detail how you did it. In the proper order. Don't forget anything. The details, above all the details. Go on!"

"You had gone away and I fell down in the cellar, sir—"

"Did you have a fit or did you sham one?"

"Of course, I shammed, sir. I shammed it all. Went down the steps quietly, I did, to the very bottom, lay down quietly, and as soon as I lay down, sir, I starts screaming. Writhing in convulsions till they carried me out."

"Just a moment! Were you shamming all the time after-wards? At the hospital, too?"

"Why, no, sir. The next morning, before they took me to hospital, I had a real fit and such a violent one as I hadn't had for years. I was quite unconscious for two days."

"All right, all right. Go on."

"Well, sir, they puts me on the bed behind the partition as I knew all along they would, for whenever I was ill Marfa Igna-tievna used to put me to bed for the night behind that same partition in their cottage. Very kind to me she's always been, sir, ever since I was born. I moaned that night, only quiet-like. I was expecting your brother Dmitri Fyodorovich to come all the time."

"Expecting him to come? To you?"

"Why should he have come to me, sir? No, I was expecting him to come to the house, for, you see, sir, I had no doubt at all that he'd come that night, for seeing as how I wasn't there to meet him and having had no news, he would be sure to get into the house by climbing over the fence, as he knew how to, and do what had to be done."

"And if he hand't come?"

"Then nothing would have happened, sir. Without him, I'd never have made up my mind to do what I did."

"All right, all right—speak more clearly. Don't hurry and, above all, don't miss anything!"

"I expected that he'd murder Fyodor Pavlovich— Yes, I

was quite sure of that. For, you see, sir, I'd prepared him for it—during the last few days and—the chief thing was that he knew about the signals. With his suspiciousness and towering rage, which had been growing in him during all those days, he was quite sure to try to get into the house with the help of them signals. That was certain, sir. I was expecting him to do it."

"Stay," Ivan interrupted, "if he'd murdered him, he'd have taken the money and carried it off. That's exactly what you must have thought would happen? Well, what would you have got out of it? I don't see it."

"You see, sir, he'd never have found the money. It was only me that told him that the money was under the mattress. But that wasn't true. No, sir. At first the money had been in a casket, that's where it was, sir. But afterwards I suggested to Fyodor Pavlovich, who trusted me more than anyone in the world, to put the envelope with the money behind the icons in the corner, for no one would never have thought of looking for it there, especially if he was in a hurry. So that's where the envelope was, sir, in the corner behind the icons. You see, sir, it would have been silly to keep it under the mattress. He should at least have kept it in a casket under lock and key. But here they all believes now that it was under the mattress. Quite a stupid notion, sir. So if Dmitri Fyodorovich had done the murder, he'd have found nothing and would either have made away quickly, afraid of any sound, as is always the case with murderers, or he'd have been arrested. So the next morning, or even on that same night, I could always go into the bedroom, and get the money from behind the icons, and Dmitri Fyodorovich would have been held responsible for it all. Yes, sir, I could always count on that."

"But what if he didn't murder him but only gave him a beating?"

"If he didn't murder him, then, of course, I wouldn't have dared to take the money and the whole thing would have fallen through. But, you see, sir, there was always the possibility that he'd beat him unconscious, so that I'd have time to take the money and then report that no one but Dmitri Fyodorovich had taken the money after beating him."

"Wait—I'm getting all mixed up. So it was Dmitri, after all, who murdered him and you only took the money?"

"No, sir, he didn't. You see, sir, I could, of course, have told you even now that he done it—but I don't want to tell you any lies now, because—because if you really, as I can see, haven't understood nothing till now and haven't been pretending to me so as to throw your undoubted guilt on me to my face, still it's you, sir, who're responsible for everything what's happened, for you knew about the murder and entrusted it to me, and went away knowing all about it. That's why I want to prove to you to your face this evening that you, you alone, are the real murderer, though I did the killing. Yes, sir, it's you who's the rightful murderer!"

"But why, why am I the murderer? Good God!" Ivan cried, unable to restrain himself any longer and forgetting that he had put off all discussion about himself till the end of their talk. "You're still harping on that Chermashnya? Stay, tell me what you needed my consent for, if you took Chermashnya for consent? How will you explain that now?"

"Well, sir, if I was sure of your consent, I'd have known that when you came back you wouldn't raise a hullabaloo about the missing three thousand, even if for some reason the police suspected me instead of Dmitri Fyodorovich, or thought that I was his accomplice. On the contrary, you'd have protected me from the others— And having obtained your inheritance, you might have rewarded me as soon as possible afterwards, and for the rest of my life, for it would be, after all, through me that you'd have got it, seeing as how otherwise your father would have married Agrafena Alexandrovna, and you wouldn't have got a brass farthing."

"Oh, so you intended to torment me afterwards—for the rest of my life, did you?" Ivan snarled. "And what if I hadn't gone away then but had told the police about you?"

"What could you have told them? That I was persuading you to go to Chermashnya? Why, sir, that's just a lot of nonsense. Besides, you'd either have gone after our conversation, or stayed on. If you'd stayed on, nothing would have happened, and I'd have known that you didn't want it to come about and I wouldn't have undertaken anything. But as you did go, it could only mean that you assured me that you wouldn't dare give evidence against me in court and that you wouldn't mind me keeping the three thousand. And, anyway, sir, you couldn't possibly have taken me to court afterwards, for I'd have told it all in court, not that I'd stolen the money or committed the murder—I shouldn't have told them that—but that you, sir, had incited me to steal and commit murder and that I wouldn't agree to it. That's why, sir, I had to have your consent then, so that you couldn't drive me into a corner afterwards, for where could you have got your proof? But I could always drive you into a corner by disclosing how eager you was for your father's death. And let me tell you, sir, the public would have believed it and you'd have been disgraced for the rest of your life."

"So I was thirsting for it, was I?" Ivan again snarled.

"Yes, sir, without a doubt you was, and by your consent at the time you gave your silent approval for me to carry on with it," said Smerdyakov, looking firmly at Ivan. He was very weak and he spoke in a faint and exhausted voice, but was driven by something, buried deep within him, evidently harbouring some intention—Ivan felt that.

"Continue," he said. "Tell me what happened that night."

"Well, sir, what is there to tell? So I lay there and I fancied I hears the master shout. Before that, Grigori Vassilievich all of a sudden got up and went out, and suddenly I heard him yelling outside and after that it was all quiet and dark. I lay there waiting, my heart's pounding, and I couldn't bear it no longer. So I got up at last, went out—saw that the bedroom window on the left was open, so I stole up still closer to the left to listen whether he was still alive there, and I heard the master rushing about the room and moaning—so he was alive all right. Damn! I thought to myself. I went up to the window and shouted to the master: 'It's me, sir!' And he said to me, 'He's been here, he's been and run off!' That is, Dmitri Fyodorovich had been and gone. 'He's murdered Grigori,' he said to me. 'Where?' I whispered. 'Over there, in the corner of the garden.' Whispering, too, he was. 'Wait, sir,' I says. So I went to the corner of the garden to look for Grigori Vassilievich, and then I stumbled over him, lying by the wall, all bloodied up and unconscious. So it's true, then, that Dmitri Fyodorovich has been here, it came into my head sudden-like, and it was just then, sir, that I made up my mind on the spot to finish it all without delay, for Grigori Vassilievich, even if he was alive, wouldn't see nothing of it, lying there unconscious. The only risk was that Marfa Ignatievna might suddenly wake up. I was aware of that at the moment, only I was so dead set on going through with it that I could scarcely breathe. So off I went back to the bedroom window and said to the master: 'She's here,' I says, 'she's come, Agrafena Alexandrovna has,' I said, 'and she wants to be let in.' Well, sir, he just gave a start like a baby. 'Where's she? Where?' he fairly gasped, but still didn't yet believe it. 'There she is,' I says, 'open the door.' He looks at me out of the window and he didn't know whether to believe me or not, but he was afraid to open the door. Yes, I thinks to myself, he's afraid of me now. And, you know, sir, a funny thing: I suddenly took it into my head to tap out the signals that Grushenka had come on the window frame before his very eyes. He didn't believe my words, but as soon as I tapped out the signal, he ran at once to open the door. So he opened it. I tried to get in, but he stood there, blocking the way. 'Where is she? Where is she?' he asked looking at me and shaking all over. Well, I thought, if he's as afraid of me as all that, it's bad! And, you know, my legs went limp with fright that he wouldn't let me in or that he'd call out or Marfa Ignatievna would run up or something or other might happen. I don't remember what exactly I was thinking just then, but I must have gone all pale as I stood before him. I whispered to him, 'Why, sir, she's there under the window! How is it you didn't see her?' 'Fetch her, then, fetch her!' 'But she's afraid,' I said. 'She's been frightened by the shouts and is hiding in the shrubbery. Go and call her yourself from the study,' I said. So off he dashed to the window, puts the candle on the windowsill. 'Grushenka,' he called out. 'Grushenka, are you there?' But though he called it out, he durstn't lean out of the window, or move away from me, because of his fear; he was so frightened of me, you see, sir, that he durstn't move away an inch from me. 'Why, sir,' I said (I walked up to the window and leaned right out of it), 'there she is, there, in that bush laughing at you, can't you see?' Well, so all of a sudden he believed me, started shaking all over—head over heels in love with her he was, sir—and leaned right out of the window. So I grabbed the iron paper-weight from his table—do you remember, sir?—it must have weighed three pounds at least—raised it and hit him from behind with the corner, right on the crown of his head. He never even cried out. Slumped down on the floor suddenly, so I hit him over the head again and a third time. The third time I knew I'd bashed it in. It's then that he fell on his back, face upwards, covered with blood. I examined my clothes—not a speck of blood on me—it didn't spurt out, you see, so I wiped the paper-weight clean, replaced it, took the money from behind the icons, and threw the envelope on the floor, the pink ribbon beside it. I went out into the garden, shaking all over. Straight to the apple-tree I went, the one with the big hollow in it—you know the hollow, sir, and I'd had a good look at it long before and put a rag and a piece of paper in it—got it ready. So I wrapped up money in the paper and then in the rag and pushed it all deep down into the hollow. There it lay for over a fortnight, all that money, sir, and I took it out only after I'd come out of hospital. Anyways, I went back to my bed, lay down, and thought to myself, fearful-like: 'Now, if Grigori Vassilievich's been killed, it may turn out bad, but if he's not killed and comes to, it will be fine, for then he'll bear witness that Dmitri Fyodorovich has been here and, therefore, must have killed him and taken his money.' So I started moaning and groaning from uncertainty and impatience so as to wake Marfa Ignatievna as soon as possible. At last, she got up, rushed up to me, but seeing all of a sudden that Grigori Vassilievich wasn't there, she ran out and I heard her screaming in the garden. Well, sir, the hue and cry was on, and it went on all through the night, and I wasn't worried about anything any more."

The speaker stopped. Ivan had listened to him in dead silence, without moving and without taking his eyes off him. Smerdyakov, on the other hand, only cast an occasional glance at him, as he went on talking, looking away most of the time.

When he had finished his story, he was evidently agitated and breathing hard. Beads of perspiration stood out on his face. It was impossible to say, however, whether he was feeling remorse or what.

"Stay," Ivan cried. "But what about the door? If he only opened the door to you, then how could Grigori have seen it open before? For Grigori saw it before you, didn't he?"

Remarkably enough, Ivan asked the question in a most peaceable voice, in quite a different tone in fact, one that bore no trace of anger, so that if anyone had opened the door just then and looked at them across the threshold, he would most certainly have concluded that they were amicably discussing some ordinary if rather interesting subject.

"As for the door and Grigori Vassilievich having seen it open, he was simply imagining things," Smerdyakov declared with a wry smile. "For let me tell you, sir, he's not a man, but just a stubborn mule: he never saw it, but only imagined he did— but you'll never shake his evidence. That's your luck and mine, sir, I mean, that he should have invented it all, for his evidence is enough to incriminate Dmitri Fyodorovich."

"Listen," said Ivan, as though his thinking was confused and he was trying hard to grasp something, "listen, I wanted to ask you lots of things, but I forget— I keep forgetting and getting muddled— Oh yes! Tell me just one thing: why did you open the envelope and leave it on the floor? Why didn't you simply take the money in the envelope away?— While you were telling me about it, I thought that you were speaking about the envelope as though that was the right thing to do— But why it was the right thing to do I can't understand—"

"Well, sir, I did that for a certain reason. For if the man had been familiar with all the circumstances, he'd have known all about it, like me, for instance, he'd have seen the money before and perhaps put it into the envelope himself and seen with his own eyes how it was sealed and addressed, in that case, sir, why should he, if that is, he had committed the murder, open the envelope afterwards, and with such great haste, too, seeing as how he knew for certain that the money must be in the envelope? On the contrary, if the burglar had been someone like me,

389

he'd simply shove the envelope into his pocket without bothering to open it and get away with it. Now, it's quite a different matter with Dmitri Fyodorovich: he knew of the envelope only from hearsay; he never saw it himself, but as soon as he'd got it out from under the mattress, for instance, he'd open it at once to make sure the money was there. And then he'd throw the envelope down on the floor because he'd have no time to think that it could serve as evidence against him, because, you see, sir, he's an inexperienced thief, who's never stolen openly before, being a gentleman born and bred. And if he made up his mind to steal now, he did so because he thought he was not stealing at all but only taking what belonged to him, for he'd already let it be known all over town and, indeed, boasted in public that he'd go and take his property from his father. I hinted as much to the public prosecutor at my interrogation, but not in so many words, just as if I did not quite understand its importance, and as if he'd thought of it himself and it was not I who prompted it to him. The public prosecutor's mouth simply watered at the hint—"

"But did you, did you really think it all up on the spot?" cried Ivan, beside himself with surprise, again looking at Smerdyakov with fright.

"Really, sir, how can one think it all up in such haste? It was all thought out beforehand."

"Well—well—it must have been the devil himself that helped you!" Ivan cried again. "No, you're not stupid. You're much more intelligent than I thought—"

He got up with the evident intention of pacing the room. He felt intensely depressed. But as the table blocked his path and he could hardly squeeze between the table and the wall, he merely turned back and resumed his seat. His inability to stretch himself must have exasperated him, for he suddenly yelled at the top of his voice, almost as fiercely as before:

"Listen, you miserable wretch! Don't you realise that if I haven't yet killed you it's only because I want to keep you intact for tomorrow's trial. God sees," said Ivan, raising his hand, "perhaps I, too, was guilty. Perhaps I really did wish in my heart that—my father were dead, but I swear to you I'm not as guilty as you think, and perhaps I didn't put you up to it at all. No, no, I didn't! It makes no difference though; I will testify against myself in court tomorrow. My mind is made up! I'll tell them everything, everything. But I'll appear in court together with you! And whatever you may say against me in court, whatever evidence you may give—I accept it, for I'm not afraid of you: I shall confirm it all myself! But you, too, must confess in court! You must, you must! We shall go there together! That's how it'll be!"

Ivan said this with impressive forcefulness, his flashing eyes speaking for his determination.

"You are ill, sir, as I can see. You're quite ill, sir. Your eyes, sir, are yellow," said Smerdyakov, without the least sarcasm, even as though with sympathy.

"We'll go together!" Ivan repeated. "And if you won't go, I shall confess alone."

Smerdyakov said nothing, as though turning the matter over in his mind.

"Nothing of the kind will happen, sir," he decided with firm finality. "You won't go, sir."

"You don't understand me!" cried Ivan reproachfully.

"You'll feel too much shame if you take it all upon yourself. And, what's more, it won't be of no use at all, sir, for I shall declare that I never said nothing of the kind to you, and that you're either suffering from some illness (and it looks like it, too) or that you're so sorry for your brother that you're sacrificing yourself to get him off and that you've invented it all against me, for all your lifetime you've thought of me as if I was a gnat, not a human being. And who will believe you? And what shred of proof have you got?"

"Listen, you showed me the money just now to convince me, I suppose."

Smerdyakov took the *Isaac the Syriac* off the bundle of notes and laid it aside.

"Take the money away with you, sir," Smerdyakov sighed.

"Of course, I will! But why are you giving it to me since you committed a murder to get it?" Ivan asked, regarding him with great surprise.

"I don't want it at all," Smerdyakov said in a trembling voice, waving a hand ruefully. "I did once have the idea of starting a new life in Moscow or, better still, abroad with that money; but that was just a dream, sir, and most of all because 'everything is permitted'. That is something you really did teach me, sir, for you said a lot to me about such things: for if there's no infinite God, there's no such thing as virtue, and there's no need for it at all. Yes, sir, this was what you taught me. That's the way I reasoned."

"Did you arrive at that yourself?" Ivan asked with a wry smile.

"With guidance from you, sir."

"And now, I suppose, you've come to believe in God since you are returning the money?"

"No, sir, I haven't," Smerdyakov whispered.

"Then why are you giving it back?"

"Why speak of that?" Smerdyakov said, with another wave of the hand. "Didn't you yourself use to say that everything was permitted, so why are you so alarmed now, sir? You even want to go and give evidence against yourself—only nothing will come of it! You won't go and testify!" Smerdyakov again decided with firm conviction.

"You'll see!" said Ivan.

"That cannot be. You're very intelligent, sir. You're fond of money, I know that. You also like to be respected, because you're very proud; you are excessively fond of the charms of women, but what you like most of all is to live in comfortable circumstances and not to have to bow and scrape to anyone—that most of all. You won't want to ruin your life for good by disgracing yourself like that in court. You, sir, are more like your father than any of his other children, with the same kind of soul, sir."

"You're no fool," said Ivan, taken aback, the blood rushing to his face. "I used to think you were a fool. You're in earnest now!" he observed, as though suddenly seeing Smerdyakov in quite a new light.

"Your pride made you think I was a fool. Take the money, sir."

Ivan took the three rolls of notes and pushed them into a pocket without wrapping them up.

"I shall produce it in court tomorrow," he said.

"Nobody will believe you, sir. You've lots of money of your own, so you could have taken it out of your casket and brought it to court."

Ivan rose from the chair.

"I repeat: if I haven't killed you now it's only because I need you for tomorrow. Remember that, don't forget it!"

"So kill me if you like. Kill me rightaway," Smerdyakov said in a queer voice, looking strangely at Ivan. "You won't even dare do it, bold as you used to be!" he added with a bitter grimace.

"Till tomorrow!" cried Ivan, preparing to leave.

"Stay, sir—let me have another look."

Ivan took out the notes and showed them to him. Smerdyakov gazed at them for some ten seconds.

"Well, you may go now," he said with a wave of the hand. "Ivan Fyodorovich!" he called out again suddenly after him.

"What is it you want?" Ivan said, turning back.

"Good-bye, sir!"

"Till tomorrow!" Ivan cried again, and left the cottage.

The snow-storm was still blowing. He took the first steps firmly, but suddenly seemed to stagger. "It's something physical," he thought, with a grin. A kind of gladness now entered his soul. He felt something like boundless determination: an end to the wavering which had tormented him so much of late! He had made up his mind, and it would not change, he thought happily. At that moment, he stumbled against something and nearly fell. Stopping short, he made out at his feet the little peasant he had knocked down, who was still lying in the same place, unconscious and motionless, the snow almost covering his face. Ivan suddenly pulled him up and dragged him along. Seeing a light in a little house on the right, he went up to it, knocked on the shutters and asked the man who had answered his knock and was the owner of the house to help him get the peasant into some house, promising to give him three roubles for the trouble. The man got ready and came out. I won't describe in detail how Ivan Fyodorovich reached his destination and arranged for the peasant to have a medical examination at once, providing liberally for the "expenses". I will only remark that the matter took a whole hour, but Ivan Fyodorovich felt quite satisfied. His thoughts wandered and his mind worked continuously: "If I hadn't made such a firm decision for tomorrow," he suddenly reflected with pleasure, "I wouldn't have wasted a whole hour looking after that peasant, but would have passed on, without caring a damn whether he froze to death or not— But how well I'm still capable of observing myself," he thought at the same moment with even greater satisfaction. "And they decided that I was going out of my mind!" On reaching his house, he stopped dead, suddenly asking himself: "Shouldn't I go and see the public prosecutor at once and tell him everything?" He replied to the question as he turned towards his house: "Tomorrow everything will be taken together!" he whispered to himself, and, strange to say, almost all his joy, all his self-satisfaction passed off instantaneously. When he entered his room, he suddenly felt as though an icy hand had clutched at his heart, as though some recollection or rather reminder of something agonising and repellent in the room, just at that very moment, which had been there before. He sank wearily on the sofa. The old woman brought in the samovar. He made the tea, but did not touch it, sending the woman away till the morning. He sat on the sofa, feeling dizzy, ill and helpless. He was on the point of dozing off, but got up and paced the room restlessly to dispel his sleepiness. At moments he imagined that he was delirious. But it was not his illness that occupied him so much; sitting down again, he began looking about himself as though trying to discern something. He did so several times. At last his glance was rivetted to a single spot. Ivan grinned, but an angry flush covered his face. He sat there for a long time, his head cupped heavily in both palms and still looking out of the corner of his eyes at the same spot, at the sofa standing against the opposite wall. There was evidently something that irritated him there, some object that worried and tormented him.

9.

The Devil. Ivan Fyodorovich's Nightmare

I am no physician, yet I feel that a time has come when I feel compelled to explain to the reader at least something of the nature of Ivan Fyodorovich's illness. Running ahead, I shall merely say that he was that night on the verge of an attack of brain fever that overcame his long-weakened organism, which had so long resisted the illness. With my ignorance of medicine, I venture to advance the theory that, by an intense effort of will, he had perhaps succeeded in staving off his illness for a time in the hope, no doubt, of coping with it completely. He knew he was ill, but he was loth to yield to illness at the time, at the approaching fateful moments of his life, when he had to present himself, speak out boldly and resolutely and "justify himself to himself". He had, however, called once on the doctor Katerina Ivanovna had summoned from Moscow, in pursuance of a whim I have already mentioned earlier. After listening to him and examining him, the doctor came to the conclusion that he was suffering from some cerebral disorder and was not at all surprised by an admission Ivan had made to him with revulsion. "In your condition," the doctor declared, "hallucinations are quite possible, though they have to be carefully verified— You must begin medical treatment in earnest, without a moment's delay, or else you'll be in a bad way." However, on taking his leave, Ivan Fyodorovich did not follow his sensible advice and refused to take to his bed and begin medical treatment: "I'm on my feet and feel strong enough to carry on; if I collapse, it will be a different matter, and anyone who likes may give me medical treatment then," he decided, dismissing the matter from his mind. And so he was sitting now, almost aware that his mind was wandering and, as I have said already, staring at some object on the sofa at the opposite wall. Someone seemed to be sitting there. Goodness only knows how he had got in, for he had not been there when Ivan Fyodorovich, on returning from Smerdyakov, had entered the room. It was a gentleman, or rather a Russian gentleman of a certain type, no longer young, *qui frisait la cinquantaine,* as the French say, with rather long, thick and dark hair, streaked with grey, and a small closely trimmed pointed beard. He was wearing a kind of brown coat of good cut but somewhat threadbare, made about three years before and now quite out of fashion, in a style that had not been worn for two years by well-to-do men about town. His linen and cravat were of the kind affected by smart gentlemen, but closer inspection revealed that his linen was somewhat soiled and the broad cravat very threadbare. The visitor's check pantaloons were of excellent cut, but again a little too light in colour and a little too tight, of the kind no longer worn, and the same was true of his white soft felt hat, he had brought with him, which was certainly out of season. In short, the impression was that of a well-bred gentleman in greatly reduced circumstances. He seemed to belong to that class of idle landowners who flourished in the times of serfdom; he had evidently been received in good and fashionable society and had once had good connections, which, he had perhaps preserved, but after a gay life in his youth and following the recent abolition of serfdom, he had gradually turned into a sort of well-bred sponger dependent on kind old friends, who received him for his agreeable disposition as well as for his being, after all, a decent fellow, who could be placed at dinner next to anyone, though, of course, at the lower end of the table. Such spongers—sociable gentlemen who know how to tell a good story, make up a fourth at cards, and most dislike accepting any commissions that may be forced upon them—are usually solitary men, either bachelors or widowers. They may have children, but these are being brought somewhere far away by aunts, whom such gentlemen hardly ever mention in good society, as though they are ashamed of such kinship. They gradually lose sight of their children, only occasionally receiving birthday or Christmas cards from them and sometimes even replying to them. The unexpected caller's face was not so much good-natured as, again, agreeable and ready to assume any amiable expression demanded by the occasion. He wore no watch, but he did have a tortoise-shell lorgnette on a black ribbon. On the middle finger of his right hand was a massive gold ring with an inexpensive opal stone. Ivan Fyodorovich was resentfully silent, unwilling to open the conversation. His visitor waited, and sat exactly like a hanger-on does who has just come downstairs from the room assigned to him, to keep his host company at tea, but is discreetly silent since the host is busy and frowningly preoccupied, but prepared to enter into any polite conversation as soon as his host begins one. Suddenly, a look of concern came over his face.

"I say," he began, "just to remind you: you went to see Smerdyakov to find out about Katerina Ivanovna, but left without finding out anything about her. I expect you must have forgotten—"

"Good Lord!" Ivan cried suddenly, and his face darkened with anxiety, "yes, I'd forgotten— Still, it makes no difference now," he muttered to himself, "everything can wait till tomorrow. As for you," he turned irritably to his visitor, "I should have remembered it myself presently, for it was what made me feel so depressed! Did you have to interfere to make me believe that it was you who reminded me of it and I didn't remember it myself?"

"You needn't believe it," the gentleman said, smiling affably. "Belief shouldn't be forced! Besides, so far as faith is concerned, no proofs are of any use, especially material ones. Thomas believed, not because he saw that Christ had risen but because he had wanted to. Now, take the spiritualists—mind you, I'm very fond of them—just imagine, they think they are useful to religion because devils show them their horns from the other world. 'That,' they maintain, 'is, as it were, material proof of the existence of another world.' The other world and material proofs—dear me! And, after all, if one can prove the existence of devils, does that prove the existence of God, too? I'd like to join an idealist society, and form an opposition in it: 'I'm a realist, so to speak, not a materialist, ha, ha!' "

"Listen," said Ivan Fyodorovich, suddenly rising from the table, "I seem to be delirious now—of course, I'm delirious—so you can talk any drivel you like for all I care! You won't drive me into a frenzy, as you did last time. I only feel ashamed of something— I feel like pacing the room— Sometimes I don't see you and I don't even hear your voice, as I did last time, but I always guess the absurd things you say because *it is I, I myself who am talking, and not you!* Only I don't know whether I was asleep last time or whether I saw you while I was awake? I'm going to dip a towel in cold water and put it on my head and perhaps you'll vanish in thin air."

Ivan Fyodorovich went into a corner of the room, took a towel and did as he had said, and, a wet towel about his head, began pacing the room.

"I'm glad we're on familiar terms now," the visitor began.

"You fool," Ivan laughed. "I'm not going to treat you with respect, am I? I'm in excellent spirits now, only I've got a pain in my temple and—and in my head— Only, please don't philosophise as you did last time. If you can't clear off, then invent something amusing. Talk gossip; you're a sponger, so talk scandal. Why should I have such a nightmare? But I'm not afraid of you. I can deal with you. They won't drag me off to a lunatic asylum!"

"*C'est charmant*—a sponger. Well, yes, I suppose I am just that. For what am I if not a sponger on this earth? By the way, I'm all ears, and can't help being a little surprised, you know: you're indeed gradually beginning to take me for something that really exists and not only as a figment of your imagination, as you insisted last time—"

"Never for a moment have I taken you for reality," Ivan even cried out in a kind of fury. "You're a lie, an illness, a phantom. I only don't know how to destroy you and I'm afraid I shall have to suffer you for a time. You are a hallucination of mine. You're an embodiment of myself, but only of one aspect of me—of my thoughts and feelings, but only the most vile and stupid. From that point of view, you might even interest me, if only I had time to waste on you—"

"Come, come, I'll catch you off balance. Some hours ago, at the lamppost, when you flew at Alyosha, you shouted to him: 'You learnt it from *him*! How did you learn that *he* comes to see me?' You were thinking of me then, weren't you? So that, for a fraction of a second, you did believe that I really existed, didn't you?" the gentleman laughed genially.

"Yes, that was a weakness of nature—but I couldn't believe in you. I don't know whether I was asleep or walking about last time. Perhaps I only saw you in a dream, not in reality—"

"Why, then, were you so severe to him, to Alyosha, I mean? He's a nice boy. I'm afraid I'm at fault with him over the *starets* Zossima."

"Don't talk to me of Alyosha! How dare you, you lackey!" Ivan laughed again.

"You abuse me and yet laugh at the same time—a good sign. Incidentally, you're much more affable to me today than last time and I know why: that great decision of yours—"

"Not a word of my decision!" Ivan cried fiercely.

"I understand, I understand, *c'est noble, c'est charmant.* You're going to defend your brother tomorrow and sacrifice yourself—*c'est chevaleresque.*"

"Shut up or I'll kick you!"

"I'll be glad in a way, for my aim will have been achieved. If you kick me, you must believe in my reality, for one doesn't kick a ghost. But joking apart, it makes no difference to me: abuse me if you like. Yet it's far better to be a little more polite, even to me. H'm, fool, lackey—the words you use!"

"In abusing you, I abuse myself!" Ivan laughed again. "You are me—me myself, only with a different mug. You're merely putting my thoughts into words—and you can't say anything new to me!"

"If my thinking coincides with yours, then it only redounds to my credit," the gentleman declared with delicate dignity.

"Except that you only take my evil thoughts, and, moreover, the stupid ones. You're stupid and vulgar. You're awfully stupid. No, I can't stand you! What am I to do? What am I to do?" cried Ivan, grinding his teeth.

"My friend, say what you like, but I prefer to be a gentleman and I want to be accepted as one," the visitor began in an access of premeditatedly compliant and good-humoured pride befitting a hanger-on. "I am poor but—I won't say very honest, but—in society it is accepted as axiomatic that I'm a fallen angel. Really, I can't imagine how I can ever have been an angel. If ever I was, it was so long ago that I can be forgiven for forgetting

399

it. The only thing I now prize is my reputation of being a decent fellow and I live as best I can, trying to be complaisant. I love people sincerely—oh, I've been terribly slandered! Here, when I come to live among them from time to time, my life does assume something like reality, and I like that most of all. For, you see, like you, I, too, suffer from the fantastic and that's why I love your terrestrial realism. With you, everything here is clear-cut, all formulas and geometry, while with us it's all some kind of indeterminate equations! Here I can walk about and dream. I like dreaming. Besides, on earth I become superstitious—don't laugh please: you see, becoming superstitious is just what I like. I adopt all your habits here: I have grown fond of going to the public baths—can you imagine that? And I enjoy a steam-bath in the company of merchants and priests. My fondest dream is to be reincarnated, but irrevocably and for good, as the fat wife of a merchant and to believe in everything she believes in. It is my ideal to go into a church and offer a candle from a pure heart—indeed, it is! That would be the end of all my sufferings. And I've also grown fond of medical treatment here: there was a small-pox epidemic in the spring and I went to a foundlings' home and got myself vaccinated—if only you knew how contented I felt that day: I donated ten roubles in aid of our Slav brothers!—But you're not listening. You know, you're not at all well today," the gentleman paused a little. "I know you went to see that doctor yesterday—well, how is your health? What did the doctor tell you?"

"You fool!" Ivan snapped.

"Ah, what a clever man you are! You're abusing me again? I wasn't asking you out of sympathy, but just out of politeness. You needn't answer if you don't want to. People begin to suffer from rheumatism again now—"

"You fool," Ivan repeated.

"You keep repeating the same thing, but I had an attack of rheumatism last year that I can't forget."

"A devil and rheumatism?"

"Why not, if I sometimes assume a human form. When I do, I suffer the consequences. *Satan sum et nihil humanum a me alienum puto.*"

"What did you say? *Satan sum et nihil humanum*—not bad for a devil!"

"I'm glad to have pleased you at last."

"You didn't get that from me," Ivan stopped dead suddenly, as though amazed. "That never entered my head—that's funny—"

"*C'est du nouveau, n'est ce pas*? This time I'll be honest and explain something to you. Listen: in dreams and particularly in nightmares caused by indigestion or whatever, a man sometimes sees such artistic things, such a complex and actual reality, such events, or even an entire world of events, woven into such a plot, full of such astonishing details, beginning with the most exalted manifestations of the human spirit down to the last button on a shirt-front that, I assure you, not even Lev Tolstoy could have thought it up, and yet such dreams are sometimes seen, not by writers but by the most ordinary people, civil servants, newspaper columnists and priests— The whole matter, in fact, presents a most difficult problem: a Cabinet minister admitted to me himself that his best ideas came to him when he was asleep. Well, that's what is happening now. Though I'm your hallucination, yet, just as in a nightmare, I say things which never entered your head before, so that I am not repeating your thoughts at all, and yet I'm only your nightmare and nothing more."

"You're lying. Your aim is to convince me that you exist as an independent entity and that you are not my nightmare. And now you admit yourself that you are a dream."

"I've adopted a special method today, my friend, I'll explain it to you later. Stay, where did I leave off? Oh yes. So I caught a cold, only not here but there—"

"What d'you mean by there? Tell me, are you going to stay here long? Can't you go away?" cried Ivan, almost in despair. He stopped pacing the room, sat down on the sofa, again put his elbows on the table and clutched his head tightly in both hands. He tore off the wet towel and flung it away in vexation: it was evidently unavailing.

"Your nerves are in rags," the gentleman remarked in a carelessly casual but very friendly tone. "You're angry with me even

401

for being able to catch cold, and yet it happened in a most natural way. I was in a hurry just then to get to a diplomatic reception given by a highly placed St. Petersburg lady, who was working to get a ministerial post for her husband. Well, of course, evening dress, white tie and tails, and gloves, but I happened to be goodness knows where at the time and to get to your earth I had to fly through space— Of course, it was only a matter of a second, but then even a ray of light from the sun takes eight minutes to get to earth, and there I was—imagine!— in evening dress and open waistcoat. Spirits do not freeze, but once you've assumed human form—anyway, I did a silly thing and set out, and, you know, in those empty spaces, in the ether, in the water that is above the firmament—why, it so freezing up there—you can hardly call it a frost—just imagine, one hundred and fifty degrees below zero! You know the sort of game village girls play: they ask a callow youth to lick an axe in thirty degrees of frost; his tongue freezes to it at once and the stupid fellow tears the skin off it so that it bleeds. Well, that is only in thirty degrees, and in one hundred and fifty you have only to put a finger to an axe and, I should think, there will be nothing left of it, if only—there could be an axe there—"

"And could there be an axe there?" Ivan Fyodorovich suddenly interrupted absently and with a sense of revulsion. He was doing his utmost not to believe in his mad dream and not go completely out of his mind.

"An axe?" the visitor repeated in surprise.

"Yes, what would happen to an axe there?" Ivan Fyodorovich suddenly cried with a kind of fierce and insistent obstinacy.

"What would happen to an axe in empty space? *Quelle idée*! If it got far enough, it would, I think, begin circling the earth like a kind of satellite with no purpose at all. The astronomers would calculate the rising and the setting of the axe, it would be recorded in the Gatzuk almanac*, and that's all."

---

*During 1870-1880 A. A. Gatzuk (1832-1891), a Moscow publisher, brought out a *Gazette* and an almanac for the coming year, with a weekly illustrated supplement.—*Tr.*

"You're stupid, terribly stupid!" Ivan said peevishly. "You'd better lie more intelligently or I won't listen. You want to get the better of me by realism, want to convince me that you do exist. But I don't want to believe that you do! I won't believe it!"

"But I'm not lying; it's all true. Unfortunately, the truth is hardly ever witty. I can see that you positively expect something extraordinary from me and, perhaps, something beautiful, too. That's a great pity, for I only give what I can—"

"Don't philosophise, you ass!"

"How can I philosophise when the whole of my right side is numb and I'm moaning and groaning. I've consulted all sorts of doctors: they can diagnose excellently; they will tell you all your symptoms; they can enumerate your illnesses, but they've no idea how you can get cured. I happened to come across a highly enthusiastic medical student: 'You may die,' he told me, 'but at least you'll have a very good idea of what illness you're dying of!' And, then again, their practice of referring you to the specialist. 'We can only diagnose your disease,' they tell you. 'But better go to such and such a specialist and he'll cure you for sure.' I tell you the old-style doctor, who used to deal with all your illnesses, is a thing of the past. Now only specialists exist, who they all advertise in the papers. If there's something wrong with your nose, they will send you to Paris: there's a European specialist there who deals with noses. You go to Paris and he examines your nose. 'I'm sorry,' he tells you, 'I can only cure your right nostril, for I don't treat left nostrils— it's not my speciality. You'd better go to Vienna, there you'll find a special expert who will treat your left nostril.' What can one do? I've tried popular remedies. A German doctor advised me to rub myself with honey and salt on a shelf in a bathhouse. I went solely to have another bath, got myself covered all over with honey and salt, but it was no good at all. In despair I wrote to Count Mattei in Milan. He sent me a book and some drops—oh, well, I don't blame him! And, just imagine, Hoff's malt extract cured me! I bought it by accident, drank a bottle and a half of it, and I was as fit as a fiddle—I could even dance if I wanted to! I decided to thank him in a letter I sent to a newspaper editor—I was prompted by a sense of gratitude. And, well, you know, things did not work out that way, for not a single newspaper would publish it! 'It would be very reactionary,' they said. 'No one will believe it. *Le diable n'existe point.* You'd better publish it anonymously,' they advised me. But what kind of gratitude is it if it's anonymous? I had a good laugh with the clerks at the newspaper office. 'Why,' I said to them, 'it's reactionary to believe in God in our age. But I'm the devil. You can believe in me.' 'Quite right,' they said, 'who doesn't believe in the devil? Yet it can't be done for it might be injurious to the trend pursued by our newspaper. It might be published as a piece of humour.' Well, I didn't think it would be very witty to treat it in jest. So it wasn't published. And, you know, I still feel upset about it. My best feelings, gratitude, for instance, are formally denied me simply because of my social status."

"Engaging in philosophy again, are you?" Ivan snarled with hatred.

"Good Lord, no, but one can't help complaining sometimes. I am a slandered person. Now, you, too, keep telling me every minute that I'm stupid. One can see you're young. My dear fellow, it isn't only brains that matter! I'm naturally kind-hearted and of a merry disposition. 'I, too, you know, write various kinds of vaudeville skits.'* I'm afraid you're set on taking me for a grey-haired Khlestakov, but my fate has been a far more serious one. By some age-old predestination, which I have never been able to make out, I was appointed 'to negate' while, in fact, I'm genuinely kind-hearted and not at all good at 'negation'. Oh, no, you go ahead and negate, for without negation there is no criticism, and what sort of periodical is it if it has no section for criticism? Without criticism there would be nothing but sheer hosannas. But hosannas alone are not enough for life, for they must be tested in the crucible of doubt, and so on in the same vein. Yet I don't want to get involved in that: I didn't create the world, so it's none of my responsibility. Well, so they have chosen their scapegoat, made me contribute to the section

*A quotation from Gogol's comedy *The Government Inspector* (1836), in which the impostor Khlestakov lays claim to absurd powers and connections to mystify his hosts.—*Tr.*

of criticism, and the outcome was most lifelike. We appreciate that comedy: for instance, I frankly and openly demand that I should be done away with. No, they say, you must go on living because there'd be nothing without you. If everything on earth were rational, nothing would take place. Without you, there would be no events, and it is essential that there should be events. So I serve with a heavy heart so that there may be happenings and, as ordered to, I create the irrational. People accept all this comedy in earnest even given their doubtless intelligence. That is their tragedy. Well, of course, they suffer, but—they live; they live a real and not an imaginary life, for suffering means living. Without suffering, what pleasure would they get out of life? Everything would turn into an endless religious service: it would be sacred but a little dull. Well, and what about me? I suffer, yet I do not live. I am the X in an indeterminate equation. I am a sort of phantom that has lost all beginnings and ends and has even forgotten his own name. You are laughing at me—no, you aren't, you're angry again. You're always angry. All you care about is intelligence. But I tell you again that I'd give up all this superstellar life, all my ranks and honours, to be reincarnated as the fat wife of a merchant and offer candles unto the Lord."

"So you, too, don't believe in God?" Ivan again sneered with hatred.

"Well, how shall I put it, if only you're in earnest—"

"Is there a God or isn't there?" cried Ivan again with fierce insistence.

"Oh, so you are in earnest! My dear fellow, I really don't know. There, I've said something outstanding."

"You don't know, and yet you see God? No, you don't exist independently. You are *me, me,* and nothing more. You are trash, my own imagination!"

"Well, if you like, I have the same philosophy as you. That will be fair. *Je pense donc je suis,* that I know for certain. As for everything else around me, all these worlds, God and even Satan himself—all that hasn't been proved to me. Does it all exist of itself or is it only an emanation of myself, a consistent development of my *I*, which has existed since the beginning of time and singularly—but I hasten to discontinue, for I see you're spoiling for a fight."

"You'd better tell me something entertaining!" Ivan said bitterly.

"I know an amusing story and on our subject, too. I mean, not really a story, but a legend. You reproach me with unbelief: 'You see,' you say, 'but you don't believe.' But, my dear fellow, I'm not alone in that. All the fellows down there feel confused, and all because of your learning. While there were still only atoms, five senses, four elements, it all still made some sense. There were atoms in the ancient world too. But as soon as our fellows learnt you'd discovered the 'chemical molecule' and the 'protoplasm' and the devil knows what else—they put their tails between their legs. There was terrible turmoil and, worst of all, superstition, scandal—you see, our people engage in scandal much as you do, even a little more—and, finally, denunciations, for you see we, too, have a special department where 'certain information' is accepted. Well, anyway, that improbable legend dates back to our middle ages—not yours, but ours—and no one believes it even among us, except the fat wives of merchants, and again I mean ours, not yours. Everything you have, we've got, too. I'm revealing one of our secrets out of friendship for you, though it is forbidden. The legend is about Paradise. There was, so it goes, a certain thinker and philosopher down here on your earth who 'rejected everything: laws, conscience, faith' and, above all, the future life. He died thinking he'd go straight to death and darkness, and, lo and behold, there was the future life before him. He was astounded and indignant. 'This,' he said, 'is against my principles.' So for that he was condemned—I'm sorry, you see, I'm only telling you what I heard myself, it's only a legend—so, you see, he was condemned to walk in darkness a quadrillion kilometres (we've gone metric, you know), and when he had completed the quadrillion, the gates of heaven would open to him and everything would be forgiven—"

"And what other torment besides the quadrillion do you have in the world to come," Ivan interrupted with strange animation.

"Torment? Oh, don't ask me. We used to have all kinds, but

the moral ones are now ever more in vogue: 'pricks of conscience' and all that rubbish. That too, we've adopted from you, from 'the growing mildness of your mores'. And who do you think has benefited? Only those with no consciences, for what do they care for pricks of conscience, when they have no conscience of any kind? On the other hand, the decent people, those with some conscience and a sense of honour left, are worse off than ever before— So that's the kind of thing that happens to reforms when the ground has not been properly laid for them and if, in addition, they've merely been copied from foreign institutions—nothing but harm results! The hell-fire of old was much better. Well, so the man who was sentenced to the quadrillion kilometres stood still, looked round and lay down across the road: 'I won't go on! I refuse to go on principle!' Now, take the soul of an enlightened Russian atheist and mix it with the soul of the prophet Jonah, the one who was in the belly of a great fish for three days and three nights, and you get the nature of the thinker who lay down across the road."

"What did he lie down on there?"

"Oh, I suppose there must have been something to lie down on. You're not joking, are you?"

"Good for you!" cried Ivan, still with the same strange animation. He was now listening with a sort of unexpected curiosity. "Well, is he lying there still?"

"That's the whole point—he isn't. He lay there for almost a thousand years, then he got up and went off."

"What a silly ass!" Ivan exclaimed with a nervous laugh, seeming to be giving deep thought to something. "What difference did it make whether he lay there for ever or walked a quadrillion versts? Why, it would take him a billion years to walk that distance, wouldn't it?"

"Much longer. I'm sorry I haven't a pencil and paper or I'd have worked it out. But, you see, he reached that place long ago, and that's where the story begins."

"Did he? But where did he get the billion years to do it in?"

"You're thinking of our earth of today! Why, our present earth has probably repeated itself a billion times. I mean, it's become extinct, frozen, cracked, fallen apart, resolved itself into its components, again the water above the firmament, then again a comet, again a sun, again an earth out of the sun—perhaps that development has already been repeated an infinite number of times, and all in one and the same way, down to the smallest detail. A most abominably boring business—"

"Well, what happened when he got there?"

"Why, the moment the gates of Paradise were opened to him and he walked in, and before he had been there for even two seconds—and that is by his watch, by his watch (though, if you ask me, his watch should have disintegrated in his pocket into its components on the way ages ago)—before he had been there two seconds, he exclaimed that for the sake of those two seconds he'd have gladly walked, not only a quadrillion but a quadrillion of quadrillions raised to a quadrillionth power! In a word, he sang a hosanna, and overdid it so much that some people there with a more elevated mode of thought even refused to shake hands with him at first: he had gone over to the conservatives a little too impetuously, they thought. The Russian temperament. I repeat, it has become a legend. I give that to you for what it's worth. So that's the sort of ideas on all these subjects that we still have down there."

"I have you on the hip now!" cried Ivan with almost childish glee, as though recalling something at last. "This amusing story about the quadrillion is something I made up myself! I was seventeen at the time, and at a Gymnasium—I made up that story then and told it to a school friend called Korovkin; that was in Moscow— The story is so characteristic that I couldn't have got it from anywhere. I seemed to have forgotten it—but I myself have recalled it subconsciously now—I did so myself, so it wasn't you who told it to me! One sometimes recalls thousands of things subconsciously even when one is being led to the execution—I've remembered it in my dream. So you are that dream! You are a dream and you don't exist!"

"Judging by the vehemence you refuse to acknowledge my existence with," the gentleman laughed, "I'm sure that you believe in me all the same."

"Not a bit! I don't believe a hundredth part in you!"

"But you do a thousandth part. Homeopathic doses, you

know, are perhaps the most potent. Confess you believe, well, a ten-thousandth part—"

"Never for a moment!" Ivan cried furiously. "I'd like to believe in you, though," he added strangely.

"Oho! That is an admission! But I'm good-natured and I'll help you there, too. Listen, it's I who have caught you out, not you me! I deliberately told you a story you had forgotten so as to make you lose faith in me completely."

"You're lying! Your appearance is designed to make me believe that you exist."

"To be sure. But hesitations, uneasiness, the conflict between belief and disbelief—why, that is sometimes such torment to a conscientious man like yourself that one would rather hang oneself. You see, knowing that you do believe in me a little bit, I made you disbelieve in me completely by telling you this story. I keep you dangling between belief and disbelief in turn, and I have a reason for it. It's the new method, sir. For when you lose your faith in me completely, you will at once begin assuring me to my face that I'm not a dream, but do really exist, I know you. And then I shall have attained my object, and that is an honourable one. I shall sow a tiny grain of faith in you and it will grow into an oak-tree—and such an oak that, as you sit on it, you will long to join 'the saintly eremites and the immaculate women'*, for that is something you yearn for at heart; you will be feeding upon locusts and you will drag yourself off into the wilderness to seek salvation!"

"So you're doing all this for the salvation of my soul, you rogue?"

"Well, one has to perform some good deed at times, you know. You are in a bad temper, I see!"

"You clown! But have you ever tried to tempt those who feed upon locusts, spend seventeen years praying in the wilderness, and are moss-grown?"

"My dear fellow, I've been doing nothing else. You will abandon the whole world and all worlds, and you will cleave to a man like that, for his price is above rubies. Why, one such soul

---

*A line from Alexander Pushkin's poem of the same title (1836).

is sometimes worth a whole galaxy of stars—you see, we have our own arithmetic. It's the conquest of such a man that is so priceless! And some of them, I assure you, are no inferior to you in intellect, though you may not believe it: they are capable of contemplating such depths of belief and disbelief at one and the same moment that you sometimes do, indeed, feel that given another hair's breadth, your man will precipitate himself 'head over heels', as the actor Gorbunov* says."

"Well, and has your nose been put out of joint?"

"My friend," the visitor observed sententiously, "sometimes it's better to have one's nose put out of joint than to have no nose at all, as an ailing marquis (he must have been treated by a specialist) said not so long ago in confessing to his spiritual Jesuit father. I was there, and it was simply delightful. 'Give me my nose back!' he said, smiting his breast. 'My son,' the Jesuit quibbled, 'in accordance with the inscrutable decrees of Providence, all things are balanced, and an obvious setback sometimes leads to extraordinary if invisible advantage. If stern destiny has deprived you of your nose, it's to your advantage, for no one, for the rest of you life, will dare tell you that your nose has been put out of joint.' 'Holy Father, that's no consolation!' the desperate man cried. 'I'd be delighted to have my nose put out of joint every day provided it was in its proper place!' 'My son,' the priest sighed, 'you must not demand all blessings at once, for that is murmuring against Providence, which has not forgotten you even in this plight; for if you cry out, as you did just now, that you'd be delighted to have your nose put out of joint for the rest of your life, your wish has already been fulfilled indirectly: for, having lost your nose, you have, as it were, had your nose put permanently out of joint *ipso facto*!'"

"How stupid!" cried Ivan.

"My friend, I only wanted to amuse you, but I swear that this is a piece of genuine Jesuit casuistry, and, I swear, it all happened just as I told you, word for word. It happened only

*I. F. Gorbunov (1831-1896)—a talented and highly successful *raconteur* of improvised stories.—*Tr.*

410

recently and it gave me a lot of trouble. On returning home, the unfortunate young man shot himself that very night. I was there with him till the last moment— As for those Jesuit confessionals, they really are my most delightful diversions at melancholy moments of life. Here's another incident that took place only the other day. A little blonde Norman girl of twenty came to an old priest. She was a beauty, plump, and buxom, and had everything Nature can lavish to tempt a man. She bent down and whispered her sin to the priest through the grating. 'Dear me, my daughter, have you fallen again already?' the priest whispered. 'O, Sancta Maria, what's this I'm hearing? Not with the same man? But how long is it to go on? And aren't you ashamed of yourself?' '*Ah mon père,*' answered the sinner, tears of repentance rolling down her cheeks, '*ça lui fait tant de plaisir et à moi si peu de peine!*' Well, just fancy an answer like that! I withdrew at this juncture: it was the cry of Nature and, if you like, better than innocence itself! I absolved her sin there and then and was about to go, but I was forced to go back at once. For I heard the priest making an assignation with her through the grating for the evening—an old man like him, so upright in his faith, and fell in a twinkling! Nature, the truth of Nature asserting itself! Why, you're turning up your nose again? Angry again? I really don't know how to please you—"

"Leave me, you are hammering at my brain like a haunting nightmare," Ivan moaned dismally, with a sense of helplessness against the apparition. "I'm bored with you, unbearably and agonisingly bored! I'd give anything to get rid of you!"

"I repeat, moderate your demands. Don't demand of me 'everything great and beautiful' and you'll see how well we shall get on together," the gentleman declared impressively. "You are really angry with me because I haven't appeared to you in a red glow, 'in thunder and lightning', with scorched wings, but have introduced myself in so unassuming a shape. You are pained, first of all, in your aesthetic feelings and, secondly, in your pride: how could such a vulgar devil come to visit such a great man? I'm afraid you do possess the romantic strain already so derided by Belinsky*. It just can't be helped, young man. I did intend, as I was on my way to you, to appear, as a joke, in the guise of a retired high-ranking official, who had served in the Caucasus, with the star of the Lion and the Sun on my frock-coat; I was positively afraid to do so because you would most certainly have beaten me black and blue for having only pinned the Lion and the Sun to my frock-coat instead of, at least, the Pole Star or Sirius**. And you go on telling me that I am stupid. But, dear Lord, I don't claim to be your equal in intellect. When he appeared to Faust, Mephistopheles introduced himself as one who desired evil but did only good. Well, that's as he pleases, but I'm quite the opposite. I'm perhaps the only man in all Nature who loves truth and sincerely desires good. I was present when the Word that died on the Cross ascended to heaven, carrying on his bosom the soul of the thief who had been crucified on his right, and I heard the joyful outcries of the cherubim, singing and shouting: hosanna, and the thunderous shouts of rapture of the seraphim, which shook heaven and all creation. And I swear by all that is sacred that I longed to join the chorus and cry hosanna with them all. The word had already escaped me—it had almost burst from my breast—you know, of course, how sentimental and artistically sensitive I am. But here, too, common sense—oh, that most unhappy trait in my make-up—kept me, within bounds, and I let the moment pass! For what, I thought at that instant, would have happened after my hosanna? Everything in the world would at once have been extinguished and no events

*Vissarion Grigorievich Belinsky (1811-1848)—a famous Russian literary critic and first representative of the *raznochinets* (non-noble) intelligentsia.—*Tr.*

**A cryptic reference. The Pole Star is a Swedish decoration. The devil is hinting at a literary almanac published in 1823-1825 by the Decembrists Ryleyev and Bestuzhev, and also Herzen and Ogarev's literary and socio-political collection, which was brought out abroad in 1855-1862 and 1869.

By Sirius, the devil is probably hinting at Voltaire, the main character in whose *Micromegas* (1752) is an "inhabitant of Sirius.". The point in this jibe is that Ivan has mistakenly seen a rebel and revolutionary in the devil, who in fact holds extreme conservative views.—*Tr.*

412

would have taken place after that. And so, solely out of a sense of duty and my social status, I was forced to suppress that good instant and carry on with my loathsome job. Somebody else takes all the credit for what is good, while all the dirty work is left to me. But I do not envy the honour of living at the expense of somebody else. I'm not ambitious. Why am I, alone of all the creatures in the world, doomed to be cursed by all decent folk and even to be kicked about? For, if I assume human form, I have to run the risk of such consequences, too, at times. I know, you see, that some secret lies here, but that secret is concealed from me because having realised what it is all about, I might roar out a hosanna, and the indispensable minus sign would disappear at once, and good sense would reign all over the world; once that happened, it would, of course, be the end of everything, even of newspapers and periodicals, for who would then care to subscribe to them? I know of course, that in the end I shall be reconciled, that I, too, shall travel my quadrillion and learn the secret. But until that comes about, I shall complainingly and reluctantly fulfil my destiny; I'll ruin thousands so that one may be saved. How many souls, for instance, have had to be ruined and how many honourable reputations discredited to get a single righteous Job, over whom I was let down so cruelly in bygone days! Yes, until the secret is revealed, there are two truths for me: theirs, of which I know nothing, and the other, my own. And there's no knowing which will turn out the worse— Are you asleep?"

"If only I were," Ivan groaned angrily. "Everything that is stupid in me, everything I experienced long ago, everything I've thrashed out in my mind and cast aside like so much carrion, you present to me as some novelty!"

"So, I've failed to please even here! And I thought I'd enchant you with my literary style: that hosanna in heaven was really not too bad, was it? Why now this sarcastic tone à la Heine, eh?"

"No, I've never been so much of a lackey! Why should my soul have begotten such a lackey as you?"

"My friend, I know a most attractive and charming young Russian gentleman: a young thinker, a great lover of literature

413

and *objets d'art,* and author of a poem of great promise entitled *The Grand Inquisitor*— I had him alone in mind."

"I forbid you to speak of *The Grand Inquisitor,*" cried Ivan, colouring all over with shame.

"Well, and what about *Geological Upheaval*? Remember? That was a lovely poem!"

"Shut up or I'll kill you!"

"Kill me? No, excuse me but I'll have my say. I've come to treat myself to that pleasure. Oh, I love the dreams of my passionate young friends, quivering with a thirst for life! 'There are new men,' you decided last spring, when you were about to come here, 'who propose to destroy everything and start all over again with anthropophagy. The fools! They didn't consult me! In my opinion, there's no need to destroy anything. What must be destroyed is the idea of God in mankind. That's what we ought to start with! Yes, we ought to start with that—oh, the blind fools, who have no understanding! Once humanity renounces God down to the last man (and I believe that period, which runs parallel to geological periods, will come to pass) the whole of the old outlook on life will collapse of itself without anthropophagy and, above all, the old morality, too, and a new era will dawn. Men will join hands to obtain whatever life can give, but only for joy and happiness in this world alone. Man will be exalted by a spirit of divine and titanic pride, and the man-god will make his appearance. Extending his conquest of Nature infinitely with every hour through his will and science, man will thereby and hourly feel so lofty a joy that it will make up for all his old hopes of heavenly bliss. Everyone will know that he is mortal, and that there is no resurrection; and he will accept death serenely and proudly like a god. His pride will make him realise that it's no use complaining that life is like the shadow of a passing bird and he will love his brother without expecting any reward. Love will satisfy only a fleeting moment of life, but that very consciousness will intensify its fire to the same extent as it is now dissipated in hopes of life eternal beyond the grave—' And so on and so forth, in the same vein. Quite charming!"

Ivan sat with his hands covering his ears and his eyes fixed

414

on the ground; he began to shiver but the voice went on:

"The question is, my young thinker thought, whether such a time will ever come to pass. If it does, everything will be resolved and mankind will achieve its goal. But since, in view of man's inveterate stupidity, it may not be achieved even in a thousand years, anyone with an awareness of the truth is entitled to carry on just as he pleases, in accordance with the new principles. In that sense 'everything is permitted' to him. Moreover, even if such a time does not come round, and since there is neither God nor immortality, anyway, the new man has a right to become a man-god, though he may be alone in the wide world, and, having attained that new rank, he may light-heartedly jump over every barrier of the old moral code of the former man-slave, if he deems it necessary. To God no law exists! God's place is wherever he stands! Wherever I may stand, will at once be the foremost place—'everything is permitted!' and that's all there is to it! All that is very charming; only, if you wish to live a life of deceit, why should you need the sanction of truth? But that's what our Russian of today is like: without that sanction he can't make up his mind to engage in deceit—he is so much in love with truth—"

The visitor talked on, evidently carried away by his eloquence, raising his voice more and more, and casting mocking glances at his host, but he did not succeed in finishing his speech: Ivan suddenly grabbed a glass from the table and hurled it with all his might at the speaker.

"*Ah, mais c'est bête enfin!*" the visitor exclaimed, jumping up from the sofa and flicking away the drops of tea from his clothes. "You've recalled Luther's ink-well*! You think I am a dream and throw glasses at a dream! How just like a woman! I knew very well that you were only pretending to stop up your ears, but that you were listening all the time—"

At the moment there was a loud and persistent knock on

---

*There is an apocryphal legend that the devil appeared to tempt Luther when he was translating the Bible into German in the castle of Wartburg in Thuringia, where he found refuge from persecution by the Papists. The reformer drove him off by throwing an ink-well at him.—*Tr.*

the window-frame. Ivan Fyodorovich jumped up from the sofa.

"Do you hear? You'd better let him in," cried the visitor. "It's your brother Alyosha, who has come to tell you a most surprising and interesting piece of news, I promise you!"

"Shut up, you swindler! I knew it was Alyosha before you spoke and, of course, he hasn't come without reason—of course, he's come with some 'news'," cried Ivan, beside himself.

"Let him in. There's a snow-storm raging, and he's your brother. *Monsieur, sait-il le temps qu'il fait? C'est à ne pas mettre un chien dehors—*"

The knocking continued. Ivan was about to rush up to the window, but something suddenly seemed to fetter his hands and feet. He tried with all his might to break the fetters, but could not. The knocking at the window grew louder and louder. At last, the fetters snapped and Ivan Fyodorovich jumped up from the sofa. He looked wildly about himself. The two candles had almost burnt out, the glass, which he had only just flung at his visitor, stood before him on the table, and there was no one on the sofa opposite. The knocking at the window, though it still went on persistently, was not as loud as it had seemed in his dream. On the contrary, it was subdued.

"It wasn't a dream! No, I swear it wasn't a dream! It all happened!" cried Ivan Fyodorovich and, rushing up to the window, he opened it.

"Alyosha, I told you not to come here, didn't I?" he shouted to his brother fiercely. "Tell me quick what do you want? Quick, do you hear?"

"Smerdyakov hanged himself an hour ago," Alyosha replied from the yard.

"Come round to the front door. I'll open it at once," said Ivan and went to open the door to Alyosha.

10.

"It Was He Who Said That!"

When he came in, Alyosha told Ivan Fyodorovich that just over an hour before Maria Kondratievna had come running to his place to let him know that Smerdyakov had committed suicide. "I went into his room," she said, "to clear away the tea things and there he was hanging from a nail in the wall." When Alyosha asked her whether she had informed the police, she replied that she had not but had first come straight to him, running all the way. She was beside herself, Alyosha said, and was shaking like an aspen leaf. And when Alyosha ran with her to the cottage, he found Smerdyakov still hanging. On the table was a note: "I've put an end to my life of my own free will and no one is to blame for it." Alyosha left the note on the table and went straight to the uyezd chief of police where he made a statement, "and from there I've come straight to you", concluded Alyosha, looking intently into Ivan's face. He had not taken his eyes off him while he was telling his story, as though struck by something in the expression of his face.

"Brother," he cried suddenly, "you must be terribly ill! You are looking at me, but don't seem to understand what I'm saying!"

"It's good of you to have come," said Ivan, as though he were thinking of something else and had not heard Alyosha's remarks. "I knew he had hanged himself."

"Who from?"

"I don't know who from. But I knew. Did I know? Yes, he told me. He told me just now—"

Ivan was standing in the middle of the room, and spoke still in the same pensive tone, his eyes fixed on the floor.

"Who is *he*?" asked Alyosha, looking round involuntarily.

"He's slipped away."

Ivan raised his head and smiled gently.

"He got frightened of you, of a gentle dove like you. You are 'a pure cherub'. Dmitri calls you a cherub. A cherub—the thunderous shout of rapture of the seraphim! What is a seraph? A whole constellation, perhaps. And, perhaps, the whole of that constellation is just a sort of chemical molecule— Is there a constellation of the Lion and the Sun—do you know?"

"Sit down, brother!" said Alyosha in alarm. "For God's sake, sit down on the sofa. You're delirious. Put your head on the pillow—so. Shall I put a wet towel on your head? You'll feel better, perhaps."

"Yes, give me the towel. It's there on the chair. I threw it down there a little while ago."

"It isn't there. Don't bother, I know where it is—here," said Alyosha, finding a clean towel, still folded and unused, at the other end of the room by Ivan's wash-stand. Ivan looked strangely at the towel; his memory seemed to have returned to him in an instant.

"Just a moment," he said, rising from the sofa. "About an hour ago I took that same towel from there and wetted it. I put it on my head and threw it down here—why is it dry? There was no other towel."

"You put this towel on your head?" asked Alyosha.

"Yes, and walked about with it about an hour ago— Why have the candles burnt down like that? What's the time?"

"Nearly twelve."

"No, no, no!" cried Ivan suddenly. "It was not a dream! He was here, sitting there, on that sofa. When you knocked at the window, I threw a glass at him—that one— Just a moment: I was asleep before, but this was no dream. It's happened before, too. You see, Alyosha, I have dreams now—but they are not really dreams. I'm actually awake. I walk about, talk and see things and—and yet I'm asleep. But he was sitting there— he was there—on that sofa— He's awfully stupid, Alyosha, awfully stupid," Ivan laughed suddenly and began pacing the room.

"Who is stupid? Who are you talking about, brother?" Alyosha asked again, sadly.

"The devil! He's taken to visiting me. He's been here twice, almost three times. He taunted me for being angry that he's just a devil and not Satan with scorched wings, appearing in thunder and lightning. But he is not Satan. He's telling lies about that. He's an impostor. He's just a devil, a rotten, insignificant devil. He goes to the baths. Undress him and you'll be sure to find a tail, a long smooth tail, like a Great Dane's, a yard long, brown in colour— Alyosha, you're cold. You've been out in the snow. Would you like some tea? What? It's cold, is it? Shall I tell her to make some? *C'est à ne pas mettre un chien dehors—*"

Alyosha ran to the wash-stand, wetted the towel, persuaded Ivan to sit down again and put the wet towel about his head. He sat down at his side.

"What were you telling me about Lise last time?" Ivan began again. (He was becoming very talkative.) "I like Lise. I said something bad about her. I was lying. I like her— I'm afraid for Katya tomorrow, I'm afraid for her more than anything. For the future. She'll jilt me tomorrow and trample me under foot. She thinks I'm ruining Mitya because I'm jealous of her! Yes, she thinks that! But it's not true. Tomorrow the cross, but not the gallows. No, I shan't hang myself. Do you know, Alyosha, that I could never commit suicide? Is it because I am a rotter? I'm no coward. It's because of my craving for life! How did I know that Smerdyakov had hanged himself? Yes, it was *he* who told me that—"

"And are you quite sure that someone was sitting here?" asked Alyosha.

"Yes, on that sofa, in the corner. You would have chased him off. Why, you did chase him off: he vanished as soon as you appeared. I love your face, Alyosha. Did you know that I love your face? But *he* is me, Alyosha, me! All that is base, rotten, and contemptible in me! Yes, I'm 'romantic,' and he noticed it—though it's a slander. He's awfully stupid, but that's his strong point. He's cunning, just like some animal and he knew how to madden me. He kept taunting me with my belief in him, and that's how he made me listen to him. He fooled me as if I were an urchin. Still, he told me a great deal that was true about myself. I would never have said it to myself. You know, Alyosha, you know," Ivan added very earnestly and as though confidentially, "I'd have liked very much that he should really be *he* and not me!"

"He has tired you out," said Alyosha, looking with compassion at his brother.

"Taunted me! And, you know, cleverly, very cleverly: 'Conscience! What is conscience? I invent it myself. Why, then, am I so unhappy? From habit. From the universal habit of mankind over the past seven thousand years. Let us cast off our habits and become gods.' It was he who said that. It was he who said that!"

"But not you, not you?" Alyosha could not help crying out, looking serenely at his brother. "Well, let him, give him up, forget all about him! Let him take away with him all that you curse now, and don't let him return!"

"Yes, but he's spiteful. He mocked at me. He was insolent, Alyosha," Ivan said with a shudder of resentment. "But he slandered me; he slandered me about lots of things. He told lies about me to my face. 'Oh, you're going to perform a feat of virtue! You're going to declare that it was you who murdered your father, that the servant murdered him at your instigation—' "

"Stay, brother!" Alyosha interrupted. "Don't say that. It wasn't you who did it. It's not true!"

"It was he who said that, he, and he knows it. 'You're going to perform a feat of virtue, yet you don't believe in virtue—that's what aggravates and torments you and makes you so vindictive.' That was what he said to me about myself, and he knows what he is talking about—"

"It's you who say that, not he!" Alyosha cried, sorrowfully. "And you say it because you are ill and delirious, and tormenting yourself!"

"No, he knows what he is talking about. You are going, he says, out of pride. You'll stand up and say: 'It was I who did it. Why do you look so horror-stricken? You are lying! I despise your opinion, I despise your horror.' He says that about me, and then he suddenly says: 'But you know you'd like very much to be praised by them: "He's a criminal, a murderer, but what magnanimous sentiments he has. Wanted to save his brother, and confessed!" ' That's a damn lie, Alyosha!" Ivan suddenly cried, with flashing eyes. "I don't want the common folk to praise me! He was lying, Alyosha! I swear he was lying! That's why I threw the glass at him, and it broke against his ugly mug."

"Calm yourself, brother! Desist!" Alyosha besought him.

"Yes, he knows how to torment me; he's cruel," Ivan went on, without listening. "I always knew why he came. 'All right,' he said, 'suppose you go out of pride, but there was still the hope that they would convict Smerdyakov and sentence him to penal servitude in Siberia, that they would acquit Mitya and find you only *morally* culpable—(You hear? he laughed at this point!) and others will laud you. But now Smerdyakov is dead; he has hanged himself, so who will believe you alone in court now? But you're going, you're going there. You will go for all that; you've made up your mind to go. Why should you go there after that?' That is frightful, Alyosha. I can't bear such questions. Who dares ask me such questions?"

"Brother," interrupted Alyosha, faint with terror, though still seeming hopeful of bringing Ivan to his senses, "how could he have told you about Smerdyakov's death before I came when no one knew about it and there was no time for any-one to learn of it?"

"He did tell me," Ivan said firmly, precluding all doubt. "He spoke of nothing but that, as a matter of fact. 'It would be all right,' he said, 'if you believed in virtue: don't let them believe me, I'm going for the principle of the thing. But you're a swine like your father; what do you care for virtue? What then do you want to drag yourself off there for, if your sacrifice won't be of any use? The fact is you don't know yourself what you are going there for! Oh, you'd give a lot to learn why you should go! And have you really made up your mind? No, you have not! You'll be sitting here all night trying to make up your mind whether to go or not. But you will go all the same, and you know it. You know yourself that, whatever you decide, the decision no longer depends on you. You will go because you won't dare not to go. Why you won't dare, you can guess for yourself—there's a riddle for you!' Then he got up and went away. You came, and he left. He called me a coward, Alyosha! *Le mot de l'énigme* is that I *am* a coward. 'It is not for such eagles to soar above the earth!' It was he who added that! It was he! And Smerdyakov said the same. He must be killed! Katya despises me, I've seen it for a month. And Lise, too, is beginning to despise me. 'You are going for people to praise you'—that is a cruel lie! And you, too, despise me, Alyosha. Now I shall hate you again. And I hate the monster, I hate the

421

monster! I don't want to save the monster; let him rot in Siberia! He has begun singing a hymn. Oh, I'll go tomorrow, stand before them, and spit in their faces!"

He jumped up in a frenzy, flung off the towel and began pacing the room again. Alyosha remembered the words he had uttered a short while before: "I seem to be awake in my sleep— I walk about, I talk and I see things, and yet I am asleep." Just as it seems to be happening now. Alyosha did not leave him. It flashed through his mind that he should run for a doctor and come back with him, but he was afraid to leave his brother alone: there was no one to leave him with. Little by little, Ivan began to lose consciousness. He went on talking; he spoke without stopping, but quite incoherently. He even articulated his words with difficulty and suddenly he staggered violently. But Alyosha was in time to support him. Ivan allowed himself to be led to his bed. Alyosha managed to undress him and put him to bed. He sat by his bedside for another two hours. The sick man slept soundly, without stirring, breathing softly and evenly. Alyosha took a pillow and lay down on the sofa without undressing. Before he fell asleep, he said a prayer for Mitya and Ivan. He began to understand Ivan's illness: "The agony of a proud decision, deep-lying conscience!" God, in whom he did not believe, and his truth, had gained possession of his heart, which still refused to yield. "Yes," the thought passed through Alyosha's head, as he fell back on the pillow, "yes, now that Smerdyakov is dead, no one will believe Ivan's evidence. But he will go and give it!" Alyosha smiled softly: "God will conquer!" he thought. "Ivan will either rise up in the light of truth or— perish in hate, avenging on himself and on everyone else his having served something he does not believe in," Alyosha added bitterly, and again he prayed for Ivan.

BOOK TWELVE

A Miscarriage of Justice

1.

The Fateful Day

At ten o'clock in the morning of the day following the events I have described, our district court opened its session and the trial of Dmitri Karamazov began.

Let me make it quite clear at once that I in no way consider myself capable of describing what took place in the courtroom, not only in full detail but also in its proper order. It seems to me that if one were to recall and explain everything properly, it would fill a whole volume, and a large one at that. And so I trust that my readers will not complain if I describe only what struck me personally and what has become embedded in my mind. I may well have taken what was of only secondary importance to be the primary at the trial, and even completely omitted the most outstanding and essential facts— However, I see it will be best for me to offer no apologies. I shall do my best and my readers will themselves realise that I have done everything in my power.

Before we enter the courtroom, I must begin by mentioning what surprised me particularly that day. As a matter of fact, I was not alone in being surprised. As it appeared afterwards, the surprise was general. What I mean is this: it was common knowledge that the case had aroused the interest of too many people, that all were burning with impatience for the trial to begin, and that it had given rise to a great deal of talk, conjecture, excitement, and wild fancies in our society during the last two months. It was common knowledge, too, that the case had come to the public notice all over Russia, but it was not yet realised, as came to light that day in court, to what a feverish and startling degree it had come as a shock to all and sundry, not only in our town but all over the country. People had arrived for the trial, not only from the principal city in our gubernia but also from several other Russian cities, as well as from Moscow and St. Petersburg. Among them were lawyers and a number of distinguished personages, as well as women of society. All the tickets of admission had been snatched up. The most distinguished gentlemen had had special seats reserved behind the table at which the judges sat: an entire row of arm-chairs had appeared there occupied by various personages, something which had never been previously allowed. There were a particularly large number of ladies, both from our town and visitors, comprising not less than half of the public, I believe. There were so many lawyers alone that seats could not be provided for all of them, since all tickets had long been distributed, sought after, and even craved for. I myself saw a special enclosure hurriedly put up at the end of the courtroom, beyond the raised platform, to which all the jurist arrivals were admitted, considering themselves fortunate to have at least standing room, for all the chairs had been removed to make more room, and the close crowd of lawyers had to stand thus, shoulder to shoulder, throughout the trial. Though some of the ladies, especially those who had arrived from other towns, appeared in the gallery very smartly dressed, most of them had even forgotten such things as dressing up. Their faces revealed intense, hysterical, and even morbid curiosity. A feature that marked the entire public gathered in the courtroom, one that must be noted, was that almost all the ladies in the courtroom—in fact, the vast major-ity—stood for Mitya and his acquittal. Perhaps, the main reason was that he had the reputation of a lady-killer. It was known that two women would appear as rivals in the case. One of them, Katerina Ivanovna, was of particular interest to all: a var-iety of extraordinary tales were told about her and her passion for Mitya, this even despite his crime. Her pride (she made prac-tically no social calls in our town) and her "aristocratic connec-tions" were particularly stressed. It was said that she intended to appeal to the government to give her permission to accompa-ny the criminal to Siberia and marry him somewhere in the mines. The court appearance of Grushenka as Katerina Ivanov-na's rival was looked forward to with no less excitement. The encounter between the two rivals—the proud aristocratic girl and the "hetaera"—was awaited with excruciating curiosity.

Grushenka, though, was better known to our ladies than Katerina Ivanovna. They had seen her, the woman who had been "the ruin of Fyodor Pavlovich Karamazov and his unfortunate son" before, and all without exception wondered how father and son could have fallen so passionately in love with this "very ordinary low-class girl with no looks at all". In short, there was a great deal of talk. I know for certain that there were several serious family quarrels on account of Mitya in our town alone. Many ladies had quarrelled violently with their husbands over differences of opinion about this dreadful case, and it was only natural that the husbands came into the courtroom, not only ill-disposed towards the accused but even hostile towards him. On the whole, it can be stated positively that, in contrast with the feminine section of the public, the masculine was frankly antagonistic to the accused. Severely frowning faces were to be seen, with others even vindictive, these being quite numerous. It is, of course, true that during his stay in our town Mitya had managed to give offence to many of them. Of course, many of the people in court looked almost cheerful and felt no concern for Mitya's fate, though not over the case as such; they were all interested in the outcome, most of the men being most certainly in favour of a conviction, except perhaps the jurists, who cared, not for the moral aspect of the case but only, as it were, for its modern legal aspect. There was a general stir over the arrival of the famous Fetyukovich, whose talent was generally known; it was not the first time that he had appeared in the provinces to act as counsel for the defence in sensational criminal cases. After his defence, such cases always became famous all over Russia and were long remembered. There were also several amusing stories about our public prosecutor and the presiding judge. It was said that our public prosecutor was so afraid of an encounter with Fetyukovich (they had been enemies ever since the beginning of their careers in St. Petersburg) that the vain man, who always considered himself badly treated in St. Petersburg, where his talents had not been properly appreciated, had plucked up courage over the Karamazov case. He even dreamed of this case restoring his diminishing reputation, but he was apprehensive only of Fetyukovich.

425

The views expressed about his fear of Fetyukovich, however, were not quite fair. Our public prosecutor was not one of those who lose courage in the face of danger; on the contrary, he was of those whose self-confidence rises and soars as danger grows. In general, it should be noted that our public prosecutor was far too excitable and morbidly impressionable. He would put heart and soul into some case and conduct it as though his entire life and fortune depended on its outcome. This gave rise to some banter in legal circles, for it was by this quality in him that our public prosecutor had gained him a certain reputation, which, if not universal, was at least far greater one than might have been justified by his modest standing in our courts. His passion for psychology evoked particular amusement. This was all mistaken, as I see it: our public prosecutor, both as man and as character, was, I think, far more serious than was generally supposed. But, from the very outset of his legal career, this ailing man had been unable to show his true worth, this continuing for the rest of his life.

As for the president of our court, all that can be said about him is that he was an educated and humane person, with a good grasp of his duties and abreast of the most progressive ideas of our times. Though somewhat vain, he was not very concerned about his career. It was the main purpose of his life to be regarded as a man of progressive views. Besides, he had excellent connections and a considerable fortune. As later emerged, he felt a keen interest in the Karamazov case, but only in a general sense. He saw it as a social phenomenon calling for classification as a product of our social foundations and reflecting the Russian national character, etc., etc. As for the personal aspect of the case, its tragic nature, as well as the personalities of the people involved, beginning with the accused, his attitude was somewhat indifferent and abstract, as perhaps it should be.

The courtroom was full to capacity long before the trial opened. Our courtroom is the finest hall in the town, spacious, lofty, and with excellent acoustics. To the right of the members of the court, who occupied a dais, a table and two rows of chairs had been reserved for the jury. To the left sat the accused and his counsel. In the middle of the courtroom, close

426

to the dais, stood a table with the exhibits: Fyodor Karamazov's bloodstained white silk dressing-gown; the fatal brass pestle, with which the murder had allegedly been committed; Mitya's shirt with its bloodstained sleeve; his frock-coat with blood-stained patches at the back above the pocket in which he had put his blood-soaked handkerchief; the handkerchief itself, stiff with blood and by now quite yellow; the pistol Mitya had loaded at Perkhotin's and had intended to commit suicide with, which the Mokroye innkeeper had surreptitiously taken from him; the envelope with the inscription which had contained the three thousand for Grushenka; the narrow pink ribbon it had been tied up with, and many other articles I cannot recall. At some distance, in the body of the hall, were the seats for the public, but before the balustrade there were a few chairs for those of the witnesses who would remain in court after testifying. At ten o'clock the judges made their appearance: the president, another judge, and an honorary Justice of the Peace. The public prosecutor, of course, came in immediately afterwards. The president was a burly man of fifty, under medium height, with a sallow face, dark, greying, closely cropped hair, and the red ribbon of some decoration, I don't remember which. The public prosecutor struck me—and not me alone—as looking extraordinarily pale and almost greenish. For some reason, he seemed to have suddenly grown much thinner, perhaps in a single night, for I had seen him looking his usual self only two days before. The president opened the proceedings by asking the tipstaff whether all the members of the jury were present. I can see, however, that I am not in a position to continue in this vein, partly because there were some things I did not hear, others that I failed to grasp the significance of, and yet others I have forgotten, but mainly because, as I have already said, were I to recall everything that was said and took place, I would literally have neither time nor space to record it all. All I know is that counsel for the defence and the public prosecutor raised few objections to the make-up of the jury. I remember the make-up of the twelve jurymen: four were civil servants in our town, two were merchants, and six peasants and townspeople. Long before the trial, I remember, the better circles in our town, especially the ladies, had been asking with some surprise: "How can such a delicate, complex and psychological case be submitted for a fateful decision to petty civil servants and, worse still, to some peasants. What can such a civil servant, let alone a peasant, make of it?" Indeed, the four civil servants on the jury were grey-haired people of no consequence and low rank, only one of them being somewhat younger. They were unknown in our society, existed on extremely low salaries, probably had elderly and unpresentable wives and lots of children, who perhaps even ran about barefoot. Their only diversion in their leisure time was probably a game of cards, and they certainly had never read a single book in their lives. The two merchants looked respectable enough, but were rather strangely taciturn and stodgy: one of them was close-shaven and wore European-style clothes; the other had a greying little beard and wore some medal on a red ribbon round his neck. There is no need to dwell on the townspeople and the peasants. Our Skotoprigonyevsk townspeople are practically peasants, and even till the soil. Two of them also wore European-style dress, and, perhaps for that reason, looked more unprepossessing and slovenly than the other four. One really could not help wondering as I did, for instance, as soon as I had a good look at them: "What can such people make of a case like this?" Nevertheless, their faces produced a strangely impressive and almost menacing impact, were severe and forbidding.

The presiding judge finally declared the case of the murder of the retired titular councellor Fyodor Pavlovich Karamazov open—I do not quite remember his exact words. The tipstaff was ordered to bring in the accused, and Mitya made his appearance. A dead silence fell on the courtroom, one could have heard a pin drop. I cannot vouch for others, but I do know that Mitya made a most disagreeable impression on me. The worst of it was that he came into court in spick and span attire: in a brand-new frock-coat. I learnt afterwards that he had had it made in Moscow expressly for the occasion, by his tailor, who had his measurements. His black kid gloves were brand-new and his linen exquisite. He marched in with his yard-long strides, staring straight ahead of him, and sat down on his chair with an air of complete unconcern. Fetyukovich, the celebrated barrister, entered immediately after him, his appearance evoking a subdued hum in court. He was a tall, spare man, with thin, long legs, extraordinarily long, thin, pale fingers, a close-shaven face, unpretentiously brushed short hair, and thin lips, which from time to time twisted into something between a sneer and a smile. He looked about forty. His face would have been rather pleasant were it not for his eyes, in themselves small and inexpressive, but set so extraordinarily close together that the only thing that divided them was the thin line of his long thin nose. In short, there was something curiously birdlike about his face—the first thing one was struck by. He wore a dress-coat and a white tie. I remember the presiding judge's first questions to Mitya: his name, his rank, and so on. Mitya replied brusquely but in an unexpectedly loud voice, so that the presiding judge even reared his head and looked at him almost in surprise. Then followed the reading of the list of names of those summoned to attend the trial, that is to say, the witnesses and the experts. It was a long list; four of the witnesses failed to appear: Miusov, who happened to be in Paris at the time but had testified at the preliminary investigation, Madame Khokhlakov and the landowner Maximov, who were both ill, and Smerdyakov, because of his sudden death, about which a statement from the police was presented. The news of Smerdyakov's death caused a stir and led to much whispering in court. Of course, many members of the public knew nothing of his sudden suicide. But what really created a sensation in court was Mitya's unexpected outburst. As soon as the statement was read out, he shouted in a loud voice from his seat:

"A fitting death for a cur!"

I remember his counsel dashing up to him and the presiding judge admonishing him, threatening to take severe measures if such an outburst were repeated. Mitya, nodding his head but showing no sign of repentance, repeated several times in an abrupt undertone to his counsel:

"I won't, I won't! It just escaped me! I won't do it again!"

And, of course, this brief episode did not produce a favourable impression on the jury or the public: his character was plain to all and spoke for itself. It was under this impression that the indictment was read out by the clerk of the court.

It was short but circumstantial, stating only the main reasons why so-and-so had been arrested and brought to trial, and so on. It did, nevertheless, produce a strong impression on me. The clerk read it distinctly in a loud and clear voice. The whole tragedy seemed again to have suddenly presented itself to everyone in distinct relief, tersely, and in a fateful and unsparing light. I remember, how immediately after it had been read, the presiding judge asked Mitya, loudly and impressively:

"Prisoner in the dock, do you plead guilty or not guilty?"

Mitya suddenly rose from his seat.

"I plead guilty to drunkenness and loose living," he exclaimed again in a sort of unexpected and almost frenzied voice, "to idleness and debauchery. I had decided to become an honest man for the rest of my life just at the very moment I was struck down by fate! But I am not guilty of the death of the old man, my father and my enemy! No, no, I am not guilty of robbing him, and could not possibly be guilty of it: Dmitri Karamazov may be a blackguard but he is no thief!"

Having shouted this, he resumed his seat, visibly trembling all over. The presiding judge again addressed him with a brief but edifying admonition to reply only to questions put to him and not to indulge in irrelevant and frenzied exclamations. He then ordered that the trial should begin. The witnesses were brought in to take the oath. It was then that I saw them all together. The prisoner's brothers, however, were not sworn in. After a brief address by the priest and the presiding judge, the witnesses were led away and were given seats as far away from each other as possible. They were then summoned one by one.

2.

Dangerous Witnesses

I do not know whether the witnesses for the prosecution and for the defence were purposely separated into groups by the presiding judge, or in what order they were supposed to be summoned. I suppose all that had been prearranged. All I know is that the witnesses for the prosecution were the first to be called to testify. I repeat: it is not my intention to give a full account of how all the witnesses were examined. Besides, such an account would be partly superfluous, since the speeches of the public prosecutor and the counsel for the defence brought to a focus and in a vivid light the entire course and significance of the evidence before the court. I took down the two addresses—both outstanding—at least in part, practically verbatim, and will quote from them in due course, as well as an extraordinary and quite unexpected incident at the trial, which suddenly occurred before the pleadings, and undoubtedly predetermined its dreadful and fateful outcome. I will only observe that, from the very first moments of the trial, a certain feature of the "case" became manifest and was generally noted, namely, the unusual strength of the prosecution as compared with the evidence produced by the defence. That feature was generally realised in the courtroom as soon as, in the hostile atmosphere of the court, the facts began to arrange themselves about a focal point, and all the horror and all that blood gradually emerged. The public quite possibly realised at the very outset that there could be no differences of opinion about the case, that the issue was never in doubt, that in fact no speeches for the defence or for the prosecution were necessary, and were merely a matter of form, and that the criminal was guilty, obviously guilty, guilty beyond the shadow of doubt. I cannot help thinking that even the ladies in the courtroom, who were without exception so eager for the acquittal of the fascinating accused man, were at the same time fully convinced of his undeniable guilt. Moreover, it seems to me that they would have been greatly disappointed if his guilt had not been so fully established, for then the effect of the final scene of the criminal's acquittal would not have been so sensational. That he would be acquitted was, strange to say, something all the ladies were absolutely convinced of almost until the very last moment: "He is guilty, but he will be acquitted on humane grounds, in accordance with the new ideas, the new sentiments now in vogue", etc., etc. That was why they had all gathered there with such eagerness. Their menfolk, on the contrary, were more interested in the contest between the public prosecutor and the celebrated Fetyukovich. And all were asking themselves in surprise what even so talented a lawyer as Fetyukovich could possibly make of a case that was obviously so hopeless and quite certainly lost—which was why his performance was followed, step by step, with the keenest attention. But to the very end, up to his address to the jury, Fetyukovich remained an enigma to all: men of experience felt that he had some system of his own, that he had already formed some idea of how he would conduct the case, that he had already set himself an aim, but one that was almost impossible to guess. There could, however, be no doubt whatever of his confidence and self-assurance. Besides, everyone at once noted with satisfaction that, during his brief stay with us, in only about three days perhaps, he had gained a thorough grasp of the case and "had it at his fingertips". People enjoyed relating afterwards, for instance, how cleverly he had managed to "outwit" the witnesses for the prosecution at the right moment and fluster them, as much as possible, and, above all, besmirch their good names and, consequently, their evidence, too. It was generally believed, however, that he did it rather as a stratagem, as it were, to display his forensic adroitness, and show that nothing had been neglected in the whole range of accepted legal methods: it was the general conviction that no tangible or conclusive advantage could result from these attempts to "besmirch" witness. Indeed, it was quite likely that he himself realised that better than anyone else, but was keeping some idea of his own up his sleeve, some concealed weapon of defence, which he could suddenly brandish when the right time came. Meanwhile, conscious of his strength, he seemed just to be playing and amusing himself. Thus, during the cross-examination of Grigori, Karamazov's former manservant, who had given some highly important evidence about "the open door into the garden", the defence counsel, when his turn came to cross-examine the witness, simply pounced on the man. It should be noted that when Grigori Vassilievich appeared in the courtroom, he behaved with composure and almost impressively, without being in the least overawed by the majesty of the law or the concourse listening to him. He gave his evidence with as much assurance as though he were talking to his wife Marfa Ignatievna, only, of course, more respectfully. He was not to be shaken. At first, the public prosecutor questioned him in detail about the Karamazov family life, a complete picture thus emerging. One could see and hear that the witness was guileless and unbiassed. Despite his profound deference for the memory of his late master, he declared, for instance, that the latter had been unfair to Mitya and had not "brought up his children properly. But for me," he added, speaking of Mitya's early childhood, "he would have been infested with lice when he was a little boy. It wasn't right, either, of the father to wrong his son over his mother's family estate." Asked by the public prosecutor to state his reasons for asserting that Fyodor Pavlovich had wronged his son in money matters, Grigori, to everyone's surprise, could proffer no convincing evidence, but insisted that Fyodor Pavlovich's settlement with his son was "unjust" and that he ought to have "paid him several thousand roubles more". I must observe, incidentally, that the public prosecutor insistently put the question whether Fyodor Pavlovich had really held back money from Mitya, to the pertinent witnesses, including Alyosha and Ivan, but could obtain no satisfactory information from any of them; they all bore out the fact, but could advance no firm evidence. When Grigori described the scene at the dinner-table when Dmitri had burst into the room and fallen on his father, threatening to come back and kill him, this made a very sombre impression in court, particularly as the old servant was sparing of words in his dispassionate account which was in a style all his own and most telling. He went on to say he bore Mitya no grudge and had long forgiven him for striking him in the face and knocking him down. Of the late Smerdyakov he observed, crossing himself, that the lad was not without ability, but retarded and depressed by illness, and, worse still, was godless, something he had learnt from Fyodor Pavlovich and his second son. But he asserted almost with warmth that he had no doubt whatever to Smerdyakov's honesty and, to prove it, told the court how a long time ago Smerdyakov, on finding some money his master had mislaid, had returned it to his master, who had given him "a gold ten-rouble piece" and trusted him implicitly from that time on. He maintained emphatically that the door into the garden had been open. However, he was asked so many questions that I find it quite impossible to recall them all. When the defence counsel finally began his cross-examination, he first of all wanted to know about the envelope in which Karamazov's three thousand for "a certain person" had "supposedly" been concealed. "Did you see it yourself, you who, for so many years, were your master's confidant?" Grigori replied that he had not seen the money and had not even heard of it from anyone "up to the very moment when everyone began talking about it". Fetyukovich put the same question about the envelope to every witness he could, and just as insistently as the public prosecutor asked the question about the division of the estate. He received one and the same answer, to the effect that none of them had seen the envelope, though many had heard of it. The defence counsel's insistence on this point was generally noted.

"Now, sir," Fetyukovich asked quite unexpectedly, "may I, if you don't mind, ask you what that balsam or rather that tincture consisted of, which, as appears from the preliminary inquiry, you rubbed into your painful back that night before going to bed, in the hope it would bring you relief."

Grigori looked stolidly at the questioner and, after a short silence, muttered:

"There was sage in it, sir."

"Only sage? Can you remember anything else?"

"There was milfoil in it, too."

"And pepper, perhaps?" Fetyukovich queried.

"Yes, sir, and pepper as well."

"And so on. And what did you steep it in? Vodka, I suppose?"

"No, sir. Spirits of alcohol."

There was a ripple of laughter in court.

"Well, well, so it was even in alcohol. And then after rubbing it into your back, you drank what remained in the bottle, to the accompaniment of a certain pious prayer known only to your wife, didn't you?"

"Yes, sir."

"About how much did you drink? Roughly speaking? A wineglass or two?"

"About a tumblerful."

"A tumblerful! Are you sure it wasn't a tumbler and a half?"

Grigori made no reply. Something seemed to have dawned on him.

"A tumbler and a half of neat spirits—not so bad, don't you think? You might have seen 'in heaven an open door' let alone the door into the garden, mightn't you?"

Grigori said nothing. There was some laughter in court and the presiding judge stirred in his seat.

"Are you quite sure," Fetyukovich persisted, "you were not asleep when you saw the open garden door?"

"I was standing on my feet, sir."

"That doesn't prove that you were not asleep (more laughter in court). Could you, for instance, have answered at the moment, had you been asked, say, what year it was?"

"I'm afraid I don't know, sir."

"And can you say what year it is now—*anno Domini*?"

Looking bewildered, Grigori stared steadily at his tormentor. It was certainly strange that he did not seem to know what year it was.

"But perhaps you can tell us how many fingers there are on your hands?"

"I'm a servant, sir," Grigori said suddenly in a loud and distinct voice. "If my betters think fit to make mock of me, that's something I must put up with."

Fetyukovich seemed a little taken aback, but at this point the presiding judge intervened, admonishing the defence counsel to make his questions more relevant. Fetyukovich gave a dignified bow in reply, and declared that he had no more questions to ask. However, both the public and the jury might very well have been left with some doubt in their minds regarding the testimony of one able to see "in heaven an open door" under the influence of some medicine, and moreover ignorant of the year he was living in. Thus, the defence counsel was able to achieve his aim. But another incident occurred before Grigori left the witness stand. Turning to the accused, the presiding judge asked him if he had anything to say about the evidence of the witness.

"With the exception of the door," Mitya cried in a loud voice, "all he said is true. I thank him for combing the lice out of my hair and I thank him for forgiving my blows. The old man has been honest all his life and as faithful to my father as seven hundred poodles."

"Prisoner at the bar, be more careful in your choice of words," the presiding judge said severely.

"I'm no poodle," Grigori muttered.

"Well, I'm a poodle, then, I am!" cried Mitya. "If I've said anything offensive, I accept the blame and I beg his pardon: I was brutal and cruel to him! I was cruel to Aesop, too."

"What Aesop?" the presiding judge again took Mitya up severely.

"I mean, that Pierrot—my father, Fyodor Pavlovich."

The presiding judge repeated his caution to Mitya in severe and impressive tones, telling him to be careful in his choice of words.

"You are harming yourself in the opinion of your judges."

The defence counsel used much the same adroit tactics in his cross-examination of the witness Rakitin. I shall observe that Rakitin was one of the most important witnesses and one the public prosecutor attached great significance to. Rakitin seemed to know everything—his knowledge was amazing: he had been everywhere, seen everything, spoken to everyone, and knew every detail in the biographies of Fyodor Pavlovich and all the Karamazovs. It was true, though, that it was only from Mitya himself that he had heard of the envelope with the three thousand. On the other hand, he gave a detailed description of Mitya's exploits in the Metropolis Inn, and all his compromising words and actions and told the story of Captain Snegiryov's "tow-beard". As to the special matter of Mitya's inheritance and whether or not Fyodor Pavlovich owed Mitya anything in settlement of that account, even Rakitin could say nothing definite; confining himself to generalities of a contemptuous nature: "Who could say which of them was to blame, or find out which of them was in debt to the other, considering the bungling way in which the Karamazovs attended to their affairs, which no one could make out and settle." He depicted the whole tragedy of the case as the result of outmoded morals born of the serf-owning system and to the untidy condition of Russia, a country suffering from a lack of the appropriate institutions. In fact, he was allowed to air his views. The trial gave Mr. Rakitin his first opportunity to display himself and attract public attention. The public prosecutor was aware that Rakitin was preparing an article on the case for a periodical, and, in his speech (as we shall see below), quoted several ideas from the article, which, of course, meant that he, the prosecutor, was acquainted with it. The picture drawn by the witness was a sombre and sinister one and greatly enhanced the "case for the prosecution". On the whole, however, Rakitin's account appealed to the public in its independent thinking and its flight of lofty sentiment. There were two or three outbreaks of applause at passages of his evidence, in which he made mention of the serf-owning system and the untidy condition of Russia. However, Rakitin's youthful outspokenness resulted in a slip, which the defence counsel at once made skilful use of. In reply to certain questions about Grushenka, and carried away by his success, of which he was, of course, aware, and the lofty heights to which he had soared, he allowed himself to speak somewhat contemptuously of Agrafena Alexandrovna as "the merchant Samsonov's kept woman". He would have given a lot afterwards to be able to retract his words, for Fetyukovich at once seized on them. And it was all because it never occurred to Rakitin that Fetyukovich could have gained such a close knowledge of the case in so short a time.

"May I," the counsel for the defence began with a most affable and even respectful smile, when his turn came to question the witness, "may I ask if you are the same Mr. Rakitin whose pamphlet, issued by the diocesan authorities under the title of *The Life of the Late Starets Father Zossima,* so full of profound and religious reflections and containing such an excellent and devout dedication to the bishop, I recently read with so much pleasure?"

"I didn't write it for publication—" Rakitin murmured, as though suddenly taken aback and almost ashamed. "It was brought out later."

"Oh, that's excellent! A thinker like you can and, I suppose, should take the broadest possible view of any social problem. Thanks to the bishop's patronage, your highly instructive pamphlet has had a wide circulation and rendered some service— But what I'm mainly interested in is this: you have just declared that you have been very closely acquainted with Miss Svetlov (N.B. Grushenka's surname was Svetlov, as I learnt for the first time on that day, in the course of the trial), haven't you?"

"I can't be held responsible for all my acquaintances— I am a young man—how can one answer for all the people one meets," replied Rakitin, his face flushing.

"I understand, I fully understand!" cried Fetyukovich, as though he, too, was embarrassed and hastened to apologise. "You, like anyone else, might be interested, too, in an acquaintance with a beautiful young woman, who so willingly received the pick of the youth of this town, but—all I want you to tell me is this: we know that two months ago Miss Svetlov was very eager to be introduced to Alexei Fyodorovich, the youngest Karamazov, and promised you twenty-five roubles just for bringing him over to her home in his monastic vestment, for that alone. That, we know, actually took place on the evening of the day which ended in the tragic disaster leading up to the present proceedings. You brought Alexei Karamazov to Miss Svetlov, but did you get the promised reward of twenty-five roubles? That's what I would like to learn from you."

"It was merely a joke— I don't see why you should be so interested in it. I took it in jest and—and I intended to return it later—"

"So you did take the money, didn't you? And you haven't returned it as yet—or have you?"

"Oh, it's of no consequence—" Rakitin muttered. "I can't

438

reply to such questions— I shall return it, of course."

The presiding judge intervened but counsel stated that he had no more questions to ask Mr. Rakitin, who left the witness-stand somewhat discredited. The impression produced by the lofty sentiments in his speech was rather marred, and, as he watched him leave, Fetyukovich seemed to be intimating to the public: "That's the kind of people your high-minded accusers are like!" Neither did this, as I remember, pass off without incident on the part of Mitya: infuriated by the way in which Rakitin had referred to Grushenka, he suddenly shouted: "You Bernard!" and when, after Rakitin's cross-examination the presiding judge asked the accused if he had anything to say, Mitya shouted in a ringing voice:

"He's been cadging money from me since I was arrested! He's contemptible Bernard and a careerist. He doesn't believe in God, and he cheated the bishop!"

Mitya was, of course, again called to order for the violence of his epithets, but that was the end of Mr. Rakitin. Nor was Captain Snegiryov's evidence any more telling, but for a quite different reason. He appeared in tattered and dirty clothes, muddy boots and, despite all precautions and the preliminary medical "examination", he suddenly proved much the worse for drink. He refused to reply to the question of how Mitya had mistreated him.

"It doesn't matter, sir. Ilyusha told me not to. God will repay."

"Who told you not to? Who are you talking about?"

"Ilyusha, my little son. 'Daddy, Daddy, how he humiliated you!' He said that at the rock. Now he is dying—"

Snegiryov suddenly burst into tears and fell at the feet of the presiding judge. He was quickly led away amidst general laughter. The impression staged by the public prosecutor did not come off.

The counsel for the defence, on the other hand, went on exploiting every opportunity, evoking ever greater amazement by his intimate knowledge of the case, down to the minutest details. Thus, the evidence of the Mokroye innkeeper at first produced a strong impression and was, of course, highly unfavourable to Mitya. He had, in fact, counted up almost on his fingertips that Mitya could not possibly have spent less than three thousand or "at least very little less during his first visit to Mokroye, a month before the murder. The money he had squandered on the Gypsy girls alone! As for our lousy peasants, he didn't fling them just half a rouble in the street but gave them at least twenty-five-rouble notes each, no less. And how much was simply filched from him, sir! For no thief left a receipt, so how was one to catch him, the thief, sir, when the money was being thrown about regardless! For our peasants, sir, are just robbers; they don't care for the salvation of their souls. And the money he wasted on our village girls! Aye, they've grown rich since then. Yes, sir! Before that, they were as poor as poor can be!" In short, he recalled every item of expenditure and added it all up as though on an abacus. Thus, the supposition that Mitya had spent only fifteen hundred and put the rest away in his "amulet" could not hold water. "I saw it myself, sir, I saw three thousand in his hands with my own eyes, sir. Me not know how to count money, sir?" the innkeeper kept exclaiming, doing his utmost to please the "authorities". But when the defence counsel began his cross-examination, he did not even attempt to refute the innkeeper's evidence. Instead he recalled something that took place when Mitya had first come to Mokroye a month before his arrest: the coachman Timofei and another peasant named Akim had picked up a hundred-rouble note from the floor in the passageway of the inn, which the drunken Mitya had dropped, and had given it to the innkeeper, who had tipped them a rouble each. "Well," the counsel for the defence asked, "did you return the hundred roubles to Mr. Karamazov that night?" Despite all his shilly-shallying, the innkeeper, after the two peasants had testified to having picked up the money, admitted to receiving it, but added that he had returned it to Mitya that very night "in all honesty, but I expect, sir, that, being in liquor at the time, he wouldn't remember it". But as he had flatly denied receiving the money until the two peasants had disproved his assertion, his evidence about having returned the money to the tipsy Mitya naturally became highly suspect. Thus, a most dangerous witness for the prosecution left the witness-box under a cloud of suspicion and with a greatly tarnished reputation. It was the same with the Poles, who appeared with a proud and independent mien. They both bore witness loudly that, in the first place, both had been "servants of the Crown" and that Mitya had offered them three thousand to sell their honour, and that they had seen a large sum of money in his possession. Musialowicz interlarded his speech with many Polish words and, seeing that this raised him in the estimation of the presiding judge and the public prosecutor, grew terribly puffed up so that he switched over completely to Polish. But Fetyukovich caught them too in his snares: however much the Mokroye innkeeper tried to twist and turn, he had finally to admit that Wróblewski had substituted his pack of cards for his own and that, when dealing, Musialowicz had cheated. That was confirmed by Kalganov's evidence and the two Poles left the court somewhat in disgrace, and even to laughter from the public.

It was exactly the same with almost all the other more dangerous witnesses. Fetyukovich succeeded in morally besmirching every one of them and dismissing them with their noses somewhat out of joint. Laymen and the jurists were only lost in admiration of Fetyukovich, but merely wondered what important and ultimate purpose it could all serve, for, I repeat, the public felt that prosecution's case was waterlight, as was becoming more and tragically obvious. But the "wizard's" air of confidence showed he felt undisturbed, and the public were all in a state of expectancy: surely he was not the kind of man to come down from St. Petersburg in vain, or to return there empty-handed.

3.

The Opinion of the Medical Experts. The Pound of Nuts

The medical evidence, too, was of little help to the accused. In fact, Fetyukovich himself did not seem to be counting heavily on it as, indeed, it later transpired. The medical line of defence had emerged primarily on the initiative of Katerina Ivanovna, who had called in a celebrated specialist from Moscow. The defence, of course, could lose nothing by it and, with luck, even stood to gain thereby. However, the outcome was somewhat comical, owing to a difference of opinion among the doctors. The medical experts were: the celebrated Moscow doctor, then our local doctor, Herzenstube, and, finally, the young doctor Varvinsky. The latter two also appeared as witnesses for the prosecution. The first to testify as an expert was Dr. Herzenstube, an old man of seventy, grey-haired and balding, of medium height and sturdy build, who was held in high esteem and respect in our town. He was a conscientious medical practitioner, an excellent and pious man, and member of the Herrnhuter community or the Moravian Brethren,* I don't quite remember which. He had been resident in our town for a great many years and his comportment was most dignified. A kind-hearted and humane man, he treated his poor patients and peasants free of charge, visiting hovels and huts and leaving behind money for medicine, but, for all his goodness, he was as stubborn as a mule. Once an idea had entered his head, it could not be dislodged. Incidentally, it became common knowledge in our town that, during the two or three days of his stay with us, the Moscow celebrity passed some exceedingly unflattering remarks about Dr. Herzenstube's medical skill. For although the Moscow doctor charged a fee of no less than twenty-five roubles for a visit, several people in our town were overjoyed at his arrival, did not grudge the expense, and rushed to consult him. All these patients, of course, had been previously treated by Dr. Herzenstube, and the famous doctor criticised his treatment with extreme harshness. In the end, indeed the first thing he asked on calling on a patient was: "Well, who has been messing about with you? Herzenstube? Ha, ha!" Dr. Herzenstube, of course, got to learn of all this. And now all the three doctors

---

*The Herrnhuter movement—a religious social trend that arose in the 18th century in the settlement of Herrnhut in Saxony, and spread to Russia in the 18th and 19th centuries.—Tr.

appeared in turn to testify. Dr. Herzenstube declared forthright that "the abnormality of the mental faculties of the accused is self-evident". Then, after producing the grounds for his statement, which I shall omit here, he added that the abnormality could be mainly diagnosed, not only from the prisoner's numerous previous actions but even from his behaviour just now, at that moment, in court. Asked to explain how he could diagnose it at that very moment, the old doctor, with his blunt way of putting things, pointed out that, on entering the courtroom, the accused had "an extraordinary and, considering the circumstances, very strange air", that he had "marched in like a soldier with his eyes fixed straight ahead of himself, when he should really have been looking leftwards, where the ladies were sitting, for he was a great admirer of the fair sex and should have been giving much thought to what the ladies would be saying about him now", the old man concluded in his peculiar style. It should be added that, though he was very talkative in Russian, every sentence of his somehow had a German smack to it, which, however, never embarrassed him, for he had a lifelong foible for thinking that his Russian was perfect, and that it was "even better than with the Russians"; he was given to using Russian proverbs, maintaining all the time that they were the finest and most forceful of all proverbs in the world. I shall note, besides, that in conversation his absent-mindedness perhaps often led him to forget the most ordinary words, which he knew perfectly well but had, for some reason, escaped his memory. Incidentally, it was the same when he spoke German; every time that happened, he waved a hand in front of his face as though trying to clutch at the lost word, and he could not be induced to continue until he had found it. His remark that the accused, on entering the courtroom, should have looked at the ladies aroused a whisper of amusement in the public. Our ladies were all very fond of the old man. It was known, too, that, a confirmed bachelor, he was religious and chaste, regarding women as superior and ideal creatures. That was why his unexpected remark struck everyone as being very strange.

When his turn came to be questioned, the Moscow doctor confirmed with brusque insistence that he considered the mental condition of the accused abnormal, even "in the highest degree". He spoke at length and sapiently of "temporary unsoundness of mind" and "mania" and drew the conclusion that, according to all the facts available, the accused had certainly been in a morbid state of temporary aberration several days before his arrest, and that if he had committed the crime, he had done so almost involuntarily, though he might have been aware of it, being utterly powerless to curb or overcome the morbid compulsion that had overcome him. But, apart from the temporary aberration, the doctor also established mania which, in his opinion, would quite certainly lead to complete insanity in future. (N.B. I am reporting his evidence in my own words, for the doctor set forth his views in very learned and highly professional language.) "All his actions," he went on, "ran counter to common sense and logic. Quite apart from what I have not seen for myself, that is to say, the crime and the disaster itself, the accused had an inexplicable fixed stare in his eyes during my talk with him the day before yesterday, and was given to outbursts of laughter that were quite out of place. He displayed unaccountable and continual irritability and used such strange words as 'Bernard, ethics,' and the like which were quite irrelevant too." But the doctor attached special significance, as indicative of mania, to the accused being unable to speak about the three thousand roubles he considered himself to have been cheated of without a kind of extreme irritation, though he can speak quite freely about all his other setbacks and grievances. Finally, according to inquiries he had made, the accused had, just as before, flown almost into a frenzy every time the three thousand roubles was mentioned, and yet he was reported to be unselfish and far from grasping in money matters. "As for the view expressed by my learned colleague," the Moscow doctor added ironically in conclusion, "that, on entering the court, the accused should have looked at the ladies and not straight ahead of himself, all I can say is that, apart from the playfulness of such a conclusion, it is, moreover, fundamentally erroneous, for though I quite agree that, on entering a courtroom where his fate is being decided, the accused should not have looked so fixedly ahead of himself, which could, in fact, be considered a symptom of an abnormal mental condition at the moment; I affirm at the same time that he should not have looked leftward at the ladies, but, on the contrary, towards the right to locate his counsel, on whose aid he must pin all his hopes and on whose defence his whole future depends." The doctor expressed his opinion vigorously and emphatically. But the comic aspect of the difference of opinion between the two learned experts was greatly enhanced by the quite unexpected conclusion submitted by Dr. Varvinsky, who was the last to be questioned. In his view, the accused was of quite sound mind, just as he had been previously, and though he must no doubt have been in a nervous and highly excited condition prior to his arrest, that could have been due to many most obvious reasons: jealousy, anger, continual heavy drinking, and the like. But that nervous condition had nothing whatever to do with "temporary unsoundness of mind", as had just been asserted. As to the question whether the accused ought to have looked to the left or the right on entering the courtroom, he, in the doctor's "humble opinion", should, on entering the courtroom, have most certainly looked straight ahead of himself as, in fact, he had done, for it was there that the president and the members of the court were seated, on whom his whole fate now depended, "so that by looking straight before him", the young doctor concluded his "humble" evidence with some warmth, "he proved the perfectly normal state of his mind at the moment".

"Bravo, doc!" cried Mitya from his seat. "You're quite right!"

Mitya was, of course, cut short, but the young doctor's opinion had a most decisive influence on the bench as well as the public, for, as it afterwards transpired, there was general agreement with him. However, Dr. Herzenstube, when questioned again, but this time as a witness, quite unexpectedly came out in Mitya's favour. As an old inhabitant of our town, with a long knowledge of the Karamazov family, he gave some evidence of great interest to the "prosecution", but suddenly, as though recalling something, he added:

"And yet the poor young man might have got a far better

lot in life, for he had a good heart both in childhood and afterwards, and I know it. But as the Russian proverb says: "One head is good, but if another clever man calls, it will be better still, for there will be two heads and not just one—"

"Two heads are better than one," the public prosecutor prompted him impatiently, for he had long been aware of the old man's way of talking in a slow and ponderous way, in disregard of the impression he was creating, or of keeping others waiting till he had finished, but, on the contrary, with a high opinion of his own turgidly heavy and always blithely complacent German wit. The old man was given to witticisms.

"Oh, yes, that's what I said," he went on stubbornly. "One head is good, but two are far better. But no one with a good head on his shoulders came to him, so his own head went—how is it said: his head went off? I'm afraid I've forgotten the word for it," he went on, waving a hand before his eyes. "Oh, yes, *spazieren.*"

"Went off for a walk."

"Yes, yes, went off for a walk, that's what I said. So his head went for a walk and came to so deep a place that it got lost. And yet he was such a grateful and sensitive youth. Oh, I remember him very well as a little chap neglected by his father in the back-yard, where he used to run about in the mud without boots, his little breeches suspended by a single button—"

A note of feeling and tenderness suddenly came into the honest old man's voice. Fetyukovich gave a start as though anticipating something, and was now all ears.

"Oh, yes, I was a young man myself then— I—well, I was forty-five at the time, and I had only just arrived here. And I felt sorry for the little boy and asked myself why I shouldn't buy him a pound of—yes, a pound of— What do you call it? I're forgotten the name—a pound of something children are very fond of—now—" the doctor began waving his hands again. "It grows on a tree and it's gathered and given as a present to everyone—"

"Apples?"

"Oh, no, no! A pound, a pound! You buy apples by the dozen, not by the pound— No, there are lots of them, and

446

they're all very small, you put them in the mouth and c-c-rack!"

"Nuts?"

"Oh, yes, nuts, that's what I said," the doctor confirmed in the calmest way, as though he had never been seeking the word. "And I bought him a pound of nuts, for no one had ever bought the little boy a pound of nuts before, and I raised a finger and said to him: 'Little boy! *Gott der Vater'*, he laughed and repeated after me: *'Gott der Vater, Gott der Sohn.'* He laughed again and prattled *'Got der Sohn, Gott der heilige Geist.'* Then he laughed again and said as best as he could, *'Gott der heilige Geist.'* So I went off. Two days later, I passed that way again, and he shouted to me himself: 'Uncle, *Gott der Vater, Gott der Sohn,'* and he had only forgotten *Gott der heilige Geist,* so I reminded him, and I again felt very sorry for him. But he was taken away somewhere, and I did not see him again. And then, twenty-three years later, I was sitting in my office one morning, my hair already white and suddenly a young man, looking the picture of health, whom I would never have recognised, walked in. He raised a finger and said laughingly, *'Gott der Vater, Gott der Sohn und Gott der heilige Geist!* I've just arrived and have come to thank you for the pound of nuts, for no one had ever bought me a pound of nuts, and you were the only one to do it.' And then I remembered the happy days of my youth and the poor boy barefoot in the yard, and my heart was moved and I said: 'You are a grateful young man, for you have remembered all your life the pound of nuts I gave you in your childhood.' And I embraced him and blessed him. And I wept. He laughed, but he also wept—for a Russian often laughs when he should be weeping. But he wept, I saw it. And now, alas—!"

"I'm weeping now, too, German! I'm weeping now, too, you saintly man!" Mitya suddenly shouted from his seat.

Be that as it may, but the story produced a certain favourable impression on the public in the courtroom. But the chief effect in Mitya's favour was created by Katerina Ivanovna's evidence, which I will describe presently. And, as a matter of fact, when the witnesses *à décharge,* that is to say, the witnesses called by the defence, began to testify, fortune seemed suddenly to smile on Mitya in good earnest, and what was so remarkable, to the surprise even of the counsel for the defence. But before Katerina Ivanovna was called, Alyosha was questioned, and he suddenly recalled a fact which seemed to furnish positive evidence against one of the most important points made by the prosecution.

4.

Fortune Smiles on Mitya

It came as a great surprise even to Alyosha himself: he was not required to take the oath and, as I remember from the very beginning of his examination, both sides treated him with gentle sympathy. His good name had clearly preceded him. He gave his evidence modestly and with restraint, but his warm sympathy for his unhappy brother was manifest in his words. In reply to a question, he characterised his brother as a man of perhaps violent temper and carried away by his passions, but also as an honourable, proud, and magnanimous man, prepared to make any sacrifice demanded of him. He admitted, however, that, because of his passion for Grushenka and his rivalry with his father, his brother had been in an intolerable position of late. But he indignantly rejected the suggestion that his brother was capable of murder for the sake of robbery, though he could but admit that the three thousand roubles had grown into a kind of obsession with Mitya, who regarded it as part of the inheritance he had been cheated out of by his father, and that, though he was quite indifferent to money, he could not even speak of the three thousand without flying into a fury. As for the rivalry between the two "ladies", as the public prosecutor had put it, that is to say, between Grushenka and Katerina, he answered evasively and was even reluctant to answer one or two questions altogether.

"Did your brother at least tell you that he intended to murder his father?" the public prosecutor asked, adding: "You need not answer the question if you don't wish to."

"He never spoke of it directly."

"Oh? Did he do so indirectly?"

"He spoke to me once of his personal hatred of Father and that he was afraid that—at an extreme moment—at a moment of loathing, he—he might perhaps murder him."

"And did you believe him when he said so?"

"I'm afraid to say that I did. But I was always convinced that some higher feeling would always save him at the critical moment, just as it actually did, because it was *not he* who killed my father," Alyosha concluded firmly in a loud voice that could be heard all over the courtroom. The public prosecutor reared his head like a war-horse at the sound of the trumpet.

"Let me assure you that I fully believe in the absolute sincerity of your conviction, without attempting to explain it by, or identify it with, your affection for your unhappy brother. Your singular view of the whole tragic episode in your family is known to us already from the preliminary investigation. I will not conceal from you that it is highly personal and contradicts all the rest of evidence obtained by the prosecution. And that is why I must insist on asking you: what facts have led you to this firm conviction of your brother's innocence and of the guilt of some other person you indicated directly at the preliminary investigation?"

"I merely answered the questions put to me at the preliminary investigation," Alyosha said quietly and calmly. "I did not myself make any accusation against Smerdyakov."

"But you did name him, didn't you?"

"I did so because of what my brother Dmitri had told me. Even before my interrogation, I was told what took place during his arrest and that he had pointed to Smerdyakov as the murderer. I believe absolutely that my brother is innocent. And if he did not commit the murder, then—"

"Then Smerdyakov did? But why Smerdyakov? And why are you so conclusively sure of your brother's innocence?"

"I couldn't but believe my brother. I know he wouldn't lie to me. His face told me he wasn't lying to me."

"Only his face? Is that all the proof you have?"

"I have no other proof."

"And you have no proof whatever of Smerdyakov's guilt except your brother's words and the expression on his face?"

"No, I have no other proof."

The public prosecutor discontinued the examination at this point. The impression Alyosha's replies made on the public was most disappointing. Even prior to the trial, people had been talking about Smerdyakov; someone had heard something; someone else had been indicating something; it was said that Alyosha had gathered some extraordinary proof of his brother's innocence and of the servant's guilt, and yet now nothing had been forthcoming—no proofs except certain moral convictions, which were so natural in a brother of the accused.

But it was now Fetyukovich's turn to cross-examine. To his questions exactly when the accused had told him, Alyosha, that he hated his father and that he had felt like killing him, and whether he heard it from him, for instance, at his last meeting before the murder, Alyosha seemed suddenly to start as he replied as though he had only just recalled and realised something.

"I've just called to mind a circumstance, I had quite forgotten, whose full significance I did not grasp at the time but now—"

And, evidently struck by an idea just at that very moment, Alyosha recalled with animation how, at his last meeting with Mitya, that evening under the tree, on the road towards the monastery, Mitya, smiting his breast—"the upper part of the breast"—had repeated several times that he had a means of restoring his honour, and that it lay there, there, on his breast—"I thought at the time that, by striking his breast, he was referring to his heart," Alyosha went on, "and that he meant he could find strength in his heart to escape from some terrible disgrace which threatened him and which he did not dare even confess to me. I must admit that I did think then he was referring to Father and that he was shuddering, as though it were a disgrace, at the thought of going to see Father and doing some violence to him. And yet he seemed to be indicating something on his breast, so that, as I remember, the thought occurred to me that the heart actually lay, not in that part of his breast but lower down, and that he had struck himself much higher up, just here, below the neck, and kept pointing to that spot. The thought seemed absurd to me at the time, but I expect perhaps he must have been indicating the little bag he had sewn the fifteen hundred roubles up in!—"

"Yes! That's right, Alyosha!" Mitya suddenly cried from his place. "I did strike it then with my fist."

Fetyukovich rushed up to him, entreating him to calm down, and at the same moment simply pounced on Alyosha. The latter, carried away by his recollection, warmly voiced his theory that what Mitya had meant by his disgrace was most probably the fifteen hundred roubles he had on his person, a sum he could have returned to Katerina Ivanovna as half of what he owed her; however, he had made up his mind not to return it to her, but to use it for some other purpose, to wit, to elope with Grushenka, if she agreed—

"Yes, it was so, it most certainly was so," Alyosha cried with sudden excitement. "My brother kept telling me that half—half of his disgrace (he repeated *half* several times!) could be removed at once, but that, realising how weak his character was, he would never do so—that he knew beforehand that he would not, that he had not the will power to do so!"

"And you remember quite clearly that he struck himself on just that part of the breast?" Fetyukovich questioned him eagerly.

"Yes, I remember it quite clearly, I'm quite sure of it, for I thought at the time: why is he beating his breast so high up when the heart is located lower down, but at the time the thought seemed absurd to me— I remember thinking it absurd— that flashed through my mind. And that's why I've recalled it just now. And how could I have forgotten it till this moment. It was the little bag he was pointing to when he said that he had the means, but that he would not return the fifteen hundred! And when he was arrested at Mokroye he cried—I know, I was told about it—that he considered it the most disgraceful act of his life that, when he had the means of repaying half (yes, half!) his debt to Katerina Ivanovna and no longer being a thief in her view, he could not bring himself to return it, but preferred to remain a thief in her view rather than part with the

451

money! And what torment he felt—what torment over that debt!" Alyosha exclaimed in conclusion.

Of course, the public prosecutor, too, intervened. He asked Alyosha to describe again how it had all happened and insisted on repeating several times his question whether the accused had really been pointing at something when he beat his breast. Perhaps, he had simply been striking the breast with his fist?

"It was not with his fist at all!" exclaimed Alyosha. "He kept pointing with his finger, and he pointed here, very high up— How could I have forgotten it so completely till this moment?"

Addressing Mitya, the presiding judge asked him what he had to say about Alyosha's evidence. Mitya confirmed that it was exactly how it had all happened and that he had been pointing to the fifteen hundred on his breast just a little below his neck, and that, of course, it was a disgrace—"a disgrace", he went on, "which I do not deny! It was the most disgraceful thing I had done in all my life!" cried Mitya. "I could have returned it, but didn't. I preferred to remain a thief in her view rather than return it. And what was the most disgraceful was that I knew beforehand that I wouldn't return it! Alyosha's right! Thank you, Alyosha!"

Thus ended Alyosha's examination. The important and remarkable thing about it was that one fact had at least emerged, one, true, very minor proof, almost a hint at proof, which nevertheless seemed to indicate, however vaguely, that the little bag had existed, that there was fifteen hundred roubles in it, and that the accused had not been lying at the preliminary inquiry when he declared at Mokroye that the fifteen hundred "were his". The delighted Alyosha returned to his seat with a flushed face. He kept repeating to himself: "How could I have forgotten it? How could I have forgotten it? And how was it that I suddenly recalled it only now?"

The examination of Katerina Ivanovna now began. Her appearance evoked something extraordinary in the courtroom. The ladies clutched their lorgnettes and opera glasses, while the men stirred in their seats, some rising to their feet to get a better view. It was generally asserted later that Mitya turned "as white as a sheet" as soon as she entered. All in black, she modestly and almost timidly approached the witness-stand. It was impossible to tell from her face that she was agitated, but there was a gleam of resolution in her dark and sombre gaze. It should be noted that a great many people asserted afterwards that she looked particularly beautiful at the moment. She began to speak in a low voice, but so clearly that it was audible throughout the courtroom. She expressed herself with the greatest composure, or, at any rate, did her utmost to be composed. The presiding judge began his questions with great caution and very deferentially, as though afraid to touch "certain chords", and with consideration for her great misfortune. But, from the very outset, Katerina Ivanovna declared firmly, in reply to a question, that she had been engaged to the accused, "till he left me of his own accord", she added in a low voice. Asked about the three thousand she had entrusted to Mitya to remit to her relations, she said firmly: "I did not give it to him merely to send off; I felt at the time that he was in great need of money—just then—I gave him the three thousand on the understanding that, if he liked, he could send it off within a month. He needn't have tormented himself so much afterwards over that debt—"

I am not repeating in detail all the questions put to her and her replies, but shall convey the gist of her evidence.

"I was positive," she went on, replying to a question, "that he would send off the money as soon as he got it from his father. I have always been convinced of his selflessness and his honesty—his scrupulous honesty in—in money matters. He was absolutely sure that he would get the three thousand from his father and told me so several times. I knew that there was a feud between him and his father, and I have always been of the opinion, and I say so now, that he had been unfairly treated by his father. I don't remember him threatening his father. In my presence, at any rate, he never said anything of the kind, and never uttered any threats. If he had come to me at the time, I should at once have set his mind at rest about the unfortunate three thousand roubles, but—he never came to see me again and—and I myself—I was placed in such a position that—that I could not ask him to come to see me— Why," she added suddenly, and there was a ring of determination in her voice, "I had no right whatever to demand repayment of that debt. I had once received a loan from him myself of more than three thousand and I accepted it though I could not foresee at the time that I would ever be in a position to repay the debt—"

There seemed to be a note of defiance in her voice. It was at that moment that Fetyukovich began to cross-examine.

"It took place not here but at the beginning of your acquaintance, did it not?" Fetyukovich suggested cautiously, at once sensing that something favourable was at hand. (I must note parenthetically that though he had been summoned from St. Petersburg partly by Katerina Ivanovna herself, he knew nothing of the episode of the five thousand Mitya had given her in that other town and of her "bowing down to the ground" to him. She had not told him of that, had withheld it—a remarkable fact! It may be confidently assumed that, down to the very last moment, she did not know herself whether she would tell about that episode in court, and was awaiting some inspiration.)

No, I can never be able to forget those moments! She began to speak, holding nothing back, of *the whole* of that episode Mitya had told Alyosha: her "bowing down to the ground" and her reasons, and about her father, and her visit to Mitya, and did not mention by a single word or hint that Mitya had himself proposed, through her sister, that "Katerina Ivanovna should be sent to him for the money". She magnanimously held that back and was not ashamed to declare in public that it was she, she herself, who had come running to the young officer, of her own impulse, hoping for something or other—to obtain the money from him. It was something shattering! I turned cold and trembled as I listened. The people in the courtroom held their breath to catch every word. There was something so unparalleled about it, so that even from so masterful and disdainfully proud a girl as she it was almost impossible to expect such utterly outspoken evidence, such self-sacrifice, such self-immolation. And to what end? For whom? To save a man who had deceived and insulted her, and to do something, however small, to bring about his acquittal by creating a good impression in his favour! And, indeed, the character of the army officer who gave up his last five thousand roubles—all he possessed in the world—and who bowed respectfully to an innocent girl, appeared in a very sympathetic and attractive light, but—my heart contracted painfully! I felt that it might give rise to slander (and it did, it actually did!). People all over our town were saying afterwards with malicious chuckles that her story was, perhaps, not quite exact, namely in her statement that the officer had let the young lady go "with allegedly only a respectful bow". It was hinted that something "was omitted here". "And even if nothing was omitted, even if it were all true," even the most esteemed of our ladies asserted, "even then it is still very doubtful whether it was proper for a young girl to behave like that, even to save her father." And, surely, with her intelligence and her keen insight, Katerina Ivanovna must have known very well that people would say things like that. She certainly must have anticipated it, yet she made up her mind to tell everything! Of course, all these sordid doubts as to the truth of her story only arose afterwards; at the first moment, all were deeply impressed. As for the members of the court, they listened to Katerina Ivanovna in reverent and, as it were, even shamefaced silence. The public prosecutor did not permit himself a single question on the matter. Fetyukovich bowed very low to her. Oh, he was almost triumphant! A great deal had been gained: a man who, on a noble impulse, gave away his last five thousand roubles, and that selfsame man murdering his own father during the night to rob him of three thousand—that was something almost incongruous. Fetyukovich could at least eliminate the charge of robbery. The "case" suddenly appeared in a quite new light.

There was a wave of sympathy for Mitya. But he—it was said that once or twice during Katerina Ivanovna's evidence he jumped up from his seat, but sank back again, his face buried in his hands. But when she had finished, he suddenly cried in a sobbing voice:

"Katya, why have you ruined me!"

And he burst into loud sobs, which could be heard all over the court. However, he controlled himself at once and shouted again:

"I am now condemned!"

Then he seemed to be petrified on his seat, his teeth clenched and his arms folded tightly across his chest. Katerina Ivanovna did not leave the courtroom but sat down on a chair reserved for her. She was pale and sat with downcast eyes. Those who were sitting near her declared that she was trembling all over as though in a fever. Next to be examined was Grushenka.

I am now coming to the disaster whose sudden advent was perhaps the real cause of Mitya's downfall. For I am quite sure—and everyone else, all the jurists, said the same thing afterwards—that, but for that episode, the accused would at least have been met with leniency. But of that in a moment. First a few words about Grushenka.

She, too, appeared in the courtroom all in black, her beautiful black shawl over her shoulders. She mounted the witness-box with the light noiseless step and slightly swaying gait sometimes to be met in women of full figure. Her eyes were fixed on the president of the court, never shifting either to the left or to the right. To my thinking, she looked particularly handsome at the moment, and not at all pale, as the ladies later declared. They asserted that her face looked somehow intent and spiteful, but it was my impression that she was merely irritated and painfully aware of the contemptuously inquisitive eyes of our scandal-loving public. Her pride made her intolerant of contempt; for she was one of those people who flare up and hit back at the least suggestion of contempt. There was also her innate timidity and a sense of shame that timidity aroused in her, so that there was nothing surprising in the uneven tone of her testimony, angry at one moment, and contemptuous and excessively rude at another, with a sincere note of self-condemnation and self-accusation appearing at times. She sometimes spoke as though she were hurling herself into some abyss: "I'll speak out whatever the consequences—" Asked about her acquaintance with Fyodor Pavlovich, she remarked curtly: "That was all nonsense! Was I to blame if he kept pestering me?" A moment later she added: "It was all my fault—I made mock of the two of them—the old man and this one here—and I brought them both to this. It all happened because of me."

A reference was made to Samsonov. "That's nobody's concern," she snapped with a sort of insolent defiance. "He was my benefactor. He took me when I was in dire need and my family had turned me out of home." The presiding judge, however, reminded her very courteously that she had to give direct answers to questions, without entering into superfluous details. Grushenka blushed, and her eyes flashed.

She had never seen the envelope with the money, but only heard from the "villain" that Fyodor Pavlovich had an envelope containing three thousand. "Only that was all nonsense. It made me laugh. I wouldn't have gone there for anything."

"Who were you referring to just now as 'villain'?" the public prosecutor asked.

"The lackey, Smerdyakov, who murdered his master and hanged himself yesterday."

She was, of course, at once asked what grounds she had for such a forthright accusation, but she, too, seemed to have no grounds for it.

"Dmitri Fyodorovich told me so himself. You must believe him. The woman who came between us has ruined him. Yes, she's the cause of it all," added Grushenka, and she seemed to be convulsed with hatred, a note of malice ringing in her voice.

She was asked who she was hinting at.

"The young lady, the Katerina Ivanovna over there. She asked me to call on her, offered me a cup of chocolate and tried to charm me. She has little true shame in her—that's the trouble—"

At this point, the presiding judge pulled her up sternly, and asked her to moderate her language. But the jealous woman's heart had flared up, and she had cast all caution to the winds—

"When the accused was arrested in the village of Mokroye," the public prosecutor recalled, "you were seen and heard to dash out of the adjacent room and cry out, 'It's all my fault! We'll go to Siberia together!' You must therefore have been certain at the moment that he had murdered his father, mustn't you?"

"I don't remember what I felt at the time," replied Grushenka. "They were all shouting that he had murdered his father, and I felt that it was my fault and that he had murdered him because of me. But when he said that he was innocent, I believed him at once, and I believe him now and always shall believe him. He isn't the kind of man to lie."

It was now Fetyukovich's turn to cross-examine. Among other things, I remember, he questioned her about Rakitin and about the twenty-five roubles "you gave him for bringing Alexei Karamazov to see you".

"There's nothing surprising about his taking the money," Grushenka smiled with angry contempt. "He was always coming to cadge money from me. He'd get thirty roubles a month sometimes and spend it on his small luxuries: he had enough for food and drink without me."

"But what was your reason for being so generous to Mr. Rakitin?" Fetyukovich was quick to ask, despite an uneasy movement on the part of the presiding judge.

"Why, he's my cousin. His mother and mine were sisters. But he has always implored me not to speak about it here. He was so terribly ashamed of me."

This new fact came as a complete surprise to the public in court. No one in the town or at the monastery, not even Mitya, had known of it. Rakitin was said to have flushed purple with shame. Before she entered the courtroom, Grushenka had somehow learnt that Rakitin had testified against Mitya, which was why she was so angry. The whole of Mr. Rakitin's speech, all its noble sentiments, all his attacks on serfdom and the political disorganisation of Russia—all its effect on the public were now finally wrecked and cast aside. Fetyukovich was satisfied: this was another windfall. In general, Grushenka was questioned quite briefly and, as a matter of fact, she could not have told them anything particularly new. She left a highly disagreeable impression on the public. Hundreds of contemptuous glances were fixed on her when, having completed her evidence, she sat down in the courtroom at some distance from Katerina Ivanovna. Throughout her examination, Mitya was silent, as though turned to stone, his eyes downcast.

Ivan Fyodorovich was the next witness.

5.

Disaster Falls

I shall note that he had been summoned prior to Alyosha, but the tipstaff informed the presiding judge that a sudden attack of illness or a kind of fit had prevented his coming, but he was ready to give his evidence as soon as he felt better. But it somehow appeared that no one had heard of it, and it only transpired later. At first, his appearance in court passed almost unnoticed: the principal witnesses, especially the two rival young women, had already been examined; curiosity was sated for the time being. There was, indeed, a general feeling of fatigue among the public. There were still several witnesses to be examined, but, in view of what had already come to light, they probably had nothing of particular importance to reveal. Time was passing. Ivan Fyodorovich mounted the witness-stand in a surprisingly slow manner, without looking at anyone and with his head sunk, as if in moody thought. He was faultlessly dressed, but his face produced, on me at least, a painful impression; there was something cadaverous about it, so that it resembled the face of a dying man. His eyes were lacklustre; he raised them and looked slowly about the courtroom. Jumping up from his seat, Alyosha moaned, "Oh!" I remember that, but few people noticed it.

The presiding judge began by informing him that, as a witness who was not on oath, he could answer questions at his discretion, but, of course, whatever evidence he gave must be according to his conscience, and so on and so forth. Ivan Fyodorovich listened and looked at him blankly, but his face suddenly began slowly to distend into a smile and as soon as the presiding judge, who eyed him with surprise, concluded, he suddenly burst into laughter.

"Well, and what else?" he asked loudly.

There was dead silence in the courtroom: it was generally felt that something extraordinary was about to happen. The presiding judge showed signs of uneasiness.

"Are you—perhaps still not feeling so well?" he asked,

looking about for the tipstaff.

"Don't worry, sir, I'm well enough and I can tell you something curious," Ivan Fyodorovich suddenly replied very calmly and respectfully.

"You have some special communication to make?" the presiding judge went on, still mistrustfully.

Ivan Fyodorovich looked down, waited a few seconds and, raising his head again, replied in a stammer, as it were.

"No, sir— I haven't, I haven't anything special."

The interrogation began. He replied rather reluctantly, with extreme brevity, even with a kind of distaste, which grew ever more marked, though his replies were rational enough. He refused to reply to many questions he pleaded ignorance of. He knew nothing of his father's money differences with Dmitri Fyodorovich. "I was not interested in them," he said. He had heard the accused threaten to kill his father and had heard from Smerdyakov about the money in the envelope.

"It's the same thing over and over again," he suddenly interrupted with a weary look. "There's nothing particular I can tell the court."

"I can see," the presiding judge began, "that you are unwell and I understand your feelings—"

He turned to the public prosecutor and the counsel for the defence and asked them to cross-examine the witness, if they thought it necessary, at which Ivan Fyodorovich suddenly asked him in an exhausted voice:

"I would like to be excused, your excellency, I feel quite ill."

Without waiting for permission, he suddenly turned round and walked towards the door. But after taking some four paces, he halted as though giving thought to something, gave a slow smile, and returned to the witness-stand.

"I'm just like that peasant girl, your excellency," he said. "You know how it goes: 'If I want to I get up, if not, I don't!' They follow her about with a sarafan or striped, homespun skirt and beg her to get up and put it on so as to go to church for her to be married, but she keeps saying: 'If I want to I get up, if not, I don't—' That seems to be a national feature of ours—"

"What do you mean by that?" the presiding judge asked severely.

"This," Ivan Fyodorovich replied suddenly, producing a sheaf of bank-notes. "Here is the money—the same notes that lay in that envelope—" (he motioned to the table with the "exhibits") "and for which my father was murdered. Where shall I put it? Tipstaff, take it."

The tipstaff rose from his seat, took the money and handed it to the president of the court.

"In what way could this money be in your possession if—if it's the same?" the presiding judge asked in surprise.

"I got it from Smerdyakov, from the murderer, yesterday—I went to see him before he hanged himself. It was he and not my brother who murdered my father. He murdered him, and it was I who prompted him to do it— Who doesn't wish for his father's death?"

"Are you in your right mind?" the presiding judge cried involuntarily.

"Yes, that's the trouble that I'm in my right mind—and in the same vile mind as you yourself and all these—ugly faces!" he turned suddenly to the public. "My father has been murdered and they make a pretence of fright," he snarled with furious contempt. "Putting on airs to one another! The liars! They all wish their fathers dead. One viper devours the other— Had there been no patricide, that would have angered all of them, and they'd have gone home in a bad temper— Circuses! 'Bread and circuses!' Yet I'm no better! Is there any water here? For Christ's sake let me have a drink of water!" he cried, suddenly clutching at his head.

The usher at once approached him. Alyosha suddenly jumped up and shouted: "He's ill! Don't believe him! He's delirious!" Katerina Ivanovna rose impetuously from her seat and, horror-stricken, gazed at Ivan Fyodorovich. Mitya got up, looked at his brother and listened eagerly to him with a kind of wild and twisted smile.

"Calm yourselves; I'm not mad, but only a murderer!" Ivan began again. "You can't expect eloquence from a murderer, can you?—" he added suddenly for some reason, and laughed wryly.

Obviously taken aback, the public prosecutor leaned towards the presiding judge. The members of the bench whispered agitatedly to one another. Fetyukovich pricked up his ears. There was a hush of expectancy in the courtroom. The presiding judge seemed suddenly to recollect himself.

"Witness, your words are incomprehensible and unacceptable here. Calm yourself, if you can, and tell us all about it if—if you really have something to say. How can you confirm your confession, if—if you are not raving?"

"The trouble is that I have no witnesses. That cur of a Smerdyakov will not provide you with evidence from the other world in—in an envelope. All you want are envelopes, but one's enough. I have no witnesses— Except, perhaps, one," he smiled pensively.

"Who is your witness?"

"He has a tail, sir. I'm afraid you wouldn't consider him a proper witness. *Le diable n'existe point!* Take no notice of him," he added, suddenly in earnest, and as though confidentially, "it's a paltry little devil. He's probably here somewhere—there under that table with the exhibits. Where else should he be sitting if not there? D'you see him? Listen, I told him I wouldn't be silent and he started talking about geological upheavals—what nonsense! Well, set the monster free—he's been singing a hymn. That's because he doesn't care! He's just like a drunken rascal bawling at the top of his voice how 'Vanka's gone to St. Petersburg', but I'd give a quadrillion of quadrillions for two seconds of joy! You don't know me at all! Oh, how stupid everything is here! Well, take me instead of him! I've come here for something after all— Why, why is everything in the world so stupid?"

And he began again to look about the courtroom slowly and as though thoughtfully. But already the courtroom was in turmoil. Alyosha rushed towards him, but the usher had already seized Ivan Fyodorovich by the arm.

"What d'you mean by that?" Ivan cried, staring the usher in the face and, suddenly grabbing the man by the shoulders, he flung him bodily to the floor. He was seized by the guards, and it was then that he uttered a piercing scream. And, shouting incoherently, he went on screaming while he was being carried out.

The court was thrown into confusion. I cannot recall the exact course of events, for I was too agitated myself to see what was going on. All I know is that afterwards, when order had been restored and it was generally realised what had happened, the usher was taken severely to task, but he quite explained to the judges at length that the witness had been well all the time, a doctor had attended him when he had a slight attack of giddiness an hour earlier but he had spoken coherently before entering the courtroom, so that it had been quite impossible to foresee anything; on the contrary, he himself had insisted on giving evidence. But before things had calmed down and order restored, another scene followed immediately: Katerina Ivanovna had an attack of hysterics. She shrieked loudly and burst into sobs, but refused to leave the courtroom; she struggled, entreated them not to remove her, and suddenly shouted to the presiding judge:

"I must give you some more evidence, at once—at once!—Here's a document, a letter—take it and read it quickly, quickly! It's a letter from that monster—that one over there!" she pointed to Mitya. "It is he who murdered his father, as you will see presently. He wrote to me how he would kill his father! But the other one is ill, ill—he's got brain fever! I could see for the last three days that he was ill!"

So she kept shrieking, beside herself. The usher took the document which she held out to the presiding judge, and she herself collapsed on her chair and burying her face, began sobbing convulsively and noiselessly, trembling and stifling every moan for fear that she should be forced to leave the courtroom. The document she had given to the usher was the letter Mitya had sent her from the Metropolis Inn, which Ivan Fyodorovich had described as a document of "mathematical" significance. Alas, its "mathematical" nature was at once established; but for that letter Mitya would not have been ruined, or, at any rate, not have been ruined so terribly! I repeat, it was difficult to keep track of every detail. Even now, the whole thing seems utterly confused in my memory. I suppose the presiding judge must at once have communicated the new document to the other members of the bench, the public prosecutor, the counsel for the defence, and the jury. I only remember how they began examining the witness. Asked gently by the presiding judge whether she was sufficiently composed to give evidence, Katerina Ivanovna cried impulsively:

"I'm ready, quite ready! I'm quite able to answer your questions," she added, evidently still terribly afraid that for some reason they would refuse to listen to her. She was asked to explain in more detail what kind of letter it was and under what circumstances she had received it.

"I received it on the day before the murder, and he wrote it the day before that at the town inn, so that it was written two days before he committed the crime. Look, it is written on some kind of bill!" she exclaimed breathlessly. "He hated me at the time because he had behaved so vilely and was running after that hussy—and also because he owed me the three thousand roubles!— Oh, he resented owing me that money just because of his vileness. Here is how the matter of the three thousand came about— I beg and entreat you to hear me out: three weeks before he murdered his father, he came to see me one morning. I knew he needed money and I knew what for—yes, to win that hussy and carry her off. I knew at the time that he had been false to me and wanted to jilt me, and I, I myself offered him the money, I gave it to him on the pretext of sending it to my sister in Moscow—and when I gave it to him, I looked him in the face and said that he could send it whenever he liked, 'even in a month's time'. How then, how then, could he have failed to understand that I was practically telling him to his face: 'You need money to betray me with that hussy of yours, so here it is, I'm giving it to you myself! Take it if you're so dishonourable as to do so!'— I wanted to expose him, and what did he do? He took the money. He took it and squandered it there with that hussy in a single night— But he realised, he realised, I assure you—he realised very well that, by giving him that money, I was only testing him: I was trying to see whether he really was so dishonourable as to take it from me. I looked him in the eye and he looked back at me and understood everything—everything, and took the money! Took my money and made off with it!"

"That's true, Katya!" Mitya suddenly roared. "I looked into your eyes and knew that you were trying to degrade me, yet I took your money! Despise the blackguard, despise me, all of you! I've deserved it!"

"Prisoner in the dock," exclaimed the presiding judge, "another word from you and I'll have you removed!"

"That money tormented him," Katerina Ivanovna went on with convulsive haste. "He wanted to give it back to me: he wanted to, true, but he also needed money for that hussy. So he murdered his father, but didn't return the money to me all the same, instead, he went off with her to the village where he was arrested. There again he squandered the money he had stolen from the father he had murdered. And he wrote me this letter the day before the murder, he wrote it while he was drunk, I saw that at once. He wrote it out of spite and knowing, knowing for sure that I wouldn't show the letter to anyone, even if he did commit murder. Otherwise, he wouldn't have written. He knew I wouldn't wish to avenge myself and ruin him! But read it, please, read it carefully, as carefully as you can, please, and you will see that he described everything in writing, everything in advance: how he would kill his father and where the money was kept. Please, look and don't miss anything. There's a sentence in it: 'I'll kill him as soon as Ivan leaves.' And that means that he had thought out beforehand how he would kill him," Katerina Ivanovna suggested to the court with gloating venom. Oh, it was clear that she had studied every line in that fateful letter, knew every word of it. "If he hadn't been drunk, he wouldn't have written to me. But look, everything is described there beforehand, everything just as it happened, how he committed the murder, the entire programme!"

She was beside herself as she spoke, and, of course, heedless of all the consequences, though she had anticipated them perhaps a month before, when, probably carried away by anger, she had wondered whether or not she should read out the letter in court. She had now cast the die. It was just at this point, as

I remember, that the clerk read the letter aloud, and it created an overwhelming impression. "Do you admit that you wrote this letter?" Mitya was asked.

"It's mine, mine all right!" Mitya exclaimed. "If I hadn't been drunk, I wouldn't have written it!— We've hated each other for many things, Katya, but I swear, I swear, I loved you even while I hated you, but you never loved me!"

He sank back on his seat, wringing his hands in despair. The public prosecutor and the counsel for the defence began the cross-examination, mainly with a view to finding out what had induced her to hold back a document and previously testify in a quite different fashion.

"Yes, yes. I was lying then," Katerina cried like one possessed. "I was telling lies all the time, against my honour and my conscience, but I wanted to save him because he had hated and despised me so much. Oh, he has despised me terribly, always despised me and, you know, you know he has done so ever since the moment I bowed down to the ground before him for the money. I saw that at once— I felt it but I refused to believe it for a long time. How many times have I read in his eyes: 'But you came to me yourself that time all the same.' Oh, he didn't understand—he didn't understand anything! He didn't understand why I came running to him then! He is capable of suspecting only base motives! He was using his own yardstick; he thought that everyone else was like him," Katerina Ivanovna cried furiously, completely beside herself. "And the only reason he wanted to marry me was because I had come into a fortune. Because of that, only that! I always suspected it! Oh, he is a brute! He was always convinced that I'd be trembling with shame because I came to him then, that he could always despise me for that, and ride roughshod over me—that's why he wanted to marry me! Yes, that's why! I tried to conquer him with love—a love that was boundless. I even tried to put up with his betrayal of me, but he understood nothing at all! And how can he be expected to understand anything? He is a monster! I only received this letter the following evening. It was brought to me from the inn, and even that very morning I wanted to forgive him everything, everything, even his betrayal!"

The presiding judge and the public prosecutor, of course, tried to calm her. I am sure all of them felt perhaps ashamed to take advantage of her frenzy and listen to such admissions. I remember hearing them say to her: "We realise how painful this is to you! Rest assured we are able to feel for you," etc., etc. And yet they extracted the evidence from the maddened and hysterical woman. Finally, she described with extraordinary clarity, which so often, if momentarily, appears during such an overwrought condition, how Ivan Fyodorovich had almost gone out of his mind during the past two months in an attempt to save his brother, that "monster and murderer".

"He tormented himself," she exclaimed, "wishing to minimise his brother's guilt. He confessed to me that he had no love for his father, and perhaps wished him dead himself. Oh, he has a sensitive, a most tender conscience! It is his conscience that has driven him out of his mind! He told me everything, everything. He called on me daily and spoke to me as his only friend. I have the honour to be his only friend!" she exclaimed suddenly, with flashing eyes, in a kind of defiance. "He had been to see Smerdyakov twice. One day he came to me and said that if Smerdyakov and not his brother had committed the murder (for lots of people here spread the silly story that Smerdyakov did it), then he, too, was guilty, because Smerdyakov knew that he had no love for his father and perhaps thought that he desired his death. Then I produced the letter and showed it to him, which fully convinced him that his brother had committed the murder, and that drove him out of his mind. He could not endure the thought that his own brother was a parricide! I could see already a week ago that it was making him ill. When he came to see me during the last few days, he was raving. I saw that he was going out of his mind. He walked about raving; he was seen talking to himself in the street. At my request, a Moscow doctor examined him the day before yesterday and told me that he was on the verge of losing his reason—and all because of him, all because of that monster! And yesterday he learnt that Smerdyakov was dead, and that was such a violent shock to him that he went mad—and all because of that monster—all because he wanted to save that monster!"

467

Oh, no doubt, such words and confessions can come once in a lifetime—at the hour of death, for instance, when mounting the scaffold. But Katya was true to herself at that moment in her life. It was the same impetuous Katya who had rushed to the young rake of an officer to save her father; the same Katya who, proud and chaste, had just sacrificed herself and her maidenly modesty to all that crowd of people by telling them about Mitya's "noble act", so as to mitigate his lot. And now she was sacrificing herself in exactly the same way, but this time for another, and perhaps it was only now, only at that moment, that she felt and fully realised how dear that other man was to her! She had sacrificed herself because she was terrified for him, for it suddenly occurred to her that he had ruined himself by testifying that he, not his brother, had committed the murder—she had sacrificed herself to save him, his good name and his reputation! And yet one could not but harbour some horrible doubt: was she lying in describing her former relations with Mitya?—that was the question. No, no, she was not slandering Mitya intentionally when she cried out that he despised her for bowing down to the ground to him! She believed it herself. She had been firmly convinced, perhaps ever since the time she had bowed down to the ground before him, that the simple-hearted Mitya, who had adored her even then, was making mock of her and despised her. Only her pride, her wounded and lacerated pride, had made her become attached to him with an hysterical love that was more like vengeance than love. Oh, perhaps that anguish-ridden love of hers might eventually have grown into real love, perhaps Katya wished for nothing but that. But Mitya's infidelity had insulted her to the depths of her soul, and there was no forgiveness in that soul now. The moment of revenge, however, had overcome her suddenly, and everything that had so long and so agonisingly accumulated in the breast of the wronged woman burst out suddenly and, again, quite unexpectedly. She betrayed Mitya, but then, she betrayed herself, too! Indeed, as soon as she had given vent to her feelings the tension was broken and she was overwhelmed with shame. Another attack of hysterics came on and she collapsed, sobbing and screaming, and had to be carried

468

out. At that moment, Grushenka rushed up from her seat to Mitya so impetuously that there was no stopping her.

"Mitya!" she cried, "your serpent has ruined you! Now she has shown you what she's really like!" she shouted to the judges, trembling with anger. At a sign from the presiding judge, she was seized to be removed from the courtroom. She resisted and struggled to get back to Mitya, who began to shout and also tried to get to her. He was overpowered.

Yes, I think our ladies must have been quite satisfied: the show had certainly been most magnificent. Then, I remember, the Moscow doctor put in an appearance. It seems that the presiding judge had sent the court usher with instructions that Ivan Fyodorovich was to be given medical aid. The doctor informed the court that Ivan Fyodorovich was suffering from a most dangerous attack of brain fever and should be taken away at once. Replying to the public prosecutor and the defence counsel, he confirmed that the sick man had consulted him of his own accord two days before and had been warned of the imminence of such an attack, but had declined medical treatment: "He was most decidely not in his right mind and told me himself that he saw visions when awake, met people in the street who had long been dead, and that Satan visited him every evening," the doctor concluded. The celebrated physician withdrew after giving his evidence. The letter produced by Katerina Ivanovna was adduced to the exhibits. After some deliberation, the members of the court decided that the trial would proceed and that the two unexpected pieces of evidence given by Katerina Ivanovna and Ivan Fyodorovich should be put on record.

I shall not go into the testimony of the rest of the witnesses, which merely repeated and confirmed what had already been said, albeit with some individual features. But, I repeat, it was all to be summed up in the public prosecutor's speech, which I shall pass on to at once. The public in the courtroom were greatly excited, electrified by the new disaster and eagerly awaiting the final outcome: the speeches for the prosecution and for the defence, and the sentence. Fetyukovich was evidently greatly shaken by Katerina Ivanovna's evidence. The public prosecutor, by contrast, was jubilant. When the testimony had all been heard, the court was adjourned for almost an hour. At last, the presiding judge called upon the public prosecutor and the counsel for the defence to speak. I believe that Ippolit Kirillovich began his speech at exactly eight o'clock.

6.

The Public Prosecutor's Speech.
A Character Study

When the public prosecutor began his speech, he was trembling all over with nervousness, his forehead in a cold sweat, and feeling hot and cold in turn, as he himself later said. He regarded this speech as his *chef d'oeuvre,* the acme of his lifetime, his swan song. Indeed, he died of galloping consumption nine months later, so that he could really have compared himself to a swan singing its last song, had he foreseen his impending decease. He put into the speech his whole heart and as much intellect as he possessed, and quite unexpectedly proved that within him was a keen sense of civic duty and of the "burning" questions of the day, at least to the best of our poor Ippolit Kirillovich's capacity. The chief reason for the powerful impact of his address lay in its sincerity: he firmly believed that the accused was guilty; it was not merely out of a sense of official duty that he accused the latter, calling for "retribution", but was passionately moved by a desire to "protect society". Even our ladies, who were, ultimately, hostile to the public prosecutor, had to admit that he produced a tremendous impression on them. He began in a cracked and faltering voice, but very soon his voice grew stronger and rang all throughout the courtroom, until the end of his speech. But he almost swooned as soon as he had concluded.

"Gentlemen of the jury," he began, "this case has created a sensation all over Russia. But, after all, what is there to be surprised at or be so horrified by, it would seem, particularly to us? We have become used to such things! The monstrosity of it all lies in such heinous deeds almost ceasing to horrify us! No doubt, the cause for horror is not some individual crime but the fact that we have grown used to crimes. Where are we to seek the causes of our indifference, our almost lukewarm attitude to such crimes, to such signs of the times, which forecast our unenviable future? Is it in our cynicism, in the premature impoverishment of the intellect and the imagination of our society, which is still so young and yet has grown so decrepit before it has aged? Is it to be sought in our moral principles, which have been shaken to their very foundations or, ultimately, in our total lack of such principles? I am not seeking to resolve these questions, but they are nevertheless agonising, so that every citizen must, is in duty bound, to feel the deepest concern over them. Our incipient and as yet timid press has rendered some good service to society, for without it we would never have learnt with any fullness about those horrors of unbridled licence and moral turpitude which are constantly reported in its pages to the public at large, and not only to those who attend the new public courts granted to us in the present reign. And what do we read almost daily? Oh, continually about things beside which even this case pales into insignificance and appears almost commonplace. But what is even more significant is that a multitude of our Russian and national crimes of violence testify to something that is universal, a kind of widespread calamity which has struck root among us and, as a universal evil, is hard to strike at. There is the instance of a brilliant young army officer, who moved in the best society and practically at the very beginning of his life and career, foully murdered, without any qualms of conscience, a petty civil servant, who had in a way been his benefactor, and the latter's maidservant, with the purpose of recovering his promissory note he had given him, as well as stealing his victim's ready cash: 'It will prove useful for my pleasures in society and my future career.' After murdering the two, he left, after putting pillows under their heads. Elsewhere, a young hero, decorated for gallantry, brutally murders and robs the mother of his chief and benefactor on the highway and, to urge his accomplices to join him, assures them that she loves him 'like a son' and 'will therefore follow his advice and take no precautions'. He is a monster, true, but I cannot dare to say, now, in our times, that he is an exceptional monster. Someone else may not actually commit murder, but will think and feel exactly like him, and be just as dishonourable at heart. In the dead of night, alone with his conscience, he may perhaps ask himself: 'What does honour mean? Isn't the sentiment against the spilling of blood a prejudice?' Perhaps people will cry out against me and say that I'm morbid and hysterical, that this is some monstrous slander, and that I'm raving, exaggerating. Let them, let them do so, and, good Lord, I'd be the first to rejoice if that were true! Oh, you need not believe me, you may regard me as a sick man, but remember my words all the same: for if only a tenth or a twentieth part of what I say is true—even that is dreadful! Look, gentlemen, look at the way young people put bullets through their brains in our country, without even asking themselves Hamlet's questions about 'something *after death*', or even a hint at any such questions, just as though this matter of the soul and what awaits us beyond the grave have long disappeared from their being, buried for good and all. Finally, consider our vice and our lechers. Fyodor Pavlovich Karamazov, the unfortunate victim in this case, was almost a babe in arms compared with some of them. And yet we all knew him—'he lived among us'—* Yes, the leading minds both in our country and in Europe will perhaps one day make a study of the psychology of Russian crime, for the subject deserves it. But that study will come some time later when the whole tragic mess of the current minute will recede into the distant past and can be scrutinised more intelligently and more impartially than, for instance, people like me can do. We are now either horrified or pretend to be horrified, while actually relishing the spectacle, like lovers of strong and eccentric sensations, which titillate our cynical apathy, or, finally, like little children, we shoo the fearful phantoms away and hide our heads under the pillow until the dreadful apparition is gone, so as to forget it at once in our merry games. But one day we, too, must begin our lives in sober thought; we, too, must cast a glance at ourselves as a society; we, too, must at least gain some

*The first line in Alexander Pushkin's poem dedicated to the Polish poet Adam Mickiewicz.—*Tr.*

idea of our social life or at least make a beginning of trying to understand it. In the finale of his greatest novel, a great writer of the preceding epoch,* in personifying Russia as a dashing Russian troika, galloping towards some unknown destination, exclaims: 'Oh, troika, you fleet troika, who has invented you?' and adds, with proud admiration that all the nations step aside respectfully to make way for the troika galloping at breakneck speed. Well, gentlemen, let them, let them step aside, respectfully or not, but in my humble opinion, the great creative artist concluded in that fashion either in an onset of childish sincerity or simply because in fear of the then censorship. For if his own characters, the Sobakeviches, the Nozdryovs and the Chichikovs, were harnessed in his troika, you would not reach any proper destination with such horses, whoever the driver may be! And those were horses of former times, horses which stand in no comparison with those of today—ours are in far better trim—"

At this point, the public prosecutor's speech was interrupted by applause. The liberalism in the simile of the Russian troika was to the liking of the public. True, the applause was confined to a small group, so that the presiding judge did not even deem it necessary to admonish the public with the threat of "clearing the court", but only looked sternly in the direction of those who had applauded. But the public prosecutor felt encouraged: he had never been applauded before! A man who had been refused a hearing for so many years was suddenly given an opportunity of speaking his mind to the whole of Russia!

"Indeed," he went on, "who are the Karamazov family, who have suddenly gained such regrettable notoriety even throughout Russia? I may be exaggerating, but it seems to me that certain general and fundamental elements of our contemporary educated society can to some extent be discerned in the picture of this family—oh, not all the elements, and these are reflected only microscopically, 'like the sun in a drop of water', yet something has been reflected, something of the kind has made

*Nikolai Gogol (1809-1852)—novelist, short-story writer and dramatist.—*Tr.*

itself felt. Consider this unfortunate, licentious and depraved old man, this 'paterfamilias', who has come to such a sad end. A nobleman born, who began his life as an impoverished hanger-on and who, by the accident of an unexpected marriage came into a small fortune by means of his wife's dowry, at first a petty rogue and a fawning clown, with an embryo of mental faculties, which were fairly good, and, above all, a usurer. With the passage of the years, that is to say, with the growth of his capital, he grew bolder. His obsequiousness and servility vanished and what remained was a sarcastic and evil-minded cynic and lecher. The spiritual aspect had dwindled away, while his thirst for life was quite extraordinary. As a result, he saw nothing in life but sensual enjoyment, and it was this that he taught his children. He knew nothing of a father's spiritual duties. He made mock of them, brought up his children in the back-yard and was glad to be rid of them. Indeed, he even forgot them completely. The old man's moral principles could be summed up in a single sentence: *après moi le déluge*. He was the reverse of the idea of citizenship, a complete and even hostile divorcement from society: 'The world can burn for all I care, if things are all right for me alone.' And they were all right; he was completely satisfied, eager to go on living in the same way for another twenty or thirty years. He cheated his own son and used his son's money, left to him by his mother, and which he refused to return, to win over the son's mistress. No, I do not want to yield the defence of the accused to the highly talented advocate from St. Petersburg. I will speak the truth myself, and can very well understand the sum of the resentment that the father built up in his son's heart. But enough, enough of that unhappy old man; he has got his deserts. But let us, however, recall that he was a father, and of our own times. Shall I offend society by saying that he was even one of many of present-day fathers? Alas, there are so many present-day fathers who merely do not speak out with such cynicism as he, for they have been better brought up and are better educated, but at bottom their philosophy is almost the same as his. But perhaps I'm a pessimist; I may be. We have agreed that you will forgive that. Let us reach an understanding in advance: you don't have to believe me, you don't have to: I shall go on speaking, but you need not believe me. But yet let me have my say, and yet do not forget something of what I say to you. However, let us turn to the children of this old man, this head of a family: one of them is here in the dock before you. I shall speak of him at length presently; of the other two I shall now say a few words. The elder of the two is one of our modern young men with an excellent education and a fairly powerful intellect who, however, no longer believes in anything; like his father, he has already rejected and erased too much in life. We have all heard him; he was given a friendly reception in our society. He made no secret of his opinions; even the reverse, quite the reverse, which emboldens me to speak somewhat frankly of him now, not, of course, as a private person, but as a member of the Karamazov family. Yesterday there died here, by his own hand, in the outskirts of the town, a sickly idiot, who is closely involved in this case, a servant and, perhaps, also the natural son of Fyodor Pavlovich Karamazov, to wit, Smerdyakov. At the preliminary investigation, he told me with hysterical tears how the young Ivan Fyodorovich Karamazov had horrified him by his spiritual unrestraint. 'With him,' he said, 'everything is permitted, everything in the world, and nothing should be forbidden in future—that's what he taught me all the time.' It seems that the idiot was completely driven out of his mind by this thesis which had been inculcated on him, though, of course, his epilepsy and all the terrible tragedy that had befallen the house also affected his reason. But this idiot let drop a highly curious remark indeed, one that would have done credit to a far more intelligent observer, which is why I shall even mention it. 'If,' he said to me, 'any of the sons most resembles Fyodor Pavlovich Karamazov in nature, it is Ivan Fyodorovich!' With this observation I shall break off the characterisation I have begun, thinking it indelicate to continue. Oh, I do not wish to draw any further conclusions and croak like a raven, promising only the ruination of a young man's future. We've seen today, in this courtroom, that the immediate force of the truth still lives in his young heart, and that the feeling of family attachment has not yet been stamped out by his disbelief and moral cynicism, which he has rather inherited than arrived at through genuine anguish of thought. Then there is the other son—oh, he is still very young, devout and humble—who, contrary to his brother's gloomy and corrupting world-view, seems to cling, as it were, to the 'folk roots', or to whatever is meant by that curious expression in some theorising circles of our thinking intelligentsia. He, you see, clung to a monastery; he almost became a monk himself. In him, as I see it, there has found early and unconscious expression that timid despair by which so many people in our poor society, who are fearful of cynicism and its corrupting influence and mistakenly attribute all evil to European enlightenment, are driven back to their 'native soil', into the maternal embrace, so to speak, of their native land; like children frightened by ghosts, they long to fall peacefully asleep at the withered breasts of their frail mother, and to sleep there all their lives, if only to avoid the sight of the horrors that terrify them. For my part, I wish that his youthful sincerity and his striving towards the folk roots may not, as so often happens, develop, in the moral sense, into gloomy mysticism, and in the civic sense, into obtuse chauvinism—two qualities that perhaps threaten the nation with an evil even greater than the early corruption resulting from a mis-understood and gratuitous adoption of European enlightenment in the way his elder brother has been affected."

Two or three people applauded at the mention of chauvinism and mysticism. The public prosecutor had, no doubt, been carried away and, besides, all this had little to do with the matter in hand, to say nothing of the fact that it was all rather vague, but the consumptive and embittered man was far too eager to have his say at least once in his lifetime. It was later asserted in our town that in his characterisation of Ivan Karamazov he was prompted by a sentiment that was even indelicate, since Ivan had on one or two occasions outargued him publicly, the remembrance of which had made the public prosecutor anxious for revenge. But I do not know whether such a conclusion could be drawn. In any case, all this was only by way of introduction, after which his speech bore more closely and directly on the case.

"And now for the third son of the head of a present-day

family," the public prosecutor went on. "There he is, in the dock before you. We also have his exploits, his life and actions before us: the hour has struck and everything has been laid bare and revealed. As distinct from 'Europeanism' and the 'folk roots' of his brothers, he seems to represent the immediate Russia—oh, not all of it, not all of it—God forfend that it should be all of it! And yet, here she is, our dear old Russia; here we have the very odour of our dear old mother; here are her very sounds. Oh, we are all impulse, an amazing blend of good and evil; we are lovers of enlightenment and Schiller and at the same time we engage in tavern brawls and pluck out the beards of drunkards, our fellow-drinkers. Oh, we can be good and noble too, but only when things are going well for us. Conversely, we are violently overcome—yes, overcome—by the loftiest ideals, but only if they come of themselves, if they fall from heaven for us, and, above all, if they come gratis, gratis, without having to be paid for. For we simply hate paying for anything, but are very fond of receiving, and that goes for everything. Oh, give us, give us every possible good thing in life (every possible thing; we won't stand for anything less) and, most especially, do not curb our natures in any way whatever, and then we will show that we, too, can be good and noble. We are not avaricious, good heavens, no! But provide us with money, lots and lots of more money, as much as possible, and you will see how magnanimously, with what contempt for filthy lucre, we shall squander it in a single night of unbridled dissipation. And if we are not given the money, we shall show how able we shall be to obtain it when we want to very much. But of that later. Let us take things in their due order. To begin with, we have before us a poor and neglected child running about 'in the backyard barefoot', in the words of our worthy and esteemed fellow-citizen who, alas, is of foreign extraction! I shall again repeat: I shall not yield the defence of the accused to anyone! I am his prosecutor, but also his defender. Yes, we, too, have human feelings and we, too, shall be able to weigh how character can be influenced by the first impressions of home and childhood. But the boy is already a youth, already a young man, an army officer. For his riotous behaviour and a challenge to a duel he is exiled to an outlying town in our bounteous Russia. There he served in his regiment, and went on with his dissipation and, to be sure, a great ship asks deep waters. He needed money, money first and foremost, and so, after long arguments, he agreed with his father to settle his remaining claim for six thousand, and the money was remitted to him. Note that he signed a document, which still exists, in which he almost renounced his claim to the rest and agreed to settle his dispute with his father over his inheritance on receipt of the six thousand. It was at this point that he met a young lady of high character and good education. Oh, I wouldn't dare to repeat the details; you have just heard them: questions of honour and self-sacrifice are involved here, and I am silent. We see fleeting before us in a most attractive light the figure of a young man, frivolous and dissipated, who pays homage to true nobility and a higher ideal. But suddenly after that the reverse of that medal has been shown to us quite unexpectedly in this very courtroom. Again, I will not venture to conjecture, and will refrain from an analysis of why this came about. But there were reasons for it to come about. With tears of long-suppressed indignation, the same young lady told us that it was he, he in the first place, who despised her for her incautious and, perhaps, impulsive action which, however, was lofty and magnanimous for all that. It was he, the girl's fiancé, who was the first to look at her with that mocking smile which she could not endure from him alone. Knowing that he had already been faithless to her (faithless in the conviction that now she had to put up with anything from him, even infidelity)—knowing that, she deliberately offered him three thousand roubles and intimated clearly, all too clearly, that she was offering the money for him to deceive her. 'Well, will you take it or not? Will you be as cynical as that?' was the silent question in her searching and accusing eyes. He looked back at her, saw clearly what was in her mind (he himself admitted here to you that he understood it all), unhesitatingly appropriated the three thousand and squandered it in two days with his new lady-love. What are we now to believe? The first legend, the impulse of high-minded nobility, consisting in the sacrifice of all of a man's substance in homage to virtue, or the reverse of the medal, which is so revolting? It usually happens in life that, given two extremes, the truth should be sought somewhere in between; in the present case, that is literally not so. It is most probable that he was sincerely noble in the first instance, and, in the second, just as genuinely base. But why? Because the Karamazovian nature is broad and reckless—that is just what I'm leading up—and capable of harbouring all kinds of opposites and contemplating at one and the same time the two abysses—the abyss above us, the abyss of supreme ideals, and the abyss below us, the abyss of the lowest and most malodorous degradation. Remember the brilliant thought expressed by Mr. Rakitin, the young observer, who has made a first-hand and profound study of the Karamazov family: 'A sense of the lowest degradation is as necessary to these unbridled and irrepressible natures as is a sense of supreme nobility.' And that is true: they stand in constant and unremitting need of this unnatural mixture. Two abysses, gentlemen, two abysses at one and the same moment: without them we are unfortunate and dissatisfied, and our existence is incomplete. We are expansive and unrestrained, as is Mother Russia. We can harbour anything and live together with anything! Incidentally, we have just touched upon the three thousand roubles and I will permit myself to run somewhat ahead. Can you only imagine that a man like that, after receiving such a sum and in such a way, at the cost of so much shame, so much ignominy and through the last degree of humiliation, can you only imagine that he could have been capable, on that very day, of setting aside half that sum, sewing it up in a little bag and of being firm-minded enough to carry it about his neck for a whole month, despite all temptations and his extraordinary need of it? Neither during his drunken orgies at the taverns, nor when he had to hastily leave the town to get, goodness only knows how, the money he needed so badly to take his lady-love away from the cajolery of his rival, his own father, did he dare to touch that little bag. It was just because he was so anxious to keep his lady-love away from the temptations of the old man he was so jealous of that he ought to have untied the little bag, and stayed on to keep constant watch over her, in expectation of the moment she would say, 'I'm yours', so as to go off with her as far as possible from the present fateful situation. But no, gentlemen, he did not touch the amulet, and on what pretext? The original pretext, as I've just said, was that when she would say: 'I'm yours, take me away wherever you wish', he had to have the wherewithal to do so. But that first pretext, according to the accused himself, paled beside the second. 'Whilst I carry that money about on me,' he declared, 'I'm a blackguard, not a thief, for I can always go to my affronted fiancée and, by placing before her half of the sum I have fraudulently appropriated, I can always say to her: 'You see, I've squandered half of your money and proved weak and immoral and, if you like, a blackguard (I'm using the prisoner's own expression), but, though a blackguard, I'm not a thief, for if I'd been a thief, I would not have brought you this half of the money but would have appropriated it as I did the first half.' An astonishing explanation of the fact! This most violent but weak man, who was unable to resist the temptation of accepting three thousand roubles through such disgrace—this same man suddenly senses such stoical firmness within himself, and carries fifteen hundred roubles about his neck without daring to touch it! Is that at all in keeping with the character we have analysed? No, it is not and I shall permit myself an account of how the real Dmitri Karamazov would have behaved in a case like that, even if he had really made up his mind to sew his money up in a little bag. At the first temptation—well, just to entertain his new lady-love, with whom he had already squandered the first half of the money—he would have undone his little bag and extracted, well, let us say, just a hundred roubles to start with, for why, indeed, should he return half the sum without fail, that is, fifteen hundred roubles? Fourteen hundred would have done just as well, for the outcome would be the same: 'I'm a blackguard but not a thief, for I've brought back fourteen hundred, while a thief would have taken it all, and returned nothing.' Then, after some time, he would have undone the bag again and extracted another hundred, and then a third and a fourth, so that by the end of the month he would have extracted the last hundred but one, for even if he had returned only one hundred, he could still assert that he was a blackguard but not a thief. He had squandered two thousand nine hundred roubles, but returned the last hundred; a thief would not have returned even that. Finally, after squandering the last hundred but one, he would have looked at the last hundred and said to himself: 'Why, it really isn't worth while to return a single hundred; I'll squander that too!' That's how the real Dmitri Karamazov, as we know him, would have acted! As for the legend about the little bag, nothing more contrary to reality can be imagined. One can assume anything but that. But we shall return to that later."

After summarising what had come to the knowledge of the court about the property disputes and family relations between father and son, and again and again drawing the conclusion that, according to all the available facts, there was not the slightest possibility of deciding who had cheated whom in the sharing of the property of Mitya's mother, to wit, Mitya's fixed idea about the three thousand roubles, the public prosecutor referred to the testimony of the medical experts.

7.

An Historical Review

"The medical experts have tried to prove to us that the accused is *non compos mentis,* and a maniac. I maintain that he is of sound mind, which is so much the worse: had he been of unsound mind, he would perhaps have proved far cleverer. As for his being a maniac, I would agree with that only on one point: that indicated by the medical experts, namely, his view on the three thousand he claims his father failed to pay him. Yet one could find a far closer viewpoint to account for the invariable frenzy of the accused in respect of the money than his proneness to insanity. For my part, I fully agree with the opinion voiced by the young physician who has found that the accused has been in full possession of his mental faculties, but has merely been irritated and embittered. That is the crux of the matter: his constant and frenzied bitterness has not stemmed from the three thousand, from that sum; there has been a special reason for his anger. That reason was jealousy!"

Here Ippolit Kirillovich gave a lengthy depiction of the fateful passion of the accused for Grushenka. He began with the moment when the accused had gone to see "the young person" in order "to give her a thrashing", to use his own words, the public prosecutor explained, "but instead of thrashing her, he remained prostrate at her feet—that was the beginning of that love. It was at the same time that the old man, the father of the accused, cast an eye on the same person—an amazing and fateful coincidence, for both hearts were suddenly set ablaze with passion at one and the same time, though both had known and met her before—and both hearts were kindled with the most unbridled and most Karamazovian of passions. Here we have her own admission: 'I was making mock of both of them,' she said. Yes, she suddenly felt like making mock of both of them; she had not felt that way before, but now the intention suddenly occurred to her, and it ended by both of them lying conquered at her feet. The old man, who worshipped money as one worships God, at once prepared three thousand roubles only for her to visit his house, but soon reached a point when he would be happy to lay his whole fortune and his name at her feet if only she agreed to become his lawful wife. We have firm evidence of that. As for the accused, his tragedy is obvious; it stands before us. But such was the young person's 'game'. The temptress gave the unfortunate young man no hope, for hope, real hope, was given him only at the very last moment when, on his knees before his tormentress, he stretched out to her hands that were already stained with the blood of his father and rival: it was in that posture that he was arrested. 'Send me to penal servitude in Siberia with him; I've brought him to this. I'm more to blame than anybody,' this woman herself exclaimed, already with genuine remorse, at the moment of his arrest. A talented young man who has undertaken to describe this case, the same Mr. Rakitin I have already referred to, has defined the character of this heroine in a few succinct and characteristic sentences: 'Early disillusionment, early betrayal and downfall, the treachery of her lover who had seduced and jilted her, then poverty, her being cursed by her respectable family and, finally, the protection of a rich old man, whom she still regards as her benefactor. Her young heart, in which there was perhaps much that was good, came to harbour resentment at a time when she was still very young. All this led to the moulding of a calculating character, given to money-grubbing. She grew sarcastic, with a grudge against society.' After such a characterisation, one can understand that she might make mock of both of them simply for amusement, malicious amusement. And so during that month of hopeless love, moral degradation, betrayal of his fiancée, the appropriation of money entrusted to his honour, the accused was driven almost to frenzy, almost to madness, by continual jealousy—and of whom? His own father! And the worst of it was that the crazy old man was enticing and tempting the object of his passion with the very three thousand his son considered as belonging to him, as part of his maternal inheritance, for which he was reproaching his father. Yes, I agree: it was hard to bear! Even mania might well have appeared. What mattered was not the money, but the fact of his happiness being ruined by that money with such revolting cynicism!"

Then Ippolit Kirillovich went over to how the idea of parricide gradually took shape in the accused, and cited facts to trace its development.

"At first he only clamoured about it at taverns—and that for a whole month. Oh, he enjoyed company and publicly airing his ideas, even the most infernal and dangerous; he loved to share his thoughts with others and, for some unknown reason, he immediately demanded their fullest sympathy, that they should take up all his worries and troubles, that they should humour him in everything, and not oppose his whims. Otherwise he would fly into a rage and wreck the place." (There followed an account of the incident with Captain Snegiryov.) "Those who had seen and heard the accused during that month finally realised that it was not just a matter of vociferation and threats against his father, but that a man in such a frenzy might well translate threats into action." (Here the public prosecutor described the family gathering at the monastery, the conversations with Alyosha, and the shocking scene in his father's house when the accused had burst in after dinner.) "It is not my intention to insistently affirm," Ippolit Kirillovich went on, "that, prior to that disgraceful scene, the accused deliberately planned with premeditation to put an end to his father by murdering him. Nevertheless, the idea presented itself to him several times and he contemplated it with firm intent: we have facts to bear that out, as well as witnesses and his own admission. I must confess, gentlemen of the jury," Ippolit Kirillovich added, "that even to this very day I hesitated to attribute to the accused full and conscious premeditation of a crime that had gripped his mind. I was firmly convinced that his mind had many a time contemplated the impending moment of fate, but merely contemplated it, merely pictured it as a possibility, but with no definite idea as to the timing or circumstances of the murder. But I was in two minds about it only till today, until the fateful document presented to the court today by Miss Verkhovtsev. You yourselves, gentlemen, heard her exclamation, 'That is the plan, the programme of the murder!' That is how she described the unhappy 'drunken' letter of the unfortunate accused man. And, indeed, the letter bears the stamp of premeditation and a programme. It was written two days prior to the crime, and so we now know for a fact that, two days before giving effect to his dreadful plan, the accused swore that, if he could not get the money the next day, he would murder his father to get the money 'in the envelope with the red ribbon, if only Ivan goes away'. Do you hear that: 'If only Ivan goes away!'? Here, therefore, everything had been thought out and the circumstances weighed. And, to be sure: he then carried out everything just as he had written it! There can be no doubt about the premeditation and deliberateness of a crime which was to be committed with the purpose of robbery; that is clearly stated, written down and undersigned. The accused does not deny his signature. It will be said: it was written by a man in his cups. But that does not detract from its significance; it actually enhances it, for he wrote when drunk what he had planned when sober. Had he not planned it when sober, he would not have written it when drunk. It may perhaps be asked then: why did he shout in the taverns that he was going to kill his father? A man who *deliberately* intends to do such a thing is silent about it and keeps it to himself. That is true, but he shouted about it at a time when there were no plans or intentions as yet, but only a desire, and the idea was merely burgeoning. He shouted less about it later. On the evening he wrote that letter, after getting drunk at the Metropolis Inn, he was quite unusually silent: he did not play billiards, sat in solitude, spoke to no one, and only drove a local shop-assistant out of his seat, but he did that almost unconsciously, out of habit, because he could not enter a tavern without picking a quarrel. It is true that, having reached a final decision, the accused must have felt apprehensive about having been publicly too outspoken about his plan, which might lead to his arrest and conviction after he had carried out his purpose. But there was nothing he could do about it; the thing had come to the public notice, and that could not be retracted; after all, something had always turned up whenever he had been in trouble, and the same was bound to happen again. He counted on his good luck, gentlemen! I must admit, however, that he did a lot to evade the fatal moment, and did all he could to eschew the spilling of blood. 'Tomorrow I'll try and raise three thousand from someone or other,' as he wrote in his peculiar language, 'and if I don't get it, blood will be spilt.' And again, he wrote it when he was drunk and, again, he carried out his preconceived plan when he was sober!"

Here Ippolit Kirillovich proceeded to give a detailed account of Mitya's efforts to raise the money so as to avoid committing the crime. He described the happening at Samsonov's, and his journey to the Lurcher—all in accordance with documentary evidence. "Exhausted, derided, hungry, selling his watch to raise the fare for the journey (though he had fifteen hundred roubles on himself but did he have it, oh, did he?), tortured by jealousy of the young woman he loved, whom he had left behind in the town, suspecting that she might go to his father whilst he was away, he finally returned. Thank goodness! She had not gone to Fyodor Pavlovich. In fact, he had himself seen her to her protector Samsonov. (Strange to say, he is not jealous of Samsonov, a highly characteristic psychological feature in this affair!) Then he dashed back to his observation post beyond his father's garden and there—there he learnt that Smerdyakov had had an epileptic fit and that the other servant was ill—the coast was clear and he knew the 'signals'—what a temptation! Yet, he still resisted it. He went to see Madame Khokhlakov, a lady highly esteemed by us all, who is temporarily in residence here. This lady, who had long felt compassion for him, offered him most sensible advice: give up his life of dissipation, his disgraceful love affair, his idling at taverns, the waste of his youthful energies, and set off to Siberia to the gold-mines: 'There you will find an outlet for your tempestuous energies and your romantic character, your thirst for adventure.'" After describing the outcome of that talk and the moment when the accused suddenly learned that Grushenka had not been to Samsonov's, and then depicting the sudden frenzy of the unfortunate, nerve-racked and jealous man at the thought that she had deceived him and was now with his father, the public prosecutor concluded by calling attention to the momentous role of the fortuitous: "had the maid had time to tell him that his lady-love was at Mokroye with her 'former' and 'rightful' lover, nothing would have happened. But she was terror-stricken, swore that she knew nothing; if the accused did not kill her on the spot, it was because he rushed off headlong in search of the woman who had betrayed him. But note: enraged as he was, he did not forget to grab the brass pestle. Why the pestle? Why not some other weapon? But if he had contemplated the scene for a whole month and prepared for it, he would grab at the first object that caught the eye as a possible weapon. During that month he had pictured to himself the kind of object that could serve as a weapon. That was why he immediately and unhesitatingly saw that it would serve his purpose! Again, that was why it was no unconscious and involuntary act when he seized the fatal pestle. Shortly afterwards, he was in his father's garden: the coast was clear; there were no witnesses; it was the dead of night, and there was darkness and jealousy. The suspicion that she was there in the house with him, his rival, in his arms and, perhaps, making mock of him at that moment—all this rendered him breathless. And it was not mere suspicion, either: the time for suspicion had gone, the deception was plain and obvious: she was there, in that lit-up room; she was there with him, behind the screen—and the unfortunate man stole up to the window, deferentially looked in, well-behavedly curbed himself, and discreetly withdrew, for fear that something dangerous and immoral might come about—at least that's what they would have us believe, us, who know the nature of the accused, and understand his state of mind as shown by the facts: the main thing is that he knew the signals by which he could at once gain entry into the house!" Here, apropos of "the signals", Ippolit Kirillovich briefly broke off his accusation, finding it necessary to dwell on the Smerdyakov episode so as to end with the suspicion that Smerdyakov had committed the murder, and dismiss the idea once and for all. He did so in great detail, and it was generally realised that, despite the contempt he had expressed for that conjecture, he considered it of the utmost importance.

8.

A Treatise on Smerdyakov

"In the first place, whence the possibility of that suspicion?" was the question Ippolit Kirillovich began with. "The accused himself was the first to cry out that Smerdyakov was the murderer, and he did so at the moment of his arrest, but he has not yet adduced a single fact to confirm the charge; moreover, not even a hint to that will make sense. Then, the accusation has been maintained by three persons only; the two brothers of the accused and Miss Svetlov. But the elder brother of the accused voiced his suspicion only today, when he was ill, of unquestionably unsound mind, and with brain fever, whilst previously, for two whole months, as we positively know, he fully shared the conviction of his brother's guilt and did not even seek to raise any objection to the idea. But we shall go into that specifically later. Then the younger brother of the accused has himself told us that he possesses no facts, not the slightest, to support his theory of Smerdyakov's guilt, and has reached this conclusion only from the words of the accused and 'the expression on his face'—yes, that colossal proof has been adduced twice today by his brother. Miss Svetlov has expressed herself in an even more colossal manner: 'You must believe what the accused tells you; he is not the kind of man to lie.' Those are all the actual proofs of Smerdyakov's guilt as produced by these three persons, who all have a personal interest in the fate of the accused. And yet the accusation against Smerdyakov has been bruited abroad and has been maintained. Is it credible, is it conceivable?"

Here Ippolit Kirillovich found it necessary to give a brief outline of the late Smerdyakov's character, "who put an end to his life in an attack of morbid mental alienation and insanity". He depicted the man as feeble-minded, with rudimentary education, disorientated by philosophical ideas above his understanding, and frightened by certain present-day doctrines on one's duties and obligations inculcated on him in practice by the dissolute life of his master and perhaps father Fyodor Pavlovich, and in theory from various strange conversations with his master's second son, Ivan Fyodorovich, who readily permitted himself this diversion, probably out of boredom or a need to deride somebody, which had not been put to better use. "He himself told me about his state of mind during the last days of his stay at his master's house," Ippolit Kirillovich explained, "but others, too, have borne witness to it: the accused himself, his brother, and even the servant Grigori, that is to say, all who should know him well. Besides, depressed by his epileptic fits, Smerdyakov was 'chicken-hearted'. 'He fell at my feet and kissed them,' the accused himself stated in his evidence at a time when he was not yet aware of the damaging nature of such a statement. 'He is an epileptic chicken,' he described him in characteristic language. And it was him that the accused chose as his confidant (as he himself stated) and intimidated him so much that he finally consented to act as his spy and informer. In this capacity of domestic spy, he betrayed his master and informed the accused of the existence of the envelope with the money and of the signals ensuring entry into the house—and, indeed, how could he help telling him? 'He'd have killed me, sir, I knew he would have killed me,' he declared during the investigation, trembling with fear even with us, though the tormentor who had scared him out of his wits was himself under arrest at the time, and could not come and punish him. 'He suspected me every minute, sir. Seeing as how I was in fear and trembling for my life, I hastened to tell him every secret to appease his anger, so that he might see for himself that I was honest, and let me off alive.' Those are his very words, I took them down and remember them. 'The moment he started yelling at me I'd just go down on my knees to him.' Being by nature a very honest young fellow and having thus gained the confidence of his master, who had taken note of his honesty in returning some money he had lost, the unhappy Smerdyakov, I suppose, must have suffered terribly from remorse at having betrayed his master, to whom he was greatly attached as his benefactor. People who suffer severely from epilepsy, so the leading psychiatrists tell us, are always predisposed to constant and, needless to say, morbid self-accusation. They are tormented by a sense of 'guilt' for something and to somebody, and by remorse, often groundlessly; they exaggerate and even invent all kinds of faults and crimes they have committed. And such an individual actually becomes guilty of a crime out of terror and intimidation. He had, besides, a strong presentiment that something untoward was likely to happen in the circumstances that were developing before his eyes. When Karamazov's second son, Ivan Fyodorovich, was leaving for Moscow before the very disaster, Smerdyakov begged him to stay on, but, being a coward, he had not the courage to tell him of his fears clearly and categorically. He merely confined himself to hints, which were not understood. It must be noted that he regarded Ivan Fyodorovich as a kind of protector, a guarantor that, as long as he was at home, no misfortune would happen. Remember the expression in Dmitri Karamazov's 'drunken' letter: 'I shall kill the old man if only Ivan goes away.' So Ivan Fyodorovich's presence was seen by all as a sort of guarantee of peace and calm in the house. But he went off, and barely an hour after the young master's departure Smerdyakov had an epileptic fit. But that can be readily understood. I must mention here that, oppressed by fears and, in a way, by despair, Smerdyakov had felt, especially during those last few days, that he would probably have an epileptic fit, which had always come on previously at moments of moral stress and shock. Of course, the day and hour of such attacks cannot be anticipated, but any epileptic prone to such attacks can sense its approach. That is what medicine tells us. And as soon as Ivan Fyodorovich had left the house, Smerdyakov, under the impression of his, so to speak, helpless and defenceless condition, went to the cellar for something and descended the steps with the thought: 'Will I have a fit or not, and what if it comes on just now?' And it was just that mood of his, that fear of an attack, the questions he had been asking himself that brought on the spasm in his throat that always precedes an epileptic fit, and down he fell headlong, unconscious, to the bottom of the cellar. And there are people who, in this perfectly natural occurrence, contrive to see something suspicious, a kind of indication, a kind of hint that he was *deliberately* feigning to be ill! But if that was done deliberately, the question arises: whatever for? What was the motive, the aim? I am not referring to what medicine has to say: science, it may be said, is often wrong and makes mistakes; doctors are not always able to distinguish between truth and pretence—let that be so, but answer the question: why should he have been shamming? Was it not with the aim, after devising the murder, of drawing the attention of all in the house to himself by having the fit in advance? You see, gentlemen of the jury, there were or had been five people at Fyodor Pavlovich's house on the night of the crime: in the first place, Fyodor Pavlovich himself—but he did not kill himself, that's clear; secondly, his servant Grigori, but he almost got killed himself; thirdly, the maid, Grigori's wife, Marfa Ignatievna, but to imagine her murdering her master would be simply shameful. Consequently, two persons remain in our purview: the accused and Smerdyakov. But as the accused maintains that he did not commit the murder, then Smerdyakov must have done it. There is no other alternative, for no one else is to be found—no other killer fits the pattern. So that's how this wily and quite extraordinary accusation arose against the unfortunate idiot who committed suicide yesterday! Yes, indeed. It arose simply because no other suspect could be found! Had there been a shadow of suspicion against anyone else, against some sixth person, I'm sure even the accused would have been ashamed to point at Smerdyakov, but would have indicated that sixth person, for to accuse Smerdyakov of the murder is the height of absurdity.

"Gentlemen, let's discard psychology, let's discard medicine, and even logic, and turn only to the facts, to nothing but the facts, and let us see what they tell us. Suppose Smerdyakov committed the murder, but how did he do it? Alone, or together with the accused? Let's consider the first alternative, that is to say, that Smerdyakov did it alone. Of course, if he did it, he must have done so for some reason, for some advantage to himself. But without the faintest motive for the murder that the accused had, to wit: hatred, jealousy, and so on, Smerdyakov, no doubt, could only have done it for the sake of money, in order to appropriate the three thousand he had seen his master put in the envelope. And yet, having devised the murder, he tells another person, moreover, one with a supreme personal interest, namely the accused, all the circumstances about the money and the signals: where the envelope lay, the inscription on it, what it was wrapped up in, and, above all, above all, told him of the 'signals' that would give him entry into the house. Did he do it just to give himself away? Or to find a rival who might himself want to enter the house and acquire the envelope? Oh, I will be told: but he gave the information out of fear. Did he really? A man who did not hesitate to devise such a bold and brutal crime and then carry it out actually told another of things he alone in the whole world knew and, were he to keep silent about them, no one in the whole world would ever have guessed at. No, however cowardly a man may be, if he has planned such a crime, he will never tell anyone of it, at least not about the envelope and the signals, for that would have meant giving himself away beforehand. He would have deliberately thought up something, and invented some lie if certain information were to be demanded of him, but he would have kept silent about that! On the contrary, I repeat, if he had kept silent about the money at least and then committed murder and appropriated the money, no one in the world would ever have accused him, at any rate, of murder for the sake of robbery, for no one besides him had seen the money or knew of its existence in the house. Even had he been accused, it would most certainly have been thought that he had committed it for some other motive. But as no one had ever observed any such motives in him previously, but, on the contrary, his master was seen to be fond of him and honour him with his confidence, he would, of course, have been the last to be suspected; suspicion would have fallen, in the first place, on one who had the motives, and himself had clamoured that he had those motives, made no secret of them but disclosed them to all and sundry: in a word, on Dmitri Fyodorovich, the murdered man's son. Smerdyakov might have killed and robbed, but the son would have been accused, and that surely would have been to the advantage of killer-Smerdyakov, wouldn't it? Well, and so, having devised the murder, Smerdyakov informed the son Dmitri in advance about the money, the envelope and the signals—how logical, how clear that is!

"The day of the murder devised by Smerdyakov came round, so he went and fell down the cellar steps in a *sham* epileptic fit. What for? Why, of course, to make sure, first of all, that the servant Grigori, who was making ready to take his medical treatment, might put it off and be on the alert, seeing that there was no one to be on watch in the house. Secondly, of course, to see to it that his master, since there was no one to keep on watch in the house, and in terror of his son's coming, which he did not conceal—might redouble his vigilance and his precautions. And, finally and above all, of course, the aim was that he, Smerdyakov, incapacitated by the fit, should at once be transferred from the kitchen, where he always slept away from the others and could come and go as he pleased, to the other end of the lodge, to Grigori and Marfa Ignatievna's room, behind the partition, three paces from their own bed, as was invariably done when he had an epileptic fit, in accordance with the arrangement made by his master and the kind-hearted Marfa Ignatievna. There, lying behind the partition, he would, of course, most likely have begun moaning, to maintain his pretence of illness, that is, to keep them awake all night (which he actually did, according to the evidence of Grigori and his wife), and all that, all that to make it more convenient for him to suddenly get up and then murder his master!

"But I may be told that he feigned his illness to escape suspicion, and that he informed the accused of the money and the signals with the express purpose of tempting him to come and commit the murder; when he had murdered his father and made off with the money, after probably making a lot of noise and waking the witnesses, then he, Smerdyakov, would get up too and go—to do what? Why, he would go to kill his master a second time, and carry off the money which had already gone. Does that make you laugh, gentlemen? I feel ashamed to advance such suggestions, and yet, just imagine, that is exactly what the accused alleges: 'After me,' he declares, 'after I had left the house, knocked down Grigori and raised the alarm, he got up, went and killed his master, and stole the money.' I need hardly ask how Smerdyakov could have possibly devised and foreseen it all beforehand, that is to say, that the exasperated and enraged son would come with the sole purpose of taking a deferential peep through the window and, though he knew the signals, beating a hasty retreat leaving all the spoils to Smerdyakov! Gentlemen, I ask you in all earnest: at what precise moment could Smerdyakov have committed his crime? Indicate that moment, for otherwise there can be no accusation.

" 'But, perhaps, the epileptic fit was genuine. The sick man suddenly came to, heard a shout, went out'— Well, and what then? Did he look about himself and think: 'I'll go and murder the master?' But how was he to know what had happened? Had he not been lying unconscious till that very moment? Incidentally, gentlemen, there is a limit even to flights of fancy.

" 'Well,' some shrewd people may say, 'but what if the two acted in collusion, two committed the murder together, and shared the money, what then?'

"Indeed, that is a momentous suspicion: in the first place, there is a mass of evidence to bear it out: one of them takes up himself all the trouble of committing the murder, while the other accomplice, lies in bed, shamming an epileptic fit, with the sole purpose of arousing general suspicion in advance, and alarming his master as well as Grigori. I wonder what motives could have led the two accomplices to invent such a crazy plan? But, perhaps, there was no active complicity on the part of Smerdyakov, whose role was, so to speak, passive and sympathetic: the terror-stricken Smerdyakov may have consented only not to resist the murder and, anticipating that he might be accused of allowing his master be murdered and failing to cry out or offer resistance, he first obtained Dmitri Karamazov's permission to stay in bed as though in an epileptic fit, 'and you may murder him just as you like; it's no concern of mine'. But if that was so, then, again, since the epileptic fit was bound to throw the house into commotion, and realising that, Dmitri Karamazov could never have agreed to such an arrangement. But I shall yield on that point: supposing he did agree. In that case, it would still follow that Dmitri Karamazov was the murderer, the actual murderer and instigator, while Smerdyakov was merely a passive accomplice—not even an accomplice, but one who merely connived at the crime out of fear and against his will, something the court would most certainly have been able to establish. But what do we actually see? No sooner is the accused taken in custody than he at once casts the blame on Smerdyakov, and accuses him *alone*. He accuses him, not of complicity but of the crime itself: 'He did it alone,' he declares. 'He murdered and robbed. It was his doing!' But what kind of accomplices are they who at once start to accuse each other? That never happens! And note the risk Karamazov was running: he was the principal murderer, while the other accomplice, who was secondary and the conniver, and lying behind the partition, so he now cast all the blame on the sick man. But Smerdyakov would have resented that, and, out of a sense of self-preservation alone, disclose the whole truth: the two of us were involved, but I did not commit the murder but only connived and let it happen out of fear. For he, Smerdyakov, could realise that the court would at once establish the degree of his guilt so that he could assume that were he to be punished, it would be infinitely less than the principal murderer would be, who had wished to cast all the blame on him. But then, consequently, he would have involuntarily made a confession. We have not seen that however. Smerdyakov did not so much as hint at any complicity though the murderer kept on accusing him, naming him as the sole murderer. Moreover, it was Smerdyakov who disclosed, during the investigation, that *he himself* had told the accused of the envelope with the money, and the signals, but for which the latter would have learnt nothing about them. Had he really been guilty of complicity, would he have so readily spoken of that during the preliminary investigation, I mean, his having himself informed the accused of everything? On the contrary, he would have tried to deny it and would most certainly have distorted the facts and minimised them. But he neither distorted nor minimised them. That is the action only of an innocent man, who is not afraid of being charged with complicity. And now, in a fit of morbid melancholy caused by his epilepsy and all this disaster, he hanged himself yesterday. He left a note couched in his peculiar style: 'I am destroying myself of my own free will and wish, and no one is to be blamed for it.' He might well have added: 'I, not Karamazov, am the murderer.' But he did not add that: did his conscience suffice for one action, but not the other?

"Then what happened? A short while ago, a sum of money, three thousand roubles, was produced in court. 'It's that very money,' we were told, 'which lay in the envelope, the one on the table with the other exhibits. I got it from Smerdyakov yesterday,' was the claim. But, gentlemen of the jury, you yourselves remember the recent painful scene. I will not repeat the details but shall permit myself to voice only two or three considerations, choosing the minor ones just because they are minor and, therefore, may not occur to anyone and be forgotten. To begin with, and again: Smerdyakov returned the money yesterday out of remorse, and hanged himself. (For if he had felt no remorse, he wouldn't have returned the money.) And, of course, it was only yesterday evening that he first confessed to Ivan Karamazov that he had committed the crime, as Ivan Karamazov himself has declared, or why else should he have kept silent till now? And so he confessed, but why, I repeat, did he not let us know the whole truth in the letter he left behind, knowing that an innocent man is to face trial for murder on the morrow? The money alone is no proof. A week ago, for instance, it came to the knowledge of myself and two other persons in this court that Ivan Fyodorovich Karamazov had sent two five per cent coupons worth five thousand roubles each, that is, ten thousand in all, to the gubernia capital to be exchanged. I mention that only to show that anyone can have had cash in hand on a certain date, and that bringing the three thousand here is no proof that it is the same money that was in a certain drawer or envelope. Finally, after receiving such an important communication from the actual murderer yesterday, Ivan Karamazov revealed full quietude. Why couldn't he have reported it at once? Why did he put it off till the morning? I think I'm entitled to conjecture why: he had been in poor health for over a week; he admitted to a doctor and some close friends that he was suffering from hallucinations and was meeting phantoms of the dead in the street. He was on the verge of the brain fever to which he succumbed today; therefore, on suddenly learning of Smerdyakov's death, he at once said to himself: 'The man is dead; I can say he did it and so save my brother. I have the money: I'll take a sheaf of notes and say that Smerdyakov gave it to me before his death.' Will you say that this is dishonourable, dishonourable to lie about the dead even to save a brother? But what if he lied unconsciously? What if he imagined it had been so, because his mind had become finally unhinged by the news of the servant's sudden death? You witnessed the recent scene and saw the man's condition. He was on his feet and talking, but where was his mind? The evidence recently given by this sick man was followed by a document, a letter sent by the accused to Miss Verkhovtsev and written two days before the crime, with a detailed advance programme of the crime. Why, then, are we looking for the programme and its compilers? Everything was carried out in precise accordance with that programme, and carried out by no one else but its author. Yes, gentlemen of the jury, it was done 'according to plan!' And he did not make off deferentially and fearfully from his father's window at a moment when he was firmly convinced that his lady-love was with him. No, that is both absurd

496

and unbelievable. He went in and—finished the business. Most probably he committed the murder in a rage, burning with resentment, as soon as he saw his hated rival but after the murder, which he must have effected with a single blow of the brass pestle, and convincing himself after a careful search that she was not there, he did not, however, forget to put his hand under the pillow and take the envelope with the money—the opened envelope now lying on that table with the other exhibits. I say so for you to take note of a circumstance which, in my opinion, is highly characteristic. Had it been a hardened murderer, a murderer, that is, whose sole object was robbery, would he have left the envelope on the floor, where it was found beside the dead body? Had it been Smerdyakov, for instance, who was committing a murder for robbery—why, he would have simply carried off the envelope with the money, without bothering to open it over his victim's dead body; for he knew for certain that the money was in the envelope—it had been inserted and sealed in his presence—and had he taken the envelope away with him, no one would have known whether there had been a robbery. I ask you, gentlemen of the jury, would Smerdyakov have acted like that? Would he have left the envelope behind on the floor? No, that is the behaviour of a man in a frenzy, a murderer who had lost his presence of mind, a murderer who is no thief, and has never stolen anything, and who, even when he snatched the money from under the mattress, not as a thief, but as one who recovers what is his own from a thief, for that was Dmitri Karamazov's idea of the three thousand, an idea which had become obsessive. And so, having taken the envelope, which he had never seen before, he tore it open to make sure that the money was there, and then made off with the money in his pocket, even forgetting to consider that he had left a most damning piece of evidence against himself in that torn envelope on the floor. And because he was Karamazov and not Smerdyakov, he did not stop to think or consider. How could he? He made off, heard a loud outcry from the servant who was overtaking him; the man caught hold of him, stopped him, and fell to the ground, struck down with the brass pestle. The accused jumped down to him out of pity. Just imagine: he assures

497

us that he jumped down out of pity, out of compassion, to see whether he could do anything to help him. But was that the moment to show such compassion? No, he jumped down to see whether the only witness to his crime was alive or dead. Any other sentiment, any other motive would have been unnatural! Please note that he went to some trouble over Grigori: he wiped his head with his handkerchief and, satisfying himself that he was dead, ran back to the house of his lady-love, dazed and bloodstained—how was it he never thought that he was all bloodstained and that he would at once give himself away? Yet the accused himself assures us that he did not even notice that he was all bloodstained. That we may well believe; that is very possible, and that always happens with criminals at such moments. They reveal diabolical cunning in one respect, and a lack of caution in another. But at that moment his only thought was: where is *she*? He had to find out her whereabouts at once, and so he ran to her lodgings and learnt an unexpected and most shattering piece of news: she had gone off to Mokroye to her 'former' and 'rightful' lover!"

9.

Psychology with a Vengeance.
The Galloping Troika.
The Public Prosecutor's Peroration

At this point in his speech, Ippolit Kirillovich, who had evidently chosen the strictly historical method of exposition so often resorted to by all high-strung speakers, who purposely seek a strictly chosen framework so as to keep their impetuosity in check—Ippolit Kirillovich now set about expatiating on Grushenka's "former" and "rightful" lover, voicing several ideas on the theme, which were quite entertaining in their way. "Karamazov, who had been insanely jealous of everyone, suddenly wilted and stood down to the 'former' and 'rightful' one. And that was all the stranger for his having practically ignored this new danger to himself, which had suddenly appeared in the person of his unexpected rival. But he had imagined it to be still far off, and a Karamazov always lives only in the present. He probably considered him even a fiction. However, he at once submitted the moment he realised, in his wounded heart, that the woman may have kept the new rival a secret and had deceived him, Mitya, so recently, because to her the newly arrived rival meant everything, all her hope in life, and was no fiction or play of fancy. Well, gentlemen of the jury, I cannot pass over in silence this unexpected trait in the soul of the accused, a trait, which, it would seem, he was quite incapable of manifesting. He suddenly revealed an irresistible need of the truth, a respect for woman, and a recognition of her heart's rights, and when did he do that? At the very moment when he had steeped his hands in his father's blood for her! It is also true that the spilt blood was at that moment already crying out for vengeance, for he, who had ruined his soul and his whole earthly future, could but have felt and asked at that moment what he meant and what he could *now* mean to her, a being dearer to him than his own soul, in comparison with her 'former' and 'rightful' lover, who had repented and returned to her, the woman he had once ruined, with fresh love, and honourable offers, and an avowal of a reborn and, this time, happy life? And he, unhappy man, what could he give her *now,* what could he offer her? Karamazov understood all this; he understood that his crime had blocked all roads to him, and that he was merely a criminal awaiting judgement, and not a man with a life to live! It was this thought that crushed and destroyed him utterly. And so he at once hit upon a frantic plan which, to a man of Karamazov's character, could not but seem the sole and fateful way out of his dreadful situation. That solution was suicide. He ran for the pistols he had pledged with the civil servant Perkhotin, and on the way pulled out of his pocket all the money for the sake of which he had steeped his hands in his father's blood. Oh, he now needed money more than anything: Karamazov was to die, Karamazov would shoot himself, and that was going to be remembered! It was not in vain that he was a poet; it was not fortuitous that he had frittered away all his life, burnt the candle at both ends. 'To her, to her! And there I'll throw a spree without parallel, one that will be remembered and talked of for a long time to come! Amid the wild outcries and frenzied Gypsy songs and dancing, I'll raise my glass and toast the woman I adore and congratulate her upon her new-found happiness and, then and there, at her feet, I shall blow my brains out and put an end to my life! She will remember Mitya Karamazov some time! She will see how Mitya loved her! She will be sorry for Mitya!' There is a great deal of picturesque and romantic frenzy in all this, a great deal of wild and unbridled Karamazovian recklessness and sentimentality, and yet, something else, gentlemen of the jury, was clamouring in his soul, throbbing incessantly in his mind and poisoning his heart unto death— that *something* was his conscience, gentlemen of the jury, its judgement and source of boundless torment! But the pistol would settle all accounts; it was the only solution, and no other, but there—I don't know whether Karamazov thought at that moment '*what will happen there*' or whether Karamazov can, like Hamlet, think of what will happen there. No, gentlemen of the jury: over there, they have their Hamlets, while as yet we have our Karamazovs!"

Here Ippolit Kirillovich unfolded a most detailed picture of Mitya's preparations, the scene at Perkhotin's, at the shop, and with the drivers. He adduced a great number of words, utterances and gestures, all confirmed by witnesses, and the picture he drew had a telling impact on his audience. It was the totality of all these facts that exerted the main influence. The guilt of this frantically harassed man, who no longer had any thought for himself, was irrefutably demonstrated. "There was no need for him to give thought to himself," said Ippolit Kirillovich. "He was on the verge of fully confessing on two or three occasions, almost hinted at it, and had it on the tip of his tongue." (Here followed the testimony of the witnesses.) "He even cried out to the coachman on the way to Mokroye: 'Do you know you are driving a murderer?' Yet, it was impossible for him to come clean: he had first to get to the village of Mokroye and complete his poem there. But what was in store for the unhappy man? The fact is that, from the very first moment in Mokroye, he saw and at last fully realised that his 'rightful' rival was not so 'rightful' after all, and that his congratulations upon their new-found happiness and his toast to their health were unwanted and unacceptable. But you already know the facts, gentlemen of the jury, from the court investigation. Karamazov's triumph over his rival was unquestionable and here—oh, here a quite new phase began in his soul, perhaps the most terrible phase it had gone through, or ever will! It may be positively said, gentlemen of the jury," Ippolit Kirillovich exclaimed, "that outraged nature and a criminal heart bring in their wake a retribution far more bitter than earthly justice can! Moreover, justice and earthly punishment even mitigate punishment meted out by nature, and are even necessary to the criminal's soul at such moments as salvation from despair, for I cannot even conceive Karamazov's horror and his moral anguish on learning that she loved him, was rejecting her 'former' and 'rightful' lover for his sake, was calling on him, him, 'Mitya', to follow her to a new life, and held out a promise of happiness—and all this, when? When everything was over for him and nothing was possible! Incidentally, I shall make, in passing, an observation highly important to you in explaining the real essence of the condition of the accused at the moment: this woman, this love of his, had been up to the very last moment, the instant of his arrest, a being utterly beyond his reach, passionately desired by him but unattainable. But why, why didn't he shoot himself then? Why did he abandon his decision, and even forgot where his pistol was? What held him back was just this passionate thirst for love and the hope of assuaging it there and then. In the intoxication of the revelry, he clung to his beloved, who was sharing in the revels and whom he thought more lovely and more seductive than ever. He did not leave her side for a moment, feasted his eyes on her and completely forwent his own self. This passionate desire for her could, momentarily, not only stifle his fear of arrest but also his qualms of conscience. But for an instant, oh, a fleeting instant! I can picture the criminal's state of mind at the time as being undoubtedly in the complete grip of three elements, which crushed it utterly: first, the influence of drink, the sound and fury of the junketing, the beat of the dance and the shrill sounds of the songs, and of her, of her, flushed with wine, singing and dancing, drunk and laughing to him! Secondly, the comforting thought in the recesses of his mind that the fateful denouncement was still far off, or at least not quite at hand, and that he was unlikely to be taken away until the next day, the following morning. So there were still several hours, and that was a lot, such a lot! One can think up so many things in a few hours. I imagine he must have experienced something resembling what a criminal feels when he's being taken to his execution, to the scaffold: there is still a long, long street to traverse and at a walking pace, too, past thousands of people; then there will be a turn into another street, only at the end of which stands the dreadful square! It seems to me that, at the beginning of the journey, the condemned man, sitting in his shameful tumbril, must feel that there is infinite life ahead of him. But the houses recede, the tumbril moves on and on—oh, it's all right: there's still a long way to the turning into the other street, and he casts confident glances right and left at all those thousands of uninvolved but curious people, whose eyes are fixed on him, and he still fancies that he is just a man like any other. But here already is the turning into another street—oh, things are not so bad as yet—there is still a whole street ahead of him. And no matter how many houses may have passed his eyes, he will still think: 'There are still so many houses to pass!' And thus to the very end, to the square itself. That I imagine, how it was with Karamazov then. 'They haven't yet got down to action there,' he must have thought. 'Something can yet be hit upon; there's still time to draw up some plan of defence, and to think of a proper rebuff, but now, now—now she is so lovely!' His soul is dark and full of dread, but he still manages to set aside half of his money and hide it somewhere—I cannot otherwise explain the disappearance of half of the three thousand he had just taken from under his father's pillow. He had been in Mokroye before, on a spree that lasted two days. He was familiar with the tavern, a spacious old building, with all its sheds and verandas. It is my surmise that part of the money was hidden there shortly before his arrest, in some chink, some crevice, under the floor-boards, in some corner, or the attic. Why? Well, disaster may fall at any moment! Of course, he hadn't yet considered how it was to be met: he hadn't the time, his head was throbbing and all the time he was being drawn to her; as for the money, why, the money was indispensable in any situation. A man with money is always on top. Perhaps such a calculation at such a minute may seem unnatural to you. But, then, he himself has assured us that a month before, at a moment of the greatest anxiety and alarm to him, he set aside half of the three thousand and sewed it up in a little bag, and if, of course, that is untrue, as we shall prove presently, the idea did occur to Karamazov, and he had been turning it over in his mind. Moreover, when he later assured the court investigator that he had set aside fifteen hundred in a little bag (which never existed), he must have thought up the little bag on the spot because two hours earlier he had set aside half the money and hidden it somewhere in Mokroye, just in case, till the morning, so as not to have it about himself, on a sudden inspiration. Here we have two abysses, gentlemen of the jury; recall that Karamazov can contemplate two abysses, and both at one and the same time! We have searched that house, but haven't found the money. It may still be there; on the other hand, it may have disappeared on the next day and is now in the possession of the accused. Anyway, he was at her side, on his knees before her when he was arrested. She was lying on the bed, and he was holding out his hands to her; he was so oblivious of everything at the moment that he did not even hear the approach of those who had come to arrest him. His mind was totally unprepared to make any reply. Both he and his mind were caught off their guard.

"And now he confronts his judges, the arbiters of his fate. There are moments, gentlemen of the jury, when, in the performance of our duties, we feel almost appalled by a man, and fearful for him! These are moments of contemplation of the grisly fear in the criminal, who already sees that all is lost but still fights on, and still intends to fight you. These are minutes when all instincts of self-preservation surge up in him, and, seeking to save himself, he looks at you with a piercing look, questioning and suffering, catches your eye and studies your face and your thoughts, anticipates the direction of your thrust, and instantaneously draws up thousands of schemes in his distracted mind, yet is afraid to speak, afraid to give himself away. These humiliating moments for the human soul, this ordeal, this blind urge to survive—all these are dreadful, and sometimes evoke horror and compassion for the criminal even in a court investigator! We witnessed all this at the time. At first, he was stunned, and several highly compromising words escaped him in his terror: 'Blood! I've deserved this!' But he rapidly regained his self-control. What to say; how to answer our questions—he had not got it all ready yet. A flat denial was all he had ready: 'I'm not guilty of my father's death!' That was so far the first barrier he put up, after which he might perhaps think up something, put up some barricade. Anticipating our questions, he hastened to explain his first compromising exclamations by declaring that he only considered himself guilty of the death of the servant Grigori. 'I'm guilty of shedding his blood, but who has killed my father, gentlemen, who has killed him? Who can have killed him, *if I did not*?' Do you hear that? He was asking us, us, who had come to ask him that very question! Do you hear those anticipatory words, 'if I did not', that low cunning, that naivety and that typically Karamazovian impatience? 'I did not kill him and you should not think I did: I meant to kill him, gentlemen, I meant to,' he was in a hurry to admit (he was in a hurry, oh, he was in a terrible hurry), 'but still I'm not guilty; it was not I who killed him!' He concedes that he meant to kill him: you can see for yourselves, he seems to say, how truthful I am; well, then, you should all the more readily believe that I didn't kill him. Oh, in such cases a criminal sometimes becomes incredibly unthinking and gullible. And at that point, he was asked the simplest question: 'Are you sure it wasn't Smerdyakov who murdered him?' The result was what we had expected: he grew terribly angry at our having anticipated him, and caught him off his guard before he had time to prepare himself and choose and grasp at the best moment to involve Smerdyakov. As was to be expected from a man of his nature, he at once rushed to the other extreme and began assuring us that Smerdyakov could not have killed him, and was incapable of committing a murder. But don't believe him; that was merely a stratagem: he had no intention, none at all of giving up the Smerdyakov idea; on the contrary, he was going to bring him forward, for whom could he bring forward but Smerdyakov, but he would do that at another moment because that cat would not jump for the time being. He would bring him forward only on the next day or perhaps, even a few days later, seeking for the right moment to exclaim to us: 'You see, I denied Smerdyakov's guilt more than you did—you remember that yourselves, don't you? But now I am convinced: it was he, and nobody else, who committed the murder!' But for the time being, he resorted to a gloomy and irritable denial; impatience and anger prompted him, however, to use the most clumsy and improbable explanation of how he had looked through his father's window and retired with deference. The main thing was that he did not as yet know of the circumstances, and the degree of the testimony given by Grigori, who had recovered. We proceeded to examine and search him. This angered but also encouraged him: all the three thousand was not found, but only fifteen hundred. And, of course, it was at that moment of angry silence and denial that the idea of the little bag first leapt to his mind. He doubtlessly realised the sheer improbability of his invented story and took pains, great pains, to make it sound plausible, like some convincing novel. In such cases, it is the prime and foremost task of the prosecution, to prevent the criminal from preparing a defence, to catch him off his guard so as to make him reveal his innermost thoughts in all their naked simplicity, improbability, and contradictoriness. The criminal, however, can be made to speak by the sudden and apparently casual communication of some new fact, some circumstance in the case, which is of the utmost importance, but he hitherto had no idea of and could not possibly have foreseen. We had such a fact in readiness, oh, in readiness for a long time: it was the evidence of the servant Grigori about the open door, through which the accused had made off. He had completely forgotten about that door and had never even supposed that Grigori could have seen it. The impact was tremendous. He jumped to his feet and shouted: 'It was Smerdyakov who killed him, Smerdyakov!' thus betraying his secret and basic idea in its most improbable form, for Smerdyakov could have committed the murder only after he had felled Grigori and run off. When we told him that Grigori had seen the open door before he was knocked down and that, as he left his bedroom, he heard Smerdyakov moaning behind the partition, Karamazov was utterly crushed. My colleague, our esteemed and resourceful Nikolai Parfenovich, later told me that he felt deeply sorry for him at the moment. And it was just then that, to correct matters, the accused hastened to tell us about that famous little bag of his: all right, then, now listen to this tale! Gentlemen of the jury, I have already explained to you why I consider this invention about the money sewn up in a little bag a month before the murder, not only absurd but also the most improbable fabrication that could have been conceived in this case. Even if one were to wager what more improbable story could have been produced, one could hardly think of anything worse than that. The main thing here is that the triumphant story-teller can be confounded and reduced to dust with certain details, those details that actual life is so rich in and are always neglected by these unfortunate and involuntary story-tellers as insignificant and unneeded trifles, and never even occur to them. Oh, at that minute they have other cares on their minds, which are bent on inventing some vast edifice, and here they are offered such trifles! But that's how they are caught! The accused was asked: 'Well, and where did you get the stuff for your little bag? Who made it for you?' 'I made it myself.' 'And where did you get the stuff?' The accused took offence, considering it almost insulting to be questioned about such a trifle and, will you believe it, he was sincere, quite sincere about it! But they are all like that. 'I tore it off my shirt.' 'Capital! So we shall find that shirt of yours among your linen tomorrow with a piece torn off.' And just think, gentlemen of the jury, if we had really found that shirt (and how could we have failed to find it in his portmanteau or his chest of drawers if such a shirt really existed?), then that would have been a fact, a tangible fact in favour of the truth of his evidence! But that is something he cannot grasp. 'I don't remember, perhaps it wasn't off my shirt. I sewed it up in my landlady's cap.' 'What kind of cap was it?' 'I got it from her. It was lying about. An old cotton rag.' 'And do you remember it clearly?' 'No, I don't remember it clearly.' And he is angry, very angry, and yet can you imagine him failing to remember? At the most dreadful moments of a man's life, when he is being led to the execution, for instance, it is just such trifles that come to mind. He will forget everything but some green roof that has caught his eyes on the way, or a jackdaw perched on a cross—that he will remember. Why, he had to keep away from the people in the house while sewing up his little bag, so he must have remembered how humiliating it was to be afraid lest someone should come in and find him needle in hand, how at the first knock on his door he would jump to his feet and dash behind the partition (there is such a partition in his room)—But, gentlemen of the jury, why am I telling you all this, all these details, all these trifles?" Ippolit Kirillovich suddenly exclaimed. "Why, just because, to this very moment, the accused stubbornly insists on this absurdity! During all these two months, ever since that disastrous night, he has not explained anything, or added a single real and explanatory fact to his former fantastic testimony: all these are trifles, he says, so we must have faith in his honour. Oh, we are glad to do that, eager to do so, even if it's only his word. Are we jackals thirsting for human blood? Give us, show us a single fact in favour of the accused and we shall rejoice, but it has to be a tangible and real fact, and not some conclusion drawn by his own brother from the expression on the face of the accused, or the statement that, when he smote his breast, he must have been pointing to the little bag, and in the darkness, too. We shall rejoice at any new fact; we shall be the first to withdraw our charge; we shall hasten to withdraw it. But justice clamours out, and we persist; we can withdraw nothing." Ippolit Kirillovich now proceeded to the peroration. He seemed in a fever, calling passionately for retribution for a father's blood spilt by his own son "with the base motive of robbery". He emphatically cited the tragic and outrageous sum of the facts. "And whatever you may

hear from the defence counsel, with his celebrated talent"
(he could not refrain from saying), "and however eloquent and
touching his words may be when he appeals to your emotions, remember that at this moment you are in a temple of our
justice. Remember that you are defenders of our truth, defenders of our holy Russia, her fundamentals, her family standards,
of everything that she holds sacred! Yes, here, at this moment,
you represent Russia, and your verdict will resound, not only
in this courtroom but throughout Russia, and all Russia will
hear you as her champions and judges, and will be encouraged
or disheartened by your verdict. Do not keep Russia and her expectations in suspense; our fateful troika is galloping furiously
on and on, perhaps towards destruction. And the people of Russia have for so long been stretching forth their hands and calling for a halt to its furious and breakneck career. And if, for
the time being, other nations fall back from the galloping troika,
that may be, not at all out of respect, as the poet would have
us believe, but simply out of horror—mark that. Out of horror,
and perhaps disgust as well, and it is good that they hold aloof,
for perhaps one day they will no longer hold aloof but will
stand like a stone wall before the onrushing apparition and will
themselves halt the frenzied spate of our unbridled wilfulness so
as to safeguard their own security, enlightenment, and civilisa-
tion! We have already heard these alarmed voices coming from
Europe. They are already beginning to resound. Do not tempt
them; do not swell their chorus of mounting hatred by a verdict justifying the murder of a father by his own son!"

In a word, though he had given vent to a stream of exhorta-
tion, Ippolit Kirillovich concluded on a note of pathos, the
overall impact being extraordinary. On ending his speech, he
hastened out of the courtroom and, I repeat, almost swooned
in the adjoining room. There was no applause, but the serious-
minded were pleased. Only the ladies were not so well pleased,
but they, too, liked his eloquence, the more so for their having
no fears as to the outcome of the trial, and placed full reliance
on Fetyukovich: "He will, at last, start to speak and, of course,
carry everything before him!" All kept looking at Mitya;
throughout the public prosecutor's speech he had sat in silence,

his hands tightly clasped, his teeth clenched and his eyes lowered. From time to time he merely raised his head and listened. Especially when Grushenka was being spoken of. When the public prosecutor quoted Rakitin's opinion of her, a contemptuous and spiteful smile came over his face and he muttered quite audibly: "These Bernards!" When Ippolit Kirillovich described how he had interrogated and tormented him at Mokroye, Mitya raised his head and listened with intense curiosity. At one point in the speech, he even seemed about to jump to his feet and cry out something but he controlled himself and only shrugged his shoulders in contempt. There was some talk in our town afterwards about the public prosecutor's peroration and his prowess at Mokroye during the interrogation of the accused, and people poked fun at Ippolit Kirillovich. "The man could not resist showing off his cleverness," it was said. The hearing was adjourned, but only briefly; for a quarter of an hour, or twenty minutes at most. There was a great deal of talk and forthright remarks among the public. I remember some of them:

"A telling speech," a gentleman in one of the groups observed with a frown.

"He simply piled up the psychology," said another voice.

"But it was all true, irrefutably true!"

"Yes, he knows his business."

"He gave the sum and substance."

"And that in respect of us all, too," a third voice added. "At the beginning of his speech, remember, when he said that we were all just like Fyodor Pavlovich."

"And at the end as well. Only he was all wrong then."

"Yes, there were a lot of inclarities."

"Got carried away a little."

"It's unfair, sir, quite unfair."

"Well, no, it was skilful all the same. He's had to wait for his hour a long time, poor fellow, and now he's had his chance, ha, ha!"

"What will the counsel for the defence have to say?"

In another group:

"He shouldn't have made that jab at the man from St. Petersburg: 'Appealing to your emotions'. Remember?"

"Yes, that was clumsy of him."

"He was in too great haste."

"A nervous man, sir."

"We are chaffing here, but what can the accused be feeling?"

"Yes, sir, poor Mitya! What must he be feeling?"

"And what will the counsel for the defence have to say?"

In yet another group:

"Who's that lady over there, with lorgnette? The fat one. Sitting at the end of the row."

"That's the wife of a general. A divorcée. I happen to know her."

"Oh, so that accounts for the lorgnette."

"There's a common look about her."

"Not at all, quite a tasty morsel."

"There's a little blonde two seats away from her. She's much better."

"Caught him tripping quite cleverly at Mokroye, didn't they?"

"I suppose so. Boasted of it again. He's been telling the story all over the town hundreds of times."

"Couldn't resist doing it again now. There's vanity for you!"

"A man with a grievance, tee-hee!"

"And very touchy. Lots of rhetoric, too. Goes in for long periods."

"Trying to intimidate us, note, intimidate us all the time. Remember his troika? 'There they have their Hamlets, but we still have our Karamazovs.' That was well put."

"That was done to get on the right side of the liberals. He's afraid of them!"

"He's afraid of the defence counsel, too."

"Indeed, what will Mr. Fetyukovich say?"

"Whatever he says, he won't get round our peasants."

"Think so?"

In another group, the fourth:

"He put it neatly about the troika. I mean, when he was referring to other nations."

510

"And, you know, he was quite right when he said that the nations won't wait."

"Meaning what?"

"Why, in the British House of Commons a member got up last week and, referring to the nihilists, asked the Minister whether it was not high time to intervene in the affairs of a barbarous nation and try to educate us. Ippolit had him in mind. I know he did. He was speaking about it last week."

"More easily said than done."

"D'you think so? Why?"

"We'll close Kronstadt down and won't let them have any wheat. Where else will they get it?"

"But what about America? They'll get it from America now."

"Rubbish."

But the bell rang and they all hastened to resume their seats. Fetyukovich mounted the rostrum.

10.

The Speech for the Defence. An Argument That Cuts Both Ways

A hush fell over the courtroom when the first words of the celebrated orator rang out. All eyes in the audience were fixed on him. He began very straightforwardly, simply and with conviction, but without the slightest trace of arrogance. There was not the least attempt at eloquence, pathos, or emotion-charged wording. He was a man speaking in an intimate circle of sympathisers. His voice was well-modulated, carried well, and was pleasing, and something even sincere and open-hearted seemed to sound in his very voice. But it was at once generally realised that the speaker could suddenly rise to true pathos and "thrill their hearts with incredible force", as the poet has it. He spoke perhaps less correctly than the public prosecutor, but without any long sentences and even with greater precision. One thing, though, the ladies did not like: he kept bending his back, especially at the beginning of his speech, not so much in bowing to his listeners as rushing forward impetuously towards them, his long spine bent almost double as though there was a hinge in the middle which enabled him to bend almost at a right angle. At the beginning of his speech, he seemed to speak in a discursive manner, as though with no system, taking up random facts, but an overall pattern ultimately emerged. His speech fell into two parts: the first half contained a criticism and refutation of the charge, at times biting and sarcastic. But in the second half he seemed to have suddenly changed his tone and even his manner, and instantly rose to pathos. The public seemed to have anticipated that, and simply quivered with delight. He went straight to the point and began by explaining that, though he was based in St. Petersburg, this was not his first visit to other Russian cities as defence counsel, but he took up cases only when he was convinced that the accused were innocent, or else he had a presentiment that they were. "It has been the same in this particular instance," he explained. "Even from the first newspaper reports alone, I was struck by something which greatly predisposed me in favour of the accused. In short, what interested me most was a certain legal fact, which though frequent in law practice, has never, I believe, appeared with such plenitude and characteristic features as in the present case. I should have formulated that fact at the end of my speech when I conclude it, but I shall do so at the very outset for I have a propensity to attack a subject head-on, without keeping any effects up my sleeve, or playing down the impressions. That may be uncalculating on my part, but then I am sincere. This thought of mine, this formula, is as follows: the overwhelming sum of the facts is against the accused, yet there is not a single fact that can stand up to criticism, if considered singly, by itself! From the newspapers and from the rumours about the case, I became more and more confirmed in my impression, and then I suddenly received an invitation from the relatives of the accused to take up his defence. I at once hastened here, and here I became finally convinced. So it was to destroy this dreadful accumulation of facts and to show that each incriminating fact, taken separately, was unproved and fantastic that I undertook the defence of this case."

The counsel for the defence began in this vein, and then he suddenly declared:

"Gentlemen of the jury, I'm a newcomer here and all the impressions have had an unprejudiced recipient in me. The accused, a man of violent and unbridled temper, has never previously offended me as he has, perhaps, many people in this town, which explains why so many people are prejudiced against him in advance. Of course, I, too, admit that the moral sentiment of local society has been aroused on good grounds: the accused is a violent and turbulent man. Yet he was received in society here. Indeed, he was even received and treated with every consideration in the family of the very learned public prosecutor." (N.B.: at these words, there were two or three laughs in the audience, quickly suppressed, but noticed by all. We all knew that the public prosecutor had received Mitya against his will, and solely because the latter had for some reason been found of interest by his wife—a highly esteemed and virtuous lady, but fanciful and self-willed, who, in some cases, liked to oppose her husband, especially in trifles. Mitya, however, was a rare caller.) "Nevertheless," the counsel for the defence went on, "I venture to assume that even a man with so independent a mind and so high a sense of justice as my learned friend could have formed a certain mistaken prejudice against my unhappy client. Oh, that is so natural: the unfortunate man has done so much to deserve being regarded even with prejudice. Injured moral and, still more, aesthetic feeling is sometimes remorseless. Of course, in the highly talented speech for the prosecution, we all heard a rigorous analysis of the character and conduct of the accused and a rigorously critical attitude towards the case as a whole; most of all, such depths of psychology were gone into to explain the substance of the case to us that, to reach them was quite out of the question given any deliberate or malicious prejudice against the person of the accused. But, then, there are things which are even worse and more ruinous in such cases than the most malicious and deliberate attitude to the matter. That holds, for instance, if we are overcome by some, so to speak, artistic urge, a drive towards

513

artistic creativity, towards writing some novel, especially if the Lord has endowed our abilities with a wealth of psychological gifts. While still preparing for my journey to your town, I was cautioned in St. Petersburg—and I was aware of that without being told—that in my opponent here I would find a profound and most refined psychologist, who had won a certain special reputation in our still young legal world through this quality in him. But, gentlemen of the jury, profound as psychology may be, it is still a weapon that cuts both ways (suppressed laughter in court). Oh, you will, I'm sure, forgive me my trivial comparison; I'm afraid I'm not much good at making eloquent speeches. However, I will take an example, the first example that occurs to me from the public prosecutor's speech. While running out of the garden at night, the accused climbed over the fence and with a brass pestle felled the servant, who had caught hold of his leg. Then he at once jumped back into the garden and concerned himself for five full minutes with the prostrate man, trying to find out whether he had killed him or not. Now, the public prosecutor refuses to believe that the accused was telling the truth when he stated that he had jumped down to Grigori out of compassion. 'No,' he says, 'can there be any such sentimentality at such a moment? That is unnatural; he jumped down to see whether the only witness to his crime was alive or dead and thereby proved that he had committed the crime, for he could not possibly have jumped down into the garden with any other motive, consideration, or feeling.' There is psychology for you: but let us take the same psychology and apply it to the case the other way round, and the result will be no less believable. The murderer jumped down as a precaution to see whether the witness to his crime was alive or not, and yet, as the public prosecutor himself asserts, he had left in the study of his murdered father a most damning piece of evidence against himself in the shape of a torn envelope with an inscription that it contained three thousand roubles. 'Had he taken the envelope away with him, no one would have known that such an envelope with the money existed and, hence, that the money had been stolen by the accused.' Those are the public prosecutor's own words. Well, so the accused was lacking in caution in one respect, you see: he must have lost his head, got frightened and ran off, leaving that piece of incriminating evidence on the floor, yet only two minutes later, he attacked and murdered another man, at once displaying a most inhuman and calculating sense of precaution—all this at our service. But let us assume that this is what actually happened: after all, the entire subtlety in psychological analysis lies in its showing that under such circumstances I'm as bloodthirsty and keen-sighted as a Caucasian eagle at one moment, and at the next as blind and timid as the humble mole. But if I'm so bloodthirsty and cruelly calculating that, having murdered a man, I ran back to him for the sole purpose of making sure whether the witness to my crime was alive or not, then why should I busy myself for five minutes over my new victim and, perhaps, run the risk of acquiring new witnesses? Why steep my handkerchief in blood, while wiping it off his head, so that it may serve as evidence against me later? If he were really so calculating and cold-hearted as that, would it not have been wiser to hit the victim again and again on the head with the same pestle so as to make quite sure he was dead, and having eliminated the witness, relieve his own heart of all anxiety? And, finally, he jumped down to make sure whether the witness against him was alive or not, and left another witness on the path, namely the brass pestle he had taken from the two women which they could always identify afterwards as theirs and testify that he had taken it from them. And it isn't as if he forgot it on the path, dropped it through absent-mindedness or because of his confused state; no, he flung it aside, for it was found within fifteen paces of the place where Grigori had been felled. Why did he do that, it may be asked? Well, he did so because it was a harrowing experience to have killed a man, an old servant, which was why he cast the pestle away in vexation and with a curse as a weapon a murder had been committed with; it could not be otherwise, for why should he have thrown it away with such force? But if he was capable of feeling pain and compassion for a man having been killed, it was surely because he had not murdered his father. Had he murdered his father, he wouldn't have jumped down to attend to another victim out of pity; in that case, it would have been

515

another feeling: he would not have bothered with pity but would have been thinking of self-preservation, and that, for a certainty. On the contrary, I repeat, he would have bashed in the man's skull and not busied himself with him for about five minutes. There was room for pity and kindliness in his heart just because his conscience had been clear. So here you have another kind of psychology. I have purposely resorted to psychology myself, gentlemen of the jury, to show clearly that anything can be deduced from it. It all depends on what hands it is in. Psychology leads even the most serious people to indulge in romancing, and that quite involuntarily. I'm speaking, gentlemen of the jury, of superfluous psychology, of a certain misuse of it."

Here again there was approving laughter in court, and all at the expense of the public prosecutor. I will not report the speech of the counsel for the defence in detail, but will only cite some passages from it, some of the highlights.

11.

There Was No Money.
Neither Was There Any Robbery

There was a point in the speech of the counsel for the defence which came as a surprise to all, to wit, his flat denial of the existence of the fateful three thousand roubles and, consequently, the possibility of their having been stolen.

"Gentlemen of the jury," the counsel for the defence began, "any fresh and unprejudiced man will be struck by a characteristic feature in this case, namely, the charge of robbery and, at the same time, the utter impossibility of actually indicating exactly what was stolen. We are told that money was stolen, namely three thousand roubles, but no one seems to know whether it ever existed. Consider: in the first place, how have we come to know that there was three thousand roubles; who saw it? The only person who did see it and declared it had been put in an envelope with an inscription was the servant Smerdyakov.

It was he who informed the accused and his brother Ivan Fyodorovich of it prior to the catastrophe. Miss Svetlov, too, was told about it. But none of these three persons actually saw the money; again it was only Smerdyakov who saw it, but here the question arises: if it is true that it did exist and that Smerdyakov saw it, then when did he see it last? What if his master had taken the money from under the mattress and put it back in his casket without telling Smerdyakov? Note that, according to the latter, the money was under the mattress; the accused would have had to get it from under the mattress, yet the bed had not in any way been disturbed, which is carefully recorded in the official record. How could the accused have left the bedding completely undisturbed and, moreover, how could he have failed to soil with his bloodstained hands the fine and spotless linen the bed had been purposely made with? But, I shall be asked, what about the envelope on the floor? Well, it deserves a few words. I must say I was a little surprised just now: my highly talented opponent in speaking of the envelope, himself—listen, gentlemen—himself stated in that part of his speech that referred to the absurdity of supposing that Smerdyakov was the murderer: 'Had it not been for that envelope, had it not been left on the floor as a clue, had the robber carried it away with him, no one in the world would have known that an envelope had been there or that there had been money in it, and that, consequently, the accused must have stolen the money.' Thus, even as admitted by the prosecutor himself, only that torn scrap of paper with its inscription has served to substantiate the accused being charged with robbery, for otherwise no one would have learnt of the robbery or that there had been any money. But surely, the mere fact that that scrap of paper was lying on the floor is no proof that it had contained money and that the money had been stolen. 'But,' it will be objected, 'Smerdyakov saw the money in the envelope.' But when did he last see it—that's what I'm asking. I spoke to Smerdyakov, who told me that he had seen it two days before the murder. But why can't I suppose, for instance, that old Fyodor Pavlovich locked himself in at his home and, in impatient and hysterical expectation of his lady-love, suddenly took it into his head, for want of some other occupation, to pull out the envelope and open it. 'The envelope alone,' he may have said to himself, 'may not work the trick. She may not believe there's any money in it. But if I show her thirty rainbow-coloured hundred-rouble notes in a roll, it will, I'm sure, make a far stronger impression on her, and make her mouth water'; so he tore the envelope open, extracted the money, and threw the envelope on the floor as the lawful possessor of the money and, of course, without any fear of leaving any incriminating evidence behind. Listen, gentlemen of the jury; is there anything more possible than such a supposition and such a fact? Why was it impossible? But if anything of the kind could have taken place, then the charge of robbery must collapse, for if there was no money, there could be no robbery. If the envelope on the floor is evidence that it contained money, then why can't I assert the reverse, namely that the envelope was on the floor because there was already no money in it, for it had been extracted previously by the owner himself? 'Yes, but where, in that case, could the money have gone if Fyodor Pavlovich took it out of the envelope, and it was not found during the search of the house?' First of all, part of the money was found in his casket and, secondly, he might have taken it out that morning or even the night before, made some other arrangements for it, given it to someone, sent it off, or, finally, radically changed his mind, his plan of action, without finding it necessary to inform Smerdyakov about it in advance? And if there exists only the possibility of such a supposition, how can the accused be so firmly and insistently charged with murder for robbery and, indeed, with having committed the robbery? We are thereby entering the realm of fiction. For if it is maintained that a certain thing has been stolen, then that thing must be produced or, at any rate, it must be proved beyond doubt that it existed. And yet no one even saw it. Not so long ago, a lad of eighteen, a pedlar, entered a St. Petersburg moneychanger's shop in broad daylight with an axe, and with extraordinary and typical callousness murdered the shopkeeper and carried off fifteen hundred roubles. He was arrested some five hours later and all the fifteen hundred was found on him except for fifteen roubles, which he had already managed to spend. Moreover, on returning to the shop after the murder, the shop-assistant informed the police, not only of the sum stolen, but even what it consisted of, that is to say, how many hundred-rouble, ten-rouble, and five-rouble notes, and how many gold coins and of what denominations there were, and those notes and coins were found on the murderer. In addition to all this, there was a full and frank confession by the murderer himself. That, gentlemen of the jury, is what I call firm evidence! There I know, see and feel the money, and I cannot say that it never existed. Is that the case in the present instance? And yet, this is a matter of life and death, of a man's fate. 'That is all very well,' it will be said, 'but he was having a high old time that night, squandering money. Fifteen hundred roubles was found on him—where did he get it?' But, then, the very fact that only fifteen hundred was found on him and the other half of the sum could nowhere be found or discovered—that very fact proves that the money may not have been the same, and that it had never been in any envelope. The most rigorous preliminary official investigation into the movements of the accused and the timing has shown beyond any doubt that, after leaving the two maids on the night of the crime, he went straight to see the civil servant Perkhotin, without going home or anywhere else, and that after that he was in the company of others all the time, so that, consequently, he could not have put aside half of the three thousand and hidden it somewhere in town. It was this very consideration that led the prosecution to assume that he must have hidden it in some crevice at Mokroye. But why not in the dungeons of the Castle of Udolpho, gentlemen? Isn't this assumption too fantastic and too romantic for words? And please note that if that single assumption breaks down, the whole charge of robbery dissolves in thin air, for where could the fifteen hundred have got to? By what miracle could it have disappeared, since it has been proved that the accused went nowhere else? And, are we prepared to ruin a man's life with such romantic tales? It will be said that, nevertheless, the accused has been unable to explain where he got the fifteen hundred found on him and that, moreover, he is known to have had no money previously to that night. But who knew that? The accused has given a clear and firm account of where he got that money, and if you please, gentlemen of the jury, if you please, nothing could be more probable than that statement, quite apart from its being entirely in character. The prosecutor is pleased with his own romantic tale. A man of weak will, who had made up his mind to accept the three thousand so humiliatingly offered by his finacée, could not, he claims, have set aside half and sewn it up in a little bag; on the contrary, had he done so, he would have unstitched it every second day and kept dipping into it for a hundred at a time and thus would have spent it all in a single month. You will remember that all this was put to you in a tone that brooked no contradiction. Well, and what if things did not develop like that at all? What if you've invented a story featuring quite a different person? That's the snag: you've thought up a quite different person! I shall be told, perhaps, that there are witnesses that he squandered all the three thousand he had received from Miss Verkhovtsev, in the village of Mokroye a month before the disaster and, at one go, down to the last copeck, so that he could not have set aside half of it. But who are these witnesses? The trustworthiness of the testimony of these witnesses has already revealed itself in this court. Besides, a hunk of bread always seems larger in another man's hands. And, last but not least, none of these witnesses counted the money, but merely judged by sight. Did not the witness Maximov testify that the accused had twenty thousand in his possession? As you see, gentlemen of the jury, psychology is a double-edged weapon, so let me apply the other edge now and we shall see what happens.

"A month before the disaster, the accused was entrusted by Miss Verkhovtsev with three thousand roubles to be remitted by post. But the question arises: is it true that it was entrusted to him in a manner so offensive and humiliating as was alleged here just now? Miss Verkhovtsev's first testimony on the subject contained a different version, one quite different; in her second testimony all we heard were outcries of bitter resentment and vengeance, outcries of long-held hatred. But the very fact that the witness gave false testimony the first time entitles us to conclude that her second testimony, too, may have been false. The prosecutor does not want—he dare not (those were his own words)—to touch upon that love affair. Very well, I won't touch upon it, either, but I shall venture to observe that if so pure and highly moral a person as the highly esteemed Miss Verkhovtsev undoubtedly is, if such a person, I say, permits herself suddenly and so sweepingly to contradict her first testimony in court with the direct aim of ruining the accused, then her second testimony has obviously been made neither impartially nor dispassionately. Are we therefore to forfeit the right to conclude that the vengeful woman may have exaggerated very much? Yes, indeed, she may have exaggerated the shame and disgrace of offering him the money. On the contrary, I suggest that it was offered in a manner acceptable even to a man as frivolous as the accused. The important point is that he expected shortly to get from his father the three thousand still owing to him, according to his calculation. This may be thoughtless of him, but then it was because he was thoughtless enough to be quite sure that his father would let him have the money and that he could, therefore, always send off the money entrusted to him by Miss Verkhovtsev, and thus settle his debt. But the prosecutor will not admit that he could have set aside half of the money on the day he received it and sewn it up in a little bag. That is not in his character, he claims; he could not have held such feelings. But didn't you yourself give voice regarding the expansive Karamazovian nature of the accused, and the two abysses that a Karamazov can contemplate? Yes, Karamazov is just such a double nature, one standing between two abysses, a nature which, when impelled by an irresistible urge for dissipation, can come to a halt if something astounds it from the other side. And that other side was love, a new love that flared up like tinder, and for that love he needed money, ah, far more than even for a riotous time with his lady-love. If she were to say to him, 'I'm yours; I don't want Fyodor Pavlovich', he would seize her at once and take her away—but for that he needed the wherewithal. That was far more important than revelry. Could a Karamazov fail to have understood that? Why, that was the prime cause of his concern and anxiety, so what is there so improbable about his setting aside that money and concealing it for an emergency? But time passed and Fyodor Pavlovich did not let the accused have the three thousand; on the contrary, there was talk that his father had set the money aside to entice the woman he, the accused, loved. 'If Fyodor Pavlovich doesn't let me have the money,' he thought, 'Katerina Ivanovna will see me as a thief.' And so he conceived the idea of going to Miss Verkhovtsev, placing before her the fifteen hundred roubles, he still carried in the little bag round his neck, and saying to her: 'I'm a blackguard but not a thief.' Herein, therefore, lay the twofold reason for guarding the money like the apple of his eye, not opening the little bag and abstracting a hundred roubles at a time from it. Why should you deny the accused a sense of honour? Yes, he has a sense of honour, though perhaps a mistaken one, and very often a false one, but it does exist; he believes in it passionately, and has proved it. However, the affair grew more complex, his torments of jealousy reached a climax, and the same two questions assumed a more and more agonising shape in the fevered brain of the accused. 'If I return the money to Katerina Ivanovna, where shall I find the means to carry Grushenka off?' If he behaved like a madman, if he got drunk and created disturbances at taverns all that month, it was perhaps because he felt sick at heart himself and was unable to bear it any longer. These two questions at last grew so acute that they drove him to despair. He sent his younger brother to his father to beg him for the last time for the three thousand, but, without waiting for a reply, forced his way into the house, and ended by assaulting the old man in the presence of witnesses. After that, there was no one to get the money from, for the father he had fallen upon would not let him have it. The same evening he beat himself on the breast—the upper part of his breast where the little bag was—and swore to his brother that he had a way of avoiding being a blackguard, but that he would remain a blackguard for all that, for he realised he would not use that means, and that he would not have the strength of mind or character to do so. Why, doesn't the prosecution believe Alexei Karamazov's evidence given so frankly and sincerely, so spontaneously and convincingly? Why, on the other hand, does it oblige me to believe in money hidden in some crack, in the dungeons of the Castle of Udolpho? After his talk with his brother that evening, the accused wrote that fateful letter, and that letter is the main and most damning evidence that the accused was guilty of robbery! 'I shall beg from anyone, and if they refuse, I shall kill my father and shall take the envelope with the pink ribbon from under the mattress if only Ivan goes away.' A full programme of the murder, we are told, so it must have been he, mustn't it? 'It all took place as he wrote it,' the prosecution exclaims. But, in the first place, the letter was written when the accused was drunk and in a state of the utmost irritation; secondly, he wrote of the envelope from Smerdyakov's words for he had not seen the envelope himself, and, thirdly, he certainly did write the letter, but how can it be proved that it all took place as written? Did the accused get the envelope from under the pillow, did he find the money, did it exist at all? Moreover, was it for the money that the accused had come in such haste? Recollect that, recollect that! He came in violent haste, not to rob but only to find out where she was, the woman who had bowled him over, so that he came, not to carry out some programme, or because of what he had written, consequently not to commit premeditated robbery, but on a sudden impulse and in a frenzy of jealousy! Yes, I shall be told, yet he did come running there and murdered his father, and then took the money as well. But did he or didn't he murder him? The charge of robbery I repudiate with indignation: a man cannot be accused of robbery if it cannot be shown definitely what he has stolen—that is an axiom! But did he commit murder, murder without robbery? Has that been proved? Isn't that, too, a piece of fiction?"

12.

Neither Was There Any Murder

"Permit me, gentlemen of the jury, to point out that a man's life is at stake and that caution must be exercised. We have heard the prosecutor himself admit that until the very last day, till today, the day of the trial, he was hesitant about bringing a charge of wilful and premeditated murder; he hesitated till the moment the fateful 'drunken' letter was produced in court today. 'It all followed the pattern!' But let me repeat once again: he ran to her and for her, solely to find out where she was. That is an unquestionable fact. Had she been at home, he would not have gone anywhere else, but would have remained with her and not have carried out what he had promised in his letter. He ran off accidentally and on the spur of the moment and, perhaps, did not even remember his 'drunken' letter at the time. 'He grabbed the pestle,' the prosecutor pointed out, and you will remember how from that pestle alone an entire psychological treatise was deduced for us: why he should have regarded the pestle as a weapon and grabbed it as such, and so on and so forth. A most ordinary thought comes to mind at this juncture: what if the pestle had not been lying about so prominently, on the shelf whence the accused grabbed it, but put away in a cupboard—then it would not have caught the eye of the accused, who would have dashed off weaponless and empty-handed, and then, perhaps, he would not have murdered anybody. How, then, can I conclude that the use of the pestle for wilful murder has been proved? Indeed, he did clamour at the taverns that he would murder his father, but two days before, in the evening he wrote his drunken letter, he was quiet and only quarrelled with a shop-assistant 'because, being a Karamazov, he could not help picking a quarrel'. To which I shall reply that if he was really contemplating such a murder, and according to plan, too, in keeping with what he had written, he most certainly would not have quarrelled with the shop-assistant and, perhaps, would not have gone to the tavern at all, for a man planning such a crime seeks quiet and self-effacement, seeks to disappear, so as not to be seen or heard: 'Forget me if you can,' he seems to be saying and he does so, not deliberately but instinctively. Gentlemen of the jury, psychology can cut both ways and we, too, are capable of understanding psychology. As for all those outcries at the taverns during that whole month, don't we often hear children, or drunkards emerging from their taverns quarrelling with one another and shouting 'I'll kill you', but they don't kill, do they? And that fateful letter itself—isn't it just the result of drunken irritability, too? Isn't it just the yell of a man leaving a tavern: 'I'll kill you, I'll kill the lot of you'? Why, why shouldn't it have been like that in this case? Why is that letter so fateful; why isn't it, on the contrary, simply ridiculous? It is because the dead body of his father was found, because a witness saw the accused in the garden, armed and running away, and was himself felled by him, and so everything had happened as had been written, and therefore the letter, too, is not ridiculous but fateful. Thank goodness, we now come to the crux of the matter: 'if he was in the garden, he committed the murder'. The entire prosecution rests on those few words: 'Since he *was* there, that *means* he did it.' But supposing it does not *mean* that, though he was there? Oh, I agree that the totality of the facts, the coincidence of the facts, is indeed quite eloquent. But consider all these facts separately, without letting yourselves be impressed by their totality: why, for instance, does the prosecution flatly refuse to acknowledge the truth of the testimony of the accused that he made off from his father's window? Remember, too, the sarcastic remarks indulged in by the prosecutor about the deference and the 'pious' sentiments which suddenly came over the accused. But what if there really was something of the kind, that is to say, if not respectfulness of sentiments, then at least piety of sentiments? 'I suppose my mother must have been praying for me at the moment,' the accused stated during the preliminary investigation: he ran off the moment he realised that Miss Svetlov was not at his father's house. 'But,' the prosecution objects, 'he could not possibly have seen that by looking through the window.' Why couldn't he? The window was open to the signals given by the accused. Some word or cry coming from Fyodor Pavlovich would have sufficed to instantly convince the accused that Miss Svetlov was not there. Why should we assume what we have imagined or set out to imagine? Thousands of things may flash past in actual life which elude observation by the subtlest of novelists. 'Yes, but Grigori saw the open door, so that the accused must certainly have been

in the house and, therefore, must have murdered his father.'
Now for that door, gentlemen of the jury— You see, we have
evidence about the open door from only one witness, who at
the time was in such a condition that—but let us say that the
door was open; let us say that the accused has denied it, lied
about it out of a sense of self-preservation, so understandable
in his condition; let us say that he did gain entry into the house,
and was in the house—so what? Why does it follow therefrom
that he committed the murder? He may have burst in, rushed
through the rooms, pushed his father aside and even struck him,
but, having made certain that Miss Svetlov was not there, he ran
off, rejoicing that she was not there and that he had made off
without killing his father. That was perhaps why, a moment
later, he jumped down from the fence to attend to Grigori,
whom he had felled in his worked-up state. He did so because
he was capable of a pure feeling, a feeling of compassion and
pity, because he had escaped the temptation of killing his
father, and because he felt within himself a pure heart and joy
at not having killed his father. The prosecutor described to us
with awesome eloquence the state of the accused man's mind
in the village of Mokroye when love was again revealed to him
calling him to a new life, and that at a time when he had no
longer any right to love because behind him was the bloodstained corpse of his father, and beyond that corpse lay punishment. Yet the prosecutor did allow him that love, which in
accordance with his psychological approach he explained as
'the state of intoxication of a criminal being taken to the execution, the long road to be travelled', and so on and so forth.
But have you not created a different person, I again ask the prosecutor. Is the accused so uncouth and callous that he could still
think of love at such a moment and of prevaricating at his trial
if his hands were really steeped in his father's blood? No, no,
and again no! As soon as he discovered that she loved him,
called on him to go away with her, and promised him a new
happiness, oh, then, I swear, he must have felt his urge to commit suicide doubled and trebled, and he would most certainly
have killed himself if behind him lay his father's corpse! Oh,
no, he wouldn't have forgotten where his pistols were! I know

the accused: the brutal and callous heartlessness imputed to him by the prosecution is not in keeping with his nature. He would have killed himself, that is certain; he did not do so because his 'mother had been praying for him' and because he was innocent of his father's blood. He was tormented and grief-stricken that night at Mokroye only over old Grigori whom he had felled and he was praying to God that the old man would come to himself and arise, that his blow had not been fatal, and that he would escape retribution for it. Why not accept such an interpretation of the events? What firm proof do we have that the accused is lying to us? But, we shall again be told, what about his father's dead body: he ran off without committing murder, so who did murder the old man?

"I repeat, herein lies the entire logic of the prosecution: who murdered him if not he? There's no one to place in his stead. Gentlemen of the jury, is that so? Is there really and positively no one to place in his stead? We have heard the public prosecutor count on his fingers all the persons who were or had been in that house. There were five. Three of them, I agree, cannot possibly have been responsible: the murdered man himself, old Grigori, and his wife. There remain, therefore, the accused and Smerdyakov, and so the counsel for the prosecution exclaims dramatically that the accused pointed at Smerdyakov for want of someone else and that, had there been a sixth person or even the ghost of a sixth person, the accused would at once have withdrawn his accusation against Smerdyakov, felt ashamed of it, and would have pointed at that sixth person. But, gentlemen of the jury, why may not I assume the reverse to be true? Here we have two men: the accused and Smerdyakov. Why can't I say that you are accusing my client simply because you have no one else to accuse? And there is no one else only because your preconceived notion has led you to preclude any suspicion of Smerdyakov. It is true, of course, that only the accused himself, his two brothers, and Miss Svetlov have testified against Smerdyakov. But there are others, too, who have done so: there is a rather vague sense of dissatisfaction among people in this town, a kind of suspicion; there is evidence of some vague rumours, there is a kind of expectancy in the air. Finally, we have the evidence of a certain comparison of facts, something highly significant, though, I admit, vague: in the first place, that fit of epilepsy on the very day of the disaster, a fit which the prosecutor has for some reason felt constrained to defend and justify. Then we have Smerdyakov's sudden suicide on the eve of the trial. Then the no less startling evidence in court today by the elder brother of the accused, who previously believed in his guilt, but suddenly produced the three thousand roubles and also named Smerdyakov as the murderer! Oh, I'm entirely of the same opinion as the court and the prosecution that Ivan Karamazov is a sick man in a state of fever and that his evidence could really be a desperate attempt, devised in a delirium, to save his brother by shifting the blame onto the dead man. Nevertheless, Smerdyakov's name has been uttered, and again we seem to have something mysterious. Something, gentlemen of the jury, has been left unsaid, left uncompleted. Perhaps it may yet be said. But we won't go into that for the time being; that still lies ahead. The court has decided to continue the hearing of the case, but for the time being I could, however, comment, for instance, on the characteristic of the late Smerdyakov, sketched with subtlety and talent by the prosecutor. But while admiring his talent, I cannot entirely agree with the essence of that character study. I visited Smerdyakov, saw him and spoke to him, and he produced a quite different impression on me. True, he was frail of health, but in character, in spirit—oh, no, he was not by any means the feeble man the prosecution made him out to be. I certainly found no timidity in him, the timidity the counsel for the prosecution has so characteristically described. Neither was there any simple-mindedness in him; on the contrary, I found in him extreme distrust under a cloak of artlessness, and an intelligence capable of contemplating a great many things. Oh, the prosecution has been far too naive in considering him feeble-minded. He produced a very definite impression on me: I left with the conviction that he was a most spiteful man, immensely ambitious, vindictive, and inordinately envious. I collected some information: he loathed his origin, was ashamed of it, and gnashed his teeth every time he recalled that he 'was the son of Smelly Lizaveta'. He had no respect for the servant Grigori and his wife, who had been his childhood benefactors. He cursed and jeered at Russia. It was his ambition to go to France and become a Frenchman. He had talked a lot about it and often used to say that he lacked the means to do so. I believe he loved no one but himself and that he was strangely self-opinionated. He saw enlightenment in the wearing of good clothes, clean shirtfronts, and polished boots. Believing himself to be Fyodor Pavlovich's natural son (and there are facts to confirm it), he might well have hated his status as compared with that of his master's legitimate sons: they had everything while he had nothing; they enjoyed all rights and would get the inheritance, while he was only a cook. He disclosed to me that he himself, together with Fyodor Pavlovich, had put the money in the envelope. The purpose of that money—a sum that might well have made his career—was, of course, hateful to him. Besides, he saw three thousand roubles in bright rainbow-coloured notes (I asked him about it on purpose). Oh, never show an ambitious and envious man a large sum of money all at once; this was the first time he had ever seen such a sum held in one hand. The sight of the wad of rainbow-coloured notes might well have inflamed his imagination, with no consequences at the beginning. The highly talented prosecutor has outlined with extraordinary subtlety all the arguments for and against the supposition that Smerdyakov could be charged with murder, and, in particular, asked why he should have staged his epileptic fit. But he need not have feigned it at all; the fit may well have come on quite naturally and it may well have passed quite naturally, and the sick man could have come to himself. He might not have recovered completely, but he could have regained consciousness sometime, as happens with epileptics. The prosecution asks at what moment Smerdyakov committed the murder. But that moment can be indicated with the greatest ease. He might have come to, got up from his deep sleep (for he was merely asleep: an attack of epilepsy is always succeeded by profound slumber) just at the instant old Grigori caught hold of the prisoner's leg and shouted at the top of his voice: 'Parricide!' The shout must have been very loud in the stillness and dark of the night, and it could have wakened Smerdyakov, whose sleep at that time might not have been very deep: naturally, he might have started coming out of his sleep an hour before. Getting out of bed, he went almost unconsciously and without any definite purpose in the direction the shout had come from, to see what the matter was. He still felt somewhat dazed and his mind was still only half awake, but in the garden he went up to the lighted windows and heard the dreadful news from his master, who was, of course, very glad to see him. His mind at once began working feverishly. From his frightened master he learnt all the details and so gradually an idea took shape in his disordered and sick brain—a terrible, but tempting and irresistibly logical idea: to murder his master, take the three thousand and afterwards put the whole blame on his young master: for who else but he would be implicated, who else could be but the young master accused in the light of the evidence? He had been there at the money. A terrible lust for the money, for gain, could have overcome him, together with an awareness of his impunity. Oh, such sudden and irresistible impulses come so often when a favourable opportunity presents itself and, what is important above all, they come on the spur of the moment to murderers who but a minute before did not know they were capable of murder. And so Smerdyakov may well have entered his master's quarters and carried out his plan. With what weapon? Why, with any stone that came to hand in the garden. But what for, with what aim? And, after all, the three thousand meant a career to him! Oh I'm not contradicting myself: the money may well have existed. And perhaps Smerdyakov alone knew where it could be found, and where his master kept it. And the sheaf of money, the torn envelope on the floor? While speaking of that envelope a short while ago, the prosecutor expressed a most subtle consideration to the effect that only an inexperienced thief, such as Karamazov, would have left it on the floor, but not Smerdyakov, who would never have left behind such incriminating evidence against himself; and, gentlemen of the jury, as I listened I couldn't help suddenly thinking that I was hearing something very familiar. And, imagine, I had heard from Smerdyakov himself exactly two days

530

before the very same consideration, the conjecture of what Karamazov would have done with the envelope. Moreover, he quite amazed me: it seemed to me that he was pretending to be naive; was running ahead and imposing the idea on me in a way to make me think I myself had drawn that conclusion, and was prompting me, as it were. Did he not suggest the same idea to the investigating authorities, too? Did he not foist it on the highly talented prosecutor, too? It will be said: and what about the old woman, Grigori's wife? She heard the sick man moaning next door to her all night. She did, indeed, but that is a most shaky consideration. I once knew a woman who complained bitterly that she had been kept awake all night by a dog in the yard. And yet the poor dog, as it appeared later, had barked only once or twice during the night. And that is natural: if anyone is asleep and suddenly hears a groan, he wakes up, annoyed at being awakened, but instantly falls asleep again. Two hours later, there is another groan; he wakes up and falls asleep again; finally, there is another groan again two hours later. In all, this happened three times during the night. The sleeper gets up the next morning and complains that someone has been groaning all night and kept waking him. And that is how it must have seemed to him; he was awakened at two-hour intervals but there is little he remembers; he only remembers the moments of awakening and so believes that he has been wakened all night long. But why, why, the prosecutor exclaims, did Smerdyakov not confess in his last message? His conscience made him confess to one thing but not to the other. But remember: conscience means repentance, and the suicide may have felt not repentance but only despair. Despair and repentance are two quite different things. Despair may be spiteful and irreconcilable, and the suicide, at the moment he lays hands on himself, may feel a redoubled hatred for those he has envied all his life. Gentlemen of the jury, beware of a miscarriage of justice! I put it to you: is there anything improbable in what I have just brought forward and depicted? Find an error in my account, find what is impossible and absurd in it. And if there is at least a mite of possibility, a shade of verisimilitude in my suppositions, refrain from condemning the man.

And is there only a shade here? I swear by everything I hold sacred that I fully believe in the interpretation of the murder I have just put to you. But what troubles and disturbs me most is the selfsame thought that, in all this mass of facts as piled up by the prosecution against the accused, there is not one that is in any way precise or incontrovertible, and that the unfortunate man may be utterly ruined simply because of the totality of these facts. Yes, that totality is awesome: the blood, the blood dripping from the fingers, the bloodstained linen, the dark night that resounded to the cry of 'parricide!' and the man who had uttered that cry sinking to the ground with a broken head, and then that mass of utterances, statements, gestures, and out- cries—oh, it all exerts so much influence, can win opinions over! But, gentlemen of the jury, can it win your opinions over? Remember, you have been given boundless authority, the power to bind or to loose. But the greater the power, the more awe- some is its application! I do not retract a jot of what I have just said, but let me, let me for a moment agree with the prosecution that my unhappy client crimsoned his hands in his father's blood. That is merely an assumption. I repeat I do not for a moment doubt his innocence, but just let me assume that the prisoner is guilty of parricide, but listen to what I have to say, even if I make that assumption. I feel an urge to say something to you, for I have a feeling that a great struggle is going on both in your hearts and minds— Forgive me, those words, gentlemen of the jury, about your hearts and minds. But I want to be truthful and sincere to the end. Let us all be sincere—"

At this point the counsel for the defence was interrupted by quite loud applause. Indeed, he uttered his last words on a note of such sincerity that all felt that he really might have something to say, and that what he was about to say was of the utmost importance. But, on hearing the applause, the presiding judge threatened in a loud voice "to clear the court" if "a similar incident" reoccurred. A hush fell on the courtroom and Fetyukovich began in a kind of new voice, full of feeling and quite unlike the one he had spoken with before.

13.

Debasers of Thought

"It is not the totality of the facts alone that dooms my client, gentlemen of the jury," he declared. "No, what really dooms my client is a single fact: the dead body of his old father! Had this been an ordinary murder, you, in view of the paltriness and the unsubstantiated and fantastic nature of the facts if regarded individually and not in their totality would have thrown out the charge or at least would have hesitated to wreck a man's life merely out of the prejudice against him, which, alas, he has so well deserved! But here we are dealing, not with an ordinary murder but with parricide! That impresses, and to such a degree that the very paltriness and unsubstantiated nature of the incriminating facts already become less paltry and unsubstantiated and that even to the most unprejudiced mind. How is such an accused to be acquitted? What if he did commit the murder and escapes punishment! That is what anyone feels at heart almost involuntarily and instinctively. Yes, it is a dreadful thing to shed a father's blood, the blood of the man who has begotten you, the blood of one who has loved you, the blood of a man who has not spared his life for you, has worried over your illnessses since the days of your childhood, has felt concern for your happiness all his life, and has lived only in your joys and your successes! Oh, to murder such a father—why, it's unthinkable! Gentlemen of the jury, what is a father, a genuine father? What kind of lofty word is it! What an awesome idea is contained in the name! I have just pointed out only in part what it means and what a true father ought to be like. But in the present case, in which we are all now so deeply involved and over which we grieve so much—in the present case, the father, the late Fyodor Pavlovich Karamazov wholly failed to live up to the concept of a father which has now appealed to us so strongly. That is a misfortune. Yes, indeed, some fathers are a misfortune. Let us examine this misfortune at closer range, for, in view of the importance of your impending decision, gentlemen of the jury, nothing should be feared. In particular we must have no fear and, so to speak, wave aside some idea as children or timid women do, as the highly talented prosecutor has so felicitously put it. But in his ardent speech my esteemed opponent (my opponent even before I first spoke) exclaimed several times: 'No, I shall not yield the defence of the accused to anyone; I shall not yield it to the advocate who has come down from St. Petersburg—I am his accuser, and I am his defender!' That is what he exclaimed several times, yet he forgot to mention that if this dreadful man has been so grateful for twenty-three years for only a pound of nuts he received from the only man who was kind to him as a child at his father's house, then, conversely, such a man could not but remember for twenty-three years how he ran about barefoot in his father's back-yard 'in his little trousers hanging by a single button', to quote the kind-hearted Doctor Herzenstube. Oh, gentlemen of the jury, why should we examine 'misfortune' at closer range, and repeat what is common knowledge? What did my client meet with when he arrived here at his father's house? And why, why depict my client as an unfeeling and selfish monster? He is unbridled, reckless and violent, for which he is standing trial, but who bears responsibility for his fate? Who is responsible for his having received such an absurd upbringing despite his excellent propensities and his noble and sensitive heart? Did anyone teach him to be reasonable? Did he get any proper education? Did anyone love him just a little in his choldhood? My client grew up by the grace of God, that is to say, like a wild animal. He may have been eager to see his father after years of separation. Recalling his childhood a thousand times perhaps, though like a dream, he may have driven away the loathsome phantoms that haunted his childhood dreams, and longed with all his heart to justify and to embrace his father! But what actually happened? He was met with cynical sneers, suspicion and chicanery over some money in dispute; all he heared was sickening talk and hackneyed precepts delivered daily 'over the brandy', and finally saw his father trying to entice away his mistress from him, his son, and with his own money. Oh, gentlemen of the jury, that was both revolting and cruel! And that same old man was complaining to all and sundry of his son's disrespect and cruelty, besmirching his name in society, injuring him, slandering him, and buying up his promissory notes to get him landed in prison! Gentlemen of the jury, such souls, these outwardly cruel-hearted, violent and uncontrollable men, such as my client, are more often than not exceedingly tender-hearted, only they don't display it. Do not laugh, do not laugh at my idea! The talented prosecutor mercilessly made fun of my client a short while ago, pointing out that he loved Schiller, loved 'the beautiful and the sublime'. I would not have sneered at that in his stead, as a prosecutor! Yes, such hearts—oh, let me speak up in defence of such hearts, so often and so unfairly misunderstood, hearts that so often long for the tender, beautiful, and just, and they do so, as it were, in contrast with themselves, their violence, and their cruelty—they yearn for it unconsciously—yes, they yearn for it. Outwardly passionate and cruel, they are capable, for instance, of falling in love with a woman to a degree where it becomes a torment to them, and their love is invariably high-minded and spiritual. Again, do not laugh at me: that is more often than not the case with men with such natures! Only they cannot conceal their passionateness, which is sometimes very coarse—and that is what strikes people, what they notice, but they do not see what takes place within such men. All their passions, on the contrary, are quickly spent, but at the side of a noble and beautiful creature such an apparently coarse and cruel man seeks for regeneration, a chance of changing himself, becoming a better, nobler, and more honourable man, seeks 'the sublime and the beautiful', however much such words may be ridiculed! I said a short while ago that I would not venture to touch upon my client's love affair with Miss Verkhovtsev. But I think I can briefly say this: what we heard just now was not testimony but the screaming of a frenzied and vengeful woman, and it is not for her to reproach him with betrayal, for she herself has betrayed him! Had she had a little time to think things over, she would not have come forward with such testimony. Oh, place no belief in her! My client is not a 'monster', as she has called him. Preparing for the Cross, the crucified Lover of mankind said: 'I am the good shepherd, and I lay down my life for the sheep, so that not one of them might be lost—' Let us, too, not wreck a man's soul. I asked just now: what is a father, and I said that it was a lofty word, a precious name. But, gentlemen of the jury, words must be used honestly, and I venture to call a thing by its proper name, the right word: such a father as the murdered old Karamazov cannot and is unworthy to be called a father. Love for a father who is undeserving of that love is an absurdity, an impossibility. One cannot create love out of nothing; only God can create out of nothing. 'Fathers, distress not your children!'* the apostle writes from a heart burning with love. It is not for the sake of my client that I quote those sacred words, but as a reminder to all fathers. Who has authorised me to preach to fathers? No one. But as a man and a citizen, I make my appeal: *vivos voco*! We are not on earth for long; we do many evil deeds and say many evil words. Let us, therefore, grasp the auspicious minute of our communion here to say a kind word to one another. That is what I am doing: while I stand here, I take advantage of my minute. It is with good reason that this tribune has been vouchsafed to us by the supreme authority: from it the whole of Russia hears us. I am not speaking only for the fathers in these parts, but I cry out to all fathers: 'Fathers, distress not your children!' Let us first carry out Christ's precept ourselves, and only then permit ourselves to demand it of our children as well. Otherwise, we are no fathers, but enemies to our children, and they are not our children but our enemies, and we ourselves have made them our enemies! 'With what measure ye mete, it shall be measured to you again.' Those are not my words, but an injunction of the Gospels: measure according to the same measure as is measured to you. How, then, can we blame our children if they measure us according to our own measure? In Finland a girl, a housemaid, was recently suspected of having secretly given birth to a child. She was watched, and behind some bricks in the loft was found a box of hers that no one knew anything about. It was

*An inexact quotation from the Epistle to the Colossians, III, 21, which runs: "Fathers, provoke not your children *to anger*, lest they be discouraged."—*Tr.*

opened and there inside it was the body of a newborn baby she had murdered. In the same box were found the skeletons of two other babies she had done away with, as she herself confessed, at the moment of their birth. Gentlemen of the jury, was she a mother to her children? It is true, she gave birth to them, but was she a mother to them? Would any one of you make so bold as to confer on her the sacred name of mother? Let us be bold, gentlemen of the jury, let us be daring even, for it is our duty to be so at this moment and not be afraid of certain words and ideas, like the Moscow merchants' wives who are afraid to hear certain words they do not understand. No, let us, on the contrary, prove that the progress of recent years has affected our development too, and let us say frankly: a man who begets a child does not become its father unless he both begets it and shows himself deserving of the name. Oh, no doubt, there's another meaning, another interpretation, of the word 'father', which demands that my father, though he be a monster, though he may maltreat his children, is yet my father simply by having begotten me. But that meaning is, so to speak, something mystical, which I cannot grasp in my mind, but can only accept by faith, or, better still, *on faith,* like many other things which I do not understand but religion bids me believe. But, in that case, let it remain beyond the sphere of actual life. In that sphere, which not only has its own rights but itself imposes great duties—in that sphere, if we want to be humane and, indeed, Christians, we must and are obliged to act upon convictions justified by reason and experience, conducted through the crucible of analysis; in short, we must act reasonably and not recklessly, as though in a dream or delirium, so as to cause harm to no man and so as to torment and ruin no man. Only then will that be real Christian work, only not mystical but reasonable and displaying true love of man—"

At this point there was loud applause in many parts of the courtroom but Fetyukovich waved his hands as though imploring them not to interrupt but to let him complete his speech. A hush at once fell over the court. The speaker went on:

"Do you think, gentlemen of the jury, that such questions can pass our children by, let us say, when they are in their youth and begin to reason? No, they cannot, and we shall not demand impossible restraint from them! The sight of an unworthy father involuntarily evokes painful questions in a youth's mind, especially when he compares him to the worthy fathers of other children of the same age as he. He is given the standard answer to this question: 'He begot you and you are his flesh and blood; therefore, it is your duty to love him.' The youth cannot help reflecting: 'But did he love me when he begot me?' he asks, wondering more and more. 'Was it for my sake that he begot me? He did not know me, nor even my sex, at that moment, at that moment of passion, perhaps under the influence of drink, and, I suppose, all he has passed down to me is his proneness to drink—those are all the benefits I have got from him—Why, then, should I love him? Only for having begot me and not caring for me later all his life long?' Oh, you may think these questions crude and cruel, but do not demand of a young mind a restraint that is impossible! 'Drive nature out of the door and it will fly in through the window', and most of all, most of all, let us not be afraid of certain specific words; let us decide the matter as dictated by reason and humaneness and not as enjoined by mystical notions. How, then, is it to be decided? Why, like this: let the son confront his father and ask him: 'Tell me, Father, why should I love you? Father, prove to me that I should love you!' And if the father is able and in a condition to reply, and prove it to him, then we are dealing with a genuine and normal family, one based, not merely on mystical prejudice but on reasonable, responsible, and strictly humane foundations. Conversely, if the father cannot prove it, the family at once falls apart: he is no father, and the son is free and entitled, in future, to consider his father a stranger, even his enemy. Our tribune, gentlemen of the jury, should be a school of truth and wholesome notions!"

Here the speaker was interrupted by irrepressible and almost frenzied applause. Of course, the applause did not come from the entire courtroom, but yet a good half did applaud. The fathers and the mothers applauded. Shrieks and screams were to be heard from the gallery where the ladies were sitting. Handkerchiefs were waved. The presiding judge began ringing his bell with all his might. He was visibly annoyed by the behaviour of the public, but dared not "clear" the court, as he had threatened to do earlier: even the eminent personages, old men with decorations on their frock-coats, who were sitting behind the rostrum on specially reserved seats, applauded and waved their handkerchiefs, so that when the noise died down, the presiding judge confined himself to repeating his stern promise to "clear" the court, and Fetyukovich, triumphant and agitated, continued his address.

"Gentlemen of the jury, you remember the dreadful night so much has been spoken of today, when the son climbed over the fence, got into the house and, finally confronted, face to face, the man who had begotten him, his enemy and his tormentor. I insist with all the force at my command that he had not come at that moment for the money: the charge of robbery is absurd, as I have already explained. And it was not to murder him that he broke into the house—oh no! If he had devised that deliberately, he would at least have provided himself with a weapon beforehand, for he instinctively grabbed the brass pestle without knowing why. Let us suppose that he deceived his father by the signals and got into the house—I have said already that I do not for a moment believe that story, but, never mind, let us for a moment assume it to be true! Gentlemen of the jury, I swear to you by all that is sacred that if his tormentor had been not his father but a complete stranger he would have dashed through the rooms and, after making sure that the woman was not there, would have rushed off without causing any harm to his rival, except that he might have struck him or pushed him aside, but nothing more, for he had no thought or time for that; he had to find out where she was. But his father, his father—oh, the sight of his father, the man who had hated him since his childhood, his enemy, his tormentor, and now his monstrous rival, was the cause of everything! He was involuntarily overcome by a feeling of hatred—irresistibly, for there was no time for reflection: it all surged up in him in an instant. It was an impulse of frenzy and madness, but an impulse of nature, avenging the violation of its eternal laws irresistibly and unconsciously, like everything in nature. But even then the accused did not kill him—I firmly maintain that; I cry that aloud—no, he merely brandished the pestle at him in an outburst of indignant revulsion, without wishing to kill, not knowing that he would kill. But for that fateful pestle in his hand, he would, perhaps, have only assaulted his father, but not killed him. As he ran away, he did not know whether the old man he had felled was dead or not. Such a murder is no murder. No, the murder of such a father cannot be called parricide. Such a murder can only be considered parricide by prejudice. But did such a murder actually take place? I conjure you again and again from the bottom of my heart! Gentlemen of the jury, if we condemn him, he will say to himself: 'These people have done nothing for me, for my upbringing, or my education; they have done nothing to make me better, make a man of me. These people have not given me food or drink; they have not visited me in my prison nakedness and now they have sent me to penal servitude. I am quits; I owe them nothing now, and I don't owe anything to anyone for ever and ever. They are spiteful and I shall be spiteful, too. They are cruel, and I shall be cruel, too.' That's what he will say, gentlemen of the jury. And I assure you that, by your verdict of guilty, you will only make things easier for him; you will ease his conscience; he will curse the blood he has shed, but not regret it. And at the same time, you will destroy in him the man he could have become, for he will remain blind and unforgiving all his life. Should you not rather punish him fearfully, terribly, with the most dreadful punishment imaginable, but in a way that will save and regenerate his soul for ever? If so, then crush him with your mercy! You will see, you will hear, now his soul will flinch back in horror: 'Is it for me to endure this mercy? Do I deserve so much love? Am I worthy of it?'—that is what he will exclaim! Oh, I know, I know that heart, that reckless but noble heart, gentlemen of the jury. It will bow down to your magnanimity. It thirsts after a great act of love; it will blaze up and revive for ever! There are men who narrow-mindedly accuse the whole world. But crush such a soul with mercy, show it love, and it will curse its own actions, for there are a great many potentialities for good in it. The soul will dilate and will see that God is merciful, and that men are just and fair-minded. It will be horror-stricken, crushed by remorse and the great debt to be repaid henceforth. Then such a man will say not, 'I'm quits,' but, 'I am guilty in the eyes of all men and I am the most unworthy of all.' With tears of repentance and poignant and tender emotion, he will cry out: 'Others are better than I am, for they have wanted to save me, not to ruin me!' Oh, you can do that, perform that act of mercy with such ease, for in the absence of evidence in any way resembling the truth you will find it too hard to pronounce: 'Yes, he is guilty!' Better release ten that are guilty than punish a single innocent man—do you hear, do you hear that majestic voice from the past century of our glorious history? Is it for so insignificant a person as I am to remind you that Russian courts do not exist for punishment alone, but also for the salvation of the lost man? Let other nations adhere to the letter of the law and to punishment; we will adhere to its spirit and meaning: the salvation and regeneration of the lost. And if that is so, if Russia and her courts of justice are really such, then let her advance along that road, and do not, do not frighten us with your frenzied troikas from which all nations stand aloof with revulsion! Not a furious troika, but the majestic Russian chariot will, with solemn majesty, reach its destination. The fate of my client is in your hands, and in your hands is the fate of our Russian truth. You will save it, vindicate it, and prove that there are men to maintain it, and that it is in good hands!'"

14.

The Muzhiks Stand up for Themselves

It was thus that Fetyukovich wound up his speech, and this time the enthusiasm of his listeners was as irrepressible as a tempest. It was already quite impossible to curb it: women wept, many men wept, too, and even a couple of important personages shed tears. The presiding judge yielded and was even slow to ring his bell: "To encroach upon such enthusiasm," as our ladies cried out afterwards, "would be encroaching upon something sacred." The speaker himself was sincerely moved. And it was at such a moment that our public prosecutor rose again "to raise some objections". He was met with looks of hatred. "What? What is he up to? How dare he object?" the ladies murmured. But even if the ladies of the entire world, headed by the public prosecutor's wife herself, had murmured, he could not have been held back at that moment. He was pale, and trembling with excitement; the first words, the first sentences he uttered were even unintelligible: he was gasping for breath, his delivery poor, and the wording shaky. However, he soon regained control of himself. But I will quote only a few sentences from his second speech.

"...I'm reproached with having woven pieces of fiction. But what about the counsel for the defence? Hasn't he been piling one romance on top of another? All that was lacking was verses. In expectation of his mistress, Fyodor Pavlovich tears the envelope open and throws it on the floor. Even what he said on this remarkable occasion had been quoted. Is that not a poem? And where is the proof that he did extract the money? Who heard what he said? The feeble-minded idiot Smerdyakov who has been transformed into a kind of Byronic hero and avenges himself on society for his illegitimate birth—isn't that a poem in the Byronic spirit? And the son who bursts into his father's house, murders him and yet does not murder him—that is not even a romance or poem, but a sphinx setting a riddle which, needless to say, he cannot himself solve. If he did murder him, he did so, but how could he have murdered him and yet not murdered him—who can understand that? Then we are admonished that ours is a tribune of truth and wholesome notions, and from this tribune of 'wholesome notions' an axiom is proclaimed, backed with a solemn enjoinder that to call the murder of a father 'patricide' is simply a prejudice! But what will become of us if parricide is a prejudice, if any child will ask his father: 'Father, why should I love you?' Then what will become of us, what will become of the foundations of society? Whither the family? Parricide, you see, is just a bogey word to frighten Moscow merchants' wives of their wits with. The most precious, the most sacred precepts concerning the

542

purpose and the future of Russian justice are presented in a perverted and frivolous form with the sole aim of justifying what is unjustifiable. Oh, the counsel for the defence exclaims: crush him with mercy. But that is all the criminal wants, and tomorrow it will be seen how crushed he will be! And is not the counsel for the defence too modest in demanding only the acquittal of the accused? Why not demand the founding of a scholarship named after the parricide to commemorate the exploit for posterity and with the younger generation? Religion and the Gospels are amended: that is all mysticism, we are told, but ours, you see, is the only true Christianity, which has stood up to the test of analysis by reason and wholesome ideas. And so a false image of Christ is set up before us. *'With what measure ye mete, it shall be measured to you again,'* the counsel for the defence exclaims, and in the same breath draws the conclusion that Christ teaches to measure as is measured to us—and that from the tribune of truth and wholesome notions! He consults the Gospels only on the eve of his speeches so as to parade his acquaintance with what is, after all, a quite original work, which can come in useful and serve to create an impression when and as required! But Christ commands us not act in that way but to eschew acting thus, because that is what the wicked world does, while we should forgive and turn the other cheek, and not mete out in the same measure in which those who offend us measure to us. That is what God teaches us, and not that it is a prejudice to forbid the murder of fathers. And we will not, from the tribune of truth and wholesome notions, amend the Gospels of our Lord, whom the counsel for the defence deigns to call only the 'crucified Lover of mankind', contrary to all of Orthodox Russia, which calls out to him 'For thou art the Lord our God!'—"

At this the presiding judge intervened to curb the over-zealous prosecutor, asking him not to exaggerate, to keep within proper bounds and so on, as presiding judges always do in such instances. Besides, the public, too, were getting restive. People were stirring in their seats and there were even outcries of indignation. Fetyukovich did not even object. He mounted the tribune, a hand pressed to his heart, only to pronounce, in an injured tone, a few words full of dignity. He merely again touched lightly and ironically upon "fiction" and "psychology" and at a certain point very appropriately remarked, "Jupiter, thou art wrathful, therefore thou art wrong", which provoked a burst of approving laughter in the courtroom, for our public prosecutor certainly bore no resemblance to Jupiter. As for the accusation that he permitted the younger generation to murder their fathers, Fetyukovich observed with great dignity that he would not even rebut it. As for the public prosecutor's remark about "the false image of Christ" and that he had not deigned to refer to Christ as our Lord, but had called him only "the crucified Lover of mankind", which was "contrary to Orthodoxy" and should not have been spoken from the tribune of truth and wholesome notions, Fetyukovich hinted at an "insinuation" and that, in coming to that place, he had at least counted on that tribune being a safeguard against accusations "dangerous to my person as a citizen and loyal subject—" But at these words, the presiding judge cut him short, too, and Fetyukovich concluded his reply with a bow, and returned to his seat to the accompaniment of a general murmur of approval in the courtroom. In the opinion of our ladies, the public prosecutor had been "crushed for good".

Then the accused was asked if he had anything to say. Mitya rose to his feet but said very little. He was utterly exhausted both morally and physically. The air of strength and independence with which he had appeared in court in the morning was almost gone. He seemed to have lived through an experience that day that would last all his life long and had taught him and inculcated in him something highly important he had not previously understood. His voice was weak; he no longer shouted as before. There was something new, submissive, defeated and dispirited in his words.

"What am I to say, gentlemen of the jury? My hour of judgement has come and I feel the hand of God upon me. The end has come to a dissolute man! But, as confessing to God, I say to you: 'No, I am guiltless of my father's blood!' I repeat for the last time: 'It was not I who murdered him!' I have been dissolute, but I have loved goodness. At every moment I have striven to reform, but I have lived like a wild beast. I thank the prosecutor; he has told me many things about myself that I did not know, but it is untrue that I murdered my father. There he was mistaken. I thank the counsel for the defence, too. I wept as I listened to him, but it is untrue that I murdered my father and there was no need even to assume that! And don't believe the doctors either: I am of sound mind but my heart is heavy. If you spare me, if you acquit me, I will pray for you. I will be a better man. I give you my word. I give it to you before God. And if you condemn me, I shall break my sword over my head myself and kiss the pieces! But spare me. Do not deprive me of my God. I know myself, I shall murmur against him! My heart is heavy, gentlemen—spare me!"

He almost fell back in his seat; his voice faltered, and he could scarcely articulate the last sentence. Then the court proceeded to formulate the questions and both sides were asked to sum up their conclusions. But I will not describe the details. Finally, the jury rose to retire. The presiding judge looked very jaded and, therefore, his summing up was rather weak. "Try to be impartial," he said. "Do not be swayed by the eloquence of the counsel for the defence. Yet weigh the evidence carefully. Remember that a great responsibility has been laid upon you", and so on. The jury withdrew and the hearing was adjourned. It was now possible to get up, stretch one's legs, exchange one's impressions, and take refreshments at the buffet. It was very late, almost an hour after midnight, but no one thought of leaving. The public were so keyed up that there could be no lull. There was an atmosphere of throbbing expectancy, though it was not universal. The ladies were merely hysterically impatient, but untroubled at heart: "Acquittal is certain." They were all prepared for a dramatic moment of general enthusiasm. I must admit that among the men, too, there were a great many who were convinced an acquittal was inevitable. Some were pleased, others frowned, and yet others walked about looking crestfallen: they did not want an acquittal! Fetyukovich himself was quite confident of success. He was surrounded by people, who congratulated him and fawned upon him.

"There are invisible threads," he said to a group, as was

545

reported afterwards, "which connect the counsel for the defence with the jury. They are established and anticipated during the speech itself. I sensed them. Those threads exist. We have won, rest assured."

"But what will our dear muzhiks say now?" a stout and pock-marked gentleman, a local landowner, said with a frown, as he approached a group of gentlemen who were engaged in conversation.

"But they aren't all muzhiks. Four of the jurymen are civil servants."

"Yes, that's true," said a member of the local agricultural board, joining the group.

"And do you know Nazaryev, Prokhor Ivanovich, that merchant with the medal, one of the jurymen?"

"What about him?"

"A smart fellow."

"But he never opens his mouth."

"He doesn't, but so much the better. He has nothing to learn from the St. Petersburg lawyer: he could teach all of St. Petersburg himself. He's the father of twelve children. Think of that!"

"But, good heavens, won't he be acquitted?" a young civil servant cried in another group.

"They're certain to acquit him," a determined voice replied.

"It would be a shame and a disgrace if he were not acquitted," the civil servant exclaimed. "Suppose he did kill him, but there are different kinds of fathers! And, after all, he was in such a state of frenzy— He really may have just brandished the pestle and the old man fell down. A pity, though, that they dragged the servant in. That was just a ridiculous episode. In Fetyukovich's stead I'd have simply said: he murdered him, but he isn't guilty, and to hell with you!"

"But he did do that, except that he did not say 'to hell with you'."

"No, Mikhail Semyonovich, he as good as said so," a third voice put in.

"But, good heavens, gentlemen, was not an actress acquitted

in our town during Lent after cutting the throat of her lover's wife."

"But she did not cut deep enough."

"It makes no difference. She started cutting it!"

"And how do you like what he said about the children? Splendid!"

"Splendid!"

"And what about mysticism? About mystical ideas, eh?"

"Oh, never mind mysticism," someone else cried. "Think of our poor public prosecutor! What do you think his life will be worth from now on? Why, his wife will scratch his eyes out tomorrow for the things he said about her dear Mitya!"

"She isn't here, is she?"

"No, of course not. If she'd been here she'd have scratched his eyes out already. She's at home with toothache. Ha, ha, ha!"

"Ha, ha, ha!"

In a third group:

"I suppose Mitya will be acquitted after all."

"I expect he'll wreck the Metropolis Inn tomorrow. He'll be drinking hard for the next fortnight."

"He's a devil!"

"Aye, the devil's involved all right. Without him, nothing would have happened. Where should he be if not here?"

"Gentlemen, eloquence is a fine thing, I grant you, but, people shouldn't bash their fathers' heads, should they? Or what are we coming to?"

"The chariot, the chariot, remember?"

"Yes, he made a chariot out of a cart."

"And tomorrow he'll make a cart out of a chariot, 'as the circumstances may require, always as the circumstances may require'."

"People are so sharp nowadays. Is there any justice in Russia, gentlemen, or doesn't it exist at all?"

But the bell rang. The jury had been absent for exactly an hour, neither more nor less. As soon as the public had resumed their seats, a deep silence fell over the courtroom. I remember the jury trooping back into the courtroom. At last! I shall not cite the questions in their due order. I've forgotten them, anyway. I only remember their reply to the first and most important question of the presiding judge, namely: "Did the accused commit the murder for the sake of robbery and with malicious intent?" (I don't remember the exact wording.) All breaths were held. The foreman of the jury, the civil servant who was the youngest member of the jury, announced in a loud and clear voice amid the dead silence in the courtroom:

"Yes, we find him guilty!"

And the same reply was forthcoming to every question: guilty, yes, guilty, and without any extenuating circumstance! That was something no one had expected, for practically all were convinced that there would at least be a recommendation for mercy. The dead silence in the courtroom was unbroken. All, both those who had longed for his conviction and those who had longed for his acquittal, seemed literally petrified, but that was only for a few minutes. After that, uproar arose. Many of the men were highly pleased. Some even rubbed their hands, without concealing their delight. Those who were displeased with the verdict seemed crushed, shrugged their shoulders, whispered among themselves, but did not seem to have fully realised what had happened. But, dear me, what came over our poor ladies! I thought they would stage a riot. At first, they did not seem to believe their ears. But suddenly loud exclamations resounded throughout the courtroom: "What's the meaning of this? What's all this?" They jumped up from their seats apparently believing that it was possible to change and reverse the verdict immediately. At that moment, Mitya rose and shouted in a heart-rending voice, stretching out his hands before him:

"I swear by God and His Last Judgement I'm not guilty of my father's blood! Katya, I forgive you! Brothers, friends, spare the other woman."

He did not go on, and burst into dreadful sobs, his voice strange and unnatural, seeming not his own, and resounding throughout the courtroom. From the farthermost corner of the gallery came a piercing shriek: it was Grushenka. She had besought someone to let her in before the addresses of counsel.

Mitya was taken away. The pronouncement of the sentence was put off for the following day. The entire court rose in a turmoil, but I did not wait or listen. I only remember a few exclamations on the steps outside the court.

"He'll get a good taste of twenty years in the mines."

"No less."

"Yes, sir, our dear muzhiks have stood up for themselves."

"And made an end of our Mitya!"

End of the fourth and last part

EPILOGUE

1.

Schemes to Save Mitya

Very early, after eight in the morning, five days after Mitya's trial, Alyosha called on Katerina Ivanovna to reach a final understanding on a matter of great moment to both of them and, besides, to deliver a message. She was seated and spoke to him in the same room in which she had once received Grushenka; in the next room lay the unconscious Ivan Fyodorovich, in a high fever. Immediately after the scene in the courtroom Katerina Ivanovna had the sick and unconscious Ivan brought to her house, ignoring the future and inevitable gossip and the public disapproval. One of the two relatives who lived with her went off to Moscow immediately after the scene in the courtroom; the other stayed on. But even if both had gone, Katerina would not have changed her mind and would have gone on nursing the sick man and sitting by his side day and night. He was attended by Varvinsky and Herzenstube; the Moscow doctor had returned home, refusing to give an opinion as to the possible outcome of the illness. Though the other two doctors reassured Katerina Ivanovna and Alyosha, it was obvious that they could not as yet hold out any firm hopes for a recovery. Alyosha visited his sick brother twice a day. But this time he had some particular and rather bothersome matter to attend to and foresaw how difficult it would be to broach it, and yet he was in great haste: he had some other urgent business to see to that morning, at a different place, and he was pressed for time. They had been talking for a quarter of an hour. Katerina Ivanovna was pale, very tired, and at the same time in a state of violent agitation: she had a presentiment of the reason for Alyosha's call.

"Don't worry about his decision," she said with firm insistence to Alyosha. "He's bound to come to it in one way or another; he's certain to arrive at that solution; he's got to make a getaway. That unfortunate man, that paragon of honour and conscience—no, not Dmitri Fyodorovich, but the other one, who is lying beyond that door, who has sacrificed himself for his brother's sake," Katerina added with flashing eyes, "told me of the entire escape plan a long time ago. You know, he has already made the contacts— I've told you something already— You see, it will probably be staged at the third prison stopover when the party of convicts is on the road to Siberia. Oh, it's still a long way off. Ivan Fyodorovich has already been to see the man who will be in charge of the prisoners at the third stop. What we don't yet know is who will be in charge of the convicts during the third stage, and that cannot be ascertained so far ahead. I may show you the entire plan in detail tomorrow; Ivan Fyodorovich left it with me on the eve of the trial, just in case— That was when—you remember—you found us quarrelling that evening; he was going down the stairs and, on seeing you, I made him return—remember? Do you know what we were quarrelling over at the time?"

"No, I don't," said Alyosha.

"Well, of course, he concealed it from you then: it was about the escape scheme. He had revealed its main features three days before, and it was then that we began and went on quarrelling for three days. It was because when he told me that, in case of his conviction, Dmitri Fyodorovich would flee abroad together with that creature, I suddenly grew furious—I can't tell you why, because I don't know myself— Oh, of course, over that creature and her fleeing abroad together with Dmitri!" Katerina Ivanovna suddenly exclaimed, her lips quivering with anger. "As soon as Ivan Fyodorovich saw that I was furious because of that creature, he immediately imagined that I was jealous of her and that therefore I still loved Dmitri. That was the reason for our first quarrel. I did not want to give any explanation and I could not ask for forgiveness; I resented such a man suspecting that I was still in love with that— And considering I myself had long before told him quite frankly that I did not love Dmitri and that I loved him alone! I was furious because of resentment over that creature. Three days later, on the evening you came, he brought me a sealed envelope and asked me to open it at once if anything happened to him. Oh, he foresaw his illness! He revealed to me that the envelope contained the details of the escape and that, if he were to die or be taken dangerously ill, I should save Mitya on my own. He then left the money with me, almost ten thousand—the bonds the public prosecutor mentioned in his speech, after learning from someone that he had sent them to be exchanged. What struck me so forcibly at the time was that Ivan Fyodorovich, though still jealous of me and still convinced that I was in love with Mitya, should not have given up his idea of rescuing his brother, and entrusted me with the scheme to save him. Oh, that was a sacrifice! No, Alexei Fyodorovich, you will never be able to fully understand such a sacrifice. I felt like falling down at his feet in reverence, but then it suddenly occurred to me that he'd take it merely as an expression of my joy that Mitya would be saved (and he'd certainly have thought that!); so exasperated was I at the time at the mere possibility of such an unjust thought on his part that I got angry again and instead of kissing his feet, I made another scene! Oh, I'm so unfortunate! Such is my nature—my awful and unfortunate nature! Oh, you will see: I shall most certainly drive him to a point when, like Dmitri, he, too, will give me up for another woman he'll find it easier to get on with, but then—oh, then I'll be unable to bear it—I'll kill myself! And when you entered that evening and I called out to you and told him to return, I was so enraged by the look of contempt and hatred he gave me that—you remember—I shouted to you that *he, he alone* had made me believe that his brother Dmitri was the murderer. I purposely said that slanderous thing about him to hurt him again, for he never, never assured me that his brother was a murderer. On the contrary, it was I, I who persuaded him. Oh, my wild rage was the cause of everything, everything! It was I, I who made that horrible scene at the trial. He wanted to prove to me that he was an honourable man and, though I might love his brother, he would not ruin him out of jealousy and revenge. That's why he appeared in court— I'm the cause of it all! I alone am to blame!"

Never before had Katya made such a confession to Alyosha, who felt that she had now reached that degree of intolerable suffering when even the proudest heart crushes its pride in anguish, and falls vanquished by grief. Oh, Alyosha knew still another terrible cause of her present agony, however much she had tried to conceal it from him all during those days since Mitya's conviction; but for some reason it would have been extremely painful to him had she decided so to abase herself as to speak to him now about that, too. She was suffering over her "treachery" at the trial, and Alyosha felt that her conscience was urging her to make a clean breast of it to him, Alyosha, especially, with tears, screams, and hysterical writhings. But he dreaded that moment and wished to spare the sufferer. It made the message he had come to give her all the more difficult. He again spoke of Mitya.

"Have no fear at all for him!" Katerina went on, with brusque insistence, "with him, everything is a fleeting thing. I know him. I know that heart only too well. Rest assured he'll agree to flee. The main thing is that it is not a matter of immediacy; there'll be time yet for him to make up his mind. Ivan Fyodorovich will have recovered by that time and will take it in hand himself, so that I won't have to do anything. Don't worry; he'll agree to flee. As a matter of fact, he has already agreed: can he give up that creature now? They won't let her join him in Siberia, so what else can he do but get away? The main thing is that he's afraid of you, afraid that, on moral grounds, you won't approve of his escape! But you must magnanimoushy *permit* it, if," Katerina added venomously, "your sanction is so essential." She paused with a bitter smile.

"He goes on talking," she began again, "about some hymns, some cross he has to bear, some duty of his. I remember Ivan Fyodorovich telling me a lot about it then, and if only you knew how he spoke about it!" Katerina suddenly exclaimed with irrepressible feeling. "If only you knew how he loved that wretched man at the moment he was telling me about him, and how he hated him, perhaps, at the very same time. And I—oh, I listened to his story and watched his tears with a haughty sneer. Oh, what a horrible creature! It is I, I who am that horrible creature! I have brought about his brain fever! But that one—the convicted man—is he ready to accept suffering? Can such as he suffer?" Katerina concluded irritably. "His kind never suffer."

There was a feeling of hatred and contemptuous distaste in her words. And yet it was she who had betrayed him. "I suppose," Alyosha thought to himself, "it is because she feels so guilty towards him that she hates him at times." He would have preferred it to be only "at times". He heard a challenge in Katerina's last words, but he did not take it up.

"I asked you to come to see me this morning," she said, "to get your promise to persuade him yourself. Or do you, too, think it dishonourable, or unheroic or, how shall I put it, un-Christian, perhaps, to flee?" Katerina added in an even more challenging tone.

"No, I don't," Alyosha murmured. "I'll tell him everything. He asked me to tell you that he'd like to see you today," he blurted out, looking firmly into her eyes.

She gave a violent start and almost recoiled from him on the sofa.

"Me? Can that be?" she murmured, turning pale.

"It can and must be!" Alyosha declared emphatically, growing greatly animated. "He needs you very badly, especially now. I wouldn't have brought it up and tormented you before the time but for the necessity. He's sick, almost out of his mind, and keeps on asking for you. It isn't to make it up with you that he wants you to come; all he wants is that you should go and show yourself. A lot has come over him since that day. He realises how boundlessly he has wronged you. It isn't your forgiveness he wants—'I can't be forgiven,' he himself says, but merely that you should show yourself at the threshold—"

"It's so sudden—" Katerina muttered. "I've had a presentiment all these days that you'd come with such a message—I knew he would ask me to come— But it's impossible!"

"It may be impossible, but do so. Remember it's the first time he's been struck by the thought that he's insulted you, the first time in his life. He's never, never realised it so fully before. He says that if you refuse to come, he'll be unhappy all his life. Do you hear? A convict sentenced to twenty years' hard labour still hopes for happiness—isn't that pitiful? Think of it: you'll be visiting a man whose life has been wrecked, though he is innocent," Alyosha blurted out, challengingly. "His hands are clean; there's no blood on them! Go and see him now for the sake of his infinite future suffering. Go, see him off into the darkness—stand in his doorway—that is all— You must, you simply *must* do it!" concluded Alyosha, with great emphasis on the word "must".

"I must, but—I can't," Katerina said, with a kind of moan. "He will look at me—I can't."

"Your eyes must meet. How can you live on if you won't make up your mind now?"

"I'd rather suffer all my life."

"You must come, you *must* come," Alyosha again emphasised remorselessly.

"But why today? Why just now?— I can't leave the sick man—"

"You can for a short while. It won't take long. If you don't come, he'll be in a fever tonight. I won't tell you an untruth. Have pity on him!"

"Have pity on *me*!" Katerina reproached him bitterly and burst into tears.

"Then you will!" Alyosha said firmly, seeing her tears. "I'll go and tell him that you'll be coming presently."

"No, don't tell him on any account," cried the frightened Katerina. "I'll come, but don't tell him in advance, because I'll come but may not go in— I don't know yet—"

Her voice failed her. She had difficulty in breathing. Alyosha got up to leave.

"But what if I should meet someone?" she suddenly said in a low voice, turning deathly pale again.

"That's why you must go now so as not to meet anyone there. There won't be anyone, you may be certain of that. We shall be expecting you," he concluded with insistence, and left the room.

2.

A Lie Becomes a Momentary Truth

He hurried off to the hospital where Mitya was now an inmate. On the second day after the verdict, he had fallen ill with a brain fever and had been placed in the convict ward of our town hospital. But at the request of Alyosha and many others (including Mrs. Khokhlakov and Lise), Dr. Varvinsky had Mitya kept, not with the convicts but in a separate cubicle, the same where Smerdyakov had been. True, a sentry was stationed at the end of the corridor, and the window was barred, so that Varvinsky could be easy in his mind about his not quite lawful indulgence, but he was a kindly and compassionate young man. He realised how hard it must be for a man like Mitya to step so suddenly into the company of thieves and murderers, which one had first to get used to. Visits by relatives and friends were sanctioned by the doctor, the prison governor, and even by the uyezd chief of police, though it was all on the quiet. However, only Alyosha and Grushenka had visited Mitya during those few days. Rakitin had made two attempts to see him, but Mitya insistently asked the doctor not to admit him.

Alyosha found him sitting on his bed in a hospital dressing-gown, slightly feverish, with a towel soaked in vinegar and water about his head. He gave Alyosha a somewhat vague look as the latter entered the room, but in his eyes there briefly appeared a kind of fear.

In general, he had grown greatly preoccupied since the trial. At times, he was silent for a full half hour, apparently pondering perplexedly over something, and quite oblivious of his visitor. If he did emerge from his reverie and begin to talk, he always did so somehow abruptly, and never said what he really wanted to. He sometimes gazed at his brother with an expression of suffering. With Grushenka, he seemed to be more at ease than with Alyosha. True, he hardly ever spoke to her, but his face lit up with happiness as soon as she entered. Alyosha sat down silently on the bed by his side. This time he had been waiting anxiously for Alyosha, but did not dare to ask him anything. He considered Katerina's consent to see him unthinkable, yet he felt her failure to come would be something quite impossible. Alyosha understood his feelings.

"Trifon," Mitya began nervously. "Trifon, I'm told, has turned his whole inn upside down: pulled up the floor-boards, torn up the planks, and picked his veranda to pieces, looking for buried treasure all the time—the fifteen hundred roubles the public prosecutor said I'd hidden there. As soon as he got back home, I'm told, he began turning the place into a shambles. Serves him right, the swindler! The hospital caretaker told me about it yesterday; he comes from over there."

"Listen," said Alyosha, "she will come, but I don't know when: perhaps today, perhaps in a few days; I don't know, but come she will, for a certainty."

Mitya started; he was about to say something, but was silent. The effect of the news was startling. He was clearly very anxious to learn the details of the talk but was afraid to ask now: any harsh and contemptuous remark by Katerina would have been a severe blow at the moment.

"Incidentally this is what she said: tell him to set his mind quite at ease about a getaway. Even if Ivan is not well by then, she'll see to it herself."

"You've already told me about that," Mitya observed musingly.

"And you've let Grushenka know of it already," observed Alyosha.

"Yes," Mitya admitted. "She won't be coming this morning," he went on, with a timid look at his brother. "She'll be here only in the evening. As soon as I told her that Katerina was taking care of things, she was silent, but made a wry face. She just whispered: "Let her!" She realised that it was something really important. I dared not try her further. By now, I should think she has realised that the other one loves Ivan and not me, hasn't she?"

"But has she?" Alyosha blurted out.

"Well, perhaps not. Only she won't be coming this morning," Mitya hastened to point out again. "I've asked her to do something for me. Listen, Alyosha, Ivan will soon surpass us all.

It is he, not we, who should go on living. He will recover."

"Just imagine, though Katerina trembles for him, she has hardly any doubt that he will recover," said Alyosha.

"That means she's sure he'll die. It's her fear that makes her so sure he'll recover."

"Ivan's is of a strong constitution," Alyosha observed anxiously. "I, too, have every hope that he will recover."

"Yes, he will. But she's certain he'll die. She's tasted so much grief—"

There was a moment of silence; something very important was tormenting Mitya.

"Alyosha," he said suddenly in a trembling and tearful voice, "I love Grushenka terribly."

"They won't let her join you *there*," Alyosha at once put in.

"And there's something else I wanted to tell you," Mitya went on in a suddenly ringing voice, "if they start flogging me on the way or *there*, I won't let them. I'll kill someone and be shot. And that is for twenty years! Even here they talk to me with familiarity. The guards do. I've been lying here all night passing judgement on myself: I'm not ready! I can't take it! I wanted to sing a 'hymn', but I can't put up with the familiarity of the guards! I can put up with anything for Grushenka's sake, anything—except beatings. But she won't be allowed to join me *there*."

Alyosha smiled gently. "Listen, brother, once and for all," he said. "This is what I think of the matter. You know I won't lie to you. Listen: you're not ready and such a cross is not for you. Moreover, since you're not prepared for it, you don't need such a martyr's cross. Had you murdered Father, I'd regret your rejection of your cross. But you're innocent and such a cross is too much for you. You wanted, through torment, to regenerate another man in you; as I see it, it will suffice for you to remember that other man always, all your life long, and wherever you may flee— Your not having accepted the great anguish of the cross will only serve to enhance your sense of duty, and by that unending feeling you will help your future regeneration throughout your lifetime, perhaps more than if you went *there*. For there, you won't be able to endure it and will rebel, and may end up by finally saying, 'I'm quits!' The lawyer was speaking the truth in this instance. It is not for everyone to bear heavy burdens; for some they are impossible—Those are my thoughts if you need them so much. If others—officers or soldiers—would be held responsible for your escape, I wouldn't 'permit' it," Alyosha smiled. "But they say (the man in charge of the stopover arrangement for the convicts himself told Ivan) that, provided everything is properly arranged, the reprimand won't be severe and that they can get off easily. Of course, bribing is dishonest even in such a case, but here it is not for me to pass judgement; for, in fact, if I were instructed by Ivan or Katerina to make all the necessary arrangements for your getaway, I know I would go and bribe whoever had to be bribed; I must tell you the whole truth. And that's why I cannot set myself up as a judge of your actions. But know that I shall never condemn you. And it would be strange if I were to judge you in this, wouldn't it? Well, I think I've gone into everything."

"But I shall condemn myself!" cried Mitya. "I shall flee—that has been decided without you: could Mitya Karamazov fail to get away? But I shall condemn myself for it and there I shall expiate my sin for ever. That's what the Jesuits say, isn't it? Just as we are doing now—eh?"

"Yes," Alyosha smiled gently.

"I love you for always telling the pure truth and never holding anything back," cried Mitya with a joyous laugh. "So that I've caught my Alyosha acting like a Jesuit! I ought to kiss you for that! Now listen to the rest: I shall reveal the other half of my soul to you. Here's what I've devised and decided: if I get away, even with money and a passport, even to America, I'll be buoyed up by the thought that I'm not fleeing to a life of joy and happiness, but truly for a life of no less trials and tribulations than here. No worse, Alexei, I tell in all truth, no worse. I already hate America, damn that country. I hate it already. Even if Grushenka is there with me, can you imagine her as an American? She's Russian, Russian through and through and she'll be pining for her native land. I'll see all the time that she's miserable for my sake, and that she's taken up the cross for me, but what has she done to deserve that? And do you think I could tolerate the outcasts there, even if any one of those people is a better man than me? I hate that America even now! And even if the people over there are all marvellous mechanics or whatever, down to the last man—to hell with them; they are not my own people, not people after my heart! I love Russia, Alexei; I love the Russian God, though I'm a blackguard! Why," he cried, his eyes flashing suddenly, "I'll die like a cur over there!" His voice was trembling with tears.

"So here's what I've decided," he began again, suppressing his agitation. "Listen, Alexei. As soon as Grushenka and I get there, I shall set to work, tilling the soil somewhere far away, in solitude, close to the wild bears. After all, some distant place can be found there, too! There are still Red Indians there, I'm told, somewhere beyond the horizon. Well, it's there we shall at once get down to grammar, Grushenka and I. Work and grammar, and thus for the next three years. During those three years we shall learn to speak English like any Englishman. And as soon as we've learnt it—farewell, America! We'll come running back here to Russia, as American citizens. Don't worry, we won't return here to this little town. We'll find refuge somewhere far away in the north or in the south. I shall have changed by that time. So will she. There, in America, some doctor will fix some kind of wart for me—it's not for nothing they're such fine mechanics! And if that can't be done, I shall pluck out an eye, grow a beard a yard long, a grey one (I shall turn grey, yearning for Russia)—and I'll never be recognised. And if I am, let them pack me off to Siberia. I don't care—it'll be just my bad luck! Here, too, we shall till the soil somewhere in the wilds, and I shall pretend to be an American all my life. But we'll die in our native land. That's my scheme, and it's all definite. Do you approve?"

"I do," said Alyosha, unwilling to contradict him.

Mitya was silent for a while, and said suddenly:

"And how well they got it all fixed at the trial! All done so neatly!"

"Even if they hadn't, they would have found you guilty all the same," Alyosha said with a sigh.

"Yes, the public here are fed up with me! That can't be helped, I suppose, but it's hard!" Mitya moaned miserably.

Again they were silent for a while.

"Alyosha," Mitya exclaimed suddenly, "put me out of my misery at once! Tell me: is she coming now or not? What did she say? How did she say it?"

"She said she'd come, but I don't know whether it'll be today. It's hard for her, you know!" Alyosha looked timidly at Mitya.

"I should think so! Very hard on her! Alyosha, this will drive me out of my wits. Grushenka keeps looking at me. She understands. Lord, chasten me: what is it I am asking for? I am asking for Katya! Do I realise what I'm asking for? The beastly Karamazovian spirit is so headstrong! No, I'm not capable of suffering! I'm a blackguard, and that's all there is to it!"

"Here she comes!" cried Alyosha.

At that moment, Katerina suddenly appeared in the doorway. For an instant, she stopped dead, gazing at Mitya with a kind of dazed expression. Mitya jumped up. He looked scared and turned pale, but a timid and pleading smile appeared on his lips and, suddenly, he held out his hands impulsively to Katerina. Seeing this, she flew impetuously to him. She seized him by the hands and made him sit down on the bed almost by force. She herself sat down beside him, and, without letting go of his hands, squeezed them convulsively. They made several attempts to say something, but stopped short as though unable to tear their eyes away from each other, and gazed intently and wordlessly at each other with strange smiles. Two minutes thus passed.

"Have you forgiven me or not?" Mitya murmured at last, and at the same instant, turning to Alyosha with a face distorted with joy, he cried to him:

"Do you hear what I'm asking? Do you hear?"

"It's because you're generous at heart that I loved you!" were the words that suddenly escaped Katerina. "And you don't need my forgiveness—neither do I need yours, whether you forgive me or not—you'll always be a wound in my soul and I in yours—that's how it should be!" she stopped to take breath.

"But why have I come here?" she began again, hurriedly and frenziedly. "I've come to embrace your feet, to press your hands—like this, till it hurts, as I used to do in Moscow, remember? And to tell you again that you're my god, my joy, to tell you that I love you madly," she moaned in anguish, and suddenly pressed his hand ardently to her lips. Tears gushed from her eyes.

Alyosha stood in speechless embarrassment; he had never expected what he was witnessing.

"Love is done with, Mitya," Katerina went on, "but what's done with is painfully precious to me. I want you to remember that always. But now, just for a little while, let there be what could have been," she murmured with a drawn smile, gazing happily into his eyes again. "You love another woman now and I love another man, but for all that I shall always love you and you will love me—did you know that? Do you hear?" she exclaimed with an almost menacing catch in her voice. "D'you hear: love me all your life!"

"I shall and—you know, Katerina," Mitya said, drawing a deep breath at each word, "you know, five days ago, on that evening I loved you— When you collapsed and you were carried out— All my life long! It will be so, it will be so for ever—"

So they went on babbling almost meaningless, frantic, perhaps not even truthful, words, but at that moment it was the truth, and they believed themselves implicitly.

"Katya," cried Mitya suddenly, "do you believe I murdered him? I know you don't believe it now, but you did believe it then—when you were giving evidence— Surely, surely you did not believe it!"

"I did not believe it even then! I never believed it! I hated you and I suddenly persuaded myself—just at that moment— While I was giving evidence, I persuaded myself and I believed it, but when I had ended I ceased at once from believing. I want you to know all that. I've forgotten that I came here to punish myself," she said suddenly with a kind of new expression, quite unlike her love-lorn chatter a moment before.

"It's too much for you, woman!" the words escaped Mitya somehow quite uncontrollably.

"Let me go," she whispered. "I'll come again. It's too much for me now."

She rose but suddenly uttered a loud cry and started back. Grushenka entered the room suddenly but quite noiselessly. No one had expected her. Katerina made for the door, but, as she drew level with Grushenka, she suddenly stopped and, turning as white as a sheet, moaned softly almost in a whisper:

"Forgive me!"

Grushenka stared at her and, pausing for a moment, replied in a voice full of venomous hatred:

"We're unkind, the two of us! We're both unkind. How then are we to forgive each other— Save him and I'll pray for you all my life."

"Don't you want to forgive her?" Mitya cried to Grushenka with wild reproach.

"Don't worry, I'll save him for you!" Katerina whispered rapidly and ran out of the room.

"And how could you fail to forgive her after she herself had asked for forgiveness?" Mitya exclaimed bitterly again.

"Mitya, don't dare reproach her," Alyosha cried warmly. "You have no right to."

"It's her proud lips that spoke, not her heart," said Grushenka in a tone of revulsion. "I'll forgive her everything if she saves you—"

She fell silent, as though stifling something in her soul. She could not yet regain her self-control. She had come, as later transpired, quite by chance, without suspecting anything or expecting to meet what she had met.

"Alyosha, run after her!" Mitya turned impetuously to his brother. "Tell her—I don't know what—don't let her go away like that!"

"I'll come again towards the evening," Alyosha cried, and dashed off after Katerina.

He caught up with her outside the hospital walls. She was walking fast, hurriedly, but as soon as Alyosha caught up with her she said quickly:

"No, I cannot punish myself in front of that woman. I said
'Forgive me' to her because I wanted to punish myself to the
end. She did not forgive me— I like her for that!" Katerina
added in a strangled voice, her eyes flashing with savage resentment.

"Mitya was not expecting her at all," Alyosha murmured.
"He was certain she wouldn't come."

"No doubt. We won't go into that," she snapped. "Listen,
I can't go to the funeral with you now. I've sent them flowers.
I believe they've still got some money. If necessary, tell them I'll
never abandon them. And now leave me, please. You're late as
it is—the bells are ringing for late Mass— Please, leave me!"

3.

Little Ilyusha's Funeral.
The Speech at the Stone

He really was late. They had been waiting for him and had
already decided to bear the pretty, flower-covered little coffin
into the church in his absence. It was poor little Ilyusha's
coffin. He had passed away two days after Mitya had been sentenced. Alyosha was met at the gate by the shouts of the boys,
Ilyusha's schoolmates. They had been waiting impatiently for
him and were glad that he had come at last. There were twelve
of them in all, and they had all come with their satchels and
school-bags over their shoulders. "Daddy will be crying," Ilyusha had told them as he lay dying, "stay with Daddy", and the
boys remembered it. Kolya Krasotkin was at their head.

"I'm so glad you've come, Karamazov," he cried, holding
out a hand to Alyosha. "It's awful here. It really is painful to
witness. Snegiryov isn't drunk; we know for a fact that he hasn't
had a drop today, but he looks as if he were— I'm self-con-
trolled as a rule, but this is dreadful. May I ask you a question,
Karamazov, before you go in, if I am not keeping you?"

"What is it, Kolya?" Alyosha asked.

"Is your brother innocent or guilty? Did he murder his

father or did the servant do it? As you say, so it will be. The thought of it has kept me awake for four nights."

"The servant did it; my brother is innocent," replied Alyosha.

"I say the same," the boy Smurov cried suddenly.

"So he'll perish as an innocent sacrifice for the truth!" cried Kolya. "Though he has perished he is lucky, I could almost envy him!"

"What are you saying? How can you? And why?" cried Alyosha.

"Oh, if only I, too, could some day sacrifice myself for the truth!" said Kolya with enthusiasm.

"But not in a case like this," said Alyosha. "Not with such disgrace and such horror."

"Of course—I'd like to die for all mankind, and as for the disgrace, it makes no difference to me: let our names perish! I respect your brother."

"And so do I!" the boy who had once declared that he knew who founded Troy cried suddenly and unexpectedly from the crowd and blushed crimson to the roots of his hair as he had done that time.

Alyosha went into the room. Ilyusha, his hands clasped and his eyes closed, lay in a blue coffin with a white frill of gauze round it. The features of his emaciated face had scarcely changed and, strange to say, there was almost no odour of decay from the corpse. The expression of his face was earnest and seemed thoughtful. His hands, clasped on his breast, were especially beautiful, as though carved in marble. A bunch of flowers had been placed in them, and, indeed, the whole coffin was covered, outside and within, with flowers, sent early that morning by Lise Khokhlakov. But there were also flowers from Katerina Ivanovna, and when Alyosha opened the door, Snegiryov had a bunch of flowers in his trembling hands and was scattering them again over his darling boy. He barely glanced at Alyosha when he came in, and he would not look at anyone, not even at his crazed and weeping wife, his "Mummy", who kept trying to raise herself on her crippled legs to have a closer look at her dead boy. The children had raised

Nina's chair and placed her close to the coffin. She sat with her head pressed to it and was also apparently weeping softly. There was an animated but also bewildered and, at the same time, hard look on Snegiryov's face. There was something crazy about his gestures and the words that escaped him from time to time. "Old fellow, dear old fellow!" he exclaimed from time to time, gazing at Ilyusha. It had been his wont, when Ilyusha was still alive, to call him affectionately: "Old fellow, dear old fellow!"

"Daddy, give me some flowers, too," the crazy "Mummy" begged in a whimper. "Take one from his hands—that white one, and let me have it!" She had either taken a fancy to a little white rose in Ilyusha's hands or else she wanted to have a flower from his hand to keep in memory of him, but she fidgeted about restlessly, holding out her hands for the flower.

"I won't give anything, I won't give anything!" Snegiryov cried hard-heartedly. "The flowers are his, not yours. They're all his, not yours!"

"Daddy, do give Mother a flower," Nina said suddenly, raising her tear-stained face.

"I won't give anything, to her least of all. She didn't love him. She took his little cannon away, and he made her a present of it," Snegiryov said, bursting into loud sobs as he remembered how Ilyusha had given his cannon to his mother. The poor crazed woman began to weep noiselessly, burying her face in her hands. At last, the boys, seeing that the father would not budge from the coffin and that it was time to carry it out, suddenly gathered about it in a close circle, and began to raise it.

"I don't want him to be buried in the churchyard," Snegiryov suddenly cried. "I'll bury him by the stone, by our stone! That was Ilyusha's wish! I won't let him be taken there!"

For the last three days he had been saying that he would bury the boy at the stone, but Alyosha, Krasotkin, and the landlady, as well as the landlady's sister and the boys, had intervened.

"Fancy burying him by an unhallowed stone as though he had hanged himself," the old landlady said severely. "The ground in the churchyard is hallowed. He'll be prayed for there.

The sound of the singing will reach there from the church, and the deacon reads out so clearly and so well that all the words will fly over him every time, just as though it was being read over his grave."

The captain finally yielded in despair: "Carry him wherever you like!" The boys took up the coffin, but as they carried it past the mother, they stopped and lowered for a moment so that she might bid little Ilyusha farewell. But on seeing suddenly the dear little face so close to her, which for the last three days she had only looked at from some distance, she trembled all over, her grey head hysterically twitching up and down over the coffin.

"Mother, make the sign of the cross over him, give him your blessing and kiss him," Nina called out to her.

But she went on jerking her head up and down like an automaton, without uttering a word, her face contorted with intense grief, and, then, she suddenly began beating her breast with her fist. The coffin was carried farther. Nina pressed her lips for the last time to her dead brother's lips. As he was leaving the house, Alyosha turned to the landlady with a request to keep an eye on the two sick women, but she did not let him go on.

"Of course, I'll stay with them; we are Christians, too, after all!" The old woman wept as she spoke.

The coffin did not have to be carried very far, about three hundred paces, no more. It was a calm and clear day, with a touch of frost in the air. The bells were ringing for the service. Snegiryov ran fussily and forlornly after the coffin in his short, old and thin summer overcoat, his head bare, his wide-brimmed old felt hat in his hand. He seemed to be in the grip of bewildered anxiety, now suddenly stretching out a hand to support the head of the coffin and thus hampering the bearers, now running alongside to find some place for himself there. A flower dropped on the snow and he rushed to pick it up as though goodness only knew what depended on the loss of the flower.

"And the crust of bread—we've forgotten the crust of bread!" he suddenly cried out in a terrible panic. But the boys at once reminded him that he had taken the crust of bread, which was in his pocket. He instantly pulled it out and, reassured, calmed down.

"Ilyusha told me to—Ilyusha," he at once explained to Alyosha. "He was lying awake one night and I was sitting beside him, and all of a sudden he said to me, 'Daddy, while my grave is being filled, crumble a crust of bread over it so that the sparrows may fly down. I shall hear them and it will cheer me up not to be lying there alone.' "

"That will be very good," said Alyosha. "That must be done as often as possible."

"Every day, every day!" Snegiryov murmured, brightening up.

They at last reached the church and the coffin was placed in the middle of it. All the boys surrounded it, remaining standing reverently all through the service. The church was very old and rather poor, and many of the icons were without settings, but somehow one prays more fervently in such churches. Snegiryov seemed to calm down a little during the service, though the same unconscious and seemingly perplexed anxiety came over him from time to time: he kept going up to the coffin to adjust the pall or a wreath, and when a candle fell out of the candlestick he hurried to put it back and busied himself a long time with it. Then he calmed down and stood still at the head of the coffin with a blank, worried, and bewildered expression on his face. After the reading from the Apostles, he suddenly whispered to Alyosha, who was standing beside him, that it had not been read *properly,* but he did not explain what he meant. During the hymn *Like Unto the Cherubim,* he tried to join in the singing, but did not carry on with it and, kneeling, pressed his head to the stone floor and lay like that for a long time. At last, the funeral service began and candles were handed round. Again the distracted father started fidgeting, but the deeply moving and heart-rending funeral chants stirred and thrilled his soul. He seemed suddenly to wilt, and burst into rapid, short sobs, at first stifling his voice, but in the end whimpering loudly. As they began taking leave of the dead boy and closing the coffin, he threw his arms round it as though he would not let them cover up Ilyusha, and began avidly to kiss his dead boy on the lips. He was at last persuaded to desist and was led down the steps, but he suddenly stretched out a hand impulsively and snatched a few flowers from the coffin. He looked at them and a new idea seemed to come over him, so that he apparently forgot what was happening all round him for a moment. Little by little, he seemed to fall into a reverie and offered no resistance when the coffin was raised and carried to the grave near the wall, close to the church. It was an expensive site, paid for by Katerina Ivanovna. After the customary rites, the grave-diggers lowered the coffin. Snegiryov bent down so low over the grave with the flowers in his hands that the boys had to catch hold of him by his coat and pull him back. He no longer seemed to realise clearly what was happening. As the grave was being filled, he suddenly began pointing anxiously at the falling earth and even started saying something, but no one could make out what he meant, and soon he fell silent himself. Then he was reminded to crumble the bread and he grew terribly excited, pulled out the crust of bread and began tearing off bits of it and scattering them on the grave: "Now, then, come on, little birdies, fly down, little sparrows!" he mumbled anxiously. One of the boys observed that he must find it hard to crumble the bread with the flowers in his hands and suggested that he should let someone hold them for a while. But he would not let them and even seemed suddenly alarmed for his flowers, as though they wanted to take them away from him. Then, casting a last look at the grave and having made sure that everything had been done and the bread scattered, he all of a sudden turned round unexpectedly and, with the utmost composure, walked off home. But his steps grew faster and more hurried, and soon he was almost at the run. The boys and Alyosha kept up with him.

"The flowers for Mummy! The flowers for Mummy! We've hurt Mummy's feelings!" he suddenly began to exclaim.

Someone called out to him to put on his hat as it was very cold, but, at these words, he flung his hat on the snow as though in anger and kept repeating: "I don't want the hat, I don't want the hat!" One of the boys, Smurov, picked it up and carried it after him. The boys were all in tears and most of all

Kolya and the boy who had discovered Troy. Though Smurov, with the captain's hat in his hands, was also weeping bitterly, he managed, while running, to pick up a piece of red brick lying on the snow of the path and fling it at a passing flight of sparrows. Of course, he missed and went on crying as he ran. Halfway to his house, Snegiryov suddenly stopped, stood still for half a minute as though struck by a thought and suddenly turned back to the church, running towards the grave they had just left. But the boys at once overtook him and held him from all sides. Then, as though bereft of strength and as though struck down, he fell on the snow, and struggling, wailing and sobbing, began crying out: "Ilyusha, old fellow, dear old fellow!" Alyosha and Kolya began raising him from the ground and did their best to persuade him to go home with them.

"Come, Captain," Kolya murmured, "a brave man must show courage!"

"You'll ruin the flowers," Alyosha said. "Remember 'Mummy' is expecting them, she's sitting there crying because you didn't give her any of Ilyusha's flowers. And Ilyusha's bed is still there—"

"Yes, yes, let's go back to Mummy," Snegiryov suddenly recollected. "They'll take his little bed away, they'll take his little bed away!" he added, as though afraid that they would indeed take it away, and he jumped up and ran home again. But it was not far off now and they all arrived together. Snegiryov hurriedly opened the door and shouted to his wife, whom he had just treated so hard-heartedly:

"Mummy, oh, my poor crippled darling, Ilyusha has sent you these flowers!" and he held out the little bunch of flowers, frozen and broken while he was struggling in the snow. But at that same moment, he caught sight of Ilyusha's little boots, which the landlady had tidily placed in a corner by the bed—a pair of patched old boots that had gone discoloured and stiff. Seeing them, he raised his hands and, rushing up to them, fell on his knees, pressed his lips against them, and began kissing them avidly, crying: "Ilyusha, old fellow, darling Ilyusha, where are your little feet?"

"Where have you carried him off to? Where?" the crazy

woman screamed in a heart-rending voice.

At this point, Nina, too, burst out sobbing. Kolya rushed out of the room, followed by the other boys. At last Alyosha, too, went out.

"Let them have a good cry," he said to Kolya. "They can't be comforted now. Let's wait a little and then go back."

"No, they can't," Kolya agreed. "It's awful. Do you know, Karamazov," he lowered his voice suddenly so that no one could hear him, "I feel awfully sad and I'd give anything in the world to restore him to life if that were possible."

"Oh dear, so would I," said Alyosha.

"What do you think, Karamazov? Ought we to come back here tonight? He'll be sure to get drunk."

"Perhaps he will. Let's come back together, you and I but no one else, to spend an hour with them, with the mother and Nina," Alyosha suggested. "For if we all come together, we'll remind them again of everything."

"The landlady is laying the table there now. There's going to be a wake, I suppose, and the priest is coming. Shall we go back there now, Karamazov?"

"Yes, certainly," said Alyosha.

"It's all so strange, Karamazov. Such sorrow and, all of a sudden, pancakes—that's all so unnatural in our religion!"

"They're going to have salmon, too," the boy who discovered Troy suddenly observed in a loud voice.

"I'll thank you, Kartashov, not to interrupt again with your stupid remarks, especially when no one is talking to you or even cares to know whether you exist or not," Kolya snapped irritably.

The boy flushed crimson, but he dared not say anything in reply. Meanwhile, they were all walking slowly along the path, and suddenly Smurov exclaimed:

"Here's Ilyusha's stone, the one they wanted to bury him under!"

They all stopped in silence at the big stone. Alyosha looked at it and the picture suddenly came back to him of what Snegiryov had told him the other day of how Ilyusha, crying and embracing his father, exclaimed, "Daddy, Daddy, how he has humiliated you!" Something seemed to give way in his soul. He looked round with a serious glance and a grave expression at the sweet bright faces of the schoolboys, Ilyusha's friends, and suddenly said to them:

"Boys, I would like to say something to you here, at this place."

The boys crowded about him and at once bent their eager, expectant gaze on him.

"Boys, we shall soon part, I'm staying here at present with my two brothers, one of whom is going to exile in Siberia, and the other is dangerously ill. But I shall leave this town soon, perhaps for some time. So we shall be parting. Let us, therefore, agree here, at Ilyusha's stone, never to forget, first, little Ilyusha, and, secondly, one another. And whatever may befall us later in life even if we do not meet again for another twenty years, we shall always remember how we buried the poor boy we once threw stones at by that little bridge—remember?—and how we all loved him so much afterwards. He was a good boy, kind-hearted and brave and felt deeply for his father's honour and the cruel insult offered to him, against which he rose up. So, first of all, boys, let us remember him throughout our lives. And though we may be engaged with most important things, win honours or fall upon evil days, let us never forget how happy we were here, when we were all together, united by such a good and kindly feeling, which made us, too, while we loved the poor boy, better men, perhaps, than we are. My dear boys—let me call you so—my heart goes out to you as I look at your kind and dear faces. My dear children, perhaps you will not understand what I'm going to say to you now, for I often speak very incomprehensibly, but I'm sure you will remember, and then sometimes agree with my words. Know that there's nothing loftier, stronger, more wholesome and more useful in life ahead than some dear memory, especially when it goes back to the days of your childhood, to the days of your life at home. You are told a lot about your upbringing, but some beautiful and sacred memory, preserved since childhood, is perhaps the best upbringing of all. If a man accumulates many such memories, he is saved for the rest of his life. And even if a single dear recollection remains in our hearts, it may also be the instrument of our salvation some day. Perhaps we may later become wicked and be unable to resist some evil action, may mock at men's tears and at those who say, as Kolya has just said: 'I want to suffer for all mankind'—we may even jeer spitefully at such people. And yet, however wicked we may become, which God forbid, as soon as we recall how we buried Ilyusha, how we loved him during these last days, and how we have been talking like friends together at this stone, the most cruel and the most derisive of us—if we do become so—will not dare to laugh inwardly at having been so good and kind at this moment! Moreover, perhaps this memory alone will keep such a man from great evil, and he will stop to give thought, saying, 'Yes, I was good, bold and honest then.' Let him sneer inwardly—never mind, a man often laughs at what is good and kind; that is only out of thoughtlessness, but I assure you that, as soon as he makes mock of something kindly and good, he will at once say in his heart: 'No, I've acted badly in being derisive, for one should not sneer at such things!' "

"It will certainly be so, Karamazov!" Kolya exclaimed with flashing eyes. "I understand you, Karamazov!" The boys grew agitated and wanted to say something, too, but held themselves in check and looked intently and with emotion at the speaker.

"I am speaking out of fear lest we become bad," Alyosha went on, "but why should we become bad—isn't that so, boys? Let us be, first and above all, kindly, then honest, and then—don't let us ever forget each other. I say that again. I give you my word, boys, that I will never forget any one of you. Even after thirty years I shall remember every face that is looking at me now. Kolya said to Kartashov a moment ago that we did not care whether he existed or not. But how can I forget that Kartashov exists and that he isn't blushing now as when he did when he discovered Troy, but is looking at me with his dear, kind, happy eyes? Boys, my dear boys, let us all be magnanimous and brave as Ilyusha, as intelligent, brave, and generous as Kolya, who, I'm sure, will grow much cleverer when he grows up, and let us be as modest but also clever and kind as Kartashov. But why am I talking only about these two? You're all dear to me from now on. Boys, I will find a place for you all in my heart and I beg you to find a place for me in your hearts, too! Well, and who has united us in this good and kindly feeling, which we shall intend to and shall remember throughout our lives? Who has done that, if not Ilyusha, the good boy, the dear boy, dear to us for ever and ever! Don't let us, then, ever forget him; may his memory live in our hearts for ever and ever!"

"Yes, yes, for ever and ever!" all the boys cried in their ringing voices, looking deeply moved.

"Let us remember his face and his clothes and his poor little boots, and his coffin, and his unfortunate and sinful father, for whom he so bravely stood up alone against his whole class!"

"We will, we will remember!" the boys cried again. "He was brave; he was kindly!"

"Oh, how I loved him!" exclaimed Kolya.

"Oh, my dear children, my dear friends, do not be afraid of life! How good life is when you do something that is good and just!"

"Yes, yes," the boys repeated enthusiastically.

"Karamazov, we love you!" a voice, probably Kartashov's, cried impulsively.

"We love you, we do love you," the other boys echoed. There were tears in the eyes of many of them.

"Three cheers for Karamazov!" Kolya shouted enthusiastically.

"And may the dead boy's memory live for ever!" Alyosha again added feelingly.

"May it live for ever!" the boys echoed again.

"Karamazov," cried Kolya, "is it really true that, as our religion tells us, we shall all rise from the dead and come to life and see one another again, all of us, and Ilyusha as well?"

"We shall certainly rise again; we shall certainly see one another, and shall tell one another gladly and joyfully everything that has been," Alyosha replied, half laughing, half rapturously.

"Oh, how wonderful it will be!" Kolya cried.

"Well, now let us make an end of talking and go to the wake. Don't be put out by our eating pancakes. It's an age-old custom and there's something good about it," Alyosha laughed. "Well, come along! And now we shall go arm in arm."

"That's how it will always be, arm in arm throughout life! Three cheers for Karamazov!" Kolya again cried with enthusiasm, and once again all the boys burst into cheers.

THE END

REQUEST TO READERS

Raduga Publishers would be glad to have your opinion of this book, its translation and design, and any suggestions you may have for future publications.
Please send all your comments to 17, Zubovsky Boulevard, Moscow, USSR.

13 ⁵⁰(2)